October 20, 1992

Keith,

Happy Birthday
man who I have shared
many adventures ~ and will have
many more... and who has
the hat to fit the adventure.

adventure. I love you!!
Linda 🙂

HIGH ADVENTURE

HIGH ADVENTURE

TALES OF EXPLORATION, ESCAPE, AND INTRIGUE

EDITED BY

CYNTHIA MANSON
& CHARLES ARDAI

BARNES
&NOBLE
BOOKS
NEW YORK

This edition published by Marboro Books Corp.,
a division of Barnes & Noble, Inc.,
by arrangement with Bantam Doubleday Dell Publishing Group, Inc.

Book design by Charles Ziga, Ziga Design

1992 Barnes & Noble Books

ISBN 0-88029-826-X

Printed and bound in the United States of America

M 9 8 7 6 5 4 3 2 1

ACKNOWLEDGMENTS

Grateful acknowledgment is made to the following for permission to use their copyrighted material:

From Zaire to Eternity by Charles Ardai, copyright © 1989 by Davis Publications, Inc., reprinted by permission of the author; *Like a Dog in the Street* by Lawrence Block, copyright © 1977 by Davis Publications, Inc., reprinted by permission of Henry Morrison, Inc.; *The Hidden Saboteur* by David Braly, copyright © 1984 by Davis Publications, Inc., reprinted by permission of the author; *Dogs* by Loren D. Estleman, copyright © 1987 by Davis Publications, Inc., reprinted by permission of the author; all stories previously appeared in *Alfred Hitchcock's Mystery Magazine,* published by Dell Magazines (a division of Bantam Doubleday Dell Publishing Group, Inc.).

Icewater Mansions by Doug Allyn, copyright © 1991 by Davis Publications, Inc., reprinted by permission of James Allen, the agent; *Pay-Off Girl* by James M. Cain, copyright © 1952 by Esquire Inc., renewed 1980 by Alice M. Piper, reprinted by permission of Harold Ober Associates, Inc.; *Brothers* by John F. Dobbyn, copyright © 1989 by Davis Publications, Inc., reprinted by permission of the author; *The Living Daylights* by Ian Fleming, copyright © 1962 by Ian Fleming, © renewed 1990 by the Executors of the estate of Ian Fleming, reprinted by permission of Glidrose Publications, Ltd. (This story is included in the book *Octopussy*—first published in 1966 in the USA by NAL and in the UK by Jonathan Cape Ltd.); *The Dakar Run* by Clark Howard, copyright © 1988 by Davis Publications, Inc., reprinted by permission of the author; *Discovery* by Patrick Ireland, copyright © 1988 by Davis Publications, Inc., reprinted by permission of the author; *Hooray for Hollywood* by Robert Twohy, copyright © 1980 by Davis Publications, Inc., reprinted by permission of the author; *The Phantom of the Subway* by Cornell Woolrich, copyright © 1945 by Gold Medal Books, renewed 1973, reprinted by permission of Scott Meredith Literary Agency, Inc.; all stories previously appeared in *Ellery Queen's Mystery Magazine,* published by Dell Magazines (a division of Bantam Doubleday Dell Publishing Group, Inc.).

Rescue Run by Anne McCaffrey, copyright © 1991 by Anne McCaffrey, reprinted by permission of the author and the author's agent, Virginia Kidd; previously appeared in *Analog Science Fiction & Fact,* published by Dell Magazines (a division of Bantam Doubleday Dell Publishing Group, Inc.).

Trapalanda by Charles Sheffield, copyright © 1987 by Charles Sheffield, reprinted by permission of the author; *On the Border* by Lucius Shepard, copyright © 1987 by Davis Publications, Inc., reprinted by permission of the author; *Superwine* by Harry Turtledove, copyright © 1987 by Davis Publications, Inc., reprinted by permission of Scott Meredith Literary Agency, Inc.; all stories previously appeared in *Isaac Asimov's Science Fiction Magazine,* published by Dell Magazines (a division of Bantam Doubleday Dell Publishing Group, Inc.).

Frost and Thunder by Randall Garrett, copyright © 1979 by Davis Publications, Inc., reprinted by permission of the Blackstone Literary Agency, Inc.; *Davidson, Shadow Slayer* by John Kelly, copyright © 1979 by Davis Publications, Inc., reprinted by permission of Scott Meredith Literary Agency, Inc.; both stories previously appeared in *Asimov's SF Adventure Magazine,* previously published by Davis Publications, Inc.

CONTENTS

Men on the Run—Men Caught in a Trap

Across Time & Space

INTRODUCTION

A meteor streaks across the sky, the forest primeval rumbles under the tread of stampeding elephants, a man on horseback gallops over the edge of a cliff, bullets fly as the Sultan's palace erupts into flames, fortune hunters converge on the hiding place of an ancient treasure . . . and you are in the world of *High Adventure*.

It's a world you know well if you grew up on *Argosy All Story* magazine and Buster Crabbe movie serials ("Buck Rogers," "Flash Gordon"), novels by Edgar Rice Burroughs and Jules Verne, comic books such as *The Avenger* and *New Adventure Comics*—or, for that matter, if you're a few years younger and grew up on *Raiders of the Lost Ark, Jewel of the Nile,* and *Star Wars*. Indiana Jones lives in this world, side by side with Tarzan, Lord of Apes, James Bond, Zorro, and all the other grand masters of derring-do.

Here are swashbucklers and sinister spies, danger and excitement, ingenious escapes, and two-fisted action. It's the world we all wanted to visit when we were kids—and which those of us fortunate enough never to have grown up still return to through movies, daydreams, and stories like the ones you are about to read.

In this collection we have attempted to cover the entire spectrum of adventure fiction. There are outlaws on the run, adventurers seeking riches, detectives fighting for their lives, foolhardy explorers going to the four corners of the earth, and one or two adventurers who go beyond the planet entirely. Venture inside an Egyptian pyramid, a Roman catacomb, and (most dangerous of all) the subway tunnels of New York City. Sail into the heart of a typhoon off the coast of China and plumb the depths of the bottomless crevasses of the Yukon. And before you are done, look deep into the heart of human greed and cunning and know the meanings of loyalty and strength, and, above all, of resourcefulness and daring.

Your guides along the way will be some of the best adventure writers who have ever lived: Jack London, Ian Fleming, Edgar Rice Burroughs, Cornell Woolrich, Anne McCaffrey, O. Henry, Robert Louis Stevenson, Joseph Conrad, Lucius Shepard, Arthur Conan Doyle, and many more—all authors to keep your pulse pounding and to make your imagination soar.

The stories are arranged in six sections:

In "Explorers, Travelers, and Fortune Hunters" there are tales of classical-style adventurers such as the archaeologist heroes of Patrick Ireland's

"Discovery," Arthur Conan Doyle's "The New Catacomb," and the team of explorers in Charles Sheffield's "Trapalanda."

In "On The High Seas," you will leave the safety of *terra firma* behind and experience the terrors and dangers of life on the water. The power of the sea threatens all who try to best her, from the crew of a Norwegian fishing boat in Edgar Allan Poe's "A Descent into the Malestrom" to the captain of the biggest ship ever built in David Braly's "The Hidden Saboteur."

The frozen reaches of the north offer a beautiful but deadly backdrop to the stories in section three, "Lands of Snow and Ice." From the great ice plains of modern-day Lake Huron (Doug Allyn's "Icewater Mansions") to the Yukon in the days of the great Gold Rush (Jack London's "The Fearless One" and John Dobbyn's "Brothers"), treasure lies just out of reach for those brave enough to search for it.

"The Living Daylights," the James Bond novelette on which the movie was based, heads off the section "Spies, Tough Guys, and Private Eyes." There you'll meet detectives and diamond smugglers, international terrorists, members of the underworld, and other uniquely seedy characters. Best-selling mystery novelists Lawrence Block, Loren D. Estleman, and James M. Cain lead the pack in exploring this world of vice and crime.

In "Men on the Run—Men Caught in a Trap" you will find stories about heroes and villains trying to get away from their pursuers . . . or their captors. In "Caught," O. Henry follows a fleeing South American president, on the run with all his country's money; and Honoré de Balzac writes of a man who has to choose between survival and the most awful crime imaginable in "The Executioner." Even Tarzan turns up to rescue a trapped member of his ape tribe in Edgar Rice Burroughs' "Tarzan's First Love."

Finally, there are four otherworldly adventures in "Across Time and Space." Randall Garrett explores the consequences of a time warp in "Frost and Thunder"; Harry Turtledove tells a tale of intrigue in an alternate universe in "Superwine"; John Kelly sends a space-traveling fugitive to hide on a devastated future Earth in "Davidson, Shadow Slayer"; and Anne McCaffrey describes the rediscovery of the lost colony of Pern in "Rescue Run."

We hope you enjoy all of these splendid stories. That's what high adventure is about, after all—pure entertainment. So pack up your pistol and bullwhip, gas up the jeep, sharpen your sword, and strap on your pith helmet. Your own high adventure is about to begin.

—The Editors

EXPLORERS, TRAVELERS & FORTUNE HUNTERS

TRAPALANDA

Charles Sheffield

John Kenyon Martindale seldom did things the usual way. Until a first-class return air ticket and a check for $10,000 arrived at my home in Lausanne I did not know he existed. The enclosed note said only: "For consulting services of Klaus Jacobi in New York, June 6–7." It was typed on his letterhead and initialed, JKM. The check was drawn on the Riggs Bank of Washington, D.C. The tickets were for Geneva–New York on June 5, with an open return.

I did not need work. I did not need money. I had no particular interest in New York, and a trans-Atlantic telephone call to John Kenyon Martindale revealed only that he was out of town until June 5. Why would I bother with him? It is easy to forget what killed the cat.

The limousine that met me at Kennedy Airport drove to a stone mansion on the East River, with a garden that went right down to the water's edge. An old woman with the nose, chin, and hairy moles of a storybook witch opened the door. She took me upstairs to the fourth floor, while my baggage disappeared under the house with the limousine. The mansion was amazingly quiet. The elevator made no noise at all, and when we stepped out of it the deeply carpeted floors of the corridor were matched by walls thick with oriental tapestries. I was not used to so much silence. When I was ushered into a long, shadowed conservatory filled with flowering plants and found myself in the presence of a man and woman, I wanted to shout. Instead I stared.

Shirley Martindale was a brunette, with black hair, thick eyebrows, and a flawless, creamy skin. She was no more than five feet three, but full-figured and strongly built. In normal company she would have been a center of attention; with John Kenyon Martindale present, she was ignored.

He was of medium height and slender build, with a wide, smiling mouth. His hair was thin and wheat-colored, combed straight back from his face. Any other expression he might have had was invisible. From an inch below his eyes to two inches above them, a flat, black shield extended across his whole face. Within that curved strip of darkness colored shadows moved, little darting points and glints of light that flared red and green and electric blue. They were hypnotic, moving in patterns that could be followed but never quite predicted, and they drew and held the attention. They were so striking that it took me a few moments to realize that John Kenyon Martindale must be blind.

He did not act like a person without sight. When I came into the room he at once came forward and confidently shook my hand. His grip was firm, and surprisingly strong for so slight a man.

"A long trip," he said, when the introductions were complete. "May I offer a little refreshment?"

Although the witch was still standing in the room, waiting, he mixed the drinks himself, cracking ice, selecting bottles, and pouring the correct measures slowly but without error. When he handed a glass to me and smilingly said "There! How's that?" I glanced at Shirley Martindale and replied, "It's fine; but before we start the toasts I'd like to learn what we are toasting. Why am I here?"

"No messing about, eh? You are very direct. Very Swiss—even though you are not one." He turned his head to his wife, and the little lights twinkled behind the black mask. "What did I tell you, Shirley? This is the man." And then to me. "You are here to make a million dollars. Is that enough reason?"

"No. Mr. Martindale, it is not. It was not money that brought me here. I have enough money."

"Then perhaps you are here to become a Swiss citizen. Is that a better offer?"

"Yes. If you can pay in advance." Already I had an idea what John Martindale wanted of me. I am not psychic, but I can read and see. The inner wall of the conservatory was papered with maps of South America.

"Let us say, I will pay half in advance. You will receive five hundred thousand dollars in your account before we leave. The remainder, and the Swiss citizenship papers, will be waiting when we return from Patagonia."

"We? Who are 'we'?"

"You and I. Other guides if you need them. We will be going through difficult country, though I understand that you know it better than anyone."

I looked at Shirley Martindale, and she shook her head decisively. "Not me, Klaus. Not for one million dollars, not for ten million dollars. This is all John's baby."

"Then my answer must be no." I sipped the best pisco sour I had tasted since I was last in Peru, and wondered where he had learned the technique. "Mr. Martindale, I retired four years ago to Switzerland. Since then I have not set foot in Argentina, even though I still carry those citizenship papers. If you want someone to lead you through the *echter Rand* of Patagonia, there must now be a dozen others more qualified than I. But that is beside the point. Even when I was in my best condition, even when I was so young and cocky that I thought nothing could kill me or touch me—even then I would have refused to lead a blind man to the high places that you display on your walls. With your wife's presence and her assistance to you for personal matters, it might barely be possible. Without her—have you any idea at all what conditions are like there?"

"Better than most people." He leaned forward. "Mr. Jacobi, let us perform a little test. Take something from your pocket, and hold it up in front of you. Something that should be completely unfamiliar to me."

I hate games, and this smacked of one; but there was something infinitely persuasive about that thin, smiling man. What did I have in my pocket? I reached in, felt my wallet, and slipped out a photograph. I did not look at it, and I was not sure myself what I had selected. I held it between thumb and forefinger, a few feet away from Martindale's intent face.

"Hold it very steady," he said. Then, while the points of light twinkled and shivered, "It is a picture, a photograph of a woman. It is your assistant, Helga Korein. Correct?"

I turned it to me. It was a portrait of Helga, smiling into the camera. "You apparently know far more about me than I know of you. However, you are not quite correct. It is a picture of my wife, Helga Jacobi. I married her four years ago, when I retired. You are not blind?"

"Legally, I am completely blind and have been since my twenty-second year, when I was foolish enough to drive a racing car into a retaining wall." Martindale tapped the black shield. "Without this, I can see nothing. With it, I am neither blind nor seeing. I receive charge-coupled diode inputs directly to my optic nerves, and I interpret them. I see neither at the wavelengths nor with the resolution provided by the human eye, nor is what I reconstruct anything like the images that I remember from the time before I became blind; but I see. On another occasion I will be happy to tell you all that I know about the technology. What you need to know tonight is that I will be able to pull my own weight on any journey. I can give you that assurance. And now I ask again: will you do it?"

It was, of course, curiosity that killed the cat. Martindale had given me almost no information as to where he wanted to go, or when, or why. But something was driving John Martindale, and I wanted to hear what it was.

I nodded my head, convinced now that he would see my movement.

"We certainly need to talk in detail; but for the moment let us use that fine old legal phrase, and say there is agreement in principle."

There is agreement in principle. With that sentence, I destroyed my life.

Shirley Martindale came to my room that night. I was not surprised. John Martindale's surrogate vision was a miracle of technology, but it had certain limitations. The device could not resolve the fleeting look in a woman's eye, or the millimeter jut to a lower lip. I had caught the signal in the first minute.

We did not speak until it was done and we were lying side by side in my bed. I knew it was not finished. She had not relaxed against me. I waited. "There is more than he told you," she said at last.

I nodded. "There is always more. But he was quite right about that place. I have felt it myself, many times."

As South America narrows from the great equatorial swell of the Amazon Basin, the land becomes colder and more broken. The great spine of the Andean cordillera loses height as one travels south. Ranges that tower to twenty-three thousand feet in the tropics dwindle to a modest twelve thousand. The land is shared between Argentina and Chile, and along their border, beginning with the chill depths of Lago Buenos Aires (sixty miles long, ten miles wide; bigger than anything in Switzerland), a great chain of mountain lakes straddles the frontier, all the way south to Tierra del Fuego and the flowering Chilean city of Puntas Arenas.

For fourteen years, the Argentina-Chile borderland between latitude 46 and 50 South had been my home, roughly from Lago Buenos Aires to Lago Argentina. It had become closer to me than any human, closer even than Helga. The east side of the Andes in this region is a bitter, parched desert, where gale-force winds blow incessantly three hundred and sixty days of the year. They come from the snow-bound slopes of the mountains, freezing whatever they touch. I knew the country and I loved it, but Helga had persuaded me that it was not a land to which a man could retire. The buffeting wind was an endless drain, too much for old blood. Better, she said, to leave in early middle age, when a life elsewhere could still be shaped.

When the time came for us to board the aircraft that would take me away to Buenos Aires and then to Europe, I wanted to throw away my ticket. I am not a sentimental man, but only Helga's presence allowed me to leave the Kingdom of the Winds.

Now John Martindale was tempting me to return there, with more than money. At one end of his conservatory-study stood a massive globe, about six feet across. Presumably it dated from the time before he had acquired his artificial eyes, because it differed from all other globes I had ever seen in one important respect; namely, it was a relief globe. Oceans were all smooth surface, while mountain ranges of the world stood out from the surface of the flattened sphere. The degree of relief had been exaggerated, but everything was in proportion. Himalayan and Karakoram ranges projected a few tenths of an inch more than the Rockies and the Andes, and they in turn were a little higher than the Alps or the volcanic ranges of Indonesia.

When my drink was finished Martindale had walked me across to that globe. He ran his finger down the backbone of the Americas, following the continuous mountain chains from their beginning in Alaska, through the American Rockies, through Central America, and on to the rising Andes and northern Chile. When he finally came to Patagonia his fingers slowed and stopped.

"Here," he said. "It begins here."

His fingertip was resting on an area very familiar to me. It was right on the Argentina–Chile border, with another of the cold mountain lakes at the center of it. I knew the lake as Lago Pueyrredon, but as usual with bodies of water that straddle the border there was a different name—Lago Cochrane —in use on the Chilean side. The little town of Paso Roballo, where I had spent a dozen nights in a dozen years, lay just to the northeast.

If I closed my eyes I could see the whole landscape that lay beneath his finger. To the east it was dry and dusty, sustaining only thornbush and tough grasses on the dark surface of old volcanic flows; westward were the tall flowering grasses and the thicketed forests of redwood, cypress, and Antarctic beech. Even in the springtime of late November there would be snow on the higher ground, with snow-fed lake waters lying black as jet under a Prussian-blue sky.

I could see all this, but it seemed impossible that John Martindale could do so. His blind skull must hold a different vision.

"What begins here?" I asked, and wondered again how much he could receive through those arrays of inorganic crystal.

"The anomalies. This region has weather patterns that defy all logic and all models."

"I agree with that, from personal experience. That area has the most curious pattern of winds of any place in the world." It had been a long flight and a long day, and by this time I was feeling a little weary. I was ready to defer discussion of the weather until tomorrow, and I wanted time to reflect on our "agreement in principle." I continued, "However, I do not see why those winds should interest you."

"I am a meteorologist. Now wait a moment." His sensor array must have caught something of my expression. "Do not jump to a wrong conclusion. Mine was a perfect profession for a blind man. Who can see the weather? I was ten times as sensitive as a sighted person to winds, to warmth, to changes in humidity and barometric pressure. What I could not see was cloud formations, and those are consequences rather than causes. I could deduce their appearance from other variables. Eight years ago I began to develop my own computer models of weather patterns, analyzing the interaction of snow, winds, and topography. Five years ago I believed that my method was completely general, and completely accurate. Then I studied the Andean system; and in one area—only one—it failed." He tapped the globe. "Here. Here there are winds with no sustaining source of energy. I can define a circulation pattern and locate a vortex, but I cannot account for its existence."

"The area you show is known locally as the Kingdom of the Winds."

"I know. I want to go there."

And so did I.

When he spoke I felt a great longing to return, to see again the *altiplano* of the eastern Andean slopes and hear the banshee music of the western wind. It was all behind me. I had sworn to myself that Argentina existed only in my past, that the Patagonian spell was broken forever. John Martindale was giving me a million dollars and Swiss citizenship, but more than that he was giving me an *excuse*. For four years I had been unconsciously searching for one.

I held out my glass. "I think, Mr. Martindale, that I would like another drink."

Or two. Or three.

Shirley Martindale was moving by my side now, running her hand restlessly along my arm. "There is more. He wants to understand the winds, but there is more. He hopes to find Trapalanda."

She did not ask me if I had heard of it. No one who spends more than a week in central Patagonia can be ignorant of Trapalanda. For three hundred years, explorers have searched for the "City of the Caesars," *Trapalanda,* the Patagonian version of El Dorado. Rumor and speculation said that Trapalanda would be found at about 47 degrees South, at the same latitude as Paso Roballo. Its fabled treasure-houses of gold and gemstones had drawn hundreds of men to their death in the high Andes. People did not come back, and say, "I sought Trapalanda, and I failed to find it." They did not come back at all. I was an exception.

"I am disappointed," I said. "I had thought your husband to be a wiser man."

"What do you mean?"

"Everyone wants to find Trapalanda. Four years of my life went into the search for it, and I had the best equipment and the best knowledge. I told your husband that there were a dozen better guides, but I was lying. I know that country better than any man alive. He is certain to fail."

"He believes that he has special knowledge. And you are going to do it. You are going to take him there. For Trapalanda."

She knew better than I. Until she spoke, I did not know what I would do. But she was right. Forget the "agreement in principle." I would go.

"You want me to do it, don't you?" I said. "But I do not understand *your* reasons. You are married to a very wealthy man. He seems to have as much money as he can ever spend."

"John is curious, always curious. He is like a little boy. He is not doing this for money. He does not care about money."

She had not answered my implied question. I had never asked for John Kenyon Martindale's motives, I had been looking for *her* reasons why he should go. Then it occurred to me that her presence, here in my bed, told me all I needed to know. He would go to the Kingdom of the Winds. If he found what he was looking for, it would bring enormous wealth. Should he fail to return, Shirley Martindale would be a free and very wealthy widow.

"Sex with your husband is not good?" I asked.

"What do you think? I am here, am I not?" Then she relented. "It is worse than not good, it is terrible. It is as bad with him as it is exciting with you. John is a gentle, thoughtful man, but I need someone who takes me and does not ask or explain. You are a strong man, and I suspect that you are a cold, selfish man. Since we have been together, you have not once spoken my name, or said a single word of affection. You do not feel it is necessary to pretend to commitments. And you are sexist. I noticed John's reaction when you said, 'I married Helga.' He would always say it differently, perhaps 'Shirley and I got married.'" Her hands moved from my arm, and were touching me more intimately. She sighed. "I do not mind your attitude. What John finds hard to stand, I *need*. You saw what you did to me here, without one word. You make me shiver."

I turned to bring our bodies into full contact. "And John?" I said. "Why did he marry you?" There was no need to ask why she had married him.

"What do you think," she said. "Was it my wit, my looks, my charm? Give me your hand." She gently moved my fingers along her face and breasts. "It was five years ago. John was still blind. We met, and when we said goodnight he felt my cheek." Her voice was bitter. "He married me for my pelt."

The texture was astonishing. I could feel no roughness, no blemish, not even the most delicate of hairs. Shirley Martindale had the warm, flawless skin of a six-month-old baby. It was growing warm under my touch.

Before we began she raised herself high above me, propping herself on straight arms. "Helga. What is she like? I cannot imagine her."

"You will see," I said. "Tomorrow I will telephone Lausanne and tell her to come to New York. She will go with us to Trapalanda."

Trapalanda. Had I said that? I was very tired, I had meant to say Patagonia.

I reached up to touch her breasts. "No talk now," I said. "No more talk." Her eyes were as black as jet, as dark as mountain lakes. I dived into their depths.

Shirley Martindale did not meet Helga; not in New York, not anywhere, not ever. John Kenyon Martindale made his position clear to me the next morning as we walked together around the seventh floor library. "I won't allow her to stay in this house," he said. "It's not for my sake or yours, and certainly not for Shirley's. It is for her sake. I know how Shirley would treat her."

He did not seem at all annoyed, but I stared at the blind black mask and revised my ideas about how much he could see with his CCD's and fiber optic bundles.

"Did she tell you last night why I am going to Patagonia?" he asked, as he picked out a book and placed it in the hopper of an iron pot-bellied stove with electronic aspirations.

I hesitated, and told the truth. "She said you were seeking Trapalanda."

He laughed. "I wanted to go to Patagonia. The easiest way to do it without an argument from Shirley was to hold out a fifty billion dollar bait. The odd thing, though, is that she is quite right. I am seeking Trapalanda." And he laughed again, more heartily than anything he had said would justify.

The black machine in front of us made a little purr of contentment, and a pleasant woman's voice began to read aloud. It was a mathematics text on the foundations of geometry. I had noticed that although Martindale described himself as a meteorologist, four-fifths of the books in the library were mathematics and theoretical physics. There were too many things about John Martindale that were not what they seemed.

"Shirley's voice," he said, while we stood by the machine and listened to a mystifying definition of the intrinsic curvature of a surface. "And a very pleasant voice, don't you think, to have whispering sweet epsilons in your ear? I borrowed it for use with this optical character recognition equipment, before I got my eyes."

"I didn't think there was a machine in the world that could do that."

"Oh, yes." He switched it off, and Shirley halted in mid-word. "This isn't even state-of-the-art any more. It was, when it was made, and it cost the earth. Next year it will be an antique, and they'll give this much capability out in cereal packets. Come on, let's go and join Shirley for a pre-lunch aperitif."

If John Martindale were angry with me or with his wife, he concealed it well. I realized that the mask extended well beyond the black casing.

Five days later we flew to Argentina. When Martindale mentioned his idea of being in the Kingdom of the Winds in time for the winter solstice, season of the anomaly's strongest showing, I dropped any thoughts of a trip back to Lausanne. I arranged for Helga to pack what I needed and meet us in Buenos Aires. She would wait at Ezeiza Airport without going into the city proper, and we would fly farther south at once. Even if our travels went well, we would need luck as well as efficiency to have a week near Paso Roballo before solstice.

It amused me to see Martindale searching for Helga in the airport arrival lounge as we walked off the plane. He had seen her photograph, and I had assured him that she would be there. He could not find her. Within seconds, long before it was possible to see her features, I had picked her out. She was staring down at a book on her lap. Every fifteen seconds her head lifted for a rapid radar-like scan of the passenger lounge, and returned to the page. Martindale did not notice her until we were at her side.

I introduced them. Helga nodded but did not speak. She stood up and led the way. She had rented a four-seater plane on open charter, and in her usual efficient way she had arranged for our luggage to be transferred to it.

Customs clearance, you ask? Let us be realistic. The Customs Office in Argentina is no more corrupt than that of, say, Bolivia or Ecuador; that is quite sufficient. Should John Martindale be successful in divining the legendary treasures of Trapalanda, plenty of hands would help to remove them illegally from the country.

Helga led the way through the airport. She was apparently not what he had expected of my wife, and I could see him studying her closely. Helga stood no more than five feet two, to my six-two, and her thin body was not quite straight. Her left shoulder dipped a bit, and she favored her left leg a trifle as she walked.

Since I was the only one with a pilot's license I sat forward in the co-pilot's chair, next to Owen Davies. I had used Owen before as a by-the-day hired pilot. He knew the Kingdom of the Winds, and he respected it. He would not take risks. In spite of his name he was Argentina born—one of the many Welshmen who found almost any job preferable to their parents' Argentinian sheep-farming. Martindale and Helga sat behind us, side-by-side in the back, as we flew to Comodoro Rivadavia on the Atlantic coast. It was the last real airfield we would see for a while unless we dipped across the Chilean border to Cochrane. I preferred not to try that. In the old days, you risked a few machine-gun bullets from frontier posts. Today it is likely to be a surface-to-air missile.

We would complete our supplies in Comodoro Rivadavia, then use dry dirt airstrips the rest of the way. The provisions were supposed to be waiting for us. While Helga and Owen were checking to make sure that the delivery included everything we had ordered, Martindale came up to my side.

"Does she never talk?" he said. "Or is it just my lack of charm?" He did not sound annoyed, merely puzzled.

"Give her time." I looked to see what Owen and Helga were doing. They were pointing at three open chests of supplies, and Owen was becoming rather loud.

"You noticed how Helga walks, and how she holds her left arm?"

The black shield dipped down and up, making me suddenly curious as to what lay behind it. "I even tried to hint at a question in that direction," he said. "Quite properly she ignored it."

"She was not born that way. When Helga walked into my office nine years ago, I assumed that I was looking at some congenital condition. She said nothing, nor did I. I was looking for an assistant, someone who was as interested in the high border country as I was, and Helga fitted. She was only twenty-one years old and still green, but I could tell she was intelligent and trainable."

"Biddable," said Martindale. "Sorry, go on."

"You have to be fit to wander around in freezing temperatures at ten thousand feet," I said. "As part of Helga's condition of employment, she had to take a full physical. She didn't want to. She agreed only when she saw that the job depended on it. She was in excellent shape and passed easily; but the doctor—quite improperly—allowed me to look at her X-rays."

Were the eyebrows raised, behind that obsidian visor? Martindale cocked his head to the right, a small gesture of inquiry. Helga and Owen Davies were walking our way.

"She was put together like a jigsaw puzzle. Almost every bone in her arms and legs showed marks of fracture and healing. Her ribs, too. When she was small she had been what these enlightened times call 'abused.' Tortured. As a very small child, Helga learned to keep quiet. The best thing she could hope for was to be ignored. You saw already how invisible she can be."

"I have never heard you angry before," he said. "You sound like her father, not her husband." His tone was calm, but something new hid behind that mask. "And is that," he continued, "why in New York—"

He was interrupted. "Tomorrow," said Owen from behind him. "He says he'll have the rest then. I believe him. I told him he's a fat idle bastard, and if we weren't on our way by noon I'd personally kick the shit out of him."

Martindale nodded at me. Conversation closed. We headed into town for Alberto McShane's bar and the uncertain pleasures of nightlife in Comodoro Rivadavia. Martindale didn't give up. All the way there he talked quietly to Helga. He may have received ten words in return.

It had been five years. Alberto McShane didn't blink when we walked in. He took my order without comment, but when Helga walked past him he reached out his good arm and gave her a big hug. She smiled like the sun. She was home. She had hung around the *Guanaco* bar since she was twelve years old, an oil brat brought here in the boom years. When her parents left, she stayed. She hid among the beer barrels in McShane's cellar until the plane took off. Then she could relax for the first time in her life. Poverty and hard work were luxury after what she had been through.

The decor of the bar hadn't changed since last time. The bottle of dirty black oil (the first one pumped at Comodoro Rivadavia, if you believe McShane) hung over the bar, and the same stuffed guanaco and rhea stood beside it. McShane's pet armadillo, or its grandson, ambled among the tables looking for beer heel-taps.

I knew our search plans, but Helga and Owen Davies needed briefing. Martindale took Owen's 1:1,000,000 scale ONC's, with their emendations and local detail in Owen's careful hand, added to them the 1:250,000 color photomaps that had been made for him in the United States, and spread the collection out to cover the whole table.

"From here, to here," he said. His fingers tapped the map near Laguna del Sello, then moved south and west until they reached Lago Belgrano.

Owen studied them for a few moments. "All on this side of the border," he said. "That's good. What do you want to do there?"

"I want to land. Here, and here, and here." Martindale indicated seven points, on a roughly north-south line.

Owen Davies squinted down, assessing each location. "Lago Gio, Paso Roballo, Lago Posadas. Know 'em all. Tough landing at two, and that last point is in the middle of the Perito Moreno National Park; but we can find a place." He looked up, not at Martindale but at me. "You're not in the true high country, though. You're twenty miles too far east. What do you want to do when you get there?"

"I want to get out, and look west," said Martindale. "After that, I'll tell you where we have to go."

Owen Davies said nothing more, but when we were at the bar picking up more drinks he gave me a shrug. *Too far east,* it said. *You're not in the high country. You won't find Trapalanda there, where he's proposing to land. What's the story?*

Owen was an honest man and a great pilot, who had made his own failed attempt at Trapalanda (sometimes I thought that was true of everyone who lived below 46 degrees South). He found it hard to believe that anyone could succeed where he had not, but he couldn't resist the lure.

"He knows something he's not telling us," I said. "He's keeping information to himself. Wouldn't you?"

Owen nodded. Barrels of star rubies and tons of platinum and gold bars shone in his dark Welsh eyes.

When we returned to the table John Martindale had made his breakthrough. Helga was talking and bubbling with laughter. "How did you *do* that," she was saying. "He's untouchable. What did you *do* to him?" McShane's armadillo was sitting on top of the table, chewing happily at a piece of apple. Martindale was rubbing the ruffle of horny plates behind its neck, and the armadillo was pushing itself against his hand.

"He thinks I'm one of them." Martindale touched the black screen across his eyes. "See? We've both got plates. I'm just one of the family." His face turned up to me. I read satisfaction behind the mask. *And should I do to your wife, Klaus, what you did to mine?* it said. *It would be no more than justice.*

Those were not Martindale's thoughts. I realized that. They were mine. And that was the moment when my liking for John Kenyon Martindale began to tilt toward resentment.

At ground level, the western winds skim off the Andean slopes at seventy knots or more. At nine thousand feet, they blow at less than thirty. Owen was an economy-minded pilot. He flew west at ten thousand until we were at the preferred landing point, then dropped us to the ground in three sickening sideslips.

He had his landing already planned. Most of Patagonia is built of great level slabs, rising like terraces from the high coastal cliffs on the Atlantic Ocean to the Andean heights in the west. The exception was in the area we were exploring. Volcanic eruptions there have pushed great layers of basalt out onto the surface. The ground is cracked and irregular, and scarred by the scouring of endless winds. It takes special skill to land a plane when the wind speed exceeds the landing airspeed, and Owen Davies had it. We showed an airspeed of over a hundred knots when we touched down, light as a dust mote, and rolled to a perfect landing. "Good enough," said Owen.

He had brought us down on a flat strip of dark lava, at three o'clock in the afternoon. The sun hung low on the northwest horizon, and we stepped out into the teeth of a cold and dust-filled gale. The wind beat and tugged and pushed our bodies, trying to blow us back to the Atlantic. Owen, Helga, and I wore goggles and helmets against the driving clouds of grit and sand.

Martindale was bare-headed. He planted a GPS transponder on the ground to confirm our exact position, and faced west. With his head tilted upward and his straw-colored hair blowing wild, he made an adjustment to the side of his visor, then nodded. "It is there," he said. "I knew it must be."

We looked, and saw nothing. "What is there?" said Helga.

"I'll tell you in a moment. Note these down. I'm going to read off heights and headings." Martindale looked at the sun and the compass. He began to turn slowly from north to south. Every fifteen degrees he stopped, stared at the featureless sky, and read off a list of numbers. When he was finished he nodded to Owen. "All right. We can do the next one now."

"You mean that's *it*? *The whole thing*? All you're going to do is stand there?" Owen is many good things, but he is not diplomatic.

"That's it—for the moment." Martindale led the way back to the aircraft.

I could not follow. Not at once. I had lifted my goggles and was peering with wind-teared eyes to the west. The land there fell upward to the dark-blue twilight sky. It was the surge of the Andes, less than twenty miles away, rolling up in long, snow-capped breakers. I walked across the tufts of bunch grass and reached out a hand to steady myself on an isolated ten-foot beech tree. Wind-shaped and stunted it stood, trunk and branches curved to the east, hiding its head from the deadly western wind. It was the only one within sight.

This was my Patagonia, the true, the terrible.

I felt a gentle touch on my arm. Helga stood there, waiting. I patted her hand in reply, and she instinctively recoiled. Together we followed Martindale and Davies back to the aircraft.

"I found what I was looking for," Martindale said, when we were all safely inside. The gale buffeted and rocked the craft, resenting our presence. "It's no secret now. When the winds approach the Andes from the Chilean side, they shed all the moisture they have picked up over the Pacific; and they accelerate. The energy balance equation is the same everywhere in the world. It depends on terrain, moisture, heating, and atmospheric layers. The same equation everywhere—except that *here*, in the Kingdom of the Winds, something goes wrong. The winds pick up so much speed that they are thermodynamically impossible. There is a mechanism at work, pumping energy into the moving air. I knew it before I left New York City; and I knew what it must be. There had to be a long, horizontal line-vortex, running north to south and transmitting energy to the western wind. But that too was impossible. First, then, I had to confirm that the vortex existed." He nodded vigorously. "It does. With my vision sensors I can see the patterns of compression and rarefaction. In other words, I can see direct evidence of the vortex. With half a dozen more readings, I will pinpoint the exact origin of its energy source."

"But what's all that got to do with finding . . ." Owen trailed off and looked at me guiltily. I had told him what Martindale was after, but I had also cautioned him never to mention it.

"With finding Trapalanda?" finished Martindale. "Why, it has everything to do with it. There must be one site, a specific place where the generator exists to power the vortex line. Find that, and we will have found Trapalanda."

Like God, Duty, or Paradise, Trapalanda means different things to different people. I could see from the expression on Owen's face that a line-vortex power generator was not *his* Trapalanda, no matter what it meant to Martindale.

I had allowed six days; it took three. On the evening of June 17, we sat around the tiny table in the aircraft's rear cabin. There would be no flying tomorrow, and Owen had produced a bottle of *usquebaugh australis;* "southern whiskey," the worst drink in the world.

"On foot," John Martindale was saying. "Now it has to be on foot—and just in case, one of us will stay at the camp in radio contact."

"Helga," I said. She and Martindale shook heads in unison. "Suppose you have to carry somebody out?" she said. "I can't do that. It must be you or Owen."

At least she was taking this seriously, which Owen Davies was not. He had watched with increasing disgust while Martindale made atmospheric observations at seven sites. Afterward he came to me secretly. "We're working for a madman," he said. "We'll find no treasure. I'd almost rather work for Diego."

Diego Luria—"Mad Diego"—believed that the location of Trapalanda could be found by a correct interpretation of the Gospel According to Saint John. He had made five expeditions to the altiplano, four of them with Owen as pilot. It was harder on Owen than you might think, since Diego sometimes said that human sacrifice would be needed before Trapalanda could be discovered. They had found nothing; but they had come back, and that in itself was no mean feat.

Martindale had done his own exact triangulation, and pinpointed a place on the map. He had calculated UTM coordinates accurate to within twenty meters. They were not promising. When we flew as close as possible to his chosen location we found that we were looking at a point halfway up a steep rock face, where a set of broken waterfalls cascaded down a near-vertical cliff.

"I am sure," he said, in reply to my implied question. "The data-fit residuals are too small to leave any doubt." He tapped the map, and looked out of the aircraft window at the distant rock face. "Tomorrow. You, and Helga, and I will go. You, Owen, you stay here and monitor our transmission frequency. If we are off the air for more than twelve hours, come and get us."

He was taking this *too* seriously. Before the light faded I went outside again and trained my binoculars on the rock face. According to Martindale, at that location was a power generator that could modify the flow of winds along two hundred and fifty miles of mountain range. I saw nothing but the blown white spray of falls and cataracts, and a grey highland fox picking its way easily up the vertical rock face.

"Trust me." Martindale had appeared suddenly at my side. "I can *see* those wind patterns when I set my sensors to function at the right wavelengths. What's your problem?"

"Size." I turned to him. "Can you make your sensors provide telescopic images?"

"Up to three-inch effective aperture."

"Then take a look up there. You're predicting that we'll find a machine which produces tremendous power—"

"Many gigawatts."

"—more power than a whole power station. And there is nothing there, nothing to see. That's impossible."

"Not at all." The sun was crawling along the northern horizon. The thin daylight lasted for only eight hours, and already it was fading. John Kenyon Martindale peered off westward and shook his head. He tapped his black visor. "You've had a good look at this," he said. "Suppose I had wanted to buy something that could do what this does, say, five years ago. Do you know what it would have weighed?"

"Weighed?" I shook my head.

"At least a ton. And ten years ago, it would have been impossible to build, no matter how big you allowed it to be. In another ten years, this assembly will fit easily inside a prosthetic eye. The way is toward miniaturization, higher energy densities, more compact design. I expect the generator to be small." He suddenly turned again to look right into my face. "I have a question for you, and it is an unforgivably personal one. Have you ever consummated your marriage with Helga?"

He had anticipated my lunge at him, and he backed away rapidly. "Do not misunderstand me," he said. "Helga's extreme aversion to physical contact is obvious. If it is total, there are New York specialists who can probably help her. I have influence there."

I looked down at my hands as they held the binoculars. They were trembling. "It is—total," I said.

"You knew that—and yet you married her. Why?"

"Why did you marry *your* wife, knowing you would be cuckolded?" I was lashing out, not expecting an answer.

"Did she tell you it was for her skin?" His voice was weary, and he was turning away as he spoke. "I'm sure she did. Well, I will tell you. I married Shirley—because she wanted me to."

Then I was standing alone in the deepening darkness. Shirley Martindale had warned me, back in New York. He was like a child, curious about everything. Including me, including Helga, including me and Helga.

Damn you, John Martindale. I looked at the bare hillside, and prayed that Trapalanda would somehow swallow him whole. Then I would never again have to endure that insidious, probing voice, asking the unanswerable.

The plane had landed on the only level piece of ground in miles. Our destination was a mile and a half away, but it was across some formidable territory. We would have to descend a steep scree, cross a quarter mile of boulders until we came to a fast-moving stream, and follow that watercourse upward, until we were in the middle of the waterfalls themselves.

The plain of boulders showed the translucent sheen of a thin ice coating. The journey could not be done in poor light. We would wait until morning, and leave promptly at ten.

Helga and I went to bed early, leaving Martindale with his calculations and Owen Davies with his *usquebaugh australis*. At a pinch the aircraft would sleep four, but Helga and I slept outside in a small reinforced tent brought along for the purpose. The floor area was five feet by seven. We had pitched the tent in the lee of the aircraft, where the howl of the wind was muted. I listened to Helga's breathing, and knew after half an hour that she was still awake.

"Think we'll find anything?" I said softly.

"I don't know." And then, after maybe one minute. "It's not that. It's you, Klaus."

"I've never been better."

"That's the problem. I've seen you, these last few days. You love it here. I should never have taken you away."

"I'm not complaining."

"That's part of the problem, too. You never complain. I wish you would." I heard her turn to face me in the dark, and for one second I imagined a hand was reaching out towards me. It was an illusion. She went on, "When I said I wanted to leave Patagonia and live in Europe, you agreed without an argument. But your heart has always been here."

"Oh, well, I don't know . . ." The lie stuck in my throat.

"And there's something else. I wasn't going to tell you, because I was afraid that you would misunderstand. But I will tell you. John Martindale tried to touch me."

I stirred, began to sit up, and felt the rough canvas against my forehead. Outside, the wind gave a sudden scream around the tent. "You mean he tried to—to—"

"No. He reached out, and tried to touch the back of my hand. That was all. I don't know why he did it, but I think it was just curiosity. He watches everything, and he has been watching us. I pulled my hand away before he got near. But it made me think of you. I have not been a wife to you, Klaus. You've done your best, and I've tried my hardest but it hasn't improved at all. Be honest with yourself, you know it hasn't. So if you want to stay here when this work is finished . . ."

I hated to hear her sound so confused and lost. "Let's not discuss it now," I said.

In other words, I can't bear to talk about it.

We had tried so hard at first, with Helga gritting her teeth at every gentle touch. When I finally realized that the sweat on her forehead and the quiver in her thin limbs was a hundred percent fear and zero percent arousal, I stopped trying. After that we had been happy—or at least, I had. I had not been faithful physically, but I could explain that well enough. And then, with this trip and the arrival on the scene of John Kenyon Martindale, the whole relationship between Helga and me felt threatened. And I did not know why.

"We ought to get as much sleep as we can tonight," I said, after another twenty seconds or so. "Tomorrow will be a tough day."

She said nothing, but she remained awake for a long, long time.

And so, of course, did I.

The first quarter mile was easy, a walk down a gently sloping incline of weathered basalt. Owen Davies had watched us leave with an odd mixture of disdain and greed on his face. We were not going to find anything, he was quite sure of that—but on the other hand, if by some miracle we *did* and he was not there to see it . . .

We carried minimal packs. I thought it would be no more than a two-hour trek to our target point, and we had no intention of being away overnight.

When we came to the field of boulders I revised my estimate. Every square millimeter of surface was coated with the thinnest and most treacherous layer of clear ice. In principle its presence was impossible. With an atmosphere of this temperature and dryness, that ice should have sublimed away.

We picked our way carefully across, concentrating on balance far more than progress. The wind buffeted us, always at the worst moments. It took another hour and a half before we were at the bottom of the waterfalls and could see how to tackle the rock face. It didn't look too bad. There were enough cracks and ledges to make the climb fairly easy.

"That's the spot," said Martindale. "Right in there."

We followed his pointing finger. About seventy feet above our heads one of the bigger waterfalls came cascading its way out from the cliff for a thirty-foot vertical drop.

"The waterfall?" said Helga. Her tone of voice said more than her words. *That's supposed to be a generator of two hundred and fifty miles of gale-force winds?* she was saying. *Tell me another one.*

"Behind it." Martindale was walking along the base of the cliff, looking for a likely point where he could begin the climb. "The coordinates are actually *inside* the cliff. Which means we have to look *behind* the waterfall. And that means we have to come at it from the side."

We had brought rock-climbing gear with us. We did not need it. Martindale found a diagonal groove that ran at an angle of thirty degrees up the side of the cliff, and after following it to a vertical chimney, we found another slanting ledge running the other way. Two more changes of route, neither difficult, and we were on a ledge about two feet wide that ran up to and right behind our waterfall.

Two feet is a lot less when you are seventy feet up and walking a rock ledge slippery with water. Even here, the winds plucked restlessly at our clothes. We roped ourselves together, Martindale leading, and inched our way forward. When we were a few feet from the waterfall Martindale lengthened the rope between him and me, and went on alone behind the cascading water.

"It's all right." He had to shout to be heard above the crash of water. "It gets easier. The ledge gets wider. It runs into a cave in the face of the cliff. Come on."

We were carrying powerful electric flashlights, and we needed them. Once we were in behind the screen of water, the light paled and dwindled. We shone the lights toward the back of the cave. We were standing on a flat area, maybe ten feet wide and twelve feet deep. So much for Owen's dream of endless caverns of treasure; so much for my dreams, too, though they had been a lot less grandiose than his.

Standing about nine feet in from the edge of the ledge stood a dark blue cylinder, maybe four feet long and as thick as a man's thigh. It was smooth-surfaced and uniform, with no sign of controls or markings on its surface. I heard Martindale grunt in satisfaction.

"Bingo," he said. "That's it."

"The whole thing?"

"Certainly. Remember what I said last night, about advanced technology making this smaller? There's the source of the line-vortex—the power unit for the whole Kingdom of the Winds." He took two steps towards it, and as he did so Helga cried out, "Look out!"

The blank wall at the back of the cave had suddenly changed. Instead of damp grey stone, a rectangle of striated darkness had formed, maybe seven feet high and five feet wide.

Martindale laughed in triumph, and turned back to us. "Don't move for the moment. But don't worry, this is exactly what I hoped we might find. I suspected something like this when I first saw that anomaly. The winds are just an accidental by-product—like an eddy. The equipment here must be a little bit off in its tuning. But it's still working, no doubt about that. Feel the inertial dragging?"

I could feel something, a weak but persistent force drawing me toward the dark rectangle. I leaned backward to counteract it and looked more closely at the opening. As my eyes adjusted I realized that it was not true darkness there. Faint blue lines of luminescence started in from the edges of the aperture and flew rapidly toward a vanishing point at the center. There they disappeared, while new blue threads came into being at the outside.

"Where did the opening come from?" said Helga. "It wasn't there when we came in."

"No. It's a portal. I'm sure it only switches on when it senses the right object within range." Martindale took another couple of steps forward. Now he was standing at the very edge of the aperture, staring through at something invisible to me.

"What is it?" I said. In spite of Martindale's words I too had taken a couple of steps closer, and so had Helga.

"A portal—a gate to some other part of the Universe, built around a gravitational line singularity." He laughed, and his voice sounded half an octave lower in pitch. "Somebody left it here for us humans, and it leads to the stars. You wanted Trapalanda? This is it—the most priceless discovery in the history of the human race."

He took one more step forward. His moving leg stretched out forever in front of him, lengthening and lengthening. When his foot came down, the leg looked fifty yards long and it dwindled away to the tiny, distant speck of his foot. He lifted his back foot from the ground, and as he leaned forward his whole body rippled and distorted, stretching away from me. Now he looked his usual self—but he was a hundred yards away, carried with one stride along a tunnel that ran as far as the eye could follow.

Martindale turned, and reached out his hand. A long arm zoomed back towards us, still attached to that distant body, and a normal-sized right hand appeared out of the aperture.

"Come on." The voice was lower again in tone, and strangely slowed. "Both of you. Don't you want to see the rest of the Universe? Here's the best chance that you will ever have."

Helga and I took another step forward, staring in to the very edge of the opening. Martindale reached out his left hand too, and it hurtled toward us, growing rapidly, until it was there to be taken and held. I took another step, and I was within the portal itself. I felt normal, but I was aware of that force again, tugging us harder toward the tunnel. Suddenly I was gripped by an irrational and irresistible fear. I had to get away. I turned to move back from the aperture, and found myself looking at Helga. She was thirty yards away, drastically diminished, standing in front of a tiny wall of falling water.

One more step would have taken me outside again to safety, clear of the aperture and its persistent, tugging field. But as I was poised to take that step, Helga acted. She closed her eyes and took a long, trembling step forward. I could see her mouth moving, almost as though in prayer. And then the action I could not believe: she leaned forward to grasp convulsively at John Martindale's outstretched hand.

I heard her gasp, and saw her shiver. Then she was taking another step forward. And another.

"Helga!" I changed my direction and blundered after her along that endless tunnel. "This way. I'll get us out."

"No." She had taken another shivering step, and she was still clutching Martindale's hand. "No, Klaus." Her voice was breathless. "He's right. This is the biggest adventure ever. It's worth everything."

"Don't be afraid," said a hollow, booming voice. It was Martindale, and now all I could see of him was a shimmering silhouette. The man had been replaced by a sparkling outline. "Come on, Klaus. It's almost here."

The tugging force was stronger, pulling on every cell of my body. I looked at Helga, a shining outline now like John Martindale. They were dwindling, vanishing. They were gone. I wearily turned around and tried to walk back the way we had come. Tons of weight hung on me, wreathed themselves around every limb. I was trying to drag the whole world up an endless hill. I forced my legs to take one small step, then another. It was impossible to see if I was making progress. I was surrounded by that roaring silent pattern of rushing blue lines, all going in the opposite direction from me, every one doing its best to drag me back.

I inched along. Finally I could see the white of the waterfall ahead. It was growing in size, but at the same time it was losing definition. My eyes ached. By the time I took the final step and fell on my face on the stone floor of the cave, the waterfall was no more than a milky haze and a sound of rushing water.

Owen Davies saved my life, what there is of it. I did my part to help him. I wanted to live when I woke up, and weak as I was, and half-blind, I managed to crawl down that steep rock face. I was dragging myself over the icy boulders when he found me. My clothes were shredding, falling off my body, and I was shivering and weeping from cold and fear. He wrapped me in his own jacket and helped me back to the aircraft.

Then he went off to look for John Martindale and Helga. He never came back. I do not know to this day if he found and entered the portal, or if he came to grief somewhere on the way.

I spent two days in the aircraft, knowing that I was too sick and my eyes were too bad to dream of flying anywhere. My front teeth had all gone, and I ate porridge or biscuits soaked in tea. Three more days, and I began to realize that if I did not fly myself, I was not going anywhere. On the seventh day I managed a faltering, incompetent takeoff and flew northeast, peering at the instruments with my newly purblind eyes. I made a crash landing at Comodoro Rivadavia, was dragged from the wreckage, and flown to a hospital in Bahia Blanca. They did what they could for me, which was not too much. By that time I was beginning to have some faint idea what had happened to my body, and as soon as the hospital was willing to release me I took a flight to Buenos Aires, and on at once to Geneva's Lakeside Hospital. They removed the cataracts from my eyes. Three weeks later I could see again without that filmy mist over everything.

Before I left the hospital I insisted on a complete physical. Thanks to John Martindale's half-million deposit, money was not going to be a problem. The doctor who went over the results with me was about thirty years old, a Viennese Jew who had been practicing for only a couple of years. He looked oddly similar to one of my cousins at that age. "Well, Mr. Jacobi," he said (after a quick look at his dossier to make sure of my name), "there are no organic abnormalities, no cardiovascular problems, only slight circulation problems. You have some osteo-arthritis in your hips and your knees. I'm delighted to be able to tell you that you are in excellent overall health for your age."

"If you didn't know," I said, "how old would you think I am?"

He looked again at his crib sheet, but found no help there. I had deliberately left out my age at the place where the hospital entry form required it. "Well," he said. He was going to humor me. "Seventy-six?"

"Spot on," I said.

I had the feeling that he had knocked a couple of years off his estimate, just to make me feel good. So let's say my biological age was seventy-eight or seventy-nine. When I flew with John Martindale to Buenos Aires, I had been one month short of my forty-fourth birthday.

At that point I flew to New York, and went to John Kenyon Martindale's house. I met with Shirley—briefly. She did not recognize me, and I did not try to identify myself. I gave my name as Owen Davies. In John's absence, I said, I was interested in contacting some of the mathematician friends that he had told me I would like to meet. Could she remember the names of any of them, so I could call them even before John came back? She looked bored, but she came back with a telephone book and produced three names. One was in San Francisco, one was in Boston, and the third was here in New York, at the Courant Institute.

He was in his middle twenties, a fit-looking curly haired man with bright blue eyes and a big smile. The thing that astonished him about my visit, I think, was not the subject matter. It was the fact that I made the visit. He found it astonishing that a spavined antique like me would come to his office to ask about this sort of topic in theoretical physics.

"What you are suggesting is not just *permitted* in today's view of space and time, Mr. Davies," he said. "It's absolutely *required*. You can't do something to *space*—such as making an instantaneous link between two places, as you have been suggesting—without at the same time having profound effects on *time*. Space and time are really a single entity. Distances and elapsed times are intimately related, like two sides of the same coin."

"And the line-vortex generator?" I said. I had told him far less about this, mainly because all I knew of it had been told to us by John Martindale.

"Well, if the generator in some sense approximated an infinitely long, rapidly rotating cylinder, then yes. General relativity insists that very peculiar things would happen there. There could be global causality violations—'before' and 'after' getting confused, cause and effect becoming mixed up, that sort of thing. God knows what time and space look like near the line singularity itself. But don't misunderstand me. Before any of these things could happen, you would have to be dealing with a huge system, something many times as massive as the Sun."

I resisted the urge to tell him he was wrong. Apparently he did not accept John Martindale's unshakable confidence in the idea that with better technology came increase in capability *and* decrease in size. I stood up and leaned on my cane. My left hip was a little dodgy and became tired if I walked too far. "You've been very helpful."

"Not at all." He stood up, too, and said, "Actually, I'm going to be giving a lecture at the Institute on these subjects in a couple of weeks. If you'd like to come . . ."

I noted down the time and place, but I knew I would not be there. It was three months to the day since John Martindale, Helga, and I had climbed the rock face and walked behind the waterfall. Time—my time—was short. I had to head south again.

The flight to Argentina was uneventful. Comodoro Rivadavia was the same as always. Now I am sitting in Alberto McShane's bar, drinking one last beer (all that my digestion today will permit) and waiting for the pilot. McShane did not recognize me, but the armadillo did. It trundled to my table, and sat looking up at me. *Where's my friend John Martindale?* it was saying.

Where indeed? I will tell you soon. The plane is ready. We are going to Trapalanda.

It will take all my strength, but I think I can do it. I have added equipment that will help me to cross that icy field of boulders and ascend the rock face. It is September. The weather will be warmer, and the going easier. If I close my eyes I can see the portal now, behind the waterfall, its black depths and shimmering blue streaks rushing away toward the vanishing point.

Thirty-five years. That is what the portal owes me. It sucked them out of my body as I struggled back against the gravity gradient. Maybe it is impossible to get them back. I don't know. My young mathematician friend insisted that time is infinitely fluid, with no more constraints on movement through it than there are on travel through space. I don't know, but I want my thirty-five years. If I die in the attempt, I will be losing little.

I am terrified of that open gate, with its alien twisting of the world's geometry. I am more afraid of it than I have ever been of anything. Last time I failed, and I could not go through it. But I will go through it now.

This time I have something more than Martindale's scientific curiosity to drive me on. It is not thoughts of danger or death that fill my mind as I sit here. I have that final image of Helga, reaching out and taking John Martindale's hand in hers. Reaching out, to grasp his hand, voluntarily. I love Helga, I am sure of that, but I cannot make sense of my other emotions; fear, jealousy, resentment, hope, excitement. She was *touching* him. Did she do it because she wanted to go through the portal, wanted it so much that every fear was insignificant? Or had she, after thirty years, finally found someone whom she could touch without cringing and loathing?

The pilot has arrived. My glass is empty. Tomorrow I will know.

DISCOVERY

Patrick Ireland

Caught in the brilliant beam of Holloway's flashlight, the earthenware jar stood distinctly apart from the centuries-old litter of artifacts that crowded the stone shelf. The chamber smelled of ages passed in underground solitude, the last eyes to behold this scene having been dust for two dozen centuries.

Holloway, transfixed by the full impact of this notion, stood breathless, simply staring at the jar. It was about fourteen inches tall, somewhat wider than that at the middle, giving it the shape of a giant onion, and beautifully enameled with geometric patterns that drew the eye into it like a whirlpool. The sheet-lead seal was still intact. Fascinated by its beauty and antiquity, he extended a reverent hand to its curving surface. It was cool to the touch, its glassy smoothness recalling to his mind the brandy snifter he'd held two weeks earlier as Sabeth had listened to his explanation of the need for money.

"You know I do my best work alone, dear," he'd told her. "Besides, Dr. Wilson insists that expeditionary funding be used only to develop proven sites. With just a few thousand, I can solo on this one."

"But, Eric, why didn't you show him the map? If it was enough to convince you, surely—"

He'd waved his meerschaum impatiently. "If I'm ever to rise above Associate Professor, I need to earn credit for my own discoveries. As Department Head, Wilson could easily claim this find as his own. I've worked too hard to let that happen, Sabeth. That's why you've got to talk to your father. Convince him to lend me the money."

"He won't agree to that, Eric, and you know it. He's never been very fond of you." She'd seen the anger surge into his eyes. "I'm sorry, but it's true."

"But this would prove to him that I'm not the screwball he thinks! I'm certain this is a prime site. And he'll share the glory. So will you." But she had just sat there, shaking her head, refusing to meet his eyes.

Caressing the jar now, Holloway smiled. Now it would be different. Now they would all see, the fools. Absently, he adjusted the wire-rimmed spectacles on his aquiline nose and placed the flashlight under his arm to allow both hands to encircle the base of the ancient jar. Careful as a surgeon with a beating heart in his hand, he lifted the jar from the shelf and cradled it.

He realized he had been holding his breath, and exhaled with satisfaction. The flashlight slipped from beneath his arm and clattered to the stone floor, winking out and leaving Holloway in total darkness. He heard the flashlight rolling down the slope away from him and suddenly his pulse was hammering in his ears. Despite the coolness, a trickle of sweat coursed down his spine. He struggled to compose himself. He absolutely could not afford to panic. Blinking and squinting, he strove desperately to detect some measure of light. It was useless. There could be no random light in this chamber, deep beneath the surface of the desert.

Cautiously he sank to his knees and eased the jar to the floor. Backing away from it, he crawled along the sloping plane, blindly searching for the flashlight, praying it wasn't broken.

The sounds of his progress seemed unnaturally loud in the inky blackness. He swept both hands in wide arcs along the gritty stone floor, stirring the dust of ages. Though near the edge of hysteria, his mind persisted in worrying about the damage he was doing to the knees of his trousers.

His fumbling right hand brushed against something smooth, warm, tubular—the flashlight! He clutched it and flicked the switch back and forth. Damn, it was broken after all!

He took several deep breaths, striving to master the rising panic, willing himself to concentrate. Of course! He had a book of matches in his shirt pocket! With a sigh of relief, he congratulated himself for having clung to the habit of pipe-smoking even though Sabeth despised it and drew the matchbook from his pocket, opened it, and counted the matches. One, two —His breath caught. Two? Only two matches?

What could he do? He had to think. He had to overcome the urge to light either of the precious matches until he could settle on a plan. Feverishly, he searched his other pockets. His notebook! The pages would burn, of course. But for how long? Surely not long enough to light his way back out of this deathtrap. Drawing back his shirtsleeve, he consulted the luminous face of his wristwatch and calculated. It had taken him just under four hours to work his way in to this point—but that included wandering down many fruitless corridors and he'd marked the twistings and turnings with his grease pencil, so the return trip would be much quicker. With adequate light, call it forty minutes.

Without adequate light, he could forget it.

Think, damn it! What else might be found that would burn? He could recall having seen nothing combustible as he'd worked his way in. The ancients had carved this catacomb into solid rock and had needed no shoring timbers. What artifacts he'd found were all pottery or carven stone.

Forty minutes. The pages of his notebook wouldn't last five. He felt a crawling coldness and his thoughts drifted back to the moment when he'd realized that the money he needed for this expedition was right there under his nose. In the form of a Declaration of Power of Attorney.

It had been stupid of him not to have seen it sooner. Grandmother was becoming more senile every day—well taken care of in the rest home, but dependent on him to conduct her business and pay her bills with the little income she had: Social Security, retirement annuity, and a bit of interest on savings. She'd assigned him power of attorney a couple of years earlier so that he could endorse her checks and he had become so used to doing it that it hadn't occurred to him at first. Of course, he wouldn't touch the principal. After all, he only needed a few thousand. But how convenient that this dividend check had popped up just when he was at wit's end.

The teller at Grandmother's bank hadn't batted an eyelash when he'd presented the check—just counted out the forty-four hundred and change with a smile. And thanked him. Holloway had almost laughed at that. Almost. Anyway, he'd be repaying Grandmother's account soon enough. With a bounce in his step, he'd left the bank and taken the subway to a travel agency. Plane ticket (first class, of course), luggage, hotel reservations in Cairo, rental car, a few necessaries, and he was soon on his way to the realization of his ambition.

Several boring hours into the flight, his enthusiasm had begun to pall as the gravity of his act penetrated his conscience. But he'd smothered his misgivings by reminding himself of the fame he was sure to win and by the time he'd checked into the hotel his resolve was firmer than ever.

In the cool darkness beneath the desert floor, Holloway now was forced to reflect on his rashness in mounting a solo expedition with borrowed money. Borrowed—he sneered at himself. Why try to justify it now? The courts wouldn't call it borrowing, would they? The law would have no sympathy for a man who had embezzled from his aged grandmother, no matter how important the reason. Well, he needn't worry about the law now. He would suffer the consequences of his conceit right here, in this trap he'd unwittingly set for himself.

Slowly, bitterness rising in his throat, he made his way back to the earthenware jar he'd left on the floor of the chamber. His smug disregard for convention and propriety had led him here, alone. And here, it seemed, he would remain, his body perhaps ultimately to be discovered by one of the colleagues he had intended to humiliate.

He found the jar and caressed its smooth surface, wondering what might be inside. Though it hardly mattered now, he should at least open the seal and examine its contents. He owed it to himself to learn what he had made the ultimate sacrifice for.

Opening his pocket knife, he sliced into the thin lead sheet, carefully working the blade around the circumference of the jar's mouth. He discarded the circle of lead and gingerly felt inside the vessel. What was this? It seemed to be a sheaf of— His fingers stiffened. Papyrus! Dozens of sheets of papyrus! The paper of the ancient Egyptians, so difficult to manufacture that it was used only to record the most important information. Any student of Egyptology knew that the majority of written words were carved in sandstone tablets. Here must be something of unique significance.

Trembling now, Holloway ripped several pages from his notebook and crumpled them together, forming a small cone, which he ignited with one priceless match. The resulting yellow glare blinded him for a moment. Then, as his eyes adjusted to the dancing light of his makeshift torch, he eagerly pulled the ancient pages from the jar and scanned them. They were covered with orderly lines of beautiful hieroglyphs, rendered in various colors of ink. He strained to make sense of them. Translation could be difficult under the best of conditions, and his sense of urgency didn't help.

The flames guttered, threatening to go out, and Holloway rapidly tore a few more pages from his notebook, feeding them carefully into the diminishing blaze. After a few minutes of eye-straining study, he realized that these records bore evidence that would set the science of Egyptology on its ear. This amazing document was a trade agreement—the long-argued link between ancient Egypt and Atlantis. Far more than enough to validate his conclusions, it would make the finder immortal as the Sphinx! Or would have, were he not trapped here with it far beneath the surface of the earth. He fed the last few pages of his notebook into the fire and tried to read further, only to find his eyesight blurred by tears of frustration. Moments later, his little fire was no more than a few glowing embers winking beneath a curling thread of acrid smoke.

So, this was it, then. All his lofty aspirations had led him to this ancient chamber, where, with a monumental discovery in his hand, he must perish. Consumed with an agony of futility and grief, he wept.

* * *

After a time, Holloway's senses returned. It dawned on him that papyrus must certainly burn. And, of course, one match remained. He shuffled numbly through the thick sheaf of ancient pages. Yes, if he were careful enough and burned only one page at a time, there was probably enough fuel here to light his way to safety. But what awaited him back on the surface, with or without his discovery?

Holloway fingered the matchbook.

THE NEW CATACOMB

Arthur Conan Doyle

Look here, Burger," said Kennedy, "I do wish that you would confide in me."

The two famous students of Roman remains sat together in Kennedy's comfortable room overlooking the Corso. The night was cold, and they had both pulled up their chairs to the unsatisfactory Italian stove which threw out a zone of stuffiness rather than of warmth. Outside under the bright winter stars lay the modern Rome, the long, double chain of the electric lamps, the brilliantly lighted cafés, the rushing carriages, and the dense throng upon the footpaths. But inside, in the sumptuous chamber of the rich young English archaeologist, there was only old Rome to be seen. Cracked and timeworn friezes hung upon the walls, grey old busts of senators and soldiers with their fighting heads and their hard, cruel faces peered out from the corners. On the centre table, amidst a litter of inscriptions, fragments, and ornaments, there stood the famous reconstruction by Kennedy of the Baths of Caracalla, which excited such interest and admiration when it was exhibited in Berlin. Amphorae hung from the ceiling, and a litter of curiosities strewed the rich red Turkey carpet. And of them all there was not one which was not of the most unimpeachable authenticity, and of the utmost rarity and value; for Kennedy, though little more than thirty, had a European reputation in this particular branch of research, and was, moreover, provided with that long purse which either proves to be a fatal handicap to the student's energies, or, if his mind is still true to its purpose, gives him an enormous advantage in the race for fame. Kennedy had often been seduced by whim and pleasure from his studies, but his mind was an incisive one, capable of long and concentrated efforts which ended in sharp reactions of sensuous languor. His handsome face, with its high, white forehead, its aggressive nose, and its somewhat loose and sensual mouth, was a fair index of the compromise between strength and weakness in his nature.

Of a very different type was his companion, Julius Burger. He came of a curious blend, a German father and an Italian mother, with the robust qualities of the North mingling strangely with the softer graces of the South. Blue Teutonic eyes lightened his sun-browned face, and above them rose a square, massive forehead, with a fringe of close yellow curls lying round it. His strong, firm jaw was clean-shaven, and his companion had frequently remarked how much it suggested those old Roman busts which peered out from the shadows in the corners of his chamber. Under its bluff German strength there lay always a suggestion of Italian subtlety, but the smile was so honest, and the eyes so frank, that one understood that this was only an indication of his ancestry, with no actual bearing upon his character. In age and in reputation, he was on the same level as his English companion, but his life and his work had both been far more arduous. Twelve years before, he had come as a poor student to Rome, and had lived ever since upon some small endowment for research which had been awarded to him by the University of Bonn. Painfully, slowly, and doggedly, with extraordinary tenacity and single-mindedness, he had climbed from rung to rung of the ladder of fame, until now he was a member of the Berlin Academy, and there was every reason to believe that he would shortly be promoted to the Chair of the greatest of German Universities. But the singleness of purpose which had brought him to the same high level as the rich and brilliant Englishman, had caused him in everything outside their work to stand infinitely below him. He had never found a pause in his studies in which to cultivate the social graces. It was only when he spoke of his own subject that his face was filled with life and soul. At other times he was silent and embarrassed, too conscious of his own limitations in larger subjects, and impatient of that small talk which is the conventional refuge of those who have no thoughts to express.

And yet for some years there had been an acquaintanceship which appeared to be slowly ripening into a friendship between these two very different rivals. The base and origin of this lay in the fact that in their own studies each was the only one of the younger men who had knowledge and enthusiasm enough to properly appreciate the other. Their common interests and pursuits had brought them together, and each had been attracted by the other's knowledge. And then gradually something had been added to this. Kennedy had been amused by the frankness and simplicity of his rival, while Burger in turn had been fascinated by the brilliancy and vivacity which had made Kennedy such a favourite in Roman society. I say "had," because just at the moment the young Englishman was somewhat under a cloud. A love-affair, the details of which had never quite come out, had indicated a heartlessness and callousness upon his part which shocked many of his friends. But in the bachelor circles of students and artists in which he preferred to move there is no very rigid code of honour in such matters, and though a head might be shaken or a pair of shoulders shrugged over the flight of two and the return of one, the general sentiment was probably one of curiosity and perhaps of envy rather than of reprobation.

"Look here, Burger," said Kennedy, looking hard at the placid face of his companion, "I do wish that you would confide in me."

As he spoke he waved his hand in the direction of a rug which lay upon the floor. On the rug stood a long, shallow fruit-basket of the light wicker-work which is used in the Campagna, and this was heaped with a litter of objects, inscribed tiles, broken inscriptions, cracked mosaics, torn papyri, rusty metal ornaments, which to the uninitiated might have seemed to have come straight from a dustman's bin, but which a specialist would have speedily recognized as unique of their kind. The pile of odds and ends in the flat wicker-work basket supplied exactly one of those missing links of social development which are of such interest to the student. It was the German who had brought them in, and the Englishman's eyes were hungry as he looked at them.

"I won't interfere with your treasure-trove, but I should very much like to hear about it," he continued, while Burger very deliberately lit a cigar. "It is evidently a discovery of the first importance. These inscriptions will make a sensation throughout Europe."

"For every one here there are a million there!" said the German. "There are so many that a dozen savants might spend a lifetime over them, and build up a reputation as solid as the Castle of St. Angelo."

Kennedy sat thinking with his fine forehead wrinkled and his fingers playing with his long, fair moustache.

"You have given yourself away, Burger!" said he at last. "Your words can only apply to one thing. You have discovered a new catacomb."

"I had no doubt that you had already come to that conclusion from an examination of these objects."

"Well, they certainly appeared to indicate it, but your last remarks make it certain. There is no place except a catacomb which could contain so vast a store of relics as you describe."

"Quite so. There is no mystery about that. I *have* discovered a new catacomb."

"Where?"

"Ah, that is my secret, my dear Kennedy. Suffice it that it is so situated that there is not one chance in a million of anyone else coming upon it. Its date is different from that of any known catacomb, and it has been reserved for the burial of the highest Christians, so that the remains and the relics are quite different from anything which has ever been seen before. If I was not aware of your knowledge and of your energy, my friend, I would not hesitate, under the pledge of secrecy, to tell you everything about it. But as it is I think that I must certainly prepare my own report of the matter before I expose myself to such formidable competition."

Kennedy loved his subject with a love which was almost a mania—a love which held him true to it, amidst all the distractions which come to a wealthy and dissipated young man. He had ambition, but his ambition was secondary to his mere abstract joy and interest in everything which concerned the old life and history of the city. He yearned to see this new underworld which his companion had discovered.

"Look here, Burger," said he, earnestly, "I assure you that you can trust me most implicitly in the matter. Nothing would induce me to put pen to paper about anything which I see until I have your express permission. I quite understand your feeling and I think it is most natural, but you have really nothing whatever to fear from me. On the other hand, if you don't tell me I shall make a systematic search, and I shall most certainly discover it. In that case, of course, I should make what use I liked of it, since I should be under no obligation to you."

Burger smiled thoughtfully over his cigar.

"I have noticed, friend Kennedy," said he, "that when I want information over any point you are not always so ready to supply it."

"When did you ever ask me anything that I did not tell you? You remember, for example, my giving you the material for your paper about the temple of the Vestals."

"Ah, well, that was not a matter of much importance. If I were to question you upon some intimate thing would you give me an answer, I wonder! This new catacomb is a very intimate thing to me, and I should certainly expect some sign of confidence in return."

"What you are driving at I cannot imagine," said the Englishman, "but if you mean that you will answer my question about the catacomb if I answer any question which you may put to me I can assure you that I will certainly do so."

"Well, then," said Burger, leaning luxuriously back in his settee, and puffing a blue tree of cigar-smoke into the air, "tell me all about your relations with Miss Mary Saunderson."

Kennedy sprang up in his chair and glared angrily at his impassive companion.

"What the devil do you mean?" he cried. "What sort of a question is this? You may mean it as a joke, but you never made a worse one."

"No, I don't mean it as a joke," said Burger, simply. "I am really rather interested in the details of the matter. I don't know much about the world and women and social life and that sort of thing, and such an incident has the fascination of the unknown for me. I know you, and I knew her by sight

—I had even spoken to her once or twice. I should very much like to hear from your own lips exactly what it was which occurred between you."

"I won't tell you a word."

"That's all right. It was only my whim to see if you would give up a secret as easily as you expected me to give up my secret of the new catacomb. You wouldn't, and I didn't expect you to. But why should you expect otherwise of me? There's Saint John's clock striking ten. It is quite time that I was going home."

"No; wait a bit, Burger," said Kennedy; "this is really a ridiculous caprice of yours to wish to know about an old love-affair which has burned out months ago. You know we look upon a man who kisses and tells as the greatest coward and villain possible."

"Certainly," said the German, gathering up his basket of curiosities, "when he tells anything about a girl which is previously unknown he must be so. But in this case, as you must be aware, it was a public matter which was the common talk of Rome, so that you are not really doing Miss Mary Saunderson any injury by discussing her case with me. But still, I respect your scruples, and so good night!"

"Wait a bit, Burger," said Kennedy, laying his hand upon the other's arm; "I am very keen upon this catacomb business, and I can't let it drop quite so easily. Would you mind asking me something else in return—something not quite so eccentric this time?"

"No, no; you have refused, and there is an end of it," said Burger, with his basket on his arm. "No doubt you are quite right not to answer, and no doubt I am quite right also—and so again, my dear Kennedy, good night!"

The Englishman watched Burger cross the room, and he had his hand on the handle of the door before his host sprang up with the air of a man who is making the best of that which cannot be helped.

"Hold on, old fellow," said he; "I think you are behaving in a most ridiculous fashion; but still; if this is your condition, I suppose that I must submit to it. I hate saying anything about a girl, but, as you say, it is all over Rome, and I don't suppose I can tell you anything which you do not know already. What was it you wanted to know?"

The German came back to the stove, and, laying down his basket, he sank into his chair once more.

"May I have another cigar?" said he. "Thank you very much! I never smoke when I work, but I enjoy a chat much more when I am under the influence of tobacco. Now, as regards this young lady, with whom you had this little adventure. What in the world has become of her?"

"She is at home with her own people."

"Oh, really—in England?"

"Yes."

"What part of England—London?"

"No, Twickenham."

"You must excuse my curiosity, my dear Kennedy, and you must put it down to my ignorance of the world. No doubt it is quite a simple thing to persuade a young lady to go off with you for three weeks or so, and then to hand her over to her own family at—what did you call the place?"

"Twickenham."

"Quite so—at Twickenham. But it is something so entirely outside my own experience that I cannot even imagine how you set about it. For example, if you had loved this girl your love could hardly disappear in three weeks, so I presume that you could not have loved her at all. But if you did not love her why should you make this great scandal which has damaged you and ruined her?"

Kennedy looked moodily into the red eye of the stove.

"That's a logical way of looking at it, certainly," said he. "Love is a big word, and it represents a good many different shades of feeling. I liked her, and—well, you say you've seen her—you know how charming she could look. But still I am willing to admit, looking back, that I could never have really loved her."

"Then, my dear Kennedy, why did you do it?"

"The adventure of the thing had a great deal to do with it."

"What! You are so fond of adventures!"

"Where would the variety of life be without them? It was for an adventure that I first began to pay my attentions to her. I've chased a good deal of game in my time, but there's no chase like that of a pretty woman. There was the piquant difficulty of it also, for, as she was the companion of Lady Emily Rood, it was almost impossible to see her alone. On the top of all the other obstacles which attracted me, I learned from her own lips very early in the proceedings that she was engaged."

"Mein Gott! To whom?"

"She mentioned no names."

"I do not think that anyone knows that. So that made the adventure more alluring, did it?"

"Well, it did certainly give a spice to it. Don't you think so?"

"I tell you that I am very ignorant about these things."

"My dear fellow, you can remember that the apple you stole from your neighbour's tree was always sweeter than that which fell from your own. And then I found that she cared for me."

"What—at once?"

"Oh, no, it took about three months of sapping and mining. But at last I won her over. She understood that my judicial separation from my wife made it impossible for me to do the right thing by her—but she came all the same, and we had a delightful time, as long as it lasted."

"But how about the other man?"

Kennedy shrugged his shoulders.

"I suppose it is the survival of the fittest," said he. "If he had been the better man she would not have deserted him. Let's drop the subject, for I have had enough of it!"

"Only one other thing. How did you get rid of her in three weeks?"

"Well, we had both cooled down a bit, you understand. She absolutely refused, under any circumstances, to come back to face the people she had known in Rome. Now, of course, Rome is necessary to me, and I was already pining to be back at my work—so there was one obvious cause of separation. Then, again, her old father turned up at the hotel in London, and there was a scene, and the whole thing became so unpleasant that really —though I missed her dreadfully at first—I was very glad to slip out of it. Now, I rely upon you not to repeat anything of what I have said."

"My dear Kennedy, I should not dream of repeating it. But all that you say interests me very much, for it gives me an insight into your way of looking at things, which is entirely different from mine, for I have seen so little of life. And now you want to know about my new catacomb. There's no use my trying to describe it, for you would never find it by that. There is only one thing, and that is for me to take you there."

"That would be splendid."

"When would you like to come?"

"The sooner the better. I am all impatience to see it."

"Well, it is a beautiful night—though a trifle cold. Suppose we start in an hour. We must be very careful to keep the matter to ourselves. If anyone saw us hunting in couples they would suspect that there was something going on."

"We can't be too cautious," said Kennedy. "Is it far?"

"Some miles."

"Not too far to walk?"

"Oh, no, we could walk there easily."

"We had better do so, then. A cabman's suspicions would be aroused if he dropped us both at some lonely spot in the dead of the night."

"Quite so. I think it would be best for us to meet at the Gate of the Appian Way at midnight. I must go back to my lodgings for the matches and candles and things."

"All right, Burger! I think it is very kind of you to let me into this secret, and I promise you that I will write nothing about it until you have published your report. Good-bye for the present! You will find me at the Gate at twelve."

The cold, clear air was filled with the musical chimes from that city of clocks as Burger, wrapped in an Italian overcoat, with a lantern hanging from his hand, walked up to the rendezvous. Kennedy stepped out of the shadow to meet him.

"You are ardent in work as well as in love!" said the German, laughing.

"Yes; I have been waiting here for nearly half an hour."

"I hope you left no clue as to where we were going."

"Not such a fool! By Jove, I am chilled to the bone! Come on, Burger, let us warm ourselves by a spurt of hard walking."

Their footsteps sounded loud and crisp upon the rough stone paving of the disappointing road which is all that is left of the most famous highway of the world. A peasant or two going home from the wine-shop, and a few carts of country produce coming up to Rome, were the only things which they met. They swung along, with the huge tombs looming up through the darkness upon each side of them, until they had come as far as the Catacombs of St. Calistus, and saw against a rising moon the great circular bastion of Cecilia Metella in front of them. Then Burger stopped with his hand to his side.

"Your legs are longer than mine, and you are more accustomed to walking," said he, laughing. "I think that the place where we turn off is somewhere here. Yes, this is it, round the corner of the trattoria. Now, it is a very narrow path, so perhaps I had better go in front and you can follow."

He had lit his lantern, and by its light they were enabled to follow a narrow and devious track which wound across the marshes of the Campagna. The great Aqueduct of old Rome lay like a monstrous caterpillar across the moonlit landscape, and their road led them under one of its huge arches, and past the circle of crumbling bricks which marks the old arena. At last Burger stopped at a solitary wooden cow-house, and he drew a key from his pocket.

"Surely your catacomb is not inside a house!" cried Kennedy.

"The entrance to it is. That is just the safeguard which we have against anyone else discovering it."

"Does the proprietor know of it?"

"Not he. He had found one or two objects which made me almost certain that his house was built on the entrance to such a place. So I rented it from him, and did my excavations for myself. Come in, and shut the door behind you."

It was a long, empty building, with the mangers of the cows along one wall. Burger put his lantern down on the ground, and shaded its light in all directions save one by draping his overcoat round it.

"It might excite remark if anyone saw a light in this lonely place," said he. "Just help me to move this boarding."

The flooring was loose in the corner, and plank by plank the two savants raised it and leaned it against the wall. Below there was a square aperture and a stair of old stone steps which led away down into the bowels of the earth.

"Be careful!" cried Burger, as Kennedy, in his impatience, hurried down them. "It is a perfect rabbits'-warren below, and if you were once to lose your way there the chances would be a hundred to one against your ever coming out again. Wait until I bring the light."

"How do you find your own way if it is so complicated?"

"I had some very narrow escapes at first, but I have gradually learned to go about. There is a certain system to it, but it is one which a lost man, if he were in the dark, could not possibly find out. Even now I always spin out a ball of string behind me when I am going far into the catacomb. You can see for yourself that it is difficult, but every one of these passages divides and subdivides a dozen times before you go a hundred yards."

They had descended some twenty feet from the level of the byre, and they were standing now in a square chamber cut out of the soft tufa. The lantern cast a flickering light, bright below and dim above, over the cracked brown walls. In every direction were the black openings of passages which radiated from this common centre.

"I want you to follow me closely, my friend," said Burger. "Do not loiter to look at anything upon the way, for the place to which I will take you contains all that you can see, and more. It will save time for us to go there direct."

He led the way down one of the corridors, and the Englishman followed closely at his heels. Every now and then the passage bifurcated, but Burger was evidently following some secret marks of his own, for he neither stopped nor hesitated. Everywhere along the walls, packed like the berths upon an emigrant ship, lay the Christians of old Rome. The yellow light flickered over the shrivelled features of the mummies, and gleamed upon rounded skulls and long, white armbones crossed over fleshless chests. And everywhere as he passed Kennedy looked with wistful eyes upon inscriptions, funeral vessels, pictures, vestments, utensils, all lying as pious hands had placed them so many centuries ago. It was apparent to him, even in those hurried, passing glances, that this was the earliest and finest of the catacombs, containing such a storehouse of Roman remains as had never before come at one time under the observation of the student.

"What would happen if the light went out?" he asked, as they hurried onwards.

"I have a spare candle and a box of matches in my pocket. By the way, Kennedy, have you any matches?"

"No; you had better give me some."

"Oh, that is all right. There is no chance of our separating."

"How far are we going? It seems to me that we have walked at least a quarter of a mile."

"More than that, I think. There is really no limit to the tombs—at least, I have never been able to find any. This is a very difficult place, so I think that I will use our ball of string."

He fastened one end of it to a projecting stone and he carried the coil in the breast of his coat, paying it out as he advanced. Kennedy saw that it was no unnecessary precaution, for the passages had become more complex and tortuous than ever, with a perfect network of intersecting corridors. But these all ended in one large circular hall with a square pedestal of tufa topped with a slab of marble at one end of it.

"By Jove!" cried Kennedy in an ecstasy, as Burger swung his lantern over the marble. "It is a Christian altar—probably the first one in existence. Here is the little consecration cross cut upon the corner of it. No doubt this circular space was used as a church."

"Precisely," said Burger. "If I had more time I should like to show you all the bodies which are buried in these niches upon the walls, for they are the early popes and bishops of the Church, with their mitres, their croziers, and full canonicals. Go over to that one and look at it!"

Kennedy went across, and stared at the ghastly head which lay loosely on the shredded and mouldering mitre.

"This is most interesting," said he, and his voice seemed to boom against the concave vault. "As far as my experience goes, it is unique. Bring the lantern over, Burger, for I want to see them all."

But the German had strolled away, and was standing in the middle of a yellow circle of light at the other side of the hall.

"Do you know how many wrong turnings there are between this and the stairs?" he asked. "There are over two thousand. No doubt it was one of the means of protection which the Christians adopted. The odds are two thousand to one against a man getting out, even if he had a light; but if he were in the dark it would, of course, be far more difficult."

"So I should think."

"And the darkness is something dreadful. I tried it once for an experiment. Let us try it again!" He stooped to the lantern, and in an instant it was as if an invisible hand was squeezed tightly over each of Kennedy's eyes. Never had he known what such darkness was. It seemed to press upon him and to smother him. It was a solid obstacle against which the body shrank from advancing. He put his hands out to push it back from him.

"That will do, Burger," said he, "let's have the light again."

But his companion began to laugh, and in that circular room the sound seemed to come from every side at once.

"You seem uneasy, friend Kennedy," said he.

"Go on, man, light the candle!" said Kennedy impatiently.

"It's very strange, Kennedy, but I could not in the least tell by the sound in which direction you stand. Could you tell where I am?"

"No; you seem to be on every side of me."

"If it were not for this string which I hold in my hand I should not have a notion which way to go."

"I dare say not. Strike a light, man, and have an end of this nonsense."

"Well, Kennedy, there are two things which I understand that you are very fond of. The one is an adventure, and the other is an obstacle to surmount. The adventure must be the finding of your way out of this catacomb. The obstacle will be the darkness and the two thousand wrong turns which make the way a little difficult to find. But you need not hurry, for you have plenty of time, and when you halt for a rest now and then, I should like you just to think of Miss Mary Saunderson, and whether you treated her quite fairly."

"You devil, what do you mean?" roared Kennedy. He was running about in little circles and clasping at the solid blackness with both hands.

"Good-bye," said the mocking voice, and it was already at some distance. "I really do not think, Kennedy, even by your own showing that you did the right thing by that girl. There was only one little thing which you appeared not to know, and I can supply it. Miss Saunderson was engaged to a poor ungainly devil of a student, and his name was Julius Burger."

There was a rustle somewhere, the vague sound of a foot striking a stone, and then there fell silence upon that old Christian church—a stagnant, heavy silence which closed round Kennedy and shut him in like water round a drowning man.

Some two months afterwards the following paragraph made the round of the European Press:

"One of the most interesting discoveries of recent years is that of the new catacomb in Rome, which lies some distance to the east of the well-known vaults of St. Calixtus. The finding of this important burial-place, which is exceeding rich in most interesting early Christian remains, is due to the energy and sagacity of Dr. Julius Burger, the young German specialist, who is rapidly taking the first place as an authority upon ancient Rome. Although the first to publish his discovery, it appears that a less fortunate adventurer had anticipated Dr. Burger. Some months ago Mr. Kennedy, the well-known English student, disappeared suddenly from his rooms in the Corso, and it was conjectured that his association with a recent scandal had driven him to leave Rome. It appears now that he had in reality fallen a victim to that fervid love of archaeology which had raised him to a distinguished place among living scholars. His body was discovered in the heart of the new catacomb, and it was evident from the condition of his feet and boots that he had tramped for days through the tortuous corridors which make these subterranean tombs so dangerous to explorers. The deceased gentleman had, with inexplicable rashness, made his way into this labyrinth without, as far as can be discovered, taking with him either candles or matches, so that his sad fate was the natural result of his own temerity. What makes the matter more painful is that Dr. Julius Burger was an intimate friend of the deceased. His joy at the extraordinary find which he has been so fortunate as to make has been greatly marred by the terrible fate of his comrade and fellow-worker."

THE MAN WHO WOULD BE KING

Rudyard Kipling

*Brother to a Prince and fellow to a beggar
if he be found worthy.*

The Law, as quoted, lays down a fair conduct of life, and one not easy to follow. I have been fellow to a beggar again and again under circumstances which prevented either of us finding out whether the other was worthy. I have still to be brother to a Prince, though I once came near to kinship with what might have been a veritable King, and was promised the reversion of a Kingdom—army, law-courts, revenue, and policy all complete. But, to-day, I greatly fear that my King is dead, and if I want a crown I must go hunt it for myself.

The beginning of everything was in a railway train upon the road to Mhow from Ajmir. There had been a Deficit in the Budget, which necessitated travelling, not Second-class, which is only half as dear as First-class, but by Intermediate, which is very awful indeed. There are no cushions in the Intermediate class, and the population are either Intermediate, which is Eurasian, or Native, which for a long night journey is nasty, or Loafer, which is amusing though intoxicated. Intermediates do not buy from refreshment-rooms. They carry their food in bundles and pots, and buy sweets from the native sweetmeat-sellers, and drink the roadside water. That is why in the hot weather Intermediates are taken out of the carriages dead, and in all weathers are most properly looked down upon.

My particular Intermediate happened to be empty till I reached Nasirabad, when a big black-browed gentleman in shirt-sleeves entered, and, following the custom of Intermediates, passed the time of day. He was a wanderer and a vagabond like myself, but with an educated taste for whisky. He told tales of things he had seen and done, of out-of-the-way corners of the Empire into which he had penetrated, and of adventures in which he risked his life for a few days' food.

'If India was filled with men like you and me, not knowing more than the crows where they'd get their next day's rations, it isn't seventy millions of revenue the land would be paying—it's seven hundred millions,' said he; and as I looked at his mouth and chin I was disposed to agree with him.

We talked politics—the politics of Loaferdom, that sees things from the underside where the lath and plaster is not smoothed off—and we talked postal arrangements because my friend wanted to send a telegram back from the next station to Ajmir, the turning-off place from the Bombay to the Mhow line as you travel westward. My friend had no money beyond eight annas, which he wanted for dinner, and I had no money at all, owing to the hitch in the Budget before mentioned. Further, I was going into a wilderness where, though I should resume touch with the Treasury, there were no telegraph offices. I was, therefore, unable to help him in any way.

'We might threaten a Station-master, and make him send a wire on tick,' said my friend, 'but that'd mean inquiries for you and for me, and I've got my hands full these days. Did you say you are travelling back along this line within any days?'

'Within ten,' I said.

'Can't you make it eight?' said he. 'Mine is rather urgent business.'

'I can send your telegram within ten days if that will serve you,' I said.

'I couldn't trust the wire to fetch him, now I think of it. It's this way. He leaves Delhi on the 23rd for Bombay. That means he'll be running through Ajmir about the night of the 23rd.'

'But I'm going into the Indian Desert,' I explained.

'Well *and* good,' said he. 'You'll be changing at Marwar Junction to get into Jodhpore territory—you must do that—and he'll be coming through Marwar Junction in the early morning of the 24th by the Bombay Mail. Can you be at Marwar Junction on that time? 'Twon't be inconveniencing you because I know that there's precious few pickings to be got out of these Central India States—even though you pretend to be correspondent of the *Backwoodsman.*'

'Have you ever tried that trick?' I asked.

'Again and again, but the Residents find you out, and then you get escorted to the border before you've time to get your knife into them. But about my friend here. I *must* give him a word o' mouth to tell him what's come to me or else he won't know where to go. I would take it more than kind of you if you was to come out of Central India in time to catch him at Marwar Junction, and say to him: "He has gone South for the week." He'll know what that means. He's a big man with a red beard, and a great swell he is. You'll find him sleeping like a gentleman with all his luggage round him in a second-class compartment. But don't you be afraid. Slip down the window, and say: "He has gone South for the week," and he'll tumble. It's only cutting your time of stay in those parts by two days. I ask you as a stranger—going to the West,' he said with emphasis.

'Where have *you* come from?' said I.

'From the East,' said he, 'and I am hoping that you will give him the message on the Square—for the sake of my Mother as well as your own.'

Englishmen are not usually softened by appeals to the memory of their mothers, but for certain reasons, which will be fully apparent, I saw fit to agree.

'It's more than a little matter,' said he, 'and that's why I asked you to do it—and now I know that I can depend on you doing it. A second-class carriage at Marwar Junction, and a red-haired man asleep in it. You'll be sure to remember. I get out at the next station, and I must hold on there till he comes or sends me what I want.'

'I'll give the message if I catch him,' I said, 'and for the sake of your Mother as well as mine I'll give you a word of advice. Don't try to run the Central India States just now as the correspondent of the *Backwoodsman*. There's a real one knocking about there, and it might lead to trouble.'

'Thank you,' said he simply, 'and when will the swine be gone? I can't starve because he's ruining my work. I wanted to get hold of the Degumber Rajah down here about his father's widow, and give him a jump.'

'What did he do to his father's widow, then?'

'Filled her up with red pepper and slippered her to death as she hung from a beam. I found that out myself, and I'm the only man that would dare going into the State to get hush-money for it. They'll try to poison me, same as they did in Chortumna when I went on the loot there. But you'll give the man at Marwar Junction my message?'

He got out at a little roadside station, and I reflected. I had heard, more than once, of men personating correspondents of newspapers and bleeding small Native States with threats of exposure, but I had never met any of the caste before. They lead a hard life, and generally die with great suddenness. The Native States have a wholesome horror of English newspapers which may throw light on their peculiar methods of government, and do their best to choke correspondents with champagne, or drive them out of their mind with four-in-hand barouches. They do not understand that nobody cares a straw for the internal administration of Native States so long as oppression and crime are kept within decent limits, and the ruler is not drugged, drunk, or diseased from one end of the year to the other. They are the dark places of the earth, full of unimaginable cruelty, touching the Railway and the Telegraph on one side, and, on the other, the days of Harun-al-Raschid. When I left the train I did business with divers Kings, and in eight days passed through many changes of life. Sometimes I wore dress-clothes and consorted with Princes and Politicals, drinking from crystal and eating from silver. Sometimes I lay out upon the ground and devoured what I could get, from a plate made of leaves, and drank the running water, and slept under the same rug as my servant. It was all in the day's work.

Then I headed for the Great Indian Desert upon the proper date, as I had promised, and the night mail set me down at Marwar Junction, where a funny, little, happy-go-lucky, native-managed railway runs to Jodhpore. The Bombay Mail from Delhi makes a short halt at Marwar. She arrived as I got in, and I had just time to hurry to her platform and go down the carriages. There was only one second-class on the train. I slipped the window and looked down upon a flaming red beard, half covered by a railway rug. That was my man, fast asleep, and I dug him gently in the ribs. He woke with a grunt, and I saw his face in the light of the lamps. It was a great and shining face.

'Tickets again?' said he.

'No,' said I. 'I am to tell you that he has gone South for the week. He has gone South for the week!'

The train had begun to move out. The red man rubbed his eyes. 'He has gone South for the week,' he repeated. 'Now that's just like his impidence. Did he say that I was to give you anything? Cause I won't.'

'He didn't,' I said, and dropped away, and watched the red lights die out in the dark. It was horribly cold because the wind was blowing off the sands. I climbed into my own train—not an Intermediate carriage this time —and went to sleep.

If the man with the beard had given me a rupee I should have kept it as a memento of a rather curious affair. But the consciousness of having done my duty was my only reward.

Later on I reflected that two gentlemen like my friends could not do any good if they forgathered and personated correspondents of newspapers, and might, if they blackmailed one of the little rat-trap states of Central India or Southern Rajputana, get themselves into serious difficulties. I therefore took some trouble to describe them as accurately as I could remember to people who would be interested in deporting them; and succeeded, so I was later informed, in having them headed back from the Degumber borders.

Then I became respectable, and returned to an office where there were no Kings and no incidents outside the daily manufacture of a newspaper. A newspaper office seems to attract every conceivable sort of person, to the prejudice of discipline. Zenana-mission ladies arrive, and beg that the Editor will instantly abandon all his duties to describe a Christian prize-giving in a back-slum of a perfectly inaccessible village; Colonels who have been overpassed for command sit down and sketch the outline of a series of ten, twelve, or twenty-four leading articles on Seniority *versus* Selection; Missionaries wish to know why they have not been permitted to escape from their regular vehicles of abuse and swear at a brother-missionary under special patronage of the editorial We; stranded theatrical companies troop up to explain that they cannot pay for their advertisements, but on their return from New Zealand or Tahiti will do so with interest; inventors of patent punkah-pulling machines, carriage couplings, and unbreakable swords and axle-trees, call with specifications in their pockets and hours at their disposal; tea-companies enter and elaborate their prospectuses with the office pens; secretaries of ball-committees clamour to have the glories of their last dance more fully described; strange ladies rustle in and say, 'I want a hundred lady's cards printed *at once,* please,' which is manifestly part of an Editor's duty; and every dissolute ruffian that ever tramped the Grand Trunk Road makes it his business to ask for employment as a proof-reader. And, all the time, the telephone-bell is ringing madly, and Kings are being killed on the Continent, and Empires are saying, 'You're another,' and Mister Gladstone is calling down brimstone upon the British Dominions and the little black copy-boys are whining, *'kaa-pi chay-ha-yeh'* [copy wanted] like tired bees, and most of the paper is as blank as Modred's shield.

But that is the amusing part of the year. There are six other months when none ever comes to call, and the thermometer walks inch by inch up to the top of the glass, and the office is darkened to just above reading-light, and the press-machines are red-hot of touch, and nobody writes anything but accounts of amusements in the Hill-stations or obituary notices. Then the telephone becomes a tinkling terror, because it tells you of the sudden deaths of men and women that you knew intimately, and the prickly-heat covers you with a garment, and you sit down and write: 'A slight increase of sickness is reported from the Khuda Janta Khan District. The outbreak is purely sporadic in its nature, and, thanks to the energetic efforts of the District authorities, is now almost at an end. It is, however, with deep regret we record the death, etc.'

Then the sickness really breaks out, and the less recording and reporting the better for the peace of the subscribers. But the Empires and the Kings continue to divert themselves as selfishly as before, and the Foreman thinks that a daily paper really ought to come out once in twenty-four hours, and all the people at the Hill-stations in the middle of their amusements say: 'Good gracious! Why can't the paper be sparkling? I'm sure there's plenty going on up here.'

That is the dark half of the moon, and, as the advertisements say, 'must be experienced to be appreciated'.

It was in that season, and a remarkably evil season, that the paper began running the last issue of the week on Saturday night, which is to say Sunday morning, after the custom of a London paper. This was a great convenience, for immediately after the paper was put to bed, the dawn would lower the temperature from 96° to almost 84° for half an hour, and in that chill—you have no idea how cold is 84° on the grass until you begin to pray for it—a very tired man could get off to sleep ere the heat roused him.

One Saturday night it was my pleasant duty to put the paper to bed alone. A King or a courtier or courtesan or a Community was going to die or get a new Constitution, or do something that was important on the other side of the world, and the paper was to be held open till the latest possible minute in order to catch the telegram.

It was a pitchy black night, as stifling as a June night can be, and the *loo*, the red-hot wind from the westward, was booming among the tinder-dry trees and pretending that the rain was on its heels. Now and again a spot of almost boiling water would fall on the dust with the flop of a frog, but all our weary world knew that was only pretence. It was a shade cooler in the press-room than the office, so I sat there, while the type ticked and clicked, and the night-jars hooted at the windows, and the all but naked compositors wiped the sweat from their foreheads, and called for water. The thing that was keeping us back, whatever it was, would not come off, though the *loo* dropped and the last type was set, and the whole round earth stood still in the choking heat, with its finger on its lip, to wait the event. I drowsed, and wondered whether the telegraph was a blessing, and whether this dying man, or struggling people, might be aware of the inconvenience the delay was causing. There was no special reason beyond the heat and worry to make tension, but, as the clock-hands crept up to three o'clock, and the machines spun their fly-wheels two or three times to see that all was in order before I said the word that would set them off, I could have shrieked aloud.

Then the roar and rattle of the wheels shivered the quiet into little bits. I rose to go away, but two men in white clothes stood in front of me. The first one said: 'It's him!' The second said: 'So it is!' And they both laughed almost as loudly as the machinery roared, and mopped their foreheads. 'We seed there was a light burning across the road, and we were sleeping in that ditch there for coolness, and I said to my friend here, "The office is open. Let's come along and speak to him as turned us back from the Degumber State," ' said the smaller of the two. He was the man I had met in the Mhow train, and his fellow was the red-haired man of Marwar Junction. There was no mistaking the eyebrows of the one or the beard of the other.

I was not pleased, because I wished to go to sleep, not to squabble with loafers. 'What do you want?' I asked.

'Half an hour's talk with you, cool and comfortable, in the office,' said the red-bearded man. 'We'd *like* some drink—the Contrack doesn't begin yet, Peachey, so you needn't look—but what we really want is advice. We don't want money. We ask you as a favour, because we found out you did us a bad turn about Degumber State.'

I led from the press-room to the stifling office with the maps on the walls, and the red-haired man rubbed his hands. 'That's something like,' said he. 'This was the proper shop to come to. Now, sir, let me introduce to you Brother Peachey Carnehan, that's him, and Brother Daniel Dravot, that is *me*, and the less said about our professions the better, for we have been most things in our time. Soldier, sailor, compositor, photographer, proof-reader, street-preacher, *and* correspondent of the *Backwoodsman* when we thought the paper wanted one. Carnehan is sober, and so am I. Look at us first, and see that's sure. It will save you cutting into my talk. We'll take one of your cigars apiece, and you shall see us light up.'

I watched the test. The men were absolutely sober, so I gave them each a tepid whisky and soda.

'Well *and* good,' said Carnehan of the eyebrows, wiping the froth from his moustache. 'Let *me* talk now, Dan. We have been all over India, mostly on foot. We have been boiler-fitters, engine-drivers, petty contractors, and all that, and we have decided that India isn't big enough for such as us.'

They certainly were too big for the office. Dravot's beard seemed to fill half the room and Carnehan's shoulders the other half, as they sat on the big table. Carnehan continued: 'The country isn't half worked out because they that governs it won't let you touch it. They spend all their blessed time in governing it, and you can't lift a spade, nor chip a rock, nor look for oil, nor anything like that, without all the Government saying, "Leave it alone, and let us govern." Therefore, such *as* it is, we will let it alone, and go away to some other place where a man isn't crowded and can come to his own. We are not little men, and there is nothing that we are afraid of except Drink, and we have signed a Contrack on that. *Therefore*, we are going away to be Kings.'

'Kings in our own right,' muttered Dravot.

'Yes, of course,' I said. 'You've been tramping in the sun, and it's a very warm night, and hadn't you better sleep over the notion? Come to-morrow.'

'Neither drunk nor sunstruck,' said Dravot. 'We have slept over the notion half a year, and require to see Books and Atlases, and we have decided that there is only one place now in the world that two strong men can Sar-a-*whack*. They call it Kafiristan. By my reckoning it's the top right-hand corner of Afghanistan, not more than three hundred miles from Peshawur. They have two-and-thirty heathen idols there, and we'll be the thirty-third and fourth. It's a mountainous country, and the women of those parts are very beautiful.'

'But that is provided against in the Contrack,' said Carnehan. 'Neither Woman nor Liqu-or, Daniel.'

'And that's all we know, except that no one has gone there, and they fight; and in any place where they fight, a man who knows how to drill men can always be a King. We shall go to those parts and say to any King we find —"D'you want to vanquish your foes?" and we will show him how to drill men; for that we know better than anything else. Then we will subvert that King and seize his Throne and establish a Dy-nasty.'

'You'll be cut to pieces before you're fifty miles across the Border,' I said. 'You have to travel through Afghanistan to get to that country. It's one mass of mountains and peaks and glaciers, and no Englishman has been through it. The people are utter brutes, and even if you reached them you couldn't do anything.'

'That's more like,' said Carnehan. 'If you could think us a little more mad we would be more pleased. We have come to you to know about this country, to read a book about it, and to be shown maps. We want you to tell us that we are fools and to show us your books.' He turned to the bookcases.

'Are you at all in earnest?' I said.

'A little,' said Dravot sweetly. 'As big a map as you have got, even if it's all blank where Kafiristan is, and any books you've got. We can read, though we aren't very educated.'

I uncased the big thirty-two-miles-to-the-inch map of India, and two smaller Frontier maps, hauled down volume INF-KAN of the *Encyclopaedia Britannica,* and the men consulted them.

'See here!' said Dravot, his thumb on the map. 'Up to Jagdallak, Peachey and me know the road. We was there with Roberts' Army. We'll have to turn off to the right at Jagdallak through Laghman territory. Then we get among the hills—fourteen thousand feet—fifteen thousand—it will be cold work there, but it don't look very far on the map.'

I handed him Wood on the *Sources of the Oxus.* Carnehan was deep in the *Encyclopaedia.*

'They're a mixed lot,' said Dravot reflectively; 'and it won't help us to know the names of their tribes. The more tribes the more they'll fight, and the better for us. From Jagdallak to Ashang—H'mm!'

'But all the information about the country is as sketchy and inaccurate as can be,' I protested. 'No one knows anything about it really. Here's the file of the *United Services' Institute.* Read what Bellew says.'

'Blow Bellew!' said Carnehan. 'Dan, they're a stinkin' lot of heathens, but this book here says they think they're related to us English.'

I smoked while the men pored over Raverty, Wood, the maps, and the *Encyclopaedia*.

'There is no use your waiting,' said Dravot politely. 'It's about four o'clock now. We'll go before six o'clock if you want to sleep, and we won't steal any of the papers. Don't you sit up. We're two harmless lunatics, and if you come tomorrow evening down to the Serai we'll say goodbye to you.'

'You *are* two fools,' I answered. 'You'll be turned back at the Frontier or cut up the minute you set foot in Afghanistan. Do you want any money or a recommendation down-country? I can help you to the chance of work next week.'

'Next week we shall be hard at work ourselves, thank you,' said Dravot. 'It isn't so easy being a King as it looks. When we've got our Kingdom in going order we'll let you know, and you can come up and help us to govern it.'

'Would two lunatics make a Contrack like that?' said Carnehan, with subdued pride, showing me a greasy half-sheet of notepaper on which was written the following. I copied it, then and there, as a curiosity:—

This Contract between me and you persuing witnesseth in the name of God— Amen and so forth.

    (One) That me and you will settle this matter together; i.e. to be Kings of Kafiristan.

    (Two) That you and me will not, while this matter is being settled, look at any Liquor, nor any Woman black, white, or brown, so as to get mixed up with one or the other harmful.

    (Three) That we conduct ourselves with Dignity and Discretion, and if one of us gets into trouble the other will stay by him.

Signed by you and me this day.

                    Peachey Taliaferro Carnehan.
                    Daniel Dravot.
                    Both Gentlemen at Large.

'There was no need for the last article,' said Carnehan, blushing modestly; 'but it looks regular. Now you know the sort of men that loafers are— we *are* loafers, Dan, until we get out of India—and *do* you think that we would sign a Contrack like that unless we was in earnest? We have kept away from the two things that make life worth having.'

'You won't enjoy your lives much longer if you are going to try this idiotic adventure. Don't set the office on fire,' I said, 'and go away before nine o'clock.'

I left them still poring over the maps and making notes on the back of the 'Contrack'. 'Be sure to come down to the Serai to-morrow,' were their parting words.

The Kumharsen Serai is the great four-square sink of humanity where the strings of camels and horses from the North load and unload. All the nationalities of Central Asia may be found there, and most of the folk of India proper. Balkh and Bokhara there meet Bengal and Bombay, and try to draw eye-teeth. You can buy ponies, turquoises, Persian pussy-cats, saddle-bags, fat-tailed sheep and musk in the Kumharsen Serai, and get many strange things for nothing. In the afternoon I went down to see whether my friends intended to keep their word or were lying there drunk.

A priest attired in fragments of ribbons and rags stalked up to me, gravely twirling a child's paper whirligig. Behind him was his servant bending under the load of a crate of mud toys. The two were loading up two camels, and the inhabitants of the Serai watched them with shrieks of laughter.

'The priest is mad,' said a horse-dealer to me. 'He is going up to Kabul to sell toys to the Amir. He will either be raised to honour or have his head cut off. He came in here this morning and has been behaving madly ever since.'

'The witless are under the protection of God,' stammered a flat-cheeked Uzbeg in broken Hindi. 'They foretell future events.'

'Would they could have foretold that my caravan would have been cut up by the Shinwaris almost within shadow of the Pass!' grunted the Yusufzai agent of a Rajputana trading-house whose goods had been diverted into the hands of other robbers just across the Border, and whose misfortunes were the laughing-stock of the bazar. 'Ohé, priest, whence come you and whither do you go?'

'From Roum have I come,' shouted the priest, waving his whirligig; 'from Roum, blown by the breath of a hundred devils across the sea! O thieves, robbers, liars, the blessing of Pir Khan on pigs, dogs, and perjurers! Who will take the Protected of God to the North to sell charms that are never still to the Amir? The camels shall not gall, the sons shall not fall sick, and the wives shall remain faithful while they are away, of the men who give me place in their caravan. Who will assist me to slipper the King of the Roos with a golden slipper with a silver heel? The protection of Pir Khan be upon his labours!' He spread out the skirts of his gaberdine and pirouetted between the lines of tethered horses.

'There starts a caravan from Peshawur to Kabul in twenty days, *Huzrut,*' said the Yusufzai trader. 'My camels go therewith. Do thou also go and bring us good luck.'

'I will go even now!' shouted the priest. 'I will depart upon my winged camels, and be at Peshawur in a day! Ho! Hazar Mir Khan,' he yelled to his servant, 'drive out the camels, but let me first mount my own.'

He leaped on the back of his beast as it knelt, and, turning to me, cried: 'Come thou also, Sahib, a little along the road, and I will sell thee a charm —an amulet that shall make thee King of Kafiristan.'

Then the light broke upon me, and I followed the two camels out of the Serai till we reached open road and the priest halted.

'What d'you think o' that?' said he in English. 'Carnehan can't talk their patter, so I've made him my servant. He makes a handsome servant. 'Tisn't for nothing that I've been knocking about the country for fourteen years. Didn't I do that talk neat? We'll hitch onto a caravan at Peshawur till we get to Jagdallak, and then we'll see if we can get donkeys for our camels, and strike into Kafiristan. Whirligigs for the Amir, oh, Lor! Put your hand under the camel-bags and tell me what you feel.'

I felt the butt of a Martini, and another and another.

'Twenty of 'em,' said Dravot placidly. 'Twenty of 'em and ammunition to correspond, under the whirligigs and the mud dolls.'

'Heaven help you if you are caught with those things!' I said. 'A Martini is worth her weight in silver among the Pathans.'

'Fifteen hundred rupees of capital—every rupee we could beg, borrow, or steal—are invested on these two camels,' said Dravot. 'We won't get caught. We're going through the Khyber with a regular caravan. Who'd touch a poor mad priest?'

'Have you got everything you want?' I asked, overcome with astonishment.

'Not yet, but we shall soon. Give us a memento of your kindness, *Brother*. You did me a service, yesterday, and that time in Marwar. Half my Kingdom shall you have, as the saying is.' I slipped a small charm compass from my watch-chain and handed it up to the priest.

'Good-bye,' said Dravot, giving me hand cautiously. 'It's the last time we'll shake hands with an Englishman these many days. Shake hands with him, Carnehan,' he cried, as the second camel passed me.

Carnehan leaned down and shook hands. Then the camels passed away along the dusty road, and I was left alone to wonder. My eye could detect no failure in the disguises. The scene in the Serai proved that they were complete to the native mind. There was just the chance, therefore, that Carnehan and Dravot would be able to wander through Afghanistan without detection. But, beyond, they would find death—certain and awful death.

Ten days later a native correspondent, giving me the news of the day from Peshawur, wound up his letter with: 'There has been much laughter here on account of a certain mad priest who is going in his estimation to sell petty gauds and insignificant trinkets which he ascribes as great charms to H.H. the Amir of Bokhara. He passed through Peshawur and associated himself to the Second Summer caravan that goes to Kabul. The merchants are pleased because through superstition they imagine that such mad fellows bring good fortune.'

The two, then, were beyond the Border. I would have prayed for them, but, that night, a real King died in Europe, and demanded an obituary notice.

The wheel of the world swings through the same phases again and again. Summer passed and winter thereafter, and came and passed again. The daily paper continued and I with it, and upon the third summer there fell a hot night, a night-issue, and a strained waiting for something to be telegraphed from the other side of the world, exactly as had happened before. A few great men had died in the past two years, the machines worked with more clatter, and some of the trees in the office garden were a few feet taller. But that was all the difference.

I passed over to the press-room, and went through just such a scene as I have already described. The nervous tension was stronger than it had been two years before, and I felt the heat more acutely. At three o'clock I cried, 'Print off,' and turned to go, when there crept to my chair what was left of a man. He was bent into a circle, his head was sunk between his shoulders, and he moved his feet one over the other like a bear. I could hardly see whether he walked or crawled—this rag-wrapped, whining cripple who addressed me by name, crying that he was come back. 'Can you give me a drink?' he whimpered. 'For the Lord's sake, give me a drink!'

I went back to the office, the man following with groans of pain, and I turned up the lamp.

'Don't you know me?' he gasped, dropping into a chair, and he turned his drawn face, surmounted by a shock of grey hair, to the light.

I looked at him intently. Once before had I seen eyebrows that met over the nose in an inch-broad black band, but for the life of me I could not recall where.

'I don't know you,' I said, handing him the whisky. 'What can I do for you?'

He took a gulp of the spirit raw, and shivered in spite of the suffocating heat.

'I've come back,' he repeated; 'and I was the King of Kafiristan—me and Dravot—crowned Kings we was! In this office we settled it—you setting there and giving us the books. I am Peachey—Peachey Taliaferro Carnehan, and you've been setting here ever since—oh, Lord!'

I was more than a little astonished, and expressed my feelings accordingly.

'It's true,' said Carnehan, with a dry cackle, nursing his feet, which were wrapped in rags. 'True as gospel. Kings we were, with crowns upon our heads—me and Dravot—poor Dan—oh, poor, poor Dan, that would never take advice, not though I begged of him!'

'Take the whisky,' I said, 'and take your own time. Tell me all you can recollect of everything from beginning to end. You got across the Border on your camels, Dravot dressed as a mad priest and you his servant. Do you remember that?'

'I ain't mad—yet, but I shall be that way soon. Of course I remember. Keep looking at me, or maybe my words will go all to pieces. Keep looking at me in my eyes and don't say anything.'

I leaned forward and looked into his face as steadily as I could. He dropped one hand upon the table and I grasped it by the wrist. It was twisted like a bird's claw, and upon the back was a ragged red diamond-shaped scar.

'No, don't look there. Look at *me*,' said Carnehan. 'That comes afterwards, but for the Lord's sake don't distrack me. We left with that caravan, me and Dravot playing all sorts of antics to amuse the people we were with. Dravot used to make us laugh in the evenings when all the people was cooking their dinners—cooking their dinners, and . . . what did they do then? They lit little fires with sparks that went into Dravot's beard, and we all laughed—fit to die. Little red fires they was, going into Dravot's big red beard—so funny.' His eyes left mine and he smiled foolishly.

'You went as far as Jagdallak with that caravan,' I said at a venture, 'after you had lit those fires. To Jagdallak where you turned off to try to get into Kafiristan.'

'No, we didn't neither. What are you talking about? We turned off before Jagdallak, because we heard the roads was good. But they wasn't good enough for our two camels—mine and Dravot's. When we left the caravan, Dravot took off all his clothes and mine too, and said we would be heathen, because the Kafirs didn't allow Mohammedans to talk to them. So we dressed betwixt and between, and such a sight as Daniel Dravot I never saw yet nor expect to see again. He burned half his beard, and slung a sheepskin over his shoulder, and shaved his head into patterns. He shaved mine, too, and made me wear outrageous things to look like a heathen. That was in a most mountainous country, and our camels couldn't go along any more because of the mountains. They were tall and black, and coming home I saw them fight like wild goats—there are lots of goats in Kafiristan. And these mountains, they never keep still, no more than the goats. Always fighting they are, and don't let you sleep at night.'

'Take some more whisky,' I said very slowly. 'What did you and Daniel Dravot do when the camels could go no farther because of the rough roads that led into Kafiristan?'

'What did which do? There was a party called Peachey Taliaferro Carnehan that was with Dravot. Shall I tell you about him? He died out there in the cold. Slap from the bridge fell old Peachey, turning and twisting in the air like a penny whirligig that you can sell to the Amir.—No; they was two for three-ha'pence, those whirligigs, or I am much mistaken and woeful sore. . . . And then these camels were no use, and Peachey said to Dravot—"For the Lord's sake let's get out of this before our heads are chopped off," and with that they killed the camels all among the mountains, not having anything in particular to eat, but first they took off the boxes with the guns and the ammunition, till two men came along driving four mules. Dravot up and dances in front of them, singing: "Sell me four mules." Says the first man: "If you are rich enough to buy, you are rich enough to rob"; but before ever he could put his hand to his knife, Dravot breaks his neck over his knee, and the other party runs away. So Carnehan loaded the mules with the rifles that was taken off the camels, and together we starts forward into those bitter cold mountaineous parts, and never a road broader than the back of your hand.'

He paused for a moment, while I asked him if he could remember the nature of the country through which he had journeyed.

'I am telling you as straight as I can, but my head isn't as good as it might be. They drove nails through it to make me hear better how Dravot died. The country was mountaineous, and the mules were most contrary, and the inhabitants was dispersed and solitary. They went up and up, and down and down, and that other party, Carnehan, was imploring of Dravot not to sing and whistle so loud, for fear of bringing down the tremenjus avalanches. But Dravot says that if a King couldn't sing it wasn't worth being King, and whacked the mules over the rump, and never took no heed for ten cold days. We came to a big level valley all among the mountains, and the mules were near dead, so we killed them, not having anything in special for them or us to eat. We sat upon the boxes, and played odd and even with the cartridges that was jolted out.

'Then ten men with bows and arrows ran down that valley, chasing twenty men with bows and arrows, and the row was tremenjus. They was fair men—fairer than you or me—with yellow hair and remarkable well built. Says Dravot, unpacking the guns: "This is the beginning of the business. We'll fight for the ten men," and with that he fires two rifles at the twenty men, and drops one of them at two hundred yards from the rock where he was sitting. The other men began to run, but Carnehan and Dravot sits on the boxes picking them off at all ranges, up and down the valley. Then we goes up to the ten men that had run across the snow too, and they fires a footy little arrow at us. Dravot he shoots above their heads and they all falls down flat. Then he walks over them and kicks them, and then he lifts them up and shakes hands all round to make them friendly like. He calls them and gives them the boxes to carry, and waves his hand for all the world as though he was King already. They takes the boxes and him across the valley and up the hill into a pine wood on the top, where there was half-a-dozen big stone idols. Dravot he goes to the biggest—a fellow they call Imbra—and lays a rifle and a cartridge at his feet, rubbing his nose respectful with his own nose, patting him on the head, and saluting in front of it. He turns round to the men and nods his head and says: "That's all right. I'm in the know too, and all these old jim jams are my friends." Then he opens his mouth and points down it, and when the first man brings him food, he says: "No"; and when the second man brings him food, he says: "No"; but when one of the old priests and the boss of the village brings him food, he says: "Yes," very haughty, and eats it slow. That was how we came to our first village, without any trouble, just as though we had tumbled from the skies. But we tumbled from one of those damned rope-bridges, you see, and—you couldn't expect a man to laugh much after that?'

'Take some more whisky and go on,' I said. 'That was the first village you came into. How did you get to be King?'

'I wasn't King,' said Carnehan. 'Dravot he was the King, and a handsome man he looked with the gold crown on his head and all. Him and the other party stayed in that village, and every morning Dravot sat by the side of old Imbra, and the people came and worshipped. That was Dravot's order. Then a lot of men came into the valley, and Carnehan and Dravot picks them off with the rifles before they knew where they was, and runs down into the valley and up again the other side and finds another village, same as the first one, and the people all falls down flat on their faces, and Dravot says: "Now what is the trouble between you two villages?" and the people points to a woman, as fair as you or me, that was carried off, and Dravot takes her back to the first village and counts up the dead—eight there was. For each dead man Dravot pours a little milk on the ground and waves his arms like a whirligig, and "That's all right," says he. Then he and Carnehan takes the big boss of each valley by the arm and walks them down into the valley, and shows them how to scratch a line with a spear right down the valley, and gives each a sod of turf from both sides of the line. Then all the people comes down and shouts like the devil and all, and Dravot says: "Go and dig the land, and be fruitful and multiply," which they did, though they didn't understand. Then we asks the names of things in their lingo—bread and water and fire and idols and such, and Dravot leads the priest of each village up to the idol, and says he must sit there and judge the people, and if anything goes wrong he is to be shot.

'Next week they was all turning up the land in the valley as quiet as bees and much prettier, and the priests heard all the complaints and told Dravot in dumb show what it was about. "That's just the beginning," says Dravot. "They think we're Gods." He and Carnehan picks out twenty good men and shows them how to click off a rifle, and form fours, and advance in line, and they was very pleased to do so, and clever to see the hang of it. Then he takes out his pipe and his baccy-pouch and leaves one at one village, and one at the other, and off we two goes to see what was to be done in the next valley. That was all rock, and there was a little village there, and Carnehan says: "Send 'em to the old valley to plant," and takes 'em there, and gives 'em some land that wasn't took before. They were a poor lot, and we blooded 'em with a kid before letting 'em into the new Kingdom. That was to impress the people, and then they settled down quiet, and Carnehan went back to Dravot, who had got into another valley, all snow and ice and most mountaineous. There was no people there and the Army got afraid, so Dravot shoots one of them, and goes on till he finds some people in a village, and the Army explains that unless the people wants to be killed they had better not shoot their little matchlocks; for they had matchlocks. We makes friends with the priest, and I stays there alone with two of the Army, teaching the men how to drill, and a thundering big Chief comes across the snow with kettle-drums and horns twanging, because he heard there was a new God kicking about. Carnehan sights for the brown of the men half a mile across the snow and wings one of them. Then he sends a message to the Chief that, unless he wished to be killed, he must come and shake hands with me and leave his arms behind. The Chief comes alone first, and Carnehan shakes hands with him and whirls his arms about, same as Dravot used, and very much surprised that Chief was, and strokes my eyebrows. Then Carnehan goes alone to the Chief, and asks him in dumb show if he had an enemy he hated. "I have," says the Chief. So Carnehan weeds out the pick of his men, and sets the two of the Army to show them drill, and at the end of two weeks the men can manoeuvre about as well as Volunteers. So he marches with the Chief to a great big plain on the top of a mountain, and the Chief's men rushes into a village and takes it; we three Martinis firing into the brown of the enemy. So we took that village too, and I gives the Chief a rag from my coat and says, "Occupy till I come"; which was scriptural. By way of a reminder, when me and the Army was eighteen hundred yards away, I drops a bullet near him standing on the snow, and all the people falls flat on their faces. Then I sends a letter to Dravot wherever he be by land or by sea.'

At the risk of throwing the creature out of train I interrupted: 'How could you write a letter up yonder?'

'The letter?—Oh!—The letter! Keep looking at me between the eyes, please. It was a string-talk letter, that we'd learned the way of it from a blind beggar in the Punjab.'

I remembered that there had once come to the office a blind man with a knotted twig and a piece of string which he wound round the twig according to some cipher of his own. He could, after the lapse of days or weeks, repeat the sentence which he had reeled up. He had reduced the alphabet to eleven primitive sounds, and tried to teach me his method, but I could not understand.

'I sent that letter to Dravot,' said Carnehan; 'and told him to come back because this Kingdom was growing too big for me to handle, and then I struck for the first valley, to see how the priests were working. They called the village we took along with the Chief, Bashkai, and the first village we took, Er-Heb. The priests at Er-Heb was doing all right, but they had a lot of pending cases about land to show me, and some men from another village had been firing arrows at night. I went out and looked for that village, and fired four rounds at it from a thousand yards. That used all the cartridges I cared to spend, and I waited for Dravot, who had been away two or three months, and I kept my people quiet.

'One morning I heard the devil's own noise of drums and horns, and Dan Dravot marches down the hill with his Army and a tail of hundreds of men, and, which was the most amazing, a great gold crown on his head. "My Gord, Carnehan," says Daniel, "this is a tremenjus business, and we've got the whole country as far as it's worth having. I am the son of Alexander by Queen Semiramis, and you're my younger brother and a God too! It's the biggest thing we've ever seen. I've been marching and fighting for six weeks with the Army, and every footy little village for fifty miles has come in rejoiceful; and more than that, I've got the key of the whole show, as you'll see, and I've got a crown for you! I told 'em to make two of 'em at a place called Shu, where the gold lies in the rock like suet in mutton. Gold I've seen, and turquoise I've kicked out of the cliffs, and there's garnets in the sands of the river, and here's a chunk of amber that a man brought me. Call up all the priests and, here, take your crown."

'One of the men opens a black hair bag, and I slips the crown on. It was too small and too heavy, but I wore it for the glory. Hammered gold it was —five pound weight, like a hoop of a barrel.

' "Peachey," says Dravot, "we don't want to fight no more. The Craft's the trick, so help me!" and he brings forward that same Chief that I left at Bashkai—Billy Fish we called him afterwards, because he was so like Billy Fish that drove the big tank-engine at Mach on the Bolan in the old days.

"Shake hands with him," says Dravot, and I shook hands and nearly dropped, for Billy Fish gave me the Grip. I said nothing, but tried him with the Fellow Craft Grip. He answers all right, and I tried the Master's Grip, but that was a slip. "A Fellow Craft he is!" I says to Dan. "Does he know the Word?"—"He does," says Dan, "and all the priests know. It's a miracle! The Chiefs and the priests can work a Fellow Craft Lodge in a way that's very like ours, and they've cut the marks on the rocks, but they don't know the Third Degree, and they've come to find out. It's Gord's Truth! I've known these long years that the Afghans knew up to the Fellow Craft Degree, but this is a miracle. A God and a Grand-Master of the Craft am I, and a Lodge in the Third Degree I will open, and we'll raise the head priests and the Chiefs of the villages."

' "It's against all the law," I says, "holding a Lodge without warrant from any one; and you know we never held office in any Lodge."

' "It's a master-stroke o' policy," says Dravot. "It means running the country as easy as a four-wheeled bogie on a down grade. We can't stop to inquire now, or they'll turn against us. I've forty Chiefs at my heel, and passed and raised according to their merit they shall be. Billet these men on the villages, and see that we run up a Lodge of some kind. The temple of Imbra will do for the Lodge-room. The women must make aprons as you show them. I'll hold a levee of Chiefs to-night and Lodge to-morrow."

'I was fair run off my legs, but I wasn't such a fool as not to see what a pull this Craft business gave us. I showed the priests' families how to make aprons of the degrees, but for Dravot's apron the blue border and marks was made of turquoise lumps on white hide, not cloth. We took a great square stone in the temple for the Master's chair, and little stones for the officers' chairs, and painted the black pavement with white squares, and did what we could to make things regular.

'At the levee which was held that night on the hillside with big bonfires, Dravot gives out that him and me were Gods and sons of Alexander, and Past Grand-Masters in the Craft, and was come to make Kafiristan a country where every man should eat in peace and drink in quiet, and 'specially obey us. Then the Chiefs come round to shake hands, and they were so hairy and white and fair it was just shaking hands with old friends. We gave them names according as they was like men we had known in India—Billy Fish, Holly Dilworth, Pikky Kergan, that was Bazar-master when I was at Mhow, and so on, and so on.

'The most amazing miracles was at Lodge next night. One of the old priests was watching us continuous, and I felt uneasy, for I knew we'd have to fudge the Ritual, and I didn't know what the men knew. The old priest was a stranger come in from beyond the village of Bashkai. The minute Dravot puts on the Master's apron that the girls had made for him, the

priest fetches a whoop and a howl, and tries to overturn the stone that
Dravot was sitting on. "It's all up now," I says. "That comes of meddling
with the Craft without warrant!" Dravot never winked an eye, not when
ten priests took and tilted over the Grand-Master's chair—which was to say
the stone of Imbra. The priest begins rubbing the bottom end of it to clear
away the black dirt, and presently he shows all the other priests the Master's
Mark, same as was on Dravot's apron, cut into the stone. Not even the
priests of the temple of Imbra knew it was there. The old chap falls flat on
his face at Dravot's feet and kisses 'em. "Luck again," says Dravot, across
the Lodge to me; "they say it's the missing Mark that no one could understand the why of. We're more than safe now." Then he bangs the butt of
his gun for a gavel and says: "By virtue of the authority vested in me by my
own right hand and the help of Peachey, I declare myself Grand-Master of
all Freemasonry in Kafiristan in this the Mother Lodge o' the country, and
King of Kafiristan equally with Peachey!" At that he puts on his crown and
I puts on mine—I was doing Senior Warden—and we opens the Lodge in
most ample form. It was a amazing miracle! The priests moved in Lodge
through the first two degrees almost without telling, as if the memory was
coming back to them. After that, Peachey and Dravot raised such as was
worthy—high priests and Chiefs of far-off villages. Billy Fish was the first,
and I can tell you we scared the soul out of him. It was not in any way
according to Ritual, but it served our turn. We didn't raise more than ten of
the biggest men, because we didn't want to make the Degree common.
And they was clamouring to be raised.

' "In another six months," says Dravot, "we'll hold another Communication, and see how you are working." Then he asks them about their
villages, and learns that they was fighting one against the other, and was
sick and tired of it. And when they wasn't doing that they was fighting with
the Mohammedans. "You can fight those when they come into our country," says Dravot. "Tell off every tenth man of your tribes for a Frontier
guard, and send two hundred at a time to this valley to be drilled. Nobody
is going to be shot or speared any more so long as he does well, and I know
that you won't cheat me, because you're white people—sons of Alexander
—and not like common, black Mohammedans. You are *my* people, and by
God," says he, running off into English at the end, "I'll make a damned
fine Nation of you, or I'll die in the making!"

'I can't tell all we did for the next six months, because Dravot did a lot I
couldn't see the hang of, and he learned their lingo in a way I never could.
My work was to help the people plough, and now and again go out with
some of the Army and see what the other villages were doing, and make
'em throw rope-bridges across the ravines which cut up the country horrid.
Dravot was very kind to me, but when he walked up and down in the pine-

wood pulling that bloody red beard of his with both fists I knew he was thinking plans I could not advise about, and I just waited for orders.

'But Dravot never showed me disrespect before the people. They were afraid of me and the Army, but they loved Dan. He was the best of friends with the priests and the Chiefs; but any one could come across the hills with a complaint, and Dravot would hear him out fair, and call four priests together and say what was to be done. He used to call in Billy Fish from Bashkai, and Pikky Kergan from Shu, and an old Chief we called Kafoozelum—it was like enough to his real name—and hold councils with 'em when there was any fighting to be done in small villages. That was his Council of War, and the four priests of Bashkai, Shu, Khawak, and Madora was his Privy Council. Between the lot of 'em they sent me, with forty men and twenty rifles and sixty men carrying turquoises, into the Ghorband country to buy those hand-made Martini rifles, that come out of the Amir's workshops at Kabul, from one of the Amir's Herati regiments that would have sold the very teeth out of their mouths for turquoises.

'I stayed in Ghorband a month, and gave the Governor there the pick of my baskets for hush-money, and bribed the Colonel of the regiment some more, and, between the two and the tribes-people, we got more than a hundred hand-made Martinis, a hundred good Kohat *jezails* that'll throw to six hundred yards, and forty man-loads of very bad ammunition for the rifles. I came back with what I had, and distributed 'em among the men that the Chiefs sent in to me to drill. Dravot was too busy to attend to those things, but the old Army that we first made helped me, and we turned out five hundred men that could drill, and two hundred that knew how to hold arms pretty straight. Even those corkscrewed, handmade guns was a miracle to them. Dravot talked big about powder-shops and factories, walking up and down in the pine-wood when the winter was coming on.

' "I won't make a Nation," says he. "I'll make an Empire! These men aren't niggers; they're English! Look at their eyes—look at their mouths. Look at the way they stand up. They sit on chairs in their own houses. They're the Lost Tribes, or something like it, and they've grown to be English. I'll take a census in the spring if the priests don't get frightened. There must be a fair two million of 'em in these hills. The villages are full o' little children. Two million people—two hundred and fifty thousand fighting men—and all English! They only want the rifles and a little drilling. Two hundred and fifty thousand men, ready to cut in on Russia's right flank when she tries for India! Peachey, man," he says, chewing his beard in great hunks, "we shall be Emperors—Emperors of the Earth! Rajah Brooke will be a suckling to us. I'll treat with the Viceroy on equal terms. I'll ask him to send me twelve picked English—twelve that I know of—to help us govern a bit. There's Mackray, Sergeant-pensioner at Segowli—many's the good dinner he's given me, and his wife a pair of trousers. There's Donkin, the Warder of Tounghoo Jail. There's hundreds that I could lay my hand on if I was in India. The Viceroy shall do it for me. I'll send a man through in the spring for those men, and I'll write for a Dispensation from the Grand Lodge for what I've done as Grand-Master. That—and all the Sniders that'll be thrown out when the native troops in India take up the Martini. They'll be worn smooth, but they'll do for fighting in these hills. Twelve English, a hundred thousand Sniders run through the Amir's country in driblets—I'd be content with twenty thousand in one year—and we'd be an Empire. When everything was shipshape, I'd hand over the crown—this crown I'm wearing now—to Queen Victoria on my knees, and she'd say: 'Rise up, Sir Daniel Dravot.' Oh, it's big! It's big, I tell you! But there's so much to be done in every place—Bashkai, Khawak, Shu, and everywhere else."

' "What is it?" I says. "There are no more men coming in to be drilled this autumn. Look at those fat, black clouds. They're bringing the snow."

' "It isn't that," says Daniel, putting his hand very hard on my shoulder; "and I don't wish to say anything that's against you, for no other living man would have followed me and made me what I am as you have done. You're a first-class Commander-in-Chief, and the people know you; but—it's a big country, and somehow you can't help me, Peachey, in the way I want to be helped."

' "Go to your blasted priests, then!" I said, and I was sorry when I made that remark, but it did hurt me sore to find Daniel talking so superior, when I'd drilled all the men, and done all he told me.

' "Don't let's quarrel, Peachey," says Daniel without cursing. "You're a King too, and the half of this Kingdom is yours; but can't you see, Peachey, we want cleverer men than us now—three or four of 'em, that we can scatter about for our Deputies. It's a hugeous great State, and I can't always tell the right thing to do, and I haven't time for all I want to do, and here's winter coming on and all." He stuffed half his beard into his mouth, all red like the gold of his crown.

' "I'm sorry, Daniel," says I. "I've done all I could. I've drilled the men and shown the people how to stack their oats better; and I've brought in those tinware rifles from Ghorband—but I know what you're driving at. I take it Kings always feel oppressed that way."

' "There's another thing too," says Dravot, walking up and down. "The winter's coming and these people won't be giving much trouble, and if they do we can't move about. I want a wife."

' "For Gord's sake, leave the women alone!" I says. "We've both got all the work we can, though I *am* a fool. Remember the Contrack, and keep clear o' women."

' "The Contrack only lasted till such time as we was Kings; and Kings we have been these months past," says Dravot, weighing his crown in his hand. "You go get a wife, too, Peachey—a nice, strappin', plump girl that'll keep you warm in the winter. They're prettier than English girls, and we can take the pick of 'em. Boil 'em once or twice in hot water and they'll come out like chicken and ham."

' "Don't tempt me!" I says. "I will not have any dealings with a woman not till we are a dam' sight more settled than we are now. I've been doing the work o' two men, and you've been doing the work o' three. Let's lie off a bit, and see if we can get some better tobacco from Afghan country and run in some good liquor; but no women."

' "Who's talking o' *women?*" says Dravot. "I said *wife*—a Queen to breed a King's son for the King. A Queen out of the strongest tribe, that'll make them your blood-brothers, and that'll lie by your side and tell you all the people thinks about you and their own affairs. That's what I want."

' "Do you remember that Bengali woman I kept at Mogul Serai when I was a platelayer?" says I. "A fat lot o' good she was to me. She taught me the lingo and one or two other things; but what happened? She ran away with the Stationmaster's servant and half my month's pay. Then she turned up at Dadur Junction in tow of a half-caste, and had the impidence to say I was her husband—all among the drivers in the running-shed too!"

' "We've done with that," says Dravot; "these women are whiter than you or me, and a Queen I will have for the winter months."

' "For the last time o' asking, Dan, do *not,*" I says. "It'll only bring us harm. The Bible says that Kings ain't to waste their strength on women, 'specially when they've got a raw new Kingdom to work over."

' "For the last time of answering, I will," said Dravot, and he went away through the pine-trees looking like a big red devil, the sun being on his crown and beard and all.

'But getting a wife was not as easy as Dan thought. He put it before the Council, and there was no answer till Billy Fish said that he'd better ask the girls. Dravot damned them all round. "What's wrong with me?" he shouts, standing by the idol Imbra. "Am I a dog or am I not enough of a man for your wenches? Haven't I put the shadow of my hand over this country? Who stopped the last Afghan raid?" It was me really, but Dravot was too angry to remember. "Who bought your guns? Who repaired the bridges? Who's the Grand-Master of the Sign cut in the stone?" says he, and he thumped his hand on the block that he used to sit on in Lodge, and at Council, which opened like Lodge always. Billy Fish said nothing and no more did the others. "Keep your hair on, Dan," said I; "and ask the girls. That's how it's done at Home, and these people are quite English."

' "The marriage of the King is a matter of State," says Dan, in a red-hot rage, for he could feel, I hope, that he was going against his better mind. He walked out of the Council-room, and the others sat still, looking at the ground.

' "Billy Fish," says I to the Chief of Bashkai, "what's the difficulty here? A straight answer to a true friend."

' "You know," says Billy Fish. "How should a man tell you who knows everything? How can daughters of men marry Gods or Devils? It's not proper."

'I remembered something like that in the Bible; but if, after seeing us as long as they had, they still believed we were Gods, 'twasn't for me to undeceive them.

' "A God can do anything," says I. "If the King is fond of a girl he'll not let her die."—"She'll have to," says Billy Fish. "There are all sorts of Gods and Devils in these mountains, and now and again a girl marries one of them and isn't seen any more. Besides, you two know the Mark cut in the stone. Only the Gods know that. We thought you were men till you showed the Sign of the Master."

'I wished then that we had explained about the loss of the genuine secrets of a Master-Mason at the first go-off; but I said nothing. All that night there was a blowing of horns in a little dark temple half-way down the hill, and I heard a girl crying fit to die. One of the priests told us that she was being prepared to marry the King.

' "I'll have no nonsense of that kind," says Dan. "I don't want to interfere with your customs, but I'll take my own wife."—"The girl's a little bit afraid," says the priest. "She thinks she's going to die, and they are a-heartening of her up down in the temple."

' "Hearten her very tender, then," says Dravot, "or I'll hearten you with the butt of a gun so you'll never want to be heartened again." He licked his lips, did Dan, and stayed up walking about more than half the night, thinking of the wife that he was going to get in the morning. I wasn't any means comfortable, for I knew that dealings with a woman in foreign parts, though you was a crowned King twenty times over, could not but be risky. I got up very early in the morning while Dravot was asleep, and I saw the priests talking together in whispers, and the Chiefs talking together too, and they looked at me out of the corners of their eyes.

' "What is up, Fish?" I says to the Bashkai man, who was wrapped up in his furs and looking splendid to behold.

' "I can't rightly say," says he; "but if you can make the King drop all this nonsense about marriage, you'll be doing him and me and yourself a great service."

' "That I do believe," says I. "But sure, you know, Billy, as well as me, having fought against and for us, that the King and me are nothing more than two of the finest men that God Almighty ever made. Nothing more, I do assure you."

' "That may be," says Billy Fish, "and yet I should be sorry if it was." He sinks his head upon his great fur cloak for a minute and thinks. "King," says he, "be you man or God or Devil, I'll stick by you to-day. I have twenty of my men with me, and they will follow me. We'll go to Bashkai until the storm blows over."

'A little snow had fallen in the night, and everything was white except them greasy fat clouds that blew down and down from the north. Dravot came out with his crown on his head, swinging his arms and stamping his feet, and looking more pleased than Punch.

' "For the last time, drop it, Dan," says I in a whisper. "Billy Fish here says that there will be a row."

' "A row among my people!" says Dravot. "Not much. Peachey, you're a fool not to get a wife too. Where's the girl?" says he with a voice as loud as the braying of a jackass. "Call up all the Chiefs and priests, and let the Emperor see if his wife suits him."

'There was no need to call any one. They were all there leaning on their guns and spears round the clearing in the centre of the pine-wood. A lot of priests went down to the little temple to bring up the girl, and the horns blew fit to wake the dead. Billy Fish saunters round and gets as close to Daniel as he could, and behind him stood his twenty men with matchlocks. Not a man of them under six feet. I was next to Dravot, and behind me was twenty men of the regular Army. Up comes the girl, and a strapping wench she was, covered with silver and turquoises, but white as death, and looking back every minute at the priests.

' "She'll do," said Dan, looking her over. "What's to be afraid of, lass? Come and kiss me." He puts his arm round her. She shuts her eyes, gives a bit of a squeak, and down goes her face in the side of Dan's flaming red beard.

' "The slut's bitten me!" says he, clapping his hand to his neck, and, sure enough, his hand was red with blood. Billy Fish and two of his matchlock-men catches hold of Dan by the shoulders and drags him into the Bashkai lot, while the priests howls in their lingo: "Neither God nor Devil but a man!" I was all taken aback, for a priest cut at me in front, and the Army behind began firing into the Bashkai men.

' "God A'mighty!" says Dan. "What is the meaning o' this?"

' "Come back! Come away!" says Billy Fish. "Ruin and Mutiny's the matter. We'll break for Bashkai if we can."

'I tried to give some sort of orders to my men—the men o' the regular Army—but it was no use, so I fired into the brown of 'em with an English Martini and drilled three beggars in a line. The valley was full of shouting, howling people, and every soul was shrieking, "Not a God nor a Devil but only a man!" The Bashkai troops stuck to Billy Fish all they were worth, but their matchlocks wasn't half as good as the Kabul breech-loaders, and four of them dropped. Dan was bellowing like a bull, for he was very wrathy; and Billy Fish had a hard job to prevent him running out at the crowd.

' "We can't stand," says Billy Fish. "Make a run for it down the valley! The whole place is against us." The matchlock-men ran, and we went down the valley in spite of Dravot. He was swearing horrible and crying out he was a King. The priests rolled great stones on us, and the regular Army fired hard, and there wasn't more than six men, not counting Dan, Billy Fish, and me, that came down to the bottom of the valley alive.

'Then they stopped firing and the horns in the temple blew again. "Come away—for God's sake come away!" says Billy Fish. "They'll send runners out to all the villages before ever we get to Bashkai. I can protect you there, but I can't do anything now."

'My own notion is that Dan began to go mad in his head from that hour. He stared up and down like a stuck pig. Then he was all for walking back alone and killing the priests with his bare hands; which he could have done. "An Emperor am I," says Daniel, "and next year I shall be a Knight of the Queen."

' "All right, Dan," says I; "but come along now while there's time."

' "It's your fault," says he, "for not looking after your Army better. There was mutiny in the midst, and you didn't know—you damned engine-driving, plate-laying, missionary's-pass-hunting hound!" He sat upon a rock and called me every name he could lay tongue to. I was too heart-sick to care, though it was all his foolishness that brought the smash.

' "I'm sorry, Dan," says I, "but there's no accounting for natives. This business is our 'Fifty-Seven. Maybe we'll make something out of it yet, when we've got to Bashkai."

' "Let's get to Bashkai, then," says Dan, "and, by God, when I come back here again I'll sweep the valley so there isn't a bug in a blanket left!"

'We walked all that day, and all that night Dan was stumping up and down on the snow, chewing his beard and muttering to himself.

' "There's no hope o' getting clear," said Billy Fish. "The priests will have sent runners to the villages to say that you are only men. Why didn't you stick on as Gods till things was more settled? I'm a dead man," says Billy Fish, and he throws himself down on the snow and begins to pray to his Gods.

'Next morning we was in a cruel bad country—all up and down, no level ground at all, and no food either. The six Bashkai men looked at Billy Fish hungry-ways as if they wanted to ask something, but they said never a word. At noon we came to the top of a flat mountain all covered with snow, and when we climbed up into it, behold, there was an Army in position waiting in the middle!

' "The runners have been very quick," says Billy Fish, with a little bit of a laugh. "They are waiting for us."

'Three or four men began to fire from the enemy's side, and a chance shot took Daniel in the calf of the leg. That brought him to his senses. He looks across the snow at the Army, and sees the rifles that we had brought into the country.

' "We're done for," says he. "They are Englishmen, these people,—and it's my blasted nonsense that has brought you to this. Get back, Billy Fish, and take your men away. You've done what you could, and now cut for it. Carnehan," says he, "shake hands with me and go along with Billy. Maybe they won't kill you. I'll go and meet 'em alone. It's me that did it. Me, the King!"

' "Go!" says I. "Go to Hell, Dan! I'm with you here. Billy Fish, you clear out, and we two will meet those folk."

' "I'm a Chief," says Billy Fish, quite quiet. "I stay with you. My men can go."

'The Bashkai fellows didn't wait for a second word, but ran off, and Dan and me and Billy Fish walked across to where the drums were drumming and the horns were horning. It was cold—awful cold. I've got that cold in the back of my head now. There's a lump of it there.'

The punkah-coolies had gone to sleep. Two kerosene lamps were blazing in the office, and the perspiration poured down my face and splashed on the blotter as I leaned forward. Carnehan was shivering, and I feared that his mind might go. I wiped my face, took a fresh grip of the piteously mangled hands, and said: 'What happened after that?'

The momentary shift of my eyes had broken the clear current.

'What was you pleased to say?' whined Carnehan. 'They took them without any sound. Not a little whisper all along the snow, not though the King knocked down the first man that set hand on him—not though old Peachey fired his last cartridge into the brown of 'em. Not a single solitary sound did those swines make. They just closed up tight, and I tell you their furs stunk. There was a man called Billy Fish, a good friend of us all, and they cut his throat, sir, then and there, like a pig; and the King kicks up the bloody snow and says: "We've had a dashed fine run for our money. What's coming next?" But Peachey, Peachey Taliaferro, I tell you, sir, in confidence as betwixt two friends, he lost his head, sir. No, he didn't neither. The King lost his head, so he did, all along o' one of those cunning rope-bridges. Kindly let me have the paper-cutter, sir. It tilted this way. They marched him a mile across that snow to a rope-bridge over a ravine with a river at the bottom. You may have seen such. They prodded him behind like an ox. "Damn your eyes!" says the King. "D'you suppose I can't die like a gentleman?" He turns to Peachey—Peachey that was crying like a child. "I've brought you to this, Peachey," says he. "Brought you out of your happy life to be killed in Kafiristan, where you was late Commander-in-Chief of the Emperor's forces. Say you forgive me, Peachey."—"I do," says Peachey. "Fully and freely do I forgive you, Dan."—"Shake hands, Peachey," says he. "I'm going now." Out he goes, looking neither right nor left, and when he was plumb in the middle of those dizzy dancing ropes —"Cut, you beggars," he shouts; and they cut, and old Dan fell, turning round and round and round, twenty thousand miles, for he took half an hour to fall till he struck the water, and I could see his body caught on a rock with the gold crown close beside.

'But do you know what they did to Peachey between two pine-trees? They crucified him, sir, as Peachey's hands will show. They used wooden pegs for his hands and his feet; and he didn't die. He hung there and screamed, and they took him down next day, and said it was a miracle that he wasn't dead. They took him down—poor old Peachey that hadn't done them any harm—that hadn't done them any—'

He rocked to and fro and wept bitterly, wiping his eyes with the back of his scarred hands and moaning like a child for some ten minutes.

'They was cruel enough to feed him up in the temple, because they said he was more of a God than old Daniel that was a man. Then they turned him out on the snow, and told him to go home, and Peachey came home in about a year, begging along the roads quite safe; for Daniel Dravot he walked before and said: "Come along, Peachey. It's a big thing we're doing." The mountains they danced at night, and the mountains they tried to fall on Peachey's head, but Dan he held up his hand, and Peachey came along bent double. He never let go of Dan's hand, and he never let go of Dan's head. They gave it to him as a present in the temple, to remind him not to come again, and though the crown was pure gold, and Peachey was starving, never would Peachey sell the same. You knew Dravot, sir! You knew Right Worshipful Brother Dravot! Look at him now!'

He fumbled in the mass of rags round his bent waist; brought out a black horsehair bag embroidered with silver thread, and shook therefrom on to my table—the dried, withered head of Daniel Dravot! The morning sun that had long been paling the lamps struck the red beard and blind sunken eyes; struck, too, a heavy circlet of gold studded with raw turquoises, that Carnehan placed tenderly on the battered temples.

'You behold now,' said Carnehan, 'the Emperor in his habit as he lived— the King of Kafiristan with his crown upon his head. Poor old Daniel that was a monarch once!'

I shuddered, for, in spite of defacements manifold, I recognized the head of the man of Marwar Junction. Carnehan rose to go. I attempted to stop him. He was not fit to walk abroad. 'Let me take away the whisky, and give me a little money,' he gasped. 'I was a King once. I'll go to the Deputy-Commissioner and ask to set in the Poorhouse till I get my health. No, thank you, I can't wait till you get a carriage for me. I've urgent private affairs—in the South—at Marwar.'

He shambled out of the office and departed in the direction of the Deputy-Commissioner's house. That day at noon I had occasion to go down the blinding hot Mall, and I saw a crooked man crawling along the white dust of the roadside, his hat in his hand, quavering dolorously after the fashion of street-singers at Home. There was not a soul in sight, and he was out of all possible earshot of the houses. And he sang through his nose, turning his head from right to left:—

> 'The Son of God goes forth to war,
> A kingly crown to gain;
> His blood-red banner streams afar!
> Who follows in his train?'

I waited to hear no more, but put the poor wretch into my carriage and drove him to the nearest missionary for eventual transfer to the Asylum. He repeated the hymn twice while he was with me, whom he did not in the least recognize, and I left him singing it to the missionary.

Two days later I inquired after his welfare of the Superintendent of the Asylum.

'He was admitted suffering from sunstroke. He died early yesterday morning,' said the Superintendent. 'Is it true that he was half an hour bare-headed in the sun at mid-day?'

'Yes,' said I, 'but do you happen to know if he had anything upon him by any chance when he died?'

'Not to my knowledge,' said the Superintendent.

And there the matter rests.

ON THE BORDER

Lucius Shepard

Chapo, handsome twenty-three-year-old, with Aztec features, black hair, adobe-colored skin. He sat on the cantina steps gazing up at the unreal fire of the border: a curtain of shimmering blood-red energy that appeared to rise halfway to the stars before merging with the night sky. So bright you could see it for miles out on the desert, a glowing seam stretching from Texas to California, and in that seam were the old towns of Tiajuana, Nuevo Laredo, Mexicali, and a dozen more, all welded into a single town of stucco bars and slums, of muzzle gleam and knife-flash, of paunchy whores and sleazy pimps and gringos on the slide from the fatlands of America: the Crust, they called it. Chapo liked thinking of himself as part of that glow, that red meanness. At least that had been the case until three days before, when he had crossed over and come back with the gringa.

Now he wasn't sure what he liked.

Somebody heaved a bottle toward the border, and Chapo tracked the arc. Violet lightnings forked away from the impact point. Throw a man into it, and you got brighter colors but the same result.

Zap!

Not even ashes.

Chapo fingered an upper from his pocket and swallowed it dry. He picked up his mesh shopping bag and headed for home. Music poured from the bars, swaying his hips, setting his fists jumping in little karate strikes. Battered old 1990s rides rumbled past, dark heads behind the wheels. Tang of marijuana, stink of fried grease. The red light shone everywhere, and shadows were sharp like they would be in Hell.

A crowd was gathered by the door of Echevarria's bar, which meant a country girl was riding the wire. The child some farmer didn't have enough money to feed, and so he'd sold her to Echevarria. A brown-skinned girl stripped naked, silver electrodes plugged to her temples. Her brains frying in a smoke of pleasure as she danced a herky-jerky path across the floor, and men touching her, laughing as she looked blindly around, trying to find them. Later when she slowed down, they'd take her upstairs and charge heavy for a short time. If he'd been smart, Chapo thought, he'd have sold the gringa to Echevarria. But the wire . . . that was where he stopped being part of the red glow. He knew he could never hand her over to that fate.

A poster with the gringa's photograph was plastered to Echevarria's wall. Blond hair and angel face. It didn't do her justice, didn't show how her eyes were. At first glance they were blue, then green, and then you saw they were all colors like fire opals, with flecks of emerald and gold and hazel. Special eyes. Beneath the photograph, big black letters spelled out her name: Anise. Just like a gringa to be named for something you drink. Even bigger letters offered a twenty-five thousand dollar reward. Everybody was looking for her now, and no way Chapo would be able to move her until things calmed down.

"Hey, Chapo!" Rafael pushed out of the crowd and came up beside him. Big chubby guy with jowls and brown frizzy hair. He was always hassling Chapo, not for any real reason, just for something to do. "You oughta see inside, man!" he said. "They gotta sweet little lady ridin' tonight!"

"Fuck it!" Chapo popped another upper. "I don't go for that shit."

"Least she gonna have fun," said Rafael, and grinned. "Least she goin' fast . . . not slow like you." He pointed to Chapo's shirt pocket, his pills.

A flash of chemical fury, and Chapo knocked him back with a slap. Rafael rubbed his mouth, and a knife materialized in his hand. "Okay," he said. "You like it fast? You got it, man."

Everybody was staring, wanting it to happen, and the pressure of all those black eyes made Chapo feel a little loose, a little casual about his life. He started to go for his own knife, but thought about the gringa and held back.

"C'mon, man!" said Rafael, dancing back and forth. "C'mon!"

"Maybe later," Chapo said.

Jeering whistles sounded behind him.

"What's the matter, Chapo?" Rafael grinned and made passes with the knife, lunging close.

Chapo half-turned, then swung his shopping bag, heavy with cans of fruit juice; the bag struck Rafael in the jaw, and he came all unhinged, falling face down in the dirt.

The whistles broke off, and as the crowd dispersed, laughing, a couple of them stopped to spit on Rafael.

*   *   *

Out on the edge of the desert, the edge of the Crust, that's where Chapo lived. A white stucco ruin with no windows, no doors. Inside, he waited a minute to make sure nobody had followed. Each of the window frames held a rectangle of golden stars and blue darkness.

When he was certain he was alone, he went into the back room. It was piled with rubble. He kneeled and knocked three times on the floor. Waited another minute. Then he lifted a heap of rubble that was glued to a round metal plate almost the size of a manhole cover. Lowered a rope ladder that had been concealed beneath the rubble. He climbed partway down, eased the metal plate back into place. "Okay," he said, climbing down the rest of the way.

A match scraped, a candle flared. Two candles. He made her out against the rear wall, sitting on a stained mattress, her legs tucked under her. Grime streaked her face, and her golden hair was getting stringy. She wore jeans and a torn white blouse.

"Got you some fruit," he said, holding up the shopping bag. "Juice."

She didn't appear to register what he'd said. The hollows in her cheeks had deepened, making her look older . . . with that wide mouth, like a model in some fashion magazine. But he figured she wasn't much over eighteen. Nineteen, maybe.

He set the shopping bag beside her and sat a couple of feet away. The candles cast tiny dancing shadows on the dirt. Dark wings fluttered behind his eyes, making the room dimmer: the uppers playing tricks.

"Please," she said wearily. "Won't you help me?"

"That's what I'm doin'," he said.

"No, I mean won't you help me get back." Her voice broke, and he hoped she wasn't going to cry again.

"I keep tellin' you," he said. "Your papa's offerin' too much money. There's guys lookin' for you all over. They see some fat ol' lady, and they go peekin' under her dress to see if the fat's for real. We'd never make it to Immigration. And you know what happens if somebody catch you? They gonna tease you, touch you . . . touch you here." He tapped his chest. "And then they say, 'Hey, why don't we taste some of that 'fore we score the money.' And once they start, they'll give everybody a taste, and pretty soon there won't be enough left to be worth the reward. That's how it goes in the Crust. People don't think ahead."

"We could call the police," she said. "We . . ."

"The police! Shit! They even worse. They hold you a while to jack up the reward. Maybe they send your papa a finger or somethin'. And when they get the money, they do you the same way. You be patient, and I'll get you out."

She stared at him a moment, hopelessness in her face. Then she reached for the shopping bag.

Sitting hunkered on the dirt floor of the cellar, gazing into nowhere, Chapo thought about the crossing. He'd been wanting to cross a long time, wanting some of that Stateside money. And Moro had given him a chance. Moro had owned one of the tubes that spat threads of light and punched holes in the red glow. Holes that spread to door-size, lasted a few seconds and then closed tight. In a single night they had stolen more money than Chapo had ever seen, and as they'd headed back to the crossing point, they'd seen the girl through a storeroom window, bound and gagged, lying on the floor. She'd been kidnapped by one of the Stateside gangs, and they were working out ransom with her rich papa. Moro had said to take her. At the crossing point, Chapo and the girl had gone through first. They'd squatted beside a dumpster, waiting for the others. But the others hadn't come through. Chapo had thought he heard a scream, but it had been hard to tell what with the hum and sizzle of the border so loud. Realizing the others were never going to show, he'd dragged the gringa to her feet and they'd made a run to Chapo's house. It had been almost dawn, the streets empty, and they'd been lucky to make it even then.

"Chapo?"

And maybe he *should* sell her. What the hell was he doing helping her? If things were reversed, she wouldn't help him. He was just a beaner to her. Just trash.

"Chapo!"

He looked up. She was smiling: it was a fake smile, but he was glad to see it. "Yeah?"

"I'm sorry," she said. "I know you're trying to help. It's just . . . I'm scared, y'know."

Chapo made a noncommittal noise.

"You can sit over here if you want." She patted the mattress.

"I'm okay."

"You can't be comfortable," she said. "Come on, please. It'll make me feel better."

"All right." He crawled over to the mattress and sat on the very end. She gave a teasing laugh, told him he could sit closer, and kept talking.

Three days without a shower, and she still smelled sweet. Out of the corner of his eye he peeked at the tented-up silver of her blouse. Her breasts weren't very big, but he could tell they had a nice shape. He could stand a taste himself. They said it was all the same, but she'd feel different.

Her body full of lazy afternoons and expensive sugars. Plush and springy, a Cadillac ride. He'd sink forever into blond flesh.

She edged a little nearer, saying she was cold, and he knew what she was doing, what was going to happen. Then her face was close to his, lips parted, dazed looking, and she said, "Oh, Chapo . . . Chapo!" And her tongue was darting into his mouth, and his hand cupped the underside of one of those breasts . . . Soft. The kind of softness that makes you dizzy, tipped with its little hard candy.

Like a fool, he pushed her away.

"We can do this," he said, his breath coming hard. "We can do this, but I ain't gonna take you out 'fore I think it's safe."

Disappointment and humiliation flooded her face.

What was the matter with him? Why didn't he just grab her and peel off the shell and pluck out the meat. That's what he wanted. But maybe not, maybe with her he wanted it real. Something he could never have. "You gotta be patient," he said.

"Patient!" She spat out the word. "For how long? Until you find some way to use me?"

He got angry, then. "What you think? You think I couldn't make money off you now? Dumbass bitch! I take you down to Avenida Juarez tonight, if that's what you think. Sell your skinny butt 'til it's wore down to gristle."

She aimed a slap at him, but he caught her wrist and shoved her away. She scooted to the end of the mattress, waiting for him to attack. For a second, he thought he might. But all he did was to repeat, "You gotta be patient."

"How long?" she asked, looking hopeless again.

"I dunno. A few weeks . . . that is, if your papa don't raise the reward."

"A few weeks." In her mouth it sounded like forever.

He couldn't figure why he wanted to save her. It might be he just wanted to save *something*, to see if anything *could* be saved. But that wasn't all of it. Trouble with words, they shrank your ideas to fit, and made you think they were what you'd meant.

She turned her face to the wall, curled up tight.

Chapo doubted she could last a few more weeks. One day she'd do something crazy, try for the border on her own. He could tie her up, drug her. But she'd get loose. Even though she cried, he could see she was strong. But her strength wasn't the kind that counted here in the Crust.

"Maybe there's a way," he said.

She didn't react. Probably didn't believe him.

"I'll check it out tomorrow," he said.

She mumbled something that he didn't catch.

What a goddamn fool he was!

He didn't want to sleep, so he did another upper. Something scrabbled in the shadows, then was still. The candles guttered low, and light seemed to be collecting around the gringa, burying her under a heap of yellow glow like an enchantment. Her breath deepened. Now and again she moaned. He studied the way the denim clung to her ass. Sleek, perfect curves. An ass Made in America. Chapo wondered what it had cost, what secrets had gone into the manufacture. And he wondered, too, what dreams were crowding that golden head. Even her nightmares would be beautiful.

The upper kicked in, and Chapo leaned back against the wall, feeling the crazy bounces of his heart, a mean wash of thoughts seeping up from the red glow of his blood.

Anise, he said to himself. What a stupid fuckin' name!

Like Chapo, Herreira lived on the backside of the Crust. An old, old man with sheet iron over his windows and big locks on his doors. He owed Chapo, owed him big. Two years before, a merchant named Ibanez had taken Herreira's granddaughter in exchange for paper he held on him, and Herreira had asked Chapo to steal the paper, so his granddaughter could get free. They hadn't talked price, but Chapo had trusted Herreira to work something out. He'd broken into Ibanez's house, and Ibanez had caught him. Chapo had opened the merchant's belly with a knife. Afterward he hadn't been able to put a price on the man's life, and he'd told Herreira that sooner or later he'd need something. Now the time had come, and he needed the old man's jeep, his maps of the desert. He'd drive the gringa across the desert to the Pacific resort of Huayacuatia. There she'd be safe.

Herreira's face was as wrinkled as tree bark, and his hair was wispy and white. But his back was unbowed, his black eyes clear. He didn't much care to risk his jeep, but a bargain was a bargain, and besides, he didn't use it anymore. It was painted white to blend in with the hardpan of the desert, and was kept in an adobe building barnacled onto the rear of the old man's house. Herreira spread his maps on the hood and showed Chapo the hiding places, how he would have to drive during the night, and by day hide the jeep and sleep in the big rocks that stuck up from the desert floor. Herreira had once been a smuggler, bringing guns from the coast into the Crust, and he told Chapo it was very dangerous to make the crossing.

"They spot you, man, and that's it." He drew a finger across his throat. "You got no place to run. It's luck if you make it, and the odds ain't good."

"What are they?" Chapo asked.

"Sixty-forty, your favor. If there's no moon, a little better. But there'll be a moon for you."

Chapo studied the map. The border was a crooked red line, and he imagined himself living there like a roach in a crack. Sixty-forty odds. It seemed no worse than what he usually faced.

"How 'bout gas?"

"You gotta extra tank," said Herreira. "Enough to cross the desert. Three nights drivin'. But you'll need more when you head up into the hills. There's a village"—he pointed—"here. San Juan de la Fiebra. Know 'bout it?"

Chapo nodded.

"Well, you can deal with 'em . . . sometimes. You get past 'em, and it's only a few hours to Huayacuatia."

Again Chapo wondered why the hell he was doing this. It didn't feel smart or even the good kind of reckless. But he pushed the question aside. Why didn't matter. He was committed, and maybe it was just in him to do.

"Bring the jeep back," said Herreira, dead-serious. "Don't sell it if you get across."

"How you know I'm plannin' to come back?"

Herreira's laugh was sneering. "Shit, Chapo! Where you gonna go? You just like me, you border meat."

"Maybe," said Chapo.

"Maybe, my ass!" Herreira scowled at Chapo. "You bring that bitch back."

The first night.

They drove south from the border. The hardpan glowed white. Every once in a while they passed huge desert rocks, indigo under the moonlight, smooth depressions in their sides like dimples made by the pressure of enormous thumbs. The shadows of smaller things—stubby cacti and little rocks—were so deep and black, they hid the objects that cast them. Chapo was tense. He could feel the blazing pinpricks of the stars on his back. The engine noise and rattles were too loud for talk, and whenever the gringa wanted to stop and pee, she had to shout. Sometimes he'd catch her looking at him, and she would smile. Not a fake smile, but one that seemed to be trying to engage him, to give him encouragement, to say something friendly, and he would nod in response and think about the smile, and then his thoughts would be worn down by the engine noise, and he would just drive.

Hours like that.

An hour before dawn he came to the first hiding place, a mountainous rock that showed chalky pink under the brightening sky. There was a niche

in the southern face large enough to hold the jeep, and after parking it
there, he covered it with brush. They crawled up to a depression, almost a
cave, from which they had a good view south and east. The gringa was
excited and wanted to talk, but Chapo told her to sleep. Later, he said, it
might be too hot to sleep. She drank a little water, chewed half a tortilla
and wrapped herself in a blanket. He had bought her a clean blouse—blue,
with a pattern of white hibiscus—and when she turned in her sleep and the
blanket slipped down from her shoulders, he could see her nipples pushing
up the clingy material. He watched them rise and fall, not thinking, just
watching, feeling mild arousal, until he began to get drowsy.

When he waked, he couldn't remember having fallen asleep. Sweat was
crawling down his sides, and the desert was rippling with heat haze; he
thought he could hear the heat humming, but the sound was in his head,
and after a second it switched off. At the base of the rock stood a green
barrel cactus. He could have sworn it hadn't been there when he'd parked
the jeep. There were supposed to be brujos in the desert: could be the
cactus was one of them in disguise. He glanced around and found the
gringa watching him.

"Good morning," she said cheerfully.

Her good spirits annoyed him. "Yeah, mornin'."

His mouth tasted like shit. He did an upper and washed it down with a
sip of water from the canteen. Shook his head to clear away the cobwebs.
He reached into his hip pocket and pulled out his wristwatch. It was nearly
one o'clock. Six, maybe seven more hours of daylight. He wished he'd slept
longer. That same old question of what he was doing here cropped up in
his mind: the desert seemed a bad answer.

"Want something to eat?" she asked.

"Un-uh."

His automatic jabbed into his back; he reached behind him and eased it
from his waistband, laid it beside his leg.

The gringa's eyes widened, but she made no comment. After a minute
she said, "Do you wanna talk or something?"

"What for?"

"Just to pass the time."

He had another sip of water. "Yeah, sure . . . all right."

She waited for him to start, and when he didn't, she said, "Why didn't
you think of this before? The jeep, I mean. It doesn't look like it's going to
be too hard."

He didn't want to tell her what Herreira had said about the odds. "I
dunno."

"Well," she said impatiently. "I'm glad you *did* think of it."

They were silent for a while, and then she said, "What do you want to be?"

"Huh?"

"What do you want to do with your life? I'm studying to be a dancer."

"You don't gotta study to do that. Dancin's just somethin' you learn natural. In the bars and shit."

"I mean formal dance."

"What's that?"

"You know . . . jazz, ballet."

He didn't know, and she tried to explain.

"Why you wanna do that?" he asked. "What's the point?"

"To make something beautiful."

For no reason he could figure, he laughed.

Irritated, she said, "I don't suppose you'd understand, but . . ."

"I understand all right!" he snapped, and let his gaze range the length of her body. "I understand beauty just fine."

She flushed and lowered her eyes. "So what do *you* wanna be?"

He had an answer, but the truth of it was all tangled up in words, hidden in snarls of black thready sentences that he would never get to come out straight. The answer wasn't a thing or a job or anything like that, but a way to be. He was angry at being unable to express himself, and out of anger, he said, "I ain't rich like you, I ain't got no choice."

"Of course you do," she said.

"Don't gimme that shit! What you know 'bout it?"

"I know you don't have to stay in the Crust. I know if you left, you might find you had other options."

He was about to snap at her again, but a thin droning sound caught his attention. He scanned the horizon.

"What is it?" she asked, alarmed.

"Airplane comin' low. Smugglers, maybe."

He spotted it, then. Silver speck glinting to the south, resolving into a twin-engine job. No more than a couple of hundred feet high. The rear door was open, showing blackly against the silver finish, and as the plane drew near, something fell from the door. Something with arms and legs that pinwheeled crazily down to land spreadeagled on the hardpan about fifty yards away, looking like an X marking buried treasure.

"Oh, Jesus!" the gringa said. "It was a man, wasn't it?"

"Could be a woman."

The plane banked toward the east and soon was lost to sight.

"Maybe he's still alive," she said. "Maybe we should go look."

"You go," he said. "You wanna see blood and bone, you go look."

She peered at the unmoving figure, her face grim, registering shock. "He *might* be alive."

"What if he is?" Chapo said. "You wanna pick him up, take him to the hospital? Nearest one's back in the Crust."

The figure seemed to be blackening and dissolving in the heat haze. The gringa continued to peer a few moments longer, then settled back into the shade, her lips thinned.

They didn't talk much after that.

The last of sunset left a red seam of fire along the western horizon, as if north had become west, and the Crust was now ahead of them. The second night was like the first, except the moon was brighter and the gringa didn't bother to smile. She rode with her head down, picking at frays in her jeans, and Chapo knew she was thinking about the dead man. He thought she might start a conversation about him, and he was glad when she kept quiet. What was there to say? That they should have checked him out? Shit! She should thank her stars it hadn't been her. The man's death had given Chapo a lucky feeling. Two nights without being spotted, and the desert had taken someone else instead of them. The signs were favorable. He realized he hadn't been concerned thus far with whether or not they would reach Huayacuatia. The concept of survival had not been part of his plan; he had simply been acting upon some mysterious inner directive. But now he wanted to make it. Now he had hope.

They didn't arrive at the second hiding place until dawn: another rock, an immense red mushroom cap a hundred feet high. The hardpan had been eroded under its eastern edge, leaving a deep overhang. Chapo drove the jeep beneath the overhang, and worked feverishly at camouflage, finishing just as the fireball cleared the horizon. He poked around in the flaky detritus and stirred up a scorpion. Crushed it with his heel. They made a meal of beans and tortillas behind the jeep, and washed the food down with canteen water. The gringa dabbed water onto her face. In the pink glow she looked tired but more beautiful than she had the previous day, her features finer, as if a layer of drab insulation had been worn away. She pulled the blanket over her shoulders and sat looking out into the new morning.

Chapo couldn't decide whether to sleep or do an upper. He was tired, but if he waited until afternoon to sleep, he'd be fresh for the night drive. He took a pill from his shirt pocket, rolled it back and forth between his thumb and forefinger.

"Hello!" somebody shouted.

Chapo jumped up, knocking his head on the overhang with such force that he went back down to one knee. He grabbed his automatic and peeked from behind the jeep. Standing about thirty feet away was a wrinkled old

Indian man wearing a straw hat and a grimy shirt and trousers of white
cotton. When he spotted Chapo, he spread his arms and called out, "Welcome to my house!"

"Who is it?" the gringa asked, leaning over Chapo's shoulder.

"Stay back!" He pushed her to the side and moved out into the sun.

"Welcome!" the old man repeated. "My name is Don Augustin. And
you?"

"Chapo."

"And the gringa . . . How is she called?"

"Anise," answered the gringa from Chapo's rear.

He spun around. "I told you to stay back!"

"Don't be afraid," said Don Augustin with a chuckle. "I won't hurt
you."

He was standing slightly forward and dead-center of a pair of large
branching cacti; they looked like two weird, pale green soldiers flanking
him. Beyond him, emptiness spread to the horizon. Chapo thought again
about brujos.

"Won't you come into my house?" Don Augustin asked. "It's been years
since I've had visitors."

"Where is it?" asked the gringa.

"My house? Behind you." Don Augustin gestured at the rock. "It's cool
inside, and there's water. You can wash and rest for your journey."

Chapo leveled the gun at him. "How you know we're on a journey?"

"Oh!" Don Augustin arched an eyebrow, and his wrinkles shifted into
lines of good humor. "You've come to see me, then? I'm honored."

"We'll stay here," said Chapo.

"I want to wash," said the gringa defiantly. Before Chapo could stop
her, she went a few steps toward the old man. "I don't understand about
your house."

"The rock's hollow," said Don Augustin. "Oh, you'll like it, Sēnorita
Anise. It's beautiful . . . Not so beautiful as you, of course." He delivered
a gallant bow and gestured toward the far side of the rock. "If you will
follow me . . ."

"No," said Chapo.

Don Augustin came a couple of paces closer. "If I wanted to harm you
would I have made so open an approach? No, I would have waited until
you were asleep and"—he made a series of wild hacking motions—
"chopped you into bits. I am a man of peace, Sēnor. When you enter my
house, you also enter my place of worship, and I permit no violence there.
And if it is magic you fear, the only magic here is the magic of this rock."

"Are you a brujo?" Chapo asked.

"That's not an easy question to answer." Don Augustin tipped back his hat and scratched his head; despite his apparent age, his hair was jet black. "Perhaps I am, and pehaps I'm not. But if I am, I have never sought the wisdom—it has simply been visited upon me, and I have no real use for it."

Chapo was inclined to believe him, but he distrusted this inclination and gave no reply.

"Please, Chapo." The gringa put her hand on his arm. "He's not going to hurt us."

"Listen to her, Chapo," said Don Augustin. "She has the wisdom of innocence, and because this place is innocent, here she must be your guide."

From these words Chapo had the idea that the old man knew everything about them, and if that were the case, if he had that much power, there was no point in being cautious. "All right," he said. "But careful, man. No tricks."

"Don't worry," said Don Augustin, and grinned. "Such a big gun! I'd never risk myself against it." And beckoning them to follow, he hustled off around the rock.

Sheltered beneath an overhang on the western side of the rock was a narrow entrance that led downward into blackness. Chapo held the gun on Don Augustin and let the gringa explore the opening. After a second she called back, "Come on! It *is* beautiful!"

"I told you," said Don Augustin with a wink.

Chapo forced him to take the lead, keeping a tight grasp on his shirt, and they entered together. Cool air washed over him, and in the moment before his eyes adjusted to the dimness he was overcome with fear; he had a sense of having intruded upon some inhuman presence, and he flung his arm around Don Augustin's neck in a chokehold. But an instant later, though that sense of alienness did not diminish, he felt secure and at peace. Gradually the interior of the rock melted up from the dark. Four kerosene lanterns were set high on the walls at what Chapo took to be the cardinal points, and in their glow he saw that the center of the hollow—which was quite large, maybe seventy across and forty feet high—was occupied by a sunken pool. The water captured a sheen of the lantern light and seemed to be radiating a golden energy. Kneeling beside it, her head turned toward them, the gringa resembled a magical creature surprised in the act of drinking.

"Isn't it wonderful?" she said, and Chapo could only nod.

Ranged along the walls were stacks of books, bulging grain sacks, bundles of kindling, a pallet, and what appeared to be an altar on which rested a glowing cube. Chapo crossed the hollow to the altar and saw that the cube contained a silver rose. From moment to moment, the rose would become opaque and then solidify; it floated in brilliant eddies of its own light and was revolving slowly.

"A hologram," said the gringa, coming up beside Chapo.

"Ah," said Don Augustin. "So that's what it was."

"Was?" said the gringa.

"Everything changes into its ideal here," replied Don Augustin. "That's why I stay." He laughed. "You should have seen me before I came. I was a truly despicable sort."

The gringa pointed at the rose. "And what is it becoming?"

Don Augustin shook his head. "Who can say? I will watch and learn. But it is already a very important something." He took the gringa by the shoulders and guided her a few steps toward the pool. "You must wash, Señorita Anise."

"But . . ." The gringa seemed flustered.

"You are concerned by lack of privacy?"

"I . . . yes . . ."

"We will marvel at your beauty . . . nothing more." Don Augustin gave her a gentle push forward, then took Chapo by the arm, led him to a pair of wicker chairs set at one end of the pallet, and urged him to sit. "Would you like some whiskey?" he asked. From behind his chair he withdrew a dusty bottle and two glasses, and poured them each half full.

Chapo could not keep his eyes from straying to the gringa. Poised on the brink of the pool, naked to the waist, her nipples showing lavender against the milky skin of her breasts.

"The feminine form," said Don Augustin, raising his glass. "Even in its most unlovely incarnation, a miracle to behold."

Chapo drank, shut his eyes against the fire burning his throat, and heard a splash. He was disappointed not to have seen the rest of the gringa.

Don Augustin smiled. "Why don't you call her by name?"

Certain now that he was in the company of a brujo, Chapo didn't bother to ask how the old man had known this. "I don't like it."

"It strikes you as artificial?"

"Yeah, I guess."

"And yet it suits her, does it not? Contemplate the meaning of the word, Chapo. A clear intoxicating liquid with a complex and tart flavor. You really should use her name. I have faith you soon will."

Before Chapo could speak, the old man produced a vial from his pocket and held it up to catch the light. Within was a quantity of brown powder. "Perhaps you'd care to try some?" Don Augustin asked.

Chapo grew suspicious. "I ain't takin' your drugs, man. You think I'm stupid?"

"Try it, Chapo, and you will receive strengthening insights." Don Augustin opened the vial and spilled a little into Chapo's glass. "Once this was a powerful drug that wrenched the soul and left the body aching for days on end. But here it has become perfected, and before Anise returns, you will also have returned. And you will understand much that now you do not . . . though you may not realize it."

Chapo felt no compulsion to drink, and yet he did: what the old man had said seemed not coercive but reasonable. He experienced a brief anxiety and a sensation of vertigo. Then he was back to normal. Standing on the verge of an underground lake in a vast cavern, its ceiling thronged with stars. Awaiting the arrival of a golden boat that would bear him to the other side. The boat drew up to shore, rowed by men with muscular torsos and the heads of eagles. Chapo boarded and sat among them as they propelled him along in long gliding strokes. Their speech was like music, and though he didn't recognize the separate words, he understood their meaning. They were counseling him to steadfastness, to resist wrong turnings, to moral wisdom. At last the boat reached the far side, and Chapo walked out into a world of such brilliance that every shape appeared to be shifting, alternately becoming larger and smaller. It was as if he were walking through a forest of living crystals that grew and changed in a rain of light. It was so bright that he could not see the companion who had met him at the landing, nor the king whose judgment he must endure.

"That wasn't so bad, was it?" said Don Augustin.

Chapo blinked to see the rough rock walls, the wicker chairs, the dimly lit pool beside which Anise was standing, doing the buttons of her blouse. "What was that place, man?" he asked.

"Making decisions is difficult even for the informed." Don Augustin removed his straw hat and ran a hand through his young man's hair. "And of course you won't think of this during the crucial moment. Just remember, Chapo. There's no such thing as happiness. Only fools like the Americans pursue it. To use strength wisely—that's the only happiness you can know."

Anise came walking up. She inclined her head and squeezed a few last drops of water from a cable of her long blond hair. Her skin shone. She looked brand new. "I had the oddest dream just now," she said. "I mean I was awake, but I could have sworn it was a dream."

The three of them sat beneath the altar of the silver rose and ate a meal of stew and tortillas that Don Augustin had prepared over a small fire; the smoke from the fire was drawn toward the roof of the cave as if by a draft, but Chapo could see no smokehole. Don Augustin told them stories of his days selling blankets at a roadside stall north of Oaxaca. How he had cheated the gringos. How he had met a magician who had been transformed into a donkey. How once he had become so drunk on pulque that he had crossed over into the world of drunkards, where sidewalks sometimes ran along the sides of walls and the metal of lampposts was often pliant, where reflections were doubled and shadows were prone to turn into an inky liquid and drain off downhill. Finally he made them a bed of empty grain sacks and advised them to rest. They lay close together, almost touching, gazing up at the hypnotic revolutions of the silver rose, bathed in its eerie light, and soon were fast asleep.

The glow of sunset was shining through the cave mouth when they waked. Don Augustin was nowhere to be seen, but as they headed outside they discovered two objects lying just inside the entrance and knew without having to be told that these were his gifts. For Chapo there was a knife with a blood-red handle, and for Anise there was a blouse embroidered with a silver rose. Without the least sign of self-consciousness, she shrugged out of the one Chapo had bought and put the new one on. Only after she had done buttoning it did she display embarrassment. To make her feel at ease, Chapo pretended not to have noticed. They walked around to the white jeep, climbed in and drove west toward a horizon brushed with streaks of slate and mauve, where the evening star was now ascending.

They reached the final hiding place several hours before dawn. It was the largest of the three rocks, resembling a miniature mountain chain with separate peaks and slopes, and it faced onto the first of a range of brown hills dotted with organpipe cactus. Centuries of wind had carved a deep bay into the rock, and they drove the jeep all the way in and covered it with mesquite. Then they climbed to the top of the lowest peak and lay down in a shallow depression from which they could see for miles in every direction. To the east, south, and north all was still. Under the full moon, the desert was a milky white plain flecked by a thousand shadows. But to the west among the hills there showed an intermittent green glow. Watching it flicker and vanish made the back of Chapo's neck prickle.

Anise edged closer to him. "What could it be?"

"That's where we gonna get gas."

"The village?" She looked horrified.

"San Juan de la Fiebra. They a buncha crazy fuckers. Some gringo come a few years back and give 'em Stateside drugs. All kinda extreme shit. And he preached this weird religion . . . like it's got Jesus, but other gods, too. You gotta watch your behavior 'round there."

She stared out at the hills, her eyes narrowing as if focusing in on something he couldn't see. "We'll be all right," she said flatly. "Ever since we met Don Augustin, I've known that."

Chapo grunted. "You can't trust how brujos make you feel."

"It's hard to believe that's what he was."

"What else?"

She thought about it. "I don't know."

Pale clouds were drifting across the stars in the west, and Chapo wondered if the clouds were above the sea. He lay flat on his stomach, watching them cruise.

"What are you gonna do after we get to Huayacuatia, Chapo?"

"Head on back, probably."

She didn't say anything, but after a couple of seconds she ran her hand along the back of his neck. The touch made him shiver. He didn't look up.

"Chapo?" She whispered it, her voice burred.

He had to look at her, then. She was smiling just enough to show a sliver of teeth as white as the desert, and the centers of her all-colored eyes were pricked with moonlight, and her golden hair was outlined in stars. He felt he was falling up toward her.

"Yeah, I . . ."

"I want you," she said.

Nobody had ever said it that way to him. Let's fuck, maybe. Let's go upstairs, or Let's see what you got, Chapo. Never "I want you." He almost didn't know what it meant, and maybe it didn't mean what he thought. He wasn't sure how to answer. "Why?" he said, and felt foolish. Acting like it was his first time. But he *couldn't* understand why. Just because he'd been helping her? That was a good reason, he guessed. But he hadn't thought it would be her reason.

She took his hand and laid it on the silver rose, on the soft weights beneath. The nipple hardened against his palm. He closed his fingers around her breast, squeezing it, and she arched her back, pressing against his hand. She let out a hissing breath. He moved his other hand beneath the blouse, then moved both hands over her breasts, cupping them, rubbing the aureoles with the balls of his thumbs, knowing their shapes. She unbuttoned the blouse, tossed it aside. It floated away like a silver wing. Veiled in her hair, he kissed the milky flesh. So much warmth, so much sweetness. He lost track of where his hands were, what his lips were doing. It was all warmth, all sweetness, and she was whispering his name, saying she wanted him, wanted him now.

Going into her was like falling into a good dream, and it *was* different with her . . . So different he couldn't say exactly how. He worried about her back on the stone, about hurting her. But soon he stopped worrying, and what he felt at the end was maybe a little stronger, a little more heat, but really was pretty much like all the other times, except for how happy he was at what *she* felt, at the way her body stiffened, her nails pricking him deep, holding him tight and still, as if were he to move, she'd break into pieces.

Afterward, becoming aware again of the cold desert wind, they got under the blanket, and Anise began talking excitedly, saying she loved him, saying he couldn't go back to the Crust, he should return to LA with her and go to school, and she loved him, and her father would help them get started, and Oh, Chapo, how much I love you, and he didn't know what to say. He had thought he'd known her before they made love, but though now he felt intimate with her, she also seemed a stranger, someone new. He realized he hadn't known her, that she had been in his eyes an emblem of foreign territory, of wealth and mysterious cities, a border he had finally crossed. Now she was no longer an emblem but real, and he was confused. Who was she? He turned on his side, pushed her gently onto her back and looked down at her, trying to find her inside her eyes, trying to understand what he felt.

"Chapo," she said, reaching up to him.

He laid a finger to her lips and studied her face.

"What are you doing?" she asked.

"Shh!"

"I know," she said after a while, "I know there's things you want to tell me, but you can't find the words."

He nodded.

"You'll find them," she said. "You will! But you have to come back with me . . . to LA."

She started talking again, but slower, her words as gentle as an easy rain, and everything she said clarified something behind her eyes, something he felt. He could see her strength, her goodness, and his recognition of those qualities seemed to make what he felt equally good and strong . . . though he couldn't put a name to his feelings. She told him about her city, the towers, the displays of light in the sky, the exotic pleasures and the roar of fifteen million souls. What she said began to make sense. He would go to LA, he would understand everything. And in that country of light, wealth would be a power, a power he could use in ways that the wealthy Americans had forgotten. He saw this was to be his destiny.

The sky paled to lavender, the stars thinned and shone gold, and they made love once again. They made love into the morning, into the blazing heat, and though he was bone-weary, Chapo could not stop making love to her. It was too beautiful to stop, too important a connection to break. And when at last they did fall asleep, they were still joined, still tangled like a knot of brown and white thread. In Chapo's dream he thought they were melting, becoming stone, and in the days to come they would be mistaken by other lovers who had climbed this high for a vaguely human shape produced from the rock by a miracle of wind and weather.

* * *

At dusk they drove into the hills and stopped on a rise above the village of San Juan de la Fiebra. At that distance it looked to be a peaceful place of white houses with red tile roofs and lights dancing in the windows. Chapo gave his pistol to Anise and told her to hide among the cactus until he returned. She begged him to take care, kissing him with such passion that when he drove away, he felt he was off on a noble mission and not simply going to find gas.

Though the rise was only a few hundred feet above San Juan de la Fiebra, the road wound through the hills, and it took Chapo half an hour to reach the village. Entering it, he passed the remains of an enormous bonfire, itself the size of a small hill, from which projected weird charred shapes that reminded him of giant insect legs, and he assumed this had been the source of the green glow. On the walls of the houses were painted horned goats and bearded corpses and creatures half fly and half man, all done in drips and spatters of red paint, making it seem they'd been rendered in a murder victim's blood. People dressed like campesinos in white cotton and straw hats came into the streets on hearing his engine. They stood in the street ahead of him, and he was forced to weave in and out among them, obscuring them in the wake of his dust. They were mostly wiry people of Indian stock, but he spotted a few with dark skin and blue eyes and a gringo cast to their features; they said nothing, only tracked him with their stares. A cold patch formed between his shoulderblades, and he had trouble swallowing.

At the far end of the village stood a Mexalina station, also adorned with grisly murals, its green pumps decorated like evil Christmas trees with garlands of cactus buds and wreaths of whitish leaves. As he approached, an amplified voice began speaking from somewhere. "GUARDIANS, AWAKE! FOR IN THE TIME OF THE FURY, THOU MUST BE EVER VIGILANT. BEWARE THE STRANGER WHO BEARS THE SEEDS OF JOY IN HIS HEART, FOR FROM HIS JOY MAY SPROUT THE FRUITS OF CORRUPTION."

Chapo pulled up to the pumps and cut the engine. A gaunt man wearing a grease-stained coverall, with coppery skin and gray streaks in his hair, ambled toward him from the door. Chapo ordered ten gallons, having to shout to make himself heard over the voice, which continued its Biblical admonitions; it was so loud, he could scarcely think. Pretending to be at ease, unconcerned, he got out of the jeep and went over to the Coke machine. Fed in coins. He uncapped the frosty bottle and took a deep drink. Looked back along the street. None of the people had moved. They were all gazing toward the station. The lights from the windows were unbelievably bright, spraying golden rays into the streets, as if each house contained a sun, and above the crown of the hill where Anise was hiding, the stars were showing this same golden color against the black sky.

". . . SHOW HIM THE MERCY OF MAD JESUS GONE SCREAM-
ING FROM THE TOMB, HIS NAILS TIPPED WITH BLOOD, HIS
THOUGHTS LIKE KNIVES . . ."

Chapo glanced into the window of the station. And froze. Sitting on the
counter beside the cash register was a hologram identical to the one belonging to Don Augustin: a silver rose revolving in its own glow. He didn't
know what to make of it, whether it was a bad sign or good.

". . . HARROW HIM, TEST HIM, FOR ONLY THUS WILL YOU
KNOW HIM . . ."

The voice was switched off. Turning, Chapo saw that six men on
motorcyles were ranged along the street facing the station. Their rides were
sleek and finished in black enamel that gleamed like chitin; they wore red
helmets, and their headlights were green and faceted like insect eyes. Pistols
at their sides. The attendant holstered the pump in its socket and came
over. Chapo fumbled for his wallet. But the attendant held up his hand to
ward off payment. "No charge, Sẽnor," he said, and smiled. His incisors
were rimmed with gold, and a red stone like a drop of blood was set into
one of the front teeth.

"It's all right," said Chapo. "I want to pay."

The attendant just kept smiling.

One of the motorcyclists revved his engine and glided to within a few
feet of Chapo. "Where are you going?" he asked.

Chapo couldn't see his face behind the black plastic of the helmet. "To
Huayacuatia," he said.

"And from where do you come?"

"The Crust."

The man shouted this information to the other motorcyclists, and they
absorbed it without reaction. He turned back to Chapo. Lifted his visor and
peered at Chapo. His face was bronzed and hawkish, and his eyes were
balled and white like a statue's eyes, with no irises or pupils. Beneath his left
ear, tracing the jawline, was a thin scar. Chapo's legs felt weak and boneless,
and gooseflesh fanned across his shoulders.

"Are you a true believer?" the man asked.

Despite those eyes, Chapo knew the man could somehow perceive him,
and he did not think he could successfully lie. "In what should I believe?"

"In the mysteries and the drugs." The man held up a vial of brown
powder that dangled from a chain around his neck, and Chapo recognized
it to be the drug he'd taken in the cave. "In the power of uncreated things,
in the light bred from the final darkness."

"I know the drug," said Chapo. "But I don't understand these other
things."

The man leaned toward him over his handlebars. "You are no seeker," he said, making it sound like an accusation.

Chapo shrugged. "I gotta be goin', man."

The man settled back on his seat. "Go, then."

As he walked back to the jeep, Chapo could sense the man's white eyes driving nails into his back. He climbed in, switched on the ignition. The needle on the gas gauge stabilized at almost three-quarters full. At least that much was all right. He gunned the engine. Then he pulled away from the pumps, swung the jeep into a U-turn and passed behind the five motorcyclists. They didn't bother to turn and watch him.

Once again he had to weave in and out among the bystanders. But this time they paid him no mind. They gazed intently toward the station as if awaiting instructions. At the site of the bonfire, people were piling cactus limbs onto the charred heap, and Chapo wondered if that was how they got it to burn a funny color, if the cactus limbs yielded a green essence. He listened for the sound of motorcycle engines as he drove into the hills, and heard nothing. Yet he didn't feel right. How could you feel right in a place where blind men could see?

He stopped on the crest of the rise, and Anise came scrambling up from a gulley. "Did you get it?" she asked breathlessly, climbing in.

"Yeah," he said, and was about to add that there might be trouble, when a shot rang out. Pinged off the hood. More shots. He pushed Anise out of the jeep and hauled her back down into the gulley, behind a boulder. Grabbed the pistol from her and trained it on the slopes. The moon was just up, and in its light the ranks of cacti looked unreal: an alien army with shadowy upraised arms. Then he heard the motorcycles. They were buzzing, swarming nearby. He glanced right. Left. That way the gulley gave out into a pitch of huge boulders. Gray shapes. Like frozen waves, melted statues. Motorcycles would never be able to penetrate them, at least not with any speed. Taking Anise's hand, he moved in a crouch along the gulley.

Raspy whine of an engine winding out, and one of the motorcycles jumped the gulley. Fire lanced down from a shadow hand, and Chapo returned the fire. Knew he'd missed.

"Who are they?" Anise clutched at his arm.

"I don't know."

He could still hear the engines buzzing as they entered the field of broken boulders, but he couldn't see any of them. Like spirits, invisible when you turned your eye on them, reappearing when you looked away. He crawled through the boulders until he found one with a cleft that offered a clear field of fire up and down slope. He drew a deep breath. Fear was stamped on Anise's face, and he couldn't think of anything to ease her. The silver rose on her chest heaved.

Fuckin' brujo!

Chapo checked his clip. Seven left. Seven bullets for six riders. He dug the red knife from his pocket, handed it to Anise. For a split-second, he thought she was going to fling it down. But then she flicked open the blade and set herself. Ready to fight. Chapo felt proud of her.

"Listen!" she said.

The engines had stopped.

He peeked out over the boulder. Spotted a couple of shadows edging toward them downslope. Maybe this wasn't such a great place to make a stand. He looked behind them. Adrenaline was pumping his heart, and his eyes were strained so wide, it seemed he could see every weed and pebble. The boulder field declined into the deep shadow of the next hill. Darkness like black gas. What the hell! There might be a cave. A trail. Something. He led the way through the rocks, keeping in a crouch. The amplified voice began to echo up from the village, the words unintelligible, booming out its nonsense. Loud enough that he couldn't hear the scrape of a boot, the rattle of a kicked pebble. The bastards might have planned it!

Halfway across the field, he began to feel a presence nearby. It was a trustworthy feeling, a Crust feeling. Tuning his senses higher.

But it didn't help.

As they passed between two of the larger boulders, a rider jumped him. Knocked him flat. Chapo lost his grip on the automatic. The rider pinned him with his knees, smashed a gloved fist into his chin, dazing him. Chapo could see his vague reflection in the visor above him. Then the rider leaped up, a red knife sprouting from his shoulder, and backhanded Anise to the ground. Chapo scrabbled for the automatic, found it. Squeezed off a round just as the rider dived at him. The bullet twisted the rider in mid-air, and he landed face down beside Chapo. Muffled wet sounds came from inside the helmet.

Chapo came to his knees. A serpent of blood trickled from the corner of Anise's mouth, black-looking. He started to stand, but something cold touched the back of his head, and a hollow voice told him to put down the gun. Three more riders stepped from behind stones and stood over Anise. Chapo dropped his eyes. Studied the weeds springing up by his knees, the pattern of pebbles. He had been waiting for this moment all his life, and now it was here, he almost welcomed it.

Anise was speaking, but Chapo was too gone into his preparation for death to hear the words. He tried to think about something good. That's what Moro had told him before they had crossed to Stateside. "If you feel it comin', man," Moro had said, "think 'bout somethin' good. 'Cause then

if you live forever, maybe you go with that good thing. And if you don't"—
Moro had grinned—"what the fuck's the difference?" Chapo called up
memories of the red glow, the border. Wild nights. None of it seemed
good. His only good thing was that one time with Anise, and that was too
much the reason for his dying to give him the peace he needed.

The last rider emerged from behind a boulder and looked down at
Chapo. No way to tell because they were all dressed alike, all hidden behind
their visors, but Chapo figured him for the one he'd talked to back at the
Mexalina station. The rider nodded, as if seeing exactly what he'd expected.
He turned and went a step toward Anise. Two of the men had hauled her
to her feet and were gripping her arms. Their leader stopped dead and
flipped up his visor. Lifted his chained vial, tapped a little powder onto his
tongue. Gazed at her chest. From where Chapo was kneeling, he could see
the rider's warrior profile. One white eye bright as new marble, set in a
stern bronze mask. The rider removed his helmet. His black hair feathered
in the breeze. He laid his hand flat against the silver rose on Anise's breast.
She squirmed, and the two men holding her applied pressure, making her
cry out. The rider tipped his head to the sky and stood absolutely still. After
a second, his hand began to tremble. He jerked it away, said something in
Indian to the two men. They let go of Anise.

She hesitated a moment. Then she scuttled to Chapo's side and kneeled
beside him, throwing an arm around his shoulder. The cold thing at the
back of Chapo's head went away. Blond hair curtained his eyes, and he
brushed it aside. The rider walked over, holding his helmet under his arm
like a knight after a tournament; the rest gathered behind him. He gestured
to the body, and two of the others picked the dead man up, propping him
erect between them. His knees were buckled, his chest a mire of blood and
charred fabric. Yet Chapo had a funny notion that he wasn't dead. Not
dead forever, anyhow. If blind men could see in San Juan de la Fiebra,
maybe the dead could be reclaimed. The careful way they were treating the
body supported that notion.

"Who are you?" asked the rider.

Chapo was still halfway to death. He didn't have an answer.

"I'm an American," said Anise tremulously, as if citizenship were at the
core of her being.

One of the men laughed. "They don't know who they are."

"Who are you?" the rider repeated.

Chapo got slowly to his feet, feeling drained. He looked into the rider's
white eyes. Depthless glowing surfaces like the desert. "Tell me why it's
important," he said.

"It's not important," said the rider. "I merely wish to know."

"I'm Chapo, and she's Anise."

Once again there was laughter, and the rider said, "These are only your names. Perhaps you *don't* know who you are."

"Well, who are you?" Anise shrilled. "Just who the hell do you think you are to go . . ." She broke off, cowed by the rider's stare.

"I am a Guardian of San Juan de la Fiebra," he said. "I am the madness of Christ, and the innocence of Moloch. I follow the northern teachings, and I have borne witness to the man in the desert . . . as have you, apparently." He indicated Anise's blouse.

"Don Augustin?" Anise looked at Chapo, then back at the rider. "Is that who you mean?"

"By his sign you may pass," said the rider. "But be warned. Do not return to San Juan de la Fiebra until you have learned who you are."

He signaled the others, and carrying their dead companion, they headed up the slope, becoming lost among the shadows of the boulder field.

Anise slumped down, leaning against Chapo. "You see?" she said. "He did help us. I *knew* he did."

Chapo watched the slope, wanting to make sure the riders had gone. "The brujo?"

"Uh-huh."

"Maybe, maybe not."

The brujo's red knife lay on the ground. Chapo wiped the blade clean on his trousers, folded it and slipped it into his pocket.

"How can you say that?" asked Anise.

"I told you . . . you can't trust brujos. The drug he gave me, the dream you had. All this might still be part of that. Could be none of it happened, or just a little of it happened, and this"—he tapped his forehead —"this did the rest."

"Why would you think that?" She stroked his hair, concern on her face.

"You believe a blind man can see? Shit! That coulda been what'cha call a hallucination."

"No it wasn't!"

"You believe in magic?"

"I don't know if I do or not. But that wasn't magic."

"What was it, then?"

"Little cameras in his eyes, wired to the optic nerves. Didn't you see his scar?" She touched Chapo's cheek beneath his left ear. "That's where they put the power source. I've seen the same thing a hundred times."

"You sure?"

"Of course." She took him by the shoulders. "Don't you start thinking none of this is real, Chapo." She kissed him, and like a slow magic, the kiss gradually brought him all the way back to life. Gold flecks seemed to have surfaced in her eyes, and everything about her seemed to have been refined. "There," she said, smiling. "Is that what you call a hallucination?"

"No," said Chapo, dazzled.

"It's all been real," she said. "That's how I know we're supposed to be together . . . because it's been so strong."

Chapo went along with her, but in his heart he wasn't so sure. Blind men with cameras in their eyes . . . That didn't sound real to him.

From a hilltop above the Pacific, Huayacuatia looked like Paradise. White sand fringed by a tame jungle of orchids and sapodilla, auguacaste and sabal palms. The trunks of the palms were bowed toward the sea, and a westerly breeze blew their fronds back from it. Half-hidden among the vegetation were villas and hotels of all colors. Pastel blues and yellows and pinks. Late afternoon sun kindled diamond fires out on the sea. As they drove into the town, music came to their ears. Soft, sweet music that seemed to be part of the wind and not issuing from a mechanical source. Laughter came from behind the high walls of the hotels, and even the policemen smiled.

They drove onto the grounds of the biggest hotel beneath a blue stucco arch with ironwork letters that spelled CASA DE MIRAGLOS. The young man who parked their jeep wore a white jacket and creased blue trousers and shiny shoes, and looked a lot like Chapo. He gave Chapo a suspicious glance, smiled at Anise, and told them they could find the manager's office beyond the swimming pool. They walked leisurely along a flagstone path past bungalows with macaws tethered to perches beside the door. Bright things darted high in the branches of fig and mango trees. Chapo thought they were birds, but then one swooped close, circling him, and he saw it was a bright blue ball with stylized yellow wings and no head. Alarmed, he swatted at it. The thing let out a warbling squeal and broke into dozens of cartoon music notes that played a melody as they faded. Not wanting to appear unsophisticated, Chapo didn't ask what it was. The things kept swooping at him, giving him starts. He smiled and pretended he'd seen them many times before.

The pool was an Olympic-sized emerald lozenge filled with swimmers, and people were sitting beneath striped umbrellas around it. One woman whose face looked about sixty years old had the body of a teenager; her hair changed color as she talked, shifting from vivid green to crimson to a striped design of black and yellow. Something silver and saucer-shaped sailed through the air and landed at Chapo's feet; tiny silver animals swarmed off it, leaped into the pool and vanished. Two kids ran over. One snatched the saucer up and sailed it across the pool toward another kid. A withered white-haired man was talking rapidly to three women, his words materializing in pale smoke above his head; when he stopped for breath, the smoke strung out into little dots, giving visible expression to his pause. Chapo felt lost. There were a hundred things going on that he didn't understand. He remembered Don Augustin's world of drunkards, and had the idea that he had stumbled into a sillier version of it.

In the manager's office, Anise placed a call to her father in the States. But he was on the border, and would be out of touch until late that night. No problem, said the manager. He'd arrange a couple of rooms and . . .

"One room will do," said Anise. "And if you could pick up some clean clothes . . . for both of us."

The manager had difficulty repressing a look of disapproval, but said it would be his pleasure.

Two hours later, dressed in fine clothes, they ate dinner in the hotel restaurant: a dimly lit room with heavy silver and candelabras and linen tablecloths. White birds of pure light winged silently above their heads. Music seemed to be everywhere, even in the conversations of the people dining nearby. In the center of the room was a pit from which a sculpture made of fire leaped and crackled, shaping itself into image after image. Jaguar, swan, serpent, and a hundred more. The waiters went about their work as silently as the birds of light, depositing new dishes and bottles of wine. Chapo was astounded, delighted. He had never seen such beauty, never tasted such food. Though he had been nervous upon entering the restaurant, he soon felt at home. They drank and laughed, laughed and drank, talking of the things they would do in LA. With their dessert, the waiter brought a note for Anise; it said her father would arrive the next morning.

"You'll like him," she told Chapo. "He's different from these people. Strong like you."

Dizzy with the wine, Chapo believed her. Disbelief was not in him. Through the silver branches of the candelabra, she seemed to sparkle. Even the things she said seemed to leave a sparkle in the air, and he was coming to think that this sparkle was emblematic of the real world.

They finished eating, and as he stood Chapo knocked over a bottle of wine. A rich red stain spread over the tablecloth. Their waiter mopped at the stain, assuring him that it was no trouble, his tone apologetic. But the other diners stared and laughed behind their hands. Chapo was frozen by those stares, feeling as if he had been caught at something.

"Don't pay any attention to them," Anise said, pulling him away.

In the central pit a fiery eagle appeared to be looking straight at Chapo, regarding him with disfavor.

* * *

Making love that night was not as good for Chapo as it had been on the
desert. The room was so large, so incomprehensible in its luxury. Everything vanished into the walls at the push of a button. Punch room service,
and the image of a beautiful woman sprang out of nowhere to take your
order. If you touched an ordinary surface, music would play or walls would
turn into windows or video screens. And as he made love to Anise, he
couldn't escape the feeling that any moment the wrong surface would be
touched and the room would fold in upon them and he, too, would vanish
or be transformed.

He waked around three o'clock, needing to go to the bathroom. But he
couldn't find the button that made the toilet appear. Finally, not wanting
to wake Anise and show what an idiot he was, he went out into the hall and
urinated in a potted plant. A couple walked past the instant he had done
zipping up, and he pretended to be examining the leaves. He returned to
the room and lay down beside Anise. She was beautiful in the half-light,
with the silken coverlet slipped down to her waist. Her breasts had the same
glistening smoothness as the material, and her face had the serenity of a
goddess. She would help him, he thought. She would teach him how to
move in her brilliant world. But the thought did not comfort him, and he
was unable to get back to sleep.

The next morning, waiting for her father, Chapo sat on the edge of a
chair, his hands clasped in his lap. He sat very still as if posing for a photograph. No thoughts occurred to him. The inside of his head might have
been poured full of cement. Anise was busy telephoning friends in the
States, and didn't notice his silence.

Suddenly the door burst open, and a lean sun-burned man with blond
hair strode in. He didn't seem old enough to be Anise's father, but she ran
to him and hugged him, talking a mile a minute. Chapo sat without moving. Anise pulled back from her father, and said, "Daddy, I want you to
meet someone."

The man looked at Chapo and smiled thinly. "Oh, yeah." Keeping an
arm around Anise, he reached into his jacket pocket and extracted a banded
stack of bills. Held them out. "Here y'are, boy. Twenty-five thousand . . .
just like advertised." His stare locked onto Chapo's, and in that exchange,
in his pose, was a world of information. *This is mine,* said the arm around
Anise. *This is yours,* said the hand holding the bills. *And that's all you're
getting,* said the stare. Chapo wasn't afraid of him. But he understood
something else from the man's attitude. He couldn't have put that sense of
ultimate distance and difference into words, and maybe the man couldn't
have done so, either. Yet they both were aware of it.

"No, Daddy," said Anise. "That's not how it is. He and I . . ."

Chapo could barely hear her. She was already receding from him, crossing the border into her own land. He got up and walked over to them and took the money. It had a good weight.

"Chapo!" Amazement, shock.

He eased past them into the hall. She cried out again, but then the door slammed shut, shearing off her voice.

The young man who brought the jeep from the parking lot extended his hand for a tip. Chapo cursed him and sped out beneath the blue arch. He sat for a moment beyond the arch, letting the engine idle, letting the warm sun soak into him. He felt empty, but the feeling was clean. A freedom from wanting, from dreams too sweet to digest. He had a final look around at Paradise. It wasn't so goddamn much! It was frail. One lapse in security, and the monkeys would come swinging back to retake the jungle, and the Devil would bask by the emerald pool, his laughter echoing through the ruins. One shot of heavy weather, and you wouldn't be able to tell it from the Crust. That was the Crust's strength: it was already down to the bone. Chapo blew out a long sighing breath, wishing he could get rid of memories as easily as bad air. Then he threw the jeep into gear and headed north along the coast, taking the legal roads home.

Back in the Crust, back in the cellar among the candles and shadows. Chapo hid the money a dozen places, two thousand dollars in each. He held back the last thousand. He'd take it and have himself a night. Spend it at La Manzanita. They had the best girls there. Young girls fresh from in the villages, still full of life, still believing the Crust was everything you could hope for. Maybe he'd have twenty-five such nights. What else could he do with the money? A bar, a business? He couldn't picture himself growing old and fat behind a counter. No, he'd have twenty-five nights to remind him of Anise. To light a thought like a blond candle, set it burning in the blackness of his skull. He wondered what had been between them. Love? Yeah, a little. But he thought it had more to do with innocence. Hers *and* his. Paring hers down, shoring his up. There was even more to it, though. You could never figure anything out, never say anything. The second you did, it became a lie, the truth shrunk to fit your words. He ran his thumb across the bills. They felt cool and slick, like strange skins. Twenty-four thousand. What if some opportunity came up, some big score?

Well, he'd have the one night, anyway.

Find a slim brown girl who'd fuck him mean and burn out the last sugars of Huayacuatia.

He swallowed one upper, then did another.

Out in the blood-red light, the wild laughter and crazy music, he walked briskly down Avenida Juarez toward the border. Every rut brimmed with shadow. In a house with black curtains a baby was screaming. Even with those curtains, crimson light penetrated and made it hard to sleep, and even when you slept, the light brought dreams that scared you awake. But the dreams made you strong, and it would be a strong baby, strong enough to dream about crossing that light.

The side wall of La Manzanita was six feet from the border. Before going in, Chapo stood an arm's length away, facing the shimmering redness. He'd seen guys jump into it, others just stroll on through. Drunks, suicides, men who believed the border was the door to a kind of afterlife. He'd had the urge himself to take that stroll. But no more. He felt satisfaction in being able to face it and not know that urge. Its hum and sizzle no longer an allure, no longer a humiliation, a weakness. Borders were everywhere, and once you recognized that, you could be strong in spite of them . . . or because of them. This unreal fire might be the least of borders. That much he'd learned on the trip to Huayacuatia, that much was true enough to say and not diminish. And having this one powerful truth was more important than having the money or Anise. It gave him a new purchase, a new perspective. He thought if he kept staring into the red glow, he would see the evolution of that truth.

He took out the brujo's knife, its enamel the same color as the border. Considered tossing it through. Magic, huh? Would it penetrate, would its flight curve around buildings and find a secret target? After a moment, he decided to hang onto it.

Save it for some special bad heart.

"Chapo!"

Rafael was coming toward him, knife in hand. His jaw still bruised from where Chapo had nailed him with the shopping bag. He dropped into a crouch, cut lazy crescents in the air.

No easy way out this time.

Chapo tried to flick the red knife open, but the blade stuck.

Brujos! Chapo silently cursed Don Augustin.

They circled each other, shoes hissing in the dirt, breath ragged. All the other sounds went away.

In the first thirty seconds Chapo took a slice on his left arm. It wasn't serious, it focused him. He sucked up the pain and studied Rafael's moves. Rafael grinned to see the blood.

Keep grinnin', asshole, Chapo said to himself.

He shook his guard arm, pretending it was bothering him.

Rafael went for the opening.

Chapo sidestepped the lunge, tripped Rafael and sent him slamming into the wall of La Manzanita. As he slumped down, the knife slipping from his fingers, Chapo grabbed him in a chokehold. Lugged him toward the border. Held him up inches away. He hadn't been angry during the fight, but now he was almost sick with anger.

Rafael was too close to the red glow to want to struggle. He twisted his head, trying to see Chapo. Even the sweat beading his forehead shone red. Dull chubby face clenched in fear. But he wasn't going to beg. Code of the Crust. He'd die stupid and macho.

That was what drained off Chapo's anger, the recognition of his own stupidity, of a poverty that left you only with a fool's pride and a talent for dying. He dragged Rafael away from the border and let him fall. Rafael couldn't believe it. He stared at Chapo, uncomprehending.

To use strength wisely—that's the only happiness you can know.

Chapo could have sworn that he heard Don Augustin's voice speaking those words, and thought that if the knife had opened, he would never have come to this moment. The brujo might have done him a favor. He studied Rafael. "Wanna go to La Manzanita?" he asked.

"La Manzanita?" Rafael blinked, confused.

"Yeah, I did some business last week. Gonna celebrate."

"You want me to go with you?"

"Yeah, sure."

"Why?" Rafael said after a pause, suspicious. "Why you doin' this?"

"'Cause this"—Chapo flourished his knife—"it's stupid. Why we gotta do it? What's the point?"

"You slugged me, man!"

Chapo displayed his bleeding arm. "We're even, okay?"

Rafael wasn't satisfied. "What kinda business give you the coin for La Manzanita?"

"Maybe I'll tell you sometime, maybe we'll do some business."

That appeared to stun Rafael. Nobody did business with him. He was too slow-witted to be slick. But, Chapo thought, maybe he could be loyal. Maybe he was born to be loyal, and no one had ever offered him a chance. It rang true. And loyalty could make up for a lot. He kicked Rafael's knife over to him. "Let's do it," he said.

Rafael picked up the knife. There was a moment. It showed in his eyes, glowing red like a little border. But the moment passed. "Okay," he said, pocketing the knife. He came to his feet, smiling. The smile was genuine, a signal as open and honest as a dog wagging its tail. Chapo wasn't ready to buy it . . . not all the way. But he did buy the concept that had produced it, and he was beginning to enjoy the feeling of control.

"La Manzanita!" said Rafael, looking at the building. "Man, I hear they got women in there can tie a knot in it, y'know. Man!"

"Let's find out," said Chapo.

"You go there a lot?" Rafael asked.

"Naw, man. Too much make you crazy . . . be bad for doin' business."
Rafael nodded sagely, like Oh, yeah, he knew all about that.

Chapo clapped him on the back, tried to steer him toward the door; but
Rafael balked, suspicion visible in his face.

"What's wrong?" Chapo asked.

"This don't make no sense, man," said Rafael.

"What you think . . . I'm gonna pay somebody to screw you to
death?"

Rafael didn't respond to the joke, engaging Chapo's eyes soberly.

"Look," said Chapo. "Just 'cause we ain't killin' each other don't mean
it don't make sense. You got anything better goin? I mean don't tell me you
ain't taken chances for a lot less reward."

Rafael's hand snaked into the pocket where he kept his knife.

All Chapo's instincts cried out for him to open Rafael up for the flies; but
he realized he had come to the end of those tactics. They brought you
temporary survival, and that had always been enough for him. But now he
wanted . . . he wasn't sure exactly what. Power for a start, and then something more. This hassle with Rafael was a test he had to pass.

"Hey," he said, throwing an arm around Rafael's shoulder. "You wanna
cut me, or you wanna lie down on silk? You wanna watch me bleed, or you
wanna hear a sugar voice sayin', 'Oh, Rafael! You so fine!' C'mon, man!
We'll have a good time tonight, and then tomorrow we can get back to
killin' each other. Or maybe not. Maybe we'll catch fire inside, maybe we'll
find out we can burn together."

Rafael's muscles relaxed, and he giggled, getting behind Chapo's rap.
"Yeah," he said. "Maybe we cross the border, cut some gringos."

"Shit!" said Chapo. "We gonna do more'n that, man." He spat at the
border, and for a second he believed his spit would dissolve the fire instead
of merely sizzling and vanishing, revealing a fabulous unknown America, a
place of golden women with jeweled eyes and occult powers. "We gonna
raid the secret tower, bring back the magic dagger. Know what I'm talkin'
'bout?"

"Yeah!" said Rafael gleefully, jittering with excitement. "Yeah!"

"We gonna dance on the moon, we gonna break the silver chains and
loose the final beast."

From behind them came a shriek, curses. An old man dressed in the
cotton trousers and shirt of a campesino was lunging toward the border,
trying to hurl himself into it, while an old woman clung to him, dragging
him back. A crowd was gathering, hemming them in against the shimmering curtain of energy. They laughed, talked, pointed. The old woman
called on God and the Virgin for help, her cries as shrill as those of a
frightened bird.

"Shit!" said Rafael, and spat. "I hate that weak shit, man! People ain't got the strength to deal, they might as well be dead, y'know."

Chapo started to say he had come to realize that what was usually considered strength sometimes was a weakness and vice versa; but on second thought, he decided it would be better for Rafael to remain ignorant of subtleties such as this. They were not friends, after all, only partners in crime. "Yeah," he said, pushing Rafael toward the entrance of the club. "Fuck 'em! We ain't got to worry 'bout bein' weak, right?"

Laughter and soft music issued from the door of La Manzanita. White light veiled the threshold. Together, Chapo and Rafael crossed over.

THE DAKAR RUN

Clark Howard

Jack Sheffield limped out of the little Theatre Americain with John Garfield's defiant words still fresh in his mind. "What are you gonna do, kill me?" Garfield, as Charley Davis, the boxer, had asked Lloyd Gough, the crooked promoter, at the end of *Body and Soul*. Then, challengingly, smugly, with the Garfield arrogance, "Everybody dies!" And he had walked away, with Lilli Palmer on his arm.

Pausing outside to look at the *Body and Soul* poster next to the box-office, Sheffield sighed wistfully. They were gone now, Garfield and Lilli Palmer, black-and-white films, the good numbers like Hazel Brooks singing "Am I Blue?" Even boxing—*real* boxing—was down the tubes. In the old days, hungry kids challenged seasoned pros. Now millionaires fought gold-medal winners.

Shaking his head at the pity of things changed, Sheffield turned up his collar against the chilly Paris night and limped up La Villette to the Place de Cluny. There was a cafe there called the Nubian, owned by a very tall Sudanese who mixed his own mustard, so hot it could etch cement. Every Tuesday night, the old-movie feature at the Theatre Americain changed and Jack Sheffield went to see it, whatever it was, and afterward he always walked to the Nubian for sausage and mustard and a double gin. Later, warm from the gin and the food, he would stroll, rain or fair, summer or winter, along the Rue de Rivoli next to the Tuileries, down to the Crazy Horse Saloon to wait for the chorus to do its last high kick so that Jane, the long-legged Englishwoman with whom he lived, could change and go home. Tuesdays never varied for Sheffield.

How many Tuesdays, he wondered as he entered the Nubian, had he been doing this exact same thing? As he pulled out a chair at the rickety little table for two at which he always sat, he tried to recall how long he had been with Jane. Was it three years or four? Catching the eye of the Sudanese, Sheffield raised his hand to signal that he was here, which was all he had to do; he never varied his order. The Sudanese nodded and walked with a camel-like gait toward the kitchen, and Sheffield was about to resume mentally backtracking his life when a young girl came in and walked directly to his table.

"Hi," she said.

He looked at her, tilting his head an inch, squinting slightly without his glasses. When he didn't respond at once, the girl gave him a wry, not totally amused look.

"I'm Chelsea," she said pointedly. "Chelsea Sheffield. Your daughter." She pulled out the opposite chair. "Don't bother to get up."

Sheffield stared at her incredulously, lips parted but no words being generated by his surprised brain.

"Mother," she explained, "said all I had to do to find you in Paris was locate a theater that showed old American movies, wait until the bill changed, and stand outside after the first show. She said if you didn't walk out, you were either dead or had been banished from France."

"Your mother was always right," he said, adding drily, "about everything."

"She also said you might be limping, after smashing up your ankle at Le Mans two years ago. Is the limp permanent?"

"More or less." He quickly changed the subject. "Your mother's well, I presume."

"Very. Like a Main Line Philadelphia doctor's wife should be. Her picture was on the society page five times last year."

"And your sister?"

"Perfect," Chelsea replied, "just as she's always been. Married to a proper young stockbroker, mother of two proper little girls, residing in a proper two-story Colonial, driving a proper Chrysler station wagon. Julie has *always* been proper. I was the foul-mouthed little girl who was too much like my race-car-driver daddy, remember?"

Sheffield didn't know whether to smile or frown. "What are you doing in Paris?" he asked.

"I came over with my boy friend. We're going to enter the Paris-to-Dakar race."

Now it was Sheffield who made a wry face. "Are you serious?"

"You better believe it," Chelsea assured him.

"Who's your boy friend—Parnelli Jones?"

"Funny, Father. His name is Austin Trowbridge. He's the son of Max Trowbridge."

Sheffield's eyebrows rose. Max Trowbridge had been one of the best race-car designers in the world before his untimely death in a plane crash. "Did your boy friend learn anything from his father?" he asked Chelsea.

"He learned plenty. For two years he's been building a car for the Paris-Dakar Rally. It's finished now. You'd have to see it to believe it: part Land Rover, part Rolls-Royce, part Corvette. We've been test-driving it on the beach at Hilton Head. It'll do one hundred and ten on hard-packed sand, ninety on soft. The engine will cut sixty-six hundred R.P.M.s."

"Where'd you learn about R.P.M.s?" he asked, surprised.

Chelsea shrugged. "I started hanging out at dirt-bike tracks when I was fourteen. Gave Mother fits. When I moved up to stock cars, she sent me away to boarding school. It didn't work. One summer at Daytona, I met Austin. We were both kind of lonely. His father had just been killed and mine—" she glanced away "—well, let's just say that Mother's new husband didn't quite know how to cope with Jack Sheffield's youngest."

And I wasn't around, Sheffield thought. He'd been off at Formula One tracks in Belgium and Italy and England, drinking champagne from racing helmets and Ferragamos with four-inch heels, looking for faster cars, getting older with younger women, sometimes crashing. Burning, bleeding, breaking—

"Don't get me wrong," Chelsea said, "I'm not being critical. Everybody's got to live his life the way he thinks best. I'm going my own way with Austin, so I can't fault you for going your own way without me."

But you do, Sheffield thought. He studied his daughter. She had to be nineteen now, maybe twenty—he couldn't even remember when her birthday was. She was plainer than she was pretty—her sister Julie had their mother's good looks, poor Chelsea favored him. Lifeless brown hair, imperfect complexion, a nose that didn't quite fit—yet there was something about her that he suspected could seize and hold a man, if he was the right man. Under the leather jacket she had unzipped was clearly the body of a woman, just as her direct grey eyes were obviously no longer the eyes of a child. There was no way, Sheffield knew, he could ever make up for the years he hadn't been there, but maybe he could do something to lessen the bad taste he'd left. Like talking her out of entering the Paris-Dakar Rally.

"You know, even with the best car in the world the Paris-Dakar run is the worst racing experience imaginable. Eight thousand miles across the Sahara Desert over the roughest terrain on the face of the earth, driving under the most brutal, dangerous, dreadful conditions. It shouldn't be called a rally, it's more like an endurance test. It's three weeks of hell."

"*You've* done it," she pointed out. "Twice."

"We already know I make mistakes. I didn't win either time, you know."

A touch of fierceness settled in her eyes. "I didn't look you up to get advice on whether to enter—Austin and I have already decided that. I came to ask if you'd go over the route map with us, maybe give us some pointers. But if you're too busy—"

"I'm not too busy," he said. Her words cut him easily.

Chelsea wrote down an address in Montmartre. "It's a rented garage. We've got two rooms above it. The car arrived in Marseilles by freighter this morning. Austin's driving it up tomorrow." She stood and zipped up her jacket. "When can we expect you?"

"Day after tomorrow okay?"

"Swell. See you then." She nodded briefly. "Good night, Father."

"Good night."

As she was walking out, Sheffield realized that he hadn't once spoken her name.

On Thursday, Sheffield took Jane with him to Montmartre, thinking at least he would have somebody on his side if Chelsea and Austin Trowbridge started making him feel guilty. It didn't work. Jane and Chelsea, who were only ten years apart in age, took to each other at once.

"Darling, you look just like him," Jane analyzed. "Same eyes, same chin. But I'm sure your disposition is much better. Jack has absolutely no sense of humor sometimes. If he wasn't so marvelous in bed, I'd leave him."

"He'll probably save you the trouble someday," Chelsea replied. "Father leaves everyone eventually."

"Why don't you two just talk about me like I'm not here?" Sheffield asked irritably.

Austin Trowbridge rescued him. "Like to take a look at the car, Mr. Sheffield?"

"Call me Jack. Yes, I would. I was a great admirer of your father, Austin. He was the best."

"Thanks. I hope I'll be half as good someday."

As soon as Sheffield saw the car, he knew Austin was already half as good, and more. It was an engineering work of art. The body was seamless, shaped not for velocity but for balance, with interchangeable balloon and radial wheels on the same axles, which had double suspension systems to lock in place for either. The steering was flexible from left-hand drive to right, the power train flexible from front to rear, side to side, corner to corner, even to individual wheels. The windshield displaced in one-eighth-inch increments to deflect glare in the daytime, while infrared sealed beams could outline night figures fifty yards distant. A primary petrol tank held one hundred liters of fuel and a backup tank carried two hundred additional liters. Everywhere Sheffield looked—carburetor, generator, distributor, voltage regulator, belt system, radiator, fuel lines—he saw imagination, innovation, improvement. The car was built for reliability and stability, power and pace. Sheffield couldn't have been more impressed.

"It's a beauty, Austin. Your dad would be proud."

"Thanks. I named it after him. I call it the 'Max One.' "

Nice kid, Sheffield thought. He'd probably been very close to his father before the tragedy. Not like Chelsea and himself.

After looking at the Max One, Sheffield took them all to lunch at a cafe on the Boulevard de la Chapelle. While they ate, he talked about the rally.

"There's no competition like it in the world," he said. "It's open to cars, trucks, motorcycles, anything on wheels. There's never any telling who'll be in—or on—the vehicle next to you: it might be a professional driver, a movie star, a millionaire, an Arab king. The run starts in Paris on New Year's Day, goes across France and Spain to Barcelona, crosses the Mediterranean by boat to Africa, then down the length of Algiers, around in a circle of sorts in Niger, across Mali, across Mauritania, up into the Spanish Sahara, then down along the Atlantic coast into Senegal to Dakar. The drivers spend fifteen to eighteen hours a day in their vehicles, then crawl into a sleeping bag for a short, badly needed rest at the end of each day's stage. From three to four hundred vehicles start the run each year. About one in ten will finish."

"We'll finish," Chelsea assured him. "We might even win."

Sheffield shook his head. "You won't win. No matter how good the car is, you don't have the experience to win."

"We don't have to win," Austin conceded. "We just have to finish well —respectably. There are some investors who financed my father from time to time. They've agreed to set me up in my own automotive-design center if I prove myself by building a vehicle that will survive Paris-Dakar. I realize, of course, that the car isn't everything—that's why I wanted to talk to you about the two rallies you ran, to get the benefit of your experience."

"You haven't been racing since you hurt your ankle," Chelsea said. "What have you been doing, Father?"

Sheffield shrugged. "Consulting, training other drivers, conducting track courses—"

"We're willing to pay you for your time to help us," she said.

Sheffield felt himself blush slightly. God, she knew how to cut.

"That won't be necessary," he said. "I'll help you all I can." He wanted to add, "After all, you *are* my daughter," but he didn't.

As he and Jane walked home, she said, "That was nice, Jack, saying you'd help them for nothing."

"Nice, maybe, but not very practical. I could have used the money. I haven't made a franc in fourteen months."

Jane shrugged. "What does that matter? I earn enough for both of us."

It mattered to Sheffield . . .

Sheffield began going to Montmartre every day. In addition to talking to

Austin about the route and terrain of the rally, he also helped him make certain modifications on Max One.

"You've got to put locks on the doors, kid. There may be times when both of you have to be away from the car at once and there are places along the route where people will steal you blind."

Holes were drilled and locks placed.

"Paint a line on the steering wheel exactly where your front wheels are aligned straight. That way, when you hit a pothole and bounce, or when you speed off a dune, you can adjust the wheels and land straight. It'll keep you from flipping over. Use luminous paint so you can see the line after dark."

Luminous paint was secured and the line put on.

A lot of Sheffield's advice was practical rather than technical. "Get rid of those blankets. It gets down to twenty degrees in the Sahara at night. Buy lightweight sleeping bags. And stock up on unsalted nuts, granola bars, high-potency vitamins, caffeine tablets. You'll need a breathing aid, too, for when you land in somebody's dust wake. Those little gauze masks painters use worked fine for me."

Most times when Sheffield went to Montmartre, Chelsea wasn't around. Austin always explained that she was running errands or doing this or that, but Sheffield could tell that he was embarrassed by the excuses. His daughter, Sheffield realized, obviously didn't want to see him any more than necessary. He tried not to let it bother him. Becoming more friendly each visit with Austin helped. The young man didn't repeat Chelsea's offer to pay him for his time, seeming to understand that it was insulting, and for that Sheffield was grateful. No one, not even Jane, knew how serious Sheffield's financial predicament was.

No one except Marcel.

One afternoon when Sheffield got back from Montmartre, Marcel was waiting for him at a table in the cafe Sheffield had to pass through to get to his rooms. "Jack, my friend," he hailed, as if the encounter were mere chance, "come join me." Snapping his fingers at the waiter, he ordered, "Another glass here."

Sheffield sat down. At a nearby table were two thugs who accompanied the diminutive Marcel everywhere he went. One was white, with a neck like a bucket and a walk like a wrestler's. The other was cafe au lait, very slim, with obscene lips and a reputation for being deadly with a straight razor. After glancing at them, Sheffield drummed his fingers silently on the table-cloth and waited for the question Marcel invariably asked first.

"So, my friend, tell me, how are things with you?"

To which Sheffield, during the past fourteen months anyway, always answered, "The same, Marcel, the same."

Marcel assumed a sad expression. Which was not difficult since he had a serious face, anyway, and had not smiled, some said, since puberty. His round little countenance would have reminded Sheffield of Peter Lorre except that Marcel's eyes were narrow slits that, despite their owner's cordiality, clearly projected danger.

"I was going over my books last week, Jack," the Frenchman said as he poured Sheffield a Pernod, "and I must admit I was a little surprised to see how terrible your luck has run all year. I mean, horse races, dog races, prizefights, soccer matches—you seem to have forgotten what it is to pick a winner. Usually, of course, I don't let anyone run up a balance so large, but I've always had a soft spot for you, Jack."

"You know about the car in Montmartre, don't you?" Sheffield asked pointedly.

"Of course," Marcel replied at once, not at all surprised by the question. "I've known about it since it arrived in Marseilles." Putting a hand on Sheffield's arm, he asked confidentially, "What do you think of it, Jack?"

Sheffield moved his arm by raising the Pernod to his lips. "It's a fine car. One of the best I've ever seen."

"I'm glad you're being honest with me," Marcel said. "I've already had a man get into the garage at night to look at it for me. He was of the same opinion. He says it can win the rally."

Sheffield shook his head. "They're a couple of kids, Marcel. They may finish—they won't win."

Marcel looked at him curiously. "What is a young man like this Austin Trowbridge able to pay you, anyway?"

"I'm not being paid."

Marcel drew back his head incredulously. "A man in your financial situation? You work for nothing?"

"I used to know the kid's father," Sheffield said. Then he added, "I used to know his girl friend's father, too."

Marcel studied the American for a moment. "Jack, let me be as candid with you as you are being with me. There are perhaps two dozen serious vehicles for which competition licenses have been secured for this year's rally. The car my associates and I are backing is a factory-built Peugeot driven by Georges Ferrand. A French driver in a French car. Call it national pride if you wish, call it practical economics—the fact is that we will have a great deal of money at risk on a Ferrand win. Of the two dozen or so vehicles that will seriously challenge Ferrand, we are convinced he will outdistance all but one of them. That one is the Trowbridge car. It is, as you said, a fine car. We have no statistics on it because it did not run in the optional trials at Cergy-Pontoise. And we know nothing about young Trowbridge himself as a driver: whether he's capable, has the stamina, whether he's *hungry*. The entire entry, car and driver, presents an unknown equation which troubles us."

"I've already told you, Marcel: the car can't win."

The Frenchman fixed him in an unblinking stare. "I want a guarantee of that, Jack." He produced a small leather notebook. "Your losses currently total forty-nine thousand francs. That's about eight thousand dollars. I'll draw a line through the entire amount for a guarantee that the Max One will not outrun Ferrand's Peugeot."

"You're not concerned whether it finishes?"

"Not in the least," Marcel waved away the consideration. "First place wins, everything else loses."

Sheffield pursed his lips in brief thought, then said, "All right, Marcel. It's a bargain."

Later, in their rooms, Jane said, "I saw you in the cafe with Marcel. You haven't started gambling again, have you?"

"Of course not." It wasn't a lie. He had never stopped.

"What did he want, then?"

"He and his friends are concerned about Austin's car. They know I'm helping the kid. They want a guarantee that the Max One won't ace out the car they're backing."

Jane shook her head in disgust. "What did you tell him?"

"That he had nothing to worry about. Austin's not trying to win, he only wants to finish."

"But you didn't agree to help Marcel in any way?"

"Of course not." Sheffield looked away. He hated lying to Jane, yet he did so regularly about his gambling. This time, though, he swore to himself, he was going to quit—when the slate was wiped clean with Marcel, he had made up his mind not to bet on anything again, not racing, not boxing, not soccer, not even whether the Eiffel Tower was still standing. And he was going to find work, too—some kind of normal job, maybe in an automobile factory, so he could bring in some money, settle down, plan for some kind of future. Jane, after all, was almost thirty; she wouldn't be able to kick her heels above her head in the Crazy Horse chorus line forever.

And his bargain with Marcel wouldn't matter to Austin and Chelsea, he emphasized to his conscience. All Austin had to do to get his design center was finish the race, not win it.

That night while Jane was at the club, Sheffield went to a bookstall on the Left Bank that specialized in racing publications. He purchased an edition of the special Paris-Dakar Rally newspaper that listed each vehicle and how it had performed in the optional trials at Cergy-Pontoise. Back home, he studied the figures on Ferrand's Peugeot and on several other cars which appeared to have the proper ratios of weight-to-speed necessary for a serious run. There was a Mitsubishi that looked very good, a factory-sponsored Mercedes, a Range Rover, a Majorette, a little Russian-built Lada, and a Belgian entry that looked like a VW but was called an Ostend.

For two hours he worked and reworked the stats on a pad of paper, dividing weights by distance, by average speeds, by days, by the hours of daylight which would be available, by the average wind velocity across the Sahara, by the number of stops necessary to adjust tire pressure, by a dozen other factors that a prudent driver needed to consider. When he finished, and compared his final figures with the figures he had estimated for Austin Trowbridge's car, Sheffield reached an unavoidable conclusion: the Max One might—just *might*—actually win the rally.

Sheffield put on his overcoat and went for a walk along the Champs-Elysees and on into the deserted Tuileries. The trees in the park were wintry and forlorn, the grass grey from its nightly frost, and the late-November air thin and cold. Sheffield limped along, his hands deep in his pockets, chin down, brow pinched. Marcel had used the word "guarantee"—and that's what Sheffield had agreed to: a guarantee that the Max One wouldn't win. But the car, Sheffield now knew, was even better than he'd thought: it *could* win. In order to secure his guarantee to Marcel, Sheffield was left with but one alternative. He had to tamper with the car.

Sheffield sat on a bench in the dark and brooded about the weaknesses of character that had brought him to his present point in life. He wondered how much courage it would take to remain on the bench all night and catch pneumonia and freeze to death. The longer he thought about it, the more inviting it seemed. He sat there until he became very cold. But eventually he rose and returned to the rooms above the cafe.

The following week, after conceiving and dismissing a number of plans, Sheffield asked Austin, "What are you going to do about oil?"

"The rally supply truck sells it at the end of every stage, doesn't it? I thought I'd buy it there every night."

"That's okay in the stages where everything goes right," Sheffield pointed out. "But the rally supply truck is only there for a couple of hours and then starts an overnight drive to the next stage. If you get lost or break down or even blow a tire, you could miss the truck and have to run on used oil the entire next day. You need to carry a dozen quarts of your own oil for emergencies."

"I hate to add the weight," Austin said reluctantly.

"I know of a garage that will seal it in plastic bags so you can eliminate the cans," Sheffield said. "That'll save you a couple of pounds."

"You really think it's necessary?"

"I'd do it," Sheffield assured him. Austin finally agreed. "Tell me the grade you want and I'll get it for you," Sheffield said.

Austin wrote down the viscosity numbers of an oil density that was perfect for the Max One's engine. On his way home, Sheffield stopped by the garage of which he had spoken. Before he ordered the bags of oil, he drew a line through some of Austin's numbers and replaced them with figures of his own—lower figures which designated less constancy in the oil's lubricating quality.

Several days later, the garage delivered to the rooms above the cafe a carton containing the bagged oil. Jane was home and accepted the delivery. The garageman gave her a message for Sheffield.

"Our mechanic said to tell Monsieur that if this oil is for a rally vehicle, it should be several grades lighter. This viscosity will reduce engine efficiency as the air temperature drops."

When the garageman left, Jane saw taped to the top bag the slip of paper with the viscosity numbers altered. When Sheffield returned from Montmartre, she asked him about it.

"Yes, I changed them," he said, his tone deliberately casual. "The oil Austin specified was too light."

"Does he know you changed his figures?"

"Sure."

"Are you lying to me, Jack?" She had been exercising and was in black leotards, hands on hips, concern wrinkling her brow.

"Why would I lie about a thing like motor oil?" Sheffield asked.

"I don't know. But I've had an uneasy feeling since I saw you with Marcel. If you're in some kind of trouble, Jack—"

"I'm not in any kind of trouble," he said, forcing a smile.

"You're not trying to get back at Chelsea for the way she's acting toward you, I hope."

"Of course not."

"Jack," she said, "I called Austin and said I thought the garage made a mistake. I read him your numbers and he said they were wrong."

"You *what?*" Sheffield stared at her. The color drained from his face. Jane sighed wearily and sat down.

"I knew it. I could feel it."

Sheffield felt a surge of relief. "You didn't call Austin."

She shook her head. "No." Her expression saddened. "Why are you doing it, Jack?"

Sheffield poured himself a drink and sat down and told her the truth. He told her about the lies of the past fourteen months, the money he'd bet and lost, the circle of desperation that had slowly been closing in on him. "I saw a way out," he pleaded.

"By hurting someone who trusts you?"

"No one will be hurt," he insisted. "Austin doesn't have to win, all he has to do—"

"Is finish," she completed the statement for him. "That's not the point, Jack. It's wrong and you know it."

"Look," he tried to explain, "when Austin uses this heavier oil, all it will do is make the Max One's engine cut down a few R.P.M.s. He probably won't even notice it. The car will slow down maybe a mile an hour."

"It's wrong, Jack. Please don't do it."

"I've *got* to do it," Sheffield asserted. "I've got to get clear of Marcel."

"We can start paying Marcel. I have some savings."

"No." Sheffield stiffened. "I'm tired of being kept by you, Jane."

"Kept by me?"

"Yes, kept! You as much as said so yourself when you told my daughter I was marvelous in bed."

"Oh, Jack—surely you don't think Chelsea took me seriously!"

"I took you seriously."

Jane stared at him. "If you think you're going to shift onto me some of the responsibility for what you're doing, you're mistaken."

"I don't want you to take any of the responsibility," he made clear, "but I don't expect you to interfere, either. Just mind your own business."

Jane's eyes hardened. "I'll do that."

In the middle of December, the Crazy Horse closed for two weeks and Jane announced that she was going back to England for the holidays. "Dad's getting on," she said, "and I haven't seen my sister's children since they were toddlers. I'd invite you along but I'm afraid it would be awkward, our not being married and all."

"I understand," Sheffield said. "I'll spend Christmas with Chelsea and Austin."

"I rather thought you would." She hesitated. "Are you still determined to go through with your plan?"

"Yes, I am."

Jane shrugged and said no more.

After she was gone, Chelsea seemed to feel guilty about Sheffield being alone for Christmas. "You're welcome to come here," she said. "I'm not the greatest cook, but—"

"Actually, I'm going to England," he lied. "Jane telephoned last night and said she missed me. I'm taking the boat train on Christmas Eve."

What he actually took on Christmas Eve was a long, lonely walk around the gaily decorated Place de la Concorde, past the chic little shops staying open late along Rue Royale. All around him holiday music played, greetings were exchanged, and the usually dour faces of the Parisiennes softened a bit. When his ankle began to ache, Sheffield bought a quart of gin, a loaf of bread, and a small basket of cold meats and cheese, and trudged back to his rooms. The cafe downstairs was closed, so he had to walk around to the alley and go up the back way. A thin, cold drizzle started and he was glad it had waited until he was almost inside.

Putting the food away, he lighted the little space heater, opened the gin, and sat trying to imagine what the future held for him. The telephone rang that night and several times on Christmas Day, but he did not answer it. He was too involved wondering about the rest of his life. And he was afraid it might be a wrong number.

Sheffield finally answered the telephone the following week when he came in one evening and found it ringing. It was Jane.

"I thought I ought to tell you, I'm staying over for a few days longer. There's a new cabaret opening in Piccadilly and they're auditioning dancers the day after New Year's. I'm going to try out. Actually, I've been thinking about working closer to home for a while. Dad's—"

"Yes, I know. Well, then. I wish you luck."

"No hard feelings?"

"Of course not. You?"

"Not any more."

"Let me know how you make out."

"Sure."

After he hung up, Sheffield got the gin out again. He drank until he passed out. It was nearly twelve hours later when he heard an incessant pounding and imagined there was a little man inside his head trying to break out through his left eye with a mallet. When he forced himself to sit upright and engage his senses, he discovered that the pounding was on his door.

He opened the door and Chelsea burst in. "Austin's broken his arm!" she announced, distraught.

On their way to Montmartre, she gave him the details. "We decided to go out for dinner last night, to celebrate finishing the last of the work on the car. We went to a little cafe on rue Lacaur—"

"That's a rough section."

"Tell me about it. On the way home, we were walking past these two guys and one of them made a comment about me. Austin said something back, and before I knew it both of them jumped him. They beat him up badly and one of them used his knee to break Austin's arm like a stick of wood. It was awful!"

In the rooms over the garage, Austin was in bed with an ice compress on his face and his right arm in a cast. "Two years of work down the tubes," he said morosely.

"It could have been worse," Sheffield told him. "People have been shot and stabbed on that street."

"I thought for a minute one of them was going to slice Austin with a razor," Chelsea said.

"A razor?" Sheffield frowned. "What kind of razor?"

"One of those barber's razors. The kind that unfolds like a pocket knife."

"A straight razor," Sheffield said quietly. An image of Marcel's two bodyguards came into focus. The thin one carried a straight razor and the other one looked strong enough to break arms.

Sheffield managed to keep his anger under control while he tried to reconcile Austin and Chelsea to the fact that it wasn't the end of the rally for them. He gave Austin the names of four drivers he knew who weren't signed up for Paris-Dakar this year and might consider an offer to make the run. Two were here in Paris, one was in Zurich, and the other at his home in Parma. "Call them and see what you can do," he said. "I'll go back to my place and see if I can think of any others."

As soon as he left the garage, he went to a telephone kiosk around the corner and called Marcel's office.

"You son of a bitch," he said when the Frenchman came on the line. "We had an arrangement that *I* was to keep Austin Trowbridge from winning."

"That is not precisely correct," Marcel said. "You agreed to take care of the *car*. I decided, because of the amount of money at risk, that it would be best to protect your guarantee with an additional guarantee."

"That wasn't necessary, you son of a bitch!"

"That's twice you've called me that," Marcel said, his tone icing. "I've overlooked it up to now because I know you're angry. Please refrain from doing it again, however. For your information—" his voice broke slightly "—my mother was a saint."

"I don't think you had a mother," Sheffield said coldly. "I think you crawled up out of a sewer!" Slamming down the receiver, he left the kiosk and stalked across the street to a bar. He had a quick drink to calm himself down, then another, which he drank more slowly as he tried to decide what to do. There was no way he could turn in Marcel's thugs without admitting his own complicity to Austin and Chelsea. And it was Marcel he wanted to get even with. But Marcel was always protected. How the hell did you take revenge on someone with the protection he had?

As Sheffield worried it over, the bartender brought him change from the banknote with which he'd paid for his drinks. Sheffield stared at the francs on the bar and suddenly thought: *Of course.* You didn't hurt a man like Marcel physically, you hurt him financially.

Leaving the second drink unfinished, something Sheffield hadn't done in years, he left the bar and hurried back to the rooms over the garage. Austin and Chelsea were at the telephone.

"The two drivers here turned us down," Austin said. "I'm about to call the one in Zurich."

"Forget it," Sheffield said flatly. "I'm driving the Max One for you . . ."

It wasn't yet dawn in the Place d'Armes where the race was to start, but a thousand portable spotlights created an artificial daylight that illuminated the four lines of vehicles in eerie silver light. A hundred thousand spectators jammed the early-morning boulevard on each side, waving flags, signs, and balloons, cheering select cars and select drivers, the women throwing and sometimes personally delivering kisses, the men reaching past the lines of gendarmes to slap fenders and shout, *"Bon courage!"*

Young girls, the kind who pursue rock stars, walked the lines seeking autographs and more while their younger brothers and sisters followed them throwing confetti. Everyone had to shout to be heard in the general din.

The Max One was in 182nd starting position, which put it in the forty-sixth row, the second car from the inside. Chelsea, in a racing suit, stood with Austin's good arm around her, both looking with great concern at Jack as he wound extra last-minute tape over the boot around his weak ankle.

"Are you absolutely sure about this, Jack?" the young designer asked. "It's not worth further damage to your ankle."

"I'm positive," Sheffield said. "Anyway, we'll be using Chelsea's feet whenever we can." Looking up, he grinned. "You just be in Dakar to receive the trophy."

"That trophy will be yours, Jack."

"The prize money will be mine," Sheffield corrected. "The trophy will be yours."

There was a sudden roar from the crowd and a voice announced through static in the loudspeaker that the first row of four vehicles had been waved to a start. The rally had begun.

"Kiss him goodbye and get in," Sheffield said, shaking hands with Austin, then leaving the couple alone for the moments they had left.

Presently father and daughter were side by side, buckled and harnessed in, adrenaline rushing, their bodies vibrating from the revving engine, their eyes fixed on the white-coated officials who moved down the line and with a brusque nod and a wave started each row of four vehicles five seconds apart.

Sheffield grinned over at Chelsea. "I wonder what your mother would say if she could see us now?"

"I know exactly what she'd say: 'Birds of a feather.' "

"Well, maybe we are," Sheffield said.

"Let's don't get sentimental, Father," Chelsea replied. "Driving together from Paris to Dakar doesn't make a relationship."

Looking at her determined young face, Sheffield nodded. "Whatever you say, kid."

A moment later, they were waved away from the starting line.

From Paris to Barcelona would have been 850 kilometers if the road had been straight. But it wasn't. It wound through Loiret, Cher, Creuse, Correze, Cantal, and more—as if the route had been designed by an aimless schoolboy on a bicycle. Nearly all the way, the roadsides were lined with cheering, waving, kiss-throwing well-wishers shouting, *"Bonne chance!"* From time to time, flowers were thrown into the cars as they bunched up in a village and were forced to slow down. Farther south, cups of *vin ordinaire*, slices of cheese, and hunks of bread were shared. The farther away from Paris one got, the more relaxed and cheerful were the French people.

Sheffield and Chelsea didn't talk much during the trip south. She was already missing Austin and Sheffield was concentrating on finding ways to relieve pressure on his weak ankle by holding his foot in various positions. These preoccupations and the increasingly beautiful French countryside kept them both silently contemplative. The Paris-to-Barcelona stage of the rally was a liaison—a controlled section of the route in which all positions remained as they had started—so it wasn't necessary to speed or try to pass. A few vehicles invariably broke down the first day, but for the most part it was little more than a tourist outing. The real race would not begin until they reached Africa.

It was after dark when they crossed the Spanish border and well into the late Spanish dinner hour when they reached Barcelona. As the French had done, the Spaniards lined the streets to cheer on the smiling, still fresh drivers in their shiny, unbattered vehicles. Because of the crowds, and the absence of adequate crowd control, the great caterpillar of vehicles inched its way down to the dock, where the Spanish ferry that would take them to Algiers waited. It was midnight when Sheffield and Chelsea finally drove onto the quay, had their papers examined, and boarded the boat. The first day, eighteen and a half hours long, was over.

Crossing the Mediterranean, Sheffield and Chelsea got some rest and nourishment and met some of the other drivers. Sheffield was well known by most of them already. (He had asked Chelsea ahead of time how she wanted to be introduced. "I don't have to say I'm your father if you'd rather I didn't," he told her. She had shrugged. "It makes no difference to me. Everyone knows we don't choose our parents." "Or our children," Sheffield added.) He introduced her simply as Chelsea and told everyone she was the vehicle designer's girl friend.

Ferrand, the French driver, Vera Kursk, a shapely but formidable-looking Russian woman, and Alf Zeebrug, a Belgian, all expressed great interest in the Max One's structural configuration. They were, Sheffield remembered from his computations, the three favorites to win the rally: Ferrand in his Peugeot, Vera Kursk in a Lada, Zeebrug in the Volkswagen lookalike called an Ostend.

As they studied the Max One, Ferrand winked at Sheffield and said, "So, you've brought in—what do you Americans call it, a ringer?"

Vera nodded her head knowingly. "I see why you passed up the trial races, Jack. Foxy."

"Let us look under the hood, Jack," pressed Zeebrug, knowing Sheffield wouldn't.

In the end, Ferrand spoke for them all when he said, "Welcome back, Jack. It's good to race with you again." Vera gave him a more-than-friendly kiss on the lips.

Later Chelsea said, "They all seem like nice people."

"They are," Sheffield said. "They're here for the race, nothing else: no politics, no nationalism, no petty jealousies. Just the race." Ferrand, Sheffield was convinced, knew nothing about Marcel's machinations in favor of the Peugeot. Had he known, Ferrand—an honorable man and an honest competitor—would have withdrawn and probably sought out Marcel for physical punishment.

Another comment Chelsea made just before they docked was, "They all seem to like and respect you, Father."

"There are some quarters in which I'm not a pariah," he replied. "Believe it or not."

In Africa, the first stage was Algiers to Ghardaia. Sheffield stuck a hand-printed list to the dashboard between them. It read:

Ferrand—Peugeot
Kursk—Lada
Zeebrug—Ostend
Sakai—Mitsubishi
Gordon—Range Rover
Smythe—Majorette

"These are the drivers and cars to beat," he told Chelsea. "I had a Mercedes on the list, too, but the driver was drinking too much on the ferry and bought a bottle of scotch to take with him when we docked. I don't think we'll have to worry about him."

Chelsea looked at him curiously. "I thought we were only in this to finish, so that Austin can get his design center."

Sheffield fixed her in a flat stare. "I'm a racer, kid. I enter races to *win*. This one is no exception. If you don't want to go along with that, you can get off here."

Chelsea shook her head determinedly. "Not on your life."

Sheffield had to look away so she wouldn't see his pleased smile.

During the first stage, it seemed to Chelsea that every car, truck, and motorcycle in the rally was passing them. "Why aren't we going faster?" she demanded.

"It's not necessary right now," Sheffield told her. "All these people passing us are the showboats—rich little boys and girls with expensive little toys. They run too fast too quickly. Most of them will burn up their engines before we get out of Algeria. Look over there—"

Chelsea looked where he indicated and saw Ferrand, Vera Kursk, and the other experienced drivers cruising along at moderate speed just as Sheffield was doing. "I guess I've got a lot to learn," she said.

At Ghardaia, their sleeping bags spread like spokes around a desert campfire, the drivers discussed the day. "Let's see," Zeebrug calculated, "three hundred forty-four vehicles started and so far one hundred eighteen have dropped out."

"Good numbers," Ferrand said.

Vera Kursk smiled. "This could turn into a race instead of a herd."

Chelsea noticed that the Russian woman and Sheffield shared a little evening brandy from the same cup and that earlier, when the sleeping bags were spread, Vera had positioned hers fairly close to Sheffield's. Commie slut, she thought. When no one was paying any attention, Chelsea moved her own sleeping bag between them.

It took a week to get out of Algeria—a week in which Sheffield and the other experienced drivers continued to drive at reasonable, safe speeds that were easy on their engines, tires, and the bodies of both car and driver. All along the route, vehicles were dropping out—throwing pistons, getting stuck in sand, blowing too many tires, sliding off soft shoulders into gullies, dropping transmissions, or the exhausted drivers simply giving up. The Mercedes quit the second day—its driver, as Sheffield had predicted, drinking too much liquor for the heat he had to endure and the stamina required to drive. A surprise dropout was the Mitsubishi. Driven by the Japanese speed-racer Sakai, it had hit a sand-concealed rock and broken its front axle. "One down, five to go," Sheffield said, drawing a line through Sakai's name on the dashboard list.

By the time they crossed into Niger, an additional sixty-three vehicles had dropped out. "That leaves one hundred sixty-three in," said Smythe, the Englishman driving the Majorette, when they camped that night. He was feeling good about the dropouts. At noon the next day, he joined them when the Majorette burned up its gearbox.

"Two down, four to go," Sheffield told Chelsea, and drew another line.

After camping one night in Chirfa, Chelsea noticed the next morning that Sheffield and Ferrand and the others shook hands all around and wished each other good luck. "What was that all about?" she asked.

"Everyone will be camping alone from now on," he said. "The socializing is over." Sheffield pointed toward a band of haze on the horizon. "We got into the Tenere Desert today. Now we start racing."

The terrain they encountered that day was hell on a back burner. The Max One was in ashlike sand up to its axles, plowing along like a man walking against a gale wind. The stink of the desert decay was unexpected and appalling to Chelsea. She gagged repeatedly. Huge white rats the size of rabbits leaped at the car windows. This stage of the rally that crossed the Tenere was a nightmare in glaring daylight no newcomer was ever prepared for.

Camped alone that night in some rocks above the desert floor, Chelsea saw Sheffield massaging his foot. "How's the ankle?" she asked.

"Just a little stiff. It'll be okay."

"Let's switch places tomorrow," she suggested. "I'll drive and you relieve." Up to then, Sheffield had done eighty percent of the driving. "Tomorrow," Sheffield told her, "we go over the Azbine Plain. It's like driving across a huge corrugated roof."

"Let me drive," she said quietly. "I can manage it."

He let her drive—and she took them across the rough terrain like a pilgrim determined to get to Mecca. Along the way, they saw Zeebrug lying at the side of the road, a rally first-aid team inflating a splint on his leg. The Ostend was nearby, upside down in a ditch, one wheel gone.

"Three and three," Sheffield said. He handed Chelsea the marker and she crossed off Zeebrug's name.

Into the second week of the race, both Jack and Chelsea began to feel the strain of the collective pressures: the usually unheated, quickly eaten food that wreaked havoc with their digestion, the constant jarring and jolting of the car that pummeled their bodies, the freezing nights sleeping on the ground, the scorching, glaring sun by day, the sand and dirt in their mouths, ears, eyes, noses, the constant headaches and relentless fatigue that the short rests could not remedy. Depression set in, underscored by the begging of poverty-stricken Africans everywhere they stopped.

"*Cadeau,*" the black children pleaded as Sheffield adjusted his tire pressure. "*Cadeau,*" they whined as Chelsea filled the radiator from a village stream.

"We have no gifts," Sheffield told them in English, in French, and by a firm shaking of his head. "Try to ignore them," he advised Chelsea, and she did try, but her eyes remained moist. As did his.

Just over the border in Mali, their physical and mental distress was displaced in priority and urgency by problems the Max One began to develop. A fuel line cracked and split, and they lost considerable petrol before Chelsea noticed the trail it was leaving behind them and they stopped to repair it. The lost fuel had to be replaced at a township pump at exorbitant cost. Later the same day, for no apparent reason, a center section of the windshield bubbled and cracked. Sheffield patched it with some of the tape he had brought for his ankle. The very next day, the odometer cable snapped and they were unable to monitor their distance to the end of the stage.

"Austin's damned car," Chelsea seethed, "is falling apart."

"It's holding up better than most." Sheffield bobbed his chin at two cars, two trucks, and a motorcycle that had dropped out at the side of the road. By then, seventy-one more vehicles had quit the rally, leaving ninety-two still in.

Near Timbuktu, Sheffield and Chelsea happened on a small water pond that no one else seemed to notice. Behind a high rise, it had a few trees, some scrub, and even a patch of Gobi grass. "We've died and gone to heaven," Chelsea said when she saw the water. She began undressing. "I hope you're not modest."

"Not if you aren't."

They took their first bath in two weeks, and when they were clean they rubbed salve on their hips and shoulders where the Max One's seatbelts and harnesses had rubbed the skin raw.

"Mother never went with you when you raced, did she?" Chelsea asked reflectively.

"No."

"Who took care of you when you got hurt?"

"Whoever was around," Sheffield said. He looked off at the distance.

Chelsea patted his head maternally. "If you get hurt in this race, *I'll* take care of you," she assured him. Then she turned away to dress, as if her words embarrassed her where her nakedness had not.

After Mali, they crossed into Mauritania. The topography of the route seemed to change every day. One stage would be a mazelike, twisting and turning trail along a dry riverbed, in turn sandy and dusty, then suddenly muddy where an unexpected patch of water appeared. Then they would encounter a long, miserable stage of deep ruts and vicious potholes, then a log-and-rock-strewn track that shook their teeth and vibrated agonizingly in Sheffield's weak ankle.

With each kilometer, his pain grew more intense. During the day he swallowed codeine tablets. At night Chelsea put wet compresses on his ankle and massaged his foot. Those days they came to a stage that was open, flat straightaway, Chelsea did the driving and Sheffield enjoyed temporary respite from the pain.

Nearly every day they caught glimpses of Ferrand, Vera Kursk, and the Australian Gordon in his Range Rover. There were no smiles, waves, or shouted greetings now—just grim nods that said, So you're still in it, are you? Well, so am I.

Into the third grueling week, the pain, fatigue, and depression evolved into recriminations. "How in hell did I let myself get into this mess anyway?" Sheffield asked as he untaped his swollen ankle one night. "I don't owe Austin Trowbridge *or* you anything."

"How did *you* get into it!" Chelsea shot back. "How did *I* get into it! I'm making the same damned mistake my mother made—getting mixed up with a man who thinks speed is some kind of religion."

"I could be back in Paris going to old movies," Sheffield lamented, "eating sausages with homemade mustard, drinking gin."

"And I could be in Philadelphia going to club meetings and playing tennis with your *other* daughter."

They caught each other's eyes in the light of the campfire and both smiled sheepishly. Chelsea came over and kneeled next to her father. "I'll do that," she said, and tended to his ankle.

Later, when he got into his sleeping bag and she was preparing to stand the first two-hour watch, flare gun at the ready, she looked very frankly at him. "You know," she said, her voice slightly hoarse from the dryness, "if we weren't blood relatives, I might find myself attracted to you."

Sheffield stayed awake most of the two hours he should have been sleeping. This was one race he would be very glad to have over—for more reasons than his swollen ankle.

From Mauritania, the route cut north across the border of the Spanish Sahara for a hundred or so kilometers of hot sand, between the wells of Tichia in the east and Bir Ganduz in the west. During that stage, with seventy-one vehicles of the original 344 still in the race, there was much jockeying for position, much cutting in, out, and around, much risky driving on soft shoulders, and much blind speeding as the dust wake of the vehicle in front reduced visibility to the length of your hood. It was a dangerous stage, driven with goggles and mouth masks, clenched jaws, white knuckles, tight sphincters, and the pedal to the metal, no quarter asked, none given.

In a one-on-one, side-by-side dash to be the first into a single lane between two enormous dunes, Chelsea at the wheel of the Max One and Gordon in his Range Rover were dead even on a thousand-yard straightaway, both pushing their vehicles to the limit, when Gordon glanced over at the Max One and smiled in his helmet at the sight of the girl, not the man, doing the driving. He had the audacity to take one hand off the wheel and wave goodbye as he inched ahead.

"You bastard," Chelsea muttered and juiced the Max One's engine by letting up on the accelerator two inches, then stomping down on it, jolting the automatic transmission into its highest gear and shooting the car forward as if catapulted. With inches to spare, she sliced in front of Gordon at the point where the dunes came together, surprising him so that he swerved, went up an embankment, and immediately slid back down, burying the Range Rover's rear end in five feet of what the nomad Arabs, translated, called "slip sand": grains that, although dry, held like wet quicksand. The Australian would, Sheffield knew, be stuck for hours, and was effectively out of the race as far as finishing up front was concerned.

"Nice work, kid," he said. Now they had only Ferrand and Vera Kursk with whom to contend.

That night they camped along with the other remaining drivers around the oasis well at Bir Ganduz. When the rally starts for the day were announced, they learned that seventeen more vehicles had fallen by the wayside on the Spanish Sahara stage, leaving fifty-four competitors: thirty-eight cars, ten trucks, and six motorcycles. Ferrand was in the lead position, one of the cyclists second, Vera Kursk third, one of the trucks fourth, another cyclist fifth, and the Max One sixth.

"Are you disappointed we aren't doing better?" Chelsea asked as they changed oil and air filters.

Sheffield shook his head. "We can pass both cyclists and the truck any time we want to. And probably will, tomorrow. It'll come down to Ferrand, Vera, and us."

"Do you think we can beat them?"

Sheffield smiled devilishly. "If we don't, we'll scare hell out of them." For a moment then he became very quiet. Presently he handed Chelsea a plastic jar. "Hustle over to the control truck and get us some distilled water."

"The battery wells aren't low—I just checked them."

"I want some extra, anyway, just in case. Go on."

As soon as she was out of sight, Sheffield reached into the car and got the flare gun. Turning to a stand of trees in deep shadows twenty feet from the car, he said. "Whoever's in there has got ten seconds to step out where I can see you or I'll light you up like the Arch of Triumph."

From out of the darkness stepped Marcel's two thugs. The one who carried a razor had a sneer on his gaunt brown face. The one with the bucket neck simply looked angry as usual. "We bring greetings from Marcel," said the thin one. "He said to tell you he is willing to be reasonable. Forget what has gone before. You and he will start fresh. He will cancel your debt and give you one hundred thousand francs if you do not overtake Ferrand."

"No deal," Sheffield replied flatly.

"I am authorized to go to a hundred and fifty thousand francs. That is twenty-five thousand dollars—"

"I can add. No deal."

The other man pointed a threatening finger. "To doublecross Marcel is not very smart—"

Sheffield cocked the flare gun. "You're the one who broke my friend's arm, aren't you? How'd you like to have a multicolored face?"

"No need for that," the thin one said quickly, holding up both hands. "We delivered Marcel's message, we have your answer. We'll go now."

"If I see you again," Sheffield warned them, "I'll tell the other drivers about you. They won't like what they hear. You'll end up either in a sandy grave or a Senegalese prison. I don't know which would be worse."

"Perhaps the young lady has an opinion," the thin man said, bobbing his chin toward the Max One, off to the side of Sheffield. It was the oldest ruse in the world, but Sheffield fell for it. He looked over to his left, and when he did the thin man leaped forward with enough speed and agility to knock the flare gun to the ground before Sheffield could resist. Then the man with the bucket neck was there, shoving him roughly until his back was against the car and driving a boot-toe hard against his painful ankle. Sheffield groaned and started to fall, but the other man held him up long enough to deliver a second brutal kick.

"That's all!" his partner said urgently. "Come on!"

They were gone, leaving Sheffield sitting on the sand clutching his ankle, tears of pain cutting lines on his dry cheeks, when Chelsea got back. She ran over to him. "My God, what happened?"

"I must have stepped in a hole. It's bad—"

The ankle swelled to thrice its normal size. For several hours, Chelsea made trips to and from the public well to draw cold water for compresses. They didn't help. By morning, Sheffield couldn't put any weight at all on the foot.

"That does it, I guess," he said resignedly. "Ferrand and Vera will have to fight it out. But at least Austin will get his design center; you can drive well enough for us to finish."

"I can drive well enough for us to win," Chelsea said. She was packing up their camp. "I proved that yesterday."

"Yesterday was on a flat desert straightaway. From here down the coast to Dakar are narrow, winding roads full of tricky curves, blind spots, loose gravel."

"I can handle it."

"You don't understand," Jack said, with the patience of a parent, "this is the final lap. This is for all the marbles—this is what the last twenty days of hell have been all about. These people still in the run are serious competitors—"

"I'm serious, too," Chelsea asserted. "I'm a racer, I'm in this run to win. If you can't accept that, if you don't want to drive with me, drop off here."

Sheffield stared incredulously at her. "You're crazy, kid. Ferrand, Vera, and the others will run you off a cliff into the Atlantic Ocean if they have to."

"They can try." She stowed their belongings on the rear deck and closed the hatchback. "You staying here?"

"Not on your life," Sheffield growled. He hopped over to the car. The passenger side.

The last lap into Dakar was a war on wheels. All caution was left behind on the Spanish Sahara. This was the heavyweight championship, the World Series, and the Kentucky Derby. No one who got this far would give an inch of track. Anything gained had to be taken.

As soon as the stage started, the Max One dropped back to eight, losing two positions as a pair of motorcycles outdistanced them. Chelsea cursed but Sheffield told her not to worry about it. "This is a good stretch for cycles. We'll probably be passed by a few more. They start falling back when we reach Akreidil; the track softens there and they can't maneuver well. Keep your speed at a steady ninety."

Chelsea glanced over. "I don't want advice on how to finish, just how to win."

"That's what you're going to get," Sheffield assured her. "You do the driving, I'll do the navigating. Deal?"

Chelsea nodded curtly. "Deal."

Sheffield tore the piece of paper from the dash and looked at the names of Ferrand and Vera Kursk. Crumbling it, he tossed it out the window.

"Litterbug," she said.

"Shut up and drive, Chelsea."

"Yes, Daddy."

They exchanged quick smiles, then grimly turned their attention back to the track.

By midmorning the Max One was back to eleventh, but Ferrand and Vera had also fallen behind, everyone being outrun by the six daredevil cyclists still in the rally. This was their moment of glory and they knew it. They would lead the last lap of the run for three magnificent hours, then— as Sheffield had predicted—start falling behind at Akreidil. From that point on, the four-wheeled vehicles overtook and passed them one by one. Ferrand moved back into first place, Vera pressed into second, and the Max One held fourth behind a modified Toyota truck. They were all sometimes mere feet apart on the dangerous track along the Mauritanian coast.

"Blind spot," Sheffield would say as they negotiated weird hairpin turns. "Hug in," he instructed when he wanted Chelsea to keep tight to the inside of the track. "Let up," he said to slow down, "Punch it" to speed up, "Drop one" to go into a lower gear as he saw Ferrand's car suddenly nose up a grade ahead.

Two of the nine trucks behind them started crowding the track south of Mederdra, taking turns ramming into the Max One's rear bumper at ninety k.p.h. "Get ready to brake," Sheffield said. Watching in a sideview mirror, he waited for exactly the right second, then yelled, "Brake!" Chelsea hit the brake and felt a jolt as one of the trucks ricocheted off the Max One's rear fender and shot across the rocky beach into the surf.

"The other one's passed us!" Chelsea shouted.

"I wanted it to," Sheffield said. "Watch."

The truck that had displaced them in fourth place quickly drew up and challenged the truck in third. For sixty kilometers they jockeyed and swerved and slammed sides trying to assert superiority. One kilometer in front of them, Ferrand and Vera held the two lead positions; behind them,

Sheffield and Chelsea kept everyone else in back of the Max One to let the trucks fight it out. Finally, on the Senegal border, the crowding truck finally forced number three off the track and moved up to take its place.

"Okay!" Sheffield yelled at Chelsea. "His body's tired but his brain is happy because he just won. The two aren't working together right now. Punch it!"

Chelsea gunned the Max One and in seconds laid it right next to the victorious truck. The driver looked over, surprised. Sheffield smiled at him. Then Sheffield put his hand over Chelsea's and jerked the steering wheel sharply. The Max One leaped to the right, the truck swerved to avoid being hit, the Max One crossed the entire track, and the truck spun around and went backward into a ditch.

"Now let's go after Vera," Sheffield said.

"With pleasure," Chelsea replied.

It became a three-car race. For more than four hundred kilometers, speeding inland along Senegal's gently undulating sandy-clay plains, the Peugeot, the Lada, and the Max One vied for position. Along straight-aways, it became clear that Austin Trowbridge's car was superior in speed to both the French and Russian vehicles. Chelsea caught up with and passed them both. "Yeeee*oh!*" she yelled as she sped into the lead.

"Don't open the champagne yet," Sheffield said.

When the straightaway ended and they once again encountered a stretch of the great continental dunes, the experienced drivers again outmaneuvered and outdistanced the Max One.

"What am I doing wrong?" Chelsea pleaded.

"Hanging out with race-car drivers."

"That's not what I mean!" she stormed, her sense of humor lost in the face of her frustration.

"We'll be on a sandstone flat when we cross the Saloum River," Sheffield calmed her. "You'll have a chance to take the lead again there."

When they reached the flat, Chelsea quickly caught up with Vera Kursk and passed her, and was pressing Ferrand for first place when the accident happened. A pack of hyenas, perhaps a dozen, suddenly ran in front of the Peugeot. Seasoned professional that he was, Ferrand did not swerve an inch as he felt the impact of his grille on the animals he hit and the rumble of his tires on those he ran over. Then one of the hyenas was spun up into the wheel well and, in a mangle of flesh and blood, jammed the axle. Ferrand's front wheels locked and his vehicle flipped end over end, landing a hundred feet out on the flats, bursting into flames.

"Stop the car!" Sheffield ordered, and Chelsea skidded to a halt on the shoulder. They unharnessed and leaped out, Sheffield grabbing the portable fire extinguisher, Chelsea helping him to balance upright on his swollen ankle. As they ran, hobbling, toward the burning car, they became aware that the Lada had also stopped and Vera Kursk was getting out.

At the fiery Peugeot, Sheffield handed Chelsea the extinguisher. "Start spraying the driver's door!" Chelsea pointed the red cylinder and shot a burst of Halon up and down the door. It immediately smothered the flames on that side and Sheffield was able to reach through the window, unstrap Ferrand, and drag him out of the car. Sheffield and Chelsea each took a hand and, Sheffield limping agonizingly, dragged the unconscious man far enough away so that when the Peugeot exploded none of them were hurt.

From overhead came the sound of a rotor. Looking up, Sheffield and Chelsea saw a rally control helicopter surveying a place to land. Paramedics wearing Red Cross armbands were in an open hatch waiting for touch-down.

"They'll take care of him," Sheffield said. He stood up, holding onto Chelsea for support, and they looked across the flat at the Max One and the Lada parked side by side. Vera Kursk was beside the Lada, peering down the track, where several kilometers back came the surviving vehicles. Smiling, she threw Sheffield and Chelsea a wave and quickly got into her car. Chelsea started running, dragging Sheffield with her. "The bitch!" she said.

"I'd do the same thing in her place," Sheffield groaned.

By the time they were harnessed back into the Max One, the Lada was half a kilometer ahead and the rest of the pack was moving up behind them very quickly. "We're almost to Dakar," Sheffield told his daughter. "If you want to win, you'll have to catch her."

Chelsea got back on the track and shot the car forward like a bullet. Into the African farming communities she sped, watching for animals, people, other vehicles, always keeping the Lada in sight. "Am I gaining on her, do you think?" she asked.

"Not yet."

Through the farmland, into the nearer outskirts, past larger villages, a soap factory, a shoe factory. "Am I gaining?" she shouted.

"Not yet."

Past a power station, a cotton mill, small handicraft shops at the side of the road, a huge open-air market, increasing lines of spectators in marvelously colored native garb. "Am I gaining?"

"Not yet."

"God*damn!*"

Then into the city of Dakar itself and on to the far end of Gann Boulevard, a wide, tree-lined thoroughfare roped off a mere one hour earlier, when the control aircraft advised the city that the first of the rally vehicles was approaching. The boulevard led straight to the finish line in the Place de l'Independence. The Lada was still half a kilometer ahead. "Punch it!" Sheffield yelled. He beat his fist on the dashboard. "Punch it! Punch it!"

Chelsea punched it.

The Max One drew up dead even on the right side of the Lada. The two women exchanged quick, appraising glances, saw only unyielding determination in the other, and, as if choreographed, both leaned into their steering wheels and tried to punch their accelerators through the floorboards. "Come *on!*" Chelsea muttered through her clenched teeth.

The Max One pulled forward an inch. Then two. Then three. Vera Kursk glanced over again, desperation in her eyes. Sheffield yelled, "All right!"

The cars sped down to the finish line next to the war memorial in the great plaza. Thousands cheered them on from a vast crowd that was but a blur of color to the drivers. Stretched across the end of the boulevard, a great banner with FINIS lettered on it fluttered in the breeze. The Max One was less than a car-length ahead, the Lada's windshield even with the American vehicle's rear bumper. Then Vera punched the Lada.

"She's pulling up!" Sheffield cried.

Chelsea saw Vera's face moving closer in the sideview mirror. In seconds, the Russian woman was next to her again. Biting down hard enough on her bottom lip to draw blood, Chelsea punched the Max One again.

The Max One crossed the finish line one and a half seconds ahead of the Lada.

At the banquet that night in the Saint Louis Hotel, Chelsea and Vera Kursk hugged each other and Austin Trowbridge read everyone a cable he had received congratulating him on the Max One and advising him that a bank account had been opened for one million dollars to start the Trowbridge Automotive Design Center. "I'd like you to come back to the States and be my partner," the young man told Sheffield. "Between the two of us, we can come up with cars nobody's ever imagined."

"I'll think about it, kid," Sheffield promised.

At midnight, Sheffield rode with Chelsea and Austin in a taxi out to Grand Dakar Airport, where they watched the Max One being rolled into the cargo hold of a Boeing 747 bound for Casablanca and New York. The young couple had seats in the passenger section of the same plane.

"Austin and I are going to be married when we get home," Chelsea told Sheffield. Austin had gone ahead, giving them time to say goodbye. "And we're going to start having babies. The first boy we have, I'm naming Jack. After a guy I recently met."

"Do yourself a favor," Sheffield said. "Raise him to be a doctor."

She shook her head. "Not on your life." She kissed him on the cheek. "Bye, Daddy."

"See you, kid."

Sheffield watched the plane rumble down the runway and climb into the starry African sky. Then he sighed and limped slowly off the observation deck and back into the terminal. When he reached the glass exit doors, he was met by the familiar face he'd been expecting.

"Hello, Marcel."

The Frenchman's two thugs were standing nearby.

"The Max One was pressing Ferrand when he crashed," Marcel accused. "You were racing to win."

"I always race to win," Sheffield replied evenly.

"Do you think you can get away with doublecrossing me?" The Frenchman's eyes were narrowed and dangerous.

Sheffield merely shrugged. "What are you going to do, Marcel, kill me?" He cocked his head in the best John Garfield tradition. "Everybody dies," he said arrogantly. And pushing through the doors, he walked painfully out into the Senegalese night.

ON THE
HIGH SEAS

THE HIDDEN SABOTEUR

David Braly

The house was palatial, with tall white walls that shone in the oppressive Arabian sun. Abdul Adr rolled up the date-tree-lined driveway in a black Mercedes driven by a chauffeur who never spoke, employed by a man whose identity Adr hadn't been told.

When they arrived at the house, the chauffeur got out and opened Adr's door. He pointed toward a long white stone stairway that led from the driveway to the second floor of the mansion. He then slid back into the car and drove away.

Adr climbed the steps. He'd been told by his superiors to come to this place, and that was the only reason he didn't panic. He was fearful, however.

A man in a blue business suit appeared at the top of the steps. He was a short, fat individual with heavy black eyebrows and dense grey hair. His jowls were wide and his skin dark. Adr knew that he was an Arab. He didn't understand why many Arab businessmen wore their native costume in the West but Western clothing in their homeland.

"It's hot today," said the man in the blue suit. The code.

"It's hot every day," responded Adr, also by prearrangement.

Adr finished the climb to find himself upon a stone porch. The man in blue motioned him into open double doors.

He passed through the doors into a hallway, followed by the other man. The floor was black and white tile, the walls red with smooth Lebanese cedar, and the ceiling bore an elaborate blue and yellow Turkish mosaic.

"Follow me, please," said the man in blue, taking the lead.

He guided Adr into a small room near the end of the hall. An Iranian carpet covered its floor, its walls were white, and its ceiling a dull blue. A large, open, multipaned window overlooked the estate and beyond to the city. The only furniture in the room was a small cedar table surrounded by several large armchairs. One of the armchairs was occupied by a man who rose to his feet when Adr entered.

Adr guessed this second man's age to be forty. He had black hair, a hooked nose, and suspicious black eyes that shifted endlessly. He, too, was dark and wore a blue suit and certainly was an Arab.

"This," said the elder man, indicating Adr, "is the representative of the Crescent Moon Strike Force." Then, indicating the other man, he said to Adr, "And this is a representative of certain Bahrain businessmen."

The two younger men nodded politely to each other.

"There is a proposition for the Crescent Moon," continued the older man. "It's necessary that a decision about it be reached before you leave this room. Do you have that sort of authority?"

"I do," said Adr.

"Good. Then I'll leave you two alone." He bowed slightly and left.

After the other two men had seated themselves, the business representative said: "I'll come right to the point. The men I am here for need some dirty work done. The sort of dirty work that the Crescent Moon is known to do occasionally for a price."

"What sort of 'dirty work,' friend?"

"Sabotage—for which we'll pay a hundred million dollars American."

"How much?"

"One hundred million."

"That is . . . that is a great amount of money."

"Then you're interested?"

"Of course."

"Have you heard of Alexis Pangalos?"

"Naturally." Who hadn't?

Adr recalled to his mind everything that he knew about Pangalos, what he'd read in the newspapers and magazines. He remembered that Pangalos had been born in southern Greece shortly after the turn of the century. He was the son of a small shipowner, a child of the lower middle class. He'd inherited his father's ship when the old man died (Alexis was about twenty, Adr thought), and expanded the business quickly. Soon he had three old freighters plying the trade routes of the eastern Mediterranean. Pangalos was twenty-four when a storm broke up the ship he was aboard. Everyone drowned except Alexis and two other men, who clung to the hull of the wreck. They drifted at sea for many days, finally being rescued by a coal carrier called the *Toltec,* named for an ancient Mexican tribe of Indians who were conquered by the Aztecs. Thereafter Pangalos named all of his ships *Toltec* this or *Toltec* that.

Pangalos saw World War II coming and sold his ships before its arrival.

He was in London when Greece was invaded, but returned home to fight in the underground.

After the war Pangalos built his first oil tanker. He built many others in the following decades. Soon the Pangalos Tanker Group had some of the world's largest supertankers.

Now Alexis was an old man and his empire was administered by his eldest son, Constantine. But it was no secret that while Constantine administered the empire, its expansion and policies were controlled by old Alexis. It'd been his decision—not Constantine's—to refuse cooperation with the Greek junta, his decision to expand the Pangalos fleet while other tanker owners retrenched, and his decision to build the *Toltec Challenger,* the world's first million-ton oil tanker, the launching of which would occur in only a few weeks.

"You may have read," said the business representative, "that Mr. Pangalos has continued to expand his tanker fleet despite economic conditions which would ordinarily have prompted such a man to retrench. To do this, he has had to borrow large sums of money from certain banks and other financial institutions in Bahrain."

"The people you represent," said Adr.

"Precisely. For collateral, the Pangalos Tanker Group has put up everything that it owns. Everything. Oil tankers, real estate in a dozen countries, office buildings, airplanes—"

"He must have borrowed hundreds of millions of dollars."

"Indeed he did."

"Can he repay it?"

The other man smiled. "That's where you come in, friend . . . Alexis Pangalos is what Westerners like to call a 'wheeler-dealer.' He juggles money, makes deals to cover deals, buys on margin, that sort of thing. A payment on the notes we hold from him will be due shortly. If he cannot make payment, we can foreclose on the entire Pangalos empire. I don't need to tell you what such a prospect means to my employers in Bahrain."

"Can he make the payment?"

"Yes. We've learned of a deal centered around the *Toltec Challenger* struck between Pangalos and several New York and Houston banks. During the ship's maiden voyage it will stop on the eastern coast of the Arabian peninsula to fill four of its five tanks with oil. This oil will be taken to South Africa and off-loaded, at which time a sum of money large enough to cover the first note payment will be deposited to the Pangalos accounts in London and Beirut. That would, of course, cost us the Pangalos properties."

"Why only four of the tanks?" asked Adr. "Why not all five?"

"I suppose it's the oil glut. Even the South Africans don't need as much oil as that monster can deliver."

Adr had read much about the "monster" during the last few months. Although the nuclear-powered ship was a technological wonder, it had serious drawbacks. Its maximum speed was eight knots. And its draft was so deep that no port in the world could receive it; oil would have to be carried to it by other, smaller tankers, then pumped aboard through long rubber hoses.

"You want us to destroy the *Toltec Challenger?*" asked Adr.

"Yes. But only after it has taken the oil aboard. We've learned that Alexis Pangalos hasn't been able to insure either the ship or the oil that it'll carry. This first million-ton vessel has the insurance companies frightened. Several would insure it, but only for premiums so high that Pangalos wouldn't pay."

"And if the tanker goes down without insurance, your chances of fore-closing are increased."

"Increased? They're guaranteed. He's gambling everything he owns on this ship, and he's already dangerously overextended." The Bahrain representative removed a folded sheet of paper from an inner pocket of his suit. "Here is the crew list. All the officers and crew are Pangalos veterans who are loyal to their employer, but you might find someone who can assist you in some manner."

He handed the paper to Adr.

"I don't know," continued the Bahrain man, "how you could destroy the ship, except perhaps by attacking it with a gunboat or airplane, without being killed yourself. If the oil aboard explodes, it would be like the blast of an atomic bomb."

"That big?"

"Many years ago a little fifty thousand ton oil tanker blew up off the coast of Mexico. The explosion was heard for fifty miles in every direction, created hurricane-force winds, and the following day, many miles away, a black rain fell from the oil that'd been shot into the air and condensed by the blast. Cattle ate the grass that it fell upon. They died."

"Fantastic." Abdul Adr looked at the crew list again. He smiled. "Yes," he said, "fantastic."

Alexis Pangalos stood beside the Japanese prime minister, smiling, nodding, and occasionally waving to the crowd below. Another triumph. Perhaps his last. He was seventy-nine now, but his age wasn't why it might be his last. His optimism and good health could see him through another ten or twenty years. No, this time the trouble was financial. The Pangalos empire was nearly bankrupt. He and a handful of his top executives knew it, as did a few other people: the bankers in Bahrain, a couple of Arab tycoons, a

Greek competitor or two, and the forty-year-old man who stood on the other side of him, his son Constantine.

To other people, Alexis Pangalos revealed nothing about his state of mind. He stood on the platform, smiling, nodding, waving, his long silver hair rustling in the warm breeze. He stood straight as the flagpole that flew the Liberian colors above the *Toltec Challenger,* a big man whose clothes looked clumsy because of his six foot six inch frame and his bulging muscles. His face was dark, deeply lined, and hard. His sea-blue eyes were outlined by bags below, thick brows above, and deep wrinkles at their sides, but they never flinched, seldom even blinked. They, too, defied age, sun, and wind, and were steady.

Constantine Pangalos shifted his feet, and alternately smiled and frowned. He looked more like a businessman than did his father. He was as tall as Alexis, but his hair was jet black, oily, and didn't blow in the breeze. His face was brown but unweathered, unlined, unwrinkled. His eyes were shielded by large, thick sunglasses. Constantine's clothes fit him perfectly. He was a good advertisement for his tailor.

Before them was the stern of the *Toltec Challenger.* It waited. The officers and crew aboard waited. The crowd waited. The press waited. The prime minister waited. Waited for the ship to be launched and begin its maiden voyage. All the speeches had been made, all the salutes fired, all the music played. The fanfare was over.

Nicholas Nasoulia waited, too. He stood against the railing in front of the bridge on the superstructure walkway and held himself as straight as the flagpole, as straight as Alexis Pangalos. He didn't mind waiting. He enjoyed ceremony. And he knew that many people were watching him stand there in his bright white uniform. Nasoulia wasn't tall like the Pangalos men. He was five nine and weighed one hundred seventy pounds, but aboard ship his authority was greater than theirs. He was the captain. The fifty-one-year-old captain of the largest ship built in the history of the world.

The First Officer, Costa Minotis, stood to the right and slightly behind Nasoulia. He was only an inch taller than Nasoulia, and he weighed the same. Costa, too, stood straight, but he didn't like it, not for so long a time. He wanted the ceremony to end so that they could be underway, could get on with the real business of running the ship.

Costa wondered how much money the delay—ten minutes now!—was costing Alexis Pangalos. Not that it would matter to Pangalos, who Costa knew had money to burn. But he wondered just the same. When he'd been told that the *Toltec Challenger* was one million dead-weight tons, Costa had figured out that its running costs would be about forty-five thousand dollars a day. That was before he learned that the ship would be nuclear. He knew too little about nuclear engines to figure the cost. He'd heard only two solid figures about the huge ship: that it had cost six hundred million dollars to build; and that the eight hundred tons of paint used to coat it had cost $148,899.27. All Costa knew was that the fixed expenses were costing Pangalos money even while the ship stood still in the water.

Suddenly the crowd on shore cheered.

Costa guessed that the woman selected to launch the ship had finally clobbered the stern with her bottle of champagne.

He was right. The great ship began to slide forward slowly.

"We'd better go inside," said Nasoulia. Costa nodded and followed the captain in.

Already the yellow and red lights on the instruments inside the long, wide bridge were on, burning steadily to light up an otherwise dark room. The instruments hummed. Five men in the room watched separate instrument panels. Costa had never seen a more beautiful bridge.

"Any problems?" Nasoulia asked a middle-aged man who had short-clipped brown hair and thick glasses.

"None," said the man, the navigator Pericles Maverrichi. "Our fears about not clearing Nagasaki harbor were groundless."

"Good. Take it to top speed as soon as we're in deep water and shoot that into the computer the course is charted on."

Costa watched the bridge activity for a few minutes, then walked over to the windows. He looked at nearby boats and distant ships, at the calm sea, and at what he could see of his own ship. Eventually he focused upon one particular seaman who was walking on the catwalk toward the superstructure. He watched him until the seaman walked beneath Costa's line of sight.

The seaman entered the superstructure and proceeded to his own cabin. His room was equipped with a television set, a multiband radio, and the usual expensive furniture that supertankers provide for their crewmen. Original oil paintings decorated the walls. He was alone in the room. Other crewmen had their wives aboard (also a common practice on modern supertankers), but his remained in Greece. He was thinking about buying a game computer at the ship's store and putting it in his room to pass the time.

There were three items in his room that he didn't get at the ship's store: a Mauser, a detonator, and a bomb.

The saboteur was aboard.

Charles Giscaret leaned back in his chair, a smile of quiet satisfaction on his face. Before him on the small formica table were the remains of two legs of chicken, a salad, a bowl of gravy-soaked mashed potatoes, and a slice of watermelon. Also an empty wine glass. Giscaret glanced around the dining room. There were only a half dozen other men still seated. That, he thought, was the trouble with people who weren't French: they ate too fast.

He felt a nudge against his right ankle. He didn't have to look down to know what was responsible for it.

The fifty-two-year-old Frenchman looked at the chicken scraps with a new sense of guilt. No meat remained on them. Tonight he'd eaten the meat right to the bone.

Giscaret bent down and spoke to the tiger-striped cat: "Sorry, *mon ami,* there's nothing for you tonight. Old Charles has been a pig."

The cat stared at him several seconds, then vigorously rubbed its head against Giscaret's leg. Giscaret repeated that he had nothing left. The cat ignored the statement and continued to rub its head against his leg.

"Ah, cats!" Giscaret took his plate of chicken bones and lowered it to where it was under the cat's head. The cat sniffed at the bones for a moment, looked up, and meowed accusingly. Giscaret shrugged his shoulders. "I have to eat, too."

The cat hurried over to another table.

For several minutes Giscaret remained at his own table, digesting his food while he thought about tomorrow's work. Work? Hardly, not aboard this ship. The nuclear engine—and everything else—worked perfectly, and Chief Engineer Giscaret looked forward to spending much of his time in the Engine Control Room (ECR) reading old magazines.

After three or four minutes of thinking about this, Giscaret decided it was time to leave. He placed his glass beside the plate and saucers on his tray and carried the tray to the warming table. He then walked across the dining room to the deck door. When he opened it, the cat suddenly reappeared and dashed out.

Giscaret walked to the port side and looked over the railing at the sea. The air was warm; they were approaching South Africa.

"Hello, Charles."

Giscaret turned and greeted Costa Minotis.

"Nice night," said the First Officer.

"Yes. I enjoy nights like these: a big yellow moon floating atop a black sea. Although I miss the motion."

"Motion?" asked Minotis. "Oh, you mean the tossing. Yes, these ships are too heavy for tossing."

Too heavy for many things, thought Minotis. Too heavy to stop fast, or to turn around, or to notice—things. Minotis had learned that last fact aboard his previous ship, the three hundred thousand ton *Toltec Runner.* Once—after an apparently peaceful, uneventful cruise—the *Runner* had put into the Hague for minor repairs. Workers found that the ship's hull had been marked by wide and long scratches, from the waterline to a height of ten feet. Obviously the *Runner* had hit and destroyed a trawler or some other boat without the tanker crew's being aware of it at the time. Not an uncommon occurrence, Costa knew, but a chill went down his spine when he caught himself wondering how big a ship the *Toltec Challenger* could destroy without the crew's being aware of it.

"If we had to stop immediately," Costa asked the engineer, "how long would it be before the ship was still?"

"From the speed we're going now, four miles."

Costa shook his head. "I hope nothing gets in our way."

Giscaret chuckled.

For several minutes they stood silently, looking out across the black waves. Then Giscaret turned and said, "I must check the indicators."

"Mind if I tag along?"

"Of course not. During our training in Japan I could tell that you were interested in nuclear engines. And they are the way of the future."

The two men walked back toward the superstructure. A young man and woman on bikes rode past them. Costa and Giscaret reached the superstructure, entered, walked half its width, and took an elevator down two stories. They talked while they walked, mostly about engines. Costa told the engineer how the nineteenth century American ship and rail tycoon Cornelius Vanderbilt had advertised his steamships as being safe from explosions, a great concern of the public at the time, by claiming that his had no boilers. Giscaret got a big laugh out of that.

When they got out of the elevator, they proceeded down a corridor to a door that bore a sign reading:

"ENGINE CONTROL ROOM—UNAUTHORIZED PERSONNEL KEEP OUT."

Costa followed Giscaret inside.

The room was large. It was also bright because of the gold light of the overhead bulbs and the red and blue flashing lights of the instruments. Everywhere there were modern, sleek computerized machines, bright, shiny, clean, operative. Their many small lights flashed off and on in a slow, normal, quiet way, and the machines hummed softly.

"Where's Saphos?" asked Giscaret.

"Who?"

"Leonidas Saphos, one of my assistants. He's supposed to be here watching the damn instruments. This room's supposed to have someone in it at all times . . . Saphos! Where the hell are you?!"

"I'll check the lavatory," said Costa.

"No, wait. Look. There's blood on the floor."

There was. For a moment the pair stood silent and motionless. The quiet was accentuated by the hum of the machinery, the silent rhythmic flashing of the dull blue and red panel bulbs.

Costa Minotis saw more blood: several drops between where they stood and a far corner of the room. The actual corner itself was blocked from view by a row of seven foot tall steel cabinets. They'd been placed there to be out of the way, but not pushed against the wall because the door into the nuclear power plant was behind them.

Costa walked the long distance to the cabinets, then stepped around them. On the floor between the cabinets and the engine door was a man's body. He was belly-down in a pool of blood.

Costa stooped down to examine him.

Suddenly the door next to him swung open. A gloved man in seaman's pants with a seaman's shirt tied around his head to hide his face leaped out and hit Costa with a metal cylindrical object. Costa went over, less from hurt than from surprise and caution.

He got up fast.

Costa ran around the cabinets in time to see his assailant hurrying out of the ECR door into the corridor. Giscaret was on the floor, apparently knocked over by a shove instead of the metal object. At least the stream of profanity coming from the chief engineer's mouth indicated that he hadn't been hurt.

"Sound an alarm!" yelled Costa as he ran by Giscaret. Then he, too, hurried out.

He saw the attacker running down the corridor. Costa pursued him. He couldn't see who he was because the man still had the shirt wrapped around his head and was otherwise dressed normally.

The attacker ran past the elevator. He hurried on, finally reaching the door that opened into a stairway and disappearing into it.

Costa ran past the elevator and continued toward the stairwell door. When he reached it, he pushed it open.

The man stood in front of him, waiting, his right hand drawn back with the metal object gripped in it.

He swung, hit Costa on the jaw. Costa fell backwards onto the floor. The man turned, ran, and the door pulled itself shut.

Although stunned badly by the blow and hurting, Costa managed to stumble to his feet. "That's two I owe you," he muttered, then he swung open the door again and stepped onto the landing. The other man wasn't in sight.

Which way to go? The man would probably seek his cabin in the area above, where the crew's quarters were located.

A loud, shrill whistle blew three times. The alert was being sounded. Instantly every crewman in his cabin would rush out and take his position for an emergency. The assailant would be only one man among many, hidden in the numbers of his fellow workers, unless Costa could catch him before he reached the area of the cabins.

Costa bounded up the stairs three steps at a time.

He passed the first deck below the main deck and kept going.

He reached the main deck, winded but with his adrenalin still pushing him forward. He threw open the stairwell door and entered the corridor. At the end of the corridor the door leading to the outside was closing itself.

Had the other man just gone out?

Costa ran toward the door.

Reached it. Threw it open. And found himself facing a young seaman—who wasn't winded.

"Did you see anyone come out of here in the last few seconds?" demanded Costa.

"Uh—well, yes, sir. I'm not sure who, but I think it was Yorgo."

"Yorgo Kamatropoulos?"

"Yes, sir. He went towards the bow, sir."

"Come with me."

Before Costa lay the great length of the ship, its bow so far away that it was invisible in the night. Costa hurried onto the catwalk and proceeded toward the bow. The catwalk stretched down the deck's middle, from the superstructure to the bow, and was raised above the deck itself, which was often underwater during turbulent weather. Thick pipes ran beside the catwalk on both sides, and there were six firefighting pump stations spread at equal distances along it.

Costa was too winded to run. He walked briskly, though, almost running. He could hardly breathe by the time he and the seaman behind him reached the empty helicopter pad halfway between the superstructure and bow.

Just past it, Costa saw movement out of the corner of his right eye, among the pipes parallel to the catwalk.

He stopped, the seaman almost walking into him. "You!" shouted Costa toward the pipes. "What are you doing down there?"

"Sir?" answered a voice from the darkness.

There was more movement. A man emerged from the darkness, coming toward Costa. He walked slowly because the deck was slanted away from the catwalk and was slippery. He climbed to the catwalk.

"Sorry, sir, I couldn't hear you."

He was Wilhelm Vogel, a thirty-seven-year-old German crewman with blond hair, a deeply-lined face, and only half his teeth remaining. Minotis knew him. Vogel had served aboard the *Toltec Runner*. He was a bully at times, but a fine seaman.

"I asked what you were doing," said Costa.

"Oh. I heard a sizzling sound down there, so I was checking it out. I was afraid that there might be trouble with one of the service pipelines . . . Didn't find a thing, though. Of course, it's pretty dark to be looking, but I couldn't hear the noise again, either. Someone should re-check it when it's light."

"Did you see or hear anyone come by here in the last few minutes?"

"No sir. But with the dark and the noise of the sea—"

"Have you see Yorgo Kamatropoulos tonight?"

"Not since dinner."

"Come with us," said Costa. He resumed walking toward the bow.

The area ahead was brightly lit. A tall pole stood at the bow, and on top of it were ten beacons, each aimed in different directions. These lit the bow as a convenience to the crew and as a warning to any boats or ships that might stray into the tanker's area.

Finally they reached the end of the catwalk. Ahead, clear under the beacon pole, were the huge machines that operated the anchors. There was one machine on each side, their winding poles thick with heavy, enormous chains.

A man stood next to the starboard machine. Like Vogel, he wore a crewman's work clothes, the same sort worn by the attacker. This man, however, had something that Vogel didn't: a metal cylindrical object balanced in his hands.

Costa leaped down the steps onto the lower bow deck, followed by Vogel and the other seaman. Only then did the man by the machine look up and see them. He straightened when he saw the First Officer, but he didn't try to run. He was about thirty-five, had a sledgehammer jaw and big floppy ears. He wasn't Yorgo; he was a veteran seaman named Stylianos Douris.

Costa approached him. "What's that?" he asked Douris.

Douris looked down at the metal object he held. It was about eighteen inches long, two inches in diameter, made of metal that had been painted black. The black paint was barely visible now, covered as it was by fresh red blood.

"I don't know," said Douris. "I was checking the forward thermometer and suddenly it came flying down and landed about twenty feet from me. I guess somebody threw it from the catwalk. I looked up, but I couldn't see anybody."

"When did this happen?"

"Oh, I guess about two, three minutes ago."

"And since that time you've just been standing here holding it?"

"Well, uh, yes sir. Trying to figure out what it is. It's covered with blood, but it don't look like a kitchen utensil to me. Looks sort of like a pipe."

Wilhelm Vogel stepped over and took the metal object from Douris. He walked to the beacon pole where he could examine it closely beneath the lights.

After several seconds, Vogel said, "It's part of a bicycle pump."

Costa took the pump, examined it a few seconds, then instructed Douris and Vogel to follow him back to the superstructure.

As Costa mounted the catwalk, he wondered where Yorgo Kamatropoulos was.

Costa Minotis stood in the ECR with Vogel and Douris, facing Captain Nasoulia, who held the bicycle pump in his gloved hands. Minotis had already explained to him everything that happened since he chased the attacker out of the ECR. Nasoulia had immediately cancelled the alert and ordered Yorgo Kamatropoulos to report to him in the ECR.

"Saphos' head was bashed in," said Nasoulia. "That explains the blood on the pump."

"I was afraid that it would," said Costa.

"Giscaret and Orakis have already made a preliminary search of the engine area. They found part of a detonator wire. Therefore, the killer is also a saboteur, and there's a bomb somewhere in there. Giscaret will direct a thorough search of the power plant and the entire engine area."

"I wonder how long we've got."

"Damned if I know. Maybe hours, maybe seconds. We have to assume that it is a time bomb, and that normally restricts the time to twenty-four hours."

Nasoulia glared at the two crewmen who'd returned with Costa. He clasped his hands behind his back, paced up and down in front of them, looking at them contemptuously. "It just came flying down, did it?"

Douris started to answer, hesitated, then nodded.

"Costa," said the captain, "I want the bow area checked at first light. If it flew down, it had to hit and bounce, and that would leave spots of blood. The sea's calm, so no water would flow over the bow to wash them away. Meanwhile, post a guard at the bow end of the catwalk to keep everyone away."

"Yes, sir."

Nasoulia next looked at Vogel. "Sizzling noise, eh?"

"That's right, sir," said the German.

"It couldn't be that you ran out on deck after you killed Saphos? That you ran to the bow to dispose of the bike pump, but found someone there and had to content yourself with throwing it onto the bow bridge instead of throwing it off the ship? That you ran back towards the superstructure, but saw Officer Minotis coming and hid among the service pipes?"

"No, sir. In fact, it makes no sense to me why the killer would run to the bow. If I had been the killer, sir, I'd have run to the edge of the ship and tossed the pump off immediately."

Costa said nothing but mentally agreed with Vogel. Why had the murderer run all the way to the bow to dispose of the murder weapon when he could have more easily hurried to either the starboard or port sides? The bow of the *Toltec Challenger* was a quarter mile from the superstructure.

The door from the corridor opened and twelve men filed in. One, in the lead, looked around the room until he saw the captain. "We were told to come down here," he said. "Something about a search."

"Go into the engine area," said Nasoulia. "The door is behind those cabinets over there. Mr. Giscaret will tell you what to do."

"Yes, sir."

"One more thing," said Nasoulia. "Don't disturb the body in front of the door."

"Uh—yes, sir."

"Good lad."

The crew glanced at each other, then headed for the cabinets.

"What are our chances of finding the bomb in a place so huge?" asked Costa.

"Almost no chance at all," said Nasoulia. "We can try, however. We'll look primarily in the area where the detonator wire was found."

"Any chance of having a bomb squad flown in from South Africa?"

"Perhaps. I'll radio the Pangalos people in London after we're through here and ask. Maybe a helicopter could fly them aboard."

The corridor door opened again. A seaman entered. He was about thirty-three, had black hair, was short but muscular, and he looked confused and nervous. Yorgo Kamatropoulos.

"Where were you," asked Nasoulia, sweeping his left hand around in order to look at his wristwatch, "a half hour ago?"

"Uh, in my cabin . . . sir."

"You were seen walking onto the main deck and proceeding toward the catwalk. Why were you outside?"

"I'm sorry, sir, but someone's made a mistake. I haven't been outside the super for two hours."

"I repeat, Mr. Kamatropoulos, that you were seen."

Kamatropoulos' face reddened, and the muscles there and in his neck stiffened. "And I repeat that I wasn't there."

Nasoulia didn't react as visibly as Kamatropoulos, but Costa could see that he didn't like the latter's attitude. Although Greek, Nasoulia had been British-trained; he put a premium on discipline.

"Do you have witnesses to prove that you were inside your cabin?" asked Nasoulia.

"No, sir. Why should I? What's going on?"

The corridor door opened again. The ship's doctor and another man entered with a gurney. "Where's the body?" asked the doctor.

"Behind those cabinets," said Nasoulia, nodding in their direction. Then he turned his attention to Kamatropoulos again. "There's the answer to your question, mister. Murder. And sabotage."

"And you think that I was involved?"

"You were seen leaving the superstructure."

"I didn't leave it! I've been in my cabin for the last two hours."

"Doing what?"

"Listening to Radio South Africa and reading a book that I checked out of the ship's library."

"Why weren't you at dinner?"

"I wasn't hungry. I ate an apple in my room." When Nasoulia looked at him disbelievingly, Kamatropoulos added: "If you wish, *sir*, you may go to my cabin and examine my trash container for the core."

Nasoulia stiffened. "Don't be impertinent."

"Sir, I'm falsely accused and I resent it."

"I don't give a damn what the bloody hell you resent! I'll not tolerate impertinence aboard my ship."

Nasoulia turned to Costa. "I'll have to occupy my time with supervising the bomb search and communicating with the London office, so I'm putting you in charge of trying to find out which of these three men murdered Saphos and planted the bomb. I don't need to tell you how important it is that we find that device immediately. Obviously if we can identify the murderer, we can question him about the location of the bomb."

Costa had no illusions about what form the "questioning" would take. Aboard a ship the captain's word was law. Nasoulia, proud to be in charge of the largest ship ever built, would not see it blasted from beneath him without trying every method to make the saboteur talk. That would include threats and torture.

"Meanwhile," continued Nasoulia, looking coldly at the three suspects, "all of you will be confined in one of the storage rooms."

Phillip Osopla shook his head slowly while he looked at the meters before him. Although he was Second Officer of the *Toltec Challenger* and had been with the Pangalos organization all of his adult life, he remained in many ways similar to the simple Greek fisherman that his father had been.

He didn't know about a lot of things, especially technological things, and he had to cover his insecurity with his humor. Fortunately, he had been blessed with an excellent sense of humor.

Osopla felt ignorant looking at the triple row of meters. Each row had fifteen meters. Although all the meters were eighteen inches in diameter, the number of needles they contained varied. So, too, Osopla suspected, did their functions. And he couldn't even guess what their functions might be.

Something about the meters bothered him.

He stood close to them—only a foot away—examining them. He wondered if they bothered him only because their function was a mystery to him. No, that couldn't be it; almost every technological item aboard was a mystery to him. Perhaps, then, it was something relating to the bomb.

Although there were three rows and many meters, there wasn't room between them for anything the size of a bomb. The spaces were too narrow and awkward.

Osopla, silently twisting one end of his handlebar mustache, stared closely at one meter. The face was white, with a small, circular row of numbers lying close to numerous lines and dashes and dots. In the center was a hole, through which protruded the needle pin. Beneath the hole he could see a few delicate copper wires. Around and beyond these wires he could see nothing. Because there was nothing to see.

He quickly examined another meter. Like the first, it appeared to be hollow between its face and back except for the center.

When Osopla examined a third meter, he saw evidence of wires, knobs, and other metal in the space between the face and the back.

Ditto for a fourth and fifth, but a sixth appeared hollow like the first and second.

"Charles!" yelled Osopla. "Come here!"

"On my way!" shouted Giscaret from a distance.

While he waited for the engineer, Osopla continued to examine the meters. He took special note of their length and width. He was sure that the amount of space between the face and back was sufficient to conceal a bomb in one of the hollow meters. He was also sure that Giscaret and the crewmen—involved in searching through several floors of gears, boxes, wires, pumps, panels, and the like—hadn't checked meters.

Giscaret came up. "What is it?"

"These," said Osopla, pointing to the meters. "Some are hollow."

"Hollow?"

"Between the faces and the backs. Just a few tiny wires."

"Of course. That's because they don't need any mechanical gears other than . . . Oh no!"

"I think we'd better have them opened, Charles. And any other meters in the engine area and power plant."

" 'Any other'? You mean 'all other.' "

"How many meters are there?"

"I don't know. Dozens of banks like this. Hundreds and hundreds of meters. And they're just one more part of this whole blasted . . ." Giscaret shook his head. "Sorry," he said.

"How many meters in the area where Orakis found the piece from the detonator wire?"

"Oh, maybe fifty or sixty."

"You'd better search them first."

The killer snapped open a folding chair and sat upon it. The other two suspects did the same.

He hadn't planned on getting trapped out on the deck like that. He'd planned to run up on deck, go to the side, and toss over the bike pump and his gun. But two men had been talking on the starboard side and a woman was staring out at the waves from the rail at the port side. He'd had to run out onto the catwalk.

Then the second problem. Not throwing the bicycle pump piece far enough. Good thing he'd worn gloves.

At least the gun had gone clear over the bow. He hadn't used the gun, of course, but possession of it would have revealed him as the killer. Even if they found it when they searched his room they would know. Guns were forbidden on board.

He was breaking a lot of rules this voyage.

He glanced at his wristwatch.

Two hours to go. Then the ship would go up. Everyone aboard would die. He would die. In two hours.

Costa was seated at his desk when the seaman knocked and entered. He handed Costa the files he'd requested. They were the personnel files on Vogel, Douris, and Kamatropoulos. Obviously the destruction of the ship would also be the destruction of the saboteur. He had to look into their histories, see if any of the three might be suicidal. Other possibilities: personal problems or some deep hatred of Pangalos or Nasoulia, a hatred so deep they would be willing to die to soothe it.

Each of the three manila folders contained—one sheet of paper!

"Wait a minute," said Costa. "Is this all?"

"Yes, sir," said the seaman. He was Nasoulia's clerk, a thin little man with dirty fingernails.

"I asked for the complete personnel records of Douris, Vogel, and Kamatropoulos. You're saying that each man has only—only a paragraph in his record!"

"At the moment, yes."

"What do you mean, 'at the moment'?"

"Well, Mr. Minotis," began the clerk, his voice acquiring an obnoxious I'm-an-expert-I'm-a-teacher tone, "there are two complete files for every employee aboard a Pangalos tanker. One file is kept at the main office in London, the other aboard the tanker. However, because the *Toltec Challenger* has only just been launched, we don't yet have our copies of the files on our men. All we have aboard are the most minuscule records, useful perhaps for the captain to make background evaluations of the crew, but nothing more."

Costa banged his fist on his desk and swore.

The clerk started to leave.

"One more thing," snapped Costa. "It feels like the ship is slowing down. Is it?"

"Yes, sir. Captain Nasoulia has ordered the ship to come to a dead stop."

"Why?"

"Instructions from London. All crewmen are to help look for the bomb. That makes them unavailable to run the ship."

The men who crowded into the engine area were confused and puzzled. They had been told to abandon work, let the ship come to a standstill, and report to the engine area above the nuclear power plant. Every man aboard ship had been told that, with only a dozen exceptions.

They stood close to each other, talking in whispers, questioning and speculating. Popular rumor said that there was a bomb aboard.

Everyone fell silent when Captain Nasoulia walked in. He hurried to a clear area near the wall.

"Men," he yelled, "we're in trouble. We have strong reason to believe that there is a bomb in this area of the ship."

The men stirred, whispered.

"We've had men searching for it, but without result. We don't know how much time we may have left. I don't need to tell you what a bomb exploding aboard this particular ship would mean, what would happen. Suffice it to say that we'd all be killed."

Nasoulia paused. The men remained silent, gloomy.

"I want every man here," continued Nasoulia, "to hunt for that bomb. Do it thoroughly, but do it quickly . . . I need not mention that you're in no greater danger here in the nuclear power plant at the stern of the ship than you would be at the bow. If the bomb goes, we all go, wherever we are . . . We have pulled as close to the coast as our draft will allow. A ship is on its way to evacuate you, other crewmen, and the women on board, and a helicopter will bring in a bomb squad. All this has been arranged by Mr. Pangalos personally. In the meantime, hunt for that bomb."

"Sir," shouted one crewman, "why can't we use the lifeboats?"

"We must make every effort to save the ship. If we haven't found the bomb by the time the rescue ship arrives, we'll evacuate. In the meantime, we'll search. That'll give us—" Nasoulia glanced at his wristwatch—"about three hours."

Costa stared down at the three sheets of paper. He was angry. And scared. There should have been more information. Bulging files on every member of the crew. Granted, the Pangalos headquarters could never antic- ipate that one of the men aboard the *Toltec Challenger* would turn into a saboteur and murderer, especially since these men were supposed to be the finest in the entire Group, but . . . but there should have been complete files on every crewman. That was standard policy.

Costa was willing to bet that some three-piece-suit man or woman in London was going to be looking for another job soon.

But enough. These thoughts were wasting his time, accomplishing noth- ing.

He lifted the first piece of paper and read:

VOGEL, WILHELM ALBERT, JR.
Level 2 tanker crewman
  B.–20.7.46, Cuxhaven, FRG; ed 10 yrs; job exp dock wrkr, crewman, freighter, joined Group 5/72 Copenhagen.
  Languages: German, Greek, English, Danish, some French, Arabic, and Spanish.
  Emergency: Blood type A; no drug allergies; dependents 0; in event of death, contact Group HQ, London; Lutheran.
  Job reports summary: strengths: leadership and mechanical, some chemi- cal, languages/weaknesses: occasionally insubordinate; occasionally in trou- ble with police for fighting and destruction of property.
  Leaves: 2/74, 7/78, 9/80, 7/81, 8/83, 4/84
  Recommendation: adv Level 1 at discretion of captain.

Costa laid aside the sheet. Since he had served aboard the *Toltec Runner* with Vogel, there was nothing in the report summary that surprised him, even though he'd never had reason to see any part of Vogel's file before.

Costa examined the next sheet:

DOURIS, STYLIANOS POPOS
  Level 4 tanker crewman
    B.–12.4.48, Agyia, Greece; ed 8 yrs; job exp crewman, freighter, yacht,
    tankers, joined Group 4/76 Athens
    Languages: Greek, English, some Bulgarian.
    Emergency: Blood type O; allergy to penicillin and aspirin; dependents 3;
  in event of death, contact Group district office Athens; G.O.
    Job reports summary: strengths: hard worker with strong sense of loyalty/
  weaknesses: poorly educated, no special skills.
    Leaves: 4/78, 2/79, 12/81, 8/82, 12/82, 12/83
    Recommendation: no adv immediate future

Except for the allergies to penicillin and aspirin and the fact that Douris had once worked on somebody's yacht, there was nothing in this report that surprised Costa, either.

He put aside Douris' sheet, and lifted that of Yorgo Kamatropoulos. He knew less about Kamatropoulos than he knew about Douris, certainly less than he knew about Vogel.

KAMATROPOULOS, YORGO
  Level 4 tanker crewman
    B.–12.12.50, Athens, Greece; ed grade and secondary, A.A. University of
    Athens, plus one year towards B.A. at same institution; job exp tanker
    crewman only, joined Group 6/74 Athens.
    Languages: Greek, English, French, some Chinese.
    Emergency: Blood type O; no allergies; dependents 0; in event of death,
  contact Group district office Athens; no religious preference.
    Job reports summary: strengths: intelligent, well-educated, takes charge
  easily/weaknesses: no mechanical or navigational skills.
    Leaves: 4-5/78, 6-8/80, 6-9/83
    Recommendation: captain's discretion for adv or not

Costa lifted the telephone receiver, putting him into contact with the still-manned Communications Center.

"Communications," said a voice.

"This is First Officer Minotis. If Captain Nasoulia or anyone else wants me, tell them I'll be talking to the sabotage suspects in Storage Room L."

"Yes, sir."

Costa glanced at the three file sheets once more. A cold shiver went up his spine. He replaced the sheets in their folders, placed the folders on the edge of his desk, and left the room.

*   *   *

Abdul Adr had once heard that the Savoy Grill served the most delicious food in London. Now he believed it. Even the lingering taste-numbness caused by his cigars couldn't kill the deliciousness of this food.

He was sure that Ahmed Panu thought the same. Panu was the chief representative of the Bahrain bankers who held the mortgages on the Pangalos empire. He was, at fifty-one, twenty years Adr's senior, a man of slow, careful movements, of sleepy olive eyes. Panu was also a man who didn't close his mouth while he ate, as the current racket coming from his face testified.

"I'm getting impatient," said Panu. "You've been telling us 'any day now' for several days."

"Don't worry so. It can't be long now. I stipulated to the man we have aboard that the ship must be blown up before it reached South Africa and off-loaded its oil."

"How long before it reaches South Africa?"

Adr smiled broadly. "Only a matter of hours, friend."

"Meaning that—" Panu stopped, glanced around the room to make sure that they weren't being observed, then resumed: "Meaning that the *Toltec Challenger* will be destroyed today?"

"Precisely."

Panu smiled, also.

Costa hesitated momentarily before he unlocked the door to Storage Room L. But only momentarily. He knew what had to be done.

He swung the door open. The three suspects stood. Costa walked in, closed the door behind him.

"How's the search going, sir?" asked Vogel.

"I don't know. That's not my department at the moment." Costa looked at Vogel, then at Douris, then at Kamatropoulos. None of the men looked more nervous or apprehensive than the others. "I want to ask each of you," said Costa, "one question."

Kamatropoulos smiled. "A trick question, sir?"

"One that'll reveal the saboteur?" asked Douris.

All three suspects chuckled uneasily. Costa did not.

"I'll ask you first, Wilhelm," said the First Officer.

"Sure," said Vogel. "Shoot."

"If you were the captain of this ship, would you continue the search or would you order everyone into the lifeboats?" Costa lifted his left wrist and glanced at the time. "Captain Nasoulia doesn't intend to abandon ship until the rescue ship arrives, and that will be another two and a half hours now."

Vogel thought about it a few seconds, and while he did he rubbed the stubble on his right cheek and his jaw. "I'd order everyone into the life-boats," he said at last. "Abandon ship immediately."

"I'm surprised, Wilhelm. You've always been a fighter."

"True, sir. But this isn't something we can fight."

"So you would just leave a six hundred million dollar ship out in the middle of the ocean without making any further effort to save it."

"Right," said Vogel. "Mind you, I'd hate to do it, sir. I mean, it is the largest ship ever to grace the waters of this world. But the lives of fifty crewmen and a number of women and journalists and observers aboard outweigh any monetary consideration."

"And you would abandon it immediately?" asked Costa. "Without any delay?"

"Right. I would forget about trying to find the bomb and leave immediately and quickly. That is to say, sir, I would get as far away from this ship as I could, as fast as I could."

"I see," said Costa. "And what about you, Yorgo?"

"I disagree with Wilhelm. I would stay and search."

"For how long?"

"At least until the rescue ships arrived. The chances are that the bomb isn't set to go off for a while and—"

"Why do you say that?"

"Because there would be too little time for the saboteur to escape."

Costa smiled. "How is he going to escape, Yorgo? It's a hundred foot drop from the railing to the sea. The lifeboats require a team effort to lower them. How is one man going to get off this ship alive all by himself?"

Kamatropoulos thought it over a minute, then shrugged.

Costa looked at Douris. "Stylianos, what do you think?"

"I agree with Wilhelm," he said. "I would abandon the ship without delay and get as far away from it as possible."

"Without waiting for the rescue ship?"

"Yes."

"You realize, of course, that our lifeboats could be swamped by the waves, whereas the rescue ship is a large vessel, entirely safe."

"Yes."

"But still you would hurry overboard in the lifeboats?"

"Yes."

Costa turned, opened the door to the corridor, stepped out, locked the door, and began to run. He had to reach Nasoulia as soon as possible. He could've phoned through the Communications Center, but he had to tell him eyeball-to-eyeball, so the captain would understand fully.

Time had run out.

*   *   *

Nasoulia was standing at the edge of the engine area above the nuclear power plant, watching the progress of the search. He slowly became aware of a large group standing a hundred feet away. Giscaret and eight other men were there, talking to each other.

It suddenly dawned upon Nasoulia that they must have found the bomb. Giscaret wasn't a man to waste time. Not in these circumstances. For the first time in years Nasoulia forgot dignity and broke into a run.

He was still twenty feet from the men when he shouted: "Where was it?"

Nobody answered. Instead, the men looked over at him, then at each other. They appeared to be confused, as though they didn't understand his question. Nasoulia, hollow in his stomach, stopped running.

"Did you find the bomb?" he asked Giscaret.

"No, captain."

"Then why the bloody hell are you just standing here talking?"

"Because," said Giscaret, "the search of the obvious places is completed. We have looked at all the readily accessible places, all the places near the Engine Control Room, and we've found nothing. The bomb cannot be found."

"But there are plenty of other places to look. You couldn't have searched the entire power plant."

"Of course not. But we've looked in all the places that can be gotten to without trouble. The other places will take too long to search. Perhaps the saboteur opened a large pipe, shoved the bomb deep into it so that it would be out of sight unless the pipe was opened and carefully examined with a flashlight. Perhaps he removed a ceiling panel and—"

"Forget the damn theories. Work on them and find the bomb!"

"Captain, to check these generally inaccessible places would take weeks. If there is a bomb aboard and it is a time bomb, there isn't enough time."

"As captain, that decision is mine."

"*Oui*, it is. If you tell us to resume looking, we shall. But as chief engineer I must tell you that the chances of our finding the bomb during the next several hours are probably one in a million. And as a simple engineer I can tell you that it's unlikely that a time bomb will allow for twelve hours, let alone twenty-four."

At that moment Costa Minotis entered the engine area in a hurry. Nasoulia realized something was happening when everyone in front of him took their eyes off him and looked past his shoulder. He turned to see Minotis closing the distance quickly.

Minotis stopped before Nasoulia, took several seconds to try (unsuccessfully) to catch a little of his breath, and then said: "We've got to abandon ship immediately."

"So I'm told," replied Nasoulia. "What's your reason for not wanting to wait for the rescue ship."

"The saboteur told me we should leave the ship now and get as far away from it as we can."

"One of the suspects has confessed?" demanded Nasoulia.

"No."

"Then how—"

"When I read over the records of the three men, I realized who the saboteur had to be. Then I asked him and the other two whether we should leave now or wait for the rescue ship. He was one of the men who said leave now."

"Naturally. If we leave now, there's no chance that we'll find his bomb. He's not going to advise us to continue searching for it. The saboteur, you'll remember, doesn't want us to find it, Costa."

Costa ignored the sarcasm. "I believe the man, sir. There isn't time to hunt. The bomb will go off before the rescue ship reaches us."

"Who is the saboteur?"

"Stylianos Douris."

"You're sure?"

"Yes, sir."

"Then I can *make* him tell us where the bomb is."

"I doubt it, sir. He has a strong reason for wanting to see this ship blown up. Perhaps you could crack him, by torture or something, but not in time. He'll hold out as long as he can. Even if you force him to talk, he'll probably gain more time by lying."

Nasoulia thought it over. "All right," he said. "We'll abandon ship. Everyone except Douris. We'll leave him aboard. If the ship blows up, he blows up with it. If he wants to live, he'll disengage the bomb."

"You can't do that," said Costa.

"I'm the captain and I can bloody well do anything I want!"

"There'll be an investigation afterward, sir. Even a captain is held responsible for—"

"Oh, never mind. Bring him along—under guard. I want two or three men holding onto him all the time. He'll have charges to answer when this thing is over."

"Why?" asked Giscaret. "Why did he do it?"

"Someone is forcing him to do it. They've taken his family hostage. He either blows up the ship or his family is killed."

"He told you that?"

"No. His file told me that. It carries no notation of mental illness or depression, no record of any grudge against the Pangalos Group or family or anyone aboard this ship. He's not suicidal, he wants us off so he's not anxious to kill everyone, so that's all that's left."

The explosion was so bright that it dimmed the sun.

Costa saw it from the lifeboat, as did the other men. First came a sharp yellow flash of light on the eastern horizon, then a great rolling mass of red, black, and watery white. Next came the sound, loud and sharp like a sonic boom multiplied fifty times, then continuous thunder.

Costa couldn't see any parts of the ship caught up in the mass of flame and smoke and water. The lifeboats were too far away, pulling farther away every second with the motors locked at full speed. But he knew that the bomb's explosion by itself hadn't caused the lighting up and the rolling smoke in the east, nor the ear-splitting bang. No bomb except a nuclear one could be that big. Instead, the bomb's blast had penetrated into the tanks, causing the oil to explode.

"It's a hell of a way for the largest ship in history to meet its end," said Nasoulia. He was seated beside Costa at the rear of the boat.

"Yes."

"And so bloody young."

"One little bomb can sure do a lot of damage."

"Where could it have been, Costa? Where could Douris have hidden it?"

"You'd have to ask Giscaret."

"He said that there were many places that a saboteur could hide a bomb if he had the time and knowledge to do a really good job."

Costa, looking toward the east, thought that the black cloud above the water resembled a horse's head. "Stylianos must have more brains than the company has given him credit for."

"Where could he have hidden it?"

Costa decided not to answer again. If he did it would only encourage Nasoulia to continue talking that way. He didn't like the way the captain sounded. Nasoulia talked like a man who was guilty of something or one entering depression.

"I was so bloody proud of that ship," continued Nasoulia. "When I first heard that I'd be the captain of the largest ship in the world, I was—Well, you can imagine my feelings."

"Yes. Similar to mine, I guess, when I learned I was going to be the First Officer."

"But I failed her."

"It wasn't your fault that a saboteur got aboard. If fault could be assigned—and I doubt that it could—it would belong to people at headquarters."

Nasoulia was silent for a minute. Then he said: "Where could that bomb have been?"

Costa ignored the remark and looked to the west. "In a few hours we'll reach land," he said. "So will the other lifeboats. Then we can ask Stylianos personally."

"Too late."

Costa thought that Nasoulia was still thinking about the ship. He worried about the depth of the captain's depression. He turned to look at the smoke again and saw that Nasoulia hadn't been referring to the ship when he said that it was too late.

In the east the ocean appeared abnormally high.

Costa stared open-mouthed at the distant water. He felt hollow in his stomach as he watched the eerie horizon.

One of the men behind him said: "Sir, on the horizon . . . That isn't . . . I mean . . ."

"Yes," said the captain. He sounded resigned to his fate. "It is. From the explosion."

Costa stood, cupped his hands over his mouth, and shouted to the men forward in the boat, who were looking west toward land instead of east toward the smoke: "Tidal wave!"

Everyone braced himself—and waited.

Everyone except Captain Nasoulia.

Nasoulia watched the rising ocean without a flicker of concern registering in his eyes. "Costa," he said easily. "There's one thing I've got to know."

"What?"

"How did you know that the saboteur was Douris?"

"All the men were sane, sir." Costa had difficulty talking because his mouth and throat were dry. Suddenly dry. "That left only the family-held-hostage scenario. Douris' file showed that he was a good team man."

"Meaning he should have been the last anyone tried to force into betrayal against his employer," said Nasoulia.

"No. Meaning he'd be ideal to recruit. Loyal to his family. And he was a good family man. His record showed that. Most crewmen take their leaves in summer or spring—after they have enough seniority to get long leaves and a choice of the seasons—but not Stylianos. His leaves were usually in December, the holidays."

"So he could be with his family," said Nasoulia.

"Yes." Costa whispered the word. He could barely breathe because of his fear. The ocean to the west was like a great blue mountain. It looked like it was only a few meters from the lifeboat, but it continued to come faster and faster, and never reached the lifeboat.

"But why not Kamatropoulos or Vogel?" asked Nasoulia, his voice still calm.

"Uh . . . Kamatropoulos and Vogel? Oh, yes, well . . . The records, sir . . . They showed . . ."

"What? What'd they show?"

"Huh?" The mountain of water grew and grew, and it roared like thunder. "Oh, yes. They, the records that is, listed the number of dependents that each man had. Kamatropoulos and Vogel had none; Stylianos Douris had three. He was the only man with a family."

"I see," said Nasoulia. "So that means—"

At that second the wave hit.

Abdul Adr left the London office of what had once been the Pangalos Tanker Group. It was damp, and even though it was afternoon a light fog enveloped the city. He began walking toward his hotel.

Adr had walked only a block when he suddenly felt that he was being followed. He looked over his shoulder and his blood ran cold.

Ten feet behind him was a man with a black beard whom he'd spotted watching him yesterday at an East End restaurant.

Adr turned and hurried on.

What next? He had few choices. The damp, foggy streets were crowded and he could see a bobby on the next block, but appealing for police protection was a bad idea for a man wanted by a dozen countries—including this one. No hope of outrunning him; the man looked younger and stronger than he. Little hope of losing him in the crowd; it was dense, but not dense enough for that.

Adr continued to hurry, to think. The only thing he could do was reach his hotel room and the Luger hidden inside his suitcase.

Who would want to kill him?

>Several rival Palestinian groups.
>Israeli agents.
>Egyptian agents.
>Lebanese agents.
>Sudanese agents.
>Moroccan agents.
>American agents.
>Rivals within the Crescent Moon.
>Several personal enemies.

Adr rushed faster.

He looked over his shoulder again. And stopped. The man with the black beard was gone.

Adr then remembered an incident that had happened in London three years earlier. Again a strange man had followed him, and Adr had feared for his life. Then too he'd been pursued through the London fog by the stranger. Only that time the man had caught up with him.

"You're an Arab," the man had said without introductions.

"Yes," said Adr, waiting for a knife thrust or gun blast.

"Say, I got me an idea for a business, see, but I don't 'ave the money to get it started, see? If you'll put up the money, I'll let you 'ave a third interest."

"A—a business?"

"Yes. A new type of electric toothbrush, you see."

"I don't understand what you're talking about."

"Well, it's the Yanks, isn't it? I mean, in the States everybody uses electric toothbrushes, see. Well, my idea is to produce a new type of electric toothbrush. It'll 'ave a radio in it."

Yes, Adr remembered the incident well. And how angry the man became when Adr told him he wouldn't give him any money.

"That's the trouble with you people what got the money!" the man had shouted after him. "You want to keep it all for yourselves. You'll steal my idea! I know you will! If you do, I'll come after you!"

That was probably what the man with the black beard was: another Englishman wanting Arab money to make him rich. That was the trouble with the English, they didn't understand about thrift, enterprise, or trade. The Arabs understood those things. Their nations had become the richest in the world because of their understanding. Oh, sure, the oil resources had helped. But the English would have to learn those values if they ever wanted to amount to anything.

He continued walking toward his hotel. Unhurried now. For a few minutes he even enjoyed the fog. But only for a few minutes.

Halfway to his hotel he became uneasy again. But when he glanced over his shoulder he didn't see any faces that looked dangerous.

He didn't quicken his pace, but his feeling of unease and of being watched never left him as he walked to the hotel. He was sure that it was the man with the black beard even though he couldn't see him.

He wished he had the Luger with him. But that was impossible. Any bobby might stop and frisk him. As a foreigner his rights were limited. If the English suspected his identity, he wouldn't have any rights at all.

He thought that maybe he should go to a phone and ask the local Crescent Moon members for protection. But what would he say to justify such an alert? That a man he saw in a restaurant later turned up walking behind him? They would think he was cracking up.

Who? Who was he?

Enemy agent? Political rival? Personal enemy?

Maybe the brother or son or cousin of someone he'd killed or ordered killed?

How many people had he ordered killed?

About seventy had died in his largest hit, the *Toltec Challenger*. About fifty crewmen and twenty wives of crewmen, journalists, and civilian observers. No one knew the exact toll. No one knew exactly how many non-crewmen had been aboard. And several crewmen had survived.

Douris wasn't one of them.

Or, if he was, no one realized that he was still alive. He could have gotten to shore by clinging to debris and swimming the way other crewmen had, then not reported his survival to the authorities.

No!

Douris was dead! As dead as his wife and twins!

All dead!

All!

Suddenly Adr heard footsteps behind him, paced identically to his own. Someone was following him. Maybe the man with the black beard. How many of his enemies had black hair? Did Douris?

Adr started to glance over his shoulder, but abruptly his fear seized control of every cell of his body. He couldn't look. He couldn't breathe. He couldn't think.

He ran.

People turned and looked at him running but he didn't care.

He had to get away.

He could hear someone running behind him, the footfalls in time with his own.

A DESCENT INTO THE MAELSTRÖM

Edgar Allan Poe

The ways of God in Nature, as in Providence, are not as our ways; nor are the models that we frame in any way commensurate to the vastness, profundity, and unsearchableness of His works, which have a depth in them greater than the well of Democritus.

—*Joseph Glanvill*

We had now reached the summit of the loftiest crag. For some minutes the old man seemed too much exhausted to speak.

"Not long ago," said he at length, "and I could have guided you on this route as well as the youngest of my sons; but, about three years past, there happened to me an event such as never happened before to mortal man—or at least such as no man ever survived to tell of—and the six hours of deadly terror which I then endured have broken me up body and soul. You suppose me a *very* old man—but I am not. It took less than a single day to change these hairs from a jetty black to white, to weaken my limbs, and to unstring my nerves, so that I tremble at the least exertion, and am frightened at a shadow. Do you know I can scarcely look over this little cliff without getting giddy?"

The "little cliff," upon whose edge he had so carelessly thrown himself down to rest that the weightier portion of his body hung over it, while he was only kept from falling by the tenure of his elbow on its extreme and slippery edge—this "little cliff" arose, a sheer unobstructed precipice of black shining rock, some fifteen or sixteen hundred feet from the world of crags beneath us. Nothing would have tempted me to be within half a dozen yards of its brink. In truth so deeply was I excited by the perilous position of my companion, that I fell at full length upon the ground, clung to the shrubs around me, and dared not even glance upward at the sky— while I struggled in vain to divest myself of the idea that the very foundations of the mountain were in danger from the fury of the winds. It was long before I could reason myself into sufficient courage to sit up and look out into the distance.

"You must get over these fancies," said the guide, "for I have brought you here that you might have the best possible view of the scene of that event I mentioned—and to tell you the whole story with the spot just under your eyes.

"We are now," he continued, in that particularizing manner which distinguished him—"we are now close upon the Norwegian coast—in the sixty-eighth degree of latitude—in the great province of Nordland—and in the dreary district of Lofoden. The mountain upon whose top we sit is Helseggen, the Cloudy. Now raise yourself up a little higher—hold on to the grass if you feel giddy—so—and look out, beyond the belt of vapor beneath us, into the sea."

I looked dizzily, and beheld a wide expanse of ocean, whose waters wore so inky a hue as to bring at once to my mind the Nubian geographer's account of the *Mare Tenebrarum*. A panorama more deplorably desolate no human imagination can conceive. To the right and left, as far as the eye could reach, there lay outstretched, like ramparts of the world, lines of horridly black and beetling cliff, whose character of gloom was but the more forcibly illustrated by the surf which reared high up against it its white and ghastly crest, howling and shrieking for ever. Just opposite the promontory upon whose apex we were placed, and at a distance of some five or six miles out at sea, there was visible a small, bleak-looking island; or, more properly, its position was discernible through the wilderness of surge in which it was enveloped. About two miles nearer the land, arose another of smaller size, hideously craggy and barren, and encompassed at various intervals by a cluster of dark rocks.

The appearance of the ocean, in the space between the more distant island and the shore, had something very unusual about it. Although, at the time, so strong a gale was blowing landward that a brig in the remote offing lay to under a double-reefed trysail, and constantly plunged her whole hull out of sight, still there was here nothing like a regular swell, but only a short, quick, angry cross dashing of water in every direction—as well in the teeth of the wind as otherwise. Of foam there was little except in the immediate vicinity of the rocks.

"The island in the distance," resumed the old man, "is called by the Norwegians Vurrgh. The one midway is Moskoe. That a mile to the northward is Ambaaren. Yonder are Islesen, Hotholm, Keildhelm, Suarven, and Buckholm. Further off—between Moskoe and Vurrgh—are Otterholm, Flimen, Sandflesen, and Stockholm. These are the true names of the places —but why it has been thought necessary to name them at all, is more than either you or I can understand. Do you hear any thing? Do you see any change in the water?"

We had now been about ten minutes upon the top of Helseggen, to which we had ascended from the interior of Lofoden, so that we had caught no glimpse of the sea until it had burst upon us from the summit. As the old man spoke, I became aware of a loud and gradually increasing sound, like the moaning of a vast herd of buffaloes upon an American prairie; and at the same moment I perceived that what seamen term the *chopping* character of the ocean beneath us, was rapidly changing into a current which set to the eastward. Even while I gazed, this current acquired a monstrous velocity. Each moment added to its speed—to its headlong impetuosity. In five minutes the whole sea, as far as Vurrgh, was lashed into ungovernable fury; but it was between Moskoe and the coast that the main uproar held its sway. Here the vast bed of the waters, seamed and scarred into a thousand conflicting channels, burst suddenly into phrensied convulsion—heaving, boiling, hissing—gyrating in gigantic and innumerable vortices, and all whirling and plunging on to the eastward with a rapidity which water never elsewhere assumes, except in precipitous descents.

In a few minutes more, there came over the scene another radical alteration. The general surface grew somewhat more smooth, and the whirlpools, one by one, disappeared, while prodigious streaks of foam became apparent where none had been seen before. These streaks, at length, spreading out to a great distance, and entering into combination, took unto themselves the gyratory motion of the subsided vortices, and seemed to form the germ of another more vast. Suddenly—very suddenly—this assumed a distinct and definite existence, in a circle of more than a mile in diameter. The edge of the whirl was represented by a broad belt of gleaming spray; but no particle of this slipped into the mouth of the terrific funnel, whose interior, as far as the eye could fathom it, was a smooth, shining, and jet-black wall of water, inclined to the horizon at an angle of some forty-five degrees, speeding dizzily round and round with a swaying and sweltering motion, and sending forth to the winds an appalling voice, half shriek, half roar, such as not even the mighty cataract of Niagara ever lifts up in its agony to Heaven.

The mountain trembled to its very base, and the rock rocked. I threw myself upon my face, and clung to the scant herbage in an excess of nervous agitation.

"This," said I at length, to the old man—"this *can* be nothing else than the great whirlpool of the Maelström."

"So it is sometimes termed," said he. "We Norwegians call it the Moskoe-ström, from the island of Moskoe in the midway."

The ordinary account of this vortex had by no means prepared me for what I saw. That of Jonas Ramus, which is perhaps the most circumstantial of any, cannot impart the faintest conception either of the magnificence, or of the horror of the scene—or of the wild bewildering sense of *the novel* which confounds the beholder. I am not sure from what point of view the writer in question surveyed it, nor at what time; but it could neither have been from the summit of Helseggen, nor during a storm. There are some passages of his description, nevertheless, which may be quoted for their details, although their effect is exceedingly feeble in conveying an impression of the spectacle.

"Between Lofoden and Moskoe," he says, "the depth of the water is between thirty-six and forty fathoms; but on the other side, toward Ver (Vurrgh) this depth decreases so as not to afford a convenient passage for a vessel, without the risk of splitting on the rocks, which happens even in the calmest weather. When it is flood, the stream runs up the country between Lofoden and Moskoe with a boisterous rapidity; but the roar of its impetuous ebb to the sea is scarce equalled by the loudest and most dreadful cataracts; the noise being heard several leagues off, and the vortices or pits are of such an extent and depth, that if a ship comes within its attraction, it is inevitably absorbed and carried down to the bottom, and there beat to pieces against the rocks; and when the water relaxes, the fragments thereof are thrown up again. But these intervals of tranquillity are only at the turn of the ebb and flood, and in calm weather, and last but a quarter of an hour, its violence gradually returning. When the stream is most boisterous, and its fury heightened by a storm, it is dangerous to come within a Norway mile of it. Boats, yachts, and ships have been carried away by not guarding against it before they were carried within its reach. It likewise happens frequently, that whales come too near the stream, and are overpowered by its violence; and then it is impossible to describe their howlings and bellowings in their fruitless struggles to disengage themselves. A bear once, attempting to swim from Lofoden to Moskoe, was caught by the stream and borne down, while he roared terribly, so as to be heard on shore. Large stocks of firs and pine trees, after being absorbed by the current, rise again broken and torn to such a degree as if bristles grew upon them. This plainly shows the bottom to consist of craggy rocks, among which they are whirled to and fro. This stream is regulated by the flux and reflux of the sea—it being constantly high and low water every six hours. In the year 1645, early in the morning of Sexagesima Sunday, it raged with such noise and impetuosity that the very stones of the houses on the coast fell to the ground."

In regard to the depth of the water, I could not see how this could have been ascertained at all in the immediate vicinity of the vortex. The "forty fathoms" must have reference only to portions of the channel close upon the shore either of Moskoe or Lofoden. The depth in the centre of the

Moskoe-ström must be unmeasurably greater; and no better proof of this
fact is necessary than can be obtained from even the sidelong glance into
the abyss of the whirl which may be had from the highest crag of Helseggen. Looking down from this pinnacle upon the howling Phlegethon below, I could not help smiling at the simplicity with which the honest Jonas
Ramus records, as a matter difficult of belief, the anecdotes of the whales
and the bears, for it appeared to me, in fact, a self-evident thing, that the
largest ships of the line in existence, coming within the influence of that
deadly attraction, could resist it as little as a feather the hurricane, and must
disappear bodily and at once.

The attempts to account for the phenomenon—some of which I remember, seemed to me sufficiently plausible in perusal—now wore a very different and unsatisfactory aspect. The idea generally received is that this, as well
as three smaller vortices among the Ferroe Islands, "have no other cause
than the collision of waves rising and falling, at flux and reflux, against a
ridge of rocks and shelves, which confines the water so that it precipitates
itself like a cataract; and thus the higher the flood rises, the deeper must the
fall be, and the natural result of all is a whirlpool or vortex, the prodigious
suction of which is sufficiently known by lesser experiments."—These are
the words of the Encyclopaedia Britannica. Kircher and others imagine that
in the centre of the channel of the maelström is an abyss penetrating the
globe, and issuing in some very remote part—the Gulf of Bothnia being
somewhat decidedly named in one instance. This opinion, idle in itself, was
the one to which, as I gazed, my imagination most readily assented; and,
mentioning it to the guide, I was rather surprised to hear him say that,
although it was the view almost universally entertained of the subject by the
Norwegians, it nevertheless was not his own. As to the former notion he
confessed his inability to comprehend it; and here I agreed with him—for,
however conclusive on paper, it becomes altogether unintelligible, and even
absurd, amid the thunder of the abyss.

"You have had a good look at the whirl now," said the old man, "and if
you will creep round this crag, so as to get in its lee, and deaden the roar of
the water, I will tell you a story that will convince you I ought to know
something of the Moskoe-ström."

I placed myself as desired, and he proceeded.

"Myself and my two brothers once owned a schooner-rigged smack of
about seventy tons burthen, with which we were in the habit of fishing
among the islands beyond Moskoe, nearly to Vurrgh. In all violent eddies at
sea there is good fishing, at proper opportunities, if one has only the courage to attempt it; but among the whole of the Lofoden coastmen, we three
were the only ones who made a regular business of going out to the islands,
as I tell you. The usual grounds are a great way lower down to the south-

ward. There fish can be got at all hours, without much risk, and therefore these places are preferred. The choice spots over here among the rocks, however, not only yield the finest variety, but in far greater abundance; so that we often got in a single day, what the more timid of the craft could not scrape together in a week. In fact, we made it a matter of desperate speculation—the risk of life standing instead of labor, and courage answering for capital.

"We kept the smack in a cove about five miles higher up the coast than this; and it was our practice, in fine weather, to take advantage of the fifteen minutes' slack to push across the main channel of the Moskoe-ström, far above the pool, and then drop down upon anchorage somewhere near Otterholm, or Sandflesen, where the eddies are not so violent as elsewhere. Here we used to remain until nearly time for slack-water again, when we weighed and made for home. We never set out upon this expedition without a steady side wind for going and coming—one that we felt sure would not fail us before our return—and we seldom made a miscalculation upon this point. Twice, during six years, we were forced to stay all night at anchor on account of a dead calm, which is a rare thing indeed just about here; and once we had to remain on the grounds nearly a week, starving to death, owing to a gale which blew up shortly after our arrival, and made the channel too boisterous to be thought of. Upon this occasion we should have been driven out to sea in spite of every thing (for the whirlpools threw us round and round so violently, that, at length, we fouled our anchor and dragged it), if it had not been that we drifted into one of the innumerable cross currents—here to-day and gone to-morrow—which drove us under the lee of Flimen, where, by good luck, we brought up.

"I could not tell you the twentieth part of the difficulties we encountered 'on the ground'—it is a bad spot to be in, even in good weather—but we make shift always to run the gauntlet of the Moskoe-ström itself without accident; although at times my heart has been in my mouth when we happened to be a minute or so behind or before the slack. The wind sometimes was not as strong as we thought it at starting, and then we made rather less way than we could wish, while the current rendered the smack unmanageable. My eldest brother had a son eighteen years old, and I had two stout boys of my own. These would have been of great assistance at such times, in using the sweeps as well as afterward in fishing—but, somehow, although we ran the risk ourselves, we had not the heart to let the young ones get into the danger—for, after all said and done, it *was* a horrible danger, and that is the truth.

"It is now within a few days of three years since what I am going to tell you occurred. It was on the tenth of July, 18—, a day which the people of this part of the world will never forget—for it was one in which blew the most terrible hurricane that ever came out of the heavens. And yet all the morning, and indeed until late in the afternoon, there was a gentle and steady breeze from the southwest, while the sun shone brightly, so that the oldest seaman among us could not have foreseen what was to follow.

"The three of us—my two brothers and myself—had crossed over to the islands about two o'clock P.M., and soon nearly loaded the smack with fine fish, which, we all remarked, were more plenty that day than we had ever known them. It was just seven, *by my watch*, when we weighed and started for home, so as to make the worst of the Ström at slack water, which we knew would be at eight.

"We set out with a fresh wind on our starboard quarter, and for some time spanked along at a great rate, never dreaming of danger, for indeed we saw not the slightest reason to apprehend it. All at once we were taken aback by a breeze from over Helseggen. This was most unusual—something that had never happened to us before—and I began to feel a little uneasy, without exactly knowing why. We put the boat on the wind, but could make no headway at all for the eddies, and I was upon the point of proposing to return to the anchorage, when, looking astern, we saw the whole horizon covered with a singular copper-colored cloud that rose with the most amazing velocity.

"In the meantime the breeze that had headed us off fell away and we were dead becalmed, drifting about in every direction. This state of things, however, did not last long enough to give us time to think about it. In less than a minute the storm was upon us—in less than two the sky was entirely overcast—and what with this and the driving spray, it became suddenly so dark that we could not see each other in the smack.

"Such a hurricane as then blew it is folly to attempt describing. The oldest seaman in Norway never experienced any thing like it. We had let our sails go by the run before it cleverly took us; but, at the first puff, both our masts went by the board as if they had been sawed off—the mainmast taking with it my youngest brother, who had lashed himself to it for safety.

"Our boat was the lightest feather of a thing that ever sat upon water. It had a complete flush deck, with only a small hatch near the bow, and this hatch it had always been our custom to batten down when about to cross the Ström, by way of precaution against the chopping seas. But for this circumstance we should have foundered at once—for we lay entirely buried for some moments. How my elder brother escaped destruction I cannot say, for I never had an opportunity of ascertaining. For my part, as soon as I had let the foresail run, I threw myself flat on deck, with my feet against the narrow gunwale of the bow, and with my hands grasping a ring-bolt near the foot of the foremast. It was mere instinct that prompted me to do this

—which was undoubtedly the very best thing I could have done—for I was too much flurried to think.

"For some moments we were completely deluged, as I say, and all this time I held my breath, and clung to the bolt. When I could stand it no longer I raised myself upon my knees, still keeping hold with my hands, and thus got my head clear. Presently our little boat gave herself a shake, just as a dog does in coming out of the water, and thus rid herself, in some measure, of the seas. I was now trying to get the better of the stupor that had come over me, and to collect my senses so as to see what was to be done, when I felt somebody grasp my arm. It was my elder brother, and my heart leaped for joy, for I had made sure that he was overboard—but the next moment all this joy was turned into horror—for he put his mouth close to my ear, and screamed out the word *'Moskoe-ström!'*

"No one ever will know what my feelings were at that moment. I shook from head to foot as if I had had the most violent fit of the ague. I knew what he meant by that one word well enough—I knew what he wished to make me understand. With the wind that now drove us on, we were bound for the whirl of the Ström, and nothing could save us!

"You perceive that in crossing the Ström *channel,* we always went a long way up above the whirl, even in the calmest weather, and then had to wait and watch carefully for the slack—but now we were driving right upon the pool itself, and in such a hurricane as this! 'To be sure,' I thought, 'we shall get there just about the slack—there is some little hope in that'—but in the next moment I cursed myself for being so great a fool as to dream of hope at all. I knew very well that we were doomed, had we been ten times a ninety-gun ship.

"By this time the first fury of the tempest had spent itself, or perhaps we did not feel it so much, as we scudded before it, but at all events the seas, which at first had been kept down by the wind, and lay flat and frothing, now got up into absolute mountains. A singular change, too, had come over the heavens. Around in every direction it was still as black as pitch, but nearly overhead there burst out, all at once, a circular rift of clear sky—as clear as I ever saw—and of a deep bright blue—and through it there blazed forth the full moon with a lustre that I never before knew her to wear. She lit up every thing about us with the greatest distinctness—but, oh God, what a scene it was to light up!

"I now made one or two attempts to speak to my brother—but in some manner which I could not understand, the din had so increased that I could not make him hear a single word, although I screamed at the top of my voice in his ear. Presently he shook his head, looking as pale as death, and held up one of his fingers, as if to say *'listen!'*

"At first I could not make out what he meant—but soon a hideous thought flashed upon me. I dragged my watch from its fob. It was not going. I glanced at its face by the moonlight, and then burst into tears as I flung it far away into the ocean. *It had run down at seven o'clock! We were behind the time of the slack, and the whirl of the Ström was in full fury!*

"When a boat is well built, properly trimmed, and not deep laden, the waves in a strong gale, when she is going large, seem always to slip from beneath her—which appears strange to a landsman—and this is what is called *riding*, in sea phrase.

"Well, so far we had ridden the swells very cleverly; but presently a gigantic sea happened to take us right under the counter, and bore us with it as it rose—up—up—as if into the sky. I would not have believed that any wave could rise so high. And then down we came with a sweep, a slide, and a plunge that made me feel sick and dizzy, as if I was falling from some lofty mountain-top in a dream. But while we were up I had thrown a quick glance around—and that one glance was all-sufficient. I saw our exact position in an instant. The Moskoe-ström whirlpool was about a quarter of a mile dead ahead—but no more like the every-day Moskoe-ström than the whirl, as you now see it, is like a mill-race. If I had not known where we were, and what we had to expect, I should not have recognized the place at all. As it was, I involuntarily closed my eyes in horror. The lids clenched themselves together as if in a spasm.

"It could not have been more than two minutes afterwards until we suddenly felt the waves subside, and were enveloped in foam. The boat made a sharp half turn to larboard, and then shot off in its new direction like a thunderbolt. At the same moment the roaring noise of the water was completely drowned in a kind of shrill shriek—such a sound as you might imagine given out by the water-pipes of many thousand steam-vessels letting off their steam all together. We were now in the belt of surf that always surrounds the whirl; and I thought, of course, that another moment would plunge us into the abyss, down which we could only see indistinctly on account of the amazing velocity with which we were borne along. The boat did not seem to sink into the water at all, but to skim like an air-bubble upon the surface of the surge. Her starboard side was next the whirl, and on the larboard arose the world of ocean we had left. It stood like a huge writhing wall between us and the horizon.

"It may appear strange, but now, when we were in the very jaws of the gulf, I felt more composed than when we were only approaching it. Having made up my mind to hope no more, I got rid of a great deal of that terror which unmanned me at first. I supposed it was despair that strung my nerves.

"It may look like boasting—but what I tell you is truth—I began to reflect how magnificent a thing it was to die in such a manner, and how

foolish it was in me to think of so paltry a consideration as my own individual life, in view of so wonderful a manifestation of God's power. I do
believe that I blushed with shame when this idea crossed my mind. After a
little while I became possessed with the keenest curiosity about the whirl
itself. I positively felt a *wish* to explore its depths, even at the sacrifice I was
going to make; and my principal grief was that I should never be able to tell
my old companions on shore about the mysteries I should see. These, no
doubt, were singular fancies to occupy a man's mind in such extremity—
and I have often thought since, that the revolutions of the boat around the
pool might have rendered me a little light-headed.

"There was another circumstance which tended to restore my self-pos-
session; and this was the cessation of the wind, which could not reach us in
our present situation—for, as you saw for yourself, the belt of the surf is
considerably lower than the general bed of the ocean, and this latter now
towered above us, a high, black, mountainous ridge. If you have never been
at sea in a heavy gale, you can form no idea of the confusion of mind
occasioned by the wind and spray together. They blind, deafen, and stran-
gle you, and take away all power of action or reflection. But we were now,
in a great measure, rid of these annoyances—just as death-condemned
felons in prison are allowed petty indulgences, forbidden them while their
doom is yet uncertain.

"How often we made the circuit of the belt it is impossible to say. We
careered round and round for perhaps an hour, flying rather than floating,
getting gradually more and more into the middle of the surge, and then
nearer and nearer to its horrible inner edge. All this time I had never let go
of the ring-bolt. My brother was at the stern, holding on to a small empty
water-cask which had been securely lashed under the coop of the counter,
and was the only thing on deck that had not been swept overboard when
the gale first took us. As we approached the brink of the pit he let go his
hold upon this, and made for the ring, from which, in the agony of his
terror, he endeavored to force my hands, as it was not large enough to
afford us both a secure grasp. I never felt deeper grief than when I saw him
attempt this act—although I knew he was a madman when he did it—a
raving maniac through sheer fright. I did not care, however, to contest the
point with him. I knew it could make no difference whether either of us
held on at all; so I let him have the bolt, and went astern to the cask. This
there was no great difficulty in doing; for the smack flew round steadily
enough, and upon an even keel—only swaying to and fro with the immense
sweeps and swelters of the whirl. Scarcely had I secured myself in my new
position, when we gave a wild lurch to starboard, and rushed headlong into
the abyss. I muttered a hurried prayer to God, and thought all was over.

"As I felt the sickening sweep of the descent, I had instinctively tight-

ened my hold upon the barrel, and closed my eyes. For some seconds I
dared not open them—while I expected instant destruction, and wondered
that I was not already in my death-struggles with the water. But moment
after moment elapsed. I still lived. The sense of falling had ceased; and the
motion of the vessel seemed much as it had been before, while in the belt of
foam, with the exception that she now lay more along. I took courage and
looked once again upon the scene.

"Never shall I forget the sensation of awe, horror, and admiration with
which I gazed about me. The boat appeared to be hanging, as if by magic,
midway down, upon the interior surface of a funnel vast in circumference,
prodigious in depth, and whose perfectly smooth sides might have been
mistaken for ebony, but for the bewildering rapidity with which they spun
around, and for the gleaming and ghastly radiance they shot forth, as the
rays of the full moon, from that circular rift amid the clouds which I have
already described, streamed in a flood of golden glory along the black walls,
and far away down into the inmost recesses of the abyss.

"At first I was too much confused to observe any thing accurately. The
general burst of terrific grandeur was all that I beheld. When I recovered
myself a little, however, my gaze fell instinctively downward. In this direction I was able to obtain an unobstructed view, from the manner in which
the smack hung on the inclined surface of the pool. She was quite upon an
even keel—that is to say, her deck lay in a plane parallel with that of the
water—but this latter sloped at an angle of more than forty-five degrees, so
that we seemed to be lying upon our beam-ends. I could not help observing, nevertheless, that I had scarcely more difficulty in maintaining my hold
and footing in this situation, than if we had been upon a dead level; and
this, I suppose, was owing to the speed at which we revolved.

"The rays of the moon seemed to search the very bottom of the profound gulf; but still I could make out nothing distinctly on account of a
thick mist in which every thing there was enveloped, and over which there
hung a magnificent rainbow, like that narrow and tottering bridge which
Mussulmen say is the only pathway between Time and Eternity. This mist,
or spray, was no doubt occasioned by the clashing of the great walls of the
funnel, as they all met together at the bottom—but the yell that went up to
the Heavens from out of that mist I dare not attempt to describe.

"Our first slide into the abyss itself, from the belt of foam above, had
carried us to a great distance down the slope; but our farther descent was
by no means proportionate. Round and round we swept—not with any
uniform movement—but in dizzying swings and jerks, that sent us sometimes only a few hundred yards—sometimes nearly the complete circuit
of the whirl. Our progress downward, at each revolution, was slow, but
very perceptible.

"Looking about me upon the wide waste of liquid ebony on which we were thus borne, I perceived that our boat was not the only object in the embrace of the whirl. Both above and below us were visible fragments of vessels, large masses of building-timber and trunks of trees, with many smaller articles, such as pieces of house furniture, broken boxes, barrels and staves. I have already described the unnatural curiosity which had taken the place of my original terrors. It appeared to grow upon me as I drew nearer and nearer to my dreadful doom. I now began to watch, with a strange interest, the numerous things that floated in our company. I *must* have been delirious, for I even sought *amusement* in speculating upon the relative velocities of their several descents toward the foam below. 'This fir-tree,' I found myself at one time saying, 'will certainly be the next thing that takes the awful plunge and disappears,'—and then I was disappointed to find that the wreck of a Dutch merchant ship overtook it and went down before. At length, after making several guesses of this nature, and being deceived in all—this fact—the fact of my invariable miscalculation, set me upon a train of reflection that made my limbs again tremble, and my heart beat heavily once more.

"It was not a new terror that thus affected me, but the dawn of a more exciting *hope*. This hope arose partly from memory and partly from present observation. I called to mind the great variety of buoyant matter that strewed the coast of Lofoden, having been absorbed and then thrown forth by the Moskoe-ström. By far the greater number of the articles were shattered in the most extraordinary way—so chafed and roughened as to have the appearance of being stuck full of splinters—but then I distinctly recollected that there were *some* of them which were not disfigured at all. Now I could not account for this difference except by supposing that the roughened fragments were the only ones which had been *completely absorbed*—that the others had entered the whirl at so late a period of the tide, or, from some reason, had descended so slowly after entering, that they did not reach the bottom before the turn of the flood came, or of the ebb, as the case might be. I conceived it possible, in either instance, that they might thus be whirled up again to the level of the ocean, without undergoing the fate of those which had been drawn in more early or absorbed more rapidly. I made, also, three important observations. The first was, that as a general rule, the larger the bodies were, the more rapid their descent—the second, that, between two masses of equal extent, the one spherical, and the other *of any other shape*, the superiority in speed of descent was with the sphere—the third, that, between two masses of equal size, the one cylindrical, and the other of any other shape, the cylinder was absorbed the more slowly. Since my escape, I have had several conversations on this subject with an old school-master of the district; and it was from him that I learned the use of the words 'cylinder' and 'sphere.' He explained to me—although I have forgotten the explanation—how what I observed was, in fact, the natural consequence of the forms of the floating fragments—and showed me how it happened that a cylinder, swimming in a vortex, offered more resistance to its suction, and was drawn in with greater difficulty than an equally bulky body, of any form whatever.[1]

"There was one startling circumstance which went a great way in enforcing these observations, and rendering me anxious to turn them to account, and this was that, at every revolution, we passed something like a barrel, or else the yard or the mast of a vessel, while many of these things, which had been on our level when I first opened my eyes upon the wonders of the whirlpool, were now high up above us, and seemed to have moved but little from their original station.

"I no longer hesitated what to do. I resolved to lash myself securely to the water-cask upon which I now held, to cut it loose from the counter, and to throw myself with it into the water. I attracted my brother's attention by signs, pointed to the floating barrels that came near us, and did every thing in my power to make him understand what I was about to do. I thought at length that he comprehended my design—but, whether this was the case or not, he shook his head despairingly, and refused to move from his station by the ring-bolt. It was impossible to reach him; the emergency admitted of no delay; and so, with a bitter struggle, I resigned him to his fate, fastened myself to the cask by means of the lashings which secured it to the counter, and precipitated myself with it into the sea, without another moment's hesitation.

"The result was precisely what I had hoped it might be. As it is myself who now tell you this tale—as you see that I *did* escape—and as you are already in possession of the mode in which this escape was effected, and must therefore anticipate all that I have farther to say—I will bring my story quickly to conclusion. It might have been an hour, or thereabout, after my quitting the smack, when, having descended to a vast distance beneath me, it made three or four wild gyrations in rapid succession, and, bearing my loved brother with it, plunged headlong, at once and forever, into the chaos of foam below. The barrel to which I was attached sunk very little farther than half the distance between the bottom of the gulf and the spot at which I leaped overboard, before a great change took place in the character of the whirlpool. The slope of the sides of the vast funnel became momently less and less steep. The gyrations of the whirl grew, gradually, less and less violent. By degrees, the froth and the rainbow disappeared, and the bottom of the gulf seemed slowly to uprise. The sky was clear, the

1 See Archimedes, *"De Incidentibus in Fluido."*—lib. 2.

winds had gone down, and the full moon was setting radiantly in the west, when I found myself on the surface of the ocean, in full view of the shores of Lofoden, and above the spot where the pool of the Moskoe-stöm *had been*. It was the hour of the slack—but the sea still heaved in mountainous waves from the effects of the hurricane. I was borne violently into the channel of the Ström, and in a few minutes, was hurried down the coast into the 'grounds' of the fishermen. A boat picked me up—exhausted from fatigue—and (now that the danger was removed) speechless from the memory of its horror. Those who drew me on board were my old mates and daily companions—but they knew me no more than they would have known a traveller from the spirit-land. My hair, which had been raven black the day before, was as white as you see it now. They say too that the whole expression of my countenance had changed. I told them my story—they did not believe it. I now tell it to *you*—and I can scarcely expect you to put more faith in it than did the merry fishermen of Lofoden."

TYPHOON

Joseph Conrad

Captain MacWhirr, of the steamer *Nan-Shan,* had a physiognomy that, in the order of material appearances, was the exact counterpart of his mind: it presented no marked characteristics of firmness or stupidity; it had no pronounced characteristics whatever; it was simply ordinary, irresponsive, and unruffled.

The only thing his aspect might have been said to suggest, at times, was bashfulness; because he would sit, in business offices ashore, sunburnt and smiling faintly, with downcast eyes. When he raised them, they were perceived to be direct in their glance and of blue colour. His hair was fair and extremely fine, clasping from temple to temple the bald dome of his skull in a clamp as of fluffy silk. The hair of his face, on the contrary, carroty and flaming, resembled a growth of copper wire clipped short to the line of the lip; while, no matter how close he shaved, fiery metallic gleams passed, when he moved his head, over the surface of his cheeks. He was rather below the medium height, a bit round-shouldered, and so sturdy of limb that his clothes always looked a shade too tight for his arms and legs. As if unable to grasp what is due to the difference of latitudes, he wore a brown bowler hat, a complete suit of a brownish hue, and clumsy black boots. These harbour togs gave to his thick figure an air of stiff and uncouth smartness. A thin silver watch chain looped his waistcoat, and he never left his ship for the shore without clutching in his powerful, hairy fist an elegant umbrella of the very best quality, but generally unrolled. Young Jukes, the chief mate, attending his commander to the gangway, would sometimes venture to say, with the greatest gentleness, "Allow me, sir"—and possessing himself of the umbrella deferentially, would elevate the ferule, shake the folds, twirl a neat furl in a jiffy, and hand it back; going through the performance with a face of such portentous gravity that Mr. Solomon Rout, the chief engineer, smoking his morning cigar over the skylight, would turn away his head in order to hide a smile. "Oh! aye! The blessed gamp. . . .

Thank 'ee, Jukes, thank 'ee," would mutter Captain MacWhirr, heartily, without looking up.

Having just enough imagination to carry him through each successive day, and no more, he was tranquilly sure of himself; and from the very same cause he was not in the least conceited. It is your imaginative superior who is touchy, overbearing, and difficult to please; but every ship Captain MacWhirr commanded was the floating abode of harmony and peace. It was, in truth, as impossible for him to take a flight of fancy as it would be for a watchmaker to put together a chronometer with nothing except a two-pound hammer and a whipsaw in the way of tools. Yet the uninteresting lives of men so entirely given to the actuality of the bare existence have their mysterious side. It was impossible in Captain MacWhirr's case, for instance, to understand what under heaven could have induced that perfectly satisfactory son of a petty grocer in Belfast to run away to sea. And yet he had done that very thing at the age of fifteen. It was enough, when you thought it over, to give you the idea of an immense, potent, and invisible hand thrust into the ant heap of the earth, laying hold of shoulders, knocking heads together, and setting the unconscious faces of the multitude towards inconceivable goals and in undreamt-of directions.

His father never really forgave him for this undutiful stupidity. "We could have got on without him," he used to say later on, "but there's the business. And he an only son, too!" His mother wept very much after his disappearance. As it had never occurred to him to leave word behind, he was mourned over for dead till, after eight months, his first letter arrived from Talcahuano. It was short, and contained the statement: "We had very fine weather on our passage out." But evidently, in the writer's mind, the only important intelligence was to the effect that his captain had, on the very day of writing, entered him regularly on the ship's articles as Ordinary Seaman. "Because I can do the work," he explained. The mother again wept copiously, while the remark, "Tom's an ass," expressed the emotions of the father. He was a corpulent man, with a gift for sly chaffing, which to the end of his life he exercised in his intercourse with his son, a little pityingly, as if upon a half-witted person.

MacWhirr's visits to his home were necessarily rare, and in the course of years he despatched other letters to his parents, informing them of his successive promotions and of his movements upon the vast earth. In these missives could be found sentences like this: "The heat here is very great." Or: "On Christmas day at 4 P.M. we fell in with some icebergs." The old people ultimately became acquainted with a good many names of ships, and with the names of the skippers who commanded them—with the names of Scots and English shipowners—with the names of seas, oceans, straits, promontories—with outlandish names of lumber ports, of rice ports, of cotton ports—with the names of islands—with the name of their son's young woman. She was called Lucy. It did not suggest itself to him to mention whether he thought the name pretty. And then they died.

The great day of MacWhirr's marriage came in due course, following shortly upon the great day when he got his first command.

All these events had taken place many years before the morning when, in the chart room of the steamer *Nan-Shan,* he stood confronted by the fall of a barometer he had no reason to distrust. The fall—taking into account the excellence of the instrument, the time of the year, and the ship's position on the terrestrial globe—was of a nature ominously prophetic; but the red face of the man betrayed no sort of inward disturbance. Omens were as nothing to him, and he was unable to discover the message of prophecy till the fulfilment had brought it home to his very door. "That's a fall, and no mistake," he thought. "There must be some uncommonly dirty weather knocking about."

The *Nan-Shan* was on her way from the southward to the treaty port of Fu-chau, with some cargo in her lower holds, and two hundred Chinese coolies returning to their village homes in the province of Fo-kien, after a few years of work in various tropical colonies. The morning was fine, the oily sea heaved without a sparkle, and there was a queer white misty patch in the sky like a halo of the sun. The foredeck, packed with Chinamen, was full of sombre clothing, yellow faces, and pigtails, sprinkled over with a good many naked shoulders, for there was no wind, and the heat was close. The coolies lounged, talked, smoked, or stared over the rail; some, drawing water over the side, sluiced each other; a few slept on hatches, while several small parties of six sat on their heels surrounding iron trays with plates of rice and tiny teacups; and every single Celestial of them was carrying with him all he had in the world—a wooden chest with a ringing lock and brass on the corners, containing the savings of his labours: some clothes of ceremony, sticks of incense, a little opium maybe, bits of nameless rubbish of conventional value, and a small hoard of silver dollars, toiled for in coal lighters, won in gambling houses or in petty trading, grubbed out of earth, sweated out in mines, on railway lines, in deadly jungle, under heavy burdens—amassed patiently, guarded with care, cherished fiercely.

A cross swell had set in from the direction of Formosa Channel about ten o'clock, without disturbing these passengers much, because the *Nan-Shan,* with her flat bottom, rolling chocks on bilges, and great breadth of beam, had the reputation of an exceptionally steady ship in a seaway. Mr. Jukes, in moments of expansion on shore, would proclaim loudly that the "old girl was as good as she was pretty." It would never have occurred to Captain MacWhirr to express his favourable opinion so loud or in terms so fanciful.

She was a good ship, undoubtedly, and not old either. She had been

built in Dumbarton less than three years before, to the order of a firm of
merchants in Siam—Messrs. Sigg and Son. When she lay afloat, finished in
every detail and ready to take up the work of her life, the builders contemplated her with pride.

"Sigg has asked us for a reliable skipper to take her out," remarked one
of the partners; and the other, after reflecting for a while, said: "I think
MacWhirr is ashore just at present." "Is he? Then wire him at once. He's
the very man," declared the senior, without a moment's hesitation.

Next morning MacWhirr stood before them unperturbed, having travelled from London by the midnight express after a sudden but undemon-
strative parting with his wife. She was the daughter of a superior couple
who had seen better days.

"We had better be going together over the ship, Captain," said the
senior partner; and the three men started to view the perfections of the
Nan-Shan from stem to stern, and from her keelson to the trucks of her
two stumpy pole masts.

Captain MacWhirr had begun by taking off his coat, which he hung on
the end of a steam windlass embodying all the latest improvements.

"My uncle wrote of you favourably by yesterday's mail to our good
friends—Messrs. Sigg, you know—and doubtless they'll continue you out
there in command," said the junior partner. "You'll be able to boast of
being in charge of the handiest boat of her size on the coast of China,
Captain," he added.

"Have you? Thank 'ee," mumbled vaguely MacWhirr, to whom the view
of a distant eventuality could appeal no more than the beauty of a wide
landscape to a purblind tourist; and his eyes happening at the moment to be
at rest upon the lock of the cabin door, he walked up to it, full of purpose,
and began to rattle the handle vigorously, while he observed, in his low,
earnest voice, "You can't trust the workmen nowadays. A brand-new lock,
and it won't act at all. Stuck fast. See? See?"

As soon as they found themselves alone in their office across the yard:
"You praised that fellow up to Sigg. What is it you see in him?" asked the
nephew, with faint contempt.

"I admit he has nothing of your fancy skipper about him, if that's what
you mean," said the elder man, curtly. "Is the foreman of the joiners on the
Nan-Shan outside? . . . Come in, Bates. How is it that you let Tait's people put us off with a defective lock on the cabin door? The Captain could
see directly he set eye on it. Have it replaced at once. The little straws, Bates
. . . the little straws. . . ."

The lock was replaced accordingly, and a few days afterwards the *Nan-
Shan* steamed out to the East, without MacWhirr having offered any further remark as to her fittings, or having been heard to utter a single word

hinting at pride in his ship, gratitude for his appointment, or satisfaction at his prospects.

With a temperament neither loquacious nor taciturn he found very little occasion to talk. There were matters of duty, of course—directions, orders, and so on; but the past being to his mind done with, and the future not there yet, the more general actualities of the day required no comment— because facts can speak for themselves with overwhelming precision.

Old Mr. Sigg liked a man of few words, and one that "you could be sure would not try to improve upon his instructions." MacWhirr satisfying these requirements, was continued in command of the *Nan-Shan*, and applied himself to the careful navigation of his ship in the China seas. She had come out on a British register, but after some time Messrs. Sigg judged it expedient to transfer her to the Siamese flag.

At the news of the contemplated transfer Jukes grew restless, as if under a sense of personal affront. He went about grumbling to himself, and uttering short scornful laughs. "Fancy having a ridiculous Noah's Ark elephant in the ensign of one's ship," he said once at the engine-room door. "Dash me if I can stand it: I'll throw up the billet. Don't it make *you* sick, Mr. Rout?" The chief engineer only cleared his throat with the air of a man who knows the value of a good billet.

The first morning the new flag floated over the stern of the *Nan-Shan* Jukes stood looking at it bitterly from the bridge. He struggled with his feelings for a while, and then remarked, "Queer flag for a man to sail under, sir."

"What's the matter with the flag?" inquired Captain MacWhirr. "Seems all right to me." And he walked across to the end of the bridge to have a good look.

"Well, it looks queer to me," burst out Jukes, greatly exasperated, and flung off the bridge.

Captain MacWhirr was amazed at these manners. After a while he stepped quietly into the chart room, and opened his International Signal Code book at the plate where the flags of all the nations are correctly figured in gaudy rows. He ran his finger over them, and when he came to Siam he contemplated with great attention the red field and the white elephant. Nothing could be more simple; but to make sure he brought the book out on the bridge for the purpose of comparing the coloured drawing with the real thing at the flagstaff astern. When next Jukes, who was carrying on the duty that day with a sort of suppressed fierceness, happened on the bridge, his commander observed:

"There's nothing amiss with that flag."

"Isn't there?" mumbled Jukes, falling on his knees before a deck locker and jerking therefrom viciously a spare lead line.

"No. I looked up the book. Length twice the breadth and the elephant exactly in the middle. I thought the people ashore would know how to make the local flag. Stands to reason. You were wrong, Jukes. . . ."

"Well, sir," began Jukes, getting up excitedly, "all I can say—" He fumbled for the end of the coil of line with trembling hands.

"That's all right." Captain MacWhirr soothed him, sitting heavily on a little canvas folding stool he greatly affected. "All you have to do is to take care they don't hoist the elephant upside down before they get quite used to it."

Jukes flung the new lead line over on the foredeck with a loud "Here you are, bo'ss'en—don't forget to wet it thoroughly," and turned with immense resolution towards his commander; but Captain MacWhirr spread his elbows on the bridge rail comfortably.

"Because it would be, I suppose, understood as a signal of distress," he went on. "What do you think? That elephant there, I take it, stands for something in the nature of the Union Jack in the flag. . . ."

"Does it!" yelled Jukes, so that every head on the *Nan-Shan's* decks looked towards the bridge. Then he sighed, and with sudden resignation: "It would certainly be a dam' distressful sight," he said, meekly.

Later in the day he accosted the chief engineer with a confidential, "Here, let me tell you the old man's latest."

Mr. Solomon Rout (frequently alluded to as Long Sol, Old Sol, or Father Rout), from finding himself almost invariably the tallest man on board every ship he joined, had acquired the habit of a stooping, leisurely condescension. His hair was scant and sandy, his flat cheeks were pale, his bony wrists and long scholarly hands were pale, too, as though he had lived all his life in the shade.

He smiled from on high at Jukes, and went on smoking and glancing about quietly, in the manner of a kind uncle lending an ear to the tale of an excited schoolboy. Then, greatly amused but impassive, he asked:

"And did you throw up the billet?"

"No," cried Jukes, raising a weary, discouraged voice above the harsh buzz of the *Nan-Shan's* friction winches. All of them were hard at work, snatching slings of cargo, high up, to the end of long derricks, only, as it seemed, to let them rip down recklessly by the run. The cargo chains groaned in the gins, clinked on coamings, rattled over the side; and the whole ship quivered, with her long grey flanks smoking in wreaths of steam. "No," cried Jukes, "I didn't. What's the good? I might just as well fling my resignation at this bulkhead. I don't believe you can make a man like that understand anything. He simply knocks me over."

At that moment Captain MacWhirr, back from the shore, crossed the deck, umbrella in hand, escorted by a mournful, self-possessed Chinaman, walking behind in paper-soled silk shoes, and who also carried an umbrella.

The master of the *Nan-Shan,* speaking just audibly and gazing at his boots as his manner was, remarked that it would be necessary to call at Fu-chau this trip, and desired Mr. Rout to have steam up tomorrow afternoon at one o'clock sharp. He pushed back his hat to wipe his forehead, observing at the same time that he hated going ashore anyhow; while overtopping him Mr. Rout, without deigning a word, smoked austerely, nursing his right elbow in the palm of his left hand. Then Jukes was directed in the same subdued voice to keep the forward tween-deck clear of cargo. Two hundred coolies were going to be put down there. The Bun Hin Company were sending that lot home. Twenty-five bags of rice would be coming off in a sampan directly, for stores. All seven-years'-men they were, said Captain MacWhirr, with a camphorwood chest to every man. The carpenter should be set to work nailing three-inch battens along the deck below, fore and aft, to keep these boxes from shifting in a seaway. Jukes had better look to it at once. "D'ye hear, Jukes?" This Chinaman here was coming with the ship as far as Fu-chau—a sort of interpreter he would be. Bun Hin's clerk he was, and wanted to have a look at the space. Jukes had better take him forward. "D'ye hear, Jukes?"

Jukes took care to punctuate these instructions in proper places with the obligatory "Yes, sir," ejaculated without enthusiasm. His brusque "Come along, John; make look see" set the Chinaman in motion at his heels.

"Wanchee look see, all same look see can do," said Jukes, who having no talent for foreign languages mangled the very pidgin English cruelly. He pointed at the open hatch. "Catchee number one piecie place to sleep in. Eh?"

He was gruff, as became his racial superiority, but not unfriendly. The Chinaman, gazing sad and speechless into the darkness of the hatchway, seemed to stand at the head of a yawning grave.

"No catchee rain down there—savee?" pointed out Jukes. "Suppose all'ee same fine weather, one piecie coolieman come topside," he pursued, warming up imaginatively. "Make so—phooooo!" He expanded his chest and blew out his cheeks. "Savee, John? Breathe—fresh air. Good. Eh? Washee him piecie pants, chowchow topside—see, John?"

With his mouth and hands he made exuberant motions of eating rice and washing clothes; and the Chinaman, who concealed his distrust of this pantomime under a collected demeanour tinged by a gentle and refined melancholy, glanced out of his almond eyes from Jukes to the hatch and back again. "Velly good," he murmured, in a disconsolate undertone, and hastened smoothly along the decks, dodging obstacles in his course. He disappeared, ducking low under a sling of ten dirty gunnybags full of some costly merchandise and exhaling a repulsive smell.

Captain MacWhirr meantime had gone on the bridge, and into the chart room, where a letter, commenced two days before, awaited termination. These long letters began with the words, "My darling wife," and the steward, between the scrubbing of the floors and the dusting of chronometer boxes, snatched at every opportunity to read them. They interested him much more than they possibly could the woman for whose eye they were intended; and this for the reason that they related in minute detail each successive trip of the *Nan-Shan*.

Her master, faithful to facts, which alone his consciousness reflected, would set them down with painstaking care upon many pages. The house in a northern suburb to which these pages were addressed had a bit of garden before the bow windows, a deep porch of good appearance, coloured glass with imitation lead frame in the front door. He paid five and forty pounds a year for it, and did not think the rent too high, because Mrs. MacWhirr (a pretentious person with a scraggy neck and a disdainful manner) was admittedly ladylike, and in the neighbourhood considered as "quite superior." The only secret of her life was her abject terror of the time when her husband would come home to stay for good. Under the same roof there dwelt also a daughter called Lydia and a son, Tom. These two were but slightly acquainted with their father. Mainly, they knew him as a rare but privileged visitor, who of an evening smoked his pipe in the dining room and slept in the house. The lanky girl, upon the whole, was rather ashamed of him; the boy was frankly and utterly indifferent in a straightforward, delightful, unaffected way manly boys have.

And Captain MacWhirr wrote home from the coast of China twelve times every year, desiring quaintly to be "remembered to the children," and subscribing himself "your loving husband," as calmly as if the words so long used by so many men were, apart from their shape, worn-out things, and of a faded meaning.

The China seas north and south are narrow seas. They are seas full of everyday, eloquent facts, such as islands, sandbanks, reefs, swift and changeable currents—tangled facts that nevertheless speak to a seaman in clear and definite language. Their speech appealed to Captain MacWhirr's sense of realities so forcibly that he had given up his stateroom below and practically lived all his days on the bridge of his ship, often having his meals sent up, and sleeping at night in the chart room. And he indited there his home letters. Each of them, without exception, contained the phrase, "The weather has been very fine this trip," or some other form of a statement to that effect. And this statement, too, in its wonderful persistence, was of the same perfect accuracy as all the others they contained.

Mr. Rout likewise wrote letters; only no one on board knew how chatty he could be pen in hand, because the chief engineer had enough imagination to keep his desk locked. His wife relished his style greatly. They were a childless couple, and Mrs. Rout, a big, high-bosomed, jolly woman of forty, shared with Mr. Rout's toothless and venerable mother a little cottage near Teddington. She would run over her correspondence, at breakfast, with lively eyes, and scream out interesting passages in a joyous voice at the deaf old lady, prefacing each extract by the warning shout, "Solomon says!" She had the trick of firing off Solomon's utterances also upon strangers, astonishing them easily by the unfamiliar text and the unexpectedly jocular vein of these quotations. On the day the new curate called for the first time at the cottage, she found occasion to remark, "As Solomon says: 'the engineers that go down to the sea in ships behold the wonders of sailor nature;' " when a change in the visitor's countenance made her stop and stare.

"Solomon. . . . Oh! . . . Mrs. Rout," stuttered the young man, very red in the face, "I must say . . . I don't. . . ."

"He's my husband," she announced in a great shout, throwing herself back in the chair. Perceiving the joke, she laughed immoderately with a handkerchief to her eyes, while he sat wearing a forced smile, and, from his inexperience of jolly women, fully persuaded that she must be deplorably insane. They were excellent friends afterwards; for, absolving her from irreverent intention, he came to think she was a very worthy person indeed; and he learned in time to receive without flinching other scraps of Solomon's wisdom.

"For my part," Solomon was reported by his wife to have said once, "give me the dullest ass for a skipper before a rogue. There is a way to take a fool; but a rogue is smart and slippery." This was an airy generalization drawn from the particular case of Captain MacWhirr's honesty, which, in itself, had the heavy obviousness of a lump of clay. On the other hand, Mr. Jukes, unable to generalize, unmarried, and unengaged, was in the habit of opening his heart after another fashion to an old chum and former shipmate, actually serving as second officer on board an Atlantic liner.

First of all he would insist upon the advantages of the Eastern trade, hinting at its superiority to the Western ocean service. He extolled the sky, the seas, the ships, and the easy life of the Far East. The *Nan-Shan*, he affirmed, was second to none as a sea boat.

"We have no brass-bound uniforms, but then we are like brothers here," he wrote. "We all mess together and live like fighting cocks. . . . All the chaps of the black squad are as decent as they make that kind, and old Sol, the Chief, is a dry stick. We are good friends. As to our old man, you could not find a quieter skipper. Sometimes you would think he hadn't sense enough to see anything wrong. And yet it isn't that. Can't be. He has been in command for a good few years now. He doesn't do anything actually foolish, and gets his ship along all right without worrying anybody. I believe he hasn't brains enough to enjoy kicking up a row. I don't take advantage of him. I would scorn it. Outside the routine of duty he doesn't seem to understand more than half of what you tell him. We get a laugh out of this at times; but it is dull, too, to be with a man like this—in the long run. Old Sol says he hasn't much conversation. Conversation! O Lord! He never talks. The other day I had been yarning under the bridge with one of the engineers, and he must have heard us. When I came up to take my watch, he steps out of the chart room and has a good look all round, peeps over at the sidelights, glances at the compass, squints upwards at the stars. That's his regular performance. By and by he says: 'Was that you talking just now in the port alleyway?' 'Yes, sir.' 'With the third engineer?' 'Yes, sir.' He walks off to starboard, and sits under the dodger on a little camp-stool of his, and for half an hour perhaps he makes no sound, except that I heard him sneeze once. Then after a while I hear him getting up over there, and he strolls across to port, where I was. 'I can't understand what you can find to talk about,' says he. 'Two solid hours. I am not blaming you. I see people ashore at it all day long, and then in the evening they sit down and keep at it over the drinks. Must be saying the same things over and over again. I can't understand.'

"Did you ever hear anything like that? And he was so patient about it. It made me quite sorry for him. But he is exasperating, too, sometimes. Of course one would not do anything to vex him even if it were worth while. But it isn't. He's so jolly innocent that if you were to put your thumb to your nose and wave your fingers at him he would only wonder gravely to himself what got into you. He told me once quite simply that he found it very difficult to make out what made people always act so queerly. He's too dense to trouble about, and that's the truth."

Thus wrote Mr. Jukes to his chum in the Western ocean trade, out of the fulness of his heart and the liveliness of his fancy.

He had expressed his honest opinion. It was not worth while trying to impress a man of that sort. If the world had been full of such men, life would have probably appeared to Jukes an unentertaining and unprofitable business. He was not alone in his opinion. The sea itself, as if sharing Mr. Jukes' good-natured forbearance, had never put itself out to startle the silent man, who seldom looked up, and wandered innocently over the waters with the only visible purpose of getting food, raiment, and house room for three people ashore. Dirty weather he had known, of course. He had been made wet, uncomfortable, tired in the usual way, felt at the time and presently forgotten. So that upon the whole he had been justified in reporting fine weather at home. But he had never been given a glimpse of immeasurable strength and of immoderate wrath, the wrath that passes exhausted but never appeased—the wrath and fury of the passionate sea. He knew it existed, as we know that crime and abominations exist; he had heard of it as a peaceable citizen in a town hears of battles, famines, and floods, and yet knows nothing of what these things mean—though, indeed, he may have been mixed up in a street row, have gone without his dinner once, or been soaked to the skin in a shower. Captain MacWhirr had sailed over the surface of the oceans as some men go skimming over the years of existence to sink gently into a placid grave, ignorant of life to the last, without ever having been made to see all it may contain of perfidy, of violence, and of terror. There are on sea and land such men thus fortunate—or thus disdained by destiny or by the sea.

II

Observing the steady fall of the barometer, Captain MacWhirr thought, "There's some dirty weather knocking about." This is precisely what he thought. He had had an experience of moderately dirty weather—the term dirty as applied to the weather implying only moderate discomfort to the seaman. Had he been informed by an indisputable authority that the end of the world was to be finally accomplished by a catastrophic disturbance of the atmosphere, he would have assimilated the information under the simple idea of dirty weather, and no other, because he had no experience of cataclysms, and belief does not necessarily imply comprehension. The wisdom of his country had pronounced by means of an Act of Parliament that before he could be considered as fit to take charge of a ship he should be able to answer certain simple questions on the subject of circular storms such as hurricanes, cyclones, typhoons; and apparently he had answered them, since he was now in command of the *Nan-Shan* in the China seas during the season of typhoons. But if he had answered he remembered nothing of it. He was, however, conscious of being made uncomfortable by the clammy heat. He came out on the bridge, and found no relief to this oppression. The air seemed thick. He gasped like a fish, and began to believe himself greatly out of sorts.

The *Nan-Shan* was ploughing a vanishing furrow upon the circle of the sea that had the surface and the shimmer of an undulating piece of grey silk. The sun, pale and without rays, poured down leaden heat in a strangely indecisive light, and the Chinamen were lying prostrate about the decks. Their bloodless, pinched, yellow faces were like the faces of bilious invalids.

Captain MacWhirr noticed two of them especially, stretched out on their backs below the bridge. As soon as they had closed their eyes they seemed dead. Three others, however, were quarrelling barbarously away forward; and one big fellow, half naked, with herculean shoulders, was hanging limply over a winch; another, sitting on the deck, his knees up and his head drooping sideways in a girlish attitude, was plaiting his pigtail with infinite languor depicted in his whole person and in the very movement of his fingers. The smoke struggled with difficulty out of the funnel, and instead of streaming away spread itself out like an infernal sort of cloud, smelling of sulphur and raining soot all over the decks.

"What the devil are you doing there, Mr. Jukes?" asked Captain MacWhirr.

This unusual form of address, though mumbled rather than spoken, caused the body of Mr. Jukes to start as though it had been prodded under the fifth rib. He had had a low bench brought on the bridge, and sitting on it, with a length of rope curled about his feet and a piece of canvas stretched over his knees, was pushing a sail needle vigorously. He looked up, and his surprise gave to his eyes an expression of innocence and candour.

"I am only roping some of that new set of bags we made last trip for whipping up coals," he remonstrated, gently. "We shall want them for the next coaling, sir."

"What became of the others?"

"Why, worn out of course, sir."

Captain MacWhirr, after glaring down irresolutely at his chief mate, disclosed the gloomy and cynical conviction that more than half of them had been lost overboard, "if only the truth was known," and retired to the other end of the bridge. Jukes, exasperated by this unprovoked attack, broke the needle at the second stitch, and dropping his work got up and cursed the heat in a violent undertone.

The propeller thumped, the three Chinamen forward had given up squabbling very suddenly, and the one who had been plaiting his tail clasped his legs and stared dejectedly over his knees. The lurid sunshine cast faint and sickly shadows. The swell ran higher and swifter every moment, and the ship lurched heavily in the smooth, deep hollows of the sea.

"I wonder where that beastly swell comes from," said Jukes aloud, recovering himself after a stagger.

"Northeast," grunted the literal MacWhirr, from his side of the bridge. "There's some dirty weather knocking about. Go and look at the glass."

When Jukes came out of the chart room, the cast of his countenance had changed to thoughtfulness and concern. He caught hold of the bridge rail and stared ahead.

The temperature in the engine room had gone up to a hundred and seventeen degrees. Irritated voices were ascending through the skylight and through the fiddle of the stokehold in a harsh and resonant uproar, mingled with angry clangs and scrapes of metal, as if men with limbs of iron and throats of bronze had been quarrelling down there. The second engineer was falling foul of the stokers for letting the steam go down. He was a man with arms like a blacksmith, and generally feared; but that afternoon the stokers were answering him back restlessly, and slammed the furnace doors with the fury of despair. Then the noise ceased suddenly, and the second engineer appeared, emerging out of the stokehold streaked with grime and soaking wet like a chimneysweep coming out of a well. As soon as his head was clear of the fiddle he began to scold Jukes for not trimming properly the stokehold ventilators; and in answer Jukes made with his hands deprecatory soothing signs meaning: "No wind—can't be helped—you can see for yourself." But the other wouldn't hear reason. His teeth flashed angrily in his dirty face. He didn't mind, he said, the trouble of punching their blanked heads down there, blank his soul, but did the condemned sailors think you could keep steam up in the Godforsaken boilers simply by knocking the blanked stokers about? No, by George! You had to get some draught, too—may he be everlastingly blanked for a swab-headed deckhand if you didn't! And the chief, too, rampaging before the steam gauge and carrying on like a lunatic up and down the engine room ever since noon. What did Jukes think he was stuck up there for, he couldn't get one of his decayed, good-for-nothing deck cripples to turn the ventilators to the wind?

The relations of the "engine room" and the "deck" of the *Nan-Shan* were, as is known, of a brotherly nature; therefore Jukes leaned over and begged the other in a restrained tone not to make a disgusting ass of himself; the skipper was on the other side of the bridge. But the second declared mutinously that he didn't care a rap who was on the other side of the bridge, and Jukes, passing in a flash from lofty disapproval into a state of exaltation, invited him in unflattering terms to come up and twist the beastly things to please himself, and catch such wind as a donkey of his sort could find. The second rushed up to the fray. He flung himself at the port ventilator as though he meant to tear it out bodily and toss it overboard. All he did was to move the cowl round a few inches, with an enormous expenditure of force, and seemed spent in the effort. He leaned against the back of the wheelhouse, and Jukes walked up to him.

"Oh, Heavens!" ejaculated the engineer in a feeble voice. He lifted his eyes to the sky, and then let his glassy stare descend to meet the horizon that, tilting up to an angle of forty degrees, seemed to hang on a slant for a while and settled down slowly. "Heavens! Phew! What's up, anyhow?"

Jukes, straddling his long legs like a pair of compasses, put on an air of superiority. "We're going to catch it this time," he said. "The barometer is tumbling down like anything, Harry. And you trying to kick up that silly row. . . ."

The word "barometer" seemed to revive the second engineer's mad animosity. Collecting afresh all his energies, he directed Jukes in a low and brutal tone to shove the unmentionable instrument down his gory throat. Who cared for his crimson barometer? It was the steam—the steam—that was going down; and what between the firemen going faint and the chief going silly, it was worse than a dog's life for him; he didn't care a tinker's curse how soon the whole show was blown out of the water. He seemed on the point of having a cry, but after regaining his breath he muttered darkly, "I'll faint them," and dashed off. He stopped upon the fiddle long enough to shake his fist at the unnatural daylight, and dropped into the dark hole with a whoop.

When Jukes turned, his eyes fell upon the rounded back and the big red ears of Captain MacWhirr, who had come across. He did not look at his chief officer, but said at once, "That's a very violent man, that second engineer."

"Jolly good second, anyhow," grunted Jukes. "They can't keep up steam," he added, rapidly, and made a grab at the rail against the coming lurch.

Captain MacWhirr, unprepared, took a run and brought himself up with a jerk by an awning stanchion.

"A profane man," he said, obstinately. "If this goes on, I'll have to get rid of him the first chance."

"It's the heat," said Jukes. "The weather's awful. It would make a saint swear. Even up here I feel exactly as if I had my head tied up in a woollen blanket."

Captain MacWhirr looked up. "D'ye mean to say, Mr. Jukes, you ever had your head tied up in a blanket? What was that for?"

"It's a manner of speaking, sir," said Jukes, stolidly.

"Some of you fellows do go on! What's that about saints swearing? I wish you wouldn't talk so wild. What sort of saint would that be that would swear? No more saint than yourself, I expect. And what's a blanket got to do with it—or the weather either. . . . The heat does not make me swear —does it? It's filthy bad temper. That's what it is. And what's the good of your talking like this?"

Thus Captain MacWhirr expostulated against the use of images in speech, and at the end electrified Jukes by a contemptuous snort, followed by words of passion and resentment: "Damme! I'll fire him out of the ship if he don't look out."

And Jukes, incorrigible, thought: "Goodness me! Somebody's put a new inside to my old man. Here's temper, if you like. Of course it's the weather; what else? It would make an angel quarrelsome—let alone a saint."

All the Chinamen on deck appeared at their last gasp.

At its setting the sun had a diminished diameter and an expiring brown, rayless glow, as if millions of centuries elapsing since the morning had brought it near its end. A dense bank of cloud became visible to the north-ward; it had a sinister dark olive tint, and lay low and motionless upon the sea, resembling a solid obstacle in the path of the ship. She went flounder-ing towards it like an exhausted creature driven to its death. The coppery twilight retired slowly, and the darkness brought out overhead a swarm of unsteady, big stars, that, as if blown upon, flickered exceedingly and seemed to hang very near the earth. At eight o'clock Jukes went into the chart room to write up the ship's log.

He copied neatly out of the rough book the number of miles, the course of the ship, and in the column for "wind" scrawled the word "calm" from top to bottom of the eight hours since noon. He was exasperated by the continuous, monotonous rolling of the ship. The heavy inkstand would slide away in a manner that suggested perverse intelligence in dodging the pen. Having written in the large space under the head of "Remarks" "Heat very oppressive," he stuck the end of the penholder in his teeth, pipe fash-ion, and mopped his face carefully.

"Ship rolling heavily in a high cross swell," he began again, and com-mented to himself, "Heavily is no word for it." Then he wrote: "Sunset threatening, with a low bank of clouds to N. and E. Sky clear overhead."

Sprawling over the table with arrested pen, he glanced out of the door, and in that frame of his vision he saw all the stars flying upwards between the teakwood jambs on a black sky. The whole lot took flight together and disappeared, leaving only a blackness flecked with white flashes, for the sea was as black as the sky and speckled with foam afar. The stars that had flown to the roll came back on the return swing of the ship, rushing downwards in their glittering multitude, not of fiery points, but enlarged to tiny discs brilliant with a clear wet sheen.

Jukes watched the flying big stars for a moment, and then wrote: "8 P.M. Swell increasing. Ship labouring and taking water on her decks. Battened down the coolies for the night. Barometer still falling." He paused, and thought to himself, "Perhaps nothing whatever'll come of it." And then he closed resolutely his entries: "Every appearance of a typhoon coming on."

On going out he had to stand aside, and Captain MacWhirr strode over the doorstep without saying a word or making a sign.

"Shut the door, Mr. Jukes, will you?" he cried from within.

Jukes turned back to do so, muttering ironically: "Afraid to catch cold, I suppose." It was his watch below, but he yearned for communion with his kind; and he remarked cheerily to the second mate: "Doesn't look so bad, after all—does it?"

The second mate was marching to and fro on the bridge, tripping down with small steps one moment, and the next climbing with difficulty the shifting slope of the deck. At the sound of Jukes' voice he stood still, facing forward, but made no reply.

"Hallo! That's a heavy one," said Jukes, swaying to meet the long roll till his lowered hand touched the planks. This time the second mate made in his throat a noise of an unfriendly nature.

He was an oldish, shabby little fellow, with bad teeth and no hair on his face. He had been shipped in a hurry in Shanghai, that trip when the second officer brought from home had delayed the ship three hours in port by contriving (in some manner Captain MacWhirr could never understand) to fall overboard into an empty coal lighter lying alongside, and had to be sent ashore to the hospital with concussion of the brain and a broken limb or two.

Jukes was not discouraged by the unsympathetic sound. "The Chinamen must be having a lovely time of it down there," he said. "It's lucky for them the old girl has the easiest roll of any ship I've ever been in. There now! This one wasn't so bad."

"You wait," snarled the second mate.

With his sharp nose, red at the tip, and his thin pinched lips, he always looked as though he were raging inwardly; and he was concise in his speech to the point of rudeness. All his time off duty he spent in his cabin with the door shut, keeping so still in there that he was supposed to fall asleep as soon as he had disappeared; but the man who came in to wake him for his watch on deck would invariably find him with his eyes wide open, flat on his back in the bunk, and glaring irritably from a soiled pillow. He never wrote any letters, did not seem to hope for news from anywhere; and though he had been heard once to mention West Hartlepool, it was with extreme bitterness, and only in connection with the extortionate charges of a boardinghouse. He was one of those men who are picked up at need in the ports of the world. They are competent enough, appear hopelessly hard up, show no evidence of any sort of vice, and carry about them all the signs of manifest failure. They come aboard on an emergency, care for no ship afloat, live in their own atmosphere of casual connection amongst their shipmates who know nothing of them, and make up their minds to leave at inconvenient times. They clear out with no words of leave-taking in some Godforsaken port other men would fear to be stranded in, and go ashore in company of a shabby sea chest, corded like a treasure box, and with an air of shaking the ship's dust off their feet.

"You wait," he repeated, balanced in great swings with his back to Jukes, motionless and implacable.

"Do you mean to say we are going to catch it hot?" asked Jukes with boyish interest.

"Say? . . . I say nothing. You don't catch me," snapped the little second mate, with a mixture of pride, scorn, and cunning, as if Jukes' question had been a trap cleverly detected. "Oh, no! None of you here shall make a fool of me if I know it," he mumbled to himself.

Jukes reflected rapidly that this second mate was a mean little beast, and in his heart he wished poor Jack Allen had never smashed himself up in the coal lighter. The far-off blackness ahead of the ship was like another night seen through the starry night of the earth—the starless night of the immensities beyond the created universe, revealed in its appalling stillness through a low fissure in the glittering sphere of which the earth is the kernel.

"Whatever there might be about," said Jukes, "we are steaming straight into it."

"*You've* said it," caught up the second mate, always with his back to Jukes. "You've said it, mind—not I."

"Oh, go to Jericho!" said Jukes, frankly; and the other emitted a triumphant little chuckle.

"You've said it," he repeated.

"And what of that?"

"I've known some real good men get into trouble with their skippers for saying a dam' sight less," answered the second mate feverishly. "Oh, no! You don't catch me."

"You seem deucedly anxious not to give yourself away," said Jukes, completely soured by such absurdity. "I wouldn't be afraid to say what I think."

"Aye, to me! That's no great trick. I am nobody, and well I know it."

The ship, after a pause of comparative steadiness, started upon a series of rolls, one worse than the other, and for a time Jukes, preserving his equilibrium, was too busy to open his mouth. As soon as the violent swinging had quieted down somewhat, he said: "This is a bit too much of a good thing. Whether anything is coming or not I think she ought to be put head on to that swell. The old man is just gone in to lie down. Hang me if I don't speak to him."

But when he opened the door of the chart room he saw his captain reading a book. Captain MacWhirr was not lying down: he was standing up with one hand grasping the edge of the bookshelf and the other holding open before his face a thick volume. The lamp wriggled in the gimbals, the loosened books toppled from side to side on the shelf, the long barometer swung in jerky circles, the table altered its slant every moment. In the midst of all this stir and movement Captain MacWhirr, holding on, showed his eyes above the upper edge, and asked, "What's the matter?"

"Swell getting worse, sir."

"Noticed that in here," muttered Captain MacWhirr. "Anything wrong?"

Jukes, inwardly disconcerted by the seriousness of the eyes looking at him over the top of the book, produced an embarrassed grin.

"Rolling like old boots," he said, sheepishly.

"Aye! Very heavy—very heavy. What do you want?"

At this Jukes lost his footing and began to flounder.

"I was thinking of our passengers," he said, in the manner of a man clutching at a straw.

"Passengers?" wondered the Captain, gravely. "What passengers?"

"Why, the Chinamen, sir," explained Jukes, very sick of this conversation.

"The Chinamen! Why don't you speak plainly? Couldn't tell what you meant. Never heard of a lot of coolies spoken of as passengers before. Passengers, indeed! What's come to you?"

Captain MacWhirr, closing the book on his forefinger, lowered his arm and looked completely mystified. "Why are you thinking of the Chinamen, Mr. Jukes?" he inquired.

Jukes took a plunge, like a man driven to it. "She's rolling her decks full of water, sir. Thought you might put her head on perhaps—for a while. Till this goes down a bit—very soon, I dare say. Head to the eastward. I never knew a ship roll like this."

He held on in the doorway, and Captain MacWhirr, feeling his grip on the shelf inadequate, made up his mind to let go in a hurry, and fell heavily on the couch.

"Head to the eastward?" he said, struggling to sit up. "That's more than four points off her course."

"Yes, sir. Fifty degrees. . . . Would just bring her head far enough round to meet this. . . ."

Captain MacWhirr was now sitting up. He had not dropped the book, and he had not lost his place.

"To the eastward?" he repeated, with dawning astonishment. "To the . . . Where do you think we are bound to? You want me to haul a full-powered steamship four points off her course to make the Chinamen comfortable! Now, I've heard more than enough of mad things done in the world—but this . . . If I didn't know you, Jukes, I would think you were in liquor. Steer four points off. . . . And what afterwards? Steer four points over the other way, I suppose, to make the course good. What put it into your head that I would start to tack a steamer as if she were a sailing ship?"

"Jolly good thing she isn't," threw in Jukes, with bitter readiness. "She would have rolled every blessed stick out of her this afternoon."

"Aye! And you just would have had to stand and see them go," said Captain MacWhirr, showing a certain animation. "It's a dead calm, isn't it?"

"It is, sir. But there's something out of the common coming, for sure."

"Maybe. I suppose you have a notion I should be getting out of the way of that dirt," said Captain MacWhirr, speaking with the utmost simplicity of manner and tone, and fixing the oilcloth on the floor with a heavy stare. Thus he noticed neither Jukes' discomfiture nor the mixture of vexation and astonished respect on his face.

"Now, here's this book," he continued with deliberation, slapping his thigh with the closed volume. "I've been reading the chapter on the storms there."

This was true. He had been reading the chapter on the storms. When he had entered the chart room, it was with no intention of taking the book down. Some influence in the air—the same influence, probably, that caused the steward to bring without orders the Captain's seaboots and oilskin coat up to the chart room—had as it were guided his hand to the shelf; and without taking the time to sit down he had waded with a conscious effort into the terminology of the subject. He lost himself amongst advancing semicircles, left- and right-hand quadrants, the curves of the tracks, the probable bearing of the centre, the shifts of wind and the readings of barometer. He tried to bring all these things into a definite relation to himself, and ended by becoming contemptuously angry with such a lot of words and with so much advice, all headwork and supposition, without a glimmer of certitude.

"It's the damnedest thing, Jukes," he said. "If a fellow was to believe all that's in there, he would be running most of his time all over the sea trying to get behind the weather."

Again he slapped his leg with the book; and Jukes opened his mouth, but said nothing.

"Running to get behind the weather! Do you understand that, Mr. Jukes? It's the maddest thing!" ejaculated Captain MacWhirr, with pauses, gazing at the floor profoundly. "You would think an old woman had been writing this. It passes me. If that thing means anything useful, then it means that I should at once alter the course away, away to the devil somewhere, and come booming down on Fu-chau from the northward at the tail of this dirty weather that's supposed to be knocking about in our way. From the north! Do you understand, Mr. Jukes? Three hundred extra miles to the distance, and a pretty coal bill to show. I couldn't bring myself to do that if every word in there was gospel truth, Mr. Jukes. Don't you expect me. . . ."

And Jukes, silent, marvelled at this display of feeling and loquacity.

"But the truth is that you don't know if the fellow is right, anyhow. How can you tell what a gale is made of till you get it? He isn't aboard here, is he? Very well. Here he says that the centre of them things bears eight points off the wind; but we haven't got any wind, for all the barometer falling. Where's his centre now?"

"We will get the wind presently," mumbled Jukes.

"Let it come, then," said Captain MacWhirr, with dignified indignation. "It's only to let you see, Mr. Jukes, that you don't find everything in books. All these rules for dodging breezes and circumventing the winds of heaven, Mr. Jukes, seem to me the maddest thing, when you come to look at it sensibly."

He raised his eyes, saw Jukes gazing at him dubiously, and tried to illustrate his meaning.

"About as queer as your extraordinary notion of dodging the ship head to sea, for I don't know how long, to make the Chinamen comfortable; whereas all we've got to do is to take them to Fu-chau, being timed to get there before noon on Friday. If the weather delays me—very well. There's your logbook to talk straight about the weather. But suppose I went swinging off my course and came in two days late, and they asked me: 'Where have you been all that time, Captain?' What could I say to that? 'Went around to dodge the bad weather,' I would say. 'It must've been dam' bad,' they would say. 'Don't know,' I would have to say; 'I've dodged clear of it.' See that, Jukes? I have been thinking it all out this afternoon."

He looked up again in his unseeing, unimaginative way. No one had ever heard him say so much at one time. Jukes, with his arms open in the doorway, was like a man invited to behold a miracle. Unbounded wonder was the intellectual meaning of his eye, while incredulity was seated in his whole countenance.

"A gale is a gale, Mr. Jukes," resumed the Captain, "and a full-powered steamship has got to face it. There's just so much dirty weather knocking about the world, and the proper thing is to go through it with none of what old Captain Wilson of the *Melita* calls 'storm strategy.' The other day ashore I heard him hold forth about it to a lot of shipmasters who came in and sat at a table next to mine. It seemed to me the greatest nonsense. He was telling them how he outmanoeuvred, I think he said, a terrific gale, so that it never came nearer than fifty miles to him. A neat piece of headwork he called it. How he knew there was a terrific gale fifty miles off beats me altogether. It was like listening to a crazy man. I would have thought Captain Wilson old enough to know better."

Captain MacWhirr ceased for a moment, then said, "It's your watch below, Mr. Jukes?"

Jukes came to himself with a start. "Yes, sir."

"Leave orders to call me at the slightest change," said the Captain. He reached up to put the book away, and tucked his legs upon the couch. "Shut the door so that it don't fly open, will you? I can't stand a door banging. They've put a lot of rubbishy locks into this ship, I must say."

Captain MacWhirr closed his eyes.

He did so to rest himself. He was tired, and he experienced that state of mental vacuity which comes at the end of an exhaustive discussion that has liberated some belief matured in the course of meditative years. He had indeed been making his confession of faith, had he only known it; and its effect was to make Jukes, on the other side of the door, stand scratching his head for a good while.

Captain MacWhirr opened his eyes.

He thought he must have been asleep. What was that loud noise? Wind? Why had he not been called? The lamp wriggled in its gimbals, the barometer swung in circles, the table altered its slant every moment; a pair of limp seaboots with collapsed tops went sliding past the couch. He put out his hand instantly, and captured one.

Jukes' face appeared in a crack of the door: only his face, very red, with staring eyes. The flame of the lamp leaped, a piece of paper flew up, a rush of air enveloped Captain MacWhirr. Beginning to draw on the boot, he directed an expectant gaze at Jukes' swollen, excited features.

"Came on like this," shouted Jukes, "five minutes ago . . . all of a sudden."

The head disappeared with a bang, and a heavy splash and patter of drops swept past the closed door as if a pailful of melted lead had been flung against the house. A whistling could be heard now upon the deep vibrating noise outside. The stuffy chart room seemed as full of draughts as a shed. Captain MacWhirr collared the other seaboot on its violent passage along the floor. He was not flustered, but he could not find at once the opening for inserting his foot. The shoes he had flung off were scurrying from end to end of the cabin, gambolling playfully over each other like puppies. As soon as he stood up he kicked at them viciously, but without effect.

He threw himself into the attitude of a lunging fencer, to reach after his oilskin coat; and afterwards he staggered all over the confined space while he jerked himself into it. Very grave, straddling his legs far apart, and stretching his neck, he started to tie deliberately the strings of his sou'-wester under his chin, with thick fingers that trembled slightly. He went through all the movements of a woman putting on her bonnet before a glass, with a strained, listening attention, as though he had expected every moment to hear the shout of his name in the confused clamour that had suddenly beset his ship. Its increase filled his ears while he was getting ready to go out and confront whatever it might mean. It was tumultuous and very loud—made up of the rush of the wind, the crashes of the sea, with that prolonged deep vibration of the air, like the roll of an immense and remote drum beating the charge of the gale.

He stood for a moment in the light of the lamp, thick, clumsy, shapeless in his panoply of combat, vigilant and red-faced.

"There's a lot of weight in this," he muttered.

As soon as he attempted to open the door the wind caught it. Clinging to the handle, he was dragged out over the doorstep, and at once found himself engaged with the wind in a sort of personal scuffle whose object was the shutting of that door. At the last moment a tongue of air scurried in and licked out the flame of the lamp.

Ahead of the ship he perceived a great darkness lying upon a multitude of white flashes; on the starboard beam a few amazing stars drooped, dim and fitful, above an immense waste of broken seas, as if seen through a mad drift of smoke.

On the bridge a knot of men, indistinct and toiling, were making great efforts in the light of the wheelhouse windows that shone mistily on their heads and backs. Suddenly darkness closed upon one pane, then on another. The voices of the lost group reached him after the manner of men's voices in a gale, in shreds and fragments of forlorn shouting snatched past the ear. All at once Jukes appeared at his side, yelling, with his head down.

"Watch—put in—wheelhouse shutters—glass—afraid—blow in."

Jukes heard his commander upbraiding.

"This—come—anything—warning—call me."

He tried to explain, with the uproar pressing on his lips.

"Light air—remained—bridge—sudden—northeast—could turn—thought—you—sure—hear."

They had gained the shelter of the weather cloth, and could converse with raised voices, as people quarrel.

"I got the hands along to cover up all the ventilators. Good job I had remained on deck. I didn't think you would be asleep, and so . . . What did you say, sir? What?"

"Nothing," cried Captain MacWhirr. "I said—all right."

"By all the powers! We've got it this time," observed Jukes in a howl.

"You haven't altered her course?" inquired Captain MacWhirr, straining his voice.

"No, sir. Certainly not. Wind came out right ahead. And here comes the head sea."

A plunge of the ship ended in a shock as if she had landed her forefoot upon something solid. After a moment of stillness a lofty flight of sprays drove hard with the wind upon their faces.

"Keep her at it as long as we can," shouted Captain MacWhirr.

Before Jukes had squeezed the salt water out of his eyes all the stars had disappeared.

III

Jukes was as ready a man as any half-dozen young mates that may be caught by casting a net upon the waters; and though he had been somewhat taken aback by the startling viciousness of the first squall, he had pulled himself together on the instant, had called out the hands and had rushed them along to secure such openings about the deck as had not been already battened down earlier in the evening. Shouting in his fresh, stentorian voice, "Jump, boys, and bear a hand!" he led in the work, telling himself the while that he had "just expected this."

But at the same time he was growing aware that this was rather more than he had expected. From the first stir of the air felt on his cheek the gale seemed to take upon itself the accumulated impetus of an avalanche. Heavy sprays enveloped the *Nan-Shan* from stem to stern, and instantly in the midst of her regular rolling she began to jerk and plunge as though she had gone mad with fright.

Jukes thought, "This is no joke." While he was exchanging explanatory yells with his captain, a sudden lowering of the darkness came upon the night, falling before their vision like something palpable. It was as if the masked lights of the world had been turned down. Jukes was uncritically glad to have his captain at hand. It relieved him as though that man had, by simply coming on deck, taken most of the gale's weight upon his shoulders. Such is the prestige, the privilege, and the burden of command.

Captain MacWhirr could expect no relief of that sort from anyone on earth. Such is the loneliness of command. He was trying to see, with that watchful manner of a seaman who stares into the wind's eye as if into the eye of an adversary, to penetrate the hidden intention and guess the aim and force of the thrust. The strong wind swept at him out of a vast obscurity; he felt under his feet the uneasiness of his ship, and he could not even discern the shadow of her shape. He wished it were not so; and very still he waited, feeling stricken by a blind man's helplessness.

To be silent was natural to him, dark or shine. Jukes, at his elbow, made himself heard yelling cheerily in the gusts, "We must have got the worst of it at once, sir." A faint burst of lightning quivered all round, as if flashed into a cavern—into a black and secret chamber of the sea, with a floor of foaming crests.

It unveiled for a sinister, fluttering moment a ragged mass of clouds hanging low, the lurch of the long outlines of the ship, the black figures of men caught on the bridge, heads forward, as if petrified in the act of butting. The darkness palpitated down upon all this, and then the real thing came at last.

It was something formidable and swift, like the sudden smashing of a vial of wrath. It seemed to explode all round the ship with an overpowering concussion and a rush of great waters, as if an immense dam had been blown up to windward. In an instant the men lost touch of each other. This is the disintegrating power of a great wind: it isolates one from one's kind. An earthquake, a landslip, an avalanche, overtake a man incidentally, as it were—without passion. A furious gale attacks him like a personal enemy, tries to grasp his limbs, fastens upon his mind, seeks to rout his very spirit out of him.

Jukes was driven away from his commander. He fancied himself whirled a great distance through the air. Everything disappeared—even, for a moment, his power of thinking; but his hand had found one of the rail stanchions. His distress was by no means alleviated by an inclination to disbelieve the reality of this experience. Though young, he had seen some bad weather, and had never doubted his ability to imagine the worst; but this was so much beyond his powers of fancy that it appeared incompatible with the existence of any ship whatever. He would have been incredulous about himself in the same way, perhaps, had he not been so harassed by the necessity of exerting a wrestling effort against a force trying to tear him away from his hold. Moreover, the conviction of not being utterly destroyed returned to him through the sensations of being half-drowned, bestially shaken, and partly choked.

It seemed to him he remained there precariously alone with the stanchion for a long, long time. The rain poured on him, flowed, drove in sheets. He breathed in gasps; and sometimes the water he swallowed was fresh and sometimes it was salt. For the most part he kept his eyes shut tight, as if suspecting his sight might be destroyed in the immense flurry of the elements. When he ventured to blink hastily, he derived some moral support from the green gleam of the starboard light shining feebly upon the flight of rain and sprays. He was actually looking at it when its ray fell upon the uprearing sea which put it out. He saw the head of the wave topple over, adding the mite of its crash to the tremendous uproar raging around him, and almost at the same instant the stanchion was wrenched away from his embracing arms. After a crushing thump on his back he found himself suddenly afloat and borne upwards. His first irresistible notion was that the whole China Sea had climbed on the bridge. Then, more sanely, he concluded himself gone overboard. All the time he was being tossed, flung, and rolled in great volumes of water, he kept on repeating mentally, with the utmost precipitation, the words: "My God! My God! My God! My God!"

All at once, in a revolt of misery and despair, he formed the crazy resolution to get out of that. And he began to thresh about with his arms and legs. But as soon as he commenced his wretched struggles he discovered that he had become somehow mixed up with a face, an oilskin coat, somebody's boots. He clawed ferociously all these things in turn, lost them, found them again, lost them once more, and finally was himself caught in the firm clasp of a pair of stout arms. He returned the embrace close round a thick solid body. He had found his captain.

They tumbled over and over, tightening their hug. Suddenly the water let them down with a brutal bang; and, stranded against the side of the wheelhouse, out of breath and bruised, they were left to stagger up in the wind and hold on where they could.

Jukes came out of it rather horrified, as though he had escaped some unparalleled outrage directed at his feelings. It weakened his faith in himself. He started shouting aimlessly to the man he could feel near him in that fiendish blackness, "Is it you, sir? Is it you, sir?" till his temples seemed ready to burst. And he heard in answer a voice, as if crying far away, as if screaming to him fretfully from a very great distance, the one word "Yes!" Other seas swept again over the bridge. He received them defencelessly right over his bare head, with both his hands engaged in holding.

The motion of the ship was extravagant. Her lurches had an appalling helplessness: she pitched as if taking a header into a void, and seemed to find a wall to hit every time. When she rolled she fell on her side headlong, and she would be righted back by such a demolishing blow that Jukes felt her reeling as a clubbed man reels before he collapses. The gale howled and scuffled about gigantically in the darkness, as though the entire world were one black gully. At certain moments the air streamed against the ship as if sucked through a tunnel with a concentrated solid force of impact that seemed to lift her clean out of the water and keep her up for an instant with only a quiver running through her from end to end. And then she would begin her tumbling again as if dropped back into a boiling cauldron. Jukes tried hard to compose his mind and judge things coolly.

The sea, flattened down in the heavier gusts, would uprise and overwhelm both ends of the *Nan-Shan* in snowy rushes of foam, expanding wide, beyond both rails, into the night. And on this dazzling sheet, spread under the blackness of the clouds and emitting a bluish glow, Captain MacWhirr could catch a desolate glimpse of a few tiny specks black as ebony, the tops of the hatches, the battened companions, the heads of the covered winches, the foot of a mast. This was all he could see of his ship. Her middle structure, covered by the bridge which bore him, his mate, the closed wheelhouse where a man was steering shut up with the fear of being swept overboard together with the whole thing in one great crash—her middle structure was like a half-tide rock awash upon a coast. It was like an outlying rock with the water boiling up, streaming over, pouring off, beating round—like a rock in the surf to which shipwrecked people cling before they let go—only it rose, it sank, it rolled continuously, without respite and rest, like a rock that should have miraculously struck adrift from a coast and gone wallowing upon the sea.

The *Nan-Shan* was being looted by the storm with a senseless, destructive fury: trysails torn out of the extra gaskets, double-lashed awnings blown away, bridge swept clean, weather cloths burst, rails twisted, light screens smashed—and two of the boats had gone already. They had gone unheard and unseen, melting, as it were, in the shock and smother of the wave. It was only later, when upon the white flash of another high sea hurling itself amidships, Jukes had a vision of two pairs of davits leaping black and empty out of the solid blackness, with one overhauled fall flying and an ironbound block capering in the air, that he became aware of what had happened within about three yards of his back.

He poked his head forward, groping for the ear of his commander. His lips touched it—big, fleshy, very wet. He cried in an agitated tone, "Our boats are going now, sir."

And again he heard that voice, forced and ringing feebly, but with a penetrating effect of quietness in the enormous discord of noises, as if sent out from some remote spot of peace beyond the black wastes of the gale; again he heard a man's voice—the frail and indomitable sound that can be made to carry an infinity of thought, resolution, and purpose, that shall be pronouncing confident words on the last day, when heavens fall, and justice is done—again he heard it, and it was crying to him, as if from very, very far —"All right."

He thought he had not managed to make himself understood. "Our boats—I say boats—the boats, sir! Two gone!"

The same voice, within a foot of him and yet so remote, yelled sensibly, "Can't be helped."

Captain MacWhirr had never turned his face, but Jukes caught some more words in the wind.

"What can—expect—when hammering through—such—Bound to leave —something behind—stands to reason."

Watchfully Jukes listened for more. No more came. This was all Captain MacWhirr had to say; and Jukes could picture to himself rather than see the broad squat back before him. An impenetrable obscurity pressed down upon the ghostly glimmers of the sea. A dull conviction seized upon Jukes that there was nothing to be done.

If the steering gear did not give way, if the immense volumes of water did not burst the deck in or smash one of the hatches, if the engines did not give up, if way could be kept on the ship against this terrific wind, and she did not bury herself in one of these awful seas, of whose white crests alone, topping high above her bows, he could now and then get a sickening glimpse—then there was a chance of her coming out of it. Something within him seemed to turn over, bringing uppermost the feeling that the *Nan-Shan* was lost.

"She's done for," he said to himself, with a surprising mental agitation, as though he had discovered an unexpected meaning in this thought. One of these things was bound to happen. Nothing could be prevented now, and nothing could be remedied. The men on board did not count, and the ship could not last. This weather was too impossible.

Jukes felt an arm thrown heavily over his shoulders; and to this overture he responded with great intelligence by catching hold of his captain round the waist.

They stood clasped thus in the blind night, bracing each other against the wind, cheek to cheek and lip to ear, in the manner of two hulks lashed stem to stern together.

And Jukes heard the voice of his commander hardly any louder than before, but nearer, as though, starting to march athwart the prodigious rush of the hurricane, it had approached him, bearing that strange effect of quietness like the serene glow of a halo.

"D'ye know where the hands got to?" it asked, vigorous and evanescent at the same time, overcoming the strength of the wind, and swept away from Jukes instantly.

Jukes didn't know. They were all on the bridge when the real force of the hurricane struck the ship. He had no idea where they had crawled to. Under the circumstances they were nowhere, for all the use that could be made of them. Somehow the captain's wish to know distressed Jukes.

"Want the hands, sir?" he cried, apprehensively.

"Ought to know," asserted Captain MacWhirr. "Hold hard."

They held hard. An outburst of unchained fury, a vicious rush of the wind absolutely steadied the ship; she rocked only, quick and light like a child's cradle, for a terrific moment of suspense, while the whole atmosphere, as it seemed, streamed furiously past her, roaring away from the tenebrous earth.

It suffocated them, and with eyes shut they tightened their grasp. What from the magnitude of the shock might have been a column of water running upright in the dark, butted against the ship, broke short, and fell on her bridge, crushingly, from on high, with a dead burying weight.

A flying fragment of that collapse, a mere splash, enveloped them in one swirl from their feet over their heads, filling violently their ears, mouths, and nostrils with salt water. It knocked out their legs, wrenched in haste at their arms, seethed away swiftly under their chins; and opening their eyes, they saw the piled-up masses of foam dashing to and fro amongst what looked like the fragments of a ship. She had given way as if driven straight in. Their panting hearts yielded, too, before the tremendous blow; and all at once she sprang up again to her desperate plunging, as if trying to scramble out from under the ruins.

The seas in the dark seemed to rush from all sides to keep her back where she might perish. There was hate in the way she was handled, and a ferocity in the blows that fell. She was like a living creature thrown to the rage of a mob: hustled terribly, struck at, borne up, flung down, leaped upon. Captain MacWhirr and Jukes kept hold of each other, deafened by the noise, gagged by the wind; and the great physical tumult beating about their bodies, brought, like an unbridled display of passion, a profound trouble to their souls. One of those wild and appalling shrieks that are heard at times passing mysteriously overhead in the steady roar of a hurricane, swooped, as if borne on wings, upon the ship, and Jukes tried to outscream it.

"Will she live through this?"

The cry was wrenched out of his breast. It was as unintentional as the birth of a thought in the head, and he heard nothing of it himself. It all became extinct at once—thought, intention, effort—and of his cry the inaudible vibration added to the tempest waves of the air.

He expected nothing from it. Nothing at all. For indeed what answer could be made? But after a while he heard with amazement the frail and resisting voice in his ear, the dwarf sound, unconquered in the giant tumult.

"She may!"

It was a dull yell, more difficult to seize than a whisper. And presently the voice returned again, half submerged in the vast crashes, like a ship battling against the waves of an ocean.

"Let's hope so!" it cried—small, lonely, and unmoved, a stranger to the visions of hope or fear; and it flickered into disconnected words: "Ship. . . . This. . . . Never—Anyhow . . . for the best." Jukes gave it up.

Then, as if it had come suddenly upon the one thing fit to withstand the power of a storm, it seemed to gain force and firmness for the last broken shouts:

"Keep on hammering . . . builders . . . good men. . . . And chance it . . . engines. . . . Rout . . . good man."

Captain MacWhirr removed his arm from Jukes' shoulders, and thereby ceased to exist for his mate, so dark it was; Jukes, after a tense stiffening of every muscle, would let himself go limp all over. The gnawing of profound discomfort existed side by side with an incredible disposition to somnolence, as though he had been buffeted and worried into drowsiness. The wind would get hold of his head and try to shake it off his shoulders; his clothes, full of water, were as heavy as lead, cold and dripping like an armour of melting ice: he shivered—it lasted a long time; and with his hands closed hard on his hold, he was letting himself sink slowly into the depths of bodily misery. His mind became concentrated upon himself in an aimless, idle way, and when something pushed lightly at the back of his knees he nearly, as the saying is, jumped out of his skin.

In the start forward he bumped the back of Captain MacWhirr, who didn't move; and then a hand gripped his thigh. A lull had come, a menacing lull of the wind, the holding of a stormy breath—and he felt himself pawed all over. It was the boatswain. Jukes recognized these hands, so thick and enormous that they seemed to belong to some new species of man.

The boatswain had arrived on the bridge, crawling on all fours against the wind, and had found the chief mate's legs with the top of his head. Immediately he crouched and began to explore Jukes' person upwards with prudent, apologetic touches, as became an inferior.

He was an ill-favoured, undersized, gruff sailor of fifty, coarsely hairy, short-legged, long-armed, resembling an elderly ape. His strength was immense; and in his great lumpy paws, bulging like brown boxing gloves on the end of furry forearms, the heaviest objects were handled like playthings. Apart from the grizzled pelt on his chest, the menacing demeanour and the hoarse voice, he had none of the classical attributes of his rating. His good nature almost amounted to imbecility: the men did what they liked with him, and he had not an ounce of initiative in his character, which was easygoing and talkative. For these reasons Jukes disliked him; but Captain MacWhirr, to Jukes' scornful disgust, seemed to regard him as a first-rate petty officer.

He pulled himself up by Jukes' coat, taking that liberty with the greatest moderation, and only so far as it was forced upon him by the hurricane.

"What is it, boss'n, what is it?" yelled Jukes, impatiently. What could that fraud of a boss'n want on the bridge? The typhoon had got on Jukes' nerves. The husky bellowings of the other, though unintelligible, seemed to suggest a state of lively satisfaction. There could be no mistake. The old fool was pleased with something.

The boatswain's other hand had found some other body, for in a changed tone he began to inquire: "Is it you, sir? Is it you, sir?" The wind strangled his howls.

"Yes!" cried Captain MacWhirr.

IV

All that the boatswain, out of a superabundance of yells, could make clear to Captain MacWhirr was the bizarre intelligence that "All them Chinamen in the fore tween-deck have fetched away, sir."

Jukes to leeward could hear these two shouting within six inches of his face, as you may hear on a still night half a mile away two men conversing across a field. He heard Captain MacWhirr's exasperated "What? What?" and the strained pitch of the other's hoarseness. "In a lump . . . seen them myself. . . . Awful sight, sir . . . thought . . . tell you."

Jukes remained indifferent, as if rendered irresponsible by the force of the hurricane, which made the very thought of action utterly vain. Besides, being very young, he had found the occupation of keeping his heart completely steeled against the worst so engrossing that he had come to feel an overpowering dislike towards any other form of activity whatever. He was not scared; he knew this because, firmly believing he would never see another sunrise, he remained calm in that belief.

These are the moments of do-nothing heroics to which even good men surrender at times. Many officers of ships can no doubt recall a case in their experience when just such a trance of confounded stoicism would come all at once over a whole ship's company. Jukes, however, had no wide experience of men or storms. He conceived himself to be calm—inexorably calm; but as a matter of fact he was daunted; not abjectly, but only so far as a decent man may, without becoming loathsome to himself.

It was rather like a forced-on numbness of spirit. The long, long stress of a gale does it; the suspense of the interminably culminating catastrophe; and there is a bodily fatigue in the mere holding on to existence within the excessive tumult; a searching and insidious fatigue that penetrates deep into a man's breast to cast down and sadden his heart, which is incorrigible, and of all the gifts of the earth—even before life itself—aspires to peace.

Jukes was benumbed much more than he supposed. He held on—very wet, very cold, stiff in every limb; and in a momentary hallucination of swift visions (it is said that a drowning man thus reviews all his life) he beheld all sorts of memories altogether unconnected with his present situation. He remembered his father, for instance: a worthy businessman who at an unfortunate crisis in his affairs went quietly to bed and died forthwith in a state of resignation. Jukes did not recall these circumstances, of course, but remaining otherwise unconcerned he seemed to see distinctly the poor man's face; a certain game of nap played when quite a boy in Table Bay on board a ship, since lost with all hands; the thick eyebrows of his first skipper; and without any emotion, as he might years ago have walked listlessly into her room and found her sitting there with a book, he remembered his mother—dead, too, now—the resolute woman, left badly off, who had been very firm in his bringing up.

It could not have lasted more than a second, perhaps not so much. A heavy arm had fallen about his shoulders; Captain MacWhirr's voice was speaking his name into his ear.

"Jukes! Jukes!"

He detected the tone of deep concern. The wind had thrown its weight on the ship, trying to pin her down amongst the seas. They made a clean breach over her, as over a deep-swimming log; and the gathered weight of crashes menaced monstrously from afar. The breakers flung out of the night with a ghostly light on their crests—the light of sea-foam that in a ferocious, boiling-up pale flash showed upon the slender body of the ship the toppling rush, the downfall, and the seething mad scurry of each wave. Never for a moment could she shake herself clear of the water; Jukes, rigid, perceived in her motion the ominous sign of haphazard floundering. She was no longer struggling intelligently. It was the beginning of the end; and the note of busy concern in Captain MacWhirr's voice sickened him like an exhibition of blind and pernicious folly.

The spell of the storm had fallen upon Jukes. He was penetrated by it, absorbed by it; he was rooted in it with a rigour of dumb attention. Captain MacWhirr persisted in his cries, but the wind got between them like a solid wedge. He hung round Jukes' neck as heavy as a millstone, and suddenly the sides of their heads knocked together.

"Jukes! Mr. Jukes, I say!"

He had to answer that voice that would not be silenced. He answered in the customary manner: ". . . Yes, sir."

And directly, his heart, corrupted by the storm that breeds a craving for peace, rebelled against the tyranny of training and command.

Captain MacWhirr had his mate's head fixed firm in the crook of his elbow, and pressed it to his yelling lips mysteriously. Sometimes Jukes would break in, admonishing hastily: "Look out, sir!" or Captain MacWhirr would bawl an earnest exhortation to "Hold hard, there!" and the whole black universe seemed to reel together with the ship. They paused. She floated yet. And Captain MacWhirr would resume his shouts. ". . . . Says . . . whole lot . . . fetched away. . . . Ought to see . . . what's the matter."

Directly the full force of the hurricane had struck the ship, every part of her deck became untenable; and the sailors, dazed and dismayed, took shelter in the port alleyway under the bridge. It had a door aft, which they shut; it was very black, cold, and dismal. At each heavy fling of the ship they would groan all together in the dark, and tons of water could be heard scuttling about as if trying to get at them from above. The boatswain had been keeping up a gruff talk, but a more unreasonable lot of men, he said afterwards, he had never been with. They were snug enough there, out of harm's way, and not wanted to do anything, either; and yet they did nothing but grumble and complain peevishly like so many sick kids. Finally, one of them said that if there had been at least some light to see each other's noses by, it wouldn't be so bad. It was making him crazy, he declared, to lie there in the dark waiting for the blamed hooker to sink.

"Why don't you step outside, then, and be done with it at once?" the boatswain turned on him.

This called up a shout of execration. The boatswain found himself overwhelmed with reproaches of all sorts. They seemed to take it ill that a lamp was not instantly created for them out of nothing. They would whine after a light to get drowned by—anyhow! And though the unreason of their revilings was patent—since no one could hope to reach the lamp room, which was forward—he became greatly distressed. He did not think it was decent of them to be nagging at him like this. He told them so, and was met by general contumely. He sought refuge, therefore, in an embittered silence. At the same time their grumbling and sighing and muttering worried him greatly, but by and by it occurred to him that there were six globe lamps hung in the tween-deck, and that there could be no harm in depriving the coolies of one of them.

The *Nan-Shan* had an athwartship coal bunker, which, being at times used as cargo space, communicated by an iron door with the fore tween-deck. It was empty then, and its manhole was the foremost one in the alleyway. The boatswain could get in, therefore, without coming out on deck at all; but to his great surprise he found he could induce no one to help him in taking off the manhole cover. He groped for it all the same, but one of the crew lying in his way refused to budge.

"Why, I only want to get you that blamed light you are crying for," he expostulated, almost pitifully.

Somebody told him to go and put his head in a bag. He regretted he could not recognize the voice, and that it was too dark to see, otherwise, as he said, he would have put a head on *that* son of a sea cook, anyway, sink or swim. Nevertheless, he had made up his mind to show them he could get a light, if he were to die for it.

Through the violence of the ship's rolling, every movement was dangerous. To be lying down seemed labour enough. He nearly broke his neck dropping into the bunker. He fell on his back, and was sent shooting helplessly from side to side in the dangerous company of a heavy iron bar—a coal-trimmer's slice probably—left down there by somebody. This thing made him as nervous as though it had been a wild beast. He could not see it, the inside of the bunker coated with coal dust being perfectly and impenetrably black; but he heard it sliding and clattering, and striking here and there, always in the neighbourhood of his head. It seemed to make an extraordinary noise, too—to give heavy thumps as though it had been as big as a bridge girder. This was remarkable enough for him to notice while he was flung from port to starboard and back again, and clawing desperately the smooth sides of the bunker in the endeavour to stop himself. The door into the tween-deck not fitting quite true, he saw a thread of dim light at the bottom.

Being a sailor, and a still active man, he did not want much of a chance to regain his feet; and as luck would have it, in scrambling up he put his hand on the iron slice, picking it up as he rose. Otherwise he would have been afraid of the thing breaking his legs, or at least knocking him down again. At first he stood still. He felt unsafe in this darkness that seemed to make the ship's motion unfamiliar, unforeseen, and difficult to counteract. He felt so much shaken for a moment that he dared not move for fear of "taking charge again." He had no mind to get battered to pieces in that bunker.

He had struck his head twice; he was dazed a little. He seemed to hear yet so plainly the clatter and bangs of the iron slice flying about his ears that he tightened his grip to prove to himself he had it there safely in his hand. He was vaguely amazed at the plainness with which down there he could hear the gale raging. Its howls and shrieks seemed to take on, in the emptiness of the bunker, something of the human character, of human rage and pain—being not vast but infinitely poignant. And there were, with every roll, thumps, too—profound, ponderous thumps, as if a bulky object of five-ton weight or so had got play in the hold. But there was no such thing in the cargo. Something on deck? Impossible. Or alongside? Couldn't be.

He thought all this quickly, clearly, competently, like a seaman, and in the end remained puzzled. This noise, though, came deadened from outside, together with the washing and pouring of water on deck above his head. Was it the wind? Must be. It made down there a row like the shouting of a big lot of crazed men. And he discovered in himself a desire for a light, too—if only to get drowned by—and a nervous anxiety to get out of that bunker as quickly as possible.

He pulled back the bolt: the heavy iron plate turned on its hinges; and it was as though he had opened the door to the sounds of the tempest. A gust

of hoarse yelling met him: the air was still; and the rushing of water overhead was covered by a tumult of strangled, throaty shrieks that produced an
effect of desperate confusion. He straddled his legs the whole width of the
doorway and stretched his neck. At first he perceived only what he had
come to seek: six small yellow flames swinging violently on the great body
of the dusk.

It was stayed like the gallery of a mine, with a row of stanchions in the
middle, and crossbeams overhead, penetrating into the gloom ahead—in-
definitely. And to port there loomed, like the caving in of one of the sides, a
bulky mass with a slanting outline. The whole place, with the shadows and
the shapes, moved all the time. The boatswain glared: the ship lurched to
starboard, and a great howl came from that mass that had the slant of fallen
earth.

Pieces of wood whizzed past. Planks, he thought, inexpressibly startled,
and flinging back his head. At his feet a man went sliding over, open-eyed,
on his back, straining with uplifted arms for nothing: and another came
bounding like a detached stone with his head between his legs and his
hands clenched. His pigtail whipped in the air; he made a grab at the
boatswain's legs, and from his opened hand a bright white disc rolled
against the boatswain's foot. He recognized a silver dollar, and yelled at it
with astonishment. With a precipitated sound of trampling and shuffling of
bare feet, and with guttural cries, the mound of writhing bodies piled up to
port detached itself from the ship's side and sliding, inert and struggling,
shifted to starboard, with a dull, brutal thump. The cries ceased. The boatswain heard a long moan through the roar and whistling of the wind; he
saw an inextricable confusion of heads and shoulders, naked soles kicking
upwards, fists raised, tumbling backs, legs, pigtails, faces.

"Good Lord!" he cried, horrified, and banged-to the iron door upon
this vision.

This was what he had come on the bridge to tell. He could not keep it to
himself; and on board ship there is only one man to whom it is worth while
to unburden yourself. On his passage back the hands in the alleyway swore
at him for a fool. Why didn't he bring that lamp? What the devil did the
coolies matter to anybody? And when he came out, the extremity of the
ship made what went on inside of her appear of little moment.

At first he thought he had left the alleyway in the very moment of her
sinking. The bridge ladders had been washed away, but an enormous sea
filling the afterdeck floated him up. After that he had to lie on his stomach
for some time, holding to a ringbolt, getting his breath now and then, and
swallowing salt water. He struggled farther on his hands and knees, too
frightened and distracted to turn back. In this way he reached the after part
of the wheelhouse. In that comparatively sheltered spot he found the sec-

ond mate. The boatswain was pleasantly surprised—his impression being that everybody on deck must have been washed away a long time ago. He asked eagerly where the Captain was.

The second mate was lying low, like a malignant little animal under a hedge.

"Captain? Gone overboard, after getting us into this mess." The mate, too, for all he knew or cared. Another fool. Didn't matter. Everybody was going by and by.

The boatswain crawled out again into the strength of the wind; not because he much expected to find anybody, he said, but just to get away from "that man." He crawled out as outcasts go to face an inclement world. Hence his great joy at finding Jukes and the Captain. But what was going on in the tween-deck was to him a minor matter by that time. Besides, it was difficult to make yourself heard. But he managed to convey the idea that the Chinamen had broken adrift together with their boxes, and that he had come up on purpose to report this. As to the hands, they were all right. Then, appeased, he subsided on the deck in a sitting posture, hugging with his arms and legs the stand of the engine-room telegraph—an iron casting as thick as a post. When that went, why, he expected he would go, too. He gave no more thought to the coolies.

Captain MacWhirr had made Jukes understand that he wanted him to go down below—to see.

"What am I to do then, sir?" And the trembling of his whole wet body caused Jukes' voice to sound like bleating.

"See first . . . Boss'n . . . says . . . adrift."

"That boss'n is a confounded fool," howled Jukes, shakily.

The absurdity of the demand made upon him revolted Jukes. He was as unwilling to go as if the moment he had left the deck the ship were sure to sink.

"I must know . . . can't leave. . . ."

"They'll settle, sir."

"Fight . . . boss'n says they fight. . . . Why? Can't have . . . fighting . . . board ship. . . . Much rather keep you here . . . case . . . I should . . . washed overboard myself. . . . Stop it . . . some way. You see and tell me . . . through engine-room tube. Don't want you . . . come up here . . . too often. Dangerous . . . moving about . . . deck."

Jukes, held with his head in chancery, had to listen to what seemed horrible suggestions.

"Don't want . . . you get lost . . . so long . . . ship isn't. . . .

Rout . . . Good man . . . Ship . . . may . . . through this . . . all right yet."

All at once Jukes understood he would have to go.

"Do you think she may?" he screamed.

But the wind devoured the reply, out of which Jukes heard only the one word, pronounced with great energy ". . . Always. . . ."

Captain MacWhirr released Jukes, and bending over the boatswain, yelled, "Get back with the mate." Jukes only knew that the arm was gone off his shoulders. He was dismissed with his orders—to do what? He was exasperated into letting go his hold carelessly, and on the instant was blown away. It seemed to him that nothing could stop him from being blown right over the stern. He flung himself down hastily, and the boatswain, who was following, fell on him.

"Don't you get up yet, sir," cried the boatswain. "No hurry!"

A sea swept over. Jukes understood the boatswain to splutter that the bridge ladders were gone. "I'll lower you down, sir, by your hands," he screamed. He shouted also something about the smokestack being as likely to go overboard as not. Jukes thought it very possible, and imagined the fires out, the ship helpless. . . . The boatswain by his side kept on yelling. "What? What is it?" Jukes cried distressfully; and the other repeated, "What would my old woman say if she saw me now?"

In the alleyway, where a lot of water had got in and splashed in the dark, the men were still as death, till Jukes stumbled against one of them and cursed him savagely for being in the way. Two or three voices then asked, eager and weak, "Any chance for us, sir?"

"What's the matter with you fools?" he said brutally. He felt as though he could throw himself down amongst them and never move any more. But they seemed cheered; and in the midst of obsequious warnings, "Look out! Mind that manhole lid, sir," they lowered him into the bunker. The boatswain tumbled down after him, and as soon as he had picked himself up he remarked, "She would say, 'Serve you right, you old fool, for going to sea.' "

The boatswain had some means, and made a point of alluding to them frequently. His wife—a fat woman—and two grown-up daughters kept a greengrocer's shop in the East-end of London.

In the dark, Jukes, unsteady on his legs, listened to a faint thunderous patter. A deadened screaming went on steadily at his elbow, as it were; and from above the louder tumult of the storm descended upon these near sounds. His head swam. To him, too, in that bunker, the motion of the ship seemed novel and menacing, sapping his resolution as though he had never been afloat before.

He had half a mind to scramble out again; but the remembrance of

Captain MacWhirr's voice made this impossible. His orders were to go and see. What was the good of it, he wanted to know. Enraged, he told himself he would see—of course. But the boatswain, staggering clumsily, warned him to be careful how he opened that door; there was a blamed fight going on. And Jukes, as if in great bodily pain, desired irritably to know what the devil they were fighting for.

"Dollars! Dollars, sir. All their rotten chests got burst open. Blamed money skipping all over the place, and they are tumbling after it head over heels—tearing and biting like anything. A regular little hell in there."

Jukes convulsively opened the door. The short boatswain peered under his arm.

One of the lamps had gone out, broken perhaps. Rancorous, gutteral cries burst out loudly on their ears, and a strange panting sound, the working of all these straining breasts. A hard blow hit the side of the ship; water fell above with a stunning shock, and in the forefront of the gloom, where the air was reddish and thick, Jukes saw a head bang the deck violently, two thick calves waving on high, muscular arms twined round a naked body, a yellow face, openmouthed and with a set wild stare, look up and slide away. An empty chest clattered turning over; a man fell head first with a jump, as if lifted by a kick; and farther off, indistinct, others streamed like a mass of rolling stones down a bank, thumping the deck with their feet and flourishing their arms wildly. The hatchway ladder was loaded with coolies swarming on it like bees on a branch. They hung on the steps in a crawling, stirring cluster, beating madly with their fists the underside of the battened hatch, and the headlong rush of the water above was heard in the intervals of their yelling. The ship heeled over more, and they began to drop off: first one, then two, then all the rest went away together, falling straight off with a great cry.

Jukes was confounded. The boatswain, with gruff anxiety, begged him, "Don't you go in there, sir."

The whole place seemed to twist upon itself, jumping incessantly the while; and when the ship rose to a sea Jukes fancied that all these men would be shot upon him in a body. He backed out, swung the door to, and with trembling hands pushed at the bolt. . . .

As soon as his mate had gone Captain MacWhirr, left alone on the bridge, sidled and staggered as far as the wheelhouse. Its door being hinged forward, he had to fight the gale for admittance, and when at last he managed to enter, it was with an instantaneous clatter and a bang, as though he had been fired through the wood. He stood within, holding on to the handle.

The steering gear leaked steam, and in the confined space the glass of the binnacle made a shiny oval of light in a thin white fog. The wind howled, hummed, whistled, with sudden booming gusts that rattled the doors and shutters in the vicious patter of sprays. Two coils of lead line and a small canvas bag hung on a long lanyard, swung wide off, and came back clinging to the bulkheads. The gratings underfoot were nearly afloat; with every sweeping blow of a sea, water squirted violently through the cracks all round the door, and the man at the helm had flung down his cap, his coat, and stood propped against the gear casing in a striped cotton shirt open on his breast. The little brass wheel in his hands had the appearance of a bright and fragile toy. The cords of his neck stood hard and lean, a dark patch lay in the hollow of his throat, and his face was still and sunken as in death.

Captain MacWhirr wiped his eyes. The sea that had nearly taken him overboard had, to his great annoyance, washed his sou'wester hat off his bald head. The fluffy, fair hair, soaked and darkened, resembled a mean skein of cotton threads festooned round his bare skull. His face, glistening with seawater, had been made crimson with the wind, with the sting of sprays. He looked as though he had come off sweating from before a furnace.

"You here?" he muttered, heavily.

The second mate had found his way into the wheelhouse some time before. He had fixed himself in a corner with his knees up, a fist pressed against each temple; and this attitude suggested rage, sorrow, resignation, surrender, with a sort of concentrated unforgiveness. He said mournfully and defiantly, "Well, it's my watch below now: ain't it?"

The steam gear clattered, stopped, clattered again; and the helmsman's eyeballs seemed to project out of a hungry face as if the compass card behind the binnacle glass had been meat. God knows how long he had been left there to steer, as if forgotten by all his shipmates. The bells had not been struck; there had been no reliefs; the ship's routine had gone down wind; but he was trying to keep her head north-northeast. The rudder might have been gone for all he knew, the fires out, the engines broken down, the ship ready to roll over like a corpse. He was anxious not to get muddled and lose control of her head, because the compass card swung far both ways, wriggling on the pivot, and sometimes seemed to whirl right round. He suffered from mental stress. He was horribly afraid, also, of the wheelhouse going. Mountains of water kept on tumbling against it. When the ship took one of her desperate dives the corners of his lips twitched.

Captain MacWhirr looked up at the wheelhouse clock. Screwed to the bulkhead, it had a white face on which the black hands appeared to stand quite still. It was half-past one in the morning.

"Another day," he muttered to himself.

The second mate heard him, and lifting his head as one grieving amongst ruins, "You won't see it break," he exclaimed. His wrists and his knees could be seen to shake violently. "No, by God! You won't. . . ."

He took his face again between his fists.

The body of the helmsman had moved slightly, but his head didn't budge on his neck—like a stone head fixed to look one way from a column. During a roll that all but took his booted legs from under him, and in the very stagger to save himself, Captain MacWhirr said austerely, "Don't you pay any attention to what that man says." And then, with an indefinable change of tone, very grave, he added, "He isn't on duty."

The sailor said nothing.

The hurricane boomed, shaking the little place, which seemed airtight; and the light of the binnacle flickered all the time.

"You haven't been relieved," Captain MacWhirr went on, looking down. "I want you to stick to the helm, though, as long as you can. You've got the hang of her. Another man coming here might make a mess of it. Wouldn't do. No child's play. And the hands are probably busy with a job down below. . . . Think you can?"

The steering gear leaped into an abrupt short clatter, stopped smouldering like an ember; and the still man, with a motionless gaze, burst out, as if all the passion in him had gone into his lips: "By Heavens, sir! I can steer forever if nobody talks to me."

"Oh! aye! All right. . . ." The Captain lifted his eyes for the first time to the man, "Hackett."

And he seemed to dismiss this matter from his mind. He stooped to the engine-room speaking tube, blew in, and bent his head. Mr. Rout below answered, and at once Captain MacWhirr put his lips to the mouthpiece.

With the uproar of the gale around him he applied alternately his lips and his ear, and the engineer's voice mounted to him, harsh and as if out of the heat of an engagement. One of the stokers was disabled, the others had given in, the second engineer and the donkeyman were firing-up. The third engineer was standing by the steam valve. The engines were being tended by hand. How was it above?

"Bad enough. It mostly rests with you," said Captain MacWhirr. Was the mate down there yet? No? Well, he would be presently. Would Mr. Rout let him talk through the speaking tube?—through the deck speaking tube, because he—the Captain—was going out again on the bridge directly. There was some trouble amongst the Chinamen. They were fighting, it seemed. Couldn't allow fighting anyhow. . . .

Mr. Rout had gone away, and Captain MacWhirr could feel against his ear the pulsation of the engines, like the beat of the ship's heart. Mr. Rout's voice down there shouted something distantly. The ship pitched headlong, the pulsation leaped with a hissing tumult, and stopped dead. Captain

MacWhirr's face was impassive, and his eyes were fixed aimlessly on the crouching shape of the second mate. Again Mr. Rout's voice cried out in the depths, and the pulsating beats recommenced, with slow strokes—growing swifter.

Mr. Rout had returned to the tube. "It don't matter much what they do," he said, hastily; and then, with irritation, "She takes these dives as if she never meant to come up again."

"Awful sea," said the Captain's voice from above.

"Don't let me drive her under," barked Solomon Rout up the pipe.

"Dark and rain. Can't see what's coming," uttered the voice. "Must—keep—her—moving—enough to steer—and chance it," it went on to state distinctly.

"I am doing as much as I dare."

"We are—getting—smashed up—a good deal up here," proceeded the voice mildly. "Doing—fairly well—though. Of course, if the wheelhouse should go . . ."

Mr. Rout, bending an attentive ear, muttered peevishly something under his breath.

But the deliberate voice up there became animated to ask: "Jukes turned up yet?" Then, after a short wait, "I wish he would bear a hand. I want him to be done and come up here in case of anything. To look after the ship. I am all alone. The second mate's lost. . . ."

"What?" shouted Mr. Rout into the engine room, taking his head away. Then up to the tube he cried, "Gone overboard?" and clapped his ear to.

"Lost his nerve," the voice from above continued in a matter-of-fact tone. "Damned awkward circumstance."

Mr. Rout, listening with bowed neck, opened his eyes wide at this. However, he heard something like the sounds of a scuffle and broken exclamations coming down to him. He strained his hearing; and all the time Beale, the third engineer, with his arms uplifted, held between the palms of his hands the rim of a little black wheel projecting at the side of a big copper pipe. He seemed to be poising it above his head, as though it were a correct attitude in some sort of game.

To steady himself, he pressed his shoulder against the white bulkhead, one knee bent, and a sweat-rag tucked in his belt hanging on his hip. His smooth cheek was begrimed and flushed, and the coal dust on his eyelids, like the black pencilling of a makeup, enhanced the liquid brilliance of the whites, giving to his youthful face something of a feminine, exotic, and fascinating aspect. When the ship pitched he would with hasty movements of his hands screw hard at the little wheel.

"Gone crazy," began the Captain's voice suddenly in the tube. "Rushed at me. . . . Just now. Had to knock him down. . . . This minute. You heard, Mr. Rout?"

"The devil!" muttered Mr. Rout. "Look out, Beale!"

His shout rang out like the blast of a warning trumpet, between the iron walls of the engine room. Painted white, they rose high into the dusk of the skylight, sloping like a roof; and the whole lofty space resembled the interior of a monument, divided by floors of iron grating, with lights flickering at different levels, and a mass of gloom lingering in the middle, within the columnar stir of machinery under the motionless swelling of the cylinders. A loud and wild resonance, made up of all the noises of the hurricane, dwelt in the still warmth of the air. There was in it the smell of hot metal, of oil, and a slight mist of steam. The blows of the sea seemed to traverse it in an unringing, stunning shock, from side to side.

Gleams, like pale long flames, trembled upon the polish of metal; from the flooring below the enormous crankheads emerged in their turns with a flash of brass and steel—going over; while the connecting rods, big-jointed, like skeleton limbs, seemed to thrust them down and pull them up again with an irresistible precision. And deep in the half-light other rods dodged deliberately to and fro, crossheads nodded, discs of metal rubbed smoothly against each other, slow and gentle, in a commingling of shadows and gleams.

Sometimes all those powerful and unerring movements would slow down simultaneously, as if they had been the functions of a living organism, stricken suddenly by the blight of languor; and Mr. Rout's eyes would blaze darker in his long sallow face. He was fighting this fight in a pair of carpet slippers. A short shiny jacket barely covered his loins, and his white wrists protruded far out of the tight sleeves, as though the emergency had added to his stature, had lengthened his limbs, augmented his pallor, hollowed his eyes.

He moved, climbing high up, disappearing low down, with a restless, purposeful industry, and when he stood still, holding the guardrail in front of the starting gear, he would keep glancing to the right at the steam gauge, at the water gauge, fixed upon the white wall in the light of a swaying lamp. The mouths of two speaking tubes gaped stupidly at his elbow, and the dial of the engine-room telegraph resembled a clock of large diameter, bearing on its face curt words instead of figures. The grouped letters stood out heavily black, around the pivot head of the indicator, emphatically symbolic of loud exclamations: AHEAD, ASTERN, SLOW, HALF, STAND BY; and the fat black hand pointed downwards to the word FULL, which, thus singled out, captured the eye as a sharp cry secures attention.

The wood-encased bulk of the low-pressure cylinder, frowning portly from above, emitted a faint wheeze at every thrust, and except for that low hiss the engines worked their steel limbs headlong or slow with a silent, determined smoothness. And all this, the white walls, the moving steel, the floor plates under Solomon Rout's feet, the floors of iron grating above his head, the dusk and the gleams, uprose and sank continuously, with one accord, upon the harsh wash of the waves against the ship's side. The whole loftiness of the place, booming hollow to the great voice of the wind, swayed at the top like a tree, would go over bodily, as if borne down this way and that by the tremendous blasts.

"You've got to hurry up," shouted Mr. Rout, as soon as he saw Jukes appear in the stokehold doorway.

Jukes' glance was wandering and tipsy; his red face was puffy, as though he had overslept himself. He had had an arduous road, and had travelled over it with immense vivacity, the agitation of his mind corresponding to the exertions of his body. He had rushed up out of the bunker, stumbling in the dark alleyway amongst a lot of bewildered men who, trod upon, asked "What's up, sir?" in awed mutters all round him; down the stokehold ladder, missing many iron rungs in his hurry, down into a place deep as a well, black as Tophet, tipping over back and forth like a seesaw. The water in the bilges thundered at each roll, and the lumps of coal skipped to and fro, from end to end, rattling like an avalanche of pebbles on a slope of iron.

Somebody in there moaned with pain, and somebody else could be seen crouching over what seemed the prone body of a dead man; a lusty voice blasphemed; and the glow under each fire door was like a pool of flaming blood radiating quietly in a velvety blackness.

A gust of wind struck upon the nape of Jukes' neck and next moment he felt it streaming about his wet ankles. The stokehold ventilators hummed: in front of the six fire doors two wild figures, stripped to the waist, staggered and stooped, wrestling with two shovels.

"Hallo! Plenty of draught now," yelled the second engineer at once, as though he had been all the time looking out for Jukes. The donkeyman, a dapper little chap with a dazzling fair skin and a tiny, gingery moustache, worked in a sort of mute transport. They were keeping a full head of steam, and a profound rumbling, as of an empty furniture van trotting over a bridge, made a sustained bass to all the other noises of the place.

"Blowing off all the time," went on yelling the second. With a sound as of a hundred scoured saucepans, the orifice of a ventilator spat upon his shoulder a sudden gush of salt water, and he volleyed a stream of curses upon all things on earth including his own soul, ripping and raving, and all the time attending to his business. With a sharp clash of metal the ardent pale glare of the fire opened upon his bullet head, showing his spluttering lips, his insolent face, and with another clang closed like the white-hot wink of an iron eye.

"Where's the blooming ship? Can you tell me? Blast my eyes! Under-water—or what? It's coming down here in tons. Are the condemned cowls gone to Hades? Hey? Don't you know anything—you jolly sailorman you . . . ?"

Jukes, after a bewildered moment, had been helped by a roll to dart through; and as soon as his eyes took in the comparative vastness, peace, and brilliance of the engine room, the ship, setting her stern heavily in the water, sent him charging head down upon Mr. Rout.

The chief's arm, long like a tentacle, and straightening as if worked by a spring, went out to meet him, and deflected his rush into a spin towards the speaking tubes. At the same time Mr. Rout repeated earnestly:

"You've got to hurry up, whatever it is."

Jukes yelled "Are you there, sir?" and listened. Nothing. Suddenly the roar of the wind fell straight into his ear, but presently a small voice shoved aside the shouting hurricane quietly.

"You, Jukes?—Well?"

Jukes was ready to talk: it was only time that seemed to be wanting. It was easy enough to account for everything. He could perfectly imagine the coolies battened down in the reeking tween-deck, lying sick and scared between the rows of chests. Then one of these chests—or perhaps several at once—breaking loose in a roll, knocking out others, sides splitting, lids flying open, and all these clumsy Chinamen rising up in a body to save their property. Afterwards every fling of the ship would hurl that tramping, yelling mob here and there, from side to side, in a whirl of smashed wood, torn clothing, rolling dollars. A struggle once started, they would be unable to stop themselves. Nothing could stop them now except main force. It was a disaster. He had seen it, and that was all he could say. Some of them must be dead, he believed. The rest would go on fighting. . . .

He sent up his words, tripping over each other, crowding the narrow tube. They mounted as if into a silence of an enlightened comprehension dwelling alone up there with a storm. And Jukes wanted to be dismissed from the face of that odious trouble intruding on the great need of the ship.

V

He waited. Before his eyes the engines turned with slow labour, that in the moment of going off into a mad fling would stop dead at Mr. Rout's shout, "Look out, Beale!" They paused in an intelligent immobility, stilled in mid-stroke, a heavy crank arrested on the cant, as if conscious of danger and the passage of time. Then, with a "Now, then!" from the chief, and the sound of a breath expelled through clinched teeth, they would accomplish the interrupted revolution and begin another.

There was the prudent sagacity of wisdom and the deliberation of enormous strength in their movements. This was their work—this patient coaxing of a distracted ship over the fury of the waves and into the very eye of the wind. At times Mr. Rout's chin would sink on his breast, and he watched them with knitted eyebrows as if lost in thought.

The voice that kept the hurricane out of Jukes' ear began: "Take the hands with you . . ." and left off unexpectedly.

"What could I do with them, sir?"

A harsh, abrupt, imperious clang exploded suddenly. The three pairs of eyes flew up to the telegraph dial to see the hand jump from FULL to STOP, as if snatched by a devil. And then these three men in the engine room had the intimate sensation of a check upon the ship, of a strange shrinking, as if she had gathered herself for a desperate leap.

"Stop her!" bellowed Mr. Rout.

Nobody—not even Captain MacWhirr, who alone on deck had caught sight of a white line of foam coming on at such a height that he couldn't believe his eyes—nobody was to know the steepness of that sea and the awful depth of the hollow the hurricane had scooped out behind the running wall of water.

It raced to meet the ship, and, with a pause, as of girding the loins, the *Nan-Shan* lifted her bows and leaped. The flames in all the lamps sank, darkening the engine room. One went out. With a tearing crash and a swirling, raving tumult, tons of water fell upon the deck, as though the ship had darted under the foot of a cataract.

Down there they looked at each other, stunned.

"Swept from end to end, by God!" bawled Jukes.

She dipped into the hollow straight down, as if going over the edge of the world. The engine room toppled forward menacingly, like the inside of a tower nodding in an earthquake. An awful racket, of iron things falling, came from the stokehold. She hung on this appalling slant long enough for Beale to drop on his hands and knees and begin to crawl as if he meant to fly on all fours out of the engine room, and for Mr. Rout to turn his head slowly, rigid, cavernous, with the lower jaw dropping. Jukes had shut his eyes, and his face in a moment became hopelessly blank and gentle, like the face of a blind man.

At last she rose slowly, staggering, as if she had to lift a mountain with her bows.

Mr. Rout shut his mouth; Jukes blinked; and little Beale stood up hastily.

"Another one like this, and that's the last of her," cried the chief.

He and Jukes looked at each other, and the same thought came into their heads. The Captain! Everything must have been swept away. Steering gear gone—ship like a log. All over directly.

"Rush!" ejaculated Mr. Rout thickly, glaring with enlarged, doubtful eyes at Jukes, who answered him by an irresolute glance.

The clang of the telegraph gong soothed them instantly. The black hand dropped in a flash from STOP to FULL.

"Now then, Beale!" cried Mr. Rout.

The steam hissed low. The piston rods slid in and out. Jukes put his ear to the tube. The voice was ready for him. It said: "Pick up all the money. Bear a hand now. I'll want you up here." And that was all.

"Sir?" called up Jukes. There was no answer.

He staggered away like a defeated man from the field of battle. He had got, in some way or other, a cut above his left eyebrow—a cut to the bone. He was not aware of it in the least: quantities of the China Sea, large enough to break his neck for him, had gone over his head, had cleaned, washed, and salted that wound. It did not bleed, but only gaped red; and this gash over the eye, his dishevelled hair, the disorder of his clothes, gave him the aspect of a man worsted in a fight with fists.

"Got to pick up the dollars." He appealed to Mr. Rout, smiling pitifully at random.

"What's that?" asked Mr. Rout, wildly. "Pick up . . . ? I don't care. . . ." Then, quivering in every muscle, but with an exaggeration of paternal tone, "Go away now, for God's sake. You deck people'll drive me silly. There's that second mate been going for the old man. Don't you know? You fellows are going wrong for want of something to do. . . ."

At these words Jukes discovered in himself the beginnings of anger. Want of something to do—indeed. . . . Full of hot scorn against the chief, he turned to go the way he had come. In the stokehold the plump donkeyman toiled with his shovel mutely, as if his tongue had been cut out; but the second was carrying on like a noisy, undaunted maniac, who had preserved his skill in the art of stoking under a marine boiler.

"Hallo, you wandering officer! Hey! Can't you get some of your slush-slingers to wind up a few of them ashes? I am getting choked with them here. Curse it! Hallo! Hey! Remember the articles: *Sailors and firemen to assist each other*. Hey! D'ye hear?"

Jukes was climbing out frantically, and the other, lifting up his face after him, howled, "Can't you speak? What are you poking about here for? What's your game, anyhow?"

A frenzy possessed Jukes. By the time he was back amongst the men in the darkness of the alleyway, he felt ready to wring all their necks at the slightest sign of hanging back. The very thought of it exasperated him. *He* couldn't hang back. They shouldn't.

The impetuosity with which he came amongst them carried them along. They had already been excited and startled at all his comings and goings— by the fierceness and rapidity of his movements; and more felt than seen in his rushes, he appeared formidable—busied with matters of life and death that brooked no delay. At his first word he heard them drop into the bunker one after another obediently, with heavy thumps.

They were not clear as to what would have to be done. "What is it? What is it?" they were asking each other. The boatswain tried to explain; the sounds of a great scuffle surprised them: and the mighty shocks, reverberating awfully in the black bunker, kept them in mind of their danger. When the boatswain threw open the door it seemed that an eddy of the hurricane, stealing through the iron sides of the ship, had set all these bodies whirling like dust; there came to them a confused uproar, a tempestuous tumult, a fierce mutter, gusts of screams dying away, and the tramping of feet mingling with the blows of the sea.

For a moment they glared amazed, blocking the doorway. Jukes pushed through them brutally. He said nothing, and simply darted in. Another lot of coolies on the ladder, struggling suicidally to break through the battened hatch to a swamped deck, fell off as before, and he disappeared under them like a man overtaken by a landslide.

The boatswain yelled excitedly: "Come along. Get the mate out. He'll be trampled to death. Come on."

They charged in, stamping on breasts, on fingers, on faces, catching their feet in heaps of clothing, kicking broken wood; but before they could get hold of him Jukes emerged waist deep in a multitude of clawing hands. In the instant he had been lost to view, all the buttons of his jacket had gone, its back had got split up to the collar, his waistcoat had been torn open. The central struggling mass of Chinamen went over to the roll, dark, indistinct, helpless, with a wild gleam of many eyes in the dim light of the lamps.

"Leave me alone—damn you. I am all right," screeched Jukes. "Drive them forward. Watch your chance when she pitches. Forward with 'em. Drive them against the bulkhead. Jam 'em up."

The rush of the sailors into the seething tween-deck was like a splash of cold water into a boiling cauldron. The commotion sank for a moment.

The bulk of Chinamen were locked in such a compact scrimmage that, linking their arms and aided by an appalling dive of the ship, the seaman sent it forward in one great shove, like a solid block. Behind their backs small clusters and loose bodies tumbled from side to side.

The boatswain performed prodigious feats of strength. With his long arms open, and each great paw clutching at a stanchion, he stopped the rush of seven entwined Chinamen rolling like a boulder. His joints cracked; he said, "Ha!" and they flew apart. But the carpenter showed the greater intelligence. Without saying a word to anybody he went back into the alleyway, to fetch several coils of cargo gear he had seen there—chain and rope. With these lifelines were rigged.

There was really no resistance. The struggle, however it began, had turned into a scramble of blind panic. If the coolies had started up after their scattered dollars they were by that time fighting only for their footing. They took each other by the throat merely to save themselves from being hurled about. Whoever got a hold anywhere would kick at the others who caught at his legs and hung on, till a roll sent them flying together across the deck.

The coming of the white devils was a terror. Had they come to kill? The individuals torn out of the ruck became very limp in the seamen's hands: some, dragged aside by the heels, were passive, like dead bodies, with open, fixed eyes. Here and there a coolie would fall on his knees as if begging for mercy; several, whom the excess of fear made unruly, were hit with hard fists between the eyes, and cowered; while those who were hurt submitted to rough handling, blinking rapidly without a plaint. Faces streamed with blood; there were raw places on the shaven heads, scratches, bruises, torn wounds, gashes. The broken porcelain out of the chests' was mostly responsible for the latter. Here and there a Chinaman, wild-eyed, with his tail unplaited, nursed a bleeding sole.

They had been ranged closely, after having been shaken into submission, cuffed a little to allay excitement, addressed in gruff words of encouragement that sounded like promises of evil. They sat on the deck in ghastly, drooping rows, and at the end the carpenter, with two hands to help him, moved busily from place to place, setting taut and hitching the lifelines. The boatswain, with one leg and one arm embracing a stanchion, struggled with a lamp pressed to his breast, trying to get a light, and growling all the time like an industrious gorilla. The figures of seamen stooped repeatedly, with the movements of gleaners, and everything was being flung into the bunker: clothing, smashed wood, broken china, and the dollars, too, gathered up in men's jackets. Now and then a sailor would stagger towards the doorway with his arms full of rubbish; and dolorous, slanting eyes followed his movements.

With every roll of the ship the long rows of sitting Celestials would sway forward brokenly, and her headlong dives knocked together the line of shaven polls from end to end. When the wash of water rolling on the deck died away for a moment, it seemed to Jukes, yet quivering from his exertions, that in his mad struggle down there he had overcome the wind somehow: that a silence had fallen upon the ship, a silence in which the sea struck thunderously at her sides.

Everything had been cleared out of the tween-deck—all the wreckage, as the men said. They stood erect and tottering above the level of heads and drooping shoulders. Here and there a coolie sobbed for his breath. Where the high light fell, Jukes could see the salient ribs of one, the yellow, wistful face of another; bowed necks; or would meet a dull stare directed at his face. He was amazed that there had been no corpses; but the lot of them seemed at their last gasp, and they appeared to him more pitiful than if they had been all dead.

Suddenly one of the coolies began to speak. The light came and went on his lean, straining face; he threw his head up like a baying hound. From the bunker came the sounds of knocking and the tinkle of some dollars rolling loose; he stretched out his arm, his mouth yawned black, and the incomprehensible gutteral hooting sounds, that did not seem to belong to a human language, penetrated Jukes with a strange emotion as if a brute had tried to be eloquent.

Two more started mouthing what seemed to Jukes fierce denunciations; the others stirred with grunts and growls. Jukes ordered the hands out of the tween-decks hurriedly. He left last himself, backing through the door, while the grunts rose to a loud murmur and hands were extended after him as after a malefactor. The boatswain shot the bolt, and remarked uneasily, "Seems as if the wind had dropped, sir."

The seamen were glad to get back into the alleyway. Secretly each of them thought that at the last moment he could rush out on deck—and that was a comfort. There is something horribly repugnant in the idea of being drowned under a deck. Now they had done with the Chinamen, they again became conscious of the ship's position.

Jukes on coming out of the alleyway found himself up to the neck in the noisy water. He gained the bridge, and discovered he could detect obscure shapes as if his sight had become preternaturally acute. He saw faint outlines. They recalled not the familiar aspect of the *Nan-Shan,* but something remembered—an old dismantled steamer he had seen years ago rotting on a mudbank. She recalled that wreck.

There was no wind, not a breath, except the faint currents created by the lurches of the ship. The smoke tossed out of the funnel was settling down upon her deck. He breathed it as he passed forward. He felt the deliberate throb of the engines, and heard small sounds that seemed to have survived the great uproar: the knocking of broken fittings, the rapid tumbling of some piece of wreckage on the bridge. He perceived dimly the squat shape of his captain holding on to a twisted bridge rail, motionless and swaying as if rooted to the planks. The unexpected stillness of the air oppressed Jukes.

"We have done it, sir," he gasped.

"Thought you would," said Captain MacWhirr.

"Did you?" murmured Jukes to himself.

"Wind fell all at once," went on the Captain.

Jukes burst out: "If you think it was an easy job—"

But his captain, clinging to the rail, paid no attention. "According to the books the worst is not over yet."

"If most of them hadn't been half dead with seasickness and fright, not one of us would have come out of that tween-deck alive," said Jukes.

"Had to do what's fair by them," mumbled MacWhirr, stolidly. "You don't find everything in books."

"Why, I believe they would have risen on us if I hadn't ordered the hands out of that pretty quick," continued Jukes with warmth.

After the whisper of their shouts, their ordinary tones, so distinct, rang out very loud to their ears in the amazing stillness of the air. It seemed to them they were talking in a dark and echoing vault.

Through a jagged aperture in the dome of clouds the light of a few stars fell upon the black sea, rising and falling confusedly. Sometimes the head of a watery cone would topple on board and mingle with the rolling flurry of foam on the swamped deck; and the *Nan-Shan* wallowed heavily at the bottom of a circular cistern of clouds. This ring of dense vapours, gyrating madly round the calm of the centre, encompassed the ship like a motionless and unbroken wall of an aspect inconceivably sinister. Within, the sea, as if agitated by an internal commotion, leaped in peaked mounds that jostled each other, slapping heavily against her sides; and a low moaning sound, the infinite plaint of the storm's fury, came from beyond the limits of the menacing calm. Captain MacWhirr remained silent, and Jukes' ready ear caught suddenly the faint, long-drawn roar of some immense wave rushing unseen under that thick blackness, which made the appalling boundary of his vision.

"Of course," he started resentfully, "they thought we had caught at the chance to plunder them. Of course! You said—pick up the money. Easier said than done. They couldn't tell what was in our heads. We came in, smash—right into the middle of them. Had to do it by a rush."

"As long as it's done . . ." mumbled the Captain, without attempting to look at Jukes. "Had to do what's fair."

"We shall find yet there's the devil to pay when this is over," said Jukes, feeling very sore. "Let them only recover a bit, and you'll see. They will fly at our throats, sir. Don't forget, sir, she isn't a British ship now. These brutes know it well, too. The damned Siamese flag."

"We are on board, all the same," remarked Captain MacWhirr.

"The trouble's not over yet," insisted Jukes, prophetically, reeling and catching on. "She's a wreck," he added, faintly.

"The trouble's not over yet," assented Captain MacWhirr, half aloud. . . . "Look out for her a minute."

"Are you going off the deck, sir?" asked Jukes, hurriedly, as if the storm were sure to pounce upon him as soon as he had been left alone with the ship.

He watched her, battered and solitary, labouring heavily in a wild scene of mountainous black waters lit by the gleams of distant worlds. She moved slowly, breathing into the still core of the hurricane the excess of her strength in a white cloud of steam—and the deep-toned vibration of the escape was like the defiant trumpeting of a living creature of the sea impatient for the renewal of the contest. It ceased suddenly. The still air moaned. Above Jukes' head a few stars shone into a pit of black vapours. The inky edge of the cloud disc frowned upon the ship under the path of glittering sky. The stars, too, seemed to look at her intently, as if for the last time, and the cluster of their splendour sat like a diadem on a lowering brow.

Captain MacWhirr had gone into the chart room. There was no light there; but he could feel the disorder of that place where he used to live tidily. His armchair was upset. The books had tumbled out on the floor; he scrunched a piece of glass under his boot. He groped for the matches and found a box on a shelf with a deep ledge. He struck one, and puckering the corners of his eyes, held out the little flame towards the barometer whose glittering top of glass and metals nodded at him continuously.

It stood very low—incredibly low, so low that Captain MacWhirr grunted. The match went out, and hurriedly he extracted another, with thick, stiff fingers.

Again a little flame flared up before the nodding glass and metal of the top. His eyes looked at it, narrowed with attention, as if expecting an imperceptible sign. With his grave face he resembled a booted and misshapen pagan burning incense before the oracle of a Joss. There was no mistake. It was the lowest reading he had ever seen in his life.

Captain MacWhirr emitted a low whistle. He forgot himself till the flame diminished to a blue spark, burnt his fingers and vanished. Perhaps something had gone wrong with the thing!

There was an aneroid glass screw above the couch. He turned that way, struck another match, and discovered the white face of the other instrument looking at him from the bulkhead, meaningly, not to be gainsaid, as though the wisdom of men were made unerring by the indifference of matter. There was no room for doubt now. Captain MacWhirr pshawed at it and threw the match down.

The worst was to come, then—and if the books were right this worst would be very bad. The experience of the last six hours had enlarged his conception of what heavy weather could be like. "It'll be terrific," he pronounced, mentally. He had not consciously looked at anything by the light of the matches except at the barometer; and yet somehow he had seen that his water bottle and the two tumblers had been flung out of their stand. It seemed to give him a more intimate knowledge of the tossing the ship had gone through. "I wouldn't have believed it," he thought. And his table had been cleared, too; his rulers, his pencils, the inkstand—all the things that had their safe appointed places—they were gone, as if a mischievous hand had plucked them out one by one and flung them on the wet floor. The hurricane had broken in upon the orderly arrangements of his privacy. This had never happened before, and the feeling of dismay reached the very seat of his composure. And the worst was to come yet! He was glad the trouble in the tween-deck had been discovered in time. If the ship had to go after all, then, at least, she wouldn't be going to the bottom with a lot of people in her fighting teeth and claw. That would have been odious. And in that feeling there was a humane intention and a vague sense of the fitness of things.

These instantaneous thoughts were yet in their essence heavy and slow, partaking of the nature of the man. He extended his hand to put back the matchbox in its corner of the shelf. There were always matches there—by his order. The steward had his instructions impressed upon him long before. "A box . . . just there, see? Not so very full . . . where I can put my hand on it, steward. Might want a light in a hurry. Can't tell on board ship *what* you might want in a hurry. Mind, now."

And of course on his side he would be careful to put it back in its place scrupulously. He did so now, but before he removed his hand it occurred to him that perhaps he would never have occasion to use that box any more. The vividness of the thought checked him and for an infinitesimal fraction of a second his fingers closed again on the small object as though it had been the symbol of all these little habits that chain us to the weary round of life. He released it at last, and letting himself fall on the settee, listened for the first sounds of returning wind.

Not yet. He heard only the wash of water, the heavy splashes, the dull shocks of the confused seas boarding his ship from all sides. She would never have a chance to clear her decks.

But the quietude of the air was startlingly tense and unsafe, like a slender hair holding a sword suspended over his head. By this awful pause the storm penetrated the defences of the man and unsealed his lips. He spoke out in the solitude and the pitch darkness of the cabin, as if addressing another being awakened within his breast.

"I shouldn't like to lose her," he said half aloud.

He sat unseen, apart from the sea, from his ship, isolated, as if withdrawn from the very current of his own existence, where such freaks as talking to himself surely had no place. His palms reposed on his knees, he bowed his short neck and puffed heavily, surrendering to a strange sensation of weariness he was not enlightened enough to recognize for the fatigue of mental stress.

From where he sat he could reach the door of a washstand locker. There should have been a towel there. There was. Good. . . . He took it out, wiped his face, and afterwards went on rubbing his wet head. He towelled himself with energy in the dark, and then remained motionless with the towel on his knees. A moment passed, of a stillness so profound that no one could have guessed there was a man sitting in that cabin. Then a murmur arose.

"She may come out of it yet."

When Captain MacWhirr came out on deck, which he did brusquely, as though he had suddenly become conscious of having stayed away too long, the calm had lasted already more than fifteen minutes—long enough to make itself intolerable even to his imagination. Jukes, motionless on the forepart of the bridge, began to speak at once. His voice, blank and forced as though he were talking through hard-set teeth, seemed to flow away on all sides into the darkness, deepening again upon the sea.

"I had the wheel relieved. Hackett began to sing out that he was done. He's lying in there alongside the steering gear with a face like death. At first I couldn't get anybody to crawl out and relieve the poor devil. That boss'en's worse than no good, I always said. Thought I would have had to go myself and haul out one of them by the neck."

"Ah, well," muttered the Captain. He stood watchful by Jukes' side.

"The second mate's in there, too, holding his head. Is he hurt, sir?"

"No—crazy," said Captain MacWhirr, curtly.

"Looks as if he had a tumble, though."

"I had to give him a push," explained the Captain.

Jukes gave an impatient sigh.

"It will come very sudden," said Captain MacWhirr, "and from over there, I fancy. God only knows though. These books are only good to muddle your head and make you jumpy. It will be bad, and there's an end. If we only can steam her round in time to meet it. . . ."

A minute passed. Some of the stars winked rapidly and vanished.

"You left them pretty safe?" began the Captain abruptly, as though the silence were unbearable.

"Are you thinking of the coolies, sir? I rigged lifelines all ways across that tween-deck."

"Did you? Good idea, Mr. Jukes."

"I didn't . . . think you cared to . . . know," said Jukes—the lurching of the ship cut his speech as though somebody had been jerking him around while he talked—"how I got on with . . . that infernal job. We did it. And it may not matter in the end."

"Had to do what's fair, for all—they are only Chinamen. Give them the same chance with ourselves—hang it all. She isn't lost yet. Bad enough to be shut up below in a gale—"

"That's what I thought when you gave me the job, sir," interjected Jukes, moodily.

"—without being battered to pieces," pursued Captain MacWhirr with rising vehemence. "Couldn't let that go on in my ship, if I knew she hadn't five minutes to live. Couldn't bear it, Mr. Jukes."

A hollow echoing noise, like that of a shout rolling in a rocky chasm, approached the ship and went away again. The last star, blurred, enlarged, as if returning to the fiery mist of its beginning, struggled with the colossal depth of blackness hanging over the ship—and went out.

"Now for it!" muttered Captain MacWhirr. "Mr. Jukes."

"Here, sir."

The two men were growing indistinct to each other.

"We must trust her to go through it and come out on the other side. That's plain and straight. There's no room for Captain Wilson's storm strategy here."

"No, sir."

"She will be smothered and swept again for hours," mumbled the Captain. "There's not much left by this time above deck for the sea to take away—unless you or me."

"Both, sir," whispered Jukes, breathlessly.

"You are always meeting trouble halfway, Jukes," Captain MacWhirr remonstrated quaintly. "Though it's a fact that the second mate is no good. D'ye hear, Mr. Jukes? You would be left alone if . . ."

Captain MacWhirr interrupted himself, and Jukes, glancing on all sides, remained silent.

"Don't you be put out by anything," the Captain continued, mumbling rather fast. "Keep her facing it. They may say what they like, but the heaviest seas run with the wind. Facing it—always facing it—that's the way to get through. You are a young sailor. Face it. That's enough for any man. Keep a cool head."

"Yes, sir," said Jukes, with a flutter of the heart.

In the next few seconds the Captain spoke to the engine room and got an answer.

For some reason Jukes experienced an access of confidence, a sensation that came from outside like a warm breath, and made him feel equal to every demand. The distant muttering of the darkness stole into his ears. He noted it unmoved, out of that sudden belief in himself, as a man safe in a shirt of mail would watch a point.

The ship laboured without intermission amongst the black hills of water, paying with this hard tumbling the price of her life. She rumbled in her depths, shaking a white plummet of steam into the night, and Jukes' thought skimmed like a bird through the engine room, where Mr. Rout—good man—was ready. When the rumbling ceased it seemed to him that there was a pause of every sound, a dead pause in which Captain MacWhirr's voice rang out startlingly.

"What's that? A puff of wind?"—it spoke much louder than Jukes had ever heard it before—"On the bow. That's right. She may come out of it yet."

The mutter of the winds drew near apace. In the forefront could be distinguished a drowsy waking plaint passing on, and far off the growth of a multiple clamour, marching and expanding. There was the throb as of many drums in it, a vicious rushing note, and like the chant of a tramping multitude.

Jukes could no longer see his captain distinctly. The darkness was absolutely piling itself upon the ship. At most he made out movements, a hint of elbows spread out, of a head thrown up.

Captain MacWhirr was trying to do up the top button of his oilskin coat with unwonted haste. The hurricane, with its power to madden the seas, to sink ships, to uproot trees, to overturn strong walls and dash the very birds of the air to the ground, had found this taciturn man in its path, and, doing its utmost, had managed to wring out a few words. Before the renewed wrath of winds swooped on his ship, Captain MacWhirr was moved to declare, in a tone of vexation, as it were: "I wouldn't like to lose her."

He was spared that annoyance.

VI

On a bright sunshiny day, with the breeze chasing her smoke far ahead, the *Nan-Shan* came into Fu-chau. Her arrival was at once noticed on shore, and the seamen in harbour said: "Look! Look at that steamer. What's that? Siamese—isn't she? Just look at her!"

She seemed, indeed, to have been used as a running target for the secondary batteries of a cruiser. A hail of minor shells could not have given her upper works a more broken, torn, and devastated aspect; and she had about her the worn, weary air of ships coming from the far ends of the world—and indeed with truth, for in her short passage she had been very far;

sighting, verily, even the coast of the Great Beyond, whence no ship ever returns to give up her crew to the dust of the earth. She was incrusted and grey with salt to the trucks of her masts and to the top of her funnel; as though (as some facetious seaman said) "the crowd on board had fished her out somewhere from the bottom of the sea and brought her in here for salvage." And further, excited by the felicity of his own wit, he offered to give five pounds for her—"as she stands."

Before she had been quite an hour at rest, a meagre little man, with a red-tipped nose and a face cast in an angry mould, landed from a sampan on the quay of the Foreign Concession, and incontinently turned to shake his fist at her.

A tall individual, with legs much too thin for a rotund stomach, and with watery eyes, strolled up and remarked, "Just left her—eh? Quick work."

He wore a soiled suit of blue flannel with a pair of dirty cricketing shoes; a dingy grey moustache drooped from his lips, and daylight could be seen in two places between the rim and the crown of his hat.

"Hallo! what are you doing here?" asked the ex-second mate of the *Nan-Shan,* shaking hands hurriedly.

"Standing by for a job—chance worth taking—got a quiet hint," explained the man with the broken hat, in jerky, apathetic wheezes.

The second shook his fist again at the *Nan-Shan.* "There's a fellow there that ain't fit to have the command of a scow," he declared, quivering with passion, while the other looked about listlessly.

"Is there?"

But he caught sight on the quay of a heavy seaman's chest, painted brown under a fringed sailcloth cover, and lashed with new manila line. He eyed it with awakened interest.

"I would talk and raise trouble if it wasn't for that damned Siamese flag. Nobody to go to—or I would make it hot for him. The fraud! Told his chief engineer—that's another fraud for you—I had lost my nerve. The greatest lot of ignorant fools that ever sailed the seas. No! You can't think . . ."

"Got your money all right?" inquired his seedy acquaintance suddenly.

"Yes. Paid me off on board," raged the second mate. " 'Get your breakfast on shore,' says he."

"Mean skunk!" commented the tall man, vaguely, and passed his tongue on his lips. "What about having a drink of some sort?"

"He struck me," hissed the second mate.

"No! Struck! You don't say?" The man in blue began to bustle about sympathetically. "Can't possibly talk here. I want to know all about it. Struck—eh? Let's get a fellow to carry your chest. I know a quiet place where they have some bottled beer. . . ."

Mr. Jukes, who had been scanning the shore through a pair of glasses, informed the chief engineer afterwards that "our late second mate hasn't been long in finding a friend. A chap looking uncommonly like a bummer. I saw them walk away together from the quay."

The hammering and banging of the needful repairs did not disturb Captain MacWhirr. The steward found in the letter he wrote, in a tidy chart room, passages of such absorbing interest that twice he was nearly caught in the act. But Mrs. MacWhirr, in the drawing room of the forty-pound house, stifled a yawn—perhaps out of self-respect—for she was alone.

She reclined in a plush-bottomed and gilt hammock-chair near a tiled fireplace, with Japanese fans on the mantel and a glow of coals in the grate. Lifting her hands, she glanced wearily here and there into the many pages. It was not her fault they were so prosy, so completely uninteresting—from "My darling wife" at the beginning, to "Your loving husband" at the end. She couldn't be really expected to understand all these ship affairs. She was glad, of course, to hear from him, but she had never asked herself why, precisely.

". . . They are called typhoons. . . . The mate did not seem to like it. . . . Not in books. . . . Couldn't think of letting it go on. . . ."

The paper rustled sharply. ". . . A calm that lasted more than twenty minutes," she read perfunctorily; and the next words her thoughtless eyes caught, on top of another page, were: "see you and the children again. . . ." She had a movement of impatience. He was always thinking of coming home. He had never had such a good salary before. What was the matter now?

It did not occur to her to turn back overleaf to look. She would have found it recorded there that between 4 and 6 A.M. on December 25, Captain MacWhirr did actually think that his ship could not possibly live another hour in such a sea, and that he would never see his wife and children again. Nobody was to know this (his letters got mislaid so quickly)—nobody whatever but the steward, who had been greatly impressed by that disclosure. So much so, that he tried to give the cook some idea of the "narrow squeak we all had" by saying solemnly, "The old man himself had a dam' poor opinion of our chance."

"How do you know?" asked, contemptuously, the cook, an old soldier. "He hasn't told you, maybe?"

"Well, he did give me a hint to that effect," the steward brazened it out.

"Get along with you! He will be coming to tell *me* next," jeered the old cook, over his shoulder.

Mrs. MacWhirr glanced farther, on the alert. ". . . Do what's fair. . . . Miserable objects. . . . Only three, with a broken leg each, and one . . .

Thought had better keep the matter quiet. . . . hope to have done the fair thing. . . ."

She let fall her hands. No: there was nothing more about coming home. Must have been merely expressing a pious wish. Mrs. MacWhirr's mind was set at ease, and a black marble clock, priced by the local jeweller at £3 18s. 6d., had a discreet stealthy tick.

The door flew open, and a girl in the long-legged, short-frocked period of existence, flung into the room. A lot of colourless, rather lanky hair was scattered over her shoulders. Seeing her mother, she stood still, and directed her pale prying eyes upon the letter.

"From Father," murmured Mrs. MacWhirr. "What have you done with your ribbon?"

The girl put her hands up to her head and pouted.

"He's well," continued Mrs. MacWhirr, languidly. "At least I think so. He never says." She had a little laugh. The girl's face expressed a wandering indifference, and Mrs. MacWhirr surveyed her with fond pride.

"Go and get your hat," she said after a while. "I am going out to do some shopping. There is a sale at Linom's."

"Oh, how jolly!" uttered the child, impressively, in unexpectedly grave vibrating tones, and bounded out of the room.

It was a fine afternoon, with a grey sky and dry sidewalks. Outside the draper's Mrs. MacWhirr smiled upon a woman in a black mantle of generous proportions armoured in jet and crowned with flowers blooming falsely above a bilious matronly countenance. They broke into a swift little babble of greetings and exclamations both together, very hurried, as if the street were ready to yawn open and swallow all that pleasure before it could be expressed.

Behind them the high glass doors were kept on the swing. People couldn't pass, men stood aside waiting patiently, and Lydia was absorbed in poking the end of her parasol between the stone flags. Mrs. MacWhirr talked rapidly.

"Thank you very much. He's not coming home yet. Of course it's very sad to have him away, but it's such a comfort to know he keeps so well." Mrs. MacWhirr drew breath. "The climate there agrees with him," she added, beamingly, as if poor MacWhirr had been away touring in China for the sake of his health.

Neither was the chief engineer coming home yet. Mr. Rout knew too well the value of a good billet.

"Solomon says wonders will never cease," cried Mrs. Rout joyously at the old lady in her armchair by the fire. Mr. Rout's mother moved slightly, her withered hands lying in black half-mittens on her lap.

The eyes of the engineer's wife fairly danced on the paper. "That captain of the ship he is in—a rather simple man, you remember, Mother?—has done something rather clever, Solomon says."

"Yes, my dear," said the old woman meekly, sitting with bowed silvery head, and that air of inward stillness characteristic of very old people who seem lost in watching the last flickers of life. "I think I remember."

Solomon Rout, Old Sol, Father Sol, the Chief, "Rout, good man"—Mr. Rout, the condescending and paternal friend of youth, had been the baby of her many children—all dead by this time. And she remembered him best as a boy of ten—long before he went away to serve his apprenticeship in some great engineering works in the North. She had seen so little of him since, she had gone through so many years, that she had now to retrace her steps very far back to recognize him plainly in the mist of time. Sometimes it seemed that her daughter-in-law was talking of some strange man.

Mrs. Rout junior was disappointed. "H'm. H'm." She turned the page. "How provoking! He doesn't say what it is. Says I couldn't understand how much there was in it. Fancy! What could it be so very clever? What a wretched man not to tell us!"

She read on without further remark soberly, and at last sat looking into the fire. The chief wrote just a word or two of the typhoon; but something had moved him to express an increased longing for the companionship of the jolly woman. "If it hadn't been that Mother must be looked after, I would send you your passage money today. You could set up a small house out here. I would have a chance to see you sometimes then. We are not growing younger. . . ."

"He's well, Mother," sighed Mrs. Rout, rousing herself.

"He always was a strong healthy boy," said the old woman, placidly.

But Mr. Jukes' account was really animated and very full. His friend in the Western Ocean trade imparted it freely to the other officers of his liner. "A chap I know writes to me about an extraordinary affair that happened on board his ship in that typhoon—you know—that we read of in the papers two months ago. It's the funniest thing! Just see for yourself what he says. I'll show you his letter."

There were phrases in it calculated to give the impression of lighthearted, indomitable resolution. Jukes had written them in good faith, for he felt thus when he wrote. He described with lurid effect the scenes in the tween-deck. ". . . It struck me in a flash that those confounded Chinamen couldn't tell we weren't a desperate kind of robbers. 'Tisn't good to part the Chinaman from his money if he is the stronger party. We need have been desperate indeed to go thieving in such weather, but what could these beggars know of us? So, without thinking of it twice, I got the hands away in a jiffy. Our work was done—that the old man had set his heart on. We cleared out without staying to inquire how they felt. I am convinced that if they had not been so unmercifully shaken, and afraid—each individual one of them—to stand up, we would have been torn to pieces. Oh! It was pretty complete, I can tell you; and you may run to and fro across the Pond to the end of time before you find yourself with such a job on your hands."

After this he alluded professionally to the damage done to the ship, and went on thus:

"It was when the weather quieted down that the situation became confoundedly delicate. It wasn't made any better by us having been lately transferred to the Siamese flag; though the skipper can't see that it makes any difference—'as long as *we* are on board'—he says. There are feelings that this man simply hasn't got—and there's an end of it. You might just as well try to make a bedpost understand. But apart from this it is an infernally lonely state for a ship to be going about the China seas with no proper consuls, not even a gunboat of her own anywhere, nor a body to go to in case of some trouble.

"My notion was to keep these Johnnies under hatches for another fifteen hours or so; as we weren't much farther than that from Fu-chau. We would find there, most likely, some sort of a man-of-war, and once under her guns we were safe enough; for surely any skipper of a man-of-war—English, French, or Dutch—would see white men through as far as a row on board goes. We could get rid of them and their money afterwards by delivering them to their Mandarin or Taotai, or whatever they call these chaps in goggles you see being carried about in sedan chairs through their stinking streets.

"The old man wouldn't see it somehow. He wanted to keep the matter quiet. He got that notion into his head, and a steam windlass couldn't drag it out of him. He wanted as little fuss made as possible, for the sake of the ship's name and for the sake of the owners—'for the sake of all concerned,' says he, looking at me very hard. It made me angry hot. Of course you couldn't keep a thing like that quiet; but the chests had been secured in the usual manner and were safe enough for any earthly gale, while this had been an altogether fiendish business I couldn't give you even an idea of.

"Meantime, I could hardly keep on my feet. None of us had a spell of any sort for nearly thirty hours, and there the old man sat rubbing his chin, rubbing the top of his head, and so bothered he didn't even think of pulling his long boots off.

" 'I hope, sir,' says I, 'you won't be letting them out on deck before we make ready for them in some shape or other.' Not, mind you, that I felt very sanguine about controlling these beggars if they meant to take charge. A trouble with a cargo of Chinamen is no child's play. I was dam' tired, too.

'I wish,' said I, 'you would let us throw the whole lot of these dollars down to them and leave them to fight it out amongst themselves, while we get a rest.'

" 'Now you talk wild, Jukes,' says he, looking up in his slow way that makes you ache all over, somehow. 'We must plan out something that would be fair to all parties.'

"I had no end of work on hand, as you may imagine, so I set the hands going, and then I thought I would turn in a bit. I hadn't been asleep in my bunk ten minutes when in rushes the steward and begins to pull at my leg.

" 'For God's sake, Mr. Jukes, come out! Come on deck quick, sir. Oh, do come out!'

"The fellow scared all the sense out of me. I didn't know what had happened: another hurricane—or what. Could hear no wind.

" 'The Captain's letting them out. Oh, he is letting them out! Jump on deck, sir, and save us. The chief engineer has just run below for his revolver.'

"That's what I understood the fool to say. However, Father Rout swears he went in there only to get a clean pocket handkerchief. Anyhow, I made one jump into my trousers and flew on deck aft. There was certainly a good deal of noise going on forward of the bridge. Four of the hands with the boss'en were at work abaft. I passed up to them some of the rifles all the ships on the China coast carry in the cabin, and led them on the bridge. On the way I ran against Old Sol, looking startled and sucking at an unlighted cigar.

" 'Come along,' I shouted to him.

"We charged, the seven of us, up to the chart room. All was over. There stood the old man with his seaboots still drawn up to the hips and in shirt-sleeves—got warm thinking it out, I suppose. Bun Hin's dandy clerk at his elbow, as dirty as a sweep, was still green in the face. I could see directly I was in for something.

" 'What the devil are these monkey tricks, Mr. Jukes?' asks the old man, as angry as ever he could be. I tell you frankly it made me lose my tongue. 'For God's sake, Mr. Jukes,' says he, 'do take away these rifles from the men. Somebody's sure to get hurt before long if you don't. Damme, if this ship isn't worse than Bedlam! Look sharp now. I want you up here to help me and Bun Hin's Chinaman to count that money. You wouldn't mind lending a hand, too, Mr. Rout, now you are here. The more of us the better.'

"He had settled it all in his mind while I was having a snooze. Had we been an English ship, or only going to land our cargo of coolies in an English port, like Hong Kong, for instance, there would have been no end of inquiries and bother, claims for damages, and so on. But these Chinamen know their officials better than we do.

"The hatches had been taken off already, and they were all on deck after a night and a day down below. It made you feel queer to see so many gaunt, wild faces together. The beggars stared about at the sky, at the sea, at the ship, as though they had expected the whole thing to have been blown to pieces. And no wonder! They had had a doing that would have shaken the soul out of a white man. But then they say a Chinaman has no soul. He has, though, something about him that is deuced tough. There was a fellow (amongst others of the badly hurt) who had had his eye all but knocked out. It stood out of his head the size of half a hen's egg. This would have laid out a white man on his back for a month: and yet there was that chap elbowing here and there in the crowd and talking to the others as if nothing had been the matter. They made a great hubbub amongst themselves, and whenever the old man showed his bald head on the foreside of the bridge, they would all leave off jawing and look at him from below.

"It seems that after he had done his thinking he made that Bun Hin's fellow go down and explain to them the only way they could get their money back. He told me afterwards that, all the coolies having worked in the same place and for the same length of time, he reckoned he would be doing the fair thing by them as near as possible if he shared all the cash we had picked up equally among the lot. You couldn't tell one man's dollars from another's, he said, and if you asked each man how much money he brought on board he was afraid they would lie, and he would find himself a long way short. I think he was right there. As to giving up the money to any Chinese official he could scare up in Fu-chau, he said he might just as well put the lot in his own pocket at once for all the good it would be to them. I suppose they thought so, too.

"We finished the distribution before dark. It was rather a sight: the sea running high, the ship a wreck to look at, these Chinamen staggering up on the bridge one by one for their share, and the old man still booted, and in his shirt-sleeves, busy paying out at the chart room door, perspring like anything, and now and then coming down sharp on myself or Father Rout about one thing or another not quite to his mind. He took the share of those who were disabled himself to them on the No. 2 hatch. There were three dollars left over, and these went to the three most damaged coolies, one to each. We turned-to afterwards, and shovelled out on deck heaps of wet rags, all sorts of fragments of things without shape, and that you couldn't give a name to, and let them settle the ownership themselves.

"This certainly is coming as near as can be to keeping the thing quiet for the benefit of all concerned. What's your opinion, you pampered mail-boat swell? The old chief says that this was plainly the only thing that could be done. The skipper remarked to me the other day, 'There are things you find nothing about in books.' I think that he got out of it very well for such a stupid man."

LANDS OF
SNOW & ICE

ICEWATER MANSIONS

Doug Allyn

t was a Christmas from hell. Sitting in a smoky lakefront saloon, listening to Bing Crosby gargle Jingle Bells from a jukebox that sounded like somebody'd stuffed it with Qualudes. The rummies hunched over the bar looked even sorrier than Bing sounded, working men in seedy clothes muttering to nobody about the Lions/Jets game on the TV, staring into their futures in the bottom of a beer mug. Two hard-eyed young studs in leather jackets were shooting pool beside a frost-rimed window that rattled with every gust of wind off Huron Bay.

The bartender's beer keg of a belly was cased in a grimy white shirt taut as a sausage skin. He wore his hair slicked back like a late-show gangster, which was appropriate since he was pocketing half the cash that came across the bar. The only woman in the room was the waitress, a treetop-tall redhead in a faded Willie Nelson tee shirt and jeans. She looked a bit like Jack Palance, high cheekbones, wide mouth, large, red-knuckled hands. She was a hard worker, waiting tables, emptying ashtrays, fighting a hopeless battle with disorder. One of the hardcase pool shooters patted her bottom as she passed. She gave him a tight grin and a left hook to the ribs that nearly dropped him to his knees. He didn't touch her again.

"You ain't drinkin' your beer, bub," the bartender said, startling me. "Something wrong with it?"

"As a matter of fact, there is. The lipstick smear on the mug isn't my shade."

He grunted, pulled a greasy rag out of his hip pocket, wiped the mauve stain off the lip of my glass, and pushed it back at me, slopping suds all over the bar.

"That does it," I said. "You know, I've been in a lot of saloons in a lot of towns, but you're the rock-bottom worst bartender I've ever seen. You're not even a good thief."

"What?"

"You heard me. If you're gonna steal, don't do it in front of the customers. Put the money in the till and rip it off after you close."

"Look, Jack, you don't like the way I run this place, don't let the door hit you in the ass on your way out."

"You're half right," I said, easing up off my stool, "I don't like the way you run this place. But I'm not the one who's leaving. You are. After you empty your pockets on the bar."

"I ain't emptyin' nothin'," he said, flushing dangerously. "What is this? You some kinda law?"

"Worse than that," I sighed. "Unfortunately, I'm the new owner, Brian Mitchell. Does the name ring a bell?"

"Maybe," he said, not giving an inch, "but I never seen you before, and you can't just walk in here and—"

"Give it up, Carney," the waitress said, "you know it's him. He looks enough like Mitch to be his brother."

"His son, actually," I said. "As in prodigal."

"I don't give a damn if you're his mother," the bartender said. "I ain't takin' no crap off you or anybody else. Hey guys, I got me a wise-ass here, need a little help!"

A couple of roughnecks stood up, brightening at the prospect of a bar war, sharks tasting blood in the water. One of the pool players sauntered toward me, carrying his cue, and I suddenly remembered my father saying that if you have to fight, try to pick on people who won't kick you to death if you fall.

"Now everybody just cool out," the waitress said, intercepting the guy with the stick. "Nobody wants any trouble."

"Especially not over this joint," I said. "You know, I worked here when I was a kid, and I don't think it's been cleaned up since. But you know what I hated most? It's always dark as a bat cave in here. The harbor's only fifty yards away and you'd never know it. No view." I picked up an empty chair, hefted it a moment to check its balance, then turned and pitched it out through the front window, smashing it out into the parking lot. The December wind howled in like a rabid Rottweiler, snapping at the curtains, spraying snow around like foam flecks.

"Gentlemen," I said, picking up another chair, "the Crow's Nest is officially under new management. And as of now, we're closed for remodeling."

"Hey! Wait a minute!" the bartender yelled, outraged, but he was overruled by the wind and the rapidly falling room temperature. His cronies knew a lost cause when it blew in and they were already gulping their drinks and heading for the door. I thought the kid with the pool cue might give me trouble but the waitress said something to him and he grinned and tossed her the stick.

"Mr. Carney," I said, setting the chair aside, "I want your key and the money in your pockets on the bar and then I want you gone. Any problem with that?"

"Hell no," he said bitterly, tossing a crumpled wad of bills on the counter. "The keys are on the desk in the office. But you ain't seen the last of me, mister. You comin', Red?"

"I don't know," the waitress said, eyeing me frankly. "How about it, Mr. Mitchell? Am I fired too?"

"Depends," I said. "At the moment I need a cleaning lady a lot more than a waitress."

"I know which end of a mop is up," Red said, "but I don't do windows. Or at least not with chairs."

"Speaking of which, I guess I'd better see about a new one," I said. "Meanwhile, why don't you find that mop you mentioned."

Small northern-Michigan towns have their pluses. A dapper, cheery little Irishman from Huron Bay Hardware and Glass showed up within the hour, looked over the job, and said if I was willing to take a unit from stock he could have an oversized bay window installed by quitting time the next day. Try getting that kind of service in a city.

The local law was only slightly less prompt. I was taping cardboard over the hole in the window when a sheriff's department black-and-white pulled into the lot. Charlie Bauer climbed out. I vaguely recalled him from the old days, his size more than anything. He stands six-six, probably close to three hundred pounds, and looks even bigger in his bulky brown uniform. He'd gone a bit jowly, soft around the middle, but still nobody to cross, square-faced, steel-grey brush cut. He sauntered over, eyed me, the chair, and the broken glass all over the ground, then picked up the chair and carried it in with him.

"What's going on here?" he said, parking the chair beside the door.

"Housecleaning," I said.

"I guess the place can use it," he nodded, glancing around. "You'd be Brian, right? Colin Mitchell's son?"

"That's right," I said, offering my hand. He ignored it.

"Didn't see you at the funeral," he said.

"I've been working as a diver on the Texas Gulf, underwater welding, whatever. Mail to the rigs gets delayed sometimes."

"I see. Anybody fill you in on what happened?"

"Not really," I said. "My father's attorney, Mr. Klein, said he was killed in an auto accident."

"Not in the wreck, exactly," Bauer said. "He got drunk, ran his pickup off the road, and froze to death in the ditch."

"You should have been a doctor," I said. "You've got a terrific bedside manner."

He shrugged. "You don't look all that broken up. And as I recall you two didn't exactly part friends."

"That was a long time ago," I said.

"Was it? Doesn't seem like it. That's one of the problems with gettin' old. Nothing that happened in your lifetime seems very long ago. Love can last a lifetime. Grudges can too."

"If it'll ease your mind, Charlie, there was nothing like that between my father and me. Hell, after all this time I'm not sure there was *anything* between us, love, hate, or otherwise."

"There was blood," Bauer said. "There was at least that, since he left you everything he had."

"I didn't ask him to."

"Most things you inherit come without asking. Like your looks. And you're of a size, you and Colin. Maybe you inherited his temper too," he said, nodding toward the broken window. "He could be mean, your old man. Hope he took that with him. You gonna be in town long?"

"I honestly don't know," I said.

"Well, if you plan to, I don't want to pick up any more furniture outa your parking lot. We understand each other?"

"Absolutely," I said.

"Good. I knew Colin a lotta years. Always expected he'd cash in early, get himself shot by a jealous husband or one of his lady friends, or maybe just dive Lake Huron a time too many. It bothers me some, him goin' like he did. He drank sometimes, who doesn't? But I never saw him so drunk he couldn't crawl out of a ditch."

"Is there any question that it was an accident?"

"I didn't say that. I just said it bothers me. Maybe because there was no class to it. Colin was no saint, but the man had style. He deserved to go out better. His truck's in the county impound lot with minor damage. You owe 'em a sixty buck towing fee. And for what it's worth, I'm sorry about your father."

"You needn't be on my account. Like you said, we didn't exactly part friends."

After Bauer left, Red and I worked like dogs scrubbing down the tables and the walls. If she had questions, she kept them to herself, which suited me just fine. The carpet was stained beyond redemption. It would have to be replaced. But underneath the grime of years, the knotty-pine walls glowed with a honey-golden patina that you couldn't buy new at any price. Which was fortunate. I had my severance pay from the oil rig, so I wasn't broke, but I wasn't exactly Diamond Jim Brady either.

Around nine we ran out of Spic and Span and I ran out of gas, a combination of jet lag and the backbreaking labor generally referred to as woman's work. We agreed to hit it hard again at ten the next morning. I climbed into my rented Ford Escort and drove—

Not home. To my father's house. It had never been a home to me. I lived with my mother in Detroit after the divorce, seeing my father only during the summers, when I worked for him rustling gear in the diving equipment shop behind the Crow's Nest and swamping out the bar. Even then I seldom stayed at the house. I usually slept on a cot in the back of the shop. His idea, and not a bad one, as it turned out.

The house was a rough-sided beachfront cottage on the tip of Ponemah Point, a fingerling peninsula that juts into the vast expanse of Lake Huron from the southern shore of Big Huron Bay.

I'd forgotten how isolated the place was, ten miles from town, the last four on a twin-rut road little better than a path, its nearest neighbor more than a mile away. The place looked eyeless and abandoned, lonely as an Aleutian lighthouse. I parked in the yard, grabbed my duffel bag out of the trunk, and was hounded to the house by the wind whining out of the dark pines that ringed the yard like sentries.

I let myself in, and promptly fell over a chain saw in the darkened entryway. The house was as cold as a witch's kiss and no more friendly. I dumped my bag in the living room, lit the LP gas stove and cranked it to the max, then trotted back outside to the generator shed. The generator's fuel tank was full and after a couple of yanks on the starter cord it settled down to a near silent hum. A string of yard lamps glowed to life, lighting my way back to the house.

The milk in the refrigerator was frozen solid, but otherwise the place seemed livable. I heated a tin of beef stew on the stove, made myself a cup of coffee, and took stock.

The cottage had two bedrooms, a kitchen, living room, and bath, all as clean and spartan as a YMCA. No art on the walls, only a few pieces of "ship's jewelry," trophies scavenged from wrecks at the bottom of Lake Huron. The Great Lakes are littered with shipwrecks, six thousand or so, from the first ship that ever sailed them, the *Griffin*, to the *Edmund Fitzgerald*. The trade in plundered artifacts is illegal of course, but that was apparently a minor point with my father. There was a wonderful walnut helm wheel over the small brick fireplace, a couple of brass running lamps, and a mint-condition brass ship's compass in one corner. With a rifle leaning against it.

I recognized the gun. It was my grandfather's old '94 Winchester, a standard deer rifle in northern Michigan. I picked it up and looked it over, remembering dusty summer afternoons, my father running me through drill with this rifle: shoulder, focus, squeeze. Never waste a shot, treat every gun as if it's loaded. This gun felt like it actually was.

I racked the action, and ejected a live round, then six more, which surprised me considerably. Guns in the house are normal up here, but not loaded. Never loaded. I put the rifle back in the rack where it belonged, picked up the cartridges, and replaced them in the box of shells that was sitting atop the compass.

Except for the Winchester, the gun rack was empty. There should have been two more guns. I found the first, my father's army .45 automatic, in a holster hanging behind the front door. It was also loaded, a full clip and a round in the chamber. His shotgun seemed to be missing, assuming he still had it after all these years. But I found something else almost as odd as the loaded weapons.

Negligees. Two of them. And a woman's embroidered silk robe in the bedroom closet. Don't get me wrong, my father liked women, in fact variety was the spice of his life. The Nest was his hunting ground and he did very well, but he almost never brought them out here. Said he liked waking up in his own place—alone. The *alone* was something he stressed a lot, the summers I worked for him.

But apparently he'd changed. Well, why not? It had been almost twenty years since I'd seen him. And now I never would again. I thought I might feel something, coming back here after all this time, a connection, a shiver of mortality, something. But I didn't. Last living relative or not, I had damn few memories of Colin Mitchell, most of them bad. And I'd covered a lot of ground since.

The bedrooms would be chilly until morning, so I unrolled my sleeping bag on the sofa near the little stove. But sleep wouldn't come. Too many images: the lawyer's office, the hassle in the Crow's Nest, Sheriff Bauer—and the guns. Loaded. Out here in the middle of nowhere. Maybe it was the creaking of the cottage in the nightwind, or maybe paranoia's hereditary, but I got up, took the .45 down off the rack, and parked it on the floor beside the sofa, near at hand. And promptly fell into the sleep of the just, deep and dreamless.

Until someone turned on the lights. Or at least that was my first impression. I blinked into dazed awareness, trying to focus, to figure out where I was, what was happening. The ship's clock on the bookcase showed a little after two A.M. And yet the room was suffused with a silvery glow, bright shafts of light bleeding around the edges of the drapes. Someone was spotlighting the house from the beach. Sharply awake now, I rolled off the sofa, jerked the .45 out of its holster. Then flattened myself against the wall beside the living room window, and swept the drapes open.

Ice. My God. Huron Bay was a crystalline, glimmering icefield that stretched unbroken to the horizon, and probably five hundred miles north to the Canadian shore. There was no spotlight out there, only the moon, three-quarters full, beaming through scudding snow clouds, refracted by a billion prisms, setting Lady Huron aglisten in a cloak of shattered diamonds.

I stared out into the glittering dark for an hour or more. Twenty years of diving in tropic seas—Viet Nam, the Caribbean, the Texas Gulf; I'd almost forgotten how the dead of winter transmuted the Great Lakes into thousands of square miles of jumbled floes and fields, as lifeless and magnificent as the valleys of the moon.

Eventually I started to wobble as exhaustion overtook me. But still I didn't go back to bed. I snuggled down in an easy chair instead, facing the bay ice with my sleeping bag wrapped around me, unwilling to give up the beauty of the night, even to sleep. I dozed, and woke, and marveled, and dozed again. And once I saw something moving out there, something large and dark and serpentine, miles offshore. And I knew I must be dreaming, nothing could live out there, and yet I saw it, and could even mark its progress past a twisted ice pillar that thrust skyward like crossed fingers. A while later the moon went down, yet the Lady continued to luminesce with a spectral phosphorescence of her own, candleglow from emerald chandeliers in the halls of her icewater mansions.

Dawn never came. I woke a bit after seven to a heavily overcast sky and a storm drifting down from Canada, snow devils swirling ahead of it like dervish scouts.

I couldn't have cared less. The cottage was snug, I didn't have to be anywhere for a few hours. I brewed up an exquisite pot of coffee, toasted a couple of cinnamon Pop Tarts, carried the lot into the living room, and ate breakfast with a view of the bay while the local AM radio station murmured Huron Harbor news in the background—farm reports, births, the Chamber of Commerce meeting. And it occurred to me that I felt like I'd come home. Too late, perhaps. But home nonetheless. For the first time in— Hell, maybe for the first time ever.

I was trying to define the feeling when I heard the faint whine of an approaching car lurching along the track. I peered through the frosty glass of the front door. A white Jag had pulled up beside my rented Escort, and a small, dark-haired woman in a chic white trenchcoat and snow boots climbed out and trotted briskly up the steps carrying a briefcase. I opened before she knocked.

"Good morning," she said coolly, "I'm Karen Stepaniak, Century Realty? I'm sorry to bother you so early, Mr. Mitchell. Your attorney, Mr. Klein, told me you were staying out here. May I come in?"

"Of course," I said. "What's this about?"

"Business," she said, glancing around like a prospective tenant. She was fortyish but wearing it well, a heart-shaped face, large, intelligent eyes. Troubled eyes. "I realize you've only just arrived and the timing is terrible, but we have an offer that I thought you should know about."

"I see. Please, sit down. Could I get you some coffee?"

"No, thank you, I really can't stay. The offer is for a hundred and sixty thousand for both properties—thirty-five down, the balance on land contract at eleven percent."

"I see," I said. "Look, I don't mean to put you on the spot, but I don't know much about local real estate values. Is this a good offer?"

"It's—fair," she said reluctantly.

"That wasn't the question," I said.

"No," she said, releasing a ragged breath. "It's not a particularly good offer. The Crow's Nest alone should be worth that. Still, it's on the table and I thought you should know."

"I appreciate your honesty," I said. "Tell me, is there any pressure involved in the offer?"

"I don't understand."

"To be blunt, how eager are the buyers?"

"Not very. They're an older couple from Detroit, looking for a business to retire to. They've made offers on several listings, all in this price range. I doubt they can go higher."

"That isn't why I asked. The truth is, I'm really not interested in selling just now and I couldn't if I wanted to. A lot of my father's papers seem to be missing."

"I see," she nodded briskly. "Well, if you change your mind, we're in the book. Thank you for your time." She turned to go, a bit hesitantly I thought.

"Miss Stepaniak? Forgive me if I'm out of line, but a lady seems to have left some clothing here. Could you do me a favor and take it with you? To drop off at Goodwill or whatever?"

"It's Mrs. Stepaniak actually," she said, reading my eyes. "I suppose I could. As a favor, of course." She took a deep breath and walked into the bedroom. I wandered out to the living room and straightened up, tossing my sleeping bag behind the couch and carrying the dishes to the sink. I glanced into the bedroom as I passed. Karen Stepaniak was sitting on the bed with her eyes closed, holding one of my father's crumpled shirts pressed over her mouth, breathing a memory. I rummaged through the chipped china mugs in the cupboard, came up with a fit-for-company Rookwood cup and saucer my father'd probably scavenged from a wreck, and poured her a cup of coffee.

She looked shaken when she came out—misty, her mouth a taut line. "Please, stay a moment," I said. "I'd like to talk to you."

She slumped down at the kitchen table, a decade older than when she arrived. She sipped her coffee gratefully and visibly knitted herself together. "So," she said after a bit, "I gather you know that your father and I were—involved."

"No, ma'am. But it does seem a bit early to talk real estate."

"The offer is legitimate," she said, stiffening a little. "Are you going to run the Crow's Nest for a while?"

"Yeah, I think I will," I said.

"Forgive me for being nosy, but Cole told me you were working as a diver in Texas or somewhere."

"I'm surprised he mentioned me at all."

"Actually he talked about you quite a bit, especially lately. Did he get in touch with you?"

"I haven't heard from him in years. Just a note when my grandfather died, and that was six months late. Why was he going to contact me?"

"I'm not really sure," she said. "He said it was family business, but he seemed uncertain about it. I take it there was some kind of trouble between you."

"Nothing complicated. The summer after I graduated from high school, I stayed out here. We weren't strangers. He taught me to dive and I'd been working for him every summer for years. But living under the same roof was a bad idea. He was drinking a lot then, and one night he brought a woman home from the bar, and they were both drunk and there was a scuffle. And, ah, I tried to rescue the damsel in distress. And got my lights punched out for my trouble. I enlisted in the navy the next day, and I've never been back."

She nodded. "I see, and that's all there was to it? A fight?"

"That and the fact that he didn't bother to contact me when my grandfather was dying. We'd had problems, but I deserved better than that."

"I suppose so. So why come back now? For the inheritance?"

"Not really." I shrugged. "I guess I was just ready for a change in my life. Midlife crisis perhaps. I've been hitting the booze a little harder than I should lately, even wound up in jail a few months ago because of it. A great place to sort out your options, jail. And it occurred to me that I'd resented my father all these years, but I'm probably more like him than I care to admit."

"You are a bit like him, you know. For instance, it seems very natural to sit here and talk with you. But you're quite different too. You're civilizing the place already for one thing," she said, indicating her cup. "You probably even sleep in beds."

"I beg your pardon?"

"It's nothing, really. I used to stop by and fix breakfast sometimes. Our schedules didn't really mesh except for mornings. Often as not I'd find him asleep in his chair in the living room. He used to sit out there all night, watching the lake, or the ice. And dream. He said sometimes he could hear her singing."

"Hear who?"

"The lady of the lake. God, what a line of blarney he had. And I'm going to miss him more than I can say. Thank you for the tea and sympathy," she said, rising briskly. "If you're going to run the Nest, take some friendly advice. Show some profit on the books. Colin always ran it in the red to avoid taxes, which made it a tough sell. I can probably get you half again as much as he was asking."

"Wait a minute. Are you saying that he was trying to sell the Nest?"

"Of course. I thought you understood that."

"No, I didn't. I guess I assumed you'd—"

"—tried to market it without a listing? Hardly. I don't need business that badly."

"Sorry. When did he list the Nest?"

"He listed both properties about six weeks ago, I believe. We—he planned to leave after the holidays for Baja, said he'd had enough snow for a lifetime, that he was getting too old for cold water." She swallowed hard and looked away.

"I'm still not sure I understand. Did you have an offer for the Nest before the accident?"

"No. I only received this offer a few days ago."

"So he was planning to leave whether the Nest sold or not? With what?"

"I'm sorry, you've lost me."

"What did he plan to live on? According to his attorney he only had a few hundred in the bank."

"I'm afraid I don't know. We never really discussed his finances. From what planning we did, I gathered that money wouldn't be a problem, especially since he could have gotten considerably more for the Nest if he'd waited for the tourist season to sell out."

"I see. Forgive me for being blunt, but I don't suppose you were planning to support him down there?"

"Mr. Mitchell," she said, straightening to her full five-three, "I realize you probably think badly of me, so let me clear the air. You mentioned a midlife crisis a minute ago. Perhaps your father was mine. I was a reasonably happily married woman before I became—involved with him. He asked me to go to Mexico with him, and I agreed. But I'm not sure I would have gone. And while I'm being frank, I hope I can count on your discretion."

"Of course," I said, "and I apologize for—well, for everything. Just one last thing, did my father seem at all uneasy the past month or so?"

"Uneasy? How do you mean?"

"I found two of his guns parked in strategic spots when I arrived last night, his pistol behind the door, a rifle in the living room. Both loaded."

"I don't recall seeing them," she said, "and I was here quite often. But uneasy? You really didn't know him well, did you?"

"No," I said, "I suppose not."

"I'm afraid that was your loss. He was a complex man, not always easy to understand, but always interesting. And he was probably the least fearful man I've ever known. I don't think he was afraid of anything on God's green earth."

"Considering how things turned out," I said, "maybe he should have been."

Lesson one for a small businessman. If you're late, everybody else will be on time, and you're paying them by the hour. Red and two workmen from the glass company were waiting none too patiently for me in the parking lot when I arrived. The glaziers promptly hung a sheet of canvas over the wall to keep the weather out, then disappeared under it to widen the opening for the new window. Red began scrubbing the walls where we'd quit the night before, and I decided to sort out the paperwork in the office. And then the wolf came to the door. Literally.

Someone began pounding on the back door, I opened it, and a wolf was sitting there, eyeing me like a potential lunch. Not a Malamute or an Alsatian. An honest-to-God Canadian grey wolf. She must've weighed close to a hundred and sixty pounds—coarse charcoal pelt, amber, intelligent eyes.

"Hey, Mitch, how you been doin'? You remember me?"

I managed to shift my gaze away from the wolf long enough to glance at her owner. A big guy in an old red-plaid hunting coat and a corduroy cap with one torn earflap. An ugly brown birthmark leaked down from his cap over one cheek—a moon-shaped face like a pimento loaf, unknown bits of stuff sticking in it.

Ratshit.

I almost said it. It was the only name I could come up with, one kids hung on him in grade school and taunted him with until his teens when he suddenly bulked up to near grizzly bear size. And temper. Radowicz. That was it. Judgment Christ Radowicz.

"Jud," I said, "how are you?"

"Good, I'm good. I heard you was back in town. I stopped by your dad's place this morning but you was already gone."

"You still live out there on the Point?"

"Yeah. In my mom's ol' shack. She died you know."

"No, I hadn't heard. I'm sorry."

"Shit happens." He shrugged, looking away. "Look, I was wonderin' if you got any work for me. My truck's broke down and I need some cash money. Any kinda manual labor, you know."

"I, ahm. . . . Do you know anything about diving gear, Jud?"

"Sure. I gofered for your dad plenty a times. I can't work more'n thirty feet down though. I got the bad ears."

"I don't want you to dive, Jud. I need somebody to clean up the dive shop out in back, straighten up the equipment, wash the walls and the shelves. It's a lot of bullwork. Six bucks an hour sound fair?"

"Damn straight." He nodded eagerly. "That'd be great. You want me to start right now?"

"Anytime you like, but you'll have to do something about the wolf."

"You mean Dog?"

"That's a dog?"

"Nah, Dog's her name. She's a cross-wolf. But you go around yellin' Wolf, people think you're nuts. You don't want her around?"

"We've got a food license, Jud. We can't have animals on the premises."

"I don't know." He frowned. "I guess I could drop her off to home. Take me a couple hours."

"Why should . . . ? You mean you walked here? From the Point?"

"Sure," he said, puzzled, "I told you my truck's broke down."

"So you did. All right, tell you what, you keep Dog in the dive shop for today, but don't bring her tomorrow. Okay?"

"Whatever you say, Mitch," he said, pumping my hand in his grimy fist. "You won't be sorry." The cross-wolf's eyes never wavered from my belly. She didn't offer to shake hands. Neither did I.

I was headed back to the office when the canvas tarp draped over the window billowed aside and a ghost stepped from beneath it—a short, compactly built man in a navy pea coat, with dark, wind-tousled hair and pirate's eyes. "I been thrown out a few saloon windows," he said, glancing around. "Don't think I've ever come in through one before. It's a lot less painful. How you been, Mitch?"

"Terry Fortier," I said, grinning, feeling my spirits lift. "I figured you'd be dead or in jail by now."

"Nah, I'm too pretty for that. But before you start blubbering how glad you are to see me, I'd better warn you. I have to beat the livin' bejesus outa you and break one of your arms."

"Why? Just because I didn't write?"

"Nope, because Joe Carney slipped me fifty bucks to bust you up."

"Only fifty? I'm insulted. Think you're up to it?"

"Oh, no doubt about it. Still, seems kinda shortsighted to whup up on a guy who just inherited a saloon. Tell you what, buy me a drink, we'll call it even."

"Buy your own drink. You're the one with the extra fifty."

"By God, you're as cheap as your old man ever was. Okay, I'll buy, you pour. In your office?"

"Sounds fair," I said. "What about Carney?"

"I guess he'll have to hire somebody to stomp the both of us now," he said, following me through to the office. "Fifty more for you, at least a grand for me. He hasn't got that kinda money. And speakin' of hirin', was that Ratshit I saw headin' back to the dive shop?"

"Do people still call him that?"

"Hell no," Terry grinned, "at least not to his face. Baggers Gant made a wisecrack about that mud pie birthmark of his and Rats beat him half to death for it. He's Mister Radowicz far as I'm concerned, but I wouldn't want him working for me. He's always been two bricks shy of a load, but since his mom died he's probably certifiable. Lives in that old shack past your father's place with a damn wolf."

"Dog," I corrected, pouring two fair-sized jolts of Courvoisier into a pair of brandy snifters.

"If that thing's a dog, Cujo was a hamster. You want to hire him, it's your lookout, but watch him. His only talent's for makin' people nervous, and rightly so."

"He said he'd been working for my father."

"Yeah, he rousted for him on his boat, did scutwork around the cottage. Colin could always handle him, kid him out of his moods and such. But no offense, Mitch, you aren't your father."

"No, I'm not," I said, raising my glass, "but I think I can probably manage Jud. Happy days."

"And happier nights," Terry said, knocking back half of his brandy with a single belt. "You know about your father's boat, right?"

"What about it?"

"I bought it off him a few weeks back. Wasn't the bill of sale in the estate papers or whatever?"

"No. Actually, quite a few papers seem to be missing, the title to the house, a few other things. They're probably filed around here somewhere."

"Well, I got a copy of the bill if you want to see it. You won't like it though. He had a four-year-old, twenty-seven-foot Bayliner. He, ah, he sold it to me for a grand."

"A grand?" I echoed, sipping my brandy, reading Terry's face. It was a good face, matinee-idol handsome. I'd known him since I was ten. Best friends back then. A long time ago. Maybe too long.

"So," I said, "why don't you tell me about it?"

"About what?"

"What my father was into. C'mon Terry, something was up. He was dumping his house and the business. He practically gave you his boat. He was getting out in a hurry. Why? What was he afraid of?"

"Your father? Hell, I don't think he was afraid of anybody. Most people were afraid of him. He had a helluva temper, your old man. He kinda mellowed some lately, though. Maybe because of his latest ladyfriend. He was always a fox in the henhouse with women, but his new lady was special. Wanted to marry her, I hear."

"Karen Stepaniak?"

"My, my, what big ears we have."

"She stopped by the house this morning. On business."

"Well I hope you got it all finished up. The lady's got a mean sumbitch husband the size of New Jersey. Hacksaw, they call him. He and your father tangled a couple months back."

"What happened?"

"Hack came to the Nest, started around the bar after Colin. Colin came up with a .45, shoved it under Hack's chin, eared back the hammer, said one more step, they'd hafta scrape his brains off the ceiling with a trowel. Man, you shoulda seen his eyes. I really thought he was gonna do it. Hack did too. He backed off. But not by much. Told your old man he'd break his back if he didn't stay away from Karen."

"And now he's dead," I said.

"But not from a broken back." Terry shrugged. "He froze to death."

"The .45 was hanging behind the door at the cottage," I said, "and my father's Winchester was in the living room. Both loaded."

"I guess maybe he took Hack seriously."

"Maybe. But I think there's more to it than a jealous husband. And more to the boat business too."

"Really? Like what?"

"Money, Terry. It comes down to the money. I can see why he'd take a low-ball price for the Nest and the cottage if he was in a hurry to get out. But not the boat. He could've sold it for double what you paid him any day of the week. So maybe you'd better tell me what else was involved. Unless you'd like to try earning Carney's fifty."

For a moment I thought he might. The competitive curiosity that always exists between friends reared its head. Who's really quicker? Who'll quit first? The dark side of affection.

"You know," Terry said slowly, "we might just get to that sometime, you and me. But not over a lousy fifty bucks. Or even a boat. I gave Colin a name."

"What kind of a name?"

"A salvage buyer's name. There's a heavy market for contraband from the deep water wrecks. Scavenging's illegal, but sometimes the money's just too good to pass up."

"And you're involved in this trade?"

"Let's just say I know people who are."

"And my father? Was he involved?"

"Not really. Oh, I'm not sayin' he wouldn't buy a brass running lamp or a ship's wheel off a diver who needed money, but he mostly turned the stuff over to the Deveraux Museum here in town. He never actually dealt in plunder as far as I know."

"Until last month."

"Could be. I just gave him the name."

"What was he trying to sell?"

"I don't know. A deal like that, I didn't ask any questions. Especially not of Colin. I've seen him in action."

"So have I," I said. "What was the dealer's name?"

"Why do you want to know?"

"It could be the gentleman owes me some money. Or a lot more."

"What, you think the buyer maybe ripped your father off? Or did him in somehow?"

"Stranger things have happened."

"I suppose it's possible. The buyer's definitely a hard-nose. Runs a couple pawnshops down in Saginaw. Supposed to be mob connected. But I don't think he and your father tangled. The buyer called me last week to ask if Colin had made a deal with somebody else. He didn't know he was dead."

"And you just took his word for that?"

"I had no reason to doubt it," Terry said evenly, "and I still don't. The guy's always been straight with me. Anyway, I doubt he'd talk to you. Too risky."

"He can either talk to me or to Sheriff Bauer. Your choice."

Terry eyed me for a moment, then shrugged. "So much for auld lang syne," he said. "Tell you what, I'll make a couple calls, see what I can find out. If anything smells wrong, we'll both take the whole thing straight to Bauer. Of course you realize that if something heavy did go down, the buyer's liable to be edgy as a pit bull on amphetamines. We could end up in the same shape as your old man."

"Then just give me his name."

"No, I hooked Colin up with him. If it went bad I'm at least partly responsible. I'll handle it. Unless you think maybe *I'm* involved in whatever happened?"

"No, of course not. How much time will you need?"

"A day or two."

"I'll give you three," I said.

"Assuming we're both still alive in three days," he sighed. I thought he was worried about trouble from the buyer. It didn't occur to me that my father might reach back to take me with him . . .

The workmen finished installing the bay window late that afternoon. And a very odd thing happened. When they swept the canvas away to reveal a Rockwell-esque view of the snowbound harbor, it was as though a new door opened in my life. And for the first time I could sense a pattern, a possible future that didn't include welding on an endless parade of drilling platforms in Texas or Alaska or God knows where. Or raw towns and strange faces and death in deep water.

"So," Red said, "what do you think?"

"I like it," I said. "I like it so much I want another one, a small one. In my office."

The workman frowned. "I doubt I've got a unit that size in stock. Might take a few days to get one."

"No rush," I said. "I'll be here."

Even the cottage looked different to me when I drove up that evening. I'd always thought of it as lonely and isolated. Now it just seemed private.

I made myself a cup of coffee, and gazed out the beachfront window, marveling at the twilight shadows on the ice and the shore, and—I noticed something odd.

The boathouse on the beach seemed to be padlocked. But according to Terry, there was no boat in there. So why lock an empty shed? Unless it was being used to store something else?

I put on a pair of my father's heavy work boots, grabbed my jacket and a flashlight, and trotted out to the boathouse, a garage-sized red metal outbuilding built over a narrow, frozen channel that led out into Huron Bay. The padlock on the side door was a combination Masterlock, brand new, impossible to cut. It took me twenty minutes to pry the hasp off with a tire iron. A waste of time. As soon as I pulled the door open I could see the shed was empty. No boat, no plunder, just the grey ice of the frozen channel and a cluttered workbench along the far wall.

As I started in I felt something brush across my shins. I hesitated. And saved my legs. I played the light down at my feet, and still nearly missed it. A tripwire, a clear monofilament fishing line, almost invisible in the dusk. I traced it with the light beam along the wall, then across the room to the workbench. To my father's shotgun, locked in the bench vise, its barrel aimed directly at the door. Sweet Jesus.

I was instantly bathed in a cold sweat, chill as an icewater shower. The line was taut across my shin. How much slack was left? I couldn't tell. Keeping the light beam on the line, I slid my left hand down my pantleg to keep the tripwire from snapping back when I stepped away. I took a shallow, ragged breath, then very slowly started shifting my feet backward a millimeter at a time, until my legs were clear of the line. Then I eased my finger back until the line returned to its original position across the open doorway.

I sidestepped out of the line of fire, sagged against the wall, and the damn gun went off, hammering a round of buckshot through the doorway beside me.

That bastard! The shot had erased the line and I stormed into the empty shed, unlocked the vise, jerked the shotgun free, and smashed it over the bench, shattering the stock. Christ, he could have killed me! What kind of a psycho would boobytrap an empty shed? He—

He wouldn't have. As my panicky heart-rate slowly subsided, that realization gradually sank in. He had a murderous temper, my father, one I'd inherited. But he wasn't crazy. At least not altogether. So what was he guarding in here? I tossed the broken shotgun aside on the bench and played the flashlight around the room. The boat entrance door was barred from the inside, so whatever it was should still be in here. But there was nothing! An empty room, nothing on the walls, only a few odd tools on the bench, the floor a frozen sheet of . . .

Ice. There were tracks on the ice, gouges. Marks of a snowmobile tread. A snowmobile had been driven in here through the channel door. And something heavy had been unloaded onto the ice, heavy enough to mark it with deep grooves in a six foot square.

Frowning, I eyed the square. It was too large. What could you carry on a snowmobile that would take up this much space? And weigh enough to make gouges like these? I knelt and ran my fingers over the grooves. They were jagged, of uneven depth. They hadn't been pressed into the ice. They'd been cut. And I only knew one way to cut through ice this thick.

I jogged back to the house and got the chain saw I'd fallen over in the entryway that first night. The chain teeth were dull, not nearly sharp enough to cut wood. But sharp enough for ice. Back in the shed it fired up with a roar. I revved the engine, getting it warm, then lowered the blade to the ice. It bit in fiercely, spraying the room with chips and splinters. The racket in the metal shed was deafening. I needed goggles and muffs and heavier gloves, but I didn't care. I was too close now, and much too pumped up.

The blade chewed through to the water beneath, and I followed the line of the square around until the slab broke free, rocking beneath my weight. I shut off the saw and set it on the bench, my head clanging like a fire alarm in the sudden silence. I stepped on one edge of the slab, tilting the opposite side up, and simply thrust it up over the rim like a sliding door.

The water was roiled from the movement of the slab and it took a few moments before I could see anything clearly. But they were down there. Wooden crates, six of them, streaked with lake-bottom mud, with wisps of sodden excelsior sticking through the slats. The top of the uppermost box had been pried off so I shucked my jacket, rolled up my sleeve, and reached down into the icy water. And retrieved a cup.

A single china cup. With a familiar pattern. Rookwood. A mate to the one in the house. I set it carefully aside, dried my arm as best I could, and slipped my jacket on. Six cases of antique china in mint condition. I wasn't sure how old the stuff was, turn-of-the-century or earlier from the look of the boxes. I'm no expert on china, but I know enough about salvage to know the crates were probably worth five or six thousand each, maybe more. But not enough.

Even at ten grand per case, this cache would barely make up the loss my father was going to take for a quick sale of the Crow's Nest. Plus, he'd kept the boxes underwater to keep the excelsior from freezing and pulverizing the china, but if these six cases were the lot, he wouldn't have bothered to store it here. He would have carried it into the cottage.

So there had to be more of it. Perhaps a whole shipload more. And maybe I even knew where it was. Or where it had been, anyway.

I'm not sure I would have called Sheriff Bauer even if there'd been a phone. In any case, I didn't try. I went back to the house and took a bearing on the crossed-finger ice spire where I'd seen movement the first night. It appeared to be about two miles out on the bay, a serious hike over the ice, but not impossible, especially since I was fairly sure there'd be a path out there. I switched on the yard light to give myself a homing beacon, then I shoved a full clip into the butt of my father's .45 automatic, slid it into my parka pocket, and set off.

Following the snowmobile tracks down the boat channel to the lake was the easy part. Once I was clear of the shore, the wind and the swirling snowdevils made walking difficult, and following the narrow tracks even harder. The ice stretched ahead and around me like a moonscape of thrusting slabs, jagged craters, and occasional ebon pools of lustrous black glass, scoured and polished by the wind. From shore the ice appears white, but out on the cap it's dappled, the skin of an ancient lady, beige patches of windblown beach sand, greyish soot smudges, and indigo shadows that stretch like fingers from every ridge and turret.

And away from shore, the lady whispers. Beneath her alabaster shroud, she moves in her dreams. Her tides follow the moon, harrying the waters of a thousand rivers ever eastward to the St. Lawrence and the sea. The floating pack responds like a lover, with gentle shifts and moans and murmurs. And occasionally a sharp crack that instantly reminds you of the depth and darkness below. And of the spirits who sleep there. For everyone who grows up in the north country knows someone who has died on the ice. Fishing, or snowmobiling. Or just walking across it.

The firmness of the pack is an illusion. It's riddled with holes, airpockets hidden by snow, gaps in the plate-seams camouflaged by a thin ice skin. I knew this of course, but I also knew that as long as I kept to the snowmobile track, I should be safe enough. Anywhere the machine had been, I could follow.

I lost the trail a number of times along the way beneath drifted snow, or where a plate had shifted and jumbled the track. But each time I was able to find it again simply by choosing the smoothest direct route. A snowmobile can sprint through broken country like a mustang, but the one I was following needed a level road for its fragile cargo.

I was nearly a mile from shore when the moon broke through, bringing the ice to life with the ghostly dancing of cloud shadows. The poignant, untouchable beauty of the night was hypnotic, and not for the first time I felt the lure of the lady below. Come down, come down to me . . . Leave your world. Sleep with me . . .

And I almost did.

I found the crossed-finger ice marker two miles out, but the track continued beyond it, northward, how far I couldn't be sure. And at that point I was so entranced by the silvery spell of the ice that I would have followed the path five hundred miles, to Canada, or oblivion. So I trudged on, nudged by the nightwind, hearing the crunch of snow beneath my boots, the murmur of the pack like low voices from another room. And then I stopped. So suddenly I surprised myself. There was a faint pattern in the ice ahead. A crude square. It could have been natural, but somehow I knew it wasn't. The snowmobile track veered sharply to the right, and ended a few feet away.

I cautiously stepped to the edge of the square and stamped my foot over the line. And punched through the crust so easily I nearly stumbled in. This was the place then.

I switched on my flashlight and played it around, not looking for anything in particular, more to be seen than to see. I found a few tracks, mud splotches on the ice where the crates had been lifted free. And I gradually felt that psychic touch, the uneasy sense that I was being watched. But I knew it wasn't true. The icepack was swimming in moonlight. I literally could see for miles in every direction, and there was nothing *to* see but ice, and snow, and shadows.

And yet, I had that feeling, as sharp and cold as an ice pack between my shoulderblades.

I played the flashlight around in ever widening circles. And suddenly caught twin reflections, eyes staring at me unblinking from fifty yards beyond the square out on the pack. A shape rose up out of the snow and began moving toward me, circling. I felt a soul-deep shiver of dread older than my life, older than words. A grey shadow, drifting across the snow silent as smoke. A wolf. No. Not a wolf.

Dog.

She made no sound—no growling, not so much as a whisper of her pads gliding over the ice, and at times she'd seem to disappear, blending into the moonshadows so perfectly I couldn't define her form until she moved again. And each time she was closer. Much closer. I grasped the butt of the .45 in my coat pocket, cold comfort indeed. In the moonlight I'd have no chance of hitting her until she was close enough to charge, and that might be too late.

I heard a faint whine from behind me, and risked a quick glance away from Dog toward the shore. Another shape was moving out there, coming toward me. But not a silent one. A snowmobile, low and black, running without lights, towing a sledge behind it, snaking through the broken surface of the pack like a slalom racer. Dog heard it too, and slowed her advance, crouching in the lee of a snow-hummock, a formless threat, invisible except for the metallic glint of her eyes.

The snowmobile whined to a halt a few yards away. Judgment Christ Radowicz unfolded himself from the machine, a hulking scarecrow figure, the night wind snapping his tattered coat. And I was glad it was him. I'd been half expecting Terry. He unstrapped a tool from the sled. A double-bitted brush axe. He didn't threaten me with it. Just held it. "Turn out the light," he said. "Somebody might see it."

"Maybe they have already," I said.

"Nah, it don't look that bright from shore. I wouldna seen it if I wasn't watchin'. I was gonna talk to you about this," he said, gesturing toward the ice patch behind me. "I was hopin' I could wait awhile, see what you was like, but it don't matter now. How did you find out? Colin leave a note or somethin'?"

"No. I saw you out here the night I arrived. I didn't know what it meant at the time."

"I been comin' out every night to bust up the ice," he said, hefting the axe. "Otherwise it'll freeze over, I'd have to use the saw again. Noise carries a long ways out here. You know what's down there?"

"A wreck," I said. "With a cargo of china."

He nodded. "Superstructure's all tore away. Only thing left is the keel. Colin tried to look her up. She might be the Victorine outa Chicago, 1891, but he couldn't be sure. I found her fishin' last fall, light was just right—seen her shape. She's fifty feet down, too deep for me—I got the bad ears—but Cole didn't have no trouble. Neither will you. We can go partners."

"Can we? Things didn't turn out very well for your last partner, Jud."

"No," he said, shaking his massive head slowly, "they didn't. It was awful, Mitch."

"What happened?"

"We had it all worked out. Colin had a guy ready to take the stuff. We figured we could make three, maybe four runs a night durin' the dark of the moon, stash the cases in his boathouse. He said there was thirty boxes down there."

"I only found six," I said.

"We only made two runs. Three cases are all the sledge'll carry and we had to get 'em ashore fast before they froze. First couple runs was no trouble, but about halfway back out after the second load, Colin fell off the sled. He was ridin' behind me, swiggin' down brandy to keep warm, and then he leaned against me for a while. I thought he was asleep. And then he just . . . fell off." He swallowed, looked away. His face was in shadow. I couldn't read it at all.

"I stopped the sled, but he was dead. Had been for a while. Already gettin' cold. I guess the water and the rides back and forth was just too much for him."

"Maybe," I said. "What about the 'accident,' Jud? How did that happen?"

"I didn't know what to do. Colin always did the thinkin', but I figured if I called an ambulance or somethin', the law'd backtrack the sled like you done, find out what we was doin'. So I got his divin' gear off, drove his truck into the ditch a ways down the road, and—God it was terrible, Mitch. The worst thing I ever been through in my life."

"I expect it was," I said, risking a quick glance over at Dog. "Why didn't you go back for the stuff in the boathouse?"

"I didn't know the combination to the lock, and anyway he had it booby-trapped."

"Why was that, Jud? Didn't he trust you?"

"He never trusted nobody. It's just how he was."

"But I can trust you, right?"

"Sure you can. Look, I waited for you, didn't I? I mean, if I wanted to cut you out I coulda got somebody else."

"Maybe. Or maybe you just didn't know anybody you could trust. Or who'd trust you."

"No, that ain't right and you know it. I been waitin' for you. You always treated me decent, never called me names, and you had more reason than any of 'em. Look," he said, starting forward, "we can work things out ashore, but right now we better bust up the hole again and get outa here before somebody spots us."

"Don't come any closer," I said, pulling the .45.

"Dammit, Mitch, don't be stupid," he said, halting. "We can't stay out here."

"We'll go," I said, "but first, toss that axe away."

"I'd never hurt you, Mitch. You must know that."

"All I know is, my father's dead. Maybe it happened the way you said. But it's also possible you and Dog just kept him from climbing out of the water long enough for him to lose consciousness. And then let the wind do the rest."

"That's crazy. Why should I do that?"

"Maybe because you heard he was taking off with his girlfriend and thought he was going to cheat you. Or maybe you just got greedy. Figuring motives is Charlie Bauer's job, not mine. But one thing I am sure of. I've got a chance for a new life up here, and I'm not gonna start out by plundering a wreck, with you or anybody else."

"No," he said, "that ain't fair. I've never had nothin'. This is the only chance I'll ever get. You can't just throw it away."

He shuffled toward me, a ragged neanderthal, axe in hand. "Jud, back off," I said, raising the .45. "I don't want to shoot anybody—"

From the corner of my eye I caught a flash of movement. Dog snaking rapidly my way, belly to the ground, fangs bared, snarling a deep rumble that seemed to emanate from the ice itself. "Call her off, Jud!" She rose suddenly and I fired a warning shot toward her, the gun blasting like a lightning strike in the darkness.

"NOO! Don't!" Jud howled, hurling himself at me. I slashed him across the temple with the gun barrel as he slammed into me chest-high, but the force of his rush hurled us backward onto the broken icefield. We came down hard together, hammering at each other, and then the ice collapsed, and we were plunged into the freezing dark.

The shock was incredible, the chill so fierce I almost cried out. Jud's weight was carrying me down. I twisted away from him, forgot about the damned gun, forgot everything but clawing my way back up to the grey jumble of ice above me, breaking through, gasping for air, then flinching backward as Dog lunged at me from the edge of the hole, her fangs clashing only inches from my face.

Jud thrashed to the surface a few feet behind me, flailing blindly about, blood streaming from the gash on his temple over the stain on his cheek, dazed, desperate. I tried to grope my way to the edge, the ice chunks breaking off in my hands, freezing to my arms like iron leeches. Dog was berserk, charging frantically back and forth, snarling, whining. Then suddenly she launched herself into the water with us, crashing into my shoulder, smashing me aside as she tried to get to Jud. God, it was horrible. She couldn't swim in the broken ice, and we were all plunging about, churning in the ice cauldron like souls in hell.

I thrust myself away from them, struggling through the broken ice chunks toward the far side. I managed to find a hold and clawed my way out, an inch at a time, my hands slipping, too numb to grip. For a moment I just knelt there, head down, panting like an animal, water streaming from my face, my clothes.

A howl from behind me brought me out of the haze. Dog was half out of the water, scrabbling at the rim with Jud clinging to her pelt, but neither of them could hold on, and they fell back. Jud lost his grip on her fur and went under, and Dog quit trying to save herself and tried to paddle to him, and something snapped in me and a *NO* came roaring up out of my subconscious. Not like this. Not like this!

I crawled on my hands and knees around the edge of the pool toward them. I groped in the water for Jud, managed to tangle my fist in his hair, and hauled his shoulders clear of the water. I didn't have strength enough to pull him out, but he weakly inched himself onto the pack, then collapsed, moaning like a child.

Dog was still struggling, going under, almost spent. I leaned out, fumbling for the scruff of her neck, but the moment I touched her she whirled and clamped onto my arm, her fangs tearing through my coat, the arm instantly afire with agony.

I roared and tried to pull free, and saved her miserable life as she came boiling up onto the ice. I hammered her face with my left hand, jabbing at her eyes, and she let go and spun away, snarling, crouching to spring again.

But she didn't. She stood her ground, glaring at me, eyes alight with fury, and if I'd had the damned gun I would have shot her on the spot. Jud tried to stand, but his legs folded and he fell, more dead than alive. And so was I. We had to get away from here. Now.

I managed to coax Jud to the sledge. He had to crawl on his own, because whenever I reached for him, Dog lunged at me, warning me off,

and there was no doubt in my mind she'd tear me apart if I touched him.
The snowmobile fired up with the first touch of the switch, thank God,
because my strength was almost gone. I flicked on the headlight and
gunned it forward, heading for the shore, with Jud unconscious on the
sledge behind and Dog trotting alongside. And she had the better of it. At
least she was moving. The nightwind howled down from the moon, sweeping across the ice, freezing my clothing to me, numbing my face, my
senses . . .

And I blacked out.

Somewhere on the trip back, I lost consciousness completely. I don't
remember smashing up the machine near shore, or crawling to my car, or
driving it until I ran into a roadsign on US 23. They tell me I did. I
honestly don't remember. I was unconscious until noon the next day,
nearly fourteen hours later.

And only then did anyone go to look for Jud.

And he wasn't there. No sign of him, Charlie Bauer said, either where
I'd wrecked the snowmobile or at the cottage. Bauer sent a Coast Guard
chopper out that afternoon, and visibility on the lake was good. But still
they didn't find him. He'd vanished as though he'd never existed. I doubt
he'll be missed much. He was big and surly and half crazy, with the mark of
Cain on him, and his only talent was for making people uneasy.

I visited his shack every day for a week, and he didn't come back there.
Still, he could have survived. He'd lived out on that point all his life, and he
was strong as a bull. Or a wolf.

And I wanted him to be alive. I needed him to be. He may have killed
my father. I need to ask him about that, and look into his eyes when he
answers. But most of all, I want to ask him about the checks. Canceled
checks that I found in a box at the Crow's Nest with my father's missing
papers. Checks paid monthly to Stella Radowicz, Jud's mother. By my
father.

Eighteen year's worth.

I think I know what they were for. We were of a size, my father, and me,
and Jud. But I'll never be sure until I look in his face, and for the first time,
try to see past that damned birthmark. But I don't think I ever will.

I think he's gone. I think the lady took him, down and down, to sleep in
the deep green halls of her icewater mansions.

In my heart, I know it's true. Because ten days after Jud disappeared,
Dog came back. I saw her on the beach at dusk, gaunt as her own ghost,
her grey pelt rimed with ice, her pads bloody and swollen. I called her but
she wouldn't come to me. She roams the point now, guarding Jud's house,

and mine. I put food out for her, and sometimes she eats it, but mostly she kills her own. She was a one-man Dog. She's all wolf now.

Sometimes I wake in the moonlight, and I see her sitting on the lake-shore, staring out over the ice, waiting for someone she's lost.

And so do I. And so do I.

THE FEARLESS ONE

Jack London

The table was of hand-hewn spruce boards, and the men who played whist had difficulties in drawing home their tricks across the uneven surface. They sat in their undershirts and the sweat beaded and oozed on their faces; yet their feet, heavily moccasined and woollen-socked, tingled with the bite of the frost—such was the difference of temperature in the small cabin between floor level and a yard or more above it. The sheet-iron Yukon stove roared red-hot; yet, eight feet away from it, on the meat-shelf placed low beside the door, lay chunks of solidly frozen moose and bacon. The door for a third of the way up from the bottom was a thick rime. In the chinking between the logs at the back of the bunks the frost showed white and glistening. A window of oiled paper furnished light. The lower portion of the paper, on the inside, was coated an inch deep with the frozen moisture of the men's breath.

They played a momentous rubber of whist, for the pair that lost was to dig a fishing hole through the seven feet of ice and snow that covered the Yukon.

"It's mighty unusual, a cold snap like this in March," remarked the man who shuffled. "What would you call it, Bob?"

"Oh, fifty-five or sixty below—all of that. What do you make it, Doc!"

Doc turned his head and glanced at the lower part of the door with a measuring eye.

"Not a bit worse than fifty. If anything, slightly under—say forty-nine. See the ice on the door? It's just about the fifty mark, but you'll notice the upper edge is ragged. The time she went seventy, the ice climbed a full four inches higher."

He picked up his hand . . . and called "Come in," to a knock on the door.

The man who entered was a big, broad-shouldered Swede, though his nationality was not obvious until he had removed his ear-flapped cap and thawed away the ice which had formed on his beard and moustache.

"I hear one doctor faller stop this camp," the Swede said at last, his face haggard and drawn from severe and long-endured pain.

"I'm the doctor. What's the matter?"

The man held up his left hand, the second finger of which was monstrously swollen. At the same time he began a rambling, disjointed history of the coming and growth of this affliction.

"Let me look at it," the doctor broke in impatiently. "Lay it on the table. There, like that."

Tenderly, as if it were a great boil, the man obeyed.

"Humph," the doctor grumbled. "A weeping sinew. You watch me, and next time do it yourself."

Without warning, squarely and savagely, the doctor brought the edge of his hand down on the swollen crooked finger. The man yelled with consternation and agony.

"That's all right," the doctor said sharply and authoritatively. "How do you feel? Better, eh? Of course. Next time you can do it yourself. . . . Go on and deal, Strothers. I think we've got you."

Slow and ox-like the face of the Swede showed gradual relief and comprehension. The pang over, the finger felt better. The pain was gone. He examined the finger curiously, with wondering eyes, slowly crooking it back and forth. He reached into his pocket and pulled out a gold-sack.

"How much?"

The doctor shook his head impatiently. "Nothing. I'm not practising. . . . Your play, Bob."

"You are good man. What your name?"

"Linday, Doctor Linday," Strothers answered, as if to save his opponent from further irritation.

"The day's half-done," Linday said to the Swede, at the end of the hand, while he shuffled. "Better rest over tonight. It's too cold for travelling. There's a spare bunk."

He was a slender dark-haired man, lean-cheeked, thin-lipped, and strong. The smooth-shaven face was a healthy sallow. All his movements were quick and precise. He did not fumble his cards. The eyes were black, direct, and piercing, with the trick of seeming to look beneath the surfaces of things. His hands, slender, fine and nervous, appeared made for delicate work, and yet gave a feeling of strength.

"Our game," he announced, drawing in the last trick. "Now for the rub and who digs the fishing hole."

A knock at the door brought a quick exclamation from him.

"Seems we just can't finish this rubber," he complained, as the door opened. "What's the matter with *you?*" he said to the stranger who entered.

The newcomer vainly strove to move his ice-bound jaws and jowls. That he had been on trail for days was patent. The skin across the cheekbones was black with repeated frost-bite. From nose to chin was a mass of solid ice perforated by the hole through which he breathed. Through this he had also spat tobacco juice, which had frozen, as it trickled, into an amber-coloured icicle, pointed like a Van Dyke beard.

He shook his head dumbly, grinned with his eyes, and went to the stove to thaw out. He assisted the process with his fingers, clawing off fragments of melting ice which rattled and sizzled on the stove.

"Nothing the matter with me," he finally announced. "But if they's a doctor in the outfit, he's sure needed. They's a man up the Little Peco that's had a ruction with a panther, an' the way he's clawed is something scand'lous."

"How far up?" Doctor Linday demanded.

"A matter of a hundred miles."

"How long since?"

"I've ben three days comin' down."

"Bad?"

"Shoulder dislocated. Some ribs broke for sure. Right arm broke. An' clawed clean to the bone most all over but the face. We sewed up two or three bad places temporary, and tied arteries with twine."

"That settles it," Linday said. "Where were they?"

"Stomach."

"He's a sight by now."

"Not on your life. Washed clean with bug-killin' dope before we stitched. Only temporary anyway. Had nothin' but linen thread, but washed that, too."

"He's as good as dead," was Linday's judgment.

"Nope. That man ain't goin' to die. He knows I've come for a doctor, an' he'll make out to live until you get there. He won't let himself die. I know him."

"Christian Science and gangrene, eh? Well, I'm not practising. Nor can I see myself travelling a hundred miles at fifty below for a dead man."

"*I* can see you, an' for a man a long ways from dead."

Linday shook his head. "Sorry you had your trip for nothing. Better stop over for the night."

"Nope. We'll be pullin' out in ten minutes."

"What makes you so cocksure?" Linday demanded testily.

Tom Daw drew himself straight and looked Linday straight in the eye.

"Because he's just goin' on livin' till you get there, if it takes you a week to make up your mind. Besides, his wife's with him, not sheddin' a tear, or nothin,' an' she's helpin' him live till you come. They think a almighty heap of each other, an' she's got a will like hisn. If he weakened, she'd just put her immortal soul into hisn an' make him live. Though he ain't weakenin' none, you can stack on that. I'll stack on it. I'll lay you three to one, in ounces, he's alive when you get there. I got a team of dawgs down the bank, an' we ought to make it back in less'n three days because the trail's broke. I'm going down to the dawgs now, an' I'll look for you in ten minutes."

Tom Daw pulled down his earflaps, drew on his mittens, and strode out.

"Damn him!" Linday exploded, glaring at the closed door.

That night, long after dark, with twenty-five miles behind them, Linday and Tom Daw made camp. It was a simple but adequate affair: a fire built in the snow; alongside, their sleeping-furs spread in a single bed on a mat of spruce boughs; behind the bed an oblong of canvas stretched to refract the heat.

Morning found the cold snap broken. Linday estimated the temperature at fifteen below and rising. Daw was worried. That day would see them in the canyon, he explained, and if the spring thaw set in, the canyon would run open water. The walls of the canyon were hundreds to thousands of feet high. They could be climbed, but the going would be slow.

Camped that evening well into the dark and forbidding gorge, over their pipes they complained of the heat, and agreed that the thermometer must be above zero—the first time in six months.

"Nobody ever heard tell of a panther this far north," Daw said next. "Rocky called it a cougar. But I shot a-many of 'em down in Curry County, Oregon, where I come from, an' we called 'em panther. Anyway, it was a bigger cat than ever I seen. Now how'd it ever stray to such out of the way huntin' range? That's the question."

Linday made no comment—he was dropping off to sleep. Propped on sticks, his moccasins steamed unheeded and unturned.

He awoke with a start and gazed at Daw, who nodded and returned the gaze. Both listened. From far off came a vague disturbance that increased to a vast roaring. It neared, ever-increasing, riding the mountain tops as well as the canyon depths, bowing the forest before it, bending the meagre, crevice-rooted pines on the walls of the gorge. A wind, strong and warm, a balmy gale, drove past them, flinging a rocket-shower of sparks from the fire. The dogs, aroused, sat on their haunches, bleak noses pointed upward, and raised the long wolf howl.

"It's the Chinook," Daw said.

"It means the river trail will be out, I suppose?"

"Sure thing. And ten miles of that is easier than one over the tops." Daw surveyed Linday for a long, considering minute. "We've just had fifteen hours of trail," he shouted above the wind, tentatively, and again waited. "Doc," he said finally, "are you game?"

For answer, Linday knocked out his pipe and began to pull on his damp moccasins. Between them in few minutes the dogs were harnessed, camp broken, and the cooking outfit and unused sleeping furs lashed on the sled. Then, through the darkness, they churned out on the trail Daw had broken a few days before. And all through the night the Chinook roared and they urged the weary dogs and spurred their own jaded muscles. Twelve hours of it they made, and stopped for breakfast after twenty-seven hours on trail.

"An hour's sleep," said Daw, when they had wolfed pounds of straight moose-meat fried with bacon.

Two hours he let his companion sleep, afraid himself to close his eyes. He occupied himself with making marks upon the soft-surfaced, shrinking snow. In two hours the snow level sank three inches. From every side, under the voice of the spring wind, came trickling of hidden waters. The Little Peco, strengthened by multitudinous streamlets, rose against the manacles of winter, riving the ice with crashings and snappings.

Daw touched Linday on the shoulder; touched him again; shook, and shook violently.

"Doc," he murmured admiringly. "You can sure go some."

The weary black eyes, under heavy lids, acknowledged the compliment.

"But that ain't the question. Rocky is clawed something scand'lous. As I said before, I helped sew up his in'ards. Doc . . ." He shook the man, whose eyes had again closed. "I say, Doc! The question is: can you go some more? Hear me? I say, can you go some more?"

The weary dogs snapped and whimpered when kicked from their sleep. The going was slow, not more than two miles an hour, and the animals took every opportunity to lie down in the wet snow.

"Twenty miles of it, and we'll be through the gorge," Daw encouraged. "After that the ice can go to blazes, for we can take to the bank, and it's only ten more miles to camp. Why, Doc, we're almost there. And when you get Rocky fixed up, you can come down in a canoe in one day."

But the ice grew more uneasy under them, breaking loose from the shore-line and rising steadily inch by inch. In places where it still held to the shore, the water overran and they waded and slushed across. The Little Peco growled and muttered.

"Get on the sled, Doc, an' take a snooze," Daw invited.

The glare from the black eyes prevented him from repeating the suggestion.

At midday they received definite warning of the beginning of the end.

Cakes of ice, borne downward in the rapid current, began to thunder beneath the ice on which they wearily walked. The dogs whimpered anxiously.

"That means open water above," Daw explained. "Pretty soon she'll jam somewheres, an' the river'll raise a hundred feet in a hundred minutes. It's us for the tops if we can find a way to climb out. Come on! Hit her up!"

At this point, the great walls of the canyon were too precipitous to scale. Daw and Linday had to keep on; and they kept on till disaster happened. With a loud explosion, the ice broke asunder midway under the team. The two animals in the middle of the string went into the fissure, and the grip of the current on their bodies dragged the lead-dog backward and in. Swept downstream under the ice, these three bodies began to drag to the edge the two whining dogs that remained.

The men held back frantically on the sled, but were slowly drawn along with it. It was all over in the space of seconds. Daw slashed the wheel-dog's traces with his sheathknife, and the animal whipped over the ice-edge and was gone. The ice on which they stood broke into a large and pivoting cake that ground and splintered against the shore ice and rocks. They got the sled ashore and up into a crevice in time to see the ice-cake up-edge and sink.

Meat and sleeping furs they made into packs, and the sled they abandoned. Linday resented Daw's taking the heavier pack, but Daw had his will.

"You got to work as soon as you get there. Come on."

It was one in the afternoon when they started to climb. At eight that evening they cleared the rim and for half an hour lay where they had fallen. Then came the fire, a pot of coffee, and an enormous feed of moosemeat. But first Linday hefted the two packs, and found his own lighter by half.

"You're an iron man, Daw," he admired.

"Who? Me? Oh, pshaw! You ought to see Rocky. He's made out of platinum, an' armour plate, an' pure gold, an' all strong things. I'm mountaineer, but he plumb beats me out. Down in Curry County I used to 'most kill the boys when we run bear. So when I hooks up with Rocky on our first hunt I had a mean idea to show 'm a few. I let out the links good an' generous, 'most nigh keepin' up with the dawgs, an' along comes Rocky a-treadin' on my heels. I knowed he couldn't last that way, and I just laid down an' did my dangdest. An' there he was, at the end of another hour, a-treadin' steady an' regular on my heels. I was some huffed. 'Mebbe you'd like to come to the front an' show me how to travel,' I says. 'Sure,' says he. An' he done it! I stayed with 'm, but let me tell you I was plumb tuckered by the time the bear tree'd.

"They ain't no stoppin' that man. He ain't afraid of nothin'. Last fall, before the freezeup, him an' me was headin' for camp about twilight. I was clean shot out—ptarmigan—an' he had one cartridge left. An' the dawgs tree'd a she grizzly. Small one. Only weighed about three hundred, but you know what grizzlies is. 'Don't do it,' says I, when he ups with his rifle. 'You only got that one shot, an' it's too dark to see the sights.'

"Climb a tree," says he. I didn't climb no tree, but when that bear come down a-cussin' among the dawgs, an' only creased, I want to tell you I was sure *hankerin'* for a tree. It was some ruction. Things come on real bad. The bear slid down a hollow against a big log. Downside, that log was four feet up an' down. Dawgs couldn't get at bear that way. Upside was steep gravel, an' the dawgs'd just naturally slide down into the bear. They was no jumpin' back, an' the bear was a-manglin' 'em fast as they come. All underbrush, gettin' pretty dark, no cartridges, nothin'.

"What's Rocky up an' do? He goes downside of log, reaches over with his knife, an' begins slashin'. But he can only reach bear's rump, an' dawgs bein' ruined fast, one-two-three time. Rocky gets desperate. He don't like to lose his dawgs. He jumps on top log, grabs bear by the slack of the rump, an' heaves over back'ard right over top of that log. Down they go, kit an' kaboodle, twenty feet, bear, dawgs, an' Rocky—slidin', cussin', an' scratchin', ker-plump into ten feet of water in the bed of stream. They all swum out different ways. He didn't get the bear, but he saved the dawgs. That's Rocky. They's no stoppin' him when his mind's set."

It was at the next camp that Linday heard how Rocky had come to be injured.

"I'd ben up the draw, about a mile from the cabin, lookin' for a piece of birch likely enough for an axe-handle. Comin' back, I heard the darndest goings-on where we had a bear trap set. Some trapper had left the trap in an old cache an' Rocky'd fixed it up. But the goings-on. It was Rocky an' his brother Harry. First I'd hear one yell and laugh, an' then the other, like it was some game. An' what do you think the fool game was? I've saw some pretty nervy cusses down in Curry County, but they beat all. They'd got a whoppin' big panther in the trap an' was takin' turns rappin' it on the nose with a light stick. But that wa'n't the point. I just come out of the brush in time to see Harry rap it. Then he chops six inches off the stick an' passes it to Rocky. You see, that stick was growin' shorter all the time. It ain't as easy as you think. The panther'd slack back an' hunch down an' spit, an' it was mighty lively in duckin' the stick. An' you never knowed when it'd jump. It was caught by the hind leg, which was curious, too, an' it had some slack I'm tellin' you.

"It was just a game of dare they was playin', an' the stick gettin' shorter an' shorter an' the panther madder 'n madder. Bimeby they wa'n't no stick left—only a nubbin, about four inches long, an' it was Rocky's turn. 'Better quit now,' says Harry. 'What for?' says Rocky. 'Because if you rap him again they won't be no stick left for me,' Harry answers. 'Then you'll quit an' I win,' says Rocky with a laugh, an' goes to it.

"An' I don't want to see anything like it again. That cat'd bunched back an' down till it had all of six feet slack in its body. An' Rocky's stick four inches long. The cat got him. You couldn't see one from t'other. No chance to shoot. It was Harry, in the end, that got his knife into the panther's jugular."

"If I'd known how he got it I'd never have come," was Linday's comment.

"That's what she said. She told me sure not to whisper how it happened."

"Is he crazy?" Linday asked coldly.

"They're all crazy. Him an' his brother are all the time devlin' each other to tom-fool things. I seen them swim the riffle last fall, bad water an' mush-ice runnin'—on a dare. They ain't nothin they won't tackle. An' she's 'most as bad. Not afraid some herself. She'll do anything Rocky'll let her. But he's almighty careful with her. Treats her like a queen. No camp-work or such for her. That's why another man an' me are hired on good wages. They've got slathers of money an' they're sure dippy on each other."

Linday's anger mounted. "I haven't any patience with fools. For two cents I'd turn back."

"No you wouldn't," Daw assured him confidently. "They ain't enough grub to turn back, an' we'll be there to-morrow. Just got to cross that last divide an' drop down to the cabin. An' they's a better reason. You're too far from home, an' I just naturally wouldn't let you turn back."

Exhausted as Linday was, the flash in his black eyes warned Daw that he had overreached himself. His hand went out.

"My mistake, Doc. Forget it. I reckon I'm gettin' some cranky what of losin' them dawgs."

Not one day, but three days later, the two men, after being snowed in on the summit by a spring blizzard, staggered up to a cabin that stood in a fat bottom beside the roaring Little Peco. Coming in from the bright sunshine to the dark cabin, Linday observed little of its occupants. He was vaguely aware of two men and a woman, but he was not interested in them. He went directly to the bunk of the injured man. The man was lying on his back, with eyes closed, and Linday noted the slender stencilling of the brows and the kinky silkiness of the brown hair. Thin and wan, the face seemed too small for the muscular neck, yet the delicate features were firmly moulded.

"What dressings have you been using?" Linday asked the woman.

"Corrosive sublimate, regular solution," came the answer.

He glanced quickly at her, shot an even quicker look at the face of the injured man, and stood erect. She breathed sharply. Linday turned to the men.

"You clear out—chop wood or something. I want to talk to his wife."

"I'm his brother," objected one of the men.

He looked at the woman, nodded reluctantly, and turned toward the door.

"Me, too?" Daw queried from the bench where he had flung himself down.

"You, too."

Linday busied himself with a superficial examination of the patient while the cabin was emptying.

"So that's your Rex Strang," he said.

She dropped her eyes to the man in the bunk, and then in silence returned Linday's gaze.

"Why don't you speak?"

She shrugged her shoulders. "What is the use? You know it is Rex Strang."

"Thank you. Though I might remind you that it is the first time I have ever seen him. Sit down." He waved her to a stool, himself taking the bench. "I'm really about all in, you know. There's no turnpike from the Yukon here."

He drew a penknife and began extracting a thorn from his thumb.

"What are going to do?" she asked.

"Eat and rest up before I start back."

"What are you going to do about . . ." She inclined her head toward the unconscious man.

"Nothing."

She went over to the bunk and rested her fingers lightly on the tight-curled hair.

"You mean you will kill him," she said slowly. "Kill him by doing nothing."

"Take it as killing if you like." He considered a moment, and stated his thought with a harsh little laugh. "From time immemorial in this weary old world it has been a not uncommon custom so to dispose of wife-stealers."

"You are unfair, Grant," she answered gently. "You forget that I was willing and that I desired. I was a free agent. Rex never stole me. It was you who lost me. I went with him willing and eager. As well accuse me of stealing him. We went together."

"A good way of looking at it," Linday conceded. "I see you are as keen as ever, Madge. That must have bothered him."

"A keen thinker can be a good lover—"

"And not so foolish," he broke in.

"Then you admit the wisdom of my course?"

He threw up his hands. "That's the devil of talking with clever women. A man always forgets and traps himself. I wouldn't wonder if you won him with a syllogism."

There was a hint of a smile in her straight-looking blue eyes.

"No, I take that back, Madge. If you'd been a numbskull you'd have won him on your looks. I ought to know—I've been through that mill, and damn it, I'm not through it yet."

His speech was quick and nervous and irritable, as it always was.

"Do you remember Lake Geneva?" she asked.

"I ought to. I was rather absurdly happy."

She nodded, and her eyes were luminous. "There is such a thing as old sake. Won't you, Grant, just remember back . . . ?"

"Now you're taking advantage," he smiled, and returned to the attack on his thumb. He drew the thorn out, inspected it critically. "No, thank you. I'm not playing the Good Samaritan."

"Yet you came here for an unknown man."

His impatience was sharp. "Do you think I'd have moved a step had I known he was my wife's lover?"

"But you are here . . . and there he lies. What are you going to do?"

"Nothing. He stole from me."

A knock came on the door.

"Get out!" he shouted.

"If you want any help—"

"Get out! Get a bucket of water! Set it down outside!"

"You are going to . . . ?" she began tremulously.

"Wash up."

She drew back from the brutality, and her lips tightened.

"Listen, Grant," she said steadily. "I shall tell his brother. I know the Strang breed. If you can forget old times, so can I. If you don't do something, he'll kill you. Why, even Tom Daw would if I asked."

"You should know me better than to threaten," he said gravely.

She closed her lips tightly, and watched his quick eyes take note of her trembling.

"It's not hysteria, Grant," she cried hastily. "You never saw me with hysteria. I've never had it. . . . I don't know what this is, but I'll control it. It's partly anger—with you. And it's fear. I don't want to lose him. I do love him, Grant. He is my king, my lover. And I have sat here beside him so many dreadful days now. Oh, Grant, please, please!"

"Just nerves," he commented drily. "Stay with it. You can beat it."

She went unsteadily back to the stool, where she watched him and fought for control. From the rough fireplace came the singing of a cricket. Outside two wolf-dogs bickered. The injured man's chest rose and fell perceptibly under the fur robes. She saw a smile, not altogether pleasant, on Linday's lips.

"How much do you love him?" he asked.

Her breast filled and rose, and her eyes shone with a proud light. He nodded in token that he was answered.

"Do you mind if I take a little time?" He stopped, thinking of a way to begin. . . . "I remember reading a story—Herbert Shaw wrote it, I think. There was a woman—young and beautiful; a man—magnificent, a lover of beauty and a wanderer. I don't know how much like your Rex Strang he was, but I imagine a resemblance. Well, this man was a painter, and a vagabond. He kissed—oh, many times and for several weeks—and rode away. She possessed for him what I thought you possessed for me . . . at Lake Geneva. And in ten years she wept the beauty out of her face. Some women turn yellow, you know, with old grief.

"Now it happened that the man went blind, and ten years after he'd left, led as a child by the hand he stumbled back to her. There was nothing left —he could no longer paint. And she was very happy, and glad he could not see her face. Remember, he worshipped beauty. And he held her in his arms and believed in her beauty . . . the memory of it was vivid in him. He never ceased to talk about it, and to lament that he could not behold it.

"One day he told her of five great pictures he wished to paint. If only his sight could be restored to paint them, he could write *finis* and be content. And then—never mind how—there came into her hands an elixir. Anointed on his eyes, it would cause his sight surely and fully to return."

Linday shrugged his shoulders.

"You see her struggle. With sight, he could paint his five pictures. Also, he would leave her. Beauty was his religion—it was impossible that he could abide her ruined face. Five days she struggled. Then she anointed his eyes."

Linday broke off and regarded her with searching eyes.

"The question is, do you love Rex Strang as much as that?"

"And if I do?" she continued.

"Do you?"

"Yes."

"You can give him up?"

Slow and reluctant—"Yes."

"And you will come with me?"

"Yes." This time her voice was a whisper. "When he is well—yes."

"You understand. It must be Lake Geneva again. You will be my wife."

She seemed to shrink and droop, but her head nodded.

"Very well." He stood up briskly, went to his pack, and began unstrapping. "I shall need help. Bring his brother in. Bring them all in. Boiling water—let there be lots of it. I've brought bandages, but let me see what you have in that line. . . . Here, Daw, build up that fire and start boiling all the water you can. . . . You," to the other man, "get that table out and under the window there. Clean it; scrub it; scald it. Clean, man, clean, as you never cleaned a thing before. You, Mrs. Strang, will be my helper. No sheets, I suppose. Well, we'll manage somehow. . . . You're his brother, sir. I'll give the anaesthetic, but you must keep it going afterward. Now listen, while I instruct you. In the first place—but before that, can you take a pulse? . . ."

Noted for his daring and success as a surgeon, through the days and weeks that followed Linday exceeded himself in daring and success. Never, because of the frightful mangling and breakage, and the long delay, had he encountered so terrible a case. But he had never had a healthier specimen of human wreck to work upon—had it not been for the patient's catlike vitality and incredible physical and mental grip on life, he would certainly have failed.

There were days of high temperature and delirium; days of heart-sinking when Strang's pulse was barely perceptible; days when he lay conscious, eyes weary and drawn, the sweat of pain on his face. Linday was indefatigable, cruelly efficient, audacious and fortunate, daring hazard after hazard, and winning. He was not content to make the man live; he devoted himself to the intricate and perilous problem of making him whole again.

"He will be a cripple?" Madge queried.

"He will not awkwardly walk and talk and be a limping caricature of his former self," Linday told her. "He shall run and leap, swim riffles, ride bears, fight panthers, and do all things to the top of his fool desire. And, I warn you, he will fascinate women just as of old. . . . Will you like that? Are you content? Remember, you will not be with him."

"Go on, go on," she breathed. "Make him whole. Make him what he was."

More than once, whenever Strang's recuperation permitted, Linday put him under the anaesthetic and did terrible things, cutting and sewing, re-wiring and connecting the disrupted organism. Later, a hitch developed in the left arm—Strang could lift it so far, and no farther. Linday applied himself to the problem. It was a case of more wires, shrunken, twisted, disconnected. Again it was cut and switch and ease and disentangle. And all that saved Strang was his tremendous vitality and the health of his flesh.

"You will kill him," his brother complained. "Let him be. For God's sake let him be. A live and crippled man is better than a whole and dead one."

Linday flamed in wrath. "You get out! Out of this cabin till you can come back and say that I make him live. Pull—by God, man, you've got to pull with me with all your soul. Your brother's travelling a razor-edge. Do you understand? A thought can topple him off. Now get out, and come back sweet and wholesome, convinced beyond all absoluteness that he will live and be what he was before you and he were fools together."

The brother, his eyes threatening, looked to Madge for counsel.

"Go, go, please," she begged. "He is right. I know he is right."

Another time, when Strang's condition seemed more promising, the brother said:

"Doc, you're a wonder, and all this time I've forgotten to ask your name."

"None of your damn business. Don't bother me. Get out."

The mangled right arm ceased from its healing, burst open again in a frightful wound.

"Necrosis," said Linday.

"That does it," groaned the brother.

"Shut up!" Linday snarled. "Take Daw and Bill. Get rabbits—live, healthy ones. Trap them."

"How many?" the brother asked.

"Forty of them—four thousand—forty thousand—all you can get. You'll help me, Mrs. Strang. I'm going to dig into that arm."

And he dug in swiftly, unerringly, scraping away disintegrating bone, ascertaining the extent of the active decay.

"It never would have happened," he told Madge, "if he hadn't had so many other things needing vitality first. Even he didn't have vitality enough to go around. That piece must go. He could manage without it, but rabbit-bone will make it what it was."

From the hundreds of rabbits brought in, he rejected, selected, tested, selected and tested again. He used the last of his chloroform and achieved the bone-graft—living bone to living bone, living man and living rabbit indissolubly bound together, their mutual processes uniting and reconstructing a perfect arm.

And through the whole trying period, especially as Strang mended, there was talk between Linday and Madge. He was not kind, nor she rebellious.

"It's a nuisance," he told her. "But the law is the law, and you'll need a divorce before we can marry again. What do you say? Shall we go to Lake Geneva?"

"As you will," she said.

And he, another time, angrily: "What in hell did you see in him anyway? I know he had money. But you and I were managing to get along with some sort of comfort. My practice was averaging around forty thousand a year—I went over the books afterward. Villas and yachts were about all that were denied you."

"Perhaps you've explained it," she answered. "Perhaps you were too interested in your practice. Maybe you forgot me."

"Humph," he sneered. "And may not your Rex be too interested in panthers and short sticks?"

He continually goaded her to explain what he chose to call her infatuation for the other man.

"There is no explanation," she replied. . . . And finally she retorted, "No one can explain love. I least of all. I only *knew* love. There was once at Fort Vancouver a baron of the Hudson Bay Company who chided the resident Church of England parson. The dominie had written home to England complaining that the Company folk, from the head factor down, were addicted to Indian wives. 'Why didn't you explain the extenuating circumstances?' demanded the baron. Replied the dominie; 'A cow's tail grows downward. I do not attempt to explain why the cow's tail grows downward. I merely cite the fact.' "

Linday snorted.

"What brought you into the Klondike, of all places?" she asked once.

"Too much money. No wife to spend it on. Wanted a rest. Possibly overwork. I tried Colorado, but their telegrams followed me, and some of them did themselves. I went on to Seattle. Same thing. Ransom ran his wife out to me in a special train. There was no escaping it. Operation successful. Local newspapers got wind of it. You can imagine the rest. I had to hide, so I ran in this direction. And—Tom Daw found me playing whist in a cabin down on the Yukon."

Came the day when Strang's bed was carried out of doors and into the sunshine.

"Let me tell him now," she said.

"No. I'm making a complete job of this. I want no set-backs. There's a slight hitch still in that left arm. It's a little thing, but I am going to remake him as God made him. Tomorrow I've planned to get into that arm and take out the kink. It will mean a couple of days on his back. I'm sorry there's no more chloroform. He'll just have to bite on a spike and hang on. He can do it. He's got grit for a dozen men."

Summer came on. The snow disappeared, save on the far peaks of the Rockies to the east. The days lengthened till there was no darkness, the sun dipping at midnight, due north, for a few minutes beneath the horizon. Linday never let up on Strang. He studied his walk, his body movements, saw to it that massage was given him without end, until he declared that Tom Daw, Bill, and the brother were properly qualified for Turkish bath and osteopathic hospital attendants.

But Linday was not yet satisfied. He put Strang through his whole reper-
toire of physical feats, searching him for hidden weaknesses. He put him on
his back again for a week, opened up his leg, played a deft trick with the
smaller veins, scraped a spot of bone no larger than a coffee grain.

"Let me tell him," Madge begged.

"Not yet," was the answer. "You will tell him when I am ready."

July passed, and most of August. He ordered Strang out on trail to get a
moose, and kept at his heels, watching him, studying him. Strang was slender, magnificent in his strength, and he walked as Linday had seen no man
walk, effortlessly, with all his body, so easy that to the eye the speed was
completely deceptive. It was the killing pace of which Tom Daw had spoken. Linday toiled behind, sweating and panting; from time to time, when
the ground favoured, making short runs to keep up. At the end of ten miles
he called a halt and threw himself down on the moss.

"Enough!" he cried. "I can't keep up with you."

He mopped his face, and Strang sat down on a spruce log, smiling at the
doctor, and, with the camaraderie of a pantheist, at all the landscape.

"Any twinges, or hurts, or aches, or hints of aches?" Linday demanded.

Strang shook his curly head and stretched his lithe body, living joyously
in every fibre of it.

"You'll do, Strang. For a winter or two you may expect to feel the cold
and damp in the old wounds. But that will pass, and perhaps you may
escape it altogether."

"God, Doctor, you have performed miracles with me. I don't know how
to thank you. I don't even know your name."

"Which doesn't matter. I've pulled you through, and that's the main
thing."

"But it's a name men must know out in the world," Strang persisted.
"I'll wager I'd recognize it if I heard it."

"I think you would," was Linday's answer. "I want one final test, and
then I'm done with you. Over the divide at the head of this creek is a
tributary of the Big Windy. Daw tells me that last year you went over, down
to the middle fork, and back again in three days. He said you nearly killed
him, too. You are to wait here and camp to-night. I'll send Daw along with
the camp outfit. Then it's up to you to go to the middle fork and back in
the same time as last year."

"Now," Linday said to Madge. "You have an hour in which to pack. I'll
go and get the canoe ready. Bill's bringing in the moose and won't get back
till dark. We'll make my cabin to-day, and in a week we'll be in Dawson."

"I was in hope . . ." She broke off proudly.

"That I'd forego the fee?"

"Oh, a compact is a compact, but you needn't have been so hateful in the collecting. You have not been fair. You have sent him away for three days, and robbed me of my last words with him."

"Leave a letter."

"I shall tell him all."

"Anything less than all would be unfair to the three of us," was Linday's answer.

When he returned from the canoe, her outfit was packed, the letter written.

"Let me read it," he said, "if you don't mind."

Her hesitation was momentary, then she passed it over. . . .

"Pretty straight," he said, when he had finished it. "Now, are you ready?"

He carried her pack down to the bank, and, kneeling, steadied the canoe with one hand while he extended the other to help her in. He watched her closely, but without a tremor she held out her hand to his and prepared to step on board.

"Wait," he said. "One moment. You remember the story I told you of the elixir. I failed to tell you the end. And when she had anointed his eyes and was about to depart, it chanced she saw in the mirror that her beauty had been restored to her. And he opened his eyes, and cried out with joy at the sight of her beauty, and folded her in his arms."

She waited, tense but controlled, for him to continue, wonder faintly beginning to show in her eyes.

"You are very beautiful, Madge." He paused, then added drily, "The rest is obvious. I fancy Rex Strang's arms won't remain long empty. Good-bye."

"Grant . . ." she said, whispering, and in her voice was all the speech that needs no words for understanding.

He stepped into the canoe and put out a slender, nervous hand.

"Good-bye," he said.

She folded both her hands about his.

"Dear, strong hand," she murmured, and bent over and kissed it.

He jerked it away, thrust the canoe out from the bank, dipped the paddle in the swift rush of the current, and entered the head of the riffle where the water poured glassily before it burst into a white madness of foam.

BROTHERS

John Dobbyn

They used to make jokes, all the boys in the bar—
Oh, I know that they meant him no harm—
But behind his big grin there was pain in his eyes,
And to end it I'd give my right arm.
My brother and me, we came north from St. Joe
To run traps 'fore the Yukon got tame—
He was normal back then, and the size of two men,
With a heart 'bout as big as his frame.
I loved that old cuss, and the best part for us
Was the freedom to roam as we will
Through a wild icy realm only God could create,
Where the world is froze breathless and still.
We learned to track beaver and seals through the ice
And to steer by the great Northern Lights
From the Eskimo nomads who'd treat us like gods
'Cause they still had no fear of the whites.
They told us of valleys locked off by the ice
And the old ones would always insist
They'd seen beaver with pelts that were white as the snow,
Though God knows if they really exist.
My brother was kind of an overgrown kid
And the thought of those pelts drove him mad—
He'd have gone it alone, and I couldn't have that,
So we sold every pelt that we had
And bought us some dogs that were bred to survive
Where a polar bear'd freeze in the womb—
We set out on a quest that I wish we'd forgot,
And we mushed into God's icy tomb.

The tale of that trek is a nightmare and more—
Even now it brings pain to recall
How we lost, one by one, every dog that we had.
But that wasn't the worst of it all.
We came too close to death just to walk away clean—
Things could never get back where they'd been.
We got out with our lives, but my brother'd been broke—
He was never quite normal again.

By the time we were physically good as we'd get,
It was clear that our wild days were done—
My brother Bill's brain wasn't up to the games
That are played by the ice, wind, and sun,
He had lost all the feeling in both of his hands,
And his fingers were rigid as wood,
The feeling was slow to come back to the palms
But the fingers were stone-cold for good.
We moved to the south, to a town that sprang up
Like so many when Gold was the cry,
And got into the business of dealing in furs
With the trappers who used to come by.
To sleep under a roof and to live in four walls—
Well, to tell you the truth, it was hell
For two wind-driven spirits whose roof was the stars,
But we tried, and the business did well.
I guess, looking back, we had three peaceful years—
Like they say, God just filled up our cup—
But it came to be clear that I'd have to go south
To look after some things that came up.
I hated the thought, 'cause it meant leaving Bill
And I wasn't quite sure he could cope,
But an offer came through that I couldn't refuse
And I figured there might be some hope.
A wrinkled old cuss with the nickname of "Doc"
Had an office for peddling pills—
No one knew if he had a license to trade,
But he treated most everyone's ills.
He had taken a shine to this brother of mine,
Always kind though my brother was slow,
So when I had to leave it was Doc who came through
With a promise to keep him in tow.
With that put to rest, I lit out for the west,

To the coast and a ship to the States.
I was plagued by the thought of my brother alone,
So I booked on the earliest dates—
Still, the journey was long and the meetings were slow—
It took weeks just to get the right deals.
By the time I mushed back through the last hundred miles,
The winter was hard on my heels.

You know how you sometimes can feel in your bones
A chill that you can't quite explain?
Just as soon as I drove past the outskirts of town,
I could sense it was under a strain.
From the men in the street to the girls by the bar,
Even kids that came up to so high,
There wasn't a one, as I drove down the street,
That could look me quite straight in the eye.
I drove straight to the man on the far side of town
Where we stabled the sled and the team—
Even Charlie, our friend, came on cold as a clam.
It was crazy—like some kind of dream.
He mumbled some stuff about feeding the dogs,
And I said, "Dang it, Charlie, hold on,
I come back to this town after two months away
And you all seem to wish I'd stayed gone."
"It ain't you," mumbled Charlie, "I guess you ain't heard—
Been a killin' that's got us undone.
Good old Doc, he was shot with a Colt .44
And the thing is, it's your brother's gun."
"You know better than that," was 'bout all I could say
'Cause it hit me like two ton of lead.
"Where's he now?" "He lit out for the north with a team—
We ain't seen him since Doc was found dead."
I kept trying to puzzle it out in my mind, but I couldn't—
My mind seemed to block.
The one thing I knew just as God is my judge,
My brother could never hurt Doc.
"Did you rent him a team? Did he say he'd be back?
Can you just give me someplace to start?"
"Well," old Charlie said, "it was no team of mine, and
Ya know, that's not the funniest part—
He came by just before this whole business came up,
'Cause we used to be sort of good friends,

And he tells me he's heard where some white beaver run
Way up north where the Bear Claw Ridge ends.
The next day he was gone—he was seen drivin' north
And that mornin' the word's around town
That old Doc has been killed and his place has been robbed
And your brother's old gun's on the ground."
My dogs needed rest, and I needed it, too,
But I guess it was not in the dice.
I knew where he went, and I'd rather be sent
Down to hell for a bucket of ice.
Those old ridges were treacherous, even in spring,
And with winter now well underway
I'd be lucky to make it back safely myself—
With my brother, there'd be hell to pay.
I laid in supplies that I'd need for the trip
And before I turned in for the night,
I dropped in for a chat with the Mountie in town
And it nearly turned into a fight.
He was stuck on the notion my brother'd killed Doc—
He was fixing to go bring him in.
I told him my brother and Doc were good friends,
But it seemed there was no way to win.
'Til I finally mentioned a fact that struck home
And I had him on our side at last—
There was no way my brother could squeeze off a round
With those fingers as stiff as a cast.
I figured that one of the trappers that camped
By the creek at the edge of the town
Had probably tried to rob Doc and been caught
And he panicked and shot old Doc down,
Then he fed my poor brother that white-beaver tale,
And he gave him a sled and a team.
When my brother lit out, he could lay blame on him,
And my brother played into his scheme.
If we found who it was that provided the dogs
For the goose-chase my brother was on,
Then we'd have us the killer and that would be that,
So I packed up to mush out at dawn.

For a man who had half of the sense God gave geese,
This whole trip was an idiot's trek—
Just inhaling the gusts of the fresh winter blasts

Felt like splinters of glass in the neck.
After three weeks, I'd moved to the crest of the ridge
At the northernmost tip of the chain—
If the furies of winter were vicious below,
At the top they could triple the pain.
Though we both took a beating—the dogs and myself—
I needed the height for the view
Of the region below where I figured he'd be,
It's the best that I thought I could do.
After three days of mushing that murderous crest,
Almost bled of the last drop of hope,
I thought that I spotted a speck in the snow,
On the face of a far-distant slope.
It was instinct, not reason, that now set the pace—
I could feel the lash making demands
That the dogs couldn't meet, but I couldn't let up,
'Cause my brother's life lay in my hands.
The couple of hours of sunlight had passed,
And only the moon and the stars
Were left for the dogs to pick paths in the snow
Between icy crevasses and bars.
By a miracle, God brought us through to the dawn
And, although they survived the terrain,
The pace was too much for a few of the dogs,
'Cause their hearts seemed to burst with the strain.
I cut loose the traces wherever they dropped
And pushed on with the dogs that hung on—
Every loss made it tougher on those that were left,
And their will to survive was near gone.
I was practically paralyzed—running on nerves—
But each time that I'd look up ahead,
There was no sign of movement, and that was the drive
To press on when my muscles were dead.

It was either next day, or the day after that—
I don't know, it's just kind of a blur—
That I got to the spot where my brother lay curled
On his sled under layers of fur.
I scrambled as fast as my muscles could crawl,
Though the dread nearly drove me insane,
There was nothing to do but to hug him and cry—
God had loosed him from all of his pain.

I think I passed out, 'cause the sun had gone down
By the time I was able to move—
I was hollow and empty in body and mind,
But I knew I had something to prove.
My brother was dead and he couldn't care less—
Even so, they had blackened his name.
I was bound and determined to set the facts straight.
If I died in the try—all the same.
I gave him a burial such as I could
And I said a few words to the Lord,
And then back to the trail—there was no time for tears,
Though his loss cut my heart like a sword.

I had only three dogs that could still pull a trace—
Only one of my brother's could stand—
But I figured that that would be more than enough
If things worked out the way that I planned.
I hitched up the three in a trace close to me
And I hitched up my brother's as lead,
Then I fashioned a sack from the furs on the sled—
It had all of the room that I'd need.
There were two main concerns. One was making it back
To the town before death pulled the shade.
The second was finding the man who killed Doc,
And I prayed that both points could be made.
I fastened the sack to the trace and climbed in,
Like a moth in a furry cocoon,
I yelled, and the dogs, without guidance from me,
Set a course for the sun at high noon.
I knew that they'd head for the place they'd been fed
And the lead dog knew just where to go—
He set them a pace like an Eskimo race
For the home that he'd known down below.
Without sled or supplies, my own weight on the trace
Was a feather they handled with ease.
In exhaustion my body cried out to go limp,
But I knew if I did I could freeze.
I kept flailing my arms and my legs in the sack
To send blood to my fingers and toes.
In my dark little cave, there was no sense of time,
Just how long it was God only knows—

I can only remember a fog rolling in,
A sweet mist that enveloped my mind,
And at some point in time I passed over the line
To a rest of a different kind.
It was bright and sublime, and it called me to climb
To a height that I couldn't believe.
I was ready to go, but some tug from below
Brought me back to the body I'd leave.
I heard rumbles and murmurs, then voices I knew,
And the mists that I loved seemed to part—
I was back in a shed on a kind of a bed
And I heard the faint beat of my heart.
They said I'd been out for a week since the day
That the dogs hauled my body back in—
I had bad signs of frost, but they got me in time
And they saved every inch of my skin.
Like I figured, the lead dog had found his way home
To the very last home that he'd known—
He came back to the trapper who traded him off
To my brother to use as his own.
The Mountie had spotted us, just as we'd planned,
And he followed us right to the door
Of that trapper who later confessed to the crime.
I figure that settled the score.

That was twenty years back—Lord, it seems like a week.
When I healed, I went back to the wild,
Like an animal caged in the prime of its life,
To run free turned me back to a child.
Together we've coursed God's majestic back yard
And we've not had one unfulfilled day.
We've been unified spirits—my brother and me—
He's been with me each step of the way.

SPIES,
TOUGH GUYS
& PRIVATE EYES

THE LIVING DAYLIGHTS

Ian Fleming

James Bond lay in the five-hundred-yard firing point of the famous Century Range at Bisley. The white peg in the grass beside him said 44, and the same number was repeated high up on the distant butt above the single six-feet-square target that, to the human eye and in the late summer dusk, looked no larger than a postage stamp. But through Bond's glass—an infrared sniperscope fixed above his rifle—the lens covered the whole canvas. He could even clearly distinguish the pale blue and beige colors in which the target was divided, and the six-inch semicircular bull's-eye looked as big as the half-moon that was already beginning to show low down in the darkening sky above the distant crest of Chobham Ridges.

James Bond's last shot had been an inner left. Not good enough. He took another glance at the yellow and blue wind flags. They were streaming across range from the east rather more stiffly than when he had begun his shoot half an hour before, and he set two clicks more to the right on the wind gauge and traversed the cross-wires on the sniperscope back to the point of aim. Then he settled himself, put his trigger finger gently inside the guard and onto the curve of the trigger, shallowed his breathing, and very, very softly squeezed.

The vicious crack of the shot boomed across the empty range. The target disappeared below ground, and at once the dummy came up in its place. Yes. The black panel was in the bottom right-hand corner this time, not in the bottom left. A bull's-eye.

"Good," said the voice of the chief range officer from behind and above him. "Stay with it."

The target was already up again, and Bond put his cheek back to its warm patch on the chunky wooden stock and his eye to the rubber eyepiece of the scope. He wiped his gun hand down the side of his trousers and took the pistol grip that jutted sharply down below the trigger guard. He splayed his legs an inch more. Now there were to be five rounds rapid. It would be interesting to see if that would produce "fade." He guessed not. This extraordinary weapon the armorer had somehow got his hands on gave one the feeling that a standing man at a mile would be easy meat.

It was mostly a .308-caliber International Experimental Target rifle built by Winchester to help American marksmen at World Championships, and it had the usual gadgets of superaccurate target weapons—a curled aluminum hand at the back of the butt that extended under the armpit and held the stock firmly into the shoulder, and an adjustable pinion below the rifle's center of gravity to allow the stock to be nailed into its grooved wooden rest. The armorer had had the usual single-shot bolt action replaced by a five-shot magazine, and he had assured Bond that if he allowed as little as two seconds between shots to steady the weapon there would be no fade even at five hundred yards.

For the job that Bond had to do, he guessed that two seconds might be a dangerous loss of time if he missed with his first shot. Anyway, M. had said that the range would be not more than three hundred yards. Bond would cut it down to one second—almost continuous fire.

"Ready?"

"Yes."

"I'll give you a countdown from five. Now! Five, four, three, two, one. Fire!"

The ground shuddered slightly and the air sang as the five whirling scraps of cupronickel spat off into the dusk. The target went down and quickly rose again, decorated with four small white discs closely grouped on the bull's-eye. There was no fifth disc—not even a black one to show an inner or an outer.

"The last round was low," said the range officer lowering his night-glasses. "Thanks for the contribution. We sift the sand on those butts at the end of every year. Never get less than fifteen tons of good lead and copper scrap out of them. Good money."

Bond had got to his feet. Corporal Menzies from the armorers' section appeared from the pavilion of the Gun Club and knelt down to dismantle the Winchester and its rest. He looked up at Bond. He said with a hint of criticism, "You were taking it a bit fast, sir. Last round was bound to jump wide."

"I know, Corporal. I wanted to see how fast I *could* take it. I'm not blaming the weapon. It's a hell of a fine job. Please tell the armorer so from me. Now I'd better get moving. You're finding your own way back to London, aren't you?"

"Yes. Good night, sir."

The chief range officer handed Bond a record of his shoot—two sighting shots and then ten rounds at each hundred yards up to five hundred.

"Damned good firing with this visibility. You ought to come back next year and have a bash at the Queen's Prize. It's open to all comers nowadays—British Commonwealth, that is."

"Thanks. Trouble is, I'm not all that much in England. And thanks for spotting for me." Bond glanced at the distant clock tower. On either side, the red danger flag and the red signal drum were coming down to show that firing had ceased. The hands stood at 9:15. "I'd like to buy you a drink, but I've got an appointment in London. Can we hold it over until that Queen's Prize you were talking about?"

The range officer nodded noncommittally. He had been looking forward to finding out more about this man who had appeared out of the blue after a flurry of signals from the Ministry of Defense and had then proceeded to score well over ninety percent at all distances. And that after the range was closed for the night and visibility was poor-to-bad. And why had he, who only officiated at the annual July meeting, been ordered to be present? And why had he been told to see that Bond had a six-inch bull's-eye at five hundred instead of the regulation fifteen-inch? And why this flummery with the danger flag and signal drum that were only used on ceremonial occasions? To put pressure on the man? To give an edge of urgency to the shoot?

Bond. Commander James Bond. The N.R.A. would surely have a record of anyone who could shoot like that. He'd remember to give them a call. Funny time to have an appointment in London. Probably a girl. The range officer's undistinguished face assumed a disgruntled expression. Sort of fellow who got all the girls he wanted.

The two men walked through the handsome façade of Club Row behind the range to Bond's car, which stood opposite the bullet-pitted iron reproduction of Landseer's famous Running Deer.

"Nice-looking job," commented the range officer. "Never seen a body like that on a Continental. Have it made specially?"

"Yes. The Mark IV's are anyway really only two-seaters. And damned little luggage space. So I got Mulliner's to make it into a real two-seater with plenty of trunk space. Selfish car, I'm afraid. Well, good night. And thanks again." The twin exhausts boomed healthily, and the back wheels briefly spat gravel.

The chief range officer watched the ruby lights vanish up King's Avenue toward the London Road. He turned on his heel and went to find Corporal Menzies on a search for information that was to prove fruitless. The corporal remained as wooden as the big mahogany box he was in the process of loading into a khaki Land Rover without military symbols.

The range officer was a major. He tried pulling his rank without success. The Land Rover hammered away in Bond's wake. The major walked mood-

ily off to the offices of the National Rifle Association to try and find out
what he wanted in the library under *Bond, J.*

James Bond's appointment was not with a girl. It was with a B.E.A. flight
to Hanover and Berlin. As he bit off the miles to London Airport, pushing
the big car hard so as to have plenty of time for a drink, three drinks, before
the takeoff, only part of his mind was on the road. The rest was reexamin-
ing, for the umpteenth time, the sequence that was now leading him to an
appointment with an airplane. But only an interim appointment. His final
rendezvous on one of the next three nights in Berlin was with a man.

He had to see this man and he had to be sure to shoot him dead.

When, at around 2:30 that afternoon, James Bond had gone in through
the double padded doors and had sat down opposite the turned-away profile on the other side of the big desk, he had sensed trouble. There was no
greeting. M's head was sunk into his stiff turned-down collar in a Churchil-
lian pose of gloomy reflection, and there was a droop of bitterness at the
corner of his lips. He swiveled his chair around to face Bond, gave him an
appraising glance as if, Bond thought, to see that his tie was straight and his
hair properly brushed, and then began speaking, fast, biting off his sentences as if he wanted to be rid of what he was saying, and of Bond, as
quickly as possible.

"Number 272. He's a good man. You won't have come across him.
Simple reason that he's been holed up in Novaya Zemlya since the war.
Now he's trying to get out—loaded with stuff. Atomic and rockets. And
their plan for a whole new series of tests. For nineteen sixty-one. To put the
heat on the West. Something to do with Berlin. Don't quite get the picture,
but the FO says if it's true it's terrific. Makes nonsense of the Geneva
Conference and all this blather about nuclear disarmament the Communist
bloc is putting out.

"He's got as far as East Berlin. But he's got practically the whole of the
KGB on his tail—and the East German security forces, of course. He's
holed up somewhere in East Berlin, and he got one message over to us.
That he'd be coming across between six and seven P.M. on one of the next
three nights—tomorrow, next day, or next day. He gave the crossing point.
Trouble is"—the downward curve of M.'s lips became even more bitter—
"the courier he used was a double. Station WB bowled him out yesterday.
Quite by chance. Had a lucky break with one of the KGB codes. The
courier'll be flown out for trial, of course. But that won't help. The KGB
knows that 272 will be making a run for it. They know when. They know
where. They know just as much as we do—and no more.

"Now, the code we cracked was a one-day-only setting on their machines. But we got the whole of that day's traffic, and that was good

enough. They plan to shoot him on the run. At this street crossing between East and West Berlin he gave us in his message. They're mounting quite an operation—Operation Extase, they call it. Put their best sniper on the job. All we know about him is that his code name is the Russian for Trigger. Station WB guesses he's the same man they've used before for sniper work. Long-range stuff across the frontier. He's going to be guarding this crossing every night, and his job is to get 272.

"Of course they'd obviously prefer to do a smoother job with machine guns and what-have-you. But it's quiet in Berlin at the moment, and apparently the word is it's got to stay so. Anyway"—M. shrugged—"they've got confidence in this Trigger operator, and that's the way it's going to be!"

"Where do I come in, sir?" But James Bond had guessed the answer, guessed why M. was showing his dislike of the whole business. This was going to be dirty work, and Bond, because he belonged to the Double-O Section, had been chosen for it. Perversely, Bond wanted to force M. to put it in black and white. This was going to be bad news, dirty news, and he didn't want to hear it from one of the section officers, or even from the Chief of Staff. This was to be murder. All right. Let M. bloody well say so.

"Where do you come in, 007?" M. looked coldly across the desk. "You know where you come in. You've got to kill this sniper. And you've got to kill him before he gets 272. That's all. Is that understood?"

The clear blue eyes remained as cold as ice. But Bond knew that they remained so only with an effort of will. M. didn't like sending any man to a killing. But, when it had to be done, he always put on this fierce, cold act of command. Bond knew why. It was to take some of the pressure, some of the guilt, off the killer's shoulders.

So now Bond, who knew these things, decided to make it easy and quick for M. He got to his feet. "That's all right, sir. I suppose the Chief of Staff has got all the gen. I'd better go and put in some practice. It wouldn't do to miss." He walked to the door.

M. said quietly, "Sorry to have to hand this to you. Nasty job. But it's got to be done well."

"I'll do my best, sir." James Bond walked out and closed the door behind him. He didn't like the job, but on the whole he'd rather have it himself than have the responsibility of ordering someone else to go and do it.

The Chief of Staff had been only a shade more sympathetic. "Sorry you've bought this one, James," he had said. "But Tanqueray was definite that he hadn't got anyone good enough on his station, and this isn't the sort of job you can ask a regular soldier to do. Plenty of top marksmen in the B.A.O.R., but a live target needs another kind of nerve. Anyway, I've been on to Bisley and fixed a shoot for you tonight at eight fifteen when the

ranges will be closed. Visibility should be about the same as you'll be getting in Berlin around an hour earlier. The armorer's got the gun—a real
target job—and he's sending it down with one of his men. You'll find your
own way. Then you're booked on a midnight B.E.A. charter flight to Berlin. Take a taxi to this address."

He handed Bond a piece of paper. "Go up to the fourth floor, and you'll
find Tanqueray's Number Two waiting for you. Then I'm afraid you'll just
have to sit it out for the next three days."

"How about the gun? Am I supposed to take it through the German
customs in a golfbag or something?"

The Chief of Staff hadn't been amused. "It'll go over in the FO pouch.
You'll have it by tomorrow midday." He had reached for a signal pad.
"Well, you'd better get cracking. I'll just let Tanqueray know everything's
fixed."

James Bond glanced down at the dim blue face of the dashboard clock.
10:15. With any luck, by this time tomorrow it would all be finished. After
all, it was the life of this man Trigger against the life of 272. It wasn't
exactly murder. Pretty near it, though.

He gave a vicious blast on his triple wind horns at an inoffensive family
sedan, took the roundabout in a quite unnecessary dry skid, wrenched the
wheel harshly to correct it, and pointed the nose of the Bentley toward the
distant glow that was London Airport.

The ugly six-story building at the corner of the Kochstrasse and the
Wilhelmstrasse was the only one standing in a waste of empty bombed
space. Bond paid off his taxi and got a brief impression of the neighborhood—waist-high weeds and half-tidied rubble walls stretching away to a
big deserted crossroads lit by a central cluster of yellowish arc lamps—
before he pushed the bell for the fourth floor and at once heard the click of
the door opener.

The door closed itself behind him, and he walked over the uncarpeted
cement floor to the old-fashioned lift. The smell of cabbage, cheap cigar
smoke, and stale sweat reminded him of other apartment houses in Germany and Central Europe. Even the sigh and faint squeal of the slow lift
were part of a hundred assignments when he had been fired off by M., like a
projectile, at some distant target where a problem waited for him, waited to
be solved by him.

At least this time the reception committee was on his side. This time
there was nothing to fear at the top of the stairs.

Number Two of Secret Service Station WB was a lean, tense man in his
early forties. He wore the uniform of his profession—well-cut, well-used,
lightweight tweeds in a dark green herringbone, a soft white silk shirt, and

an old school tie (in his case Wykehamist). At the sight of the tie, and while they exchanged conventional greetings in the small musty lobby of the apartment, Bond's spirits, already low, sank another degree.

He knew the type—backbone of the civil service . . . overcrammed and underloved at Winchester . . . a good second in P.P.E. at Oxford . . . the war, staff jobs he would have done meticulously—perhaps an O.B.E. . . . Allied Control Commission in Germany where he had been recruited into the I Branch . . . And thence—because he was the ideal staff man and A-One with Security, and because he thought he would find life, drama, romance—the things he had never had—into the Secret Service. A sober, careful man had been needed to chaperone Bond on this ugly business. Captain Paul Sender, late of the Welsh Guards, had been the obvious choice. He had bought it. Now, like a good Wykehamist, he concealed his distaste for the job beneath careful, trite conversation as he showed Bond the layout of the apartment and the arrangements that had been made for the executioner's preparedness and, to a modest extent, his comfort.

The flat consisted of a large double bedroom, a bathroom, and a kitchen containing tinned food, milk, butter, eggs, bread, and one bottle of Dimple Haig. The only odd feature in the bedroom was that one of the double beds was angled up against the curtains covering the single broad window and was piled high with three mattresses below the bedclothes.

Captain Sender said, "Care to have a look at the field of fire? Then I can explain what the other side has in mind."

Bond was tired. He didn't particularly want to go to sleep with the picture of the battlefield on his mind. But he said, "That'd be fine."

Captain Sender switched off the lights. Chinks from the streetlight at the intersection showed round the curtains. "Don't want to draw the curtains," said Captain Sender. "Unlikely, but they may be on the lookout for a covering party for 272. If you'd just lie on the bed and get your head under the curtains, I'll brief you about what you'll be looking at. Look to the left."

It was a sash window, and the bottom half was open. The mattresses, by design, gave only a little, and James Bond found himself more or less in the firing position he had been in on the Century Range. But now he was staring across broken, thickly weeded bombed ground toward the bright river of the Zimmerstrasse—the border with East Berlin. It looked about a hundred and fifty yards away. Captain Sender's voice from above him and behind the curtain began reciting. It reminded Bond of a spiritualist séance.

"That's bombed ground in front of you. Plenty of cover. A hundred and thirty yards of it up to the frontier. Then the frontier—the street—and then a big stretch of more bombed ground on the enemy side. That's why 272 chose this route. It's one of the few places in the town which is broken land

—thick weeds, ruined walls, cellars—on both sides of the frontier . . . 272 will sneak through that mess on the other side, and make a dash across the Zimmerstrasse for the mess on our side. Trouble is, he'll have thirty yards of brightly lit frontier to sprint across. That'll be the killing ground. Right?"

Bond said, "Yes." He said it softly. The scent of the enemy, the need to take care, already had him by the nerves.

"To your left, that big new ten-story block is the Haus der Ministerien, the chief brain center of East Berlin. You can see the lights are still on in most of the windows. Most of those will stay on all night. These chaps work hard—shifts all round the clock. You probably won't need to worry about the lighted ones. This Trigger chap will almost certainly fire from one of the dark windows. You'll see there's a block of four together on the corner above the intersection. They've stayed dark last night and tonight. They've got the best field of fire. From here, their range varies from three hundred to three hundred and ten yards. I've got all the figures when you want them.

"You needn't worry about much else. That street stays empty during the night—only the motorized patrols about every half an hour. Light armored car with a couple of motorcycles as escort. Last night, which I suppose is typical, between six and seven when this thing's going to be done, there were a few people that came and went out of that side door. Civil-servant types. Before that nothing out of the ordinary—usual flow of people in and out of a busy government building, except, of all things, a whole damned woman's orchestra. Made a hell of a racket in some concert hall they've got in there. Part of the block is the Ministry of Culture.

"Otherwise nothing—certainly none of the KGB people we know, or any signs of preparation for a job like this. But there wouldn't be. They're careful chaps, the opposition. Anyway, have a good look. Don't forget it's darker than it will be tomorrow around six. But you can get the general picture."

Bond got the general picture, and it stayed with him long after the other man was asleep and snoring softly with a gentle regular clicking sound. A Wykehamist snore, Bond reflected irritably.

Yes, he had got the picture. The picture of a flicker of movement among the shadowy ruins on the other side of the gleaming river of light, a pause, the wild zigzagging sprint of a man in the full glare of the arcs, the crash of gunfire—and then either a crumpled, sprawling heap in the middle of the wide street or the noise of his onward dash through the weeds and rubble of the Western Sector. Sudden death or a home run. The true gauntlet!

How much time would Bond have to spot the Russian sniper in one of those dark windows? And kill him? Five seconds? Ten?

When dawn edged the curtains with gun metal, Bond capitulated to his fretting mind. It had won. He went softly into the bathroom and surveyed the ranks of medicine bottles that a thoughtful Secret Service had provided to keep its executioner in good shape. He selected the Tuinal, chased down two of the ruby and blue depth charges with a glass of water, and went back to bed. Then, poleaxed, he slept.

He awoke at midday. The flat was empty. Bond drew the curtains to let in the gray Prussian day, and, standing well back from the window, gazed out at the drabness of Berlin, and listened to the tram noises and to the distant screeching of the U-Bahn as it took the big curve into the Zoo Station. He gave a quick, reluctant glance at what he had examined the night before, noted that the weeds among the bomb rubble were much the same as the London ones—campion, dock, and bracken—and then went into the kitchen.

There was a note propped against a loaf of bread: "My friend [a Secret Service euphemism that in this context meant Sender's chief] says it's all right for you to go out. But to be back by 1700 hours. Your gear [double-talk for Bond's rifle] has arrived and the batman will lay it out this P.M. P. Sender."

Bond lit the gas cooker, and with a sneer at his profession, burned the message. Then he brewed himself a vast dish of scrambled eggs and bacon, which he heaped on buttered toast and washed down with black coffee into which he had poured a liberal tot of whiskey. Then he bathed and shaved, dressed in the drab, anonymous, middle-European clothes he had brought over for the purpose, looked at his disordered bed, decided to hell with it, and went down in the lift and out of the building.

James Bond had always found Berlin a glum, inimical city, varnished on the Western side with a brittle veneer of gimcrack polish rather like the chromium trim on American motor cars. He walked to the Kurfür-stendamm and sat in the Café Marquardt and drank an espresso and mood-ily watched the obedient queues of pedestrians waiting for the Go sign on the traffic lights while the shiny stream of cars went through their danger-ous quadrille at the busy intersection.

It was cold outside and the sharp wind from the Russian steppes whipped at the girls' skirts and at the waterproofs of the impatient hurrying men, each with the inevitable brief case tucked under his arm. The infrared wall heaters in the café glared redly down and gave a spurious glow to the faces of the café squatters, consuming their traditional "one cup of coffee and ten glasses of water," reading the free newspapers and periodicals in their wooden racks, earnestly bending over business documents.

Bond, closing his mind to the evening, debated with himself about ways to spend the afternoon. It finally came down to a choice between a visit to that respectable-looking brownstone house in the Clausewitzstrasse known to all concierges and taxi drivers and a trip to the Wannsee and a strenuous walk in the Grunewald. Virtue triumphed. Bond paid for his coffee and went out into the cold and took a taxi to the Zoo Station.

The pretty young trees round the long lake had already been touched by the breath of autumn, and there was occasional gold among the green. Bond walked hard for two hours along the leafy paths, then chose a restaurant with a glassed-in veranda above the lake and greatly enjoyed a high tea consisting of a double portion of *Matjeshering,* smothered in cream and onion rings, and two *Molle mit Korn.* (This Berlin equivalent of a boilermaker and his assistant was a schnapps, double, washed down with draft Löwenbräu.) Then, feeling more encouraged, he took the S-Bahn back into the city.

Outside the apartment house a nondescript young man was tinkering with the engine of a black Opel Kapitan. He didn't take his head out from under the hood when Bond passed close by him and went up to the door and pressed the bell.

Captain Sender was reassuring. It was a "friend"—a corporal from the transport section of Station WB. He had fixed up some bad engine trouble on the Opel. Each night, from six to seven, he would be ready to produce a series of multiple backfires when a signal on a walkie-talkie operated by Sender told him to do so. This would give some kind of cover for the noise of Bond's shooting. Otherwise, the neighborhood might alert the police and there would be a lot of untidy explaining to be done. Their hideout was in the American Sector, and while their American "friends" had given Station WB clearance for this operation, the "friends" were naturally anxious that it should be a clean job and without repercussions.

Bond was suitably impressed by the car gimmick, as he was by the very workmanlike preparations that had been made for him in the living room. Here, behind the head of his high bed, giving a perfect firing position, a wood and metal stand had been erected against the broad window sill, and along it lay the Winchester, the tip of its barrel just denting the curtains. The wood and all the metal parts of the rifle and sniperscope had been painted a dull black, and, laid out on the bed like sinister evening clothes, was a black velvet hood stitched to a waist-length shirt of the same material. The hood had wide slits for the eyes and mouth. It reminded Bond of old prints of the Spanish Inquisition or of the anonymous operators on the guillotine platform during the French Revolution.

There was a similar hood on Captain Sender's bed, and on his section of the window sill there lay a pair of nightglasses and the microphone for the walkie-talkie.

Captain Sender, his face worried and tense with nerves, said there was no news at the Station, no change in the situation as they knew it. Did Bond want anything to eat? Or a cup of tea? Perhaps a tranquilizer—there were several kinds in the bathroom?

Bond stitched a cheerful, relaxed expression on his face and said, "No, thanks," and gave a light-hearted account of his day while an artery near his solar plexus began thumping gently as tension build up inside him like a watch spring tightening. Finally his small talk petered out and he lay down on his bed with a German thriller he had bought on his wanderings, while Captain Sender moved fretfully about the flat, looking too often at his watch and chain-smoking Kent filter-tips through (he was a careful man) a Dunhill filtered cigarette holder.

James Bond's choice of reading matter, prompted by a spectacular jacket of a half-naked girl strapped to a bed, turned out to have been a happy one for the occasion. It was called *Verderbt, Verdammt, Verraten*. The prefix *ver* signified that the girl had not only been ruined, damned, and betrayed, but that she had suffered these misfortunes most thoroughly. James Bond temporarily lost himself in the tribulations of the heroine, Gräfin Liselotte Mutzenbacher, and it was with irritation that he heard Captain Sender say that it was 5:30 and time to take up their positions.

Bond took off his coat and tie, put two sticks of chewing gum in his mouth, and donned the hood. The lights were switched off by Captain Sender, and Bond lay along the bed, got his eye to the eyepiece of the sniperscope, and gently lifted the bottom edge of the curtain back and over his shoulders.

Now dusk was approaching, but otherwise the scene (a year later to become famous as Checkpoint Charlie) was like a well-remembered photograph—the wasteland in front of him, the bright river of the frontier road, the farther wasteland, and, on the left, the ugly square block of the Haus der Ministerien with its lit and dark windows. Bond scanned it all slowly, moving the sniperscope, with the rifle, by means of the precision screws on the wooden base. It was all the same except that now there was a trickle of personnel leaving and entering the Haus der Ministrien through the door onto the Wilhelmstrasse.

Bond looked long at the four dark windows—dark again tonight—that he agreed with Sender were the enemy's firing points. The curtains were drawn back, and the sash windows were wide open at the bottom. Bond's scope could not penetrate into the rooms, but there was no sign of movement within the four oblong black gaping mouths.

Now there was extra traffic in the street below the windows. The woman's orchestra came trooping down the pavement toward the entrance. Twenty laughing, talking girls carrying their instruments—violin and wind instrument cases, satchels with their scores—and four of them with the drums. A gay, happy little crocodile. Bond was reflecting that some people still seemed to find life fun in the Soviet Sector, when his glasses picked out and stayed on the girl carrying the cello. Bond's masticating jaws stopped still, and then reflectively went on with their chewing as he twisted the screw to depress the sniperscope and keep her in its center.

The girl was taller than the others, and her long, straight, fair hair, falling to her shoulders, shone like molten gold under the arcs at the intersection. She was hurrying along in a charming, excited way, carrying the cello case as if it were no heavier than a violin. Everything was flying—the skirt of her coat, her feet, her hair. She was vivid with movement and life and, it seemed, with gaiety and happiness as she chattered to the two girls who flanked her and laughed back at what she was saying.

As she turned in at the entrance amid her troupe, the arcs momentarily caught a beautiful, pale profile. And then she was gone, and, it seemed to Bond, that with her disappearance a stab of grief lanced into his heart. How odd! How very odd! This had not happened to him since he was young. And now this single girl, seen only indistinctly and far away, had caused him to suffer this sharp pang of longing, this thrill of animal magnetism!

Morosely, Bond glanced down at the luminous dial of his watch. 5:50. Only ten minutes to go. No transport arriving at the entrance. None of those anonymous black Zik cars he had half expected. He closed as much of his mind as he could to the girl and sharpened his wits. Get on, damn you! Get back to your job!

From somewhere inside the Haus der Ministerien there came the familiar sounds of an orchestra tuning up—the strings tuning their instruments to single notes on the piano, the sharp blare of individual woodwinds—then a pause, and then the collective crash of melody as the whole orchestra threw itself competently, so far as Bond could judge, into the opening bars of what even to James Bond was vaguely familiar.

"Moussorgsky's Overture to *Boris Godunov,*" said Captain Sender succinctly. "Anyway, six o'clock coming up." And then, urgently, "Hey! Right-hand bottom of the four windows! Watch out!"

Bond depressed the sniperscope. Yes, there was movement inside the black cave. Now, from the interior, a thick black object, a weapon, had slid out. It moved firmly, minutely, swiveling down and sideways so as to cover the stretch of the Zimmerstrasse between the two wastelands of rubble. Then the unseen operator in the room behind seemed satisfied, and the weapon remained still, fixed obviously to such a stand as Bond had beneath his rifle.

"What is it? What sort of gun?" Captain Sender's voice was more breathless than it should have been.

Take it easy, dammit! thought Bond. It's me who's supposed to have the nerves.

He strained his eyes, taking in the squat flash eliminator at the muzzle, the telescopic sight, and the thick downward chunk of magazine. Yes! Absolutely for sure—and the best they had!

"Kalashnikov," he said curtly. "Submachinegun. Gas-operated. Thirty rounds in seven sixty-two millimeter. Favorite with the KGB. They're going to do a saturation job after all. Perfect for range. We'll have to get him pretty quick, or 272 will end up not just dead but strawberry jam. You keep an eye out for any movement over there in that rubble. I'll have to stay married to that window and the gun. He'll have to show himself to fire. Other chaps are probably spotting behind him—perhaps from all four windows. Much the sort of setup we expected, but I didn't think they'd use a weapon that's going to make all the racket this one will. Should have known they would. A running man will be hard to get in this light with a single-shot job."

Bond fiddled minutely with the traversing and elevating screws at his fingertips and got the fine lines of the scope exactly intersected, just behind where the butt of the enemy gun merged into the blackness behind. Get the chest—don't bother about the head!

Inside the hood Bond's face began to sweat and his eye socket was slippery against the rubber of the eyepiece. That didn't matter. It was only his hands, his trigger finger, that must stay bone-dry. As the minutes ticked by, he frequently blinked his eyes to rest them, shifted his limbs to keep them supple, listened to the music to relax his mind.

The minutes slouched on leaden feet. How old would she be? Early twenties? Say twenty-three? With that poise and insouciance, the hint of authority in her long easy stride, she would come of good racy stock—one of the old Prussian families probably or from similar remnants in Poland or even Russia. Why in hell did she have to choose the cello? There was something almost indecent in the idea of this bulbous, ungainly instrument between her splayed thighs. Of course Suggia had managed to look elegant, and so did that girl Amaryllis somebody. But they should invent a way for women to play the damned thing sidesaddle.

From his side Captain Sender said, "Seven o'clock. Nothing's stirred on the other side. Bit of movement on our side, near a cellar close to the frontier. That'll be our reception committee—two good men from the Station. Better stay with it until they close down. Let me know when they take that gun in."

"All right."

It was 7:30 when the KGB submachinegun was gently drawn back into the black interior. One by one the bottom sashes of the four windows were closed. The cold-hearted game was over for the night. 272 was still holed up. Two more nights to go!

Bond softly drew the curtain over his shoulders and across the muzzle of the Winchester. He got up, pulled off his cowl, and went into the bathroom, where he stripped and had a shower. Then he had two large whiskeys-on-the-rocks in quick succession, while he waited, his ears pricked, for the now muffled sound of the orchestra to stop. At eight o'clock it did, with the expert comment from Sender—"Borodin's *Prince Igor,* Choral Dance Number 17, I think"—who had been getting off his report in garbled language to the Head of Station.

"Just going to have another look. I've rather taken to that tall blonde with the cello," Bond said to Sender.

"Didn't notice her," said Sender, uninterested. He went into the kitchen. Tea, guessed Bond. Or perhaps Horlick's. Bond donned his cowl, went back to his firing position, and depressed the sniperscope to the doorway of the Haus der Ministerien.

Yes, there they went, not so gay and laughing now. Tired perhaps. And now here she came, less lively, but still with that beautiful careless stride. Bond watched the blown golden hair and the fawn raincoat until it had vanished into the indigo dusk up the Wilhemstrasse. Where did she live? In some miserable flaked room in the suburbs? Or in one of the privileged apartments in the hideous lavatory-tiled Stalinallee?

Bond drew himself back. Somewhere, within easy reach, that girl lived. Was she married? Did she have a lover? Anyway, to hell with it! She was not for him.

The next day, and the next night watch, were duplicates, with small variations, of the first. James Bond had his two more brief rendezvous, by sniperscope, with the girl, and the rest was a killing of time and a tightening of the tension that, by the time the third and final day came, was like a fog in the small room.

James Bond crammed the third day with an almost lunatic program of museums, art galleries, the zoo, and a film, hardly perceiving anything he looked at, his mind's eye divided between the girl and those four black squares and the black tube and the unknown man behind it—the man he was now certainly going to kill tonight.

Back punctually at five in the apartment, Bond narrowly averted a row with Captain Sender because, that evening, Bond took a stiff drink of the whiskey before he donned the hideous cowl that now stank of his sweat. Captain Sender had tried to prevent him, and when he failed, had threatened to call up Head of Station and report Bond for breaking training.

"Look, my friend," said Bond wearily, "I've got to commit a murder tonight. Not you. Me. So be a good chap and stuff it, would you? You can tell Tanqueray anything you like when it's over. Think I like this job? Having a Double-O number and so on? I'd be quite happy for you to get me sacked from the Double-O Section. Then I could settle down and make a snug nest of papers as an ordinary staffer. Right?"

Bond drank down his whisky, reached for his thriller—now arriving at an appalling climax—and threw himself on the bed.

Captain Sender, icily silent, went off into the kitchen to brew, from the sounds, his inevitable cuppa.

Bond felt the whiskey beginning to melt the coiled nerves in his stomach. Now then, Liselotte, how in hell are you going to get out of this fix?

It was exactly 6:05 when Sender, at his post, began talking excitedly. "Bond, there's something moving 'way back over there. Now he's stopped —wait, no, he's on the move again, keeping low. There's a bit of broken wall there. He'll be out of sight of the opposition. But thick weeds, yards of them, ahead of him. Now he's coming through the weeds. And they're moving. Hope to God they think it's only the wind. Now he's through and gone to ground. Any reaction?"

"No," said Bond tensely. "Keep on telling me. How far to the frontier?"

"He's only got about fifty yards to go," Captain Sender's voice was harsh with excitement. "Broken stuff, but some of it's open. Then a solid chunk of wall right up against the pavement. He'll have to get over it. They can't fail to spot him then. Now! Now he's made ten yards, and another ten. Got him clearly then. Blackened his face and hands. Get ready! Any moment now he'll make the last sprint."

James Bond felt the sweat pouring down his face and neck. He took a chance and quickly wiped his hands down his sides and then got them back to the rifle, his finger inside the guard, just lying along the curved trigger. "There's something moving in the room behind the gun. They must have spotted him. Get that Opel working."

Bond heard the code word go into the microphone, heard the Opel in the street below start up, felt his pulse quicken as the engine leaped into life and a series of ear-splitting cracks came from the exhaust.

The movement in the black cave was now definite. A black arm with a black glove had reached out and under the stock.

"Now!" called out Captain Sender. "Now! He's run for the wall! He's up it! Just going to jump!"

And then, in the sniperscope, Bond saw the head of Trigger—the purity of the profile, the golden bell of hair—all laid out along the stock of the Kalashnikov! She was dead, a sitting duck! Bond's fingers flashed down to the screws, inched them round, and as yellow flame fluttered at the snout of the submachinegun, he squeezed the trigger.

The bullet, dead-on at three hundred and ten yards, must have hit where the stock ended up the barrel, might have got her in the left hand—but the effect was to tear the gun off its mountings, smash it against the side of the window frame, and then hurl it out of the window. It turned several times on its way down and crashed into the middle of the street.

"He's over!" shouted Captain Sender. "He's over! He's done it! My God, he's done it!"

"Get down!" said Bond sharply, and threw himself sideways off the bed as the big eye of a searchlight in one of the black windows blazed on, swerving up the street toward their block and their room. Then gunfire crashed, and the bullets howled into their window, ripping the curtains, smashing the woodwork, thudding into the walls.

Behind the roar and zing of the bullets Bond heard the Opel race off down the street, and, behind that again, the fragmentary whisper of the orchestra. The combination of the two background noises clicked. Of course! The orchestra, that must have raised an infernal din throughout the offices and corridors of the Haus der Ministerien, was, as on their side the backfiring Opel, designed to provide some cover for the sharp burst of fire from Trigger. Had she carried her weapon to and fro every day in that cello case? Was the whole orchestra composed of KGB women? Had the other instrument cases contained only equipment—the big drum perhaps the searchlight—while the real instruments were available in the concert hall? Too elaborate? Too fantastic? Probably.

But there had been no doubt about the girl. In the sniperscope Bond had even been able to see one wide, heavily lashed, aiming eye. Had he hurt her? Almost certainly her left arm. There would be no chance of seeing her, seeing how she was, if she left with the orchestra. Now he would never see her again. Bond's window would be a death trap. To underline the fact, a stray bullet smashed into the mechanism of the Winchester, already overturned and damaged, and hot lead splashed down on Bond's hand, burning the skin. On Bond's emphatic oath the firing stopped abruptly and silence sang in the room.

Captain Sender emerged from beside his bed, brushing glass out of his hair. Bond and Sender crunched across the floor and through the splintered door into the kitchen. Here, because the room faced away from the street, it was safe to switch on the light.

"And damage?" asked Bond.

"No. You all right?" Captain Sender's pale eyes were bright with the fever that comes in battle. They also, Bond noticed, held a sharp glint of accusation.

"Yes. Just get an Elastoplast for my hand. Caught a splash from one of the bullets." Bond went into the bathroom.

When he came out, Captain Sender was sitting by the walkie-talkie he had fetched from the sitting room. He was speaking into it. Now he said into the microphone. "That's all for now. Fine about 272. Hurry the armored car, if you would. Be glad to get out of here, and 007 will need to write his version of what happened. Okay? Then *over* and *out.*"

Captain Sender turned to Bond. Half accusing, half embarrassed he said, "Afraid Head of Station needs your reasons in writing for not getting that chap. I had to tell him I'd seen you alter your aim at the last second. Gave Trigger time to get off a burst. Damned lucky for 272 he'd just begun his sprint. Blew chunks off the wall behind him. What was it all about?"

James Bond knew he could lie, knew he could fake a dozen reasons why. Instead he took a deep pull at the strong whiskey he had poured for himself, put the glass down, and looked Captain Sender straight in the eye.

"Trigger was a woman."

"So what? KGB has got plenty of women agents—and women gunners. I'm not in the least surprised. The Russian woman's team always does well in the World Championships. Last meeting, in Moscow, they came first, second, and third against seventeen countries. I can even remember two of their names—Donskaya and Lomova. Terrific shots. She may even have been one of them. What did she look like? Records'll probably be able to turn her up."

"She was a blonde. She was the girl who carried the cello in that orchestra. Probably had her gun in the cello case. The orchestra was to cover up the shooting."

"Oh!" said Captain Sender slowly. "I see. The girl you were keen on?"

"That's right."

"Well, I'm sorry, but I'll have to put that in my report too. You had clear orders to exterminate Trigger."

There came the sound of a car approaching. It pulled up somewhere below. The bell rang twice. Sender said, "Well, let's get going. They've sent an armored car to get us out of here." He paused. His eyes flicked over Bond's shoulder, avoiding Bond's eyes. "Sorry about the report. Got to do my duty, y'know. You should have killed that sniper whoever it was."

Bond got up. He suddenly didn't want to leave the stinking little smashed-up flat, leave the place from which, for three days, he had had this long-range, one-sided romance with an unknown girl—an unknown enemy agent with much the same job in her outfit as he had in his. Poor little bitch! She would be in worse trouble now than he was! She'd certainly be courtmartialed for muffing this job. Probably be kicked out of the KGB. He shrugged. At least they'd stop short of killing her—as he himself had done.

James Bond said wearily, "Okay. With any luck it'll cost me my Double-

O number. But tell Head of Station not to worry. That girl won't do any more sniping. Probably lost her left hand. Certainly broke her nerve for that kind of work. Scared the living daylights out of her. In my book, that was enough. Let's go."

LIKE A DOG
IN THE STREET

Lawrence Block

The capture of the man called Anselmo amounted to the gathering together of innumerable threads, many of them wispy and frail. For almost two years the terrorist had been the target of massive manhunt operations launched by not one but over a dozen nations. The sole valid photograph of him, its focus blurred and indistinct, had been reproduced and broadcast throughout the world; his features—the jagged and irregular yellow teeth, the too-small upturned nose, the underslung jaw, the bushy eyebrows grown together into a single thick dark line—were as familiar to the public as they were to counterintelligence professionals and Interpol agents.

Bit by bit, little by little, the threads began to link up. In a café in a working-class neighborhood in Milan, two men sat sipping espresso laced with anisette. They spoke of an interregional soccer match, and of the possibility of work stoppage by the truck dispatchers. Then their voices dropped, and one spoke quickly and quietly of Anselmo while the other took careful note of every word.

In a suburb of Asuncion, a portly gentleman wearing the uniform of a Brigadier General in the Paraguayan Army shared the front seat of a four-year-old Chevrolet Impala with a slender young man wearing the uniform of a chauffeur. The general talked while the chauffeur listened. While Anselmo was not mentioned by name, he was the subject of the conversation. At its conclusion the chauffeur gave the general an envelope containing currency in the amount of two thousand German marks. Three hours later the "chauffeur" was on a plane for Mexico City. The following afternoon the "general" was dead of what the attending physician diagnosed as a massive myocardial infarction.

In Paris, in the Ninth Arrondissement, three security officers, one of them French, entered an apartment which had been under surveillance for several weeks. It proved to be empty. Surveillance was continued, but no one returned to the apartment during the course of the following month. A thoroughgoing analysis of various papers and detritus found in the apartment was relayed in due course to authorities in London and Tel Aviv.

In West Berlin, a man and woman, both in their mid-twenties, both blond, fair-skinned, and blue-eyed, and looking enough alike to be brother and sister, made the acquaintance of a dark-haired and full-bodied young woman at a cabaret called Justine's. The three shared a bottle of sparkling Burgundy, then repaired to a small apartment on the Bergenstrasse where they shared several marijuana cigarettes, half a bottle of Almspach brandy, and a bed. The blond couple did certain things which the dark-haired young woman found quite painful, but she gave every indication of enjoying the activity. Later, when she appeared to be asleep, the blond man and woman talked at some length. The dark-haired woman was in fact awake throughout the conversation, and was still awake later when the other two lay sprawled beside her, snoring lustily. She dressed and left quickly, pausing only long enough to slit their throats with a kitchen knife. Her flight to Beirut landed shortly before two in the afternoon, and within an hour she was talking with a middle-aged Armenian gentleman in the back room of a travel agency.

Bits and pieces. Frail threads coming together to form a net . . .

And throughout it all the man called Anselmo remained as active as ever. A Pan-Am flight bound for Belgrade blew up in the air over Austria. A telephone call claiming credit for the deed on behalf of the Popular Front for Croatian Autonomy was logged at the airline's New York office scant minutes before the explosion shredded the jetliner.

A week earlier, rumors had begun drifting around that Anselmo was working with the Croats.

In Jerusalem, less than a quarter of a mile from the Wailing Wall, four gunmen burst into a Sephardic synagogue during morning services. They shot and killed twenty-eight members of the congregation before they themselves were rooted out and shot down by police officers. The dead gunmen proved to be members of a leftist movement aimed at securing the independence of Puerto Rico from the United States. But why should Puerto Rican extremists be mounting a terrorist operation against Israel?

The common denominator was Anselmo.

An embassy in Washington. A police barracks in Strabane, in Northern Ireland. A labor union in Buenos Aires.

Anselmo.

Assassinations. The Spanish Ambassador to Sweden, shot down in the streets of Stockholm. The sister-in-law of the Premier of Iraq. The research-and-development head of a multinational oil company. A British journalist. An Indonesian general. An African head of state.

Anselmo.

Hijacking and kidnapping. Ransom demands. Outrages.

Anselmo. Always Anselmo.

Of course it was not always his hand on the trigger. When the Puerto Rican gunmen shot up the Jerusalem synagogue, Anselmo was playing solitaire in a dimly lit basement room in Pretoria. When a firebomb roasted the Iraqi Premier's sister-in-law, Anselmo was flashing a savage yellow smile in Bolivia. It was not Anselmo's hand that forced a dagger between the ribs of General Subandoro in Jakarta; the hand belonged to a nubile young lady from Thailand—but it *was* Anselmo who had decreed that Subandoro must die and who had staged and scripted his death.

Bits and pieces. A couple of words scrawled on the back of an envelope. A scrap of conversation overheard. Bits, pieces, scraps. Threads braided together can make strong rope. Strands of rope interwoven comprise a net.

When the net finally dropped around Anselmo, Nahum Grodin held its ends in his knobby hands.

It was early summer. For three days a dry wind had been blowing relentlessly. The town of Al-dhareesh, a small Arab settlement on the West Bank of the Jordan, yielded to the wind as to a conquering army. The women tended their cooking fires. Men sat at small tables in their courtyards sipping cups of sweet black coffee. The yellow dogs that ran through the narrow streets seemed to stay more in the shadows than was their custom, scurrying from doorway to doorway, keeping their distance from passing humans.

"Even the dogs feel it," Nahum Grodin said. His Hebrew bore Russian and Polish overtones. "Look at the way they slink around."

"The wind," Gershon Meir said.

"Anselmo."

"The wind," Meir insisted. A Sabra, he had the unromantic outlook of the nativeborn. He was Grodin's immediate subordinate in the counterterror division of Shin Bet, and the older man knew there was no difference between the keenness both felt at the prospect of springing a trap on Anselmo. But Grodin felt it in the air while Meir felt nothing but the dry wind off the desert.

"The same wind blows over the whole country," Grodin said. "And yet it's different here. The way those damned yellow dogs stay in the shadows."

"You make too much of the Arabs' mongrel dogs."

"And their children?"

"What children?"

"Aha!" Grodin extended a forefinger. "The dogs keep to the shadows.

The children stay in their huts and avoid the streets altogether. Don't tell me, my friend, that the wind is enough to keep children from their play."

"So the townspeople know he's here. They shelter him. That's nothing new."

"A few know he's here. The ones planning the raid across the Jordan, perhaps a handful of others. The rest are like the dogs and the children. They sense something in the air."

Gershon Meir looked at his superior officer. He considered the set of his jaw, the reined excitement that glinted in his pale-blue eyes. "Something in the air," he said.

"Yes. You feel something yourself, Gershon. Admit it."

"I feel too damned much caffeine in my blood. That last cup of coffee was a mistake."

"You feel more than caffeine."

Gershon Meir shrugged but said nothing.

"He's here, Gershon."

"Yes, I think he is. But we have been so close to him so many times—"

"This time we have him."

"When he's behind bars, that's when I'll say we have him."

"Or when he's dead."

Again the younger man looked at Grodin, a sharp look this time. Grodin's right hand, the knuckles swollen with arthritis, rested on the butt of his holstered machine pistol.

"Or when he's dead," Gershon Meir agreed.

Whether it was merely the wind or something special in the air, the man called Anselmo felt it too. He set down his little cup of coffee—it was sweeter than he liked it and worried his chin with the tips of his fingers. With no apparent concern, he studied the five men in the room with him. They were local Arabs ranging in age from sixteen to twenty-eight. Anselmo had met one of them before in Beirut and knew two of the others by reputation. The remaining two were unequivocally guaranteed by their comrades. Anselmo did not specifically trust them—he had never in his life placed full trust in another human being—but neither did he specifically distrust them. They were village Arabs, politically unsophisticated and mentally uncomplicated, desperate young men who would perform any act and undertake any risk. Anselmo had known and used the same sort of man throughout the world. He could not function without such men.

Something in the air . . .

He went to a window and inched the burlap curtain aside with the edge of his palm. He saw nothing remarkable, yet a special perception more reliable than eyesight told him that the town was swarming with Israelis. He did not have to see them to be certain of their presence.

He turned and considered his five companions. They were to cross the river that night. By dawn they would have established their position. A school bus loaded with between fifty and sixty retarded children would slow down before making a left turn at the corner where Anselmo and his Arabs would be posted. It would be child's play—he bared his teeth in a smile at the phrase—to shoot the tires out of the bus. In a matter of minutes all of the Jewish children and their driver would be dead at the side of the road. In a few more minutes Anselmo and the Arabs would have scattered and made good their escape.

A perfect act of terror, mindless, meaningless, unquestionably dramatic. The Jews would retaliate, of course, and of course their retaliation would find the wrong target, and the situation would deteriorate.

At times, most often late at night just before his mind slipped over the edge into sleep, Anselmo could see the outline of a master plan, the way in which all the component parts of the terror he juggled moved together to make a new world. The image of the plan hovered at the perimeter of his inner vision, trembling at the edge of thought. He could almost see it, as one can almost see God in a haze of opium.

The rest of the time he saw no master plan and had no need to search for one. The existential act of terror, theatrical as thunder, seemed to him to be a perfectly satisfactory end in itself. Let the children bleed at the roadside. Let the plane explode overhead. Let the rifle crack.

Let the world take note.

He turned once more to the window but left the curtain in place, merely testing the texture of the burlap with his fingertips. Out there in the darkness were troops and police officers. Should he wait in the shadows for them to pass? No, the village was small and they could search it house by house with little difficulty. He could pass as an Arab—he was garbed as one now—but if he was the man they were looking for, they would know him when they saw him.

He could send these five out, sacrifice them in suicidal combat while he made good his own escape. It would be a small sacrifice. They were unimportant, expendable; he was Anselmo. But if the Jews had encircled the town, a diversion would have little effect.

He snapped his head back. Time was his enemy, only drawing the net tighter around him. The longer he delayed, the greater his vulnerability. Better a bad decision than no decision at all.

"Wait here for me," he told his men, his Arabic low and guttural. "I'll see how the wind blows."

He began to open the door, disturbing the rest of a scrawny, long-muzzled dog. The animal whined and took itself off to the side. Anselmo slipped through the open door and let it close behind him.

The moon overhead was just past fullness. There were no clouds to block it—the dry wind had blown them all away days ago. Anselmo reached through his loose clothing, touched the Walther automatic on his hip, the long-bladed hunting knife in a sheath strapped to his thigh, the smaller knife fastened with tape to the inside of his left forearm. Around his waist an oilcloth money-belt rested next to his skin. It held four passports in as many names and a few thousand dollars in the currencies of half a dozen countries. Anselmo could travel readily, crossing borders as another man would cross the street. If only he could first get out of Al-dhareesh.

He moved quickly and sinuously, keeping to the shadows, letting his eyes and ears perform a quick reconnaissance before moving onward. Twice he spotted armed uniformed men and withdrew before he was seen, changing direction, scurrying through a yard and down an alley.

They were everywhere.

Just as he caught sight of still another Israeli patrol on a street-corner, gunfire broke out a few hundred yards to his left. There was a ragged volley of pistol fire answered by several bursts from what he identified as an Uzi machine pistol. Then silence.

His five men, he thought. Caught in the house or on the street in front of it. If he had stayed there he'd have been caught with them. From the sound of it, they hadn't made much trouble. His lip curled and a spot of red danced in his forebrain. He only hoped the five had been shot dead so that they couldn't inform the Jews of his presence.

As if they had to. As if the bastards didn't already know . . .

A three-man patrol turned into the street a dozen houses to Anselmo's left. One of the men kicked at the earth as he walked and the dust billowed around his feet in the moonlight. Anselmo cursed the men and the moonlight and circled around the side of a house.

But there was no way out. All the streets were blocked. Once Anselmo drew his Walther and took deliberate aim at a pair of uniformed men. They were within easy range and his finger trembled on the trigger. It would be so nice to kill them, but where was the profit in it? Their companions would be on him in an instant.

If you teach a rat to solve mazes, presenting it over a period of months with mazes of increasing difficulty, and finally placing it in a maze which is truly unsolvable, the rat will do a curious thing. He will scurry about in an attempt to solve the maze, becoming increasingly inefficient in his efforts, and ultimately he will sit down in a corner and devour his own feet.

There was no way out of Al-dhareesh. The Israelis were closing in, searching the village house by house, moving ever nearer to Anselmo, cut-

ting down his space. He tucked himself into a corner where a four-foot wall
of sun-baked earth butted up against the wall of a house. He sat on his
haunches and pressed himself into the shadows.

Footsteps—

A dog scampered along close to the wall, found Anselmo, and whimpered. Was it the same dog he'd disturbed on leaving the house? Not likely,
he thought. The town was full of these craven, whining beasts. This one
poked its nose into Anselmo's side and whimpered again. The sound was
one the terrorist did not care for. He laid a hand on the back of the dog's
skull, gentling it. The whimpering continued at a slightly lower pitch. With
his free hand, Anselmo drew the hunting knife from the sheath on his
thigh. While he went on rubbing the back of the dog's head, he found the
spot between its ribs. The animal had almost ceased to whimper when he
sent the blade home, finding the heart directly, making the kill in silence.
He wiped the blade on the dog's fur and returned it to its sheath.

A calm descended with the death of the dog. Anselmo licked a finger,
held it overhead. Had the wind ceased to blow? It seemed to him that it
had. He took a deep breath and got to his feet.

He walked not in the shadows but down the precise middle of the narrow street. When the two men stepped into view ahead of him, he did not
turn aside or bolt for cover. His hand quivered, itching to reach for the
Walther, but the calm which had come upon him enabled him to master the
urge.

He threw his hands high overhead. In reasonably good Hebrew he sang
out, "I am your prisoner!" And he drew his lips back, exposing his bad
teeth in a terrible grin.

Both men trained their guns on him. He had faced guns innumerable
times in the past and did not find them intimidating. But one of the men
held his Uzi as if he was about to fire it. Moonlight glinted on the gun
barrel. Anselmo, still grinning, waited for a burst of fire and an explosion in
his chest.

It never came.

The two men sat in folding chairs and watched their prisoner through a
one-way mirror. His cell was as small and bare as the room from which they
watched him. He sat on a narrow iron bedstead and stroked his chin with
the tips of his fingers. Now and then his gaze passed over the mirror.

"You'd swear he can see us," Gershon Meir said.

"He knows we're here."

"I suppose he must. The devil's cool, isn't he? Do you think he'll talk?"

Nahum Grodin shook his head.

"He could tell us a great deal."

"He'll never tell us a thing. Why should he? The man's comfortable. He was comfortable dressed as an Arab and now he's comfortable dressed as a prisoner."

Anselmo had been disarmed, of course, and relieved of his loose-fitting Arab clothing. Now he wore the standard clothing issued to prisoners—a pair of trousers and a short-sleeved shirt of grey denim, and cloth slippers. The trousers were beltless and the slippers had no laces.

Grodin said, "He could be made to talk. No, *nahr*, I don't mean torture. You watch too many films. Pentothal, if they'd let me use it. Although I suspect his resistance is high. He has such enormous confidence."

"The way he smiled when he surrendered to us."

"Yes."

"For a moment I thought—"

"Yes?"

"That you were going to shoot him."

"I very nearly did."

"Did you suspect a trap?"

"No." Grodin interlaced his fingers, cracked knuckles. "No," he said, "I knew it was no trick. The man is a pragmatist. He knew he was trapped. He surrendered to save his skin."

"And you thought to shoot him anyway?"

"I should have done it, Gershon. I should have shot him. Something made me hesitate. And you know the saying, he who hesitates and so forth. So I hesitated and was lost. Not I, but the opportunity. I should have shot him at once—without hesitating, without thinking, without anything but an ounce of pressure on the trigger and a few punctuation marks for the night."

Gershon studied the man they were discussing. He had removed one of the slippers and was picking at his feet. Gershon wanted to look away but watched, fascinated. "You want him dead," he said.

"Of course."

"We're a progressive nation. We don't put our enemies to death any more. Life imprisonment is supposed to be punishment enough. Don't you agree?"

"No."

"You like the eye-for-an-eye stuff, eh?"

"It's not a terrible idea, you know. I wouldn't be so quick to dismiss it out of hand."

"Revenge."

"Or retribution, more accurately. You can't have revenge, my friend. Not in this case. The man's crimes are too enormous for his own personal death to balance them out. But that's not why I wish I'd killed him."

"Then I don't understand."

Nahum Grodin aimed a forefinger at the glass. "Look," he said. "What do you see?"

"A piggish lout picking his feet."

"You see a prisoner."

"Of course. I don't understand what you're getting at, Nahum."

"You think you see a prisoner. But he's not our prisoner, Gershon."

"Oh?"

"We are his prisoners."

"I don't follow you."

"No?" The older man massaged the knuckle of his right index finger. It was that finger, he thought, which had hesitated upon the trigger of the Uzi. And now it throbbed and ached. Arthritis—or the punishment it deserved for its hesitation?

"Nahum—"

"We are at his mercy," Grodin said crisply. "He's our captive. His comrades will try to bring about his release. As long as he is our prisoner he is a sword pointed at our throats."

"That's farfetched."

"Do you think so?" Nahum Grodin sighed. "I wish we were not so civilized as to have abolished capital punishment. And at this particular moment I wish we were a police state and that this vermin could be officially described as having been shot while attempting to escape. We could take him outside right now, you and I, and he could attempt to escape."

Gershon shuddered. "We couldn't do that."

"No," Grodin agreed. "We could not do that. But I could have gunned him down when I had the chance. Did you ever see a mad dog? When I was a boy in Lublin, Gershon, I saw one running wild. It is one of the earliest childhood memories I've been able to retain. They don't really foam at the mouth, you know. But I seem to remember that dog having a foamy mouth. And a policeman shot him down. I remember that he held his pistol in both hands, held it out in front of him with both arms fully extended. Do you suppose I actually saw the beast shot down or that the memory is in part composed of what I was told? I could swear I actually saw the act. I can see it now in my mind, the policeman with his legs braced and his two arms held out in front of him. And the dog charging. I wonder if that incident might have had anything to do with this profession I seem to have chosen."

"Do you think it did?"

"I'll leave that to the psychiatrists to decide." Grodin smiled, then let the smile fade. "I should have shot this one down like a dog in the street," he said. "When I had the chance."

"How is he dangerous in a cell?"

"Not as long as he will remain in that cell." Grodin sighed. "He is a leader. He has a leader's magnetism. The world is full of lunatics to whom this man is special. They'll demand his release. They'll hijack a plane, kidnap a politician, hold schoolchildren for ransom."

"We have never paid ransom."

"No."

"They've made such demands before. We've never released a terrorist in response to extortion."

"Not yet we haven't."

Both men fell silent. On the other side of the one-way mirror, the man called Anselmo had ceased picking his toes. Now he stripped to his underwear and seated himself on the bare tiled floor of his cell. His fingers interlaced behind his head and he began doing sit-ups. He exercised rhythmically, pausing after each series of five sit-ups, then, springing to his feet after he had completed six sets, he deliberately flashed his teeth at the one-way mirror.

"Look at that," Gershon Meir said.

Nahum Grodin's right forefinger resumed aching.

Grodin was right. Revolutionaries throughout the world had very strong reasons for wishing to see Anselmo released from his cell. In various corners of the globe, desperate men plotted desperate acts to achieve it.

The first attempts were not successful. Less than a week after Anselmo was taken, four men and two women stormed a building in Geneva where high-level international disarmament talks were being conducted. Two of the men were shot, one fatally. One of the women had her arm broken in a struggle with a guard. The rest were captured. In the course of interrogation, Swiss authorities determined that the exercise had had as its object the release of Anselmo. The two women and one of the men were West German anarchists. The other three men, including the one who was shot dead, were Basque separatists.

A matter of days after this incident, guerrillas in Uruguay stopped a limousine carrying the Israeli Ambassador to a reception in the heart of Montevideo. Security police were following the Ambassador's limousine at the time, and the gun battle which ensued claimed the lives of all seven guerrillas, three security policemen, the Ambassador, his chauffeur, and four bystanders. While the purpose of the attempted kidnapping was impossible to determine, persistent rumors linked the action to Anselmo.

Within the week, Eritrean revolutionaries succeeded in skyjacking an El Al 747 en route from New York to Tel Aviv. The jet with 144 passengers and crew members was diverted to the capital city of an African nation where it overshot the runway, crashed, and was consumed in flames. A handful of passengers survived. The remaining passengers, along with all crew members and the eight or ten Eritreans, were all killed.

Palestinians seized another plane, this one an Air France jetliner. The plane was landed successfully in Libya and demands were presented which called for the release of Anselmo and a dozen or so other terrorists then held by the Israelis. The demands were rejected out of hand. After several deadlines had come and gone, the terrorists began executing hostages, ultimately blowing up the plane with the remaining hostages aboard. According to some reports, the terrorists were taken into custody by Libyan authorities; according to other reports, they were given token reprimands and released.

After the affair in Libya, both sides felt they had managed to establish something. The Israelis felt they had proved conclusively that they would not be blackmailed. The loosely knit group who aimed to free Anselmo felt just as strongly that they had demonstrated their resolve to free him, no matter what risks they were forced to run, no matter how many lives—their own or others—they had to sacrifice.

"If there were *two* Henry Clays," said the bearer of that name after a bitterly disappointing loss of the Presidency, "then one of them would make the other President of the United States of America."

It is unlikely that Anselmo knew the story. He cared nothing for the past, read nothing but current newspapers. But as he exercised in his cell his thoughts often echoed those of Henry Clay.

If there were only two Anselmos, one would surely spring the other from this cursed jail.

But it didn't require a second Anselmo, as it turned out. All it took was a nuclear bomb.

The bomb itself was stolen from a NATO installation forty miles from Antwerp. A theft of this sort is perhaps the most difficult way of obtaining such a weapon. Nuclear technology is such that anyone with a good grounding in college-level science can put together a rudimentary atomic bomb in his own basement workshop, given access to the essential elements. Security precautions being what they are, it is worlds easier to steal the component parts of a bomb than the assembled bomb itself. But in this case it was necessary not merely to have the bomb but to let the world know that one had the bomb. Hence the theft by way of a daring and dramatic dead-of-night raid. While media publicity was kept to a minimum, people whose job it was to know such things knew overnight that a devastating bomb had been stolen, and that the thieves had in all likelihood been members of the Peridot Gang.

The Peridot Gang was based in Paris, although its membership was international in nature. The gang was organized to practice terrorism in the Anselmo mode. Its politics were of the left, but very little ideology lay beneath the commitment to extremist activism. Security personnel throughout Europe and the Middle East shuddered at the thought of a nuclear device in the hands of the Peridots. Clearly they had not stolen the bomb for the fun of it. Clearly they intended to make use of it, and clearly they were capable of almost any outrage.

Removing the bomb from the Belgian NATO installation had been reasonably difficult. In comparison, disassembling it and smuggling it into the United States, transporting it to New York City, reassembling it, and finally installing it in the interfaith meditation chamber of the United Nations was simplicity itself.

Once the meditation chamber had been secured, a Peridot emissary presented a full complement of demands. Several of these had to do with guaranteeing the eventual safety of gang members at the time of their withdrawal from the chamber, the U.N. Building, and New York itself. Another, directed at the General Assembly of the United Nations, called for changes in international policy toward insurgent movements and revolutionary organizations. Various individual member nations were called upon to liberate specific political prisoners, including several dozen persons belonging to or allied with the Peridot organization. Specifically, the government of Israel was instructed to grant liberty to the man called Anselmo.

Any attempt to seize the bomb would be met by its detonation. Any effort to evacuate the United Nations Building or New York itself would similarly prompt the Peridots to set the bomb off. If all demands were not met within ten days of their publication, the bomb would go off.

Authorities differed in their estimates of the bomb's lethal range. But the lowest estimate of probable deaths was in excess of one million

Throughout the world, those governments blackmailed by the Peridots faced up to reality. One after the other they made arrangements to do what they could not avoid doing. Whatever their avowed policy toward extortion, however great their reluctance to liberate terrorists, they could not avoid recognizing a fairly simple fact: they had no choice.

Anselmo could not resist a smile when the two men came into the room. How nice, he thought, that it was these two who came to him. They had captured him in the first place, they had attempted to interrogate him time and time again, and now they were on hand to make arrangements for his release.

"Well," he said. "I guess I won't be with you much longer, eh?"

"Not much longer," the older one said.

"When do you release me?"

"The day after tomorrow. In the morning. You are to be turned over to Palestinians at the Syrian border. A private jet will fly you to one of the North African countries, either Algeria or Libya. I don't have the details yet."

"It hardly matters."

The younger of the Israelis, dark-eyed and olive-skinned, cleared his throat. "You won't want to leave here in prison clothes," he said. "We can give you what you wore when you were captured or you may have western dress. It's your choice."

"You are very accommodating," Anselmo told him.

The man's face colored. "The choice is yours."

"It's of no importance to me."

"Then you'll walk out as you walked in."

"It doesn't matter what I wear." He touched his grey denim clothing. "Just so it's not this." And he favored them with a smile again.

The older man unclasped a small black bag, drew out a hypodermic needle. Anselmo raised his eyebrows. "Pentothal," the man said.

"You could have used it before."

"It was against policy."

"And has your policy changed?"

"Obviously."

"A great deal has changed," the younger man added. "A package bill passed the Knesset last evening. There was a special session called for the purpose. The death penalty has been restored."

"Ah."

"For certain crimes only. Crimes of political terrorism. Any terrorists captured alive will be brought to trial within three days after capture. If convicted, sentence will be carried out within twenty-four hours after it had been pronounced."

"Was there much opposition to this bill?"

"There was considerable debate. But when it came to a vote the margin was overwhelming for passage."

Anselmo considered this in the abstract. "It seems to me that it is an intelligent bill. I inspired it, eh?"

"You might say that."

"So you will avoid this sort of situation in the future. But of course, there is a loss all the same. You will not look good to the rest of the world, executing prisoners so quickly after capture. There will be talk of kangaroo courts, star chamber hearings, that sort of thing." He flashed his teeth.

"There's another change that did not require legislation," the older man said. "An unofficial change of policy for troops and police officers. We will have slower reflexes when it comes to noticing that a man is attempting to surrender."

Anselmo laughed aloud at the phrasing. "Slower reflexes! You mean you will shoot first and ask questions later?"

"Something along those lines."

"Also an intelligent policy. I shall make my own plans accordingly. But I don't think it will do you very much good, you know."

The man shrugged. The hypodermic needle looked small in his big gnarled hand. "The pentothal," he said. "Will it be necessary to restrain you? Or will you cooperate?"

"Why should I require restraint? We are both professionals, after all. I'll cooperate."

"That simplifies things."

Anselmo extended his arm. The younger man took him by the wrist while the other one readied the needle. "This won't do you any good either," Anselmo said conversationally. "I've had pentothal before. It's not effective on me."

"We'll have to establish that for ourselves."

"As you will."

"At least you'll get a pleasant nap out of it."

"I never have trouble sleeping," Anselmo said. "I sleep like a baby."

He didn't fight the drug but went with the flow as it circulated in his bloodstream. His consciousness went off to the side somewhere.

Then he was awake, aware of his surroundings, aware that the two men were speaking but unable to make sense of their conversation. When full acuity returned he gave no sign of it at first, hoping to overhear something of importance, but their conversation held nothing of interest to him. After a few minutes he stirred himself and opened his eyes.

"Well?" he demanded. "Did I tell you any vital secrets?"

The older one shook his head.

"I told you as much."

"So you did. You'll forgive our not taking your word, I hope."

Anselmo laughed aloud. "You have humor, old one. It's almost a pity we're enemies. Tell me your name."

"What does it matter?"

"It doesn't."

"Nahum Grodin."

Anselmo repeated the name aloud. "When you captured me," he said, "in that filthy Arab town—"

"Al-dhareesh."

"Al-dhareesh. Yes. When I surrendered, you know, I thought for a long moment that you were going to gun me down. That wind that blew endlessly, and the moon glinting off your pistol, and something in the air. Something in the way you were standing. I thought you were going to shoot me."

"I very nearly did."

"Yes, so I thought." Anselmo laughed suddenly. "And now you must wish that you did, eh? Hesitation, that's what kills men, Grodin. Better the wrong choice than no choice at all. You should have shot me."

"Yes."

"Next time you'll know better, Grodin."

"Next time?"

"Oh, there will be a next time for us, old one. And next time you won't hesitate to fire. But then next time I'll know better than to surrender, eh?"

"I almost shot you."

"I sensed it."

"Like a dog."

"A dog?" Anselmo thought of the dogs in the Arab town, the one he'd disturbed when he opened the door, the whining one he'd killed. His hand remembered the feel of the animal's skull and the brief tremor that passed through the beast when the long knife went home. It was difficult now to recall just why he had knifed the dog. He supposed he must have done it to prevent the animal's whimpering and drawing attention, but was that really the reason? The act itself had been so reflexive that one could scarcely determine its motive. If it mattered.

Outside, the sunlight was blinding. Gershon Meir took a pair of sunglasses from his breast pocket and put them on. Nahum Grodin squinted against the light. He never wore sunglasses and didn't mind the glare. And the sun warmed his bones, eased the ache in his joints.

"The day after tomorrow," Gershon Meir said. "I'll be glad to see the last of him."

"Will you?"

"Yes. I hate having to release him, but sometimes I think I hate speaking with him even more."

"I know what you mean."

They walked through the streets in a comfortable silence. After a few blocks the younger man said, "I had the oddest feeling earlier. Just for a moment."

"Oh?"

"When you gave him the pentothal. For an instant I was afraid you were going to kill him."

"With pentothal?"

"I thought you might inject an air bubble into the vein. It would have been easy enough."

"Perhaps, though I don't know that I'd be able to find a vein that easily. I'm hardly a doctor. A subcutaneous injection of pentothal, that's within my capabilities, but I might not be so good at squirting air into a vein. But do you think for a moment I'd be mad enough to kill him?"

"It was a feeling, not a thought."

"I'd delight in killing him," Grodin said. "But I'd hate to wipe out New York in the process."

"They might not detonate the bomb just for Anselmo. They want to get other prisoners out, and their other demands. If you told them Anselmo had died a natural death they might swallow it and pretend to believe it."

"You think we should call their bluff that way?"

"No. They're lunatics. Who knows what they might do?"

"Exactly," Grodin said.

"It was just a feeling, that's all." Meir pulled thoughtfully at his earlobe. "Nahum? It's a curious thing. When you and Anselmo talk I might as well not be in the room."

"I don't take your meaning, Gershon."

"There's a current that runs between the two of you. I feel utterly excluded from the company. The two of you, you seem to understand each other."

"That's interesting. You think I understand Anselmo? I don't begin to understand him. You know, I didn't expect to gain any real information from him while he was under the pentothal. But I did hope to get some insight into what motivates the man. And he gave me nothing. He likes to see blood spill, he likes loud noises. You know what Bakunin said?"

"I don't even know who Bakunin is."

"He was a Russian. 'The urge to destroy is a creative urge,' is what he said. Perhaps the context in which he said it mitigates the thought somewhat, I wouldn't know. But Anselmo is an embodiment of that philosophy. His wish to destroy *is* his life. No, Gershon, I do not understand him."

"But there is a sympathy between the two of you just the same. I'm not putting it well, but there is something."

Grodin and Meir were on hand the day that Anselmo was released. They watched from a distance while the terrorist was escorted from his cell to an armored car for transport to the Syrian lines. They followed the armored car in a vehicle of their own, Meir driving, Grodin at his side. The ceremony at the Syrian border, by means of which custody of Anselmo was transferred from his Israeli guards to a group of Palestinian commandos, was tense; nevertheless, it was concluded without incident. Just before he entered the waiting car, Anselmo turned for a last look across the border. His eyes darted around as if seeking a specific target. Then he thrust out his jaw and drew back his lips, baring his jagged teeth in a final hideous smile. He gave his head a toss and ducked into the car. The door swung shut and moments later the car sped toward Damascus.

"Quite a performance," Gershon Meir said.

"He's an actor. Everything is performance for him. His whole life is theater."

"He was looking for you."

"I think not."

"He was looking for someone. For whom else would he look?"

Grodin gave his head an impatient shake. His assistant recognized the gesture and let it drop.

On the long drive back, Nahum Grodin leaned back in his seat and closed his eyes. It seemed to him that he dreamed without quite losing consciousness. After perhaps half an hour he opened his eyes and straightened up in his seat.

"Where is he now?" he wondered aloud. "Damascus? Or is his plane already in the air?"

"I'd guess he's still on the ground."

"No matter." He sighed. "How do you feel, Gershon? Letting such a one out of our hands? Forget revenge. Think of the ability he has to work with disparate groups of lunatics. He takes partisans of one mad cause and puts them to work on behalf of another equally insane movement. He coordinates the actions of extremists who have nothing else in common. And his touch is like nobody else's. This latest devilment at the United Nations, it's almost impossible to believe that someone other than Anselmo planned it. In fact, I wouldn't be surprised to learn that he hatched the concept some time ago to be held at the ready in the event that he should ever be captured."

"I wonder if that could be true."

"It's not impossible, is it? And we had to let him go."

"We'll never have to do that again."

"No," Grodin agreed. "One good thing's come of this. The new law isn't perfect, God knows. Instant trials and speedy hangings are not what democracies ought to aspire to. But it's comforting to know that we will not be in this position again. Gershon?"

"Yes?"

"Stop the car, please. Pull off onto the shoulder."

"Is something wrong?"

"No. But there is something I've decided to tell you. Good, and turn off the engine. We'll be here a few moments." Grodin squeezed his eyes shut, put his hand to his forehead. Without opening his eyes he said, "Anselmo said he and I would meet again. But he was wrong. He'll never return to Israel. He'll meet his friends, if one calls such people friends, and he'll go wherever he has it in mind to go. And in two weeks or a month or possibly as much as two months, he will experience a certain amount of nervousness. He may be mentally depressed, he may grow anxious and irritable. It's quite possible that he'll pay no attention to these signs because they may not be very much out of the ordinary. His life is disorganized, chaotic, enervating, so this state may be no departure from the normal course of things for him."

"I don't understand, Nahum."

"Then after a day or so these symptoms will be more pronounced," Grodin went on. "He may run a fever. His appetite will wane. He'll grow very nervous. He may talk a great deal, might even become something of a chatterbox. You recall that he said he sleeps like a baby. Well, he may experience insomnia.

"Then after a couple of days, things will take a turn for the worse." Grodin took a pinseal billfold from his pocket, drew out and unfolded a sheet of paper.

"Here's a description from a medical encyclopedia. 'The agitation of the sufferer now becomes greatly increased and the countenance now exhibits anxiety and terror. There is marked embarrassment of the breathing, but the most striking and terrible feature of this state is the effect produced by attempts to swallow fluids. The patient suffers from thirst and desires eagerly to drink, but on making the effort is seized with a violent suffocative paroxysm which continues for several seconds and is succeeded by a feeling of intense alarm and distress. Indeed the very thought of drinking suffices to bring on a choking paroxysm, as does also the sound of running water.

" 'The patient is extremely sensitive to any kind of external impression— a bright light, a loud noise, a breath of cool air, anything of this sort may bring on a seizure. There also occur general convulsions and occasionally a condition of tetanic spasm. These various paroxysms increase in frequency and severity with the advance of the disease.' "

"Disease?" Gershon Meir frowned. "I don't understand, Nahum. What disease? What are you driving at?"

Grodin went on reading. " 'The individual experiences alternate intervals of comparative quiet in which there is intense anxiety and more or less constant difficulty in respiration accompanied by a peculiar sonorous exhalation which has suggested the notion that the patient barks like a dog. In many instances—' "

"A dog!"

" 'In many instances there are intermittent fits of maniacal excitement.

During this stage of the disease the patient is tormented with a viscid secretion accumulating in his mouth. From dread of swallowing this, he constantly spits about himself. He may also make snapping movements of the jaws as if attempting to bite. These are actually a manifestation of the spasmodic action which affects the muscles in general. There is no great amount of fever, but the patient will be constipated, his flow of urine will be diminished, and he will often feel sexual excitement.

" 'After two or three days of suffering of the most terrible description, the patient succumbs, with death taking place either in a paroxysm of choking or from exhaustion. The duration of the disease from the first declaration of symptoms is generally from three to five days.' "

Grodin refolded the paper, returned it to his wallet. "Rabies," he said quietly. "Hydrophobia. Its incubation period is less than a week in dogs and other lower mammals. In humans it generally takes a month to erupt. It works faster in small children, I understand. And if the bite is in the head or neck the incubation period is speeded up."

"Can't it be cured? I thought—"

"The Pasteur shots, yes. A series of about a dozen painful injections. I believe the vaccine is introduced by a needle into the stomach. And there are other less arduous methods of vaccination if the particular strain of rabies virus can be determined. But they have to be employed immediately. Once the incubation period is complete, once the symptoms manifest themselves, death is inevitable."

"God."

"By the time Anselmo has the slightest idea what's wrong with him—"

"It will be too late."

"Exactly," Grodin said.

"When you gave him the pentothal—"

"Yes. There was more than pentothal in the needle."

"I sensed something."

"So you said."

Gershon Meir shuddered. "When he realizes what you did to him and how you did it—"

"Then what?" Grodin spread his hands. "Could he be more utterly our enemy than he is already? And I don't honestly think he'll guess how he was tricked. He'll most likely suppose he was exposed to rabies from an animal source. I understand you can get it from inhaling the vapors of the dung of rabid bats. Perhaps he has hidden out in a bat-infested cave and will blame the bats for his illness. But it doesn't matter, Gershon. Let him know what I did to him. I almost hope he guesses, for all the good it will do him."

"God."

"I just wanted to tell you," Grodin said, his voice calmer now. "There's poetry to it, don't you think? He's walking around now like a time bomb. He could get the Pasteur shots and save himself, but he doesn't know that, and by the time he does—"

"Oh, God."

"Start the car, eh? We'd better be getting back." And the older man straightened up in his seat and rubbed the throbbing knuckles of his right hand. They still ached, but all the same he was smiling.

DOGS

Loren D. Estleman

Elda Chase lived in an efficiency flat in Iroquois Heights with no rugs on the hardwood floor and the handsome furniture arranged in geometric patterns like a manor house maze. That day she had the curtains open on the window overlooking the municipal park and the statue of LaSalle with his foot up on a rock scratching his head over a map he had unrolled on his knee. The view was strictly for my benefit; Elda Chase had been blind since birth.

Not that you'd have known it from the way she got around that apartment, discreetly touching this chair and brushing that lamp as she bustled to catch the whistling teapot and find the cups and place the works on a platter and bring it over and set it down on the coffee table. When I leaned forward from the sofa to pour, I was just in time to accept the full cup she extended to me. She filled the other one then and took a seat in the chair opposite. She was a tall woman in her middle fifties who wore her graying hair pinned up and lightly tinted glasses with clear plastic rims. Her ruby blouse and long matching skirt went well with her high coloring and she had on pearl earrings and white low-heeled shoes. I wondered who picked it all out.

"The Braille edition of the Yellow Pages comes so late," she said, balancing her cup and saucer on one crossed knee. "I was half afraid your number had changed."

"Not in a dozen years. Or anything else about the office, except the wallpaper."

"Anyway, thank you for coming. You were the fourth investigator I tried. The first number was disconnected and the other two men referred me to the Humane Society. I'd called them right after it happened, of course. They wanted me to put up posters around the neighborhood. As if I could go out at all without my Max."

"Max is the dog?"

"A shepherd. I've had him three years. When Lucy died I was sure I'd never have another one as good, but Max is special. He's taken me places I'd never have dared go with Lucy."

I sipped some tea and was relieved to find out it was bitter. Watching her operate I'd begun to feel inadequate. "You're sure he didn't run away?"

"Trained seeing-eye dogs don't run away, Mr. Walker. But to lay your cynicism to rest, the padlock on the kennel door had been cut. You saw it in the yard?"

"A six-foot chain link fence to keep in a dog that wouldn't run away," I confirmed.

"The fence was to protect him. It didn't do a very good job. I knew dog-stealing was a possibility, but I hate to keep a big animal cooped up indoors. The police were not encouraging."

"I'm not surprised, in this town."

"I like Iroquois Heights," she said.

"The park is nice."

She raised her face. With her sightless eyes downcast behind the colored lenses she looked like a lioness taking in the sun. "Can you find him?"

"There are markets for purebreds. I can ask some questions. I can't promise anything. My specialty's tracing two-legged mammals."

"I could have gone to someone who traces pets for a living. I don't like professional dog people. They're strident. They'd make me out the villain for not hiring a governess to look after the dog."

"Is there a picture?"

She groped for and opened a drawer in the end table next to her chair and handed me a color snapshot of herself in a wrap and gloves hanging on to a harness attached to a black and tan German shepherd.

"Marks?" I put it in my breast pocket.

"Now, how would I know that?"

"Sorry. I forgot."

"I'll take that as a compliment. He answers to his name with a sharp bark." She took a checkbook off the end table and started writing. "Seven-fifty is your retainer, I believe."

I took the check and put it in my wallet. I drank some more tea, peeled my upper lip back down, and stood, setting aside the cup and saucer. "I'll call you tomorrow. Earlier if I find out anything."

"Thank you." She hesitated. "It isn't just that I need him. If it were just that—"

"I had a dog once," I said. "I still think about him sometimes."

"You sound like someone who would."

*　　*　　*

Mrs. Chase's landlady, a thin blonde named Silcox, lived on the ground floor. Mrs. Chase was her oldest tenant and Mrs. Silcox's son, a sophomore at the University of Michigan, had built the kennel at his mother's request. Neither was home when it was broken into.

From there I went to the office of the Iroquois Heights *Spectator*. The newspaper was the flagship of a fleet owned by a local politician, but the classified section was reliable. I asked for that editor and was directed to a paunchy grayhead standing at the water cooler.

"Rube Zendt," he said when I introduced myself, and shook my hand. "Born Reuben, but trust newspaper folk to latch on to the obvious."

His hair was thin and black on top with gray sidewalls and he had a chipmunk grin that was too small for his full cheeks. He wore black-rimmed glasses and a blue tie at half-mast on a white shirt. I apologized for interrupting his break.

"This distilled stuff rusts my pipes. I only come here to watch the bubbles. Got something to sell or buy, or did you lose something or find it?"

"Close. A local woman hired me to find her dog. I thought that holding down lost and found you'd be the one to talk to about the local market."

"Dog-napping, you mean. I just take the ads. Man you want to see is Stillwell on cophouse."

"He around?"

"This time of day you can catch him at the police station."

"What time of day can I catch him anywhere else?"

The chipmunk grin widened a hundredth of an inch. "I see you know our town. But things aren't so bad down there since Mark Proust made acting chief."

"Meaning what?"

"Meaning he spends all his time in his office. Tell Stillwell Rube sent you."

The first three floors of a corner building on the main stem belonged to the city police. It was a hot day in August and the air conditioning was operating on the ground floor, but that had nothing to do with the drop in my temperature when I came in from the street. At the peak of the busing controversy in the early seventies a group of local citizens had protested the measure by overturning a bus full of schoolchildren; some of that group were in office now and they had built the city law enforcement structure from the prosecutor right down to the last meter maid.

A steely-haired desk sergeant with an exotropic eye turned the good one on me from behind his high bench when I said I was looking for Stillwell of the *Spectator* and held it on me for another minute before saying, "Over there."

The wandering eye was pointing north and I went that way. He'd never have made the Detroit department with that eye, but with his temperament he was right at home.

Two big patrolmen in light summer uniforms were fondling their saps in the corner by the men's room, leering at and listening to a man with no hair above the spread collar of his shirt and a wrinkled cotton sport coat over it.

". . . and the other guy says 'Help me find my keys and we'll *drive* out of here!' "

The cops opened a pair of mouths like buckets and roared. I approached the bald man. "Mr. Stillwell?"

The laughter stopped like a bell grabbed in mid-clang. Two pairs of cop eyes measured me and the bald man's face went guarded with the jokester's leer still in place. "Who's asking?"

"Amos Walker. Rube Zendt said to talk to you."

"Step into my office." He pushed open the men's room door and held it. The cops moved off.

The place had two urinals, a stall, and a sink. He leaned his shoulders against the stall, waiting. He was younger than the clean head indicated, around thirty. He had no eyebrows and clear blue eyes in a lineless face whose innocence could turn the oldest filthy joke into a laugh marathon. I gave him my spiel.

"Shepherd," he said. "There's not a lot of call for them without papers. No gold rushes going on in Alaska to goose the sled-dog trade."

"It's a seeing eye. That's an expensive market."

"They're handled by big organizations that train their own. They don't need to deal in stolen animals and you'd need papers and a good story to sell them one that's already schooled. Tell your client to place an ad with Rube offering a reward and stay home and wait to hear from whoever took the dog."

"Staying home is no problem."

"I guess not. Sorry I can't help."

"What about the fight game?"

"There's no fight game in this town."

"What town we talking about?"

"Yeah." He crossed his ankles then and I knew my leg had been pulled. "That racket's all pit bulls now. I can think of only one guy would even look at a shepherd."

I gave him twenty dollars.

"Henry Revere." He crumpled the bill into the side pocket of his sport coat. "Caretaker over at the old high school. He's there days."

"School board know what he does nights?"

"Everyone knows everything that goes on in this town, except the people who pay taxes to live in it."

"Thanks." I gave him a card, which he crumpled into the same pocket without looking at it. Coming out of the men's room I had the desk sergeant's errant eye. The other was on a woman in a yellow pants suit who had come in to complain about a delivery van that was blocking her Coup de Ville in her driveway.

It was a three story brick box with big mullioned windows and a steel tube that slanted down from the roof for a fire escape. When the new school was built down the road, this one had been converted into administrative offices and a place to vote in district elections. I found its only inhabitant on that summer vacation day, an old black man wearing a green worksuit and tennis shoes, waxing the gym floor. He saw me coming in from the hall and turned off the machine. "Street shoes!"

I stopped. He left the machine and limped my way. I saw that the sole of one of his sneakers was built up twice as thick as its mate.

"Mister, you know how hard it is to get black heel marks off of hardwood?"

"Sorry." I showed him my I.D. "I'm looking for a German shepherd, answers to Max. If you're Henry Revere, someone told me you deal in them."

"Someone lied. What use I got for dogs? I got a job."

"Also a lot of girlfriends. Unless those are dog hairs on your pants."

He caught himself looking, too late. His cracked face bunched like a fist. "You're trespassing."

I held up two ten-dollar bills. He didn't look at them.

"This here's a good job, mister. I got a wife with a bad cough and a boy at Wayne State. I ain't trading them for no twenty bucks. You better get out before I call the po-lice."

I put away the bills. "What are you afraid of?"

"Unemployment and welfare," he said. "Maybe you never been there."

Back in my office in downtown Detroit I made some calls. First I rang Elda Chase, who said that no one had called her yet offering to return Max for a reward. I tried the Humane Society in three counties and got a female shepherd, a mix, and a lecture about the importance of spaying and neutering one's pets at sixty bucks a crack. After that it was time for dinner. When I got back from the place down the street the telephone was ringing. I said hello twice.

"Walker?"

"This is Walker."

Another long pause. "Ed Stillwell. The *Spectator?*"

I said I remembered him. He sounded drunk.

"Yeah. Listen, what I told you 'bout Henry Revere? Forget it. Bum steer."

"I don't think so. He denied too much when I spoke to him."

There was a muffled silence on his end, as of a hand clamped over the mouthpiece. Then: "Listen. Forget it, okay? I only gave you his name 'cause I needed the twenty. I got to make a monthly spousal support payment you wouldn't believe. What I know about dogfighting you could stick in a whistle."

"Okay."

"'Kay."

A receiver was fumbled into a cradle. I hung up and sat there smoking a couple of cigarettes before I went home.

". . . believe the motive was robbery. Once again, Iroquois Heights journalist Edward Stillwell, in critical condition this morning at Detroit General Hospital after police found him beaten unconscious in an empty lot next to the *Spectator* building."

I had turned on the radio while fixing breakfast and got the end of the story. I tried all the other stations. Nothing. I turned off the stove and called the *Spectator*. I kept getting a busy signal. I settled for coffee and left home. As I swung out of the driveway, a navy blue Chrysler with twin mounted spotlights and no chrome pulled away from the curb behind me.

It was still in my mirror when I found a slot in front of the *Spectator* office. I went inside, where everyone on the floor was hunched over his desk arguing with a telephone. Rube Zendt hung his up just as I took a seat in the chair in front of his desk. "The damn *Free Press*," he said, pointing at the instrument. "They want the rundown on Stillwell before we even print it. Those city sheets think they wrote the First Amendment."

"Which desk is Stillwell's?"

"Why?"

I counted on my fingers. "Stillwell gives me a man to see about a dog. A cross-eyed sergeant at the cophouse sees us talking. I see the man. Last night Stillwell calls me, sounding sloshed and telling me to forget the man. This morning the cops scrape Stillwell out of an alley."

"Empty lot."

"In Detroit we call them alleys. I'm not finished. This morning I've got a tail that might as well have UNMARKED POLICE CAR painted in big white letters on the side. Someone's scared. I want to know what makes Stillwell so scary. Maybe he kept notes. He's a newspaperman."

"I can't let you go through his desk. Only Stillwell can do that. Or George Strong. He publishes the *Spectator.*"

"I know who Strong is. Where is he?"

"Lady, we don't *need* no warrant. We're in hot pursuit of a suspect in an assault and battery."

This was a new player. I turned in my chair and looked at a pair of hulks in strained jackets and wide ties standing just inside the front door dwarfing a skinny woman in a tailored suit. One, a crewcut blond with a neck like a leg, spotted me and pointed. "There he is."

I got up. "Back way."

Zendt jerked a thumb over his shoulder. "End of that hall. Good luck." He stuck out his hand. I took it hastily and brought mine away with a business card folded in it.

The detectives were bumping into desks and cursing behind me when I made the end of the hall and sprinted out the back door. I ran around the building to my car. One of the cops, graying with a thick mustache, had doubled back and was barreling out the front door when I got under the wheel. I scratched pavement with the car door flapping. In the mirror I saw him draw his revolver and sight down on the car. I went into a swerve, but his partner reached him then and knocked up his elbow. I was four blocks away before I heard their siren.

I backed the car into a deserted driveway and unfolded the card Zendt had given me. It was engraved with George Strong's name, telephone number, and address on Lake Shore Drive in Grosse Pointe Farms. I waited a little. When I was sure I couldn't hear the siren any more I pulled out. My head stayed sunk between my shoulder blades until I was past the city limits.

It was one of the deep walled estates facing the glass-flat surface of Lake St. Clair, with a driveway that wound through a lawn as big as a golf course, but greener, ending in front of a brownstone sprawl with windows the size of suburbs. I tucked the Chevy in behind a row of German cars and walked around the house toward the pulse of music. I should have packed a lunch.

Rich people aren't always throwing parties; it's just that that's the only time you catch them at home. This one was going on around a wallet-shaped pool with guests in bathing suits and designer-original sundresses and ascots and silk blazers. There was a small band, not more than sixteen pieces, and the partygoers outnumbered the serving staff by a good one and a half to one.

George Strong wasn't hard to spot. He had made his fortune from newspapers and cable television, and his employees had dutifully smeared his face all over the pages and airwaves during two unsuccessful campaigns for state office. His tow head and crinkled bronze face towered four inches over his tallest listener in a knot of people standing by the rosebushes. I inserted some polyester into the group and introduced myself.

"Do we know each other?" Strong looked older in person than in his ads. His chin sagged and his face was starting to bloat.

"It's about one of your reporters, Ed Stillwell."

"I heard. Terrible thing. The company will pay his bills, even though the incident had nothing to do with the newspaper. I understand he was drunk when they mugged him."

"Nobody mugged him. I think he was beaten by the police."

"Excuse us, gentlemen." He put a hand on my arm and steered me toward the house.

His study was all dark oak and red leather with rows of unread books on shelves and photographs of George Strong shaking hands with governors and presidents. When we were on opposite sides of an Empire desk I told him the story. Unconsciously he patted the loosening flesh under his chin.

"Ridiculous. The police in Iroquois Heights aren't thugs."

"Two of them tried to arrest me for Stillwell's beating in the *Spectator* office half an hour ago, without a warrant. They followed me there from my house, where they have no jurisdiction. Your classifieds editor gave me your card. Call him."

He didn't. "I won't have my reporters manhandled. You say you want to go through Stillwell's desk?"

I said yes. He took a sheet of heavy stock out of a drawer and scribbled on it with a gold pen from an onyx stand. He folded it and handed it to me. "I'll pay double what the woman's paying you to forget the dog and find out who beat up Stillwell."

"Save it for your next campaign. If my hunch is right I'll find them both in the same spot." I put the note in my pocket and took myself out.

The navy blue Chrysler was parked across the street from the newspaper office when I came around the corner from where I'd left my car. There was only one man in it, which meant his partner was watching the back door. I ducked inside a department store down the block to think.

There was a fire exit in Men's Wear with a warning sign in red. The clerk, slim and black in a gray three-piece, was helping a customer pick out a necktie by the dressing rooms. I pushed through the door.

The alarm was good and loud. Mustache had gotten out of the car and was hustling through the front door when I rounded the building and trotted across the street to the *Spectator*. The skinny woman in the tailored suit read Strong's note and pointed out Ed Stillwell's desk.

Reporters are packrats. While I was sifting through a ton of scrawled-over scrap, Rube Zendt came over and leaned on the desk. "Cops are watching the place," he said.

"Do tell."

"The older one with the mustache is Sergeant Gogol. The wrestler's Officer Joyce. They're meaner than two vice principals. When you're ready to go, hide in the toilet and I'll call in Joyce from the back—tell him Gogol's got you out front or something—and you can duck out the rear. It worked once."

"I guess you scribblers look out for each other."

"Stillwell? Can't stand the bald son of a bitch. But ink's thicker than blood." He strolled back to his desk.

Ten minutes later I found something that looked good, one half of a fifty dollar bill with a scrap of paper clipped to it and "9 P.M. 8/8 OHS" penciled on the scrap in Stillwell's crooked hand. Today was the eighth. The torn-bill gag was corny as anything, but that was Iroquois Heights for you. I pocketed it, got Zendt's attention, and went to the bathroom.

I spent the rest of the day in a Detroit motel in case the cops went to my house or office. From there I called Elda Chase to tell her I was still working and to ask if she'd heard anything. She hadn't. I watched TV, ordered a pizza for dinner, and left three slices for the maid at eight thirty.

The old high school was lit up like Homecoming when I presented myself at the open front door. A security guard in khaki asked me if I was there for the parents' meeting. I handed him the half-bill. He looked at it, dug the other half out of a shirt pocket, and matched them. Then he put both halves in the pocket. "You're Stillwell?"

"Yeah."

"I heard you was in the hospital."

"I got out." I passed him ahead of any more questions.

A meeting was going on somewhere in the building; voices droned in the linoleum and tile halls. Acting on instinct I headed away from them, stepping around a folding gate beyond which the overhead lights had been turned off. A new noise reached me: louder, not as stylized, less human. It increased as I passed through twin doors and stopped before a steel one marked BOILER ROOM. I opened it and stepped into tropical heat.

I was on a catwalk overlooking the basement, where twenty men in undershirts or no shirts at all crouched around fifteen square feet of bare concrete floor, shouting and shaking their fists at a pair of pit bulls ripping at each other in the center. From the pitch of their snarls it was still early in the fight, but already the floor was patterned with blood.

The door opened behind me while I was leaning over the pipe railing trying to get a look at the men's faces. I stepped back behind the door, crowding into a dark corner smelling of cobwebs and crumbling cement. I wished I'd brought my gun with me. I'd thought it would slow me down.

Two men came in and stood with their backs to me, close enough to breathe down their collars. I recognized Henry Revere's white head and green workclothes. The other man's hair wasn't much darker. He was taller and white, wearing a gray summerweight suit cut to disguise an advanced middle-age spread. From the back he looked familiar.

"Which dog's that?" wheezed the man in the suit. I knew that broken windpipe.

"Lord Baltimore," said Revere. "Bart. He's new."

"He doesn't have the weight to start out that hard. He'll fold in five."

"That's a bull for you. Shepherds pace theirselves."

"Shepherds are pansies. I told you not to buy any more."

"I gots to buy something. We're running out of dogs."

"Sell what you got. I'm jumping this racket."

"Man, I don't like the other. That's heat with a big *H.*"

"*I'm* the heat."

"What if one of them cons talks to the press?"

The man in the suit coughed. "Why'd he want to? What other chance he got to miss a stretch in Jackson? He should thank us."

"Not if he gets beat half to death like that reporter."

"Gogol and Joyce got carried away. They were supposed to just rough him around, maybe break something. Anyway he had his slice. He should've stood on his tongue."

"What I mean," Revere said. "If he talked, so could a con. And what about that detective?"

"I got men everyplace he goes. His wings are clipped."

"You say so, chief. I feel better when he's grounded."

A shrill yelp sheared the air. Then silence.

"There, you see?" said the man in the suit. "No distance."

The door opened again. I squeezed tight to the wall. The pair turned, and I got a good view in profile at Acting Chief of Police Mark Proust's long slack face. His complexion matched the gray of his suit.

"Chief, that guy Stillwell's here. Thought I better tell you." The security man's voice was muffled a little on the other side of the open door.

"Impossible. What'd he look like?"

"About six feet, one eighty-five, brown hair."

"That's not—"

I hit the door with my shoulder, occupying the guard while I shoved Proust into the railing. Revere moved my way, but his short leg slowed him down. I swept past him and threw a right at the guard, missing his jaw but glancing off the muscle on the side of his neck. He lost his balance. I vaulted over him.

"It's Walker!" Proust shouted. "Use your gun!"

Flying through the twin doors in the hall, I sent a late dog rooter sprawling. Behind me a shot flattened the air. The bullet shattered the glass in one of the doors. I reached the folding gate, but the opening was gone; the guard or someone had closed and locked it. The guard was coming through the broken door, behind his gun. I ducked through a square arch in the wall, stumbled on stairs in the darkness, caught my equilibrium on the run, and started taking them two at a time heading up. A bullet skidded off brick next to my right ear.

I ran out of stairs on a dark landing. Feet pounded the steps behind me. I felt for and found a doorknob. It turned.

Cool fresh air slid over me down a shaft of moonlight. I was on the roof with the lights of Iroquois Heights spread at my feet. I let the heavy door slam shut of its own weight, got my bearings, and made for the fire chute. I had a foot over the edge when the security guard piled out the door and skidded to a halt, bringing his gun up in two hands. Gravity took me.

The inside of the tube smelled of stale metal. My ears roared as I slid a long way, as if falling in a dream. Then I leveled out and my feet hit ground and inertia carried me upright and forward. Officer Joyce, standing at the bottom, pivoted his bulk and brought his right arm down with a grunt. A fuse blew in my head and I went down another chute, this one bottomless.

I awoke with a flash of nausea. My scalp stung and an inflated balloon was rubbing against the inside of my skull. I got my eyelids open despite sand in the works, only to find that I was still in darkness. This darkness stank. As I lay waiting for my pupils to catch up, I grew aware of an incessant loud yapping and that it was not in my head. Then I identified the smell. I was in a kennel.

Not quite in it, I thought, as objects around me assumed vague shape. I was lying on moist earth surrounded by wire cages with wet black muzzles pressed against the wire from inside and eyes shining farther back. These were the quiet ones. The others were setting up a racket and hurling themselves against the doors and trying to gnaw through the wire.

My arms had gone to sleep. I tried to move them, and that was when I found out my wrists were cuffed behind me. My ankles were bound, too, with something thin and strong that chafed skin; twine or insulated wire. I rolled over onto my face and worked myself up onto my knees. The balloon inside my head creaked.

Something rattled, followed by a current of air that sucked in light. The walls were gray corrugated steel. A pair of shiny black Oxfords appeared in front of me and I looked up at Mark Proust. The battery-powered lantern he was carrying shadowed the pouches in his paper-pulp face.

"Cut his legs loose," he said. "He isn't going anywhere."

Feet scraped earth behind me. A blade sawed fiber and my ankles came apart. I got up awkwardly with my wrists still bound. Circulation needled back into my lower legs.

"When was the last time, snoop? The Broderick kill?"

I said nothing. Officer Joyce joined Proust, folding a jackknife. The crewcut gave his face a planed look, like a wooden carving with the features blocked in for finishing later.

"Shut up those dogs," Proust said.

I hadn't realized Henry Revere was present. The old black man came up from behind me and kicked the cage containing the loudest of the dogs. The dog, a sixty pound pit bull, stopped barking and shrank back snarling. He kicked two more. The third dog hesitated, then lunged, fangs biting wire. Revere kicked again and it yelped and cowered. Its eyes glittered in the shadows at the rear of the cage. The rest of the animals fell into a whimpering silence. Two of the cages contained shepherds.

"Know where we are, snoop?" asked Proust.

"The Iroquois Heights Police Academy," I said. "Those are some of your new rookies."

"Funny guy. It's my little ten-acre retirement nest egg six miles out of the Heights. The old high school's nice, but it's too close to everything."

"Makes a good front, though," I said. "Like dog fighting, which is illegal but forgiveable in case someone starts prying. Maybe he won't think to look further and find the real racket."

"What's that, snoop?"

I said nothing again.

"Smart." He smirked at Joyce and Revere. "A smart private nose is what we got here. Only he just thinks he's smart. Thinks if he acts dumb we'll let him go on breathing. Which makes him dumb for real."

I shrugged. "Okay. I heard enough to know you've graduated from fighting dogs to fighting inmates, probably from downtown holding. In return for their release or a word to the judge they agree to fight each other, probably in front of a crowd that's outgrown betting on dogs. Your piece of the gate must be sweet."

"It pays the bills. Especially when we put a black in the pit with a white. A lot of the residents here left Detroit to get away from the blacks. No offense, Henry."

"I'm surprised you didn't put one in with Stillwell."

"He wouldn't have lasted two minutes. Gogol and Joyce almost killed him without even trying." He paused, tasting his next words. "I figure you for a better show."

"I was wondering when we were coming to that."

"You might win, who knows?"

"What do I win, a bullet?"

"Warm up if you want. People are still coming. I'll send someone back for you." He went out, trailing Joyce and Revere. A padlock rattled.

It was a truss barn with a high roof and some moonlight seeping through cracks between the bolted-on sections. The cage doors were latched with simple sliding bolts. I backed up to them and worked them loose, hoping the agitated dogs inside wouldn't chew off my fingers. I left them engaged just enough to keep the doors closed. A good lunge would slip any of them. I came to the shepherds last. In the gloom either of them could have been the dog in the picture Elda Chase had given me.

"Max."

One of them barked sharply. I called again. It barked again. The other looked at me and gave a rippling snarl. Just to be sure I left both cages locked. They were safer inside.

Some of the cages were empty and I sat on one. I wanted a cigarette but I didn't fidget. The last thing I wanted to do was startle a dog into breaking loose while I was still present.

After a long time of measured breathing and sweating beyond measure, I heard the lock rattle again and Gogol and Joyce came in. I stood. The detective with the mustache held his revolver on me while his partner led me out. Gogol followed with the gun.

We walked twenty yards through a jumble of cars parked on rutted earth to a steel barn bigger than the one we had just left. Henry Revere passed us coming out the door. He was going back to see to the dogs.

The interior was lit with electric bulbs strung along the tops of the walls. Crude bleachers had been erected on either side of a hole dug five feet deep and eight feet in diameter and lined with rough concrete. The bleachers were jammed with men and some women, all talking in loud voices that grew shrill when we entered. This building smelled as strong as the other, but the stink here was sharper, more foul, distinctly human. Proust sat in the middle of the front row.

We stopped at the edge of the pit and Joyce unlocked my handcuffs. Inside the pit stood a black man wearing only faded bluejeans. His hair was cropped short and his torso was slabbed with glistening muscle. He watched me with yellowish eyes under a ridge of bone.

I was rubbing circulation back into my wrists when Joyce shoved me into the pit. My opponent caught me and hurled me backward. I struck concrete, emptying my lungs. The crowd shrieked. He charged. I pivoted just in time to avoid being crushed between him and the wall. He caught himself with his hands, pushed off, and whirled. I hit him with everything, flush on the chin. He shook his head. I threw a left. He caught it in a hand the size of my office and hit me on the side of the head with his other fist. I heard a gong.

I backpedaled, buying time for my vision to clear. He followed me. I kicked him in the groin and punched him in the throat; he was no boxer and had left both unprotected. They didn't need protecting. He wrapped a hand around my neck and reared back. "Sorry, man."

The fist was coming at me when a woman in the crowd screamed. The scream was higher and louder than any of the others and it made him hesitate just an instant.

I didn't. I doubled both fists and brought them up in an uppercut that tipped his head back and snapped his teeth together and broke his grip on my neck. Then I put my head down and butted him in the chest. He staggered back, spitting teeth.

The whole crowd was screaming now, and not at us. A torn and bleeding Henry Revere had stumbled into the building trailing a pack of enraged dogs that were bounding through the audience, bellowing and slashing at limbs and throats with the madness of fear and anger and pain. One, a red-eyed pit bull, leaped over the concrete rim and landed on my dazed opponent and I clubbed it with my forearm before it could rip out his throat. Stunned, the dog sank down on all fours and fouled the pit.

"You all right?" I asked.

He got his feet under him, a hand on his throat. It came away bloody, but the skin was barely torn. "I guess."

"What'd they promise you, a clean ticket?"

"Probation."

"Give me a leg up and maybe you'll still get it."

After a moment he complied and I scrambled out of the pit, then stuck out a hand and helped him up. Most of the crowd had cleared out of the building. One of the dogs lay dead, shot through the head by one of the cops; the report had been drowned in the confusion. Another stood panting and glaze-eyed with its tongue hanging out of a scarlet muzzle. I didn't look for the others. My former opponent and I went out the door.

It was more dangerous outside now than in. Cars were swinging out of the makeshift parking lot, sideswiping one another and raking headlamps over scurrying pedestrians and dogs.

I heard sirens getting nearer. I wondered who had called the cops. I wondered which cops they had called.

A maroon Cadillac swung into the light spilling out the barn door, illuminating Proust's pale face behind the wheel. I shouted at the black man and we ran after it. His legs were longer than mine; he reached the car first and tore open the door on the driver's side and pulled Proust out with one hand. The car kept going and stalled against the corner of the other building.

The black man took a gun from under Proust's coat and hit him with it. I let him, then twisted it out of his grip from behind. His other hand was clutching the acting police chief's collar. Proust was bleeding from a cut on his forehead.

"Police! Freeze! Drop the gun!"

I did both. A county sheriff's car had pulled up alongside us and a deputy was coming out with his gun in both hands. The door on the passenger's side opened and George Strong got out.

"It's all right," he said. "That's our inside man."

The deputy kept his stance. "What about the other?"

I said, "He's with me."

Strong looked from Proust's half-conscious face to mine. "I bribed the guard at the high school for this spot. I remembered I was a newspaperman and that maybe the biggest story in years was getting away from me. What about the ones who hurt Stillwell?"

"Sergeant Gogol and Officer Joyce," I said. "APB them."

His crinkled face got wry. "Did you find the woman's dog?"

I indicated the other barn. "In there. Take it easy on him," I told the deputy. "Take it easy on all of them."

"You a dog lover or something?"

"No, just one of the dogs." I walked away to breathe.

PAY-OFF GIRL

James M. Cain

I met her a month ago at a little café called Mike's Joint, in Cottage City, Maryland, a town just over the District line from Washington, D.C. As to what she was doing in this lovely honkytonk, I'll get to it, all in due time. As to what I was doing there, I'm not at all sure that I know, as it wasn't my kind of place. But even a code clerk gets restless, especially if he used to dream about being a diplomat and he wound up behind a glass partition, unscrambling cables. And on top of that was my father out in San Diego, who kept writing me sarcastic letters telling how an A-1 canned-goods salesman had turned into a Z-99 government punk, and wanting to know when I'd start working for him again, and making some money. And on top of that was Washington, with the suicide climate it has, which to a Californian is the same as death, only worse.

Or it may have been lack of character. But whatever it was, there I sat, at the end of the bar having a bottle of beer, when from behind me came a voice: "Mike, a light in that phone booth would help. People could see to dial. And that candle in there smells bad."

"Yes, Miss, I'll get a bulb."

"I know, Mike, but when?"

"I'll get one."

She spoke low, but meant business. He tossed some cubes in a glass and made her iced coffee, and she took the next stool to drink it. As soon as I could see her I got a stifled feeling. She was blonde, a bit younger than I am, which is twenty-five, medium size, with quite a shape, and good-looking enough, though maybe no raving beauty. But what cut my wind were the clothes and the way she wore them. She had on a peasant blouse, with big orange beads dipping into the neck, black shoes with high heels and fancy latticework straps and a pleated orange skirt that flickered around her like flame. And to me, born right on the border, that outfit spelled Mexico, but hot Mexico, with chili, castanets, and hat dancing in it, which I love. I

looked all the law allowed, and then had to do eyes front, as she began
looking at her beads, at her clothes, at her feet, to see what the trouble was.

Soon a guy came in and said the bookies had sent him here to get paid
off on a horse. Mike said have a seat, the young lady would take care of
him. She said: "At the table in the corner. I'll be there directly."

I sipped my beer and thought it over. If I say I liked that she was pay-off
girl for some bookies, I'm not telling the truth, and if I say it made any
difference, I'm telling a downright lie. I just didn't care, because my throat
had talked to my mouth, which was so dry the beer rasped through it. I
watched her while she finished her coffee, went to the table, and opened a
leather case she'd been holding in her lap. She took out a tiny adding
machine, some typewritten sheets of paper, and a box of little manila envelopes. She handed the guy a pen, had him sign one of the sheets, and gave
him one of the envelopes. Then she picked up the pen and made a note on
the sheet. He came to the bar and ordered a drink. Mike winked at me. He
said: "They make a nice class of business, gamblers do. When they win they
want a drink, and when they lose they need one."

More guys came, and also girls, until they formed a line, and when they
were done at the table they crowded up to the bar. She gave some of them
envelopes, but not all. Quite a few paid her, and she'd tap the adding
machine. Then she had a lull. I paid for my beer, counted ten, swallowed
three times, and went over to her table. When she looked up I took off my
hat and said: "How do I bet on horses?"

"You sure you want to?"

"I think so."

"You know it's against the law?"

"I've heard it is."

"I didn't say it was wrong. It's legal at the tracks, and what's all right one
place can't be any howling outrage someplace else, looks like. But you
should know how it is."

"Okay, I know."

"Then sit down and I'll explain."

We talked jerky, with breaks between, and she seemed as rattled as I was.
When I got camped down, though, it changed. She drew a long trembly
breath and said: "It has to be done by telephone. These gentlemen, the
ones making the book, can't have a mob around, so it's all done on your
word, like in an auction room, where a nod is as good as a bond, and
people don't rat on their bids. I take your name, address, and phone, and
when you're looked up you'll get a call. They give you a number, and from
then on you phone in, and your name will be good for your bets."

"My name is Miles Kearny."

She wrote it on an envelope, with my phone and address, an apartment in southeast Washington. I took the pen from her hand, rubbed ink on my signet ring, and pressed the ring on the envelope, so the little coronet, with the three tulips over it, showed nice and clear. She got some ink off my hand with her blotter, then studied the impression on the envelope. She said: "Are you a prince or something?"

"No, but it's been in the family. And it's one way to get my hand held. And pave the way for me to ask something."

"Which is?"

"Are you from the West?"

"No, I'm not. I'm from Ohio. Why?"

"And you've never lived in Mexico?"

"No, but I love Mexican clothes."

"Then that explains it."

"Explains what?"

"How you come to look that way, and—how I came to fall for you. I'm from the West. Southern California."

She got badly rattled again and after a long break said: "Have you got it straight now? About losses? They have to be paid."

"I generally pay what I owe."

There was a long, queer break then, and she seemed to have something on her mind. At last she blurted out: "And do you really want in?"

"Listen, I'm over twenty-one."

"In's easy. Out's not."

"You mean it's habit-forming?"

"I mean, be careful who you give your name to, or your address, or phone."

"They give theirs, don't they?"

"They give you a number."

"Is that number yours, too?"

"I can be reached there."

"And who do I ask for?"

"Ruth."

"That all the name you got?"

"In this business, yes."

"I want in."

Next day, by the cold gray light of Foggy Bottom, which is what they call the State Department, you'd think that I'd come to my senses and forget her. But I thought of her all day long, and that night I was back, on the same old stool, when she came in, made a call from the booth, came out, squawked about the light and picked up her coffee to drink it. When she saw me she took it to the table. I went over, took off my hat, and said:

"I rang in before I came. My apartment house. But they said no calls came in for me."

"It generally takes a while."

That seemed to be all, and I left. Next night it was the same, and for some nights after that. But one night she said, "Sit down," and then: "Until they straighten it out, why don't you bet with me? Unless, of course, you have to wait until post time. But if you're satisfied to pick them the night before, I could take care of it."

"You mean, you didn't give in my name?"

"I told you, it all takes time."

"Why didn't you give it in?"

"Listen, you wanted to bet."

"Okay, let's bet."

I didn't know one horse from another, but she had a racing paper there, and I picked a horse called Fresno, because he reminded me of home and at least I could remember his name. From the weights he looked like a long shot, so I played him to win, place, and show, two dollars each way. He turned out an also-ran, and the next night I kicked in with six dollars more and picked another horse, still trying for openings to get going with her. That went on for some nights, I hoping to break through, she hoping I'd drop out, and both of us getting nowhere. Then one night Fresno was entered again and I played him again, across the board. Next night I put down my six dollars, and she sat staring at me. She said: "But Fresno won."

"Oh. Well say. Good old Fresno."

"He paid sixty-four eighty for two."

I didn't much care, to tell the truth. I didn't want her money. But she seemed quite upset. She went on: "However, the top bookie price, on any horse that wins, is twenty to one. At that I owe you forty dollars win money, twenty-two dollars place and fourteen dollars show, plus of course the six that you bet. That's eighty-two in all. Mr. Kearny, I'll pay you tomorrow. I came away before the last race was run, and I just now got the results when I called in. I'm sorry, but I don't have the money with me, and you'll have to wait."

"Ruth, I told you from the first, my weakness isn't horses. It's you. If six bucks a night is the ante, okay, that's how it is, and dirt cheap. But if you'll act as a girl ought to act, quit holding out on me, what your name is and how I get in touch, I'll quit giving an imitation of a third-rate gambler, and we'll both quit worrying whether you pay me or not. We'll start over, and—"

"What do you mean, act as a girl ought to act?"

"I mean go out with me."

"On this job how can I?"

"Somebody making you hold it?"

"They might be, at that."

"With a gun to your head, maybe?"

"They got 'em, don't worry."

"There's only one thing wrong with that. Some other girl and a gun, that might be her reason. But not you. You don't say yes to a gun, or to anybody giving you orders, or trying to. If you did, I wouldn't be here."

She sat looking down in her lap, and then, in a very low voice: "I don't say I was forced. I do say, when you're young you can be a fool. Then people can do things to you. And you might try to get back, for spite. Once you start that, you'll be in too deep to pull out."

"Oh, you could pull out, if you tried."

"How, for instance?"

"Marrying me is one way."

"Me, a pay-off girl for a gang of bookies, marry Miles Kearny, a guy with a crown on his ring and a father that owns a big business and a mother—who's your mother, by the way?"

"My mother's dead."

"I'm sorry."

We had dead air for a while, and she said: "Mr. Kearny, men like you don't marry girls like me, at least to live with them and like it. Maybe a wife can have cross-eyes or buckteeth; but she can't have a past."

"Ruth, I told you my first night here, I'm from California, where we've got present and future. There isn't any past. Too many of their grandmothers did what you do, they worked for gambling houses. They dealt so much faro and rolled so many dice and spun so many roulette wheels, in Sacramento and Virginia City and San Francisco, they don't talk about the past. You got to admit they made a good state though, those old ladies and their children. They made the best there is, and that's where I'd be taking you, and that's why we'd be happy."

"It's out."

"Are you married, Ruth?"

"No, but it's out."

"Why is it?"

"I'll pay you tomorrow night."

Next night the place was full, because a lot of them had bet a favorite that came in and they were celebrating their luck. When she'd paid them off she motioned and I went over. She picked up eight tens and two ones and handed them to me, and to get away from the argument I took the bills and put them in my wallet. Then I tried to start where we'd left off the night before, but she held out her hand and said: "Mr. Kearny, it's been wonderful knowing you, especially knowing someone who always takes off his hat. I've wanted to tell you that. But don't come any more. I won't see you any more, or accept bets, or anything. Goodbye, and good luck."

"I'm not letting you go."

"Aren't you taking my hand?"

"We're getting married, tonight."

Tears squirted out of her eyes, and she said: "Where?"

"Elkton. They got day and night service, for license, preacher and witnesses. Maybe not the way we'd want it done, but it's one way. And it's a two-hour drive in my car."

"What about—?" She waved at the bag, equipment, and money.

I said: "I tell you, I'll look it all up to make sure, but I'm under the impression—just a hunch—that they got parcel post now, so we can lock, seal, and mail it. How's that?"

"You sure are a wheedling cowboy."

"Might be, I love you."

"Might be, that does it."

We fixed it up then, whispering fast, how I'd wait outside in the car while she stuck around to pay the last few winners, which she said would make it easier. So I sat there, knowing I could still drive off, and not even for a second wanting to. All I could think about was how sweet she was, how happy the old man would be, and how happy our life would be, all full of love and hope and California sunshine. Some people went in the café, and a whole slew came out. The jukebox started, a tune called *Night and Day*, then played it again and again.

Then it came to me: I'd been there quite a while. I wondered if something was wrong, if maybe *she* had taken a powder. I got up, walked to the café, and peeped. She was still there, at the table. But a guy was standing beside her, with his hat on, and if it was the way he talked or the way he held himself, as to that I couldn't be sure, but I thought he looked kind of mean. I started in. Mike was blocking the door. He said: "Pal, come back later. Just now I'm kind of full."

"Full? Your crowd's leaving."

"Yeah, but the cops are watching me."

"Hey, what is this?"

He'd sort of mumbled, but I roared it, and as he's little and I'm big it took less than a second for him to bounce off me and for me to start past the bar. But the guy heard it, and as I headed for him he headed for me. We met a few feet from her table, and she was white as a sheet. He was tall, thin, and sporty-looking, in a light, double-breasted suit, and I didn't stop until I bumped him and he had to back up. Some girl screamed. I said: "What seems to be the trouble?"

He turned to Mike and said, "Mike, who's your friend?"

"I don't know, Tony. Some jerk."

He said to her: "Ruth, who is he?"

"How would I know?"

"He's not a friend, by chance?"

"I never saw him before."

I bowed to her and waved at Mike. I said: "I'm greatly obliged to you two for your thoughtful if misplaced effort to conceal my identity. You may now relax, as I propose to stand revealed."

I turned to the guy and said: "I am a friend, as it happens, of Ruth's, and in fact considerably more. I'm going to marry her. As for you, you're getting out."

"I am?"

"I'll show you."

I let drive with a nice one-two, and you think he went down on the floor? He just wasn't there. All that was left was perfume, a queer foreign smell, and it seemed to hang on my fist. When I found him in my sights again he was at the end of the bar, looking at me over a gun. He said: "Put 'em up."

I did.

"Mike, get me his money."

"Listen, Tony, I don't pick pockets—"

"Mike!"

"Yes, Tony."

Mike got my wallet, and did what he was told: "Take out that money, and every ten in it, hold it up to the light, here where I can see. . . . There they are, two pinholes in Hamilton's eyes, right where I put them before passing the jack to a crooked two-timing dame who was playing me double."

He made me follow his gun to where she was. He leaned down to her, said: "I'm going to kill you, but I'm going to kill him first, so you can see him fall, so get over there, right beside him."

She spit in his face.

Where he had me was right in front of the telephone booth, and all the time he was talking I was working the ring off. Now I could slip it up in the empty bulb socket. I pushed, and the fuse blew. The place went dark. The jukebox stopped with a moan, and I started with a yell. I went straight ahead, not with a one-two this time. I gave it all my weight, and when I hit him he toppled over and I heard the breath go out of him. It was dark, but I knew it was him by the smell. First, I got a thumb on his mastoid and heard him scream from the pain. Then I caught his wrist and used my other thumb there. The gun dropped, it hit my foot, it was in my hand. "Mike,"

I yelled, "the candle! In the booth! I've got his gun! But for Pete's sake, give us some light!"

So after about three years Mike found his matches and lit up. While I was waiting I felt her arms come around me and heard her whisper in my ear: "You've set me free, do you still want me?"

"You bet I do!"

"Let's go to Elkton!"

So we did, and I'm writing this on the train, stringing it out so I can watch her as she watches mesquite, sage, buttes, and the rest of the West rolling by the window. But I can't string it out much longer. Except that we're goof happy, and the old man is throwing handsprings, that's all.

Period.

New paragraph.

California, here we come.

FROM ZAIRE
TO ETERNITY

Charles Ardai

The morning mail held two surprises for Dan Reed. The first was a letter from his sister Evelyn, from whom he hadn't heard in almost a year. The second was a hundred-carat diamond.

Evelyn had been married (she wrote) on the eve of her eighteenth birthday, to an actor named Kyle Nuys. They were taking a honeymoon in Africa, to coincide with the start of the First Annual Pan-African Tennis Consortium and Tournament, upon the conclusion of which they were to return to North Hollywood and a life ever after of marital bliss.

The letter closed with a mention of bad weather, standard queries after Dan's health, and the assurance that when she returned Evelyn would insist on spending at least a week in New York with her big brother. At the bottom of the page was the parenthetical postscript, "('Evelyn Nuys'! I'm still not used to it!)"

And then there was the package.

It was not evident at first that the package contained a hundred-carat diamond. It seemed, in fact, to contain a tennis ball. Tennis balls do not rattle, however, as this one did, and they have a certain peculiar heft that this one did not. And generally, when one receives a tennis ball in the mail, it is accompanied by a note of explanation, or at least a return address. This one was not.

So, after looking at the ball for several minutes, listening to the sound it made when shaken, and tossing it from hand to hand, Dan pulled a steak knife from his lower desk drawer and sliced the ball neatly in half. A bright, glittery, *huge* cut diamond clattered onto Dan's desk. Dan dropped the remnants of the tennis ball into his trash can.

Dan had not seen many diamonds in the course of his investigations, and none of his other professions paid well enough to afford him such luxuries. He held the stone up to the light. Judging by its size, few professions would. But he knew one thing: this monster gem was no trifle.

Where had it come from? The tennis ball suggested Evelyn, who was an avid tennis fan; she had spent the previous four years traveling the world in pursuit of exotic matches, first with their mother and then alone from age sixteen on. The stamps and postmark confirmed Dan's suspicion: they matched those on the letter, both having originated in Zaire.

Zaire. Home of the world's second largest diamond-mining industry. Ditto a prominent diamond smuggling industry, mostly through South Africa. Ditto, evidently, the First Annual Pan-African Tennis Consortium and Tournament.

And ditto Evelyn Nuys, eighteen-year-old would-be diamond smuggler. Typically, without Mom around to keep an eye on her, Evelyn had gone and done something illegal. Only now, at eighteen, she was old enough to be thrown in jail, or worse.

She wouldn't be, though. Dan had confidence in his sister. Unless she was slowing down in her old age, catching Evelyn wouldn't be easy, holding her even less so. She had certainly escaped from home quickly enough, and diamond smugglers could hardly be more tenacious than her mother had been, following her all over the globe. Of course, smugglers might be more violent . . .

Dan turned the diamond this way and that, watching the light flicker off its facets. Why did she send it to me? he wondered. And how did she get it out of the country? The box the ball came in would have cloaked the rattling, but didn't the authorities notice that the ball weighed more than it should have?

For that matter, where had she gotten the diamond? Zaire might have many mines, but Dan doubted there were diamonds littering the tennis courts. And this Kyle Nuys—did he realize what he was getting into, marrying a self-proclaimed swindler, rogue, and criminal genius? Poor fellow, if he should turn out to be the quiet, sedentary sort.

A knock on the door drew Dan from his thoughts. The silhouette on the other side of the frosted glass was bulky and rectangular. Dan let his hand drop, slid the diamond into his pocket, pulled his control box out of a desk drawer, and flicked the uppermost of its six toggle switches.

On the door, the words "Dan Reed" lit up. Beneath Dan's name were six lines of text, each in a circle of neon tubing:

AAARMCHAIR DETECTIVE AGENCY

ACE COMPUTER CONSULTING

AARON LLOYD'S PATENTED SHIATSU MASSAGE

AALEXANDER THE GREAT
MAGIC/ENTERTAINMENT/
CHILDREN'S PARTIES

Dan slapped a white button on his desk to activate the intercom. "Are you Dan Reed?"

Dan said nothing. He assumed the man could read.

"Let me in," the man said. His voice was an indelicate, throaty rumble.

"What do you want?" Dan asked.

"I want to come in."

"Do you want a detective? A computer consultant? A massage? A magician?" Dan flicked the switches, highlighting each option in turn.

"*I want to come in,*" the man repeated.

"Patience. First, tell me which—"

The man raised a fist that was roughly the size of a telephone book and smashed it through the glass. He turned the knob from the inside and let himself in.

"—service you are interested in." Dan hated to leave a sentence unfinished.

The man sat in the chair next to Dan's desk. He was tremendous and dour, an overgrown, square-jawed lizard. His arms were hairy and dark, and thick like the roots of an oak. A good foot beneath his eyes, his face ended abruptly at a blunt, stubble-coated plateau. His nose, equally square, Dan could account for as the result of too many blows; but for such a square chin Dan could imagine no culprit except an unkind twist of heredity. And even sitting down, the man towered over Dan.

Dan let him tower silently, which he did for an uncomfortable minute and a half. In time, it dawned on him that Dan was not going to speak. "Did you see what I did to your door?" he asked.

Obviously this was no mental giant, as Dan was facing the wreckage. "What do you think?" Dan asked.

"I'll do the same to you."

"You'll punch my lights out, too," Dan said. "That's wonderful. I suppose you even have a reason."

"Yes," the giant said, "and you know what it is."

"Refresh my memory." The man glowered at Dan. "Do you work for Samson Grey?"

"Who's Samson Grey?"

"Never mind," Dan said. "Just someone who's ten thousand dollars poorer than he'd like to be."

"That's why you had the diamond stolen? To pay this man back?"

"No," Dan said, "I have no intention of paying him back."

"But you admit you had the diamond stolen."

Ouch. At least now Dan knew what the man was after. Was he working for the government of Zaire or for whomever Evelyn had stolen the diamond from? Dan couldn't decide. For all he knew, the government *was* whom Evelyn had stolen the diamond from.

What a situation to be thrown into unprepared! And to think he had planned a quiet afternoon. Dan jotted a note to himself on his notepad: "Thank Evelyn for the lovely gift."

"So," Dan said, "you want the diamond."

"We know the girl sent it to you."

"Why didn't you just take it from her in Zaire?"

The man reddened, turning a shade somewhere between adobe and brick. "She eluded us."

"Why didn't you stop the package from leaving the country?"

"She prevented us."

Evelyn hadn't changed, obviously. "And you figure I'll be easier to deal with."

"Mr. Reed," the man said, "anyone would be easier to deal with." For a moment he almost sounded human.

Dan rummaged through his drawers and came up with three paper cups. He turned them onto the desk in a mouth-down row. "How about a fair exchange?" Dan asked. "I keep the diamond in return for what you did to my door." The man shook his head. Dan shrugged. "Okay. Here's the diamond."

Dan tipped the middle cup back. A small plastic diamond was under it. "That's not it," the man said. Dan let the cup cover the diamond. He lifted the other two to show them empty, then stacked them over the middle cup. Misdirection, Dan knew, was the only way out of this situation, short of surrendering the diamond.

"You have five seconds," the man said, "before I start breaking bones." Dan lifted the stacked cups. An egg had appeared under them. "Four," the man said.

Dan cracked the egg and tipped a different diamond out. It was smaller than the one that had come in the mail, and it was fake, but it was the closest match he had at hand. He squeezed the halves of the eggshell in his left hand, the diamond in his right, then held his fists out. Anything to keep the man's attention diverted . . .

The man wrapped his hands tightly and significantly around Dan's. "Three," he said.

Dan turned his fists over. The man relaxed his grip and Dan opened his hands. They were empty.

"Two," the man said.

Dan pulled the diamond out of the man's ear and handed it to him. "You're a tough audience."

"I hate magic," the man growled. He put the diamond in his breast pocket. "And I hate tricks. If you're pulling a trick, I'll come back and show you 'Cutting a Magician in Half.'" At this, he laughed long and loud, as if it were the height of wit. Then he stood and left.

Go figure, Dan thought.

He opened the door behind his desk. In the back room he had a small bed, a computer, and a television. He lived in this room, saving himself the trouble of paying rent on an apartment he'd rarely use anyway.

Dan pulled a suitcase from under the bed and dug through his records. Eventually, he turned up a bill from the man who had installed his door and phoned for a replacement from the telephone by the computer. As he hung up, someone outside knocked on the front door.

Did he figure out that it's fake? Dan wondered. Is he back already? Do I have to go out?

There seemed to be no way around it. Dan returned to his desk, closing his door behind him.

Despite himself, he breathed a sigh of relief when he looked through the broken glass. The giant had not returned. (In a sudden burst of hindsight, Dan realized that if he *had* returned, he wouldn't have knocked.)

Actually, there might have been more than relief in his sigh, since his new caller was as beautiful as his previous caller had been ugly. "My name is Diana Keeper," she said in a sweet brandy voice. "May I come in?"

"Help yourself," Dan said.

Diana Keeper reached through the smashed window and opened the door. She was taller than Dan, and thin, and blessed with a soft peach complexion, bountiful black hair that showered in waves over her shoulders, and a figure that commanded attention. It didn't hurt that she accentuated her best features in a grey, zipper-front jumpsuit unzipped past the point of discretion. But most of all, she possessed the unique beauty of youth; she radiated freshness and exuberance.

Dan gauged her to be in her early twenties. It was clear from the energy in her step, in her eyes, in the way she spoke, that life was still an adventure for her, still a grand game. Dan shook his head briskly. He was a jaded and inertial thirty-four, not old by any reckoning, but weary—and old enough for capering with a twenty-year-old nymph to be unseemly. Still, his eyes lingered above her zipper. He was not unmoved.

Aware that he was staring, Dan made a show of removing a speck from the wall behind her. She tolerated this charade, for she understood his embarrassment better even than he did. After disposing of the invented speck, Dan offered her the seat so recently vacated. She elected to stand. Dan sat.

"I see Christiansen's men have been here," she said warily.

"Man," Dan corrected. "Just one big tree of a man."

"That would be Percy," Diana said.

"Percy?"

"A thug about eight feet tall, with a jaw like Dick Tracy's and a brow like a Neanderthal?"

Dan nodded.

"That's Percy," Diana said. "Percy Wheems. He hates the world. I think it's because of his name."

"And Christiansen?"

"He's a thug, too." Diana looked for a response from Dan, but received none. "He's a smuggler, a fence, specializes in diamonds and precious metals. He controls his empire from a fortress in Zaire. If anyone tries to take anything from him, he sends Percy as a warning."

"That was a warning?"

"You're still here, aren't you?"

"What does he send if he's really angry?"

Diana shuddered, a gesture Dan appreciated thoroughly. "There's a man called Cutter."

"Cutter?" Dan asked.

"It's not his name," Diana explained. "It's his job."

And I just passed a lump of plastic off as a diamond, Dan thought. Cutting a magician in half. Now I get it.

Somehow he couldn't manage a laugh.

"I suppose," he said at last, "that you want to hire me in my capacity as head of the Aaarmchair Detective Agency."

"Hire you?" Diana laughed. "I just want the diamond."

Dan reached into his desk drawer and pulled out three paper cups. Diana put her hands over his. "Don't play games," she said. "Just give me the diamond."

Diana's grip was by no means as threatening as Percy's, but in its way it was as effective.

"Who are you?" Dan asked. "What's your stake in this?"

A smile dashed across Diana's face, stopping briefly at her lips and her eyes. "I'm just in it for the money."

"I like money, too," Dan said. "Why should I give you the diamond?"

"I think I have something to offer you," Diana said. Her fingers strolled to her zipper and slid it an inch lower. Yes, she commanded attention. It wasn't enough to make him give up the diamond, and Dan got the feeling she knew that, but it was a sorely tempting start and Dan got the feeling she knew that, too. Dan went to her side, almost against his will.

Suddenly a dark form filled the space that had been Dan's door. The form, and the darkness, belonged to a gaunt man wearing a brownish-red smock. He opened the door and came into the office. Two butcher's knives hung in sheaths tied to the smock's belt. This had to be Cutter.

Dan realized that Diana was no longer standing beside him. He looked back. She was lying face down on his desk.

"Are you Dan Reed?" Cutter asked.

"No," Dan said. "I'm Aaron Lloyd." He went to his desk, slipped Diana's jumpsuit down and began to knead her shoulders. "Dan's in there." He indicated the door behind the desk.

"Very good," Cutter said. He unsnapped the strap on one of the sheaths. "Go on with what you're doing," he said, staring Dan in the eye, "no matter what you hear from in there. Do you understand?" Dan nodded. "Good."

Cutter opened the door a crack, ignoring the sign that said "Employee Only." He slipped inside the room.

For all his sinister presence, this Cutter was clearly no brighter than Percy. Dan wasn't complaining. He braced himself against the desk and shoved it up against the door. He tried not to look when Diana bounced to her feet, but he failed, and was glad—for a while, at least—that he had.

Diana yanked the front door open and ran to the stairs. Dan followed at his customary pace.

"Come on," Diana shouted. "Run!"

He reached the staircase and paused with his hand on the banister. "I don't run," he said.

From his office came the sound of his desk toppling over. "You run," Diana said.

Cutter burst through the door, a foot-long knife held high above his head. "I run," Dan said.

He ran.

They reached the first floor side by side and crashed through the staircase door. A floor behind them, they could hear Cutter clattering down the stairs in pursuit.

Dan and Diana sped out onto 34th Street, right past Percy, who was stationed by the door. Percy figured out what was happening as Cutter emerged from the building.

"Idiot!" Cutter screamed. "Get them!"

Christiansen's two goons ran after their prey, dodging across Broadway, through the crowded lobby of Herald Center, down to 32nd Street and over toward Fifth Avenue. Along the way, Diana dragged a full Dumpster into their path, gaining a half-block lead.

Dan dodged into a building labeled "6," and dragged Diana after him. Mercifully, an elevator was waiting in the lobby. Dan jabbed at the fourth floor button until the door slid shut.

"Dan," Diana said, "I think I should—"

"Not now, you shouldn't," Dan said. "We can talk later, if we lose them."

"We will," Diana said, but she fell silent.

Young and beautiful, Dan thought, also young and naive. So confident that the grand adventure would have a happy ending. There was a time when he could have looked a knife-wielding assassin in the eye and felt sure of success, but no longer. One day, she would learn. Dan hoped it wouldn't be today.

The doors opened and Dan pulled Diana into the showroom of Louis Tannen's magic shop. Ira West sent Dan a cheery wave, then dropped it when Diana bounded over the glass display cases between them. Dan took the long way around.

"What's going on, Dan?" Ira asked.

"I can't stop, Ira," Dan said. "I promise I'll explain later. For now, all you need to know is that there are two men heading up after us. Stop them, whatever it takes. Be careful—one of them's armed, and the other one doesn't need to be."

"Armed?"

Dan clapped Ira on the back and rushed past him into the storeroom. "Just knives," he said, "but they're big ones."

"Just knives, he says," Ira said. "That's all, just knives."

Dan threaded his way among rows of metal shelves and boxes overflowing with colorful props to the freight elevator. Diana followed him and they took the elevator back down to street level.

"That was a good idea," Diana said. "I hope they'll be able to handle Percy and Cutter."

"I'm not worried about Cutter," Dan said. "Ira can handle knives. I just hope they have something strong enough to hold Percy."

"If they don't, it still bought us time. Let's get out of here."

"We probably shouldn't go back to my office," Dan said.

"No. How about my hotel room?"

How about her hotel room. That sounded promising. Dan hailed a taxi.

* * *

The elevator doors opened and Percy and Cutter crashed out. Four balls of blinding orange flame came hurtling at their heads. The fireballs vanished before reaching them, but when they could see again, they were surrounded by magicians.

Ira was between them and the elevators. Two teenagers in leather and whiteface blocked the door to the stairs. A man in a tuxedo stood in the way of the storeroom entrance, flanked by his female assistants dressed in street clothes. Directly in front of Percy was a very old man in a hooded robe and sandals.

Cutter brandished one of his knives. Ira scaled a metal plate at his hand. The knife fell to the floor. One of the teenagers snagged it with a coil of fishing line and reeled it in.

Cutter pulled his second knife and advanced on the man in the tuxedo. Percy kept the others at bay. Cutter thrust at the assistants, who shrank back. A black walking stick appeared in the magician's hand, and he used it to parry Cutter's next thrust. Then he struck twice more, once at Cutter's temple and once at his wrist.

"Cutter!" Percy shouted.

Cutter spun around, but it was too late. One of the assistants brought a heavy metal wand down on his knife hand while the other pulled a burlap sack over his head. Together they took him to the floor. Despite his furious struggling, they managed to tie the neck of the bag closed and stuff him into a trunk.

Percy tried to come to Cutter's aid. He rushed the old man, who was the weakest link in the chain surrouncing him. As Percy collided with him, the man vanished, his cloak falling to the floor, empty. Percy barreled forward, lost his balance, and sprawled on the floor.

The two teenagers climbed on top of him, pulling every restraint they could find from their pockets, the walls, and the display cases. When they were through, Percy was chained from head to toe, his hands and feet were tied with stiff twine, and he had thumbcuffs on all his fingers and several hundred dollars' worth of handcuffs along his arms and legs. Percy strained against the pounds of metal confining him, but got nowhere.

Ira picked up the cloak and reset the wire frame inside it that created the illusion of mass. Rubber feet anchored the hem, while a rubber mask created the old man's face. Quite an effective illusion, he thought.

"I hate magic," Percy said. One of the teenagers gagged him. The other tied a blindfold over his eyes and slapped a steel mask over that.

"You're in the wrong place then," Ira said. He turned to the other magicians to thank them.

Dan owed him, again.

*   *   *

The taxi let them out at the New York Penta, only a few blocks away from Tannen's. Dan paid the cabbie and followed Diana up to the eleventh floor.

"They don't know you're staying here?" he asked.

"Of course not," she said. She found her room key and unlocked the door to her suite.

"I want answers," Dan said.

"All right," Diana said, "but not out here. Wait till we get in." She opened the door. When they were both inside, she turned on the lights.

A man in a grey fedora was sitting in a chair facing the door. A cigarette smoked nearly to the filter jutted from one of his hands, a pistol from the other. He took a final drag on the cigarette and stubbed it out on the arm of the chair. His pistol was aimed dead center at Diana's chest.

"Now," he said, "you are going to give me the diamond."

"Get in line," Dan said.

The gun rotated until it pointed at the obvious bulge in Dan's pocket. "You have it."

"No, I'm just glad to see you."

"Dan," Diana said, "give him the diamond."

"What is this?" Dan asked. "Do you know him?"

"No, but he's got a gun."

"I can see that," Dan said.

"Don't argue with a gun. Just give him the diamond, *please.*"

"That's right," the man said. "Give it to me. Please."

Dan eased the diamond out of his pocket and held it out. The man took it and walked carefully to the door, never lowering his aim. "That was simple, wasn't it? Now you're not going to call the cops, because you'd have to explain what you were doing with a stolen diamond in your possession. But I don't have to tell you that because we're all professionals, right? And you're not going to come after me because if you do I'll have to shoot you dead. But you already knew that, too. It's been a pleasure dealing with you." With that, he was gone.

Neither Dan nor Diana made a move for the door.

"Who are you?" Dan asked at last. "If you don't work for Christiansen, how did you know about the diamond?"

"Dan," Diana said, "there's something I should tell you."

"Why should I believe you, whatever you say? How do I know these thugs don't work for you? And if they don't, why did you make me give up the diamond?"

"Calm down. That's part of what I want to tell you."

"You'd better start talking, lady."

Diana sighed. "I made you give it up because it wasn't worth our lives. It's not even a real diamond. It's cubic zirconium."

"How do you know that?"

"I ought to know," Diana said. "I sent it to you."

"You did not send it to me. My sister sent it to me."

"That's right."

It took a moment for this to sink in. "Impossible," Dan said.

"It's me, Dan. In the flesh."

"It can't be," Dan said. "Evelyn's just . . ."

"Just what? Just a little girl? Dan, you haven't seen me in almost five years!"

"I don't buy it. Prove that you're my sister."

"I married Kyle Nuys a couple of months ago. Before that I was Evelyn Reed. You used to tease me when I was a kid by making doves appear in my bed. You had this card trick you used to do, where the back of the deck changed color and the faces went blank. I idolized you because you had moved to New York and become a detective, and I told everyone that I was going to become a criminal so that we could work together.

"You've got a wart you can't get rid of on your right foot, and once you tried burning it off with Mom's lighter. You couldn't walk for weeks. The doctor wanted Mom to take you to a psychiatrist. You wouldn't go—"

"All right, all right," Dan said. "Enough!" He examined his sister from head to toe and back again. "You've changed."

"That's puberty for you. One day you're in pigtails and overalls, and then, just like that, five years later, you're a grown woman."

"You're stunning," Dan said.

"Thank you, Dan. A compliment from you means a lot, though your reaction back in your office was clear enough."

"I didn't know," Dan sputtered, "I couldn't—"

"No, of course not. It's asking too much that you should recognize your own sister."

"You don't look quite the way I remember," Dan said.

"To be fair, I don't look at all the way you remember," Evelyn said. "For that matter, you don't look the way I remember, either. Why do you think I put on that act, vamping you, and all? I wasn't sure it was you."

"What do you mean?"

"You looked right, but I was just a kid when I saw you last. Between that and your door being smashed, I figured you might be a plant, one of Christiansen's men come to intercept my package. I thought so until Cutter showed up, at least, but even that could have been a setup. You understand, don't you? I couldn't take the chance of telling you who I was."

"When did you decide I was really me?" Dan asked.

"When you took me to Tannen's. No one else would have done that. If I had any doubts left, they were gone when the salesman called you by name. That would have been too elaborate even for Christiansen to set up."

Slowly Dan was getting over the initial shock. This made room in his head for confusion. Evelyn back from Zaire, and married, and gorgeous . . . three men, each less pleasant than the last, not to mention the mysterious kingpin, Christiansen . . . fists, knives, guns, diamonds—it was all terribly disconcerting.

And all of it for a *phony* diamond? Dan hoped Evelyn could clear things up.

"Could you do me a favor," he said, "and tell me what's going on?"

"Certainly," Evelyn said. "Christiansen sent his men after you because he thought I had sent you a diamond I stole from him."

"And he was right," Dan said.

"No, he wasn't. What I sent you was pure cubic zirconium, the biggest piece I could find. It's not worthless, but it's hardly priceless."

"And you stole that?"

"No, I bought it nice and legal, sealed it in the tennis ball right in front of a postal officer, and paid the postage in cash. I explained it was a gag gift for a friend in the States who would enjoy getting a 'smuggled diamond.' He went along with it."

"I'm surprised he did," Dan said.

"The bribe didn't hurt. Neither did a little flirting. Besides, he wasn't doing anything illegal; what harm could come of letting me mail my own CZ home any way I wanted to?"

"I suppose," Dan said. "But what good could come of it?"

"I'm surprised you haven't figured it out," Evelyn said. "You taught me the principle, after all. I'm just applying it."

"What principle is that?"

"Misdirection."

Dan grinned. Of course. "You weren't smuggling the CZ."

"No, I wasn't."

"You were smuggling the tennis ball."

"Give the man a prize."

"And why would you want to smuggle a tennis ball?"

"It wasn't an ordinary tennis ball," Evelyn said.

"I would hope not."

"Where is it now? I'll show you what's special about it."

"I threw it out," Dan said, "in my office."

Dan picked the two pieces of the tennis ball from his trash can. Evelyn took them from him and turned them inside out, so the rubber lining faced out. Burned into the rubber was an irregular pattern of lines and squares. Evelyn held the two pieces so that the patterns intersected.

"It's a map," she said, "to Christiansen's private stash. In addition to every other illegal activity he's engaged in, he's skimming off the top of his own operation. A smart thief, armed with a detailed map, could clean him out. And a smart businesswoman could sell such a map for a tidy flat fee plus percentage, with this for proof that it's authentic." Evelyn reached into her jumpsuit and withdrew from a concealed pocket a stone that looked like the one Dan had given up, only considerably smaller.

"More CZ?"

"No. That's the real thing."

Dan took it from his sister. To his eye it looked no more or less authentic than the one Evelyn had revealed to be fake. "And how did you get this one out?"

"It was all misdirection," Evelyn said. "Christiansen thought I had already mailed the stone to you, so his people gave up looking for it on me." She took the diamond back and returned it to its resting place. "Getting it past customs was a little trickier. I cut the bottom off a bottle of Grand Marnier, put the diamond in, glued the bottle shut, then declared the bottle. No one thought to check it since I was presenting it so openly, and if they had, they would have found the seal intact."

"How did you cut a glass bottle?" Dan asked. Then he realized. "The diamond, of course." She was good! It was hard to believe, but little Evie had made good on her vow to become a criminal mastermind. Dan was proud of her in the way only a brother can be.

Of course she was taking it a little too far. Being clever might net you a diamond, but it takes a lot more than cleverness for you to keep it, especially when it belongs to a man who smuggles diamonds for a living—and who employs enforcers like Percy and Cutter. There's only so long you can keep running.

"That man who took the CZ back at the hotel—who was he?" Dan asked.

As they spoke, Evelyn helped Dan right his desk. "I'm not sure. I didn't recognize him, but I'll bet he works for Christiansen."

"And that diamond you just showed me," Dan said, "you stole that from Christiansen?"

"You got it. Romanced him, robbed him, and ran. The three R's."

Dan was tempted to ask her what Kyle thought of all this, but he decided not to. "Percy, Cutter, and this third man were all trying to get the diamond that's in your pocket?"

"Right."

"But you've still got it."

"Right."

"So won't they come back?"

"Not Percy and Cutter, if your friends took care of them," Evelyn said, "but Christiansen's got plenty more where they came from."

"That's what I thought. You'll have to send the diamond back, then."

"I can't," Evelyn said. "Without it, no one will believe the map's genuine."

"I'm sorry," Dan said, "but if you don't, people will constantly be breaking my door down to get it. I can't have that." Besides, he added silently, it's for your own good.

"You could move," Evelyn said. "Get a new identity. Go underground."

Dan fixed his sister with a withering stare. "I don't want to go underground. I like it where I am."

"Come on, Dan! After everything I've gone through . . ."

Dan handed her a sheet of paper and a pen. " 'Dear Christiansen,' " he said. " 'I'm so sorry I took your diamond, but you know what jealousy can make a person do.' "

"Jealousy?"

" 'Can you ever forgive me? I'll never forget our time together.' So on and so forth, here's your diamond back, affectionately, Evelyn Nuys, or Diana Keeper, or whatever you called yourself." Dan ignored the fury in her eyes. "Got that? Now write it. And then I want to see it. I don't trust you."

Evelyn looked ready to kill. "I won't forget this."

Dan patted her on the head. "What are big brothers for?"

It was way past business hours when Dan returned to Tannen's. Ira was waiting when he got there.

Dan let Cutter out of his trunk first. Without his knives, Cutter wasn't much of a threat. Dan explained that there was a bit of a misunderstanding, and handed him a package containing the diamond and Evelyn's letter.

Cutter inhaled deeply, the stink of burlap still caught in his throat, and examined the package and its contents. Only when he seemed satisfied did Dan begin the complicated process of undoing Percy's shackles.

When Percy was finally free, he seemed set to erupt; but Dan apologized to him, and returned Cutter's knives, and this so surprised him that he forgot to beat Dan and Ira to a pulp and demolish the store as he had vowed to himself that he would.

Ira called the elevator and ushered the two men out. For the first time since the whole affair began, Ira was alone with Dan. He waggled a finger in Dan's face. "We never talk any more."

Dan laughed. "I'll tell you everything. It's a crazy story. How soon can you leave?"

Ira looked at the mess on the floor. "Fifteen minutes. Ten if you help."

"Sure," Dan said. "We don't have to meet Evelyn until eleven. That should be plenty of time to fill you in."

Percy couldn't find a thing to watch. He was sitting in a chair across from the television; every few seconds he'd stand to change channels. In the end he settled on wrestling. It was the standard routine, but at least it was something he could appreciate.

Cutter, meanwhile, had opened his briefcase on one of the room's twin beds. Inside it were two machines and the two fake diamonds Dan had foisted on them. If this was another fake . . . Cutter didn't even want to think about it.

He took the package out of one of his smock's pockets and carefully unwrapped the diamond. The machine on the left looked like a miniature tissue box with a pen-shaped probe attached to it. Cutter took the probe and touched it to the diamond. A green light lit up on the box.

Very good. The only way to tell a diamond apart from a hunk of cubic zirconium was to measure its thermal conductivity. This sample had just tested positive. Cutter returned the probe to its clip on the side of the box. The green light went off. He rewrapped the diamond and nestled it next to the probe.

Next, Cutter moved the telephone from the nightstand to the bed and lifted the cover of the second machine. Inside, the machine had a padded cradle into which the telephone receiver fit snugly. Cutter dialed an outside line, then the international code that would connect him with Zaire. While his call went through, he flipped a switch below the cradle labeled SCRAMBLE.

The call was picked up and after Cutter went through channels and delivered a half-dozen passwords, a powerful male voice issued from a loud-speaker. "This is scrambled?"

"Yes," Cutter said. "This is Cutter. Percy is with me. Newton will be with us soon. We have the diamond."

"You are certain?"

"Absolutely. The girl's brother gave it to us."

"Strange. And the girl?"

"She had him give us a note for you."

"Read it."

"Sir, are you sure?"

"*Read it.*" Cutter unfolded Evelyn's note and read it aloud, stumbling only over its most intimate passages. When he was done, he folded it up and put it in his pocket. "Very good." The voice sounded pleased. "Bring it home."

Cutter disconnected the call and closed the scrambler. "Come on," he said to Percy. He took off his smock and knives, put them in the briefcase, and locked it. "Newton's checking out for us. Let's go." Percy gladly switched off the television.

Downstairs, they collected Newton, who was still wearing his grey fedora. An unlit cigarette clung to his lower lip. Cutter relayed his conversation with Christiansen to Newton, who shook his head.

"The boss must really be hung up on this girl," Newton said. "First he doesn't want us to kill her, then he doesn't want us to kill the brother either, now he gets a 'Dear John' letter and you say he sounded happy?"

"Forget it," Cutter said. "He got the diamond, and that's what matters."

The three men left the Plaza Hotel walking towards Central Park. When they reached the park's southern edge, they tried to hail a taxi. The night was dark and noisy and full of cars, but there were no empty taxis. Cutter sent Newton out into the street to catch a cab the hard way, by standing in one's path.

From behind, Cutter felt a tap on his shoulder. "Don't make any noise," a cold voice said. "Don't call your friend. Give me your watches and your wallets."

Newton was in the street, out of reach; naturally, he was the only one with a weapon. Cutter cursed under his breath and turned around. This was New York City, not Zaire, specifically Central Park at night; he should have been more careful.

"I said, watches and wallets. Give them to me or I'll blow your heads off." Their assailant was a black man of medium build in a knit cap and a jogging suit. He was holding a small-caliber handgun. His eyes were full of fear and anger, and his finger was tight on the trigger.

Cutter chanced a look back as Percy turned around. Newton was still dodging cars, oblivious. Cutter slid his watch off his wrist and his wallet out of his pocket, and gave them to the mugger. Percy wore no watch, but he surrendered his wallet.

"You got any housekeys?"

Cutter spread his hands. "We're from out of the country."

"Fine. The briefcase."

"What?" Cutter said.

"Hand it over, man."

Cutter swung the briefcase desperately at the gun. The mugger fired, hitting Cutter in the right knee. Cutter collapsed. The gun shot caught Newton's attention and he ran to Cutter's side, but the mugger had already grabbed the briefcase and vanished into the park. At their feet, Cutter started to moan.

"Oh, God," Percy said. "How are you going to explain this to the boss?"

Newton looked at Percy, then down at Cutter, then back.

"Well?" Percy asked.

"Shut up, Wheems."

Dan and Ira met Evelyn outside the Cometeria nightclub. Dan had expected her to be angry with him still, but instead she was in a good mood. She told them that Kyle would be coming by later, and that they were all to go in ahead.

The man at the door stopped them. "You two are fine," he told the men, "but I need an I.D. for her."

Evelyn was offended, and Dan could see why. In heels and a strapless dress she hardly looked under age. "You can let her in," Dan said.

"Sure I can," the man said, "but I won't unless you show me proof that she's twenty-one."

"I'll show you proof that she's a hundred." A bill appeared at Dan's fingertips.

The man took it and examined it. "Her name's Benjamin Franklin?"

"That's right," Dan said.

"Pass." The man pocketed the bill.

"Dan," Evelyn said once they had found a table, "you didn't have to do that."

"You have to know how to deal with these people," Dan said. "You've got to speak their language. Besides, it's fake."

"Counterfeit?" Evelyn asked.

"Fake," Dan said.

Evelyn laughed. "There's hope for you yet."

Four rounds of drinks later, a black man in his late twenties approached the table. He was wearing a leather jacket with a sport shirt and black denim pants. Evelyn stood up and took his hand.

"Dan, Ira," she said, "I want you to meet my husband, Kyle."

"Your husband?" Dan asked.

"Sorry I'm late," Kyle said. He kissed Evelyn, took a seat, and ordered a Gibson martini. "I had some work to finish and then I had to change. So, what did I miss?"

"A gallon of booze." Ira indicated the empty glasses.

"Evelyn was telling us about the tournament," Dan said.

"Oh, yes," Kyle said. His eyes sparkled in the club's half-light. "I turned her on to that, actually. We're both big tennis fans, and my family's from Zaire originally, so I thought it would make an interesting honeymoon."

"Did you enjoy it?" Dan asked.

"I wouldn't go back, if that's what you mean. Some parts of the country are absolutely wretched, and the way the miners live is horrible. The tennis was good, though. And really, we didn't get out much."

"Dan just wants to know about the sex," Evelyn said. "He's like you." Kyle laughed and Dan made a throttling motion in her direction.

Shortly after midnight, the crowd started to thin and the conversation to dwindle. Evelyn and Kyle decided to call it a night. Before they left, Dan took Evelyn aside.

"About that map," he said. "You're not going to go back yourself, are you?"

"If I can't sell it to anyone else, I will."

"But Christiansen knows you! He'll recognize you!"

"You should have thought of that before you made me give the diamond back." Evelyn tousled Dan's hair. "Don't worry. I'll take care of myself."

"Don't worry, she says. I'm going back to a fortress in Zaire to steal some diamonds, but don't worry." Dan hugged his sister tight. "I'll try."

Then Dan took Kyle aside. He had to. He put his hands on Kyle's shoulders and looked him straight in the eye. "You got the diamond back, didn't you?"

"Yes," Kyle said.

They chose each other well, Dan decided. He hugged Kyle as he had hugged Evelyn. "Welcome to the family."

HOORAY FOR HOLLYWOOD

Robert Twohy

Wanting a change, I flew up to San Francisco on Friday night, and on Monday morning when I got on the plane for the return flight I had wobbly disco knees and gongs in my head, which was the whole idea of the weekend.

I cabbed from Burbank to my apartment on Orange Drive, one of Hollywood's classier streets—my lifestyle was good and on the way to getting a lot better. *Catastrophe* was expected to be the big movie of the year, with the great Bora Pelicularu directing—it was his production, the trades said he'd sunk five million of his own in it. And I had the lead role. My first really big one, after 14 years in the vineyards. *Catastrophe* would do for me what the *Falcon* did for Bogart.

As I dropped my bag on the floor, kicked off my Guccis, and fell on the couch, I had yeasty thoughts of the future that lay ahead.

The phone rang.

Half in a doze I reached for it and fell off the couch. Fortunately the rug was thick. I got the phone and, rubbing my ribs, said, "Hello."

A voice with a foreign lilt said, "So finally you are home. This is Bora. I tell Finnegan but for polite, want to give you personal the news . . . *Catastrophe* is *kaputsky*. I return to Rashpudlovik."

I took about eight breaths, finally managed, "Return to where?"

"To family estate, back in homeland. In English mean fertility, fruitfulness, things in blossom. Very poetical name."

"Yeah, really nice . . . *Catastrophe* is *kaputsky?*"

"Not right for today—and I am director for today. Understand?"

"No." All I understood was that suddenly I wasn't going to be the new Bogart. "*Catastrophe* is great! It'd rank right up there with the top detective movies—the ones that are real art. Like the *Falcon, Chinatown*—"

"Fooey on *Falcoon, Chinatown*—only one film from yesterday great for today. You know which one?"

"Which?"

"Big Schlepp."

After a few seconds I figured that one out. *"Big Sleep.* Yeah, that's another great one."

"You know why great? I tell you why. 'Cause it don't make no sense."

"Huh?"

"No sense. I see it twenty-six time and still not know who do what or why. They just do it. Everything confoozel—and that why it still great movie for today. 'Cause it got right mood for today. And that why *Falcoon*—"

"Falcon."

"Yah, Big Bird—why great film for yesterday but not today. Too much sense—just like *Catastrophe.* Not mood for today. So go back to homeland and get new creative visions. Come up with whole new contraption—"

"Conception."

"Whatever. Work up great new approach so *Catastrophe* be film for today. Call you when get back. Goo'bye."

That seemed to be that. "Thanks for your call. Have fun in Pashrudlovik."

"Rashpudlovik. Pashrudlovik means pregnant buzzard."

"Whatever."

We hung up. I needed sleep but thought I needed a drink more. I got a bottle of blackberry brandy, took it to the couch, lay down, and drank from the neck. When it was empty I went to sleep.

The movie life is total unreality but you put eight weeks into a great script, do better than you've ever done in your life, and whamo it's *kaputsky* and you're left with nothing but a big urge to drink enough to take away the taste of crumbled dreams.

But first, before I started on what I intended to rank with the classic drunks of Hollywood legend, I called my agent, Finnegan, at his home. It was about seven P.M.

I went on a while about what a soulless rat Pelicularu was and he made consoling noises, then said, "Geniuses go by their own inner voices. Forget him. Something new has come up."

His voice took on a furtive tone. I got a picture of him crouched behind his phone, shooting furtive glances in various directions. He's basically a very furtive guy. He's repulsive, but not a bad agent as the type goes. "Something very hot. Meet me at Flupo's at eight."

"By eight I'll be a slobbering drunk. Lay it on me now."

"Can't. I had to promise to play clam. Flupo's, eight sharp."

I tried to slam the phone down quicker than he did so he'd get the whack in the ear, but as always he was quicker and I got the whack. You can't beat Finnegan for fast moves with the phone.

I got to Flupo's, took a dinky little table in the bar, looked around, saw no one I recognized, just a few celebrities that weren't very celebrated and the usual mawk of tourists. Suddenly I saw a smile and damned if it didn't belong to a woman with soft reddish hair with lights in it, and green eyes with the same.

She was standing a little away from my table. She wore a glittery maroon dress that above the waist was quality rather than quantity, and her skin was California gold. Around her neck shone a lot of pearls. On her arm she carried a stole that if it wasn't pure mink I'm Laurence of Olivier. This lady was loaded, and in every way spectacularly. She said in a low voice, "May I sit down?"

I half got up, knees rubbery—and not just from the Frisco discos. I looked at my watch. It said 8:10. Finnegan was late. I hoped he'd stay that way.

She sat down. "I was passing, and recognized you. You're Randy Spear."

I'm not, really—I'm Elbert P. Hummell, originally from Sapulpa, Oklahoma. But Finnegan thought Randy Spear had a lot more pizazz, so that's who I've been since coming to Hollywood.

We looked at each other, this woman and I. Finally she murmured, "I didn't stop for an autograph. I recognized you and thought how nice it would be if you bought me a margarita."

I signaled the cocktail girl and gave her an order for a margarita and a refill of my highball. The red-gold goddess smiled at me. "The evening is young, the night is dark and beautiful, the drive to Ojai is a delight that never dulls. Don't you love that drive?"

"With a passion." I'd never driven it but had no doubt it could lead to wondrous places. "Do you live in Ojai?"

"Do I live anywhere?" It was said very low. The brightness of her eyes was dimmed by a sudden shadow.

It wasn't part of the game we'd started, the Hollywood game, which I know real good and which she seemed to know too. That shadow over her eyes wasn't Hollywood—it was reality.

Just for a second. Then it was gone and her eyes had the sparkle again. Whatever had brought on the shadow, she wanted to forget it.

Our drinks came. I took a swallow and said, "You know who I am, which puts you a square ahead."

"Barbara Bacon." She sipped her margarita, gave me back my gaze. "I was wondering—but I'm presumptuous. You were waiting for someone."

"Was I?" I'd forgotten Finnegan. He was always super-punctual—something must have come up. Perhaps an accident. "Maybe I was waiting for you."

She said, in that low voice, "Maybe you were. Maybe some things are destined."

And again her sparkle was darkened—just for a second.

Fifteen minutes later we crossed the parking lot to a blue Cad, an open convertible. I thought first it was a beautiful old model, because they haven't made convertibles for years, then saw it was this year's model. For $50,000 or in that neighborhood you can get a standard turned into a convertible, at some specialty shop up near San Jose.

She said, "D'you want to drive?" She didn't wait for the answer—she saw it in my face. She smiled, handed me keys, and got in on the passenger side.

I slid in, turned things on, and reached for the gizmo that works the folding top. She said, "Leave it open."

"It'll get nippy up coast."

"That's why I brought my stole." She'd had me put it over her as we left the restaurant. "I love to drive the coast with the top down."

It was all right by me. Everything was fine. I was driving a beautiful woman in a beautiful car to Ojai—which all I knew about was that it's 80 miles or so from L.A., and a lot of rich people live there.

With that car, the pearls, the stole, she qualified.

We got on the freeway, and it got nippier, but was beautiful—clear dark sky, thin slice of moon, glittering sea. Not many cars on the freeway, easy driving.

I glanced at her, liking the way her red hair flipped around in the breeze. "Tell me about yourself—like what do you do?"

"Not much, when my husband's in town."

Something went *THONNKKK!* in my chest. I should have known. Things don't go on as great as this evening had gone so far. There's always a stray tack somewhere in the stardust, waiting to be stepped on.

But her remark had a reverse twist. I asked, "Is he in town now?"

"No, he's in Rome."

"What's he doing in Rome?"

"Sleeping, probably. That's the most fun he has. But he's in pretty good health for a man in his seventies."

I looked the obvious question at her.

She gave a little shrug, and a crooked smile, and her hand came up and fiddled with the stole, then moved on and up to the necklace.

I drove a while. A few cars passed us, we passed a few—as I said, not much traffic. "He's rich, huh?"

"He's a banker."

"But he's in Rome."

"Far as I know."

"So you're on the lonely side."

"Only when he's home. When he's away, I stop being lonely." She looked at me full-face. "Like right now. I'm not lonely now."

I wasn't either.

Then her eyes slid from my face and the look she had been giving me was gone, and now her eyes were two gleaming circles of fear.

She whispered tautly, "Down! Get down!" And that's what she was doing—falling over sideward to the window, arms covering her red head.

She could do that, I couldn't. Not while piloting 6000 pounds of Cad along the freeway.

I looked in the rear-view mirror.

Lights were coming fast in the next lane. It was a greenish sedan. It pulled even. I turned my head, glanced at the dark shape of the driver—dark glasses, sharp profile, eyes straight ahead. He stayed there, keeping the green sedan even with us.

Something bright caught the edge of my glance, and it slid back along the car. I saw bright metal, and it stuck out of a hand that rested on the open rear window. It was a gun, looking at me.

I didn't think, just reacted—hit the brake and rode it, the Cad slewing to the right. Over the shriek of tires I heard a sharp clean pop—and something was happening to the windshield in front of me. It was spider-webbing—and caught in the middle of the sudden web was a hole.

But the skid got my full attention. I eased off the brake, went along with the skid, felt things start back under control, saw I was off the freeway on the shoulder, made a twitch of the wheel here, then there, braking down now firm and steady—and we came to a stop on the far edge of the shoulder.

The green sedan wasn't alongside any more. I looked through the cracked windshield and saw its tail-lights going away very fast down the middle lane.

I took a few deep breaths, then reached out and down and touched the mink.

"You all right?"

The mink moved, came up under my hand. "Yes."

I looked at her tight, white face. She closed her eyes a few seconds, then rubbed her cheeks, and some color came back into them.

She murmured, "Have they gone on?"

"Yes. Who were they?"

"Some of Kay's men."

"Kay?"

"A man I know."

"Kay's a man?"

She looked beyond me. The terror was out of her eyes. The shadow lay over them, but a softness showed through it. She murmured, "Yes. Kay's a man."

I looked at the hole in the windshield. "Why'd he want to kill us?"

"He didn't." She was still looking off. "It was just to—remind me."

"Of what?"

"Things of the past."

This mess I'd got into was getting nothing but thicker. Maybe Kay didn't want to kill us but that was a real hole in the windshield. An inch farther to the right and it would have been in my head, and there'd have been a hell of a car crash, and Barbara would have wound up as dead as me. I said, "Kay seems like a pretty unconventional guy."

Her lips made a slight curve. "Yes. Never dull, never predictable. But believe me—if he'd told them to kill us, we'd be dead. Snecker put the bullet just where he wanted to."

"Snecker? The gunman?"

She seemed to know all the characters involved. I was the new boy in class, knowing no one.

She said, "Can you see to drive?"

"I guess so." It was distorted through the webby windshield, but navigable.

"Then let's get on to Ojai."

I wasn't sold on that notion. The green sedan could be up ahead, pulled over to the shoulder, waiting for us. "We better take the next ramp and get back to L.A."

She said quietly, "No. They've done all they meant to do."

In this deep, I might as well go deeper, try to find out what lay at the bottom. If she was wrong and those guys wanted another try at us, they could do it as well toward L.A. as toward Ojai—so there was no big advantage to turning back. I started the car. "Tell me who Kay is, and what's going on."

"I will. When we get to Ojai."

I looked in the mirror to see if it was clear to turn onto the freeway, then heard a yell up forward, hit the brake, and saw I'd nearly piled into a panel truck pulled in front of me on the shoulder. A guy jacking up for a rear-tire change yelled, "You blind or something?"

"Fogged windshield." I pulled around him, got out on the freeway, leaving him squawking insults.

We passed the Ventura turnoffs and took the turn to Ojai, which the sign said was 13 miles. I drove steady and careful, paying attention now and seeing fairly well through the windshield. I kept checking the mirror, but I saw no green sedan.

We got near the town and she had me take a side road. We climbed a while, and it was low estate homes set in trees—this was the richest part of a rich man's town, high up over it. We came to a long stone fence and approached an open iron gate. Barbara nodded, gestured. I turned in.

We drove on a curving road through trees. There was nothing but trees —no lawn. The trees grew right up to a big two-story adobe, topped with red tile. A wide drive went off around, which would be the garage area. "You want me to put it in there?"

"No, drive on past the house—I feel like walking back."

I did as she said and stopped on the side of the curved road. I gave her the keys and we got out, and walked 200 feet back to the house. She used a key and we went in.

Stylish furnishings, oil paintings, wall hangings, everything old-Spanish style. A wide, low, very expensive and classy main room.

She took off the stole and dropped it in a chair. "It's cool and lovely out. Let's sit by the pool."

I followed her out a big oak door. We were on a patio, where there were a couple of deckchairs. It wasn't nippy like on the coast—Ojai is in a valley, inland. The thin moon was caught in the tops of some tall trees and things were shadowy, the big rectangular pool before us darkly shining.

Barbara went to a switch, flipped it, and lights sprang on from under the house eaves and from the branches of trees near the pool. That wasn't so romantic as moonlight but romance right now wasn't what I was after— that could come later, if it came. Right now I felt better with the lights on because it meant less chance the guy with the gun could come sneaking through the trees. She might be sure that the guys in the green sedan had knocked off work for the night, but I wasn't.

I sat down in one of the chairs. "Tell me about Kay."

"Kay." She stood by me, gazing at the diving tower at the far end of the pool. It was a high tower. "We met in Yugoslavia. That was years ago." The shadow was over her eyes and she had an odd smile. "I look at the diving tower," she said softly, "and I think of then."

I didn't see the connection. Maybe it would become clear. I said, "It's really a high tower." A diving board stuck out from it.

She said, "Twenty feet high."

"Are you a diver?"

"I love to dive. I used to dive off cliffs at Rijeka." So that was the connection. "A lifetime ago . . . so much since then. So very much."

She was looking down at me. Her look was the look you dream a beautiful woman will give you. It got closer. Her face was coming down on mine. Her whole body was coming down on me. Now she was all over me. I had a lapful of California gold, and her mouth had become part of mine or vice-versa. My ears thumped, my hair felt electrified, I was like disappearing under tumbling red hair. Then suddenly her soft weight was off me. I opened my eyes, saw her staring back toward the house. I craned around the back of the chair to see. A mahogany-colored giant in a seedy black suit stood there in the doorway.

"Har-Tai?" Barbara said softly. "You're back?"

The giant made a gurgling noise in his throat.

Barbara murmured to me, "Don't be frightened."

I saw no reason not to be. He was about seven feet tall and had hands in proportion. They twitched. Bright black eyes were fixed on my face.

She said, her voice brisk now, "Bring drinks, Har-Tai. The usual for me, whiskey and water for Mr. Spear."

The giant turned, lumped back in the house.

I let out a few breaths, and said, "Who's he?"

"Har-Tai. From Madagascar. They tore his tongue out."

I blinked at that. She didn't elaborate. "Excuse me, while I slip into something less formal."

As not too much of her was restricted by the maroon dress, I wondered what she had in mind. I watched her move across the patio, through the oak door.

I sat there gazing at the lighted pool and the tall tower at the end, and the trees growing close on the far side. I wondered who had torn Har-Tai's tongue out, and why, and wondered about Kay, who left reminders that ruined windshields. I didn't know how this night was going to wind up. It seemed a night for sudden happenings and odd people—and Barbara was certainly changeable, as to mood and clothes.

A snuffle sounded close behind my head. Something told me it meant trouble—I went to instinct, dived forward out of the chair, and fell flat on the tile.

Pushing up, I threw a look, saw the Madagascan just completing the follow-through of a stiff-finger jab that would have dented my skull as when you squeeze a beer can.

I scrambled to hands and knees. He was coming at me, hands spread. I had no time to ponder things—I rolled on my back, got my feet up, and kicked from the shoulders.

And damned if he didn't slip in a wet place and slide into my kick, taking it in the belly, and of course continuing his slide and bending my legs back over my head so I rolled on my shoulders all the way over, winding up on my knees with my face in the tile—and wet all over, because he'd gone belly-whacking into the pool.

He made gurgling sounds and beat his arms around. I got up and watched him slap water—he wasn't a swimmer. But he sucked in a suitcase full of air, went under, and I guess crawled along the bottom because his hands shot up and gripped the edge of the pool. I went over to stamp them loose and Barbara's voice sounded sharply, "No!"

She had come out the door, in a frothy green thing that kind of floated around her. She said, "I'll take care of him."

The Madagascan's hands were followed by head, shoulders, and chest, and he was heaving himself out of the pool. I stepped back toward the house.

Barbara stood quiet, and as he got out, shook himself, blew water, and then started for me, she said, low and compelling, "Stop, Har-Tai!"

He blinked, looked at her, stopped.

"Go. Go to trees. Spend night in trees."

His shoulders drooped, so did his head. His mahogany face kind of broke up.

"Go," said Barbara, pointing off.

He spread his hands in an appealing way, then turned, and in draggy fashion walked around the pool, and disappeared into the trees.

She gazed after him. "He'll weep all night, out of shame for losing his cool, but he'll be all right in the morning."

"Why'd he want to attack me?"

She gave me a look that held a lot of meaning, but I wasn't sure what it meant. "It doesn't matter. He won't try it again. Not tonight."

"Nothing seems to matter. Getting shot at didn't matter, now this doesn't matter—"

She said in that low voice, "Things that are over don't matter. All that matters are things still to come."

She was at the edge of the pool, staring in, her attitude one of intensity. She gestured. I came over, looked in the direction she was looking, toward the deep end—and saw a body. Face down, near the bottom. It had a white shirt, dark pants, shoes. Whoever it was hadn't gone in for a swim.

I said, "Time we called the cops."

"Yes." Her look was steady. "Tell them the Bacon place. Don't mention Kay or Har-Tai. While you're phoning, I'll pull the body out."

I was about to tell her that *she* should phone, she was the hostess here—and no need to pull this latest guest out, he could wait where he was for the cops. But she moved fast and there was a puff of filmy green, then a neat splash, and the frothy thing was on the tile and she was in the water, a smooth pink fish in a pearl necklace flashing toward the body.

I watched her go under, then turned and hurried through the oak door, thinking that if I made the call fast and short I could be back in time to help her get the body out.

I looked around the soft-lit living room and spotted the phone on a corner table. I went over, picked it up, and there was a stabby pop and the phone flew out of my hand. I hit the floor as another pop stabbed. A heavy armchair was near and I scooted behind it, staying low. The third pop went through the chair, zizzed past my nose, and thunked into the wall.

Then everything was quiet, except I heard a kind of thumping splash from outside, then quieter slurping sounds. That would be Barbara heaving the corpse out of the pool and dragging it up on the tile.

Some time passed. I got to my hands and knees, went forward a little, and peeked around the chair. Everything stayed quiet, except for the outside slurping. I got my legs under me and came up slowly behind the chair. This time the gunman couldn't have missed—so it was clear he had gone.

I took in air for a while. Then I walked across the room and out the door. Barbara, back in her green froth, was standing near the pool, rubbing her cheeks and gazing down at the body at her feet. It lay on its back and the handle of a dagger stuck out the middle of its chest.

I went over and looked down at the face of a fit-looking old man with a lot of gray hair. "Your husband?"

She nodded.

"I thought he was in Rome."

"No, he's here. Did you get the police?"

"No. The phone was shot out of my hand."

She was quiet, her full lower lip hooked by her teeth, and then she murmured, "So it's all to be settled tonight."

"What is?"

She grabbed my arm, stared up at me, and her eyes were wide and shiny with that fear I'd seen before. "Are you going to help me?"

"What do you want me to do?"

"Drive to Ojai."

"To the cops?"

"Too late for that. Drive down the road we came up till you see a sign that says Munson's Hogs. Take the road there and drive till the road ends in barbed wire. Go through the wire and there's a farmhouse with a well in front. Have you got that?"

"Farmhouse with a well."

"Find a stone, drop it in the well. Wait thirty seconds, then drop two more stones, one after the other. Then wait. Someone will come out."

"Of the well?"

"No, the farmhouse."

"Who?"

"The only one who can help me now."

"Kay?"

Her voice had a ragged undertone of hysteria. "Don't you understand that time is all we have to work with—and it's almost gone?"

Her urgency got me in motion. I went through the door, through the living room, out the front door, and started for the Cad, parked in the drive 200 feet away. The moonlight picked it out brightly. If the sharpshooter was out there in the trees I'd be an easy target. But no pop stabbed the silence.

I knew where I was going to drive. Not to Munson's hog farm—to the Ojai police station, where I'd lay it all out for the cops and they would take it from there. This whole thing had become too sinister and confusing for me to handle by myself.

I ran toward the Cad and when I was 60 feet from it there was a terrific flash, a giant concussion, and I was knocked over on my back. I scrambled up—parts of the Cad were flying around. I ran back to the house, turned, saw pieces and wheels still flying, and where the car had stood, there was only a black patch on the road.

I went through the house and out the door, yelling, "The car blew up!"

But she wasn't there, and neither was the body of her husband. The patio was deserted except for the two deckchairs.

Movement across the pool caught the edge of my glance. I looked fast, saw the giant Madagascan loping away toward the trees. Slung over his shoulder was the body of the dead man.

I shouted, "Where do you think you're going with that?"

He stopped, turned.

"Where's Barbara?" I called.

His teeth flashed at me. Then he turned, and with his soggy burden disappeared into the trees.

I went back in the house. She wasn't in the front room. I started up the stairs. The phone rang.

It had been knocked out of my hand and I hadn't hung it up afterward. But from the stairs I could see it back in its cradle on the corner table, with a bullet hole in the mouthpiece.

I watched it. It kept ringing.

I walked toward it wondering if shots would start popping. But it kept ringing. I picked it up and said, "Hello?"

I heard a whispery laugh.

I said, "Barbara?"

The laugh again.

"Who's laughing?"

A voice whispered, "Too bad for you, Peeper."

It flashed to me—this whole mess could be a mistake in identification—the shots hadn't been meant for me but somebody else. I said, "You got the wrong guy. I'm—" The phone went click.

I hung up. I stood a minute, trying to figure things out.

"Barbara?" I called again. But everything stayed quiet.

The best thing was to get to Ojai, to the cops. I started toward the front door, planning to get out on the road, flag down somebody—

I heard a scream. It came from outside, at the pool. It turned into words: "Help me! For God's sake, help me!"

I ran through the oak door, looked around the patio, saw nothing, heard nothing more.

I stared at the pool, saw something splash into it.

A drop of red.

I looked up. Drops of red were falling from the end of the high diving board, falling into the pool.

The board was bent—it hadn't been bent before.

Bright drops of red, glistening.

"Barbara?"

I couldn't see who or what lay on the diving board. I took various positions on the patio, but couldn't see. If I went in the house, up to the second story, and looked out, maybe I could see.

I stopped. A big dog was in the doorway. Not big, huge. A giant black dog.

He didn't come at me. He just stood there watching. His snout wrinkled, and from deep inside him came an ominous rumbling.

I backed away a little. I held out my hand, palms up, the way you show you're not going to throw anything.

The snarling got higher-pitched. The hairs on his face seemed to get spikier, as if he were charging himself up. More creases showed in his snout. He started to walk, slow and stiff-legged, toward me.

I backed along the side of the pool, toward the deep end. He kept walking toward me. I moved around the corner of the pool, saw his eyes get a sudden crazed look, as if he couldn't stand the anticipation any longer, and was going to make his lunge. I twisted and leaped, a standing broad jump, hoping the ladder to the tower was near enough, and it was—barely. My fingers hooked on a rung, my body swung under, and I pushed up straight and ran up the ladder, running till I was sure I was clear, then looked down. The dog was stretched as far up the ladder as he could go, front paws on the step below me, teeth snapping eight inches below my shoes.

I got a quarter from my pocket and tossed it when his jaws were open at their widest and the coin must have slid down into his throat because he gagged, got a glassy look, and fell backward off the ladder.

He got up all hunched over, choking, shoulders shaking. Finally he gave a low moan, then turned and walked away, not stiff-legged now but shaky and droop-hipped. He got to the patio door, gave me a long look, but the fire was out of him. Then he disappeared inside the house.

I looked in and over the pool. Drops of red, falling in front of me, were splashing into the pool.

"Barbara?"

I didn't want it to be Barbara, but if it was I'd better know now.

I went on up the ladder.

I put my face over the top.

She wasn't there. Nobody was.

I looked along the length of board, and a big flat chunk of iron was out there, making it bend. At the end was a small plastic bag. There were holes in it. Red stuff was leaking out of the holes, puddling around the bag, then slipping, drop by drop, from the end of the board.

I didn't know what to think.

Then I felt something stinging both my palms. It flashed on me that one time when I came home late and turned on a lamp it didn't light. I had reached under to feel if the bulb was loose and found there was no bulb. I stuck my finger in the socket and got bombed across the room. That was what I was getting now—an electric jolt from the ladder rails.

I thought I was. I wasn't. All I was getting was an electric stroke.

Now I got the jolt.

I gave a yell and snatched my hands free, which often you can't do, you just stick to what's jolting you and get cooked. I was lucky. Also I was falling, and I figured I had about 20 feet to wonder about things—then would come crash time.

I waited for the hard tile, trying to tell myself there are worse ways to go. Then I wasn't falling any more. I was lying on something, and it wasn't tile.

Maybe it was a cloud. Maybe you don't remember when you get the fatal knock, maybe your last feeling just fades out, and next thing you know you're lying on a cloud.

That was my first vague thought. Then I came full to reality and knew I wasn't on a cloud. It was something slick and slippery, and soft—I was on something rubbery.

I sat up and looked around. I saw people. They were making noises, they were laughing and whooping.

I heard Barbara's voice—"You okay?" There she was, in her frothy thing, grinning at me.

I started to pick out other faces—there were about 20 people. A foot higher than any other face was Har-Tai's. He gave me a big grin, a wave, called, "Great going!" He must have grown a new tongue.

I saw the gray-haired guy, upright, not wearing the knife in his chest. He had a drink in his hand. Most of the people seemed to have drinks in their hands.

A couple of guys came over, stuck out their hands, took mine and pulled, and I stood up in the rubbery thing, stumbled around on it, and was pulled clear. It was a thick rubber mattress.

A guy handed me a drink. I didn't know if it was bourbon or what, and didn't care. I drank it down. It was bourbon.

Barbara, bright-eyed, said, "I was afraid you'd catch on at the beginning, with the lobster truck in front of us or just behind us all the way from L.A., and pulled up in front of us with the lights out while we were parked off the freeway."

"Yeah," I said. "Lobster truck. Right." I remembered pulling around a panel truck after having the windshield shot up. I hadn't noticed it was a lobster truck. Nor had I noticed the truck on the freeway from L.A.

A furtive voice on the other side of me said, "Stroka genius. Like I said—the guy's a genius."

I turned and it was my agent, Finnegan. He was grinning but shifty-eyed as always—he'd look shifty buying cookies from a Girl Scout. "Bora said you had a great build but as an actor you stunk. Said the only way to get life in you was to have you not know you're acting. Then maybe you'd react to things like someone alive, not made of plaster—and all the other actors would go without scripts and react to your reactions. And it would be realism like it's never been done before."

"I was bugged," said Barbara. I blinked at her. "Bugged for sound. From the time we met at Flupo's."

She fingered her pearls, grinned.

"The pearls were bugged?"

She nodded. "Great natural dialogue. It's all on tape, just needs a word change here and there."

"So it all began at Flupo's, huh? With hidden cameras there?"

"Uh huh. Bora arranged it."

"And the dog was a trained dog?"

"Sure," said a guy standing near. "Mitzi wouldn't hurt a flea."

I had the picture now—or at least the general outline. The lobster truck was a film truck, and all around the pool here and in the main room were hidden cameras, as at Flupo's. But some impressions I still had to shake around till they formed up . . . I wanted another drink, and said so. A guy took my glass and scurried away.

Then suddenly across the patio came the genius himself. All five feet four of him. He bounced up to me, jumped, grabbed my neck, pulled himself up, hung on me, and gave me slobbery kisses on the cheeks.

There was cheering and applause. He continued to hang on my neck and slobber. I've had experience with emotional directors, so I put up with it. Finally he unlatched me. I wiped my sleeve over my face. "Thanks. Were the bullets real?"

"Everything real!"

The guy handed me my drink. I swallowed it and handed it back for a refill. I said to Pelicularu, "So a guy shot an inch from my head, blew a phone out of my hand—weren't you taking a big chance with real bullets?"

"No worry. Great marksman. Retired from Mafia, seek new career in pictures. I give him chance—splendid shooter. Meet Izador."

He beamed at a thin scruffy guy with a bony face who had dead blue eyes.

I said, "Hi, Izador. Good shooting."

He looked at me with his dead eyes. I smiled. He didn't. I doubt he ever had. Pelicularu gave him a pat on the back and he went away.

I drank down my third drink. "The blowup of the Cad—that was real too?"

"Yah. Terrific scene—like whole screen blow up in audience face!"

I was handed a fresh glass. Finnegan said, "Bora told me not to peep—and I was a clam." He grinned, shifting his eyes everywhere.

I said to the genius, "The ladder rails were charged?"

"Yah. Important you reach top of ladder, look over—we have zoom-boom on your face—look of fear, then poozlement. Then we give you jolt in the hands." He grinned delightedly. "Make great closing scene."

"That's the end of the picture?"

"Yah."

"I look at a leaky sack of red paint and fall off the ladder?"

"Audience not see sack of paint—just see last look on your phizoozel—the shlock, the shlock!"

"Shock."

"Whatever. Then you drop off ladder. That the end. Audience ask their-self—what he see? What give him such a look? Audience let own sick imagi-nation fill in—so they come up with more sickening finish than even Pelicu-laru could cook up for them!"

"That's genius," said Finnegan in a reverent voice. And everybody in earshot murmured that was what it was, genius.

Pelicularu didn't argue. He stared into space at private visions—probably a dozen Academy nominations.

I'd finished my drink and stuck out my glass for someone to fill it. Someone took it. I said, "What's the theme of the picture?"

He came back from space. "I dunno. Don't matter. Up to critics to figger."

Everybody murmured again about genius.

I said, "None of it seems to make any sense."

He leaped, hung on my neck again. "Right! Just like *Big Schlepp!* So is great picture for today and for evermore! Greater and greater, as world gradual go *kaputsky!*"

Everybody cheered.

I got my fresh drink and downed it.

The night went on—a party celebrating the quickest filming of a major epic in Hollywood history. Everybody got drunk—me the fastest, because of low resistance due to a pretty harrowing evening. People got loud and started singing. Then some people were saying that the most artistic part of this whole masterpiece was Barbara's informal swim, and would she give a repeat performance? I don't know if she did—just about then I passed out and fell backward onto the rubber mattress.

I spent the rest of the night there, coming to with the sun high. Everybody was gone except one guy staggering around the patio picking up empties, shaking them, then tossing them into the empty pool.

He was the driver of the lobster truck that had done the freeway filming. We walked around to the garage area, got in the truck, and he gave me a ride back to Hollywood.

That was a year ago. I'm still living in the same place on Orange Drive. I've had a few commercials, but not much else since *Catastrophe*.

It got great reviews. Critics said it had real relevance and profound meaning, and was undoubtedly a work of high cinematic art. So nobody came to see it. So they missed the car blowup, the wild dog, that great final shot of my face in shock—and Barbara's swim.

Pelicularu went back to Rashpudlovik, saying America was ten years behind his visions.

I called Barbara a few times, and we made dates, but never seemed to get together. I guess it wasn't our destiny.

Har-Tai and the wild dog, they're pretty busy in horror films.

Izador dropped out of sight.

Hooray for Hollywood.

MEN ON
THE RUN
MEN CAUGHT
IN A TRAP

THE PHANTOM OF THE SUBWAY

Cornell Woolrich

Delaney boarded an empty northbound train at 125th Street by the simple expedient of loosening a chain across the station platform that barred his way, instead of dropping a token into a turnstile. The little metal disc attached to his cap, bearing the numerals 01629, gave him the privilege of doing that. That disc was his by reason of the fact that he was a subway guard.

He pulled a folded tabloid out from behind the panel in the car vestibule and, scorning to assume duties which were still rightfully the night shift's, he sprawled comfortably on one of the seats, legs out before him. The pale pink newssheet engrossed him while the train rattled its way to the end of the line, to start back and meet the rush hour. It was full of topics that had very little bearing on himself and his daily surroundings, such as storms at sea, airplane mishaps, the shapely limbs of a Miss Beaumont who had just flown in from Hollywood, and also a great deal about a "phantom burglar" who was being besieged by the police in the Wadsworth Building, on lower Broadway.

The man had been in there ever since the small hours of the previous night, had ransacked five offices singlehanded to the tune of $500,000, killed the watchman, and they still hadn't been able to lay their hands on him. A cordon had been thrown around the place, the paper said; and it was just a matter of time—time and a mere fifty or sixty floors to cover—before they caught up with him.

Delaney, reading it, felt vaguely cheated. Up above there was always something doing; down here, below ground, nothing ever happened—you were like in your grave already.

As they pulled in at the end of the line, he put the paper back where he'd found it, stirred his stumps, and presented himself and his passbook to the factotum who detailed the personnel off the various southbound trains.

"Last section, third train out," he was told. They were all expresses this far up; the locals didn't go beyond 137th Street. The headway, during the rush hour, was a train every two minutes.

This rite—"shenanigans," Delaney termed it—attended to, he joined his mates on the benches until his own train pulled in. It was a "ghost" train, without a soul on it so far. He stepped aboard and placed himself exactly over the coupling irons of the second and third cars from the end, one foot on each platform, like a sort of Atlas astride his own little world. The time bell rang and he bore down on the pneumatic lever. Six doors in all, three to the left of him and three to the right, slid sibilantly closed. The train pulled out. Another day had begun.

One station down and the train was no longer empty. Before it dove under at Dyckman it was jammed. At 96th it was a madhouse on wheels, and at Times Square the riveted seams of the steel cars threatened to open.

That was the highwater mark, then the ebb set in. After Wall Street, Delaney himself was sitting down again, reading another tabloid that someone had left behind. This was a six A.M. edition; they hadn't caught up with the "phantom" yet. They'd got to the top of the tower by now, but he'd miraculously slipped through them somehow, and he was on his way down. But he was still in there, and the cordon down at street level had been reinforced. They were going to keep the personnel out, and they were sending in tear-gas bombs. The police order now was to give him no quarter, shoot him on sight; for he'd chalked up his second killing, one of their own, trapped in an angle of a dead-end corridor and plugged in the back.

The strangest thing about it was that nobody knew what he looked like. The only two who had caught a glimpse of him were dead before they could tell—hence the "phantom" tag. Delaney doped this out laboriously for himself while his ears hummed as he plunged under the river for the first time that day and hit Brooklyn.

At the other end of the line, with a twenty-minute relief on his hands, he changed his six A.M. edition, which was stale already, for one that had just hit the streets, hadn't been born yet when he got on the train uptown. He took it upstairs with him for a smoke and a shot of fresh air. Miss Beaumont's legs were still there, but they'd lost ground; the Phantom had shoved them from the first page back to the third. He rated a scarehead now. He'd cheated the cordon of police, got out, loot and all. From an extension onto the roof of a church next door, as closely as they could figure it. Then down into the church through a lovely stained-glass skylight, which now lay all over the floor in pieces.

The sexton had had sense enough to hide behind one of the pews, and had got a good look at him and thereby also lived to spill it. He'd watched him slip out, valise and all, and duck down the steps into the Wall Street station, which was right outside the door—with two score bluecoated backs in full view a building-length away.

By the time the sexton got over to them, and the stampede got started, they were just a flight of steps too late. The Wall Street West Side station is a single platform between the tracks, instead of a double one like most. Break one for the Phantom. There were two trains in together, going in opposite directions, which mightn't have happened all the rest of the day. Break two for the Phantom. By the time the cavalcade got down, they had their choice of tail-lights, which didn't tell them a thing.

The station agent headed the downtown one off by telephoning Clark Street, and it was held sealed when it got there and dragnetted, but the Phantom wasn't on it. They couldn't catch the uptown one in time, even by telephone, for the Fulton and Park Place Stations were too close; but when they finally stopped that train and gave it the works at Chambers Street, the Phantom didn't turn up there either. He'd had two ganged-up stations to slip off at, though none of the other passengers they quizzed remembered seeing anyone with a valise, and neither did the station agents in question.

The chase had shifted to Delaney's own domain now and his interest was whetted; a second-hand thrill was better than none at all. It was coming closer all the time.

Just before eight, the paper gave as the time the getaway into the subway had taken place. Delaney began to calculate absorbedly, sitting on an empty ginger-ale case by the station exit. He himself had made Wall Street at about eight sharp, leaving on a 7:20 headway as he had. Trains make poorer time during the rush hour, on account of the gangs getting off at every stop.

"That southbound one," he told himself disappointedly, "musta been the one right ahead of me. I musta got there two minutes after he lammed. Just my luck. It wouldn't be my train he picks—but somebody else's! I must have the Indian sign on me."

He pocketed the paper, disgusted, and reported downstairs for the return run. The fact that the guy was armed and had already killed two men in cold blood didn't lessen Delaney's sense of personal grievance. He felt that he had been dished out of the little excitement there was to be had. "Just one train up, and I coulda maybe had him riding with me!"

The time bell pealed and he slammed his section shut with a face that would have soured milk. The long haul back got under way. The outer stations came and went: Church, Sterling, President, Franklin.

Then Eastern Parkway showed up. Now at Eastern, the West Side lines do this in-bound: two branches fork together. A five-car section coming in from Flatbush Avenue, a half train, waits there for a five-car section coming in from New Lots; they're hooked together to make a full train, ten cars, and cover the rest of the route in one. Outward-bound it's reversed: at that point they split.

Delaney's half got in, waited, and its complementary half showed up behind it on the dot, kissed it with a slight jolt. The coupling crew jumped to its duty, compressed air hissed, and the two sections were joined. The second motorman, dispensed with, went off duty. Delaney's post automatically shifted one car back, to take in what had formerly been the control car. This brought him to what had been the rear platform until now, not used by passengers getting off or on.

It was when he had stepped back from leaning out between cars to catch the signal, and they were already under way, that he first saw the thing, standing by itself in the corner of the vestibule. A dingy, dog-eared cowhide valise, flush with the door. It didn't click, didn't mean a thing at first; it was traveling *in* toward Wall Street, *not* out away from there.

Yet he couldn't understand how it could have been left where it was. That end door hadn't been in use until now, and no one had got on carrying a bag like that since the return trip had begun. He would have seen it. When they did bring stuff like that on, they kept it right under their feet or close to one of the doors in operation, didn't lug it all the way out of sight to the back platform.

Whatever it was, it was in the way, blocking the door. He slurred it with his foot across to the other side of the vestibule, then stood in the doorway and gave the car in general a dirty look.

"Whose suitcase is that?" he megaphoned. "Whaddya think this is, a baggage car? Clear it outa here!"

The sprinkling of passengers looked up interestedly—but blankly. They consisted of a Western Union messenger, two matrons headed for shopping, a sleepy youth who had been ladling orangeade all night, a pair of chattering Puerto Ricans, and an old man with a long beard who believed in the second coming of the Messiah and was dropping pamphlets on everybody else's lap. No takers—none, that is, for the mysterious valise.

Delaney went back again to open for Grand Army Plaza, then when that was out of the way, stood staring at the thing, thinking it over. Suspicion became a certainty, little by little. He'd found it on the side that opened for Wall Street; almost all the rest, the whole length of the line, opened on the opposite side. No one to claim it; no one riding in with it. There was only one answer—it didn't belong on this trip. It must have been brought on during the run before, overlooked at the end of the line by the crew jumping off; and now it was starting back again. It was hard to believe, a thing that size, but maybe with that metal partition swinging loose in front of it they hadn't spotted it.

He glanced up at the car number—3334. They shuffled the cars around a good deal at the end of each run, he knew; coming back he might have been assigned to what had been the train ahead of his the last time, without knowing it. And if so, maybe that thing in the corner over there had half a million in it this very minute!

He went over to it, tried the two latches; but they were locked tight. He picked it up, tested its weight—hard to say what it had in it. Even if it was what he took it for, he still didn't get the idea. It meant this "Phantom" had sent his loot sailing at Wall Street and hadn't gone with it. That sounded screwy. Robbing five offices just to give the haul a free ride by itself on the subway? Unless he had someone working with him, waiting at the end of the line to pick it up. If he had, something had gone wrong, for here it was on its way back again, unclaimed.

Which meant it had run the gauntlet twice, not only at the end of the line when the cars were cleared, but before that at Clark Street when the police had halted the train and gone through it, looking for the murderer. It could have happened at that, incredible as it seemed. They were looking for someone fitting the sexton's description, first of all, and the valise was only incidental. Not finding him, the suitcase itself could easily have escaped their attention, hidden under people's legs in that milling, half-hysterical crowd. They'd had all the doors to watch, and ten packed cars to wade through, and not much time to do it in. There probably wasn't elbow room to bend down and peer at the floor, even if they'd thought of doing so.

Delaney was beginning to understand what must have happened. The guy dove down the steps just a leap ahead of them. There were two trains in, one on each side of him. He must have had to do his thinking fast, no time to hesitate. He couldn't even count on the trains pulling out in time; they might be stopped right where they were and held there in the station.

He didn't know the sexton had glimpsed him in the church. The only giveaway, he thought, was the valise. Separate himself from that, and he was safe. So he plunged it into the downtown train, spun around, and dove into the uptown one without it.

People are always running for trains, why should that have attracted any attention? And on the downtown car vestibule they were probably crammed so close together, all with their papers up in front of their faces, that like the police they didn't see that he'd left something on the floor. And later, each one thought it belonged to the other fellow—until the train split up, and it became the rear platform, and there weren't any left any more. And the Phantom, of course, had had sense enough to lam out of his own train at Fulton, without waiting for them to overhaul it at Chambers.

So far, so good, but then what? No one parts company with five hundred grand that easily, whether it means the chair or not. Delaney discarded the accomplice theory at this point; they wouldn't have had any way of getting in touch with each other in time. The Phantom hadn't intended powdering down the subway, he'd just done it instinctively—the only hole in the ground there was for him to hide in. But for him to send his haul barging off like that on its own, there must have been some connecting link in his mind, some trick play, by which he could catch up with it later. Delaney refused to believe he had kissed it good-bye for good, not after what he'd been through to get his hands on it.

Now just what way was there for him to connect with it again? He certainly wasn't counting on it being turned in to the lost-and-found and then showing up later to claim it: that would be putting his head into the noose for fair. "Can you identify the contents?" "Half a million in cash and securities." And he certainly was not fool enough to think that by taking a later train from farther up he could overtake the first one in time and get his hands on it again. He'd spend the rest of the day riding back and forth, always just one train too late!

But a guy like the Phantom wouldn't work that way.

No, the answer was this: he'd played a hundred-to-one shot, a thousand-to-one shot, had no other choice. He was waiting some place up the line, where this train would have to pass, waiting for that suitcase to come back to him undisturbed, overlooked! And he'd rung the bell, just this once out of a thousand times: it hadn't been taken off, it was heading back to him again! It nearly made Delaney's hair stand up to think of luck like that, of nerve to take a chance like that and have it come through!

But there was just one little remaining hitch to be smoothed away, at least in Delaney's own mind. How in the devil's name did he expect to know the right train, the right car, when it pulled up in front of him? They were all alike even to Delaney, and he spent his life on them. Had he marked the door in some way, so he'd know it again when it made the trip back? That was asking a lot, to expect a guy running for his life to have a piece of chalk or something ready in his hand for just such a purpose!

Just to convince himself, though, Delaney stepped outside at the next stop and scanned all three doors of the car. There wasn't a mark on them. But the answer came to him when he got on again—so simple that he'd overlooked it until now. How did the company officials themselves, anybody at all, tell one car from another? Why, by the number, of course—stenciled in big white numerals on the blackened lower pane of each end window. And this one was a pushover—3334. In that split second when the

Phantom had wedged the suitcase aboard, he'd lamped the number beside the door—and that was all he had to go by; that was the one slim connecting link between him and his hot half million now.

He must have good eyes, all right, to count on glimpsing it in time, one car out of ten, as it whizzed in past whatever platform he was waiting on at this very minute! Still, it could be done.

They were coming into Clark Street now. Delaney bent down and picked up the valise. "Ain't it a shame," he mused dryly, "that I caught onto his little stunt, without nobody telling me nothing! Now all I do is just move it one car over—and where is he? All his sweat and brainwork for nothing."

Abruptly Delaney set it down again. "He'll look in first," he said to himself. "If he doesn't see it, he won't get on—figure his thousand-to-one shot muffed and it was taken off at the other end." He scratched the back of his head. "I'd like to see what he looks like," he decided. "A guy as tricky and nervy as all that! Hell, I got that much coming to me, after packin' sardines in all day long."

He left the valise where it was.

He wasn't, he assured himself, endangering the money any by leaving it exposed like that. "He can get on, but he can't get it off again while I'm on the doors. I'll see to that. I just want to watch what he does—oughta be fun, break the monotony!"

A moment later, as they went under the river, he remembered that the fellow would be armed, had already killed two men who had tried to hinder him. He still left the valise where it was.

They blew into Wall Street, where the Phantom had last been seen, and nothing happened. No one at all got into Delaney's cars there, though he stretched his neck both ways; they were all going to their offices at that hour, not coming away from them. He spotted a pair of cops still hanging around, one at each end of the platform, that was all.

At least it showed they hadn't nabbed him yet. Delaney decided he must have a criminal streak in himself, the satisfaction he felt at that knowledge. Almost as if he was rooting for the guy—which of course he wasn't.

As for flagging the bluecoats and turning the valise over to them, there were several good reasons for not doing it. In the first place, he was only surmising what it was, the regulations were that it was to be turned in at the end of the line. He was working for the company, and not the police.

Wall Street dropped back, and almost immediately Fulton showed around the curve. Delaney didn't watch the platform as hard this time, was giving up hope of his theory being correct. His car hit about the center of the boat-shaped concrete "island."

There didn't seem to be anyone waiting to get on. Down at the end someone was standing shaking one of the chewing-gum slot machines, trying to get his penny back. It looked as though he was waiting for a downtown train, made no move toward this one. Delaney cautiously turned to look up the other way; there was no one at all up there.

When he turned back again, the figure had vanished.

Park Place ticked off, then the train slowed up for Chambers. The valise stayed where it was, unmolested. After Chambers would come a five-minute straightaway without breaks, all the way to 14th. Delaney gave Chambers a good once-over, up and down, from his vantage point. There were a couple of cops hanging around there too. A fat lady, whose girth would have been the pride of any sideshow, accosted him just then from the platform.

"Doth ith go to Timeth Thquare?" she queried.

"It doth," he assured her.

She scowled, and proceeded to wedge herself aboard.

The bell was pealing, and he closed the door. He hadn't calculated on how much of her there was. Most of her was on already, but not quite all. The rubber-edged door nipped her stern slightly.

A moment later, as she moved on, there was a distinct sound of rending silk. A look of alarm crossed her baby face. "Eep!" she squealed, and started revolving slowly on her axis, trying to get a look behind her.

Delaney knew the type. "Now I'm in for it," he told himself resignedly. He was.

"I'm gonna weport you for thith, young man—" she began indignantly, as he stepped down to the vestibule and tried to look unaware of her presence. "I'm gonna thue thith company!"

This probably would have continued without a letup all the way to 14th Street, but Delaney happened to look past her just then to where the valise had been. He snapped to attention with a jolt. The bag was gone!

It was traveling down the aisle, had already gotten half a car length away in the minute his back had been turned, gripped by the same slouch-hatted figure he'd seen so harmlessly tinkering with the slot machine at Fulton Street. Pretending to fuss about a penny while he waited to pounce on half a million dollars!

So that was their "Phantom," was it? Well, he didn't look like much from the back—just a wiry little fellow going some place in a hurry. But Delaney wasn't letting it go at that. He was going to get a look at his face or know the reason why.

"Hey, you!" he bawled, and his voice went booming down the car. "Drop that!"

A face flashed white over one hurrying shoulder. Even at that distance Delaney could see there wasn't any fright in it. There was only cold-blooded, grinning death. The fat lady was in his way, monumental, wedged in the inner doorway—and that probably saved Delaney's life.

Before he could get past her and leap after the man, as he was primed to, the answer to his hail came back—and not in words. There was a second flash over that shoulder—smaller, brighter this time—a whipcrack that topped the roar of the train. A white sworl powdered the glass of the vestibule door just behind Delaney. The door had slipped partly free with the motion of the train.

The fat lady promptly fainted, but fortunately sideways onto the nearest vacant seat. That cleared the aisle. But the figure in the loosely flapping topcoat had already bridged the platform into the next car. He banged the communicating door closed to hamper Delaney, and the glass shattered. Delaney came plunging at it, tore the frame out of the way, and opened the back of his hand in a thin red line.

The lights of Chambers Street had just fallen behind the last car—it was a long station and the whole thing had happened in a flash—and there had been two cops on the platform there. He leaped upward and sidewise in the second vestibule, gave the emergency cord a yank that buckled it into a long loop. If they backed up a few yards, they could get help aboard from the station.

The fugitive had increased his lead to a whole car length now. He seemed to glide between the scattering of frozen, stunned passengers, immune to touch. It was Delaney following after, capless now, with his grim face and bleeding hand, who sowed panic. Women jumped up on the seats with both feet, screaming, then herded toward the back of the train, all trying to get out of the car at once.

The express slurred to a crazy, jolting stop as the signal reached the motorman. Some of the passengers were thrown to the floor.

"Get out on the rear platform," Delaney shouted over his shoulder. "Sing out for help—they may hear you back at the station!" Whether they understood or not, he couldn't tell; he didn't wait to find out.

The fugitive was a car and a half ahead now. Half a million can weigh very little, when it's going to be all yours. The man was out of Delaney's section by this time. A weird silence had overtaken the stalled cars the minute the motion went out of them—all but the chirping at the rear. Delaney, without slowing up, megaphoned his hands and boomed ahead: "Sullivan! Stop that man! The guy with the bag!" It carried like a trumpet call through the still cars.

A minute later he cursed himself for doing it. There was another of those whip-cracks, and the smoke from it was still lazing overhead when he got to the next guard's platform. Sullivan was sprawled on his back, a hole over his eye had just begun to bleed. Delaney jumped over him, swore like a mad dog as the sight registered, went plowing on. The hysterical passengers scattered like leaves in front of him, pushed out windows with their elbows, clawed their way out the other end of the car.

The distant figure with the valise, all that he had eyes for now, had hit the first car at last, couldn't go any farther. Delaney heard himself bellowing out loud like a vindictive bull. He'd never known a guy could want to kill another guy so much, until now. He was in such a red rage that the thought of the gun was actually a come-on instead of a deterrent. A bullet right through the heart, he felt, wouldn't have been able to slow him up now.

The front car came into focus before his smoldering eyes—and the killer had vanished, wasn't in front of him any more. Just as he leaped the platform-gap, the train gave a jerk forward, then plunged into full motion again.

Damn that motorman, why did he ignore the signal like that? He was cutting them off from help at Chambers Street—with 14th Street a full five-minute run ahead! The train picked up speed as it never did under the eyes of a station timekeeper; it was in full careening flight already, rocking from side to side.

There had only been a single man in the first car. He was crouched down at seat level now, pointing terrifiedly. "He went in that little doohinky there! He's got a gun, watch y'self, man!" Then he slithered out of the way.

Delaney had known already he was in there, in the booth with the motorman. It was the only place left for him to go, unless he took a jump down forward under the whistling wheels. Delaney lunged at the metal door with his shoulder, heaved. It held fast. He must have wedged his body against it, since there was no way of locking it on the inside.

Delaney roared through the crack, "Stop the train, you fool! Cut the switch!"

It wasn't the motorman's voice that answered from the other side of the partition, cold, distinct above the tunnel-roar: "Get away from that door or I'll let him have it! You'll be on a train *without* a driver!"

And then the old fellow's voice, crazed with fear, "Delaney, for God's sake, do what he says—he's got a gun at the back of my neck!"

A green all-clear signal winked by beside the track outside. They'd have a few more of those, Delaney knew, but in a minute or two they'd be getting red ones as they overtook the train ahead. And they were bound to if they didn't stop. The headway was longer now than during the rush hour, but the rate they were going would use it up in no time.

He tried to warn the maniac in there of what would happen, continuing to heave at the door while he panted, "You can't get away with it! You'll pile us up on the train ahead!"

The panel gave slightly and the killer's voice sounded from the inside, "Show me how it works! Come on, show me how it works—and I'll do the handling!"

The train slowed momentarily, as the contact broke, then picked up speed again as it was resumed.

There was an insane laugh that froze Delaney. "That's all I need to know!" The panel fell all the way back in a flash, and as Delaney crouched to rush the opening, the old motorman toppled out into his arms, blood threading down by his ear. The booth banged shut again behind him and the train seemed to roar forward.

Delaney eased the overalled figure to the floor, dragged it back out of the way. "Pop! What'd he do, shoot you?"

But it wasn't a bullet wound, it was a vicious blow with the butt of the gun that had knocked him out. Meaning, probably, that the skunk was running low on cartridges, wanted to hang on to the few he had left.

Delaney didn't know much about guns, but he remembered that the fellow was carrying a revolver, and that six slugs was all one packed. He'd shot two off in the Wadsworth Building and two just now in the train. Unless he had a second gun or a pocketful of refills, he had only two left. But a hell of a lot of good knowing that did, with the lights of Canal Street cometing by and then another double green track-light right after that. Red was due any moment.

Delaney leaned across the prostrate motorman and stuck his head out the open upper half of one of the windows. And there it was, still way up the track, but already visible—two midget dots of warning, one above the other, at right-angles to the tunnel wall. And beyond that, almost invisible in the gloom, a cluster of even tinier ruby pinpoints, where their predecessor was slowing up as it neared 14th Street. Two, maybe three, local stops away yet, but they'd be on top of it before it could pull out again!

He let the impregnable booth go hang, turned and fled down the deserted aisle toward the back, as all the passengers had done before him. But he wasn't thinking of his own skin. The second car was empty too, but at the end of that the bolder and more curious among them were huddled, peering up ahead with blanched, tense faces. They started to scatter again as he bore down on them.

"Metal!" he shrieked. "One of you—gimme something made of metal —anything, to throw a short circuit!"

They didn't understand him, or were too frightened. Another local stop gleamed by, and beyond it the two red stop-signals were already the size of dimes.

The fat lady who had involuntarily saved his life once was hunched there, shaking and sniffling. He clawed at her throat and she gave a screech of terror, tried to waddle away. The long silk scarf she wore tucked about her whipped off in his hand, yards and yards of it. He ran back toward the first car, trailing it after him. The red light came abreast, shot past them.

He rolled the thing up into a big loose ball, ducked past the control booth with it, and dropped flat on his stomach over the lip of the open front platform. His head hung down over the edge. Up ahead, the taillights of the next train were square now and expanding every second. Either the guy deliberately intended to commit suicide rather than be caught, or he didn't know how to stop any more.

But right while Delaney lay there with the big fluffy bunch of silk poised in his hand to pitch at the shoe that gripped the third rail, and stall them, the Phantom gave him the answer. He broke out of the booth just in back of Delaney, valise still in one hand, something else now in the other. The control-key that shut off contact. He'd brought it out with him!

He pitched it at one of the windows. There was a slight crash, and it vanished. They couldn't stop now, there was no way—not from the control room, anyhow.

He streaked toward the back, gun out again to replace the key he'd thrown away. He was going to let it happen, callously sending dozens of people to death or painful injury, simply to better his chance of escaping in the resulting chaos! That was the idea, another of those thousand-to-one shots of his! To beat the crash to the end of the train, toss his suitcase off the rear platform, drop off after it himself, and if he survived the fall, make good his escape up through the nearest emergency exit.

And survive he probably would at that; it was just the kind of freak luck he'd been running in for twelve hours straight now. What would a few lacerations or bruises mean to him, living on borrowed time as he was?

The gods of blind chance would probably see him through; they seemed to be all for his kind of reckless fool.

Delaney dropped his head downward again, concentrated on the shoe gliding along the third rail, below and off to the side of him. One thing at a time—there were human lives on this train, and on that other one up front there, and they counted for more than even half a million dollars.

Three times Delaney swung his arm out ahead of him with the rumpled mass of silk, that excellent conductor, foaming out of his hand, and three times swung it under and downward—without letting go. If the rush of air deflected it, carried it harmlessly past the shoe straight down the middle of the trackbed—

But there wasn't any more time left, not even enough to hesitate. The taillights ahead were only a train length away by now. He could look up the aisle of the end car already; it was like a small lighted tunnel telescoped within a bigger black one. Let the gods of luck give somebody else a break for a change!

He opened his hand, let go, with just a fillip to the right to carry the silk off-center. It streamed out and downward, opening as it went. It hit the third rail just inches ahead of the shoe, whipped from sight, and seemed to be sucked in under the rail guard.

Then there was a warning spatter of sparks. The whole tunnel turned blue as though a giant flashlight picture had just been taken down there under the car truck. And then a report like heavy artillery that put the Phantom's puny pistol cracks to shame.

The blue glare went out again as suddenly as it had flared up, but the cars were already jarring to a sickening halt. Delaney had been given his break. He had short-circuited the train.

He nearly went sailing off through the open platform door with the suddenness of the lurch. He caught the single chain with one upflung arm and dangled there, half in and half out. He managed to squirm back in again, scrambled to his feet, and plunged down a car aisle that had turned dark now and was filled with a thin layer of acrid smoke drifting lazily rearward. The train lights had gone with the power, but a single automatic emergency bulb gleamed dully just above the vestibule of each car. He thanked God for them, for the passengers' sake if not his own.

They'd all been thrown down by the halt, and they'd reached a pitch of terror by now, some of them anyway, that was almost animal. But he wasn't concerned with them just now. He raced down the clear lane between their prone, jabbering forms that someone else had opened just ahead of him, with the wave of that deadly little gun.

He was in mid car, out of reach of the levers, when all the doors silently swung back around him. He knew who'd done it! The fellow was getting out the side instead of going all the way to the back. He must have remembered that there'd be a guard down at the end-section who might tangle with him. And now the train had stalled, it was no longer suicide to jump off at the side, in fact, easier and quicker than the other way.

Delaney spurted for the nearest controls, to try to reverse them again before the fellow had time to slip through, but by the time he'd done it, he knew it was too late. Leaning out at nearly a forty-five degree angle between cars, trying to pierce the tunnel gloom down that way, only proved the assumption to be correct. It was just the next car down that he'd made his getaway from, and the feeble radius of light from the bulb down at the vestibule momentarily outlined something moving away from it that instantly lost itself in the murk. But Delaney had seen that it was a figure holding onto a square shape and hopping awkwardly athwart the local tracks to the two-foot emergency runway niched into the side of the tunnel. And that led far down to where blue and white lights, one above the other, and a puff of gray daylight, marked an exit.

Well, he wasn't there yet! And he'd shot, maybe killed Sullivan, banged the old man on the conk, and tied up the whole line into a knot! Delaney reversed the controls a second time, and jumped down to the tracks himself.

The tunnel was black, but it looked red to him just then. Two long jumps cleared the local rails for him, and he caught the single hand-guard that hemmed the causeway, hoisted himself up onto the little narrow footpath. It was at about train level. Instantly the blue and white lights up ahead vanished. Something was between him and them.

Delaney sprinted along the straight, two-foot cement ribbon of foothold, pushing himself in toward the wall constantly with one hand on the rail that paralleled it. It was hard to make time along a place that narrow and tricky, but it was even harder if you had a valise to pack, he told himself. You'd have to scuttle along crabwise in that case, so it wouldn't trip you. He himself tripped once, went down face forward, and all but fell down to the tracks three feet below. He picked himself up and bolted on, knees and palms stinging.

The exit lights ahead slowly rose in perspective as they drew nearer, cleared the top of the silhouette that had obscured them, and hit him in the eye like two moons. For the first time, then, he saw how close he and his quarry were. There was only about ten yards between them. The thumping and slapping of the suitcase as it was borne along were now clearly audible. The cars of his own motionless train were far in back of him by now; he was traversing the pitch-black empty stretch between it and the one behind, a local, also stalled and semi-lighted. Just ahead of that, though, were the exit lights and the gush of daylight that marked safety for the killer.

But Delaney already knew he'd beat him to it. That grip was hampering the fellow something fierce. The ten yards were down to about seven now, and the man's hoarse strangled breathing seemed to fill the tunnel.

Delaney made himself audible at last, though the other must have known all along someone was after him. "Come on, give up, I've got you now!"

A second later he'd paid for his overconfidence. One foot somehow got in front of the other, and he went down a second time. He managed to stay on the runway, but was flat as a mat.

Just as the floor came up and smacked him, the figure ahead whirled. There was a bang, a flash, and a thin whistle past where Delaney's head should have been.

One bullet left, and five yards between them. They were both motionless for a minute, half strangling for air. Delaney crouched, leaped at the man from scratch in a sort of long rising tackle that brought him up to shoulder level by the time they connected. The gun exploded again, but straight at the ceiling like a sprint signal this time, but with one of Delaney's hands at the wrist that wielded it, the other at the fellow's neck, pulling it together into a flesh necktie. The gun clicked harmlessly twice more in the air, then dropped to the runway with a clash, and bounced down to the tracks below.

Delaney took away his open hand from the fellow's throat, only to bring it back again hardened into a meteorite of a fist that drove between the other's eyes as though it had come all the way from another planet.

If any consciousness survived the impact, there was no sign of it. The wrist Delaney had been gripping jerked from his grasp, the other's body went down flat over the valise that had been standing just behind him. The head missed the edge of the runway, dropped from sight, and pulled all the rest of him down to the tracks after it with a sort of acrobat's half turn and back flip, under the hand rail. The valise stayed on the ledge; but the Phantom stayed down below in an indistinguishable heap.

Delaney, about to jump down after him, was suddenly conscious of light flaring all around him, like an abrupt aurora borealis there in the tunnel. That local, not far down, was all at once blazing with light again, bleaching the tunnel walls. So was his own train, far up the other way. They'd ironed out the short-circuit and the power had come on again.

A puff of black, acrid smoke seemed to spurt from under the mound of clothes that lay on the tracks just beneath him, as though they were on fire. He turned his head away and leaned sickly up against the tunnel wall.

Later, trudging away from there, hauling the recovered valise slowly after him, the professional came to the surface in Delaney again. "Two shorts in a row," he mused despondently. "They'll can me sure when they find out it was me caused the first one."

"And did they?" asked his blindfolded train-mate Sullivan from the hospital bed that evening.

"I didn't let on it was me done it," answered Delaney, "but somebody must have tipped them off. They seemed to know it, anyway. They didn't dock me, though. Instead, all the higher-ups come around shaking hands with me. They said something about promoting me."

"Well, what're you kicking about?" the other asked. "You sound like—"

"It was bad enough before, riding the platforms," complained Delaney. "Now it'll be twice as slow, stuck behind some signal-board keeping tabs on the lights all day long! That's what a guy gets. He don't know when he's well off!"

CAUGHT

O. Henry

The plans for the detention of the flying president Miraflores and his companion at the coast line seemed hardly likely to fail. Dr. Zavalla himself had gone to the port of Alazan to establish a guard at that point. At Coralio the Liberal patriot Varras could be depended upon to keep close watch. Goodwin held himself responsible for the district about Coralio.

The news of the president's flight had been disclosed to no one in the coast towns save trusted members of the ambitious political party that was desirous of succeeding to power. The telegraph wire running from San Mateo to the coast had been cut far up on the mountain trail by an emissary of Zavalla's. Long before this could be repaired and word received along it from the capital the fugitives would have reached the coast and the question of escape or capture been solved.

Goodwin had stationed armed sentinels at frequent intervals along the shore for a mile in each direction from Coralio. They were instructed to keep a vigilant lookout during the night to prevent Miraflores from attempting to embark stealthily by means of some boat or sloop found by chance at the water's edge. A dozen patrols walked the streets of Coralio unsuspected, ready to intercept the truant official should he show himself there.

Goodwin was very well convinced that no precautions had been overlooked. He strolled about the streets that bore such high-sounding names and were but narrow, grass-covered lanes, lending his own aid to the vigil that had been intrusted to him by Bob Englehart.

The town had begun the tepid round of its nightly diversions. A few leisurely dandies, clad in white duck, with flowing neckties, and swinging slim bamboo canes, threaded the grassy by-ways toward the houses of their favored señoritas. Those who wooed the art of music dragged tirelessly at whining concertinas, or fingered lugubrious guitars at doors and windows.

An occasional soldier from the *cuartel*, with flapping straw hat, without coat or shoes, hurried by, balancing his long gun like a lance in one hand. From every density of the foliage the giant tree frogs sounded their loud and irritating clatter. Further out, where the by-ways perished at the brink of the jungle, the guttural cries of marauding baboons and the coughing of the alligators in the black estuaries fractured the vain silence of the wood.

By ten o'clock the streets were deserted. The oil lamps that had burned, a sickly yellow, at random corners, had been extinguished by some economical civic agent. Coralio lay sleeping calmly between toppling mountains and encroaching sea like a stolen babe in the arms of its abductors. Somewhere over in that tropical darkness—perhaps already threading the profundities of the alluvial lowlands—the high adventurer and his mate were moving toward land's end. The game of Fox-in-the-Morning should be coming soon to its close.

Goodwin, at his deliberate gait, passed the long, low *cuartel* where Coralio's contingent of Anchuria's military force slumbered, with its bare toes pointed heavenward. There was a law that no civilian might come so near the headquarters of that citadel of war after nine o'clock, but Goodwin was always forgetting the minor statutes.

"*Quién vive?*" shrieked the sentinel, wrestling prodigiously with his lengthy musket.

"*Americano,*" growled Goodwin, without turning his head, and passed on, unhalted.

To the right he turned, and to the left up the street that ultimately reached the Plaza Nacional. When within the toss of a cigar stump from the intersecting Street of the Holy Sepulchre, he stopped suddenly in the pathway.

He saw the form of a tall man, clothed in black and carrying a large valise, hurry down the cross-street in the direction of the beach. And Goodwin's second glance made him aware of a woman at the man's elbow on the farther side, who seemed to urge forward, if not even to assist, her companion in their swift but silent progress. They were no Coralians, those two.

Goodwin followed at increased speed, but without any of the artful tactics that are so dear to the heart of the sleuth. The American was too broad to feel the instinct of the detective. He stood as an agent for the people of Anchuria, and but for political reasons he would have demanded then and there the money. It was the design of his party to secure the imperilled fund, to restore it to the treasury of the country, and to declare itself in power without bloodshed or resistance.

The couple halted at the door of the Hotel de los Extranjeros, and the man struck upon the wood with the impatience of one unused to his entry being stayed. Madama was long in response; but after a time her light showed, the door was opened, and the guests housed.

Goodwin stood in the quiet street, lighting another cigar. In two minutes a faint gleam began to show between the slats of the jalousies in the upper story of the hotel. "They have engaged rooms," said Goodwin to himself. "So, then, their arrangements for sailing have yet to be made."

At that moment there came along one Estebán Delgado, a barber, an enemy to existing government, a jovial plotter against stagnation in any form. This barber was one of Coralio's saddest dogs, often remaining out of doors as late as eleven, post meridian. He was a partisan Liberal; and he greeted Goodwin with flatulent importance as a brother in the cause. But he had something important to tell.

"What think you, Don Frank!" he cried, in the universal tone of the conspirator. "I have to-night shaved *la barba*— what you call the 'weeskers' of the *Presidente* himself, of this countree! Consider! He sent for me to come. In the poor *casita* of an old woman he awaited me—in a verree leetle house in a dark place. *Caramba!*—el Señor Presidente to make himself thus secret and obscured! I think he desired not to be known—but, *carajo!* can you shave a man and not see his face? This gold piece he gave me, and said it was to be all quite still. I think, Don Frank, there is what you call a chip over the bug."

"Have you ever seen President Miraflores before?" asked Goodwin.

"But once," answered Estebán. "He is tall; and he had weeskers verree black and sufficient."

"Was any one else present when you shaved him?"

"An old Indian woman, Señor, that belonged with the *casa*, and one señorita—a ladee of so much beautee!—*ah, Dios!*"

"All right, Estebán," said Goodwin. "It's very lucky that you happened along with your tonsorial information. The new administration will be likely to remember you for this."

Then in a few words he made the barber acquainted with the crisis into which the affairs of the nation had culminated, and instructed him to remain outside, keeping watch upon the two sides of the hotel that looked upon the street, and observing whether any one should attempt to leave the house by any door or window. Goodwin himself went to the door through which the guests had entered, opened it and stepped inside.

Madama had returned downstairs from her journey above to see after the comfort of her lodgers. Her candle stood upon the bar. She was about to take a thimbleful of rum as a solace for having her rest disturbed. She looked up without surprise or alarm as her third caller entered.

"Ah! it is the Señor Goodwin. Not often does he honor my poor house by his presence."

"I must come oftener," said Goodwin, with the Goodwin smile. "I hear that your cognac is the best between Belize to the north and Rio to the south. Set out the bottle, Madama, and let us have the proof in *un vasito* for each of us."

"My *aguardiente*," said Madama, with pride, "is the best. It grows, in beautiful bottles, in the dark places among the banana-trees. *Si, Señor.* Only at midnight can they be picked by sailor-men who bring them, before daylight comes, to your back door. Good *aguardiente* is a verree difficult fruit to handle, Señor Goodwin."

Smuggling, in Coralio, was much nearer than competition to being the life of trade. One spoke of it slyly, yet with a certain conceit, when it had been well accomplished.

"You have guests in the house to-night," said Goodwin, laying a silver dollar upon the counter.

"Why not?" said Madama, counting the change. "Two, one señor, not quite old, and one señorita of sufficient handsomeness. To their rooms they have ascended, not desiring the to-eat nor the to-drink. Two rooms— *Número* 9 and *Número* 10."

"I was expecting that gentleman and that lady," said Goodwin. "I have important *negocios* that must be transacted. Will you allow me to see them?"

"Why not?" sighed Madama, placidly. "Why should not Señor Goodwin ascend and speak to his friends? *Está bueno.* Room *Número* 9 and room *Número* 10."

Goodwin loosened in his coat pocket the American revolver that he carried, and ascended the steep, dark stairway.

In the hallway above, the saffron light from a hanging lamp allowed him to select the gaudy numbers on the doors. He turned the knob of Number 9, entered and closed the door behind him.

If that was Isabel Guilbert seated by the table in that poorly furnished room, report had failed to do her charms justice. She rested her head upon one hand. Extreme fatigue was signified in every line of her figure; and upon her countenance a deep perplexity was written. Her eyes were gray-irised, and of that mould that seems to have belonged to the orbs of all the famous queens of hearts. Their whites were singularly clear and brilliant, concealed above the irises by heavy horizontal lids, and showing a snowy line below them. Such eyes denote great nobility, vigor, and, if you can conceive of it, a most generous selfishness. She looked up when the American entered with an expression of surprised inquiry, but without alarm.

Goodwin took off his hat and seated himself, with his characteristic deliberate ease, upon a corner of the table. He held a lighted cigar between his fingers. He took this familiar course because he was sure that preliminaries would be wasted upon Miss Guilbert. He knew her history, and the small part that the conventions had played in it.

"Good evening," he said. "Now, madame, let us come to business at once. You will observe that I mention no names, but I know who is in the next room, and what he carries in that valise. That is the point which brings me here. I have come to dictate terms of surrender."

The lady neither moved nor replied, but steadily regarded the cigar in Goodwin's hand.

"We," continued the dictator, thoughtfully regarding the neat buckskin shoe on his gently swinging foot—"I speak for a considerable majority of the people—demand the return of the stolen funds belonging to them. Our terms go very little further than that. They are very simple. As an accredited spokesman, I promise that our interference will cease if they are accepted. Give up the money, and you and your companion will be permitted to proceed wherever you will. In fact, assistance will be given you in the matter of securing a passage by any outgoing vessel you may choose. It is on my personal responsibility that I add congratulations to the gentleman in Number 10 upon his taste in feminine charms."

Returning his cigar to his mouth, Goodwin observed her, and saw that her eyes followed it and rested upon it with icy and significant concentration. Apparently she had not heard a word he had said. He understood, tossed the cigar out the window, and, with an amused laugh, slid from the table to his feet.

"That is better," said the lady. "It makes it possible for me to listen to you. For a second lesson in good manners, you might now tell me by whom I am being insulted."

"I am sorry," said Goodwin, leaning one hand on the table, "that my time is too brief for devoting much of it to a course of etiquette. Come, now; I appeal to your good sense. You have shown yourself, in more than one instance, to be well aware of what is to your advantage. This is an occasion that demands the exercise of your undoubted intelligence. There is no mystery here. I am Frank Goodwin; and I have come for the money. I entered this room at a venture. Had I entered the other I would have had it before now. Do you want it in words? The gentleman in Number 10 has betrayed a great trust. He has robbed his people of a large sum, and it is I who will prevent their losing it. I do not say who that gentleman is; but if I should be forced to see him and he should prove to be a certain high official of the republic, it will be my duty to arrest him. The house is guarded. I am offering you liberal terms. It is not absolutely necessary that I confer personally with the gentleman in the next room. Bring me the valise containing the money, and we will call the affair ended."

The lady arose from her chair, and stood for a moment, thinking deeply.

"Do you live here, Mr. Goodwin?" she asked, presently.

"Yes."

"What is your authority for this intrusion?"

"I am an instrument of the republic. I was advised by wire of the movements of the—gentleman in Number 10."

"May I ask you two or three questions? I believe you to be a man more apt to be truthful than—timid. What sort of a town is this—Coralio, I think they call it?"

"Not much of a town," said Goodwin, smiling. "A banana town, as they run. Grass huts, 'dobes, five or six two-story houses, accommodations limited, population half-breed Spanish and Indian, Caribs and blackamoors. No sidewalks to speak of, no amusements. Rather unmoral. That's an off-hand sketch, of course."

"Are there any inducements, say in a social or in a business way, for people to reside here?"

"Oh, yes," answered Goodwin, smiling broadly. "There are no afternoon teas, no hand-organs, no department stores—and there is no extradition treaty."

"He told me," went on the lady, speaking as if to herself, and with a slight frown, "that there were towns on this coast of beauty and importance; that there was a pleasing social order—especially an American colony of cultured residents."

"There is an American colony," said Goodwin, gazing at her in some wonder. "Some of the members are all right. Some are fugitives from justice from the States. I recall two exiled bank presidents, one army paymaster under a cloud, a couple of manslayers, and a widow—arsenic, I believe, was the suspicion in her case. I myself complete the colony, but, as yet, I have not distinguished myself by any particular crime."

"Do not lose hope," said the lady, dryly; "I see nothing in your actions to-night to guarantee your further obscurity. Some mistake has been made; I do not know just where. But *him* you shall not disturb to-night. The journey has fatigued him so that he has fallen asleep, I think, in his clothes. You talk of stolen money! I do not understand you. Some mistake has been made. I will convince you. Remain where you are and I will bring you the valise that you seem to covet so, and show it to you."

She moved toward the closed door that connected the two rooms, but stopped, and half turned and bestowed upon Goodwin a grave, searching look that ended in a quizzical smile.

"You force my door," she said, "and you follow your ruffianly behavior with the basest accusations; and yet"—she hesitated, as if to reconsider what she was about to say—"and yet—it is a puzzling thing—I am sure there has been some mistake."

She took a step toward the door, but Goodwin stayed her by a light touch upon her arm. I have said before that women turned to look at him in the streets. He was the viking sort of man, big, good-looking, and with an air of kindly truculence. She was dark and proud, glowing or pale as her mood moved her. I do not know if Eve were light or dark, but if such a woman had stood in the garden I know that the apple would have been eaten. This woman was to be Goodwin's fate, and he did not know it; but he must have felt the first throes of destiny, for, as he faced her, the knowledge of what report named her turned bitter in his throat.

"If there has been any mistake," he said, hotly, "it was yours. I do not blame the man who has lost his country, his honor, and is about to lose the poor consolation of his stolen riches as much as I blame you, for, by Heaven! I can very well see how he was brought to it. I can understand, and pity him. It is such women as you that strew this degraded coast with wretched exiles, that make men forget their trusts, that drag—"

The lady interrupted him with a weary gesture.

"There is no need to continue your insults," she said, coldly, "I do not understand what you are saying, nor do I know what mad blunder you are making; but if the inspection of the contents of a gentleman's portmanteau will rid me of you, let us delay it no longer."

She passed quickly and noiselessly into the other room, and returned with the heavy leather valise, which she handed to the American with an air of patient contempt.

Goodwin set the valise quickly upon the table and began to unfasten the straps. The lady stood by, with an expression of infinite scorn and weariness upon her face.

The valise opened wide to a powerful, sidelong wrench. Goodwin dragged out two or three articles of clothing, exposing the bulk of its contents—package after package of tightly packed United States bank and treasury notes of large denomination. Reckoning from the high figures written upon the paper bands that bound them, the total must have come closely upon the hundred thousand mark.

Goodwin glanced swiftly at the woman, and saw, with surprise and a thrill of pleasure that he wondered at, that she had experienced an unmistakable shock. Her eyes grew wide, she gasped, and leaned heavily against the table. She had been ignorant, then, he inferred, that her companion had looted the government treasury. But why, he angrily asked himself, should he be so well pleased to think this wandering and unscrupulous singer not so black as report had painted her?

A noise in the other room startled them both. The door swung open, and a tall, elderly, dark complexioned man, recently shaven, hurried into the room.

All the pictures of President Miraflores represent him as the possessor of a luxuriant supply of dark and carefully tended whiskers; but the story of the barber, Estebán, had prepared Goodwin for the change.

The man stumbled in from the dark room, his eyes blinking at the lamp-light, and heavy from sleep.

"What does this mean?" he demanded in excellent English, with a keen and perturbed look at the American—"robbery?"

"Very near it," answered Goodwin. "But I rather think I'm in time to prevent it. I represent the people to whom this money belongs, and I have come to convey it back to them." He thrust his hand into a pocket of his loose linen coat.

The other man's hand went quickly behind him.

"Don't draw," called Goodwin, sharply; "I've got you covered from my pocket."

The lady stepped forward, and laid one hand upon the shoulder of her hesitating companion. She pointed to the table. "Tell me the truth—the truth," she said, in a low voice. "Whose money is that?"

The man did not answer. He gave a deep, long-drawn sigh, leaned and kissed her on the forehead, stepped back into the other room and closed the door.

Goodwin foresaw his purpose, and jumped for the door, but the report of the pistol echoed as his hand touched the knob. A heavy fall followed, and some one swept him aside and struggled into the room of the fallen man.

A desolation, thought Goodwin, greater than that derived from the loss of cavalier and gold must have been in the heart of the enchantress to have wrung from her, in that moment, the cry of one turning to the all-forgiving, all-comforting earthly consoler—to have made her call out from that bloody and dishonored room—"Oh, mother, mother, mother!"

But there was an alarm outside. The barber, Estebán, at the sound of the shot, had raised his voice; and the shot itself had aroused half the town. A pattering of feet came up the street, and official orders rang out on the still air. Goodwin had a duty to perform. Circumstances had made him the custodian of his adopted country's treasure. Swiftly cramming the money into the valise, he closed it, leaned far out of the window and dropped it into a thick orange-tree in the little inclosure below.

They will tell you in Coralio, as they delight in telling the stranger, of the conclusion of that tragic flight. They will tell you how the upholders of the law came apace when the alarm was sounded—the *Comandante* in red slippers and a jacket like a head waiter's and girded sword, the soldiers with their interminable guns, followed by outnumbering officers struggling into their gold lace and epaulettes; the bare-footed policemen (the only capables in the lot), and ruffled citizens of every hue and description.

They say that the countenance of the dead man was marred sadly by the effects of the shot; but he was identified as the fallen president by both Goodwin and the barber Esteban. On the next morning messages began to come over the mended telegraph wire; and the story of the flight from the capital was given out to the public. In San Mateo the revolutionary party had seized the sceptre of government, without opposition, and the *vivas* of the mercurial populace quickly effaced the interest belonging to the unfortunate Miraflores.

They will relate to you how the new government sifted the towns and raked the roads to find the valise containing Anchuria's surplus capital, which the president was known to have carried with him, but all in vain. In Coralio Señor Goodwin himself led the searching party which combed that town as carefully as a woman combs her hair; but the money was not found.

So they buried the dead man, without honors, back of the town near the little bridge that spans the mangrove swamp; and for a *real* a boy will show you his grave. They say that the old woman in whose hut the barber shaved the president placed the wooden slab at his head, and burned the inscription upon it with a hot iron.

You will hear also that Señor Goodwin, like a tower of strength, shielded Doña Isabel Guilbert through those subsequent distressful days; and that his scruples as to her past career (if he had any) vanished; and her adventuresome waywardness (if she had any) left her, and they were wedded and were happy.

The American built a home on a little foot hill near the town. It is a conglomerate structure of native woods that, exported, would be worth a fortune, and of brick, palm, glass, bamboo and adobe. There is a paradise of nature about it; and something of the same sort within. The natives speak of its interior with hands uplifted in admiration. There are floors polished like mirrors and covered with hand-woven Indian rugs of silk fibre, tall ornaments and pictures, musical instruments and papered walls—"figure-it-to-yourself!" they exclaim.

But they cannot tell you in Coralio (as you shall learn) what became of the money that Frank Goodwin dropped into the orange-tree. But that shall come later; for the palms are fluttering in the breeze, bidding us to sport and gaiety.

THE SIRE DE MALÉTROIT'S DOOR

Robert Louis Stevenson

Denis de Beaulieu was not yet two-and-twenty, but he counted himself a grown man, and a very accomplished cavalier into the bargain. Lads were early formed in that rough, warfaring epoch; and when one has been in a pitched battle and a dozen raids, has killed one's man in an honourable fashion, and knows a thing or two of strategy and mankind, a certain swagger in the gait is surely to be pardoned. He had put up his horse with due care, and supped with due deliberation; and then, in a very agreeable frame of mind, went out to pay a visit in the grey of the evening. It was not a very wise proceeding on the young man's part. He would have done better to remain beside the fire or go decently to bed. For the town was full of the troops of Burgundy and England under a mixed command; and though Denis was there on safe-conduct, his safe-conduct was like to serve him little on a chance encounter.

It was September, 1429; the weather had fallen sharp; a flighty piping wind, laden with showers, beat about the township; and the dead leaves ran riot along the streets. Here and there a window was already lighted up; and the noise of men-at-arms making merry over supper within, came forth in fits and was swallowed up and carried away by the wind. The night fell swiftly; the flag of England, fluttering on the spire-top, grew ever fainter and fainter against the flying clouds—a black speck like a swallow in the tumultuous, leaden chaos of the sky. As the night fell the wind rose and began to hoot under archways and roar amid the tree-tops in the valley below the town.

Denis de Beaulieu walked fast and was soon knocking at his friend's door; but though he promised himself to stay only a little while and make an early return, his welcome was so pleasant, and he found so much to delay him, that it was already long past midnight before he said good-bye upon the threshold. The wind had fallen again in the meanwhile; the night was as black as the grave; not a star, nor a glimmer of moonshine, slipped through

the canopy of cloud. Denis was ill-acquainted with the intricate lanes of
Chateau Landon; even by daylight he had found some trouble in picking
his way; and in this absolute darkness he soon lost it altogether. He was
certain of one thing only—to keep mounting the hill; for his friend's house
lay at the lower end, or tail, of Chateau Landon, while the inn was up at the
head, under the great church spire. With this clue to go upon he stumbled
and groped forward, now breathing more freely in open places where there
was a good slice of sky overhead, now feeling along the wall in stifling
closes. It is an eerie and mysterious position to be thus submerged in
opaque blackness in an almost unknown town. The silence is terrifying in its
possibilities. The touch of cold window bars to the exploring hand startles
the man like the touch of a toad; the inequalities of the pavement shake his
heart into his mouth; a piece of denser darkness threatens an ambuscade or
a chasm in the pathway; and where the air is brighter, the houses put on
strange and bewildering appearances, as if to lead him farther from his way.
For Denis, who had to regain his inn without attracting notice, there was
real danger as well as mere discomfort in the walk; and he went warily and
boldly at once, and at every corner paused to make an observation.

He had been for some time threading a lane so narrow that he could
touch a wall with either hand, when it began to open out and go sharply
downward. Plainly this lay no longer in the direction of his inn; but the
hope of a little more light tempted him forward to reconnoitre. The lane
ended in a terrace with a bartisan wall, which gave an outlook between high
houses, as out of an embrasure, into the valley lying dark and formless
several hundred feet below. Denis looked down, and could discern a few
tree-tops waving and a single speck of brightness where the river ran across
a weir. The weather was clearing up, and the sky had lightened, so as to
show the outline of the heavier clouds and the dark margin of the hills. By
the uncertain glimmer, the house on his left hand should be a place of some
pretensions; it was surmounted by several pinnacles and turret-tops; the
round stern of a chapel, with a fringe of flying buttresses, projected boldly
from the main block; and the door was sheltered under a deep porch carved
with figures and overhung by two long gargoyles. The windows of the
chapel gleamed through their intricate tracery with a light as of many tapers, and threw out the buttresses and the peaked roof in a more intense
blackness against the sky. It was plainly the hotel of some great family of the
neighbourhood; and as it reminded Denis of a town house of his own at
Bourges, he stood for some time gazing up at it and mentally gauging the
skill of the architects and the consideration of the two families.

There seemed to be no issue to the terrace but the lane by which he had
reached it; he could only retrace his steps, but he had gained some notion
of his whereabouts, and hoped by this means to hit the main thoroughfare

and speedily regain the inn. He was reckoning without that chapter of accidents which was to make this night memorable above all others in his career; for he had not gone back above a hundred yards before he saw a light coming to meet him, and heard loud voices speaking together in the echoing of the lane. It was a party of men-at-arms going the night round with torches. Denis assured himself that they had all been making free with the wine-bowl, and were in no mood to be particular about safe-conducts or the niceties of chivalrous war. It was as like as not that they would kill him like a dog and leave him where he fell. The situation was inspiriting but nervous. Their own torches would conceal him from sight, he reflected; and he hoped that they would drown the noise of his footsteps with their own empty voices. If he were but fleet and silent, he might evade their notice altogether.

Unfortunately, as he turned to beat a retreat, his foot rolled upon a pebble; he fell against the wall with an ejaculation, and his sword rang loudly on the stones. Two or three voices demanded who went there—some in French, some in English; but Denis made no reply, and ran the faster down the lane. Once upon the terrace, he paused to look back. They still kept calling after him, and just then began to double the pace in pursuit, with a considerable clank of armour, and great tossing of the torch-light to and fro in the narrow jaws of the passage.

Denis cast a look around and darted into the porch. There he might escape observation, or—if that were too much to expect—was in a capital posture whether for parley or defence. So thinking, he drew his sword and tried to set his back against the door. To his surprise, it yielded behind his weight; and though he turned in a moment, continued to swing back on oiled and noiseless hinges, until it stood wide open on a black interior. When things fall out opportunely for the person concerned, he is not apt to be critical about the how or why, his own immediate personal convenience seeming a sufficient reason for the strangest oddities and revolutions in our sublunary things; and so Denis, without a moment's hesitation, stepped within and partly closed the door behind him to conceal his place of refuge. Nothing was further from his thoughts than to close it altogether; but for some inexplicable reason—perhaps by a spring or a weight—the ponderous mass of oak whipped itself out of his fingers and clanked to, with a formidable rumble and a noise like the falling of an automatic bar.

The round, at that very moment, debouched upon the terrace and proceeded to summon him with shouts and curses. He heard them ferreting in the dark corners; and the stock of a lance even rattled along the outer surface of the door behind which he stood; but these gentlemen were in too high a humour to be long delayed, and soon made off down a corkscrew pathway which had escaped Denis's observation, and passed out of sight and hearing along the battlements of the town.

Denis breathed again. He gave them a few minutes' grace for fear of accidents, and then groped about for some means of opening the door and slipping forth again. The inner surface was quite smooth, not a handle, not a moulding, not a projection of any sort. He got his finger-nails round the edges and pulled, but the mass was immovable. He shook it, it was as firm as a rock. Denis de Beaulieu frowned and gave vent to a little noiseless whistle. What ailed the door? he wondered. Why was it open? How came it to shut so easily and so effectually after him? There was something obscure and underhand about all this, that was little to the young man's fancy. It looked like a snare; and yet who would suppose a snare in such a quiet by-street and in a house of so prosperous and even noble an exterior? And yet —snare or no snare, intentionally or unintentionally—here he was, prettily trapped; and for the life of him he could see no way out of it again. The darkness began to weigh upon him. He gave ear; all was silent without, but within and close by he seemed to catch a faint sighing, a faint sobbing rustle, a little stealthy creak—as though many persons were at his side, holding themselves quite still, and governing even their respiration with the extreme of slyness. The idea went to his vitals with a shock, and he faced about suddenly as if to defend his life. Then, for the first time, he became aware of a light about the level of his eyes and at some distance in the interior of the house—a vertical thread of light, widening towards the bottom, such as might escape between two wings of arras over a doorway. To see anything was a relief to Denis; it was like a piece of solid ground to a man labouring in a morass; his mind seized upon it with avidity; and he stood staring at it and trying to piece together some logical conception of his surroundings. Plainly there was a flight of steps ascending from his own level to that of this illuminated doorway; and indeed he thought he could make out another thread of light, as fine as a needle and as faint as phosphorescence, which might very well be reflected along the polished wood of a handrail. Since he had begun to suspect that he was not alone, his heart had continued to beat with smothering violence, and an intolerable desire for action of any sort had possessed itself of his spirit. He was in deadly peril, he believed. What could be more natural than to mount the staircase, lift the curtain, and confront his difficulty at once? At least he would be dealing with something tangible; at least he would be no longer in the dark. He stepped slowly forward with outstretched hands, until his foot struck the bottom step; then he rapidly scaled the stairs, stood for a moment to compose his expression, lifted the arras and went in.

He found himself in a large apartment of polished stone. There were three doors; one on each of three sides; all similarly curtained with tapestry.

The fourth side was occupied by two large windows and a great stone chimney-piece, carved with the arms of the Malétroits. Denis recognized the bearings, and was gratified to find himself in such good hands. The room was strongly illuminated; but it contained little furniture except a heavy table and a chair or two, the hearth was innocent of fire, and the pavement was but sparsely strewn with rushes clearly many days old.

On a high chair beside the chimney, and directly facing Denis as he entered, sat a little old gentleman in a fur tippet. He sat with his legs crossed and his hands folded, and a cup of spiced wine stood by his elbow on a bracket on the wall. His countenance had a strongly masculine cast; not properly human, but such as we see in the bull, the goat, or the domestic boar; something equivocal and wheedling, something greedy, brutal, and dangerous. The upper lip was inordinately full, as though swollen by a blow or a toothache; and the smile, the peaked eyebrows, and the small, strong eyes were quaintly and almost comically evil in expression. Beautiful white hair hung straight all round his head, like a saint's, and fell in a single curl upon the tippet. His beard and moustache were the pink of venerable sweetness. Age, probably in consequence of inordinate precautions, had left no mark upon his hands; and the Malétroit hand was famous. It would be difficult to imagine anything at once so fleshy and so delicate in design; the tapered, sensual fingers were like those of one of Leonardo's women; the fork of the thumb made a dimpled protuberance when closed; the nails were perfectly shaped, and of a dead, surprising whiteness. It rendered his aspect tenfold more redoubtable, that a man with hands like these should keep them devoutly folded in his lap like a virgin martyr—that a man with so intense and startling an expression of face should sit patiently on his seat and contemplate people with an unwinking stare, like a god, or a god's statue. His quiescence seemed ironical and treacherous, it fitted so poorly with his looks.

Such was Alain, Sire de Malétroit.

Denis and he looked silently at each other for a second or two.

"Pray step in," said the Sire de Malétroit. "I have been expecting you all the evening."

He had not risen, but he accompanied his words with a smile and a slight but courteous inclination of the head. Partly from the smile, partly from the strange musical murmur with which the Sire prefaced his observation, Denis felt a strong shudder of disgust go through his marrow. And what with disgust and honest confusion of mind, he could scarcely get words together in reply.

"I fear," he said, "that this is a double accident. I am not the person you suppose me. It seems you were looking for a visit; but for my part, nothing was further from my thoughts—nothing could be more contrary to my wishes—than this intrusion."

"Well, well," replied the old gentleman indulgently, "here you are, which is the main point. Seat yourself, my friend, and put yourself entirely at your ease. We shall arrange our little affairs presently."

Denis perceived that the matter was still complicated with some misconception, and he hastened to continue his explanations.

"Your door . . ." he began.

"About my door?" asked the other, raising his peaked eyebrows. "A little piece of ingenuity." And he shrugged his shoulders. "A hospitable fancy! By your own account, you were not desirous of making my acquaintance. We old people look for such reluctance now and then; and when it touches our honour, we cast about until we find some way of overcoming it. You arrive uninvited, but believe me, very welcome."

"You persist in error, sir," said Denis. "There can be no question between you and me. I am a stranger in this countryside. My name is Denis, damoiseau de Beaulieu. If you see me in your house, it is only——"

"My young friend," interrupted the other, "you will permit me to have my own ideas on that subject. They probably differ from yours at the present moment," he added with a leer, "but time will show which of us is in the right."

Denis was convinced he had to do with a lunatic. He seated himself with a shrug, content to wait the upshot; and a pause ensued, during which he thought he could distinguish a hurried gabbling as of prayer from behind the arras immediately opposite him. Sometimes there seemed to be but one person engaged, sometimes two; and the vehemence of the voice, low as it was, seemed to indicate either great haste or an agony of spirit. It occurred to him that this piece of tapestry covered the entrance to the chapel he had noticed from without.

The old gentleman meanwhile surveyed Denis from head to foot with a smile, and from time to time emitted little noises like a bird or a mouse, which seemed to indicate a high degree of satisfaction. This state of matters became rapidly insupportable; and Denis, to put an end to it, remarked politely that the wind had gone down.

The old gentleman fell into a fit of silent laughter, so prolonged and violent that he became quite red in the face. Denis got upon his feet at once, and put on his hat with a flourish.

"Sir," he said, "if you are in your wits, you have affronted me grossly. If you are out of them, I flatter myself I can find better employment for my brains than to talk with lunatics. My conscience is clear; you have made a fool of me from the first moment; you have refused to hear my explanations; and now there is no power under God will make me stay here any longer; and if I cannot make my way out in a more decent fashion, I will hack your door in pieces with my sword."

The Sire de Malétroit raised his right hand and wagged it at Denis with the fore and little fingers extended.

"My dear nephew," he said, "sit down."

"Nephew!" retorted Denis, "you lie in your throat;" and he snapped his fingers in his face.

"Sit down, you rogue!" cried the old gentlemen, in a sudden harsh voice, like the barking of a dog. "Do you fancy," he went on, "that when I had made my little contrivance for the door I had stopped short with that? If you prefer to be bound hand and foot till your bones ache, rise and try to go away. If you choose to remain a free young buck, agreeably conversing with an old gentleman—why, sit where you are in peace, and God be with you."

"Do you mean I am a prisoner?" demanded Denis.

"I state the facts," replied the other. "I would rather leave the conclusion to yourself."

Denis sat down again. Externally he managed to keep pretty calm; but within, he was now boiling with anger, now chilled with apprehension. He no longer felt convinced that he was dealing with a madman. And if the old gentleman was sane, what, in God's name, had he to look for? What absurd or tragical adventure had befallen him? What countenance was he to assume?

While he was thus unpleasantly reflecting, the arras that overhung the chapel door was raised, and a tall priest in his robes came forth and, giving a long, keen stare at Denis, said something in an undertone to Sire de Malétroit.

"She is in a better frame of spirit?" asked the latter.

"She is more resigned, messire," replied the priest.

"Now the Lord help her, she is hard to please!" sneered the old gentleman. "A likely stripling—not ill-born—and of her own choosing, too? Why, what more would the jade have?"

"The situation is not usual for a young damsel," said the other, "and somewhat trying to her blushes."

"She should have thought of that before she began the dance. It was none of my choosing, God knows that: but since she is in it, by our Lady, she shall carry it to the end." And then addressing Denis, "Monsieur de Beaulieu," he asked, "may I present you to my niece? She has been waiting your arrival, I may say, with even greater impatience than myself."

Denis had resigned himself with a good grace—all he desired was to know the worst of it as speedily as possible; so he rose at once, and bowed in acquiescence. The Sire de Malétroit followed his example and limped, with the assistance of the chaplain's arm, towards the chapel door. The priest pulled aside the arras, and all three entered. The building had considerable architectural pretensions. A light groining sprang from six stout columns, and hung down in two rich pendants from the centre of the vault. The place terminated behind the altar in a round end, embossed and honeycombed with a superfluity of ornament in relief, and pierced by many little windows shaped like stars, trefoils, or wheels. These windows were imperfectly glazed, so that the night air circulated freely in the chapel. The tapers, of which there must have been half a hundred burning on the altar, were unmercifully blown about; and the light went through many different phases of brilliancy and semi-eclipse. On the steps in front of the altar knelt a young girl richly attired as a bride. A chill settled over Denis as he observed her costume; he fought with desperate energy against the conclusion that was thrust upon his mind; it could not—it should not—be as he feared.

"Blanche," said the Sire, in his most flute-like tones, "I have brought a friend to see you, my little girl; turn round and give him your pretty hand. It is good to be devout; but it is necessary to be polite, my niece."

The girl rose to her feet and turned towards the new comers. She moved all of a piece; and shame and exhaustion were expressed in every line of her fresh young body; and she held her head down and kept her eyes upon the pavement, as she came slowly forward. In the course of her advance, her eyes fell upon Denis de Beaulieu's feet—feet of which he was justly vain, be it remarked, and wore in the most elegant accoutrement even while travelling. She paused—started, as if his yellow boots had conveyed some shocking meaning—and glanced suddenly up into the wearer's countenance. Their eyes met; shame gave place to horror and terror in her looks; the blood left her lips; with a piercing scream she covered her face with her hands and sank upon the chapel floor.

"That is not the man!" she cried. "My uncle, that is not the man!"

The Sire de Malétroit chirped agreeably. "Of course not," he said; "I expected as much. It was so unfortunate you could not remember his name."

"Indeed," she cried, "indeed, I have never seen this person till this moment—I have never so much as set eyes upon him—I never wish to see him again. Sir," she said, turning to Denis, "if you are a gentleman, you will bear me out. Have I ever seen you—have you ever seen me—before this accursed hour?"

"To speak for myself, I have never had that pleasure," answered the young man. "This is the first time, messire, that I have met with your engaging niece."

The old gentleman shrugged his shoulders.

"I am distressed to hear it," he said. "But it is never too late to begin. I had little more acquaintance with my own late lady ere I married her; which proves," he added with a grimace, "that these impromptu marriages may often produce an excellent understanding in the long run. As the bridegroom is to have a voice in the matter, I will give him two hours to make up for lost time before we proceed with the ceremony." And he turned towards the door, followed by the clergyman.

The girl was on her feet in a moment. "My uncle, you cannot be in earnest," she said. "I declare before God I will stab myself rather than be forced on that young man. The heart rises at it; God forbid such marriages; you dishonour your white hair. Oh, my uncle, pity me! There is not a woman in all the world but would prefer death to such a nuptial. Is it possible," she added, faltering, "is it possible that you do not believe me— that you still think this"—and she pointed at Denis with a tremor of anger and contempt—"that you still think *this* to be the man?"

"Frankly," said the old gentleman, pausing on the threshold, "I do. But let me explain to you once for all, Blanche de Malétroit, my way of thinking about this affair. When you took it into your head to dishonour my family and the name that I have borne, in peace and war, for more than threescore years, you forfeited, not only the right to question my designs, but that of looking me in the face. If your father had been alive, he would have spat on you and turned you out of doors. His was the hand of iron. You may bless your God you have only to deal with the hand of velvet, mademoiselle. It was my duty to get you married without delay. Out of pure goodwill, I have tried to find your own gallant for you. And I believe I have succeeded. But before God and all the holy angels, Blanche de Malétroit, if I have not, I care not one jackstraw. So let me recommend you to be polite to our young friend; for upon my word, your next groom may be less appetising."

And with that he went out, with the chaplain at his heels; and the arras fell behind the pair.

The girl turned upon Denis with flashing eyes.

"And what, sir," she demanded, "may be the meaning of all this?"

"God knows," returned Denis gloomily. "I am a prisoner in this house, which seems full of mad people. More I know not; and nothing do I understand."

"And pray how came you here?" she asked.

He told her as briefly as he could. "For the rest," he added, "perhaps you will follow my example, and tell me the answer to all these riddles, and what, in God's name, is like to be the end of it."

She stood silent for a little, and he could see her lips tremble and her tearless eyes burn with a feverish lustre. Then she pressed her forehead in both hands.

"Alas, how my head aches!" she said wearily—"to say nothing of my poor heart! But it is due to you to know my story, unmaidenly as it must seem. I am called Blanche de Malétroit; I have been without father or mother for—oh! for as long as I can recollect, and indeed I have been most unhappy all my life. Three months ago a young captain began to stand near me every day in church. I could see that I pleased him; I am much to blame, but I was so glad that anyone should love me; and when he passed me a letter, I took it home with me and read it with great pleasure. Since that time he has written many. He was so anxious to speak with me, poor fellow! and kept asking me to leave the door open some evening that we might have two words upon the stair. For he knew how much my uncle trusted me." She gave something like a sob at that, and it was a moment before she could go on. "My uncle is a hard man, but he is very shrewd," she said at last. "He has performed many feats in war, and was a great person at court, and much trusted by Queen Isabeau in old days. How he came to suspect me I cannot tell; but it is hard to keep anything from his knowledge; and this morning, as we came from mass, he took my hand in his, forced it open, and read my little billet, walking by my side all the while. When he had finished, he gave it back to me with great politeness. It contained another request to have the door left open; and this has been the ruin of us all. My uncle kept me strictly in my room until evening, and then ordered me to dress myself as you see me—a hard mockery for a young girl, do you not think so? I suppose, when he could not prevail with me to tell him the young captain's name, he must have laid a trap for him: into which, alas! you have fallen in the anger of God. I looked for much confusion; for how could I tell whether he was willing to take me for his wife on these sharp terms? He might have been trifling with me from the first; or I might have made myself too cheap in his eyes. But truly I had not looked for such a shameful punishment as this! I could not think that God would let a girl be so disgraced before a young man. And now I have told you all; and I can scarcely hope that you will not despise me."

Denis made her a respectful inclination.

"Madam," he said, "you have honoured me by your confidence. It remains for me to prove that I am not unworthy of the honour. Is Messire de Malétroit at hand?"

"I believe he is writing in the salle without," she answered.

"May I lead you thither, madam?" asked Denis, offering his hand with his most courtly bearing.

She accepted it; and the pair passed out of the chapel, Blanche in a very drooping and shamefast condition, but Denis strutting and ruffling in the consciousness of a mission, and the boyish certainty of accomplishing it with honour.

The Sire de Malétroit rose to meet them with an ironical obeisance.

"Sir," said Denis with the grandest possible air, "I believe I am to have some say in the matter of this marriage; and let me tell you at once, I will be no party to forcing the inclination of this young lady. Had it been freely offered to me, I should have been proud to accept her hand, for I perceive she is as good as she is beautiful; but as things are, I have now the honour, messire, of refusing."

Blanche looked at him with gratitude in her eyes; but the old gentleman only smiled and smiled, until his smile grew positively sickening to Denis.

"I am afraid," he said, "Monsieur de Beaulieu, that you do not perfectly understand the choice I have to offer you. Follow me, I beseech you, to this window." And he led the way to one of the large windows which stood open on the night. "You observe," he went on, "there is an iron ring in the upper masonry, and reeved through that, a very efficacious rope. Now, mark my words; if you should find your disinclination to my niece's person insurmountable, I shall have you hanged out of this window before sunrise. I shall only proceed to such an extremity with the greatest regret, you may believe me. For it is not at all your death that I desire, but my niece's establishment in life. At the same time, it must come to that if you prove obstinate. Your family, Monsieur de Beaulieu, is very well in its way; but if you sprang from Charlemagne, you should not refuse the hand of a Malétroit with impunity—not if she had been as common as the Paris road—not if she were as hideous as the gargoyle over my door. Neither my niece nor you, nor my own private feelings, move me at all in this matter. The honour of my house has been compromised; I believe you to be the guilty person; at least you are now in the secret; and you can hardly wonder if I request you to wipe out the stain. If you will not, your blood be on your own head! It will be no great satisfaction to me to have your interesting relics kicking their heels in the breeze below my windows; but half a loaf is better than no bread, and if I cannot cure the dishonour, I shall at least stop the scandal."

There was a pause.

"I believe there are other ways of settling such imbroglios among gentlemen," said Denis. "You wear a sword, and I hear you have used it with distinction."

The Sire de Malétroit made a signal to the chaplain, who crossed the room with long silent strides and raised the arras over the third of the three doors. It was only a moment before he let it fall again; but Denis had time to see a dusky passage full of armed men.

"When I was a little younger, I should have been delighted to honour you, Monsieur de Beaulieu," said Sire Alain; "but I am now too old. Faithful retainers are the sinews of age, and I must employ the strength I have. This is one of the hardest things to swallow as a man grows up in years; but with a little patience, even this becomes habitual. You and the lady seem to prefer the salle for what remains of your two hours; and as I have no desire to cross your preference, I shall resign it to your use with all the pleasure in the world. No haste!" he added, holding up his hand, as he saw a dangerous look come into Denis de Beaulieu's face. "If your mind revolts against hanging, it will be time enough two hours hence to throw yourself out of the window or upon the pikes of my retainers. Two hours of life are always two hours. A great many things may turn up in even as little a while as that. And, besides, if I understand her appearance, my niece has still something to say to you. You will not disfigure your last hours by a want of politeness to a lady?"

Denis looked at Blanche, and she made him an imploring gesture.

It is likely that the old gentleman was hugely pleased at this symptom of an understanding; for he smiled on both, and added sweetly: "If you will give me your word of honour, Monsieur de Beaulieu, to wait my return at the end of the two hours before attempting anything desperate, I shall withdraw my retainers, and let you speak in greater privacy with mademoiselle."

Denis again glanced at the girl, who seemed to beseech him to agree.

"I give you my word of honour," he said.

Messire de Malétroit bowed, and proceeded to limp about the apartment, clearing his throat the while with that odd musical chirp which had already grown so irritating in the ears of Denis de Beaulieu. He first possessed himself of some papers which lay upon the table; then he went to the mouth of the passage and appeared to give an order to the men behind the arras; and lastly he hobbled out through the door by which Denis had come in, turning upon the threshold to address a last smiling bow to the young couple, and followed by the chaplain with a hand-lamp.

No sooner were they alone than Blanche advanced towards Denis with her hands extended. Her face was flushed and excited, and her eyes shone with tears.

"You shall not die!" she cried, "you shall marry me after all."

"You seem to think, madam," replied Denis, "that I stand much in fear of death."

"Oh no, no," she said, "I see you are no poltroon. It is for my own sake—I could not bear to have you slain for such a scruple."

"I am afraid," returned Denis, "that you underrate the difficulty, madam. What you may be too generous to refuse, I may be too proud to accept. In a moment of noble feeling towards me, you forgot what you perhaps owe to others."

He had the decency to keep his eyes upon the floor as he said this, and after he had finished, so as not to spy upon her confusion. She stood silent for a moment, then walked suddenly away, and falling on her uncle's chair, fairly burst out sobbing. Denis was in the acme of embarrassment. He looked round, as if to seek for inspiration, and seeing a stool, plumped down upon it for something to do. There he sat, playing with the guard of his rapier, and wishing himself dead a thousand times over, and buried in the nastiest kitchen-heap in France. His eyes wandered round the apartment, but found nothing to arrest them. There were such wide spaces between the furniture, the light fell so badly and cheerlessly over all, the dark outside air looked in so coldly through the windows, that he thought he had never seen a church so vast, nor a tomb so melancholy. The regular sobs of Blanche de Malétroit measured out the time like the ticking of a clock. He read the device upon the shield over and over again, until his eyes became obscured; he stared into shadowy corners until he imagined they were swarming with horrible animals; and every now and again he awoke with a start, to remember that his last two hours were running, and death was on the march.

Oftener and oftener, as the time went on, did his glance settle on the girl herself. Her face was bowed forward and covered with her hands, and she was shaken at intervals by the convulsive hiccup of grief. Even thus she was not an unpleasant object to dwell upon, so plump and yet so fine, with a warm brown skin, and the most beautiful hair, Denis thought, in the whole world of womankind. Her hands were like her uncle's; but they were more in place at the end of her young arms, and looked infinitely soft and caressing. He remembered how her blue eyes had shone upon him, full of anger, pity, and innocence. And the more he dwelt on her perfections, the uglier death looked, and the more deeply was he smitten with penitence at her continued tears. Now he felt that no man could have the courage to leave a world which contained so beautiful a creature; and now he would have given forty minutes of his last hour to have unsaid his cruel speech.

Suddenly a hoarse and ragged peal of cockcrow rose to their ears from the dark valley below the windows. And this shattering noise in the silence of all around was like a light in a dark place, and shook them both out of their reflections.

"Alas, can I do nothing to help you?" she said, looking up.

"Madam," replied Denis, with a fine irrelevancy, "if I have said anything to wound you, believe me, it was for your own sake and not for mine."

She thanked him with a tearful look.

"I feel your position cruelly," he went on. "The world has been bitter hard on you. Your uncle is a disgrace to mankind. Believe me, madam, there is no young gentleman in all France but would be glad of my opportunity to die in doing you a momentary service."

"I know already that you can be very brave and generous," she answered. "What I *want* to know is whether I can serve you—now or after-wards," she added, with a quaver.

"Most certainly," he answered with a smile. "Let me sit beside you as if I were a friend, instead of a foolish intruder; try to forget how awkwardly we are placed to one another; make my last moments go pleasantly; and you will do me the chief service possible."

"You are very gallant," she added, with a yet deeper sadness . . . "very gallant . . . and it somehow pains me. But draw nearer, if you please; and if you find anything to say to me, you will at least make certain of a very friendly listener. Ah! Monsieur de Beaulieu," she broke forth—"ah! Monsieur de Beaulieu, how can I look you in the face?" And she fell to weeping again with a renewed effusion.

"Madam," said Denis, taking her hand in both of his, "reflect on the little time I have before me, and the great bitterness into which I am cast by the sight of your distress. Spare me, in my last moments, the spectacle of what I cannot cure even with the sacrifice of my life."

"I am very selfish," answered Blanche. "I will be braver, Monsieur de Beaulieu, for your sake. But think if I can do you no kindness in the future —if you have no friends to whom I could carry your adieus. Charge me as heavily as you can; every burden will lighten, by so little, the invaluable gratitude I owe you. Put it in my power to do something more for you than weep."

"My mother is married again, and has a young family to care for. My brother Guichard will inherit my fiefs; and if I am not in error, that will content him amply for my death. Life is a little vapour that passeth away, as we are told by those in holy orders. When a man is in a fair way and sees all life open in front of him, he seems to himself to make a very important figure in the world. His horse whinnies to him; the trumpets blow and the girls look out of window as he rides into town before his company; he receives many assurances of trust and regard—sometimes by express in a letter—sometimes face to face, with persons of great consequence falling on his neck. It is not wonderful if his head is turned for a time. But once he is dead, were he as brave as Hercules or as wise as Solomon, he is soon forgotten. It is not ten years since my father fell, with many other knights around him, in a very fierce encounter, and I do not think that any one of them, nor so much as the name of the fight, is now remembered. No, no, madam, the nearer you come to it, you see that death is a dark and dusty corner, where a man gets into his tomb and has the door shut after him till the judgment day. I have few friends just now, and once I am dead I shall have none."

"Ah, Monsieur de Beaulieu!" she exclaimed, "you forget Blanche de Malétroit."

"You have a sweet nature, madam, and you are pleased to estimate a little service far beyond its worth."

"It is not that," she answered. "You mistake me if you think I am so easily touched by my own concerns. I say so, because you are the noblest man I have ever met; because I recognise in you a spirit that would have made even a common person famous in the land."

"And yet here I die in a mouse-trap—with no more noise about it than my own squeaking," answered he.

A look of pain crossed her face, and she was silent for a little while. Then a light came into her eyes, and with a smile she spoke again."

"I cannot have my champion think meanly of himself. Anyone who gives his life for another will be met in Paradise by all the heralds and angels of the Lord God. And you have no such cause to hang your head. For . . . Pray, do you think me beautiful?" she asked, with a deep flush.

"Indeed, madam, I do," he said.

"I am glad of that," she answered heartily. "Do you think there are many men in France who have been asked in marriage by a beautiful maiden—with her own lips—and who have refused her to her face? I know you men would half despise such a triumph; but believe me, we women know more of what is precious in love. There is nothing that should set a person higher in his own esteem; and we women would prize nothing more dearly."

"You are very good," he said; "but you cannot make me forget that I was asked in pity and not for love."

"I am not so sure of that," she replied, holding down her head. "Hear me to an end, Monsieur de Beaulieu. I know how you must despise me; I feel you are right to do so; I am too poor a creature to occupy one thought of your mind, although, alas! you must die for me this morning. But when I asked you to marry me, indeed, and indeed, it was because I respected and admired you, and loved you with my whole soul, from the very moment that you took my part against my uncle. If you had seen yourself, and how noble you looked, you would pity rather than despise me. And now," she went on, hurriedly checking him with her hand, "although I have laid aside all reserve and told you so much, remember that I know your sentiments towards me already. I would not, believe me, being nobly born, weary you with importunities into consent. I too have a pride of my own: and I declare before the holy mother of God, if you should now go back from your word already given, I would no more marry you than I would marry my uncle's groom."

Denis smiled a little bitterly.

"It is a small love," he said, "that shies at a little pride."

She made no answer, although she probably had her own thoughts.

"Come hither to the window," he said, with a sigh. "Here is the dawn."

And indeed the dawn was already beginning. The hollow of the sky was full of essential daylight, colourless and clean; and the valley underneath was flooded with a grey reflection. A few thin vapours clung in the coves of the forest or lay along the winding course of the river. The scene disengaged a surprising effect of stillness, which was hardly interrupted when the cocks began once more to crow among the steadings. Perhaps the same fellow who had made so horrid a clangour in the darkness not half-an-hour before, now sent up the merriest cheer to greet the coming day. A little wind went bustling and eddying among the tree-tops underneath the windows. And still the daylight kept flooding insensibly out of the east, which was soon to grow incandescent and cast up that red-hot cannon-ball, the rising sun.

Denis looked out over all this with a bit of a shiver. He had taken her hand, and retained it in his almost unconsciously.

"Has the day begun already?" she said; and then, illogically enough: "the night has been so long! Alas! what shall we say to my uncle when he returns?"

"What you will," said Denis, and he pressed her fingers in his.

She was silent.

"Blanche," he said, with a swift, uncertain, passionate utterance, "you have seen whether I fear death. You must know well enough that I would as gladly leap out of that window into the empty air as lay a finger on you without your free and full consent. But if you care for me at all do not let me lose my life in a misapprehension; for I love you better than the whole world; and though I will die for you blithely, it would be like all the joys of Paradise to live on and spend my life in your service."

As he stopped speaking, a bell began to ring loudly in the interior of the house; and a clatter of armour in the corridor showed that the retainers were returning to their post, and the two hours were at an end.

"After all that you have heard?" she whispered, leaning towards him with her lips and eyes.

"I have heard nothing," he replied.

"The captain's name was Florimond de Champdivers," she said in his ear.

"I did not hear it," he answered, taking her supple body in his arms and covering her wet face with kisses.

A melodious chirping was audible behind, followed by a beautiful chuckle, and the voice of Messire de Malétroit wished his new nephew a good morning.

THE EXECUTIONER

Honoré de Balzac

Midnight had just sounded from the belfry tower of the little town of Menda. A young French officer, leaning over the parapet of the long terrace at the further end of the castle gardens, seemed to be unusually absorbed in deep thought for one who led the reckless life of a soldier; but it must be admitted that never was the hour, the scene, and the night more favorable to meditation.

The blue dome of the cloudless sky of Spain was overhead; he was looking out over the coy windings of a lovely valley lit by the uncertain starlight and the soft radiance of the moon. The officer, leaning against an orange tree in blossom, could also see, a hundred feet below him, the town of Menda, which seemed to nestle for shelter from the north wind at the foot of the crags on which the castle itself was built. He turned his head and caught sight of the sea; the moonlit waves made a broad frame of silver for the landscape.

There were lights in the castle windows. The mirth and movement of a ball, the sounds of the violins, the laughter of the officers and their partners in the dance was borne towards him, and blended with the far-off murmur of the waves. The cool night had certain bracing effect upon his frame, wearied as he had been by the heat of the day.

The castle of Menda belonged to a Spanish grandee, who was living in it at that time with his family. All through the evening the oldest daughter of the house had watched the officer with such a wistful interest that the Spanish lady's compassionate eyes might well have set the young Frenchman dreaming. Clara was beautiful; and although she had three brothers and a sister, the broad lands of the Marqués de Légañès appeared to be sufficient warrant for Victor Marchand's belief that the young lady would have a splendid dowry. But how could he dare to imagine that the most fanatical believer in blue blood in all Spain would give his daughter to the son of a grocer in Paris?

Moreover, the French were hated. It was because the Marquis had been suspected of an attempt to raise the country in favor of Ferdinand VII that General G———, who governed the province, had stationed Victor Marchand's battalion in the little town of Menda to overawe the neighboring districts which received the Marqués de Légañès's word as law. A recent dispatch from Marshal Ney had given ground for fear that the English might soon effect a landing on the coast, and had indicated the Marquis as being in correspondence with the Cabinet in London.

In spite, therefore, of the welcome with which the Spaniards had received Victor Marchand and his soldiers, that officer was always on his guard. As he went towards the terrace, where he had just surveyed the town and the districts confided to his charge, he had been asking himself what construction he ought to put upon the friendliness which the Marquis had invariably shown him, and how to reconcile the apparent tranquillity of the country with his General's uneasiness. But a moment later these thoughts were driven from his mind by the instincts of caution and very legitimate curiosity.

It had just struck him that there was a very fair number of lights in the town below. Although it was the Feast of Saint James, he himself had issued orders that very morning that all lights must be put out in the town at the hour prescribed by military regulations. The castle alone had been excepted in this order. Plainly here and there he saw the gleam of bayonets, where his own men were at their accustomed posts; but in the town there was a solemn silence, and not a sign that the Spaniards had given themselves up to the intoxication of a festival.

He tried vainly for a while to explain this breach of the regulations on the part of the inhabitants; the mystery seemed but so much the more obscure because he had left instructions with some of his officers to make the rounds of the town.

With the impetuosity of youth, he was about to spring through a gap in the wall preparatory to a rapid scramble down the rocks, thinking to reach a small guardhouse at the nearest entrance into the town more quickly than by the beaten track, when a faint sound stopped him. He fancied that he could hear the light footstep of a woman along the graveled walk.

He turned his head and saw no one; for one moment his eyes were dazzled by the wonderful brightness of the sea, the next he saw a sight so ominous that he stood stock-still with amazement, thinking that his senses must be deceiving him. The white moonbeams lighted the horizon, so that he could distinguish the sails of ships still a considerable distance out at sea. A shudder ran through him; he tried to persuade himself that this was some optical delusion of moonlight on the waves; and even as he made the attempt, a hoarse voice called to him by name.

The officer glanced at the gap in the wall; saw a soldier's head slowly emerge from it, and knew the grenadier whom he had ordered to accompany him to the castle.

"Is that you, Commandant?"

"Yes. What is it?" returned the young officer in a low voice.

"Those beggars down there are creeping about like worms; and, by your leave, I came as quickly as I could to report my little reconnoitering expedition."

"Go on," answered Victor Marchand.

"I have just been following a man from the castle who came round this way with a lantern in his hand. I don't imagine that there was any need for that good Christian to be lighting tapers at this time of night. Says I to myself, 'They mean to gobble us up!' and I set myself to dogging his heels; and that is how I found out that there is a pile of fagots, sir, two or three steps away from here."

Suddenly a dreadful shriek rang through the town below, and cut the man short. A light flashed in the Commandant's face, and the poor grenadier dropped down with a bullet through his head. Ten paces away a bonfire flared up like a conflagration. The sounds of music ceased all at once in the ballroom; the silence of death, broken only by groans, succeeded to the rhythmical murmur of the festival. Then the roar of the cannon sounded from across the white plain of the sea.

A cold sweat broke out on the young officer's forehead. He had left his sword behind. He knew that his men had been murdered, and that the English were about to land. He knew that if he lived he would be dishonored; he saw himself summoned before a courtmartial. For a moment his eyes measured the depth of the valley; the next, just as he was about to spring down, Clara's hand caught his.

"Fly!" she cried. "My brothers are coming after me to kill you. Down yonder at the foot of the cliff you will find Juanito's Andalusian. Go!"

She thrust him away. The young man gazed at her in dull bewilderment; but obeying the instinct of self-preservation, which never deserts even the bravest, he rushed across the park in the direction pointed out to him, springing from rock to rock. He heard Clara calling to her brothers to pursue him; he heard the footsteps of the murderers; again and again he heard their balls whistling about his ears; but he reached the foot of the cliff, found the horse, mounted, and fled with lightning speed.

A few hours later the young officer reached General G——'s quarters, and found him at dinner with the staff.

"I put my life in your hands!" cried the haggard and exhausted Commandant.

He sank into a seat, and told his story. It was received with an appalling silence.

"It seems to me that you are more to be pitied than blamed," the terrible General said at last. "You are not answerable for the Spaniard's crimes, and unless the Marshal decides otherwise, I acquit you."

These words brought but cold comfort to the unfortunate officer.

"When the Emperor comes to hear about it!" he cried.

"Oh, he will be for having you shot," said the General, "but we shall see. Now we will say no more about this," he added severely, "except to plan a revenge that shall strike terror into this country, where they carry on war like savages."

An hour later a whole regiment, a detachment of cavalry, and a convoy of artillery were upon the road. The General and Victor marched at the head of the column. The soldiers had been told of the fate of their comrades, and their rage knew no bounds.

The distance between headquarters and the town of Menda was crossed at a well-nigh miraculous speed. Whole villages by the way were found to be under arms; every one of the wretched hamlets was surrounded, and their inhabitants decimated.

It so chanced that the English vessels still lay out at sea, and were no nearer the shore, a fact inexplicable until it was learned afterwards that they were artillery transports which had outsailed the rest of the fleet. So the townsmen of Menda, left without the assistance on which they had reckoned when the sails of the English appeared, were surrounded by French troops almost before they had had time to strike a blow. This struck such terror into them that they offered to surrender at discretion. An impulse of devotion, no isolated instance in the history of the Peninsula, led the actual slayers of the French to offer to give themselves up; seeking in this way to save the town, for from the General's reputation for cruelty it was feared that he would give Menda over to the flames, and put the whole population to the sword.

General G—— took their offer, stipulating that every soul in the castle from the lowest servant to the Marquis should likewise be given up to him. These terms being accepted, the General promised to spare the lives of the rest of the townsmen, and to prohibit his soldiers from pillaging or setting fire to the town. A heavy contribution was levied, and the wealthiest inhabitants were taken as hostages to guarantee payment within twenty-four hours.

The General took every necessary precaution for the safety of his troops, provided for the defense of the place, and refused to billet his men in the houses of the town. After they had bivouacked, he went up to the castle and entered it as a conqueror. The whole family of Légañès and their household were gagged, shut up in the great ballroom, and closely watched.

The staff was established in an adjoining gallery, where the General forthwith held a council as to the best means of preventing the landing of the English. An aide-de-camp was dispatched to Marshal Ney, orders were issued to plant batteries along the coast, and then the General and his staff turned their attention to their prisoners. The two hundred Spaniards given up by the townsfolk were shot down then and there upon the terrace. And after this military execution, the General gave orders to erect gibbets to the number of the prisoners in the ballroom in the same place, and to send for the hangman out of the town. Victor took advantage of the interval before dinner to pay a visit to the prisoners. He soon came back to the General.

"I am come in haste," he faltered out, "to ask a favor."

"*You!*" exclaimed the General, with bitter irony in his tones.

"Alas!" answered Victor, "it is a sorry favor. The Marquis has seen them erecting the gallows, and hopes that you will commute the punishment for his family; he entreats you to have the nobles beheaded."

"Granted," said the General.

"He further asks that they may be allowed the consolations of religion, and that they may be unbound; they give you their word that they will not attempt to escape."

"That I permit," said the General, "but you are answerable for them."

"The old noble offers you all that he has if you will pardon his youngest son."

"Really!" cried the Commander. "His property is forfeit already to King Joseph." He paused; a contemptuous thought set wrinkles in his forehead, as he added, "I will do better than they ask. I understand what he means by that last request of his. Very good. Let him hand down his name to posterity; but whenever it is mentioned, all Spain shall remember his treason and its punishment! I will give the fortune and his life to any of the sons who will do the executioner's office. . . . There, don't talk any more about them to me."

Dinner was ready. The officers sat down to satisfy an appetite whetted by hunger. Only one among them was absent from the table—that one was Victor Marchand. After long hesitation, he went to the ballroom, and heard the last sighs of the proud house of Légañès. He looked sadly at the scene before him.

Only last night, in this very room, he had seen their faces whirled past him in the waltz, and he shuddered to think that those girlish heads with those of the three young brothers must fall in a brief space by the executioner's sword. There sat the father and mother, their three sons and two daughters, perfectly motionless, bound to their gilded chairs. Eight serving men stood with their hands tied behind them.

These fifteen prisoners, under sentence of death, exchanged grave glances; it was difficult to read the thoughts that filled them from their eyes, but profound resignation and regret that their enterprise should have failed so completely was written on more than one brow.

The impassive soldiers who guarded them respected the grief of their bitter enemies. A gleam of curiosity lighted up all faces when Victor came in. He gave orders that the condemned prisoners should be unbound, and himself unfastened the cords that held Clara a prisoner. She smiled mournfully at him. The officer could not refrain from lightly touching the young girl's arm; he could not help admiring her dark hair, her slender waist. She was a true daughter of Spain, with a Spanish complexion, a Spaniard's eyes, blacker than the raven's wing beneath their long, curving lashes.

"Did you succeed?" she asked, with a mournful smile, in which a certain girlish charm still lingered.

Victor could not repress a groan. He looked from the faces of the three brothers to Clara, and again at the three young Spaniards.

The first, the oldest of the family, was a man of thirty. He was short, and somewhat ill-made; he looked haughty and proud, but a certain distinction was not lacking in his bearing, and he was apparently no stranger to the delicacy of feeling for which in olden times the chivalry of Spain was famous. His name was Juanito.

The second son, Felipe, was about twenty years of age; he was like his sister Clara; and the youngest was a child of eight. In the features of the little Manuel a painter would have discerned something of that Roman steadfastness which David has given to the children's faces in his Republican genre pictures. The old Marquis, with his white hair, might have come down from some canvas of Murillo's.

Victor threw back his head in despair after this survey; how should one of these accept the General's offer! Nevertheless he ventured to intrust it to Clara. A shudder ran through the Spanish girl, but she recovered herself almost instantly, and knelt before her father.

"Father," she said, "bid Juanito swear to obey the commands that you shall give him, and we shall be content."

The Marquesa trembled with hope, but as she leaned towards her husband and learned Clara's hideous secret, the mother fainted away. Juanito understood it all, and leaped up like a caged lion. Victor took it upon himself to dismiss the soldiers, after receiving an assurance of entire submission from the Marquis. The servants were led away and given over to the hangman and their fate.

When only Victor remained on guard in the room, the old Marqués de Légañès rose to his feet.

"Juanito," he said. For an answer Juanito bowed his head in a way that meant refusal; he sank down into his chair, and fixed tearless eyes upon his father and mother in an intolerable gaze. Clara went over to him and sat on his knee; she put her arms about him, and pressed kisses on his eyelids, saying gaily—

"Dear Juanito, if you but knew how sweet death at your hands will be to me! I shall not be compelled to submit to the hateful touch of the hangman's fingers. You will snatch me away from the evils to come and . . . Dear, kind Juanito, you could not bear the thought of my belonging to anyone—well, then?"

The velvet eyes gave Victor a burning glance; she seemed to try to awaken in Juanito's heart his hatred for the French.

"Take courage," said his brother Felipe, "or our well-nigh royal line will be extinct."

Suddenly Clara sprang to her feet. The group round Juanito fell back, and the son who had rebelled with such good reason was confronted with his aged father.

"Juanito, I command you!" said the Marquis solemnly.

The young Count gave no sign, and his father fell on his knees; Clara, Manuel, and Felipe unconsciously followed his example, stretching out suppliant hands to him who must save their family from oblivion.

"Can it be that you lack the fortitude and true sensibility of a Spaniard, my son? Do you mean to keep me on my knees? What right have you to think of your own life and of your own sufferings? Is this my son, madame?" the old Marquis added, turning to his wife.

"He will consent to it," cried the mother in agony of soul.

Mariquita, the second daughter, knelt, with her slender clinging arms about her mother; the hot tears fell from her eyes, and her little brother Manuel upbraided her for weeping. Just at that moment the castle chaplain came in; the whole family surrounded him and led him up to Juanito. Victor felt that he could endure the sight no longer, and with a sign to Clara he hurried from the room.

An hour later, a hundred of the principal citizens of Menda were summoned to the terrace by the General's orders to witness the execution of the family of Légañès. A detachment had been told to keep order among the Spanish townsfolk, who were marshaled beneath the gallows whereon the Marquis's servants hung; the feet of those martyrs of their cause all but touched the citizens' heads.

Thirty paces away stood the block; the blade of a scimitar glittered upon it, and the executioner stood by in case Juanito should refuse at the last.

The deepest silence prevailed, but before long it was broken by the sound of many footsteps, the measured tramp of a picket of soldiers, and the jingling of their weapons. Mingled with these came other noises—loud talk and laughter from the dinner-table where the officers were sitting.

All eyes turned to the castle, and beheld the family of nobles coming forth, with incredible composure, to their death. Every brow was serene and calm. One alone among them, haggard and overcome, leant on the arm of the priest, who poured forth all the consolations of religion for the one man who was condemned to live. Then the executioner, like the spectators, knew that Juanito had consented to perform his office for a day.

The old Marquis and his wife, Clara and Mariquita, and their two brothers knelt a few paces from the fatal spot. Juanito reached it, guided by the priest. As he stood at the block the executioner plucked him by the sleeve, and took him aside, probably to give him certain instructions. The confessor so placed the victims that they could not witness the executions, but one and all stood upright and fearless.

Clara sprang to her brother's side before the others.

"Juanito," she said to him, "be merciful to my lack of courage. Take me first!"

As she spoke, the footsteps of a man running at full speed echoed from the walls, and Victor appeared upon the scene. Clara was kneeling before the block; her white neck seemed to appeal to the blade to fall. The officer turned faint, but he found strength to rush to her side.

"The General grants you your life if you will consent to marry me," he murmured.

The Spanish girl gave the officer a glance full of proud disdain.

"Now, Juanito!" she said in her deep-toned voice.

Her head fell at Victor's feet. A shudder ran through the Marquesa de Léganès, a convulsive tremor that she could not control, but she gave no other sign of her anguish.

"Is this where I ought to be, dear Juanito? Is it all right?" little Manuel asked his brother. . . .

"Oh, Mariquita, you are weeping!" Juanito said when his sister came.

"Yes," said the girl; "I am thinking of you, poor Juanito; how unhappy you will be when we are gone."

Then the Marquis's tall figure approached. He looked at the block where his children's blood had been shed, turned to the mute and motionless crowd, and said in a loud voice as he stretched out his hands to Juanito—

"Spaniards! I give my son a father's blessing. Now, *Marquis,* strike 'without fear'; thou art 'without reproach.' "

But when his mother came near, leaning on the confessor's arm—"She fed me from her breast!" Juanito cried in tones that drew a cry of horror from the crowd. The uproarious mirth of the officers over their wine died away before that terrible cry. The Marquesa knew that Juanito's courage was exhausted; at one bound she sprang to the balustrade, leapt forth, and was dashed to death on the rock below. A cry of admiration broke from the spectators. Juanito swooned.

"General," said an officer, half drunk by this time, "Marchand has just been telling me something about this execution; I will wager that it was not by your orders—"

"Are you forgetting, gentlemen, that in a month's time five hundred families in France will be in mourning, and that we are still in Spain?" cried General G——. "Do you want us to leave our bones here?"

But not a man at the table, not even a subaltern, dared to empty his glass after that speech.

In spite of the respect in which all men hold the Marqués de Légañès, in spite of the title of *El Verdugo* (the executioner) conferred upon him as a patent of nobility by the King of Spain, the great noble is consumed by a gnawing grief. He lives a retired life, and seldom appears in public. The burden of his heroic crime weighs heavily upon him, and he seems to wait impatiently till the birth of a second son shall release him, and he may go to join the Shades that never cease to haunt him.

TARZAN'S FIRST LOVE

Edgar Rice Burroughs

Teeka, stretched at luxurious ease in the shade of the tropical forest, presented, unquestionably, a most alluring picture of young, feminine loveliness. Or at least so thought Tarzan of the Apes, who squatted upon a low-swinging branch in a near-by tree and looked down upon her.

Just to have seen him there, lolling upon the swaying bough of the jungle-forest giant, his brown skin mottled by the brilliant equatorial sunlight which percolated through the leafy canopy of green above him, his clean-limbed body relaxed in graceful ease, his shapely head partly turned in contemplative absorption and his intelligent, gray eyes dreamily devouring the object of their devotion, you would have thought him the reincarnation of some demigod of old.

You would not have guessed that in infancy he had suckled at the breast of a hideous, hairy she-ape, nor that in all his conscious past since his parents had passed away in the little cabin by the land-locked harbor at the jungles verge, he had known no other associates than the sullen bulls and the snarling cows of the tribe of Kerchak, the great ape.

Nor, could you have read the thoughts which passed through that active, healthy brain, the longings and desires and aspirations which the sight of Teeka inspired, would you have been any more inclined to give credence to the reality of the origin of the ape-man. For, from his thoughts alone, you could never have gleaned the truth—that he had been born to a gentle English lady or that his sire had been an English nobleman of time-honored lineage.

Lost to Tarzan of the Apes was the truth of his origin. That he was John Clayton, Lord Greystoke, with a seat in the House of Lords, he did not know, nor, knowing, would have understood.

Yes, Teeka was indeed beautiful!

Of course Kala had been beautiful—one's mother is always that—but

Teeka was beautiful in a way all her own, an indescribable sort of way which Tarzan was just beginning to sense in a rather vague and hazy manner.

For years had Tarzan and Teeka been play-fellows, and Teeka still continued to be playful while the young bulls of her own age were rapidly becoming surly and morose. Tarzan, if he gave the matter much thought at all, probably reasoned that his growing attachment for the young female could be easily accounted for by the fact that of the former playmates she and he alone retained any desire to frolic as of old.

But today, as he sat gazing upon her, he found himself noting the beauties of Teeka's form and features—something he never had done before, since none of them had aught to do with Teeka's ability to race nimbly through the lower terraces of the forest in the primitive games of tag and hide-and-go-seek which Tarzan's fertile brain evolved.

Tarzan scratched his head, running his fingers deep into the shock of black hair which framed his shapely, boyish face—he scratched his head and sighed. Teeka's new-found beauty became as suddenly his despair. He envied her the handsome coat of hair which covered her body. His own smooth, brown hide he hated with a hatred born of disgust and contempt. Years back he had harbored a hope that some day he, too, would be clothed in hair as were all his brothers and sisters; but of late he had been forced to abandon the delectable dream.

Then there were Teeka's great teeth, not so large as the males, of course, but still mighty, handsome things by comparison with Tarzan's feeble white ones. And her beetling brows, and broad, flat nose, and her mouth! Tarzan had often practiced making his mouth into a little round circle and then puffing out his cheeks while he winked his eyes rapidly; but he felt that he could never do it in the same cute and irresistible way in which Teeka did it.

And as he watched her that afternoon, and wondered, a young bull ape who had been lazily foraging for food beneath the damp, matted carpet of decaying vegetation at the roots of a near-by tree lumbered awkwardly in Teeka's direction. The other apes of the tribe of Kerchak moved listlessly about or lolled restfully in the midday heat of the equatorial jungle. From time to time one or another of them had passed close to Teeka, and Tarzan had been uninterested. Why was it then that his brows contracted and his muscles tensed as he saw Taug pause beside the young she and then squat down close to her?

Tarzan always had liked Taug. Since childhood they had romped together. Side by side they had squatted near the water, their quick, strong fingers ready to leap forth and seize Pisah, the fish, should that wary denizen of the cool depths dart surfaceward to the lure of the insects Tarzan tossed upon the face of the pool.

Together they had baited Tublat and teased Numa, the lion. Why, then, should Tarzan feel the rise of the short hairs at the nape of his neck merely because Taug sat close to Teeka?

It is true that Taug was no longer the frolicsome ape of yesterday. When his snarling-muscles bared his giant fangs no one could longer imagine that Taug was in as playful a mood as when he and Tarzan had rolled upon the turf in mimic battle. The Taug of today was a huge, sullen bull ape, somber and forbidding. Yet he and Tarzan never had quarreled.

For a few minutes the young ape-man watched Taug press closer to Teeka. He saw the rough caress of the huge paw as it stroked the sleek shoulder of the she, and then Tarzan of the Apes slipped catlike to the ground and approached the two.

As he came his upper lip curled into a snarl, exposing his fighting fangs, and a deep growl rumbled from his cavernous chest. Taug looked up, batting his blood-shot eyes. Teeka half raised herself and looked at Tarzan. Did she guess the cause of his perturbation? Who may say? At any rate, she was feminine, and so she reached up and scratched Taug behind one of his small, flat ears.

Tarzan saw, and in the instant that he saw, Teeka was no longer the little playmate of an hour ago; instead she was a wondrous thing—the most wondrous in the world—and a possession for which Tarzan would fight to the death against Taug or any other who dared question his right of proprietorship.

Stooped, his muscles rigid and one great shoulder turned toward the young bull, Tarzan of the Apes sidled nearer and nearer. His face was partly averted, but his keen gray eyes never left those of Taug, and as he came, his growls increased in depth and volume.

Taug rose upon his short legs, bristling. His fighting fangs were bared. He, too, sidled, stiff-legged, and growled.

"Teeka is Tarzan's," said the ape-man, in the low gutturals of the great anthropoids.

"Teeka is Taug's," replied the bull ape.

Thaka and Numgo and Gunto, disturbed by the growlings of the two young bulls, looked up half apathetic, half interested. They were sleepy, but they sensed a fight. It would break the monotony of the humdrum jungle life they led.

Coiled about his shoulders was Tarzan's long grass rope, in his hand was the hunting knife of the long-dead father he had never known. In Taug's little brain lay a great respect for the shiny bit of sharp metal which the ape-boy knew so well how to use. With it had he slain Tublat, his fierce foster father, and Bolgani, the gorilla. Taug knew these things, and so he came warily, circling about Tarzan in search of an opening. The latter, made

cautious because of his lesser bulk and the inferiority of his natural armament, followed similar tactics.

For a time it seemed that the altercation would follow the way of the
majority of such differences between members of the tribe and that one of
them would finally lose interest and wander off to prosecute some other
line of endeavor. Such might have been the end of it had the *casus belli*
been other than it was; but Teeka was flattered at the attention that was
being drawn to her and by the fact that these two young bulls were contemplating battle on her account. Such a thing never before had occurred in
Teeka's brief life. She had seen other bulls battling for other and older shes,
and in the depth of her wild little heart she had longed for the day when the
jungle grasses would be reddened with the blood of mortal combat for her
fair sake.

So now she squatted upon her haunches and insulted both her admirers
impartially. She hurled taunts at them for their cowardice, and called them
vile names, such as Histah, the snake, and Dango, the hyena. She threatened to call Mumga to chastise them with a stick—Mumga, who was so old
that she could no longer climb and so toothless that she was forced to
confine her diet almost exclusively to bananas and grubworms.

The apes who were watching heard and laughed. Taug was infuriated.
He made a sudden lunge for Tarzan, but the ape-boy leaped nimbly to one
side, eluding him, and with the quickness of a cat wheeled and leaped back
again to close quarters. His hunting knife was raised above his head as he
came in, and he aimed a vicious blow at Taug's neck. The ape wheeled to
dodge the weapon so that the keen blade struck him but a glancing blow
upon the shoulder.

The spurt of red blood brought a shrill cry of delight from Teeka. Ah,
but this was something worth while! She glanced about to see if others had
witnessed this evidence of her popularity. Helen of Troy was never one whit
more proud than was Teeka at that moment.

If Teeka had not been so absorbed in her own vaingloriousness she
might have noted the rustling of leaves in the tree above her—a rustling
which was not caused by any movement of the wind, since there was no
wind. And had she looked up she might have seen a sleek body crouching
almost directly over her and wicked yellow eyes glaring hungrily down
upon her, but Teeka did not look up.

With his wound Taug had backed off growling horribly. Tarzan had
followed him, screaming insults at him, and menacing him with his bran-
dishing blade. Teeka moved from beneath the tree in an effort to keep close
to the duelists.

The branch above Teeka bent and swayed a trifle with the movement of
the body of the watcher stretched along it. Taug had halted now and was

preparing to make a new stand. His lips were flecked with foam, and saliva drooled from his jowls. He stood with head lowered and arms outstretched, preparing for a sudden charge to close quarters. Could he but lay his mighty hands upon that soft, brown skin the battle would be his. Taug considered Tarzan's manner of fighting unfair. He would not close. Instead, he leaped nimbly just beyond the reach of Taug's muscular fingers.

The ape-boy had as yet never come to a real trial of strength with a bull ape, other than in play, and so he was not at all sure that it would be safe to put his muscles to the test in a life and death struggle. Not that he was afraid, for Tarzan knew nothing of fear. The instinct of self-preservation gave him caution—that was all. He took risks only when it seemed necessary, and then he would hesitate at nothing.

His own method of fighting seemed best fitted to his build and to his armament. His teeth, while strong and sharp, were, as weapons of offense, pitifully inadequate by comparison with the mighty fighting fangs of the anthropoids. By dancing about, just out of reach of an antagonist, Tarzan could do infinite injury with his long, sharp hunting knife, and at the same time escape many of the painful and dangerous wounds which would be sure to follow his falling into the clutches of a bull ape.

And so Taug charged and bellowed like a bull, and Tarzan of the Apes danced lightly to this side and that, hurling jungle billingsgate at his foe, the while he nicked him now and again with his knife.

There were lulls in the fighting when the two would stand panting for breath, facing each other, mustering their wits and their forces for a new onslaught. It was during a pause such as this that Taug chanced to let his eyes rove beyond his foe-man. Instantly the entire aspect of the ape altered. Rage left his countenance to be supplanted by an expression of fear.

With a cry that every ape there recognized, Taug turned and fled. No need to question him—his warning proclaimed the near presence of their ancient enemy.

Tarzan started to seek safety, as did the other members of the tribe, and as he did so he heard a panther's scream mingled with the frightened cry of a she-ape. Taug heard, too; but he did not pause in his flight.

With the ape-boy, however, it was different. He looked back to see if any member of the tribe was close pressed by the beast of prey, and the sight that met his eyes filled them with an expression of horror.

Teeka it was who cried out in terror as she fled across a little clearing toward the trees upon the opposite side, for after her leaped Sheeta, the panther, in easy, graceful bounds. Sheeta appeared to be in no hurry. His meat was assured, since even though the ape reached the trees ahead of him she could not climb beyond his clutches before he could be upon her.

Tarzan saw that Teeka must die. He cried to Taug and the other bulls to hasten to Teeka's assistance, and at the same time he ran toward the pursuing beast, taking down his rope as he came. Tarzan knew that once the great bulls were aroused none of the jungle, not even Numa, the lion, was anxious to measure fangs with them, and that if all those of the tribe who chanced to be present today would charge, Sheeta, the great cat, would doubtless turn tail and run for his life.

Taug heard, as did the others, but no one came to Tarzan's assistance or Teeka's rescue, and Sheeta was rapidly closing up the distance between himself and his prey.

The ape-boy, leaping after the panther, cried aloud to the beast in an effort to turn it from Teeka or otherwise distract its attention until the she-ape could gain the safety of the higher branches where Sheeta dare not go. He called the panther every opprobrious name that fell to his tongue. He dared him to stop and do battle with him; but Sheeta only loped on after the luscious tidbit now almost within his reach.

Tarzan was not far behind and he was gaining, but the distance was so short that he scarce hoped to overhaul the carnivore before it had felled Teeka. In his right hand the boy swung his grass rope above his head as he ran. He hated to chance a miss, for the distance was much greater than he ever had cast before except in practice. It was the full length of his grass rope which separated him from Sheeta, and yet there was no other thing to do. He could not reach the brute's side before it overhauled Teeka. He must chance a throw.

And just as Teeka sprang for the lower limb of a great tree, and Sheeta rose behind her in a long, sinuous leap, the coils of the ape-boy's grass rope shot swiftly through the air, straightening into a long thin line as the open noose hovered for an instant above the savage head and the snarling jaws. Then it settled—clean and true about the tawny neck it settled, and Tarzan, with a quick twist of his rope-hand, drew the noose taut, bracing himself for the shock when Sheeta should have taken up the slack.

Just short of Teeka's glossy rump the cruel talons raked the air as the rope tightened and Sheeta was brought to a sudden stop—a stop that snapped the big beast over upon his back. Instantly Sheeta was up—with glaring eyes, and lashing tail, and gaping jaws, from which issued hideous cries of rage and disappointment.

He saw the ape-boy, the cause of his discomfiture, scarce forty feet before him, and Sheeta charged.

Teeka was safe now; Tarzan saw to that by a quick glance into the tree whose safety she had gained not an instant too soon, and Sheeta was charging. It were useless to risk his life in idle and unequal combat from which no good could come; but could he escape a battle with the enraged cat? And if he was forced to fight, what chance had he to survive? Tarzan was constrained to admit that his position was aught but a desirable one. The trees were too far to hope to reach in time to elude the cat. Tarzan could but stand facing that hideous charge. In his right hand he grasped his hunting knife—a puny, futile thing indeed by comparison with the great rows of mighty teeth which lined Sheeta's powerful jaws, and the sharp talons encased within his padded paws; yet the young Lord Greystoke faced it with the same courageous resignation with which some fearless ancestor went down to defeat and death on Senlac Hill by Hastings.

From safety points in the trees the great apes watched, screaming hatred at Sheeta and advice at Tarzan, for the progenitors of man have, naturally, many human traits. Teeka was frightened. She screamed at the bulls to hasten to Tarzan's assistance; but the bulls were otherwise engaged—principally in giving advice and making faces. Anyway, Tarzan was not a real Mangani, so why should they risk their lives in an effort to protect him?

And now Sheeta was almost upon the lithe, naked body, and—the body was not there. Quick as was the great cat, the ape-boy was quicker. He leaped to one side almost as the panther's talons were closing upon him, and as Sheeta went hurtling to the ground beyond, Tarzan was racing for the safety of the nearest tree.

The panther recovered himself almost immediately and, wheeling, tore after his prey, the ape-boy's rope dragging along the ground behind him. In doubling back after Tarzan, Sheeta had passed around a low bush. It was a mere nothing in the path of any jungle creature of the size and weight of Sheeta—provided it had no trailing rope dangling behind. But Sheeta was handicapped by such a rope, and as he leaped once again after Tarzan of the Apes the rope encircled the small bush, became tangled in it and brought the panther to a sudden stop. An instant later Tarzan was safe among the higher branches of a small tree into which Sheeta could not follow him.

Here he perched, hurling twigs and epithets at the raging feline beneath him. The other members of the tribe now took up the bombardment, using such hard-shelled fruits and dead branches as came within their reach, until Sheeta, goaded to frenzy and snapping at the grass rope, finally succeeded in severing its strands. For a moment the panther stood glaring first at one of his tormentors and then at another, until, with a final scream of rage, he turned and slunk off into the tangled mazes of the jungle.

A half hour later the tribe was again upon the ground, feeding as though naught had occurred to interrupt the somber dullness of their lives. Tarzan had recovered the greater part of his rope and was busy fashioning a new noose, while Teeka squatted close beside him, in evident token that her choice was made.

Taug eyed them sullenly. Once when he came close, Teeka bared her fangs and growled at him, and Tarzan showed his canines in an ugly snarl;

but Taug did not provoke a quarrel. He seemed to accept after the manner of his kind the decision of the she as an indication that he had been vanquished in his battle for her favors.

Later in the day, his rope repaired, Tarzan took to the trees in search of game. More than his fellows he required meat, and so, while they were satisfied with fruits and herbs and beetles, which could be discovered without much effort upon their part, Tarzan spent considerable time hunting the game animals whose flesh alone satisfied the cravings of his stomach and furnished sustenance and strength to the mighty thews which, day by day, were building beneath the soft, smooth texture of his brown hide.

Taug saw him depart, and then, quite casually, the big beast hunted closer and closer to Teeka in his search for food. At last he was within a few feet of her, and when he shot a covert glance at her he saw that she was appraising him and that there was no evidence of anger upon her face.

Taug expanded his great chest and rolled about on his short legs, making strange growlings in his throat. He raised his lips, baring his fangs. My, but what great, beautiful fangs he had! Teeka could not but notice them. She also let her eyes rest in admiration upon Taug's beetling brows and his short, powerful neck. What a beautiful creature he was indeed!

Taug, flattered by the unconcealed admiration in her eyes, strutted about, as proud and as vain as a peacock. Presently he began to inventory his assets, mentally, and shortly he found himself comparing them with those of his rival.

Taug grunted, for there was no comparison. How could one compare his beautiful coat with the smooth and naked hideousness of Tarzan's bare hide? Who could see beauty in the stingy nose of the Tarmangani after looking at Taug's broad nostrils? And Tarzan's eyes! Hideous things, showing white about them, and entirely unrimmed with red. Taug knew that his own blood-shot eyes were beautiful, for he had seen them reflected in the glassy surface of many a drinking pool.

The bull drew nearer to Teeka, finally squatting close against her. When Tarzan returned from his hunting a short time later it was to see Teeka contentedly scratching the back of his rival.

Tarzan was disgusted. Neither Taug nor Teeka saw him as he swung through the trees into the glade. He paused a moment, looking at them; then, with a sorrowful grimace, he turned and faded away into the labyrinth of leafy boughs and festooned moss out of which he had come.

Tarzan wished to be as far away from the cause of his heartache as he could. He was suffering the first pangs of blighted love, and he didn't quite know what was the matter with him. He thought that he was angry with Taug, and so he couldn't understand why it was that he had run away instead of rushing into mortal combat with the destroyer of his happiness.

He also thought that he was angry with Teeka, yet a vision of her many beauties persisted in haunting him, so that he could only see her in the light of love as the most desirable thing in the world.

The ape-boy craved affection. From babyhood until the time of her death, when the poisoned arrow of Kulonga had pierced her savage heart, Kala had represented to the English boy the sole object of love which he had known.

In her wild, fierce way Kala had loved her adopted son, and Tarzan had returned that love, though the outward demonstrations of it were no greater than might have been expected from any other beast of the jungle. It was not until he was bereft of her that the boy realized how deep had been his attachment for his mother, for as such he looked upon her.

In Teeka he had seen within the past few hours a substitute for Kala—someone to fight for and to hunt for—someone to caress; but now his dream was shattered. Something hurt within his breast. He placed his hand over his heart and wondered what had happened to him. Vaguely he attributed his pain to Teeka. The more he thought of Teeka as he had last seen her, caressing Taug, the more the thing within his breast hurt him.

Tarzan shook his head and growled; then on and on through the jungle he swung, and the farther he traveled and the more he thought upon his wrongs, the nearer he approached becoming an irreclaimable misogynist.

Two days later he was still hunting alone—very morose and very unhappy; but he was determined never to return to the tribe. He could not bear the thought of seeing Taug and Teeka always together. As he swung upon a great limb Numa, the lion, and Sabor, the lioness, passed beneath him, side by side, and Sabor leaned against the lion and bit playfully at his cheek. It was a half caress. Tarzan sighed and hurled a nut at them.

Later he came upon several of Mbonga's black warriors. He was upon the point of dropping his noose about the neck of one of them, who was a little distance from his companions, when he became interested in the thing which occupied the savages. They were building a cage in the trail and covering it with leafy branches. When they had completed their work the structure was scarcely visible.

Tarzan wondered what the purpose of the thing might be, and why, when they had built it, they turned away and started back along the trail in the direction of their village.

It had been some time since Tarzan had visited the blacks and looked down from the shelter of the great trees which overhung their palisade upon the activities of his enemies, from among whom had come the slayer of Kala.

Although he hated them, Tarzan derived considerable entertainment in watching them at their daily life within the village, and especially at their dances, when the fires glared against their naked bodies as they leaped and turned and twisted in mimic warfare. It was rather in the hope of witnessing something of the kind that he now followed the warriors back toward their village, but in this he was disappointed, for there was no dance that night.

Instead, from the safe concealment of his tree, Tarzan saw little groups seated about tiny fires discussing the events of the day, and in the darker corners of the village he descried isolated couples talking and laughing together, and always one of each couple was a young man and the other a young woman.

Tarzan cocked his head upon one side and thought, and before he went to sleep that night, curled in the crotch of the great tree above the village, Teeka filled his mind, and afterward she filled his dreams—she and the young black men laughing and talking with the young black women.

Taug, hunting alone, had wandered some distance from the balance of the tribe. He was making his way slowly along an elephant path when he discovered that it was blocked with undergrowth. Now Taug, come into maturity, was an evil-natured brute of an exceeding short temper. When something thwarted him, his sole idea was to overcome it by brute strength and ferocity, and so now when he found his way blocked, he tore angrily into the leafy screen and an instant later found himself within a strange lair, his progress effectually blocked, notwithstanding his most violent efforts to forge ahead.

Biting and striking at the barrier, Taug finally worked himself into a frightful rage, but all to no avail; and at last he became convinced that he must turn back. But when he would have done so, what was his chagrin to discover that another barrier had dropped behind him while he fought to break down the one before him! Taug was trapped. Until exhaustion overcame him he fought frantically for his freedom; but all for naught.

In the morning a party of blacks set out from the village of Mbonga in the direction of the trap they had constructed the previous day, while among the branches of the trees above them hovered a naked young giant filled with the curiosity of the wild things. Manu, the monkey, chattered and scolded as Tarzan passed, and though he was not afraid of the familiar figure of the ape-boy, he hugged closer to him the little brown body of his life's companion. Tarzan laughed as he saw it; but the laugh was followed by a sudden clouding of his face and a deep sigh.

A little farther on, a gaily feathered bird strutted about before the admiring eyes of his somber-hued mate. It seemed to Tarzan that everything in the jungle was combining to remind him that he had lost Teeka; yet every day of his life he had seen these same things and thought nothing of them.

When the blacks reached the trap, Taug set up a great commotion. Seizing the bars of his prison, he shook them frantically, and all the while he roared and growled terrifically. The blacks were elated, for while they had not built their trap for this hairy tree man, they were delighted with their catch.

Tarzan pricked up his ears when he heard the voice of a great ape and, circling quickly until he was down wind from the trap, he sniffed at the air in search of the scent spoor of the prisoner. Nor was it long before there came to those delicate nostrils the familiar odor that told Tarzan the identity of the captive as unerringly as though he had looked upon Taug with his eyes. Yes, it was Taug, and he was alone.

Tarzan grinned as he approached to discover what the blacks would do to their prisoner. Doubtless they would slay him at once. Again Tarzan grinned. Now he could have Teeka for his own, with none to dispute his right to her. As he watched, he saw the black warriors strip the screen from about the cage, fasten ropes to it and drag it away along the trail in the direction of their village.

Tarzan watched until his rival passed out of sight, still beating upon the bars of his prison and growling out his anger and his threats. Then the ape-boy turned and swung rapidly off in search of the tribe, and Teeka.

Once, upon the journey, he surprised Sheeta and his family in a little overgrown clearing. The great cat lay stretched upon the ground, while his mate, one paw across her lord's savage face, licked at the soft white fur at his throat.

Tarzan increased his speed then until he fairly flew through the forest, nor was it long before he came upon the tribe. He saw them before they saw him, for of all the jungle creatures, none passed more quietly than Tarzan of the Apes. He saw Kamma and her mate feeding side by side, their hairy bodies rubbing against each other. And he saw Teeka feeding by herself. Not for long would she feed thus in loneliness, thought Tarzan, as with a bound he landed amongst them.

There was a startled rush and a chorus of angry and frightened snarls, for Tarzan had surprised them; but there was more, too, than mere nervous shock to account for the bristling neck hair which remained standing long after the apes had discovered the identity of the newcomer.

Tarzan noticed this as he had noticed it many times in the past—that always his sudden coming among them left them nervous and unstrung for a considerable time, and that they one and all found it necessary to satisfy themselves that he was indeed Tarzan by smelling about him a half dozen or more times before they calmed down.

Pushing through them, he made his way toward Teeka; but as he approached her the ape drew away.

"Teeka," he said, "it is Tarzan. You belong to Tarzan. I have come for you."

The ape drew closer, looking him over carefully. Finally she sniffed at him, as though to make assurance doubly sure.

"Where is Taug?" she asked.

"The Gomangani have him," replied Tarzan. "They will kill him."

In the eyes of the she, Tarzan saw a wistful expression and a troubled look of sorrow as he told her of Taug's fate; but she came quite close and snuggled against him, and Tarzan, Lord Greystoke, put his arm about her.

As he did so he noticed, with a start, the strange incongruity of that smooth, brown arm against the black and hairy coat of his lady-love. He recalled the paw of Sheeta's mate across Sheeta's face—no incongruity there. He thought of little Manu hugging his she, and how the one seemed to belong to the other. Even the proud male bird, with his gay plumage, bore a close resemblance to his quieter spouse, while Numa, but for his shaggy mane, was almost a counterpart of Sabor, the lioness. The males and the females differed, it was true; but not with such differences as existed between Tarzan and Teeka.

Tarzan was puzzled. There was something wrong. His arm dropped from the shoulder of Teeka. Very slowly he drew away from her. She looked at him with her head cocked upon one side. Tarzan rose to his full height and beat upon his breast with his fists. He raised his head toward the heavens and opened his mouth. From the depths of his lungs rose the fierce, weird challenge of the victorious bull ape. The tribe turned curiously to eye him. He had killed nothing, nor was there any antagonist to be goaded to madness by the savage scream. No, there was no excuse for it, and they turned back to their feeding, but with an eye upon the ape-man lest he be preparing to suddenly run amuck.

As they watched him they saw him swing into a nearby tree and disappear from sight. Then they forgot him, even Teeka.

Mbonga's black warriors, sweating beneath their strenuous task, and resting often, made slow progress toward their village. Always the savage beast in the primitive cage growled and roared when they moved him. He beat upon the bars and slavered at the mouth. His noise was hideous.

They had almost completed their journey and were making their final rest before forging ahead to gain the clearing in which lay their village. A few more minutes would have taken them out of the forest, and then, doubtless, the thing would not have happened which did happen.

A silent figure moved through the trees above them. Keen eyes inspected the cage and counted the number of warriors. An alert and daring brain figured upon the chances of success when a certain plan should be put to the test.

Tarzan watched the blacks lolling in the shade. They were exhausted. Already several of them slept. He crept closer, pausing just above them. Not a leaf rustled before his stealthy advance. He waited in the infinite patience of the beast of prey. Presently but two of the warriors remained awake, and one of these was dozing.

Tarzan of the Apes gathered himself, and as he did so the black who did not sleep arose and passed around to the rear of the cage. The ape-boy followed just above his head. Taug was eyeing the warrior and emitting low growls. Tarzan feared that the anthropoid would awaken the sleepers.

In a whisper which was inaudible to the ears of the Negro, Tarzan whispered Taug's name, cautioning the ape to silence, and Taug's growling ceased.

The black approached the rear of the cage and examined the fastenings of the door, and as he stood there the beast above him launched itself from the tree full upon his back. Steel fingers circled his throat, choking the cry which sprang to the lips of the terrified man. Strong teeth fastened themselves in his shoulder, and powerful legs wound themselves about his torso.

The black in a frenzy of terror tried to dislodge the silent thing which clung to him. He threw himself to the ground and rolled about; but still those mighty fingers closed more and more tightly their deadly grip.

The man's mouth gaped wide, his swollen tongue protruded, his eyes started from their sockets; but the relentless fingers only increased their pressure.

Taug was a silent witness of the struggle. In his fierce little brain he doubtless wondered what purpose prompted Tarzan to attack the black. Taug had not forgotten his recent battle with the ape-boy, nor the cause of it. Now he saw the form of the Gomangani suddenly go limp. There was a convulsive shiver and the man lay still.

Tarzan sprang from his prey and ran to the door of the cage. With nimble fingers he worked rapidly at the thongs which held the door in place. Taug could only watch—he could not help. Presently Tarzan pushed the thing up a couple of feet and Taug crawled out. The ape would have turned upon the sleeping blacks that he might wreak his pent vengeance; but Tarzan would not permit it.

Instead, the ape-boy dragged the body of the black within the cage and propped it against the side bars. Then he lowered the door and made fast the thongs as they had been before.

A happy smile lighted his features as he worked, for one of his principal diversions was the baiting of the blacks of Mbonga's village. He could imagine their terror when they awoke and found the dead body of their comrade fast in the cage where they had left the great ape safely secured but a few minutes before.

Tarzan and Taug took to the trees together, the shaggy coat of the fierce ape brushing the sleek skin of the English lordling as they passed through the primeval jungle side by side.

"Go back to Teeka," said Tarzan. "She is yours. Tarzan does not want her."

"Tarzan has found another she?" asked Taug.

The ape-boy shrugged.

"For the Gomangani there is another Gomangani," he said; "for Numa, the lion, there is Sabor, the lioness; for Sheeta there is a she of his own kind; for Bara, the deer; for Manu, the monkey; for all the beasts and the birds of the jungle is there a mate. Only for Tarzan of the Apes is there none. Taug is an ape. Teeka is an ape. Go back to Teeka. Tarzan is a man. He will go alone."

ACROSS
TIME & SPACE

FROST AND THUNDER

Randall Garrett

Ulglossen was dabbling in polydimensional energy flows again.
    Do not try to understand Ulglossen. Ulglossen's time was—is—will be—three million years after Homo sapiens sapiens *ruled Earth, and Ulglossen's species is no more to be understood by us than we could be understood by* Australopithecus.

To say, then, that Ulglossen built a "time machine" is as erroneous—and as truthful—as saying that a big industrial computer of the late 20th Century is a device for counting with pebbles.

Doing polydimensional vector analysis mentally was, for Ulglossen, too simple and automatic to be called child's play. Actually constructing the mechanism was somewhat more difficult, but Ulglossen went about it with the same toilsome joy that a racing buff goes about rebuilding his Ferrari. When it was finished, Ulglossen viewed it with the equivalent of pride. In doing the mental math, Ulglossen had rounded off at the nineteenth decimal place, for no greater accuracy than that was needed. But, as a result, Ulglossen's "machine" caused slight eddy currents in the time flow as it passed. The resulting effect was much the same as that of an automobile going down a freeway and passing a wadded ball of paper. The paper is picked up and carried a few yards down the freeway before it falls out of the eddy currents and is dropped again.

Ulglossen was not unaware of that fact; it was simply that Ulglossen ignored it.

The device, you see, was merely a side effect of Ulglossen's real work, which was the study of the attenuation of the universal gravitational constant over a period of millions of millenia. Ulglossen happened to be on Earth, and had some experiments to perform in the very early pre-Cambrian. Ulglossen went back to do so.

I'll try to tell this the best I can. I don't expect you to believe it because, in the first place, I haven't a shred of proof, and, in the second place, I wouldn't believe it myself if I hadn't actually experienced it.

Sure, I *might* have dreamed it. But it was too solid, too detailed, too logical, too *real* to have been a dream. So it happened, and I'm stuck with it.

It begins, I suppose, when I got the letter from Sten Örnfeld. I've known Sten for years. We've fought together in some pretty odd places, argued with each other about the damndest things, and once even quarreled over the same woman. (He won.) He's a good drinking buddy, and he'll back a friend in a pinch. What more do you want?

A few years back, Sten and I got interested in what was then the relatively new sport of combat pistol, down in southern California. It's a game that requires fast draw, fast shooting, fast reloading, and accuracy to make points. One of the rules is that you *must* use full-charge service cartridges. No half-charge wadcutters allowed.

We both enjoyed it.

Then, I didn't see Sten for some time. I didn't think much about it. Sten does a lot of traveling, but, basically, he's a Swede, and he has to go home every so often. I'm only half Swede, and I was born in the United States. Sweden is a lovely country, but it just isn't home to me.

Anyway, I got this letter addressed to me, Theodore Sorenson, with a Stockholm postmark. Sten, so he claimed, had introduced combat pistol shooting to Sweden, and had built a range on his property. He was holding a match in September, and would I come? There would be plenty of *akvavit*.

He hadn't needed to add that last, but it helped. I made plane reservations and other arrangements.

You would not believe how hard it is to get a handgun into Sweden legally. (I don't know how hard it would be to do it illegally; I've never tried.) Even though Sten Örnfeld had all kinds of connections in high places and had filed a declaration of intent or something, informing the government of his shooting match, and had gotten the government's permission, it was rough sledding. I had to produce all kinds of papers identifying the weapon, and papers showing that I had never been convicted of a felony, and on and on. Fortunately, Sten's letter had warned me about all that. Still, just filling out papers and signing my name must have used up a good liter of ink.

Eventually, they decided I could take my .45 Colt Commander into Sweden. Provided, of course, that I brought it back out again; I couldn't sell it, give it away, or, presumably, lose it, under dire penalties.

Mine isn't an ordinary, off-the-shelf Colt Commander. I had it rebuilt by

Pachmayr of Los Angeles. It has a 4½-inch barrel, a BoMar adjustable combat rear sight, a precision-fit slide with a special Micro barrel-bushing, a special trigger assembly that lets me fire the first shot double action, and a lot of other extra goodies. It's hard-chromed all over, which means it can stand up to a lot of weather without rusting. In a machine rest, I can get a three-inch group at a hundred yards with a hundred shots. When Frank Pachmayr finishes with a Colt Commander, you can damn well bet you're got one of the finest, hardest-hitting handguns in the world.

So I had no intention of selling, giving away, or losing that weapon.

Sten Örnfeld met me at Arlanda Airport and helped me get through the paperwork. My Swedish is as good as his, just as his English is as good as mine—but he knows the ins-and-outs of the local ways better than I do. Then we got in his plane, and he flew me to his little place in the woods.

Not so little, and more of a forest than woods. It was on the Österdalälven—the Österdal River—on the western slope of the Kjölen, that great ridge of mountains whose peaks separate Norway from Sweden. It was some miles northeast of a little town called Älvadalen, well away from everything.

Sten landed us in a little clearing, and said: "Theodore, we are here."

Sten always called me Theodore, another reason why he was a friend. I have never liked "Ted." My mother was an O'Malley, with red-auburn hair; my father was a blond Swede. Mine came out flaming red-orange. So I was "Ted the Red"—and worse—in school. Like the guy named Sue, it taught me to fight, but I hated it.

Of course, if Sten was speaking Swedish at the time, it came out something like "Taydor" but I didn't mind that.

He showed me through his house, an old-fashioned, sturdy place with the typical high-pitched, snow-shedding roof.

"You're the first one in," he told me. "Sit down and have a little *akvavit*. Unless you're hungry?"

I wasn't; I'd eaten pretty well on the plane. We had *akvavit* and coffee, and some *rågkakor* his mother had sent him.

"Tonight," he said, "I'll fix up the spices and the orange rind and the almonds and the raisins, and let 'em soak in the booze overnight for hot *glögg* tomorrow. And I've fixed it up for some people to drive up from Älvadalen with a *julskinka* we'll serve fourteen weeks early."

"So I'm the only one here so far?" I said.

"First arrival," he said. "Which poses a problem."

I sipped more *akvavit*. "Which is?"

"I *think*—I say I *think*—you're going to outshoot the whole lot of 'em. Now, I've got this special course laid out, and a lot of 'friend-and-foe' pop-up targets. I was going to let each of you guys run it cold. But there are some of these hard-nosed skvareheads who'd secretly think I took you over the course early so you'd be prepared. They wouldn't say anything, but they'd think it."

"So what do you figure on doing?"

"Well, I haven't set the pop-ups yet; I was going to set 'em in the morning. Instead, I'm going to take all of you over the course before the targets are set, then set 'em up while you guys watch each other here." He roared with laughter. "That will keep you all honest!"

Sten isn't your big Swede; he's a little guy, five-six or so, and I stand six-four. I must outweigh him by thirty-six kilos. I could probably whip him in a fight, but I would be in damn sad condition for a while afterward. I have seen what has happened to a couple of large galoots who thought he'd be an easy pushover. He was standing over them, begging them to get up for more fun, but they couldn't hear him.

"Hey!" he said, "How about checking me out on that fancy piece of artillery, now that we've managed to get it into the country?"

I was willing. I showed him the Pachmayr conversion of the Colt Commander, and he was fascinated. His final comment was: "God*dam*, what a gun!"

When we were glowing nicely warm inside the *akvavit*, and I could taste caraway clear back to my tonsils, Sten put the bottle away. "Got to keep the shootin' eye clear and the shootin' hand steady for tomorrow," he said. "Besides, I've got to do the *glögg* fixin's."

"Need any help?"

"Nope."

"Is there anyplace I could go hose a few rounds through the tube, just to get the feel in this climate?"

"Sure. There's a dead pine about eighty yards due south. I'm going to cut it down for winter fuel later, but I've put a few slugs in it, myself. Make damn heavy logs, I'll bet." He laughed again. Then: "Hey, you got a name for that blaster of yours yet?"

"No. Not yet." Sten had a habit of naming his weapons, but I'd never gone in for the custom much.

"Shame. Good gun should have a name. Never mind; you'll think of one. It's beginning to get late. Dark in an hour and a half. Dress warm. Good shooting."

Dressing warm was no problem. I was ready for it; I knew that the weather can get pretty chilly in the highlands of Sweden in September. Walking from Sten's little plane hangar to his lodge had told me that I wasn't properly dressed for afternoon; I knew good and well that the clothes I was wearing wouldn't be warm enough for dusk.

"What's the forecast for tomorrow, Sten?" I yelled at him in the kitchen.

"Cold and clear!" he yelled back. "Below freezing!"

"I should have known! You call me out of warm California so I can freeze my ass off trying to fire a handgun in Sweden!"

"Damn right! You got to have *some* sort of handicap! Shut up and go shoot!"

It really wasn't cold enough yet, but I decided I'd have a little practice in full insulation. I put on my Scandinavian net long johns, and an aluminized close-weave over that. I get my outdoor clothing from Herter's, in Minnesota; there's no one like them for quality and price. I wore a Guide Association Chamois Cloth tan shirt, Down Arctic pants, and Yukon Leather Pac boots. Over that went the Hudson Bay Down Artic parka with the frost-free, fur-trimmed hood.

For gloves, I had two choices: the pigskin shooting gloves or the Hudson Bay buckskin one-finger mittens. I shoved the mittens in my parka pocket and put on the shooting gloves. *Try 'em both,* I told myself.

I'd had the parka specially cut for quick-draw work, with an opening on the right side for the pistol and holster. Before I sealed up the parka, I put on the gunbelt, a special job made for me by Don Hume, of Miami, Oklahoma. It has quick-release leather pockets, five of them, for holding extra magazines. The holster is a quick-draw job made for my sidearm. When Don Hume says, "Whatever the need," he means it.

"Carry on, bartender!" I yelled from the door. "I am off to the wars!"

"Be sure that old dead pine doesn't beat you to the draw!" he yelled back.

It was cold outside, but there wasn't much wind. I saw the dead pine, and headed for it.

Night comes on slowly in the north, but it comes early east of the Kjölen. Those mountains make for a high horizon.

Sven had, indeed, used that pine for target practice; he'd painted a six-inch white circle on it. I went up to the pine, then turned to pace off twenty-five yards.

I was at twenty paces when the wind hit.

I don't know how to describe what happened. It was like a wind, and yet it wasn't. It was as if everything whirled around, and *then* the wind came.

And I was in the middle of the goddamdest blizzard I had seen since the time I nearly froze to death in Nebraska.

I stood still. Only a damn fool wanders around when he can't see where he's going. I knew I was only fifty yards from Sten's lodge, and I trusted the insulated clothing I was wearing. I wouldn't freeze, and I could wait out the storm until I got my bearings.

I put out my arms and turned slowly. My right hand touched a tree. I hadn't remembered a tree that near, but it gave me an anchor. I stepped over and stood the leeward side of it, away from the wind.

In those two steps, I noticed something impossible to believe.

The snow around my ankles was four inches deep.

There had been no snow on the ground when I started out.

And I don't believe there has *ever* been a storm which could deposit four inches of snow in less than two seconds.

I just stood there, wondering what the hell had happened. I couldn't see more than a couple of yards in front of me, and the dim light didn't help much. I waited. The howling of that sudden wind was far too loud for my voice to be heard over fifty yards. Sten would never hear me.

But he would know I was out in this mess, and he would know I would keep my head. I could wait. For a while, at least.

I looked at my watch to check the time. Very good. Then I leaned back against the relatively warm tree to wait.

My hands began to get cold. I stripped off the shooting gloves and put on the one-finger mittens. Better.

As sometimes happens in a snowstorm, the wind died down abruptly. It became a gentle breeze. Overhead, the clouds had cleared, and there came almost a dead calm as the last few snowflakes drifted down. My watch told me it had been twenty-seven minutes since the storm had started.

The sun glittered off the fresh snow.

The sun?

By now, it should have been close to the peaks of the Kjölen. It wasn't. It was almost overhead.

I looked carefully around. I should have been able to see the dead pine, and I certainly should have been able to see Sven's lodge.

I could see neither. Around me was nothing but forest. Only the distant crest of the Kjölen looked the same.

The whole thing was impossible, and I knew it. I also knew that I was seeing what I was seeing.

My mother, bless her, had told me stories when I was a kid—old Irish stories about the Folk of Faerie and the Hollow Hills.

"If you're invited beneath a Hollow Hill by the Faerie Folk, don't ever touch a drop of their drink or a bite of their food, or when you come out after the night, a hundred years will have passed."

Throw out that hypothesis. I hadn't been invited beneath any Hollow Hill, much less taken a drink or eaten a bit.

Unless Sten—

Oh, hell, *no!* That was silly.

But certainly *something* had gone wrong with time. Or with my mind. The sun was in the wrong place.

If you can't trust your own mind, what can you trust? As old Whatsisname—Descartes—said: *Cogito ergo sum.*

I think; therefore, I am.

I decided, therefore, that not only I *was,* but I was sane.

I had read about cryogenic experiments. Theoretically, if an organism is frozen properly, it can stay in a state of suspended animation for an indefinite time. Suppose that had happened to me. Suppose a sudden blizzard had frozen me stiff, and I had thawed out years later, without realizing that time had passed.

It didn't seem likely. Surely I would have been found by Sten. Or, if not, I'd have waked up flat on my back instead of standing up. No. Not likely.

But I decided to check it out. It would take a long time for Sten's lodge to deteriorate to the point where there were no traces left.

I walked over to where the lodge should have been, trudging through the ankle-deep snow. I'm a pretty good judge of distance and direction, and I checked the whole area where the lodge should have been.

Nothing. Pine needles under the snow; nothing under the pine needles but dirt. Nothing.

There was an old, broken tree stump about where Sten's living room should have been. I brushed the snow off it and sat down.

I don't think I thought for several minutes. Then I noticed that I was beginning to get a little chilled. Get some exercise and build a fire. I went out and gathered what broken bits of pine branches I could find, and built a small campfire near the stump. No rubbing two sticks together; my butane lighter still worked.

I sat there for an hour in a pale blue funk, wondering what had happened.

I know it was an hour, because I looked at my watch again. That was when I heard a quiet noise behind me.

I jerked my head around and looked. My hand went to my right hip. But I didn't draw.

Standing not ten paces from me were seven men.

They were quiet and unmoving, like frozen statues except for their eyes, which regarded me with interest, curiosity, and caution.

They were heavily clad in dark furs, like Eskimos wearing black bearskins. Each one carried a long spear and a roundshield.

They weren't Eskimos. Eskimos don't have blue eyes and blond hair. Those blue eyes regarded me with suspicion.

I lifted my hands carefully, showing them empty. I couldn't figure out the spears, but I didn't want to get in a hassle with the locals.

"Good afternoon, gentlemen," I said in Swedish. I kept my voice low and controlled. "Would you care to share the fire with me?"

There was a pause while all of them looked blank. Then one of them stepped forward and said something in an equally low and controlled voice. I couldn't understand a word of it.

Still, it sounded damned familiar.

I can speak—besides English—Swedish, Norwegian, Icelandic, and Danish very well. I speak German with a weird accent, but I can make myself understood easily. Afrikaans is a language I can almost understand, but not quite. This was like that.

"I don't understand," I said.

The man who had stepped out—obviously the leader—turned and said something to the man next to him. The second man answered. Their voices were low and so soft I couldn't get the drift. I figured the second man was second in command.

The leader turned to me again and spoke in a louder voice, very slowly, syllable by syllable.

It took me a few seconds to get it.

I don't know if I can explain it to you. Look; suppose you were in that same situation, and some fur-clad character had come up to you and said: *"hwahn-thah-tah-pree-lah-wee-thiz-show-rez-so-tah-theh-drocht-ahv-mahrch-ath-peersed-tow-theh-row-tah. . . ."*

You might feel a little left out of it, right?

Then, suddenly, it comes to you that what he is doing is too-carefully pronouncing Chaucer's *"Whan that Aprillë with his shourës sootë/The droghte of Marche hath percëd to the rootë. . . ."*

And then you have to translate that into modern English as: "When April, with his showers sweet, the drought of March has pierced to the root . . ."

It was like that to me. I got it, partly, but it was older than any Northman's tongue I had ever heard. It was more inflected and had more syllables per word than any I knew. It made Icelandic seem modern.

What he had said was: "You say you do not understand?"

I tried to copy his usage and inflection. It came out something like: "Yah. Me no understand."

I won't try to give you any more of my linguistic troubles. I'll just say that the conversation took a little longer than it should have.

"You must understand a little," he said.

"Yah. A little. Not well. I am sorry."

"Who are you, and what do you do here?"

"I called Theodore." But I pronounced it "Taydor."

"What do you do here?" he repeated. Those spears weren't pointed at me, but they were at the ready. I didn't like the looks of the chipped flint points.

"I lost," I said. "I have hunger and suffer from cold."

"Where do you come from?"

"America. Across the western sea."

They looked at each other. Then the leader looked back at me. "You are alone?"

"I am alone." It was a dangerous admission to make. A lone man is easier prey than one who has friends. But I figured a bluff of having friends around wouldn't work, and I didn't want to be caught out as a liar right off the bat. Besides, if worse came to worst, I figured I could gun the seven of them down before they could touch me. But I didn't want to do that. Not unless they attacked me without provocation.

The spears remained at the ready, but the men seemed to relax a little.

"What is your station?" the leader asked.

It took me a second. He was asking my rank in life. Was I a thrall or a freeman or a noble?

"I am a freeman and a warrior," I answered honestly. The time I'd spent in the service ought to count for something. "But I have, as you see, no spear and no shield."

"Then how do we know you are a warrior? How did you lose your spear and shield?"

"I did not lose them. I have come in peace."

That flabbergasted them. There was a lot of low talk among them. I sat quietly.

I was taking the tide as it ran. I still had no idea of what had happened to me, but I was damned if I'd be a stupid tourist in someone else's country.

Finally, the leader said: "Tay'or, you will come with us. We will give you food and drink and we will talk over your oddness."

"I will come," I said. I stood up.

They gripped their spears more tightly, and their eyes widened.

I knew why. It was something none of us had realized while I was seated. I was bigger than any of them. Not a one of them was taller than Sten Örnfeld. But they looked just as tough.

I folded my hands on my chest. "I go where you lead."

They didn't all lead. The head cheese and his lieutenant went ahead; the other five were behind me, spears still at the ready.

It was about twenty minutes' walk, which made sense. The fire I had started had attracted their attention, and the wisp of smoke had led them to me. It had just taken them a little time to decide to investigate.

We ended up at a collection of log cabins. I was marched straight to the largest one and led inside, past a curtain of bearskin. I had to duck my head to get through the doorway. Just inside, the leader stopped and said: "You are in the mead-hall of Vigalaf Wolfslayer. Conduct yourself accordingly."

There was a fire in the middle of the earth-floored room, just below a hole in the roof which was supposed to let the smoke out. Maybe eighty percent of it went out, but the other twenty percent filled the air. Underneath the smell of pine smoke was an odor of rancid fat and cooked meat.

By the fire stood a man with a great gray-blond beard, and long hair to match. He was a giant of a man, compared to the others; he must have stood a full five-eight.

I took him to be Vigalaf Wolfslayer, and, as it turned out, I was right. He said two words: "Explain, Hrotokar."

Hrotokar was the leader of the squad who'd found me. He told his story straight, emphasizing the fact that I had given no trouble.

Vigalaf looked at me for the first time. "Doff your hood in my presence, Giant Tay'or," he said—not arrogantly, but merely as a statement of his due. I peeled back the hood of my parka.

"Truly, not one of *Them*, then," he said. "The Eaters-of-Men have no such hair, nor such eyes. Are you truly one of us, Giant?"

"A distant relative, Vigalaf Wolfslayer," I said. I thought I was telling the truth, but God knows how distant the relationship was.

"You will call me Father Wolfslayer," he said. Again, no arrogance—just his due.

"I ask pardon, Father Wolfslayer," I said. "I am not familiar with your customs. Forgive me if I err."

He nodded and eased himself down on a pile of furs near the fire. "Sit," he said.

I sat. My escort did not. Evidently, they knew his order had not been addressed to them. There were no furs for me, so I planted my rump on the bare earth of the floor, crossing my legs.

"Bring him mead," he said.

By this time, my eyes had grown accustomed to the gloom in the windowless mead-hall. I saw that there were other people back in the dark corners, all wearing furs. In spite of the fire, there was still a chill; most of the heat was going out the roof hole.

From one dark corner, there was a gurgling noise. Then a figure stepped forward, bearing a horn of mead. I mean it. An honest-to-God cow's horn, ten inches long, full of liquid.

I've done a lot of drinking in a lot of places, but the one drink I'd never tried until that moment was mead. I knew it was made from honey, so I had, somewhere in the back of my mind, the notion that it was sweet, like port or sweet sherry.

No such thing. This stuff tasted like flat beer. It had a certain amount of authority, however.

Before I drank, I thought I ought to say something. I lifted the horn and said: "I thank you for your hospitality, Father Wolfslayer." I drank.

It was evidently the right thing to say. I saw his beard and mustache curl in a smile. "Truly," he said again, "not one of *Them.*"

I took the bit in my teeth. "Forgive my ignorance, Father Wolfslayer, but you speak of *Them.* Who are *They?*"

His shaggy gray eyebrows lifted. "You know not? Truly, you are from afar. *They* are the demons, the Evil Ones, the Eaters-of-Men. *They* are from the Far North, and they come to slay and to eat. *They* speak as do animals. *They* are Giants!" He paused. "Not so great as you, but Giants, nonetheless." Another pause. "And they wear frost about them instead of furs, as decent folk do."

I couldn't make any sense out of that, but I filed it away for later reference.

"I know nothing of them, Father Wolfslayer," I said. "They are certainly no friends nor kin of mine."

An enemy of these people, obviously. But the "demon" bit, and the "evil" and the "eaters-of-men" I figured as just so much propaganda.

"You speak well, Giant Tay'or," Vigalaf said. He raised a hand. "Bring him food."

The same person came out from the shadows, bearing a wooden bowl in one hand. This time, I looked more closely at who was serving me.

Me, I wear a beard. It's as red as the rest of my hair. I think shaving is a bore. The rest of the men there wore beards, too. My server was either a beardless boy or a woman. A people who use flint points on their spears find shaving more than a bore; they find it impossible. Besides, the lines around her eyes showed more character than a kid ever had. With those heavy furs on, it was hard to tell anything about her figure, but my instincts told me, more than anything else, that this was no teenage lad.

The glint in her eyes as they met mine confirmed my assessment of the situation. There was a slight smile on her lips as she handed me the bowl.

I automatically took it with my right hand. Then she held out her closed left hand toward mine. I opened my left hand, palm up. She dropped three nuts into it and turned away, going back to her dark corner.

I just sat there for a few seconds. The bowl contained some sort of porridge with a few chunks of meat in it. But there were no utensils to eat it with. And what about those nuts in my other hand?

I could feel every eye in the place on me. This was a test of some kind, but I didn't know what. What the hell should I do next?

Think, Sorenson! Think!

The mead-hall was utterly silent except for the crackling of the fire.

I don't know what sort of logic I used. All I knew was that if I failed this test I had better have my right hand free.

I closed my left hand on the nuts, put the bowl in my lap, and said: "Thank you again, Father Wolfslayer."

There was no answer. Carefully, I began to pick up the lumpy porridge with the thumb and first two fingers of my right hand, conveying the stuff to my mouth. No reaction from the audience. I ate it all. Then I put the bowl on the ground near me. Still no reaction.

It was those damn three nuts, then.

What was I supposed to do with them? Eat them? Give them back? Shove them up my nose? What?

I opened my hand slowly and looked at them. They were some kind of walnut, I guessed, but the shell on them was a lot thicker and harder than the walnuts I was used to.

I wiped my right hand off on my pantsleg. I didn't want a slick hand if I had to grab for my gun. Then I lifted my head slowly and looked at the Wolfslayer, holding his eyes.

He nodded silently and gestured with one hand.

The broad-shouldered blonde woman brought me a flat rock, laying it on the ground in front of me before she retreated to her corner.

I got it then. Every man in the place—and the woman, too—carried a little stone-headed mallet cinched at the waist.

Well, what the hell. A chance is a chance.

Frank Pachmayr will supply you, if you want them, with magazines that have a quarter-inch of rubber on the bottom, which, according to some, makes it easier to slam the magazine home on the reload. I never cared for them. Mine are steel on the bottom—no rubber. A personal idiosyncrasy.

At that moment, I thanked God for my idiosyncrasy.

I put the three walnuts on the flat rock, and drew my weapon.

A gun should never be used that way. But, then, a gun should never be used in any way unless there's need for it. It saved my life that time. I took it out, grabbed it near the muzzle, and carefully cracked nuts with the butt.

Call it instinct, call it intuition, call it what you will. It was the right thing to do. I found out later that the terrible Eaters-of-Men carried large stone axes, but not small ones. If they ever ate nuts, they cracked them by grabbing the nearest rock and slamming them. No delicacy.

The nuts, by the way, were very bitter.

As I ate the last one, there was a deep sigh that sounded all through the mead-hall. Wolfslayer said: "Giant Tay'or, will you be our guest?"

Searching back in my memory for what little I knew about the ancient history of the Northmen, I said: "I have no guest-gift for my host, Father Wolfslayer."

"Your guest-gift will be your strength, if you will give it. Will you fight against *Them* when the Demons come again?"

That was a tough one. I only knew one side of the quarrel. But, what the hell, a man who can't choose sides, even if he's wrong, isn't worth a damn. "I have no spear or shield, Father Wolfslayer," I said. And realized I was hedging.

"They will be provided."

"Then I will fight for you."

"Then you are my guest!" Suddenly, he came out with a barrel-roll laugh. "Mead! Mead for all! Come, Giant, sit by me! Here is a skin!"

The party began.

After about the fourth horn of mead, the Wolfslayer leaned over and said: "Where did you come by such a strange mallet?"

"It was made by a friend in a distant country," I said. "It was made for my hands alone." I didn't want the old boy to ask to handle my Colt.

His bushy eyebrows went up again. "Of course. Are not all such, in all places?"

"Of course, Father Wolfslayer." More information. The nutcrackers were personal gear. Fine.

That night, I slept under a bearskin, still wearing my insulated outdoor clothing. I hadn't bathed, but nobody else around there had, either. You could tell.

When I woke up, I was sweating, but my nose was cold. Around me, I could hear thunderous snores, but somebody was moving around, too. I opened one eye a crack. I should have known. The men were still sleeping; the women were preparing breakfast. Women's lib had evidently not reached these people. Which reminded me—

Just who the hell *were* these people?

I was sleeping on my left side (A holstered .45 makes a very lumpy mattress), with my right hand on the butt of my pistol. I kept my eyes closed and checked for hangover. Nope. Whoever their brewmaster was, he made a good brew.

This was the first opportunity that I had had to really think since the squad of seven had found me in the forest. Since then, I had merely been doing my best to stay alive.

I realized that I had accepted one thing: Like Twain's Connecticut Yankee or de Camp's Martin Padway, I had slipped back in time. How far? I didn't know. I still don't. I probably never will. These people weren't Christians, by a long shot, and they'd never heard of Him; I'd got that much in my conversations the previous night.

They'd never heard of Rome, either, but that didn't mean anything.

There were a lot of things they might not have heard of, way up here. Like Egypt.

Still, I think I must have been at least fifteen hundred years in my own past, and probably more. Their use of stone instead of metal certainly argued for great antiquity, and they didn't act at all like the bloodthirsty Vikings history records so vividly.

They were a hunting-and-gathering culture, with emphasis on hunting in the winter. Bear seemed to be their big game during the cold months. A hibernating bear, if you can find one, is fairly easy to kill if you can get it before it wakes up. The meat is good, and the skins are useful.

Snores were changing to snorts and snuffles; the men were waking up. I sat up and yawned prodigiously. Almost immediately, the broad-shouldered blonde of the night before was kneeling in front of me with a wooden bowl full of meat chunks and a horn of warm mead. She was really smiling this time, showing teeth. I noticed that the left upper lateral incisor was crooked. Charming. If only she'd had a bath.

"What's your name?" I asked, after thanking her for the food. As I said, I won't go into my linguistic difficulties. She didn't understand me at first, and we had to work it out.

"Brahenagenunda Vigalaf Wolfslayer's Daughter," she told me. "But you should not thank me for the food; you should thank Father Wolfslayer, for the food is his."

"I shall thank *him* for the food," I said. "I am thanking *you* for the preparing of it." After all, if she was the Wolfslayer's daughter, I was talking to a princess.

She blushed. "Excuse me. I must serve the others."

It occurred to me then that since everyone addressed the old man as "Father" maybe everyone called themselves his sons and daughters, whether they were biologically his children or not. I found out later that only his true children took the Wolfslayer's name. Brahenagenunda was his daughter, all right.

I saw a couple of the men going out, and I had a hunch I knew where they were going, so I followed them. I was right; they headed for the woods. When I returned, I felt much more comfortable. Snow is a poor substitute for toilet tissue, but it's better than nothing.

The cold was not too bitter. About minus two Celsius, I figured. The people from the other, smaller log cabins were going about their business, their breath, like mine, making white plumes in the air, as if everyone were puffing cigarettes. I was glad I'd never had the habit of smoking; I had the feeling tobacco would be hard to come by here-and-now.

Squad Leader Hrotokar was waiting for me just outside Vigalaf's mead-hall. "Hail, Tay'or."

"Hail, Hrotokar."

"We go to seek the bear, my men and I. Will you come?" Another test, I decided. "I will come."

"There is spear and shield for you." Then he looked me over and became less formal. "Are you sure those funny clothes you're wearing will keep you warm enough?"

"They'll be fine," I assured him. I wasn't going to tell him that they were probably far better than the stuff he was wearing.

"Well, they'll have to do, I guess," he said. "I've got an extra jacket and trousers, but I doubt they'd fit."

"I think you're right. How do we go about this bear hunt?"

Primarily, it turned out, what we did was look for tiny wisps of vapor coming out of a crack in the snow. It indicated that a bear was holed away underneath, breathing slowly and shallowly in hibernation. Then we checked to see if the bear was a female with cubs. We only killed males.

I won't bother telling about that day's hunt, because that's all we did—hunt. Didn't find a damned thing. But Hrotokar and I got to know each other pretty well. Unlike most hunts, we could talk; there's not much danger of waking up a hibernating bear.

The thing was, I wasn't able to get in any practice with spear and shield that day. There's a Greek friend of mine in San José who is a nut on spear-and-shield work in the manner of the ancient Greek *hoplites*. He and a bunch of his buddies worked out the technique, and practiced it, using blunt, padded spears. I practiced with them, and got pretty good at it, but trying it for real is very different indeed. I've had lots of practice with bayonet-and-rifle, too, but I've never had to use it in combat. Or against a bear, even a sleeping one.

The sun shone most of the day, but the clouds came in in the afternoon, and it was snowing again by the time we reached the settlement.

We came in empty-handed, and so did all of the other squads but one. They had a bear, which caused great rejoicing and happiness throughout the community. (I never actually counted them, but I'd estimate there were between fifty-five and sixty people in the whole settlement.) One of the other squads had seen a deer, but that was the one that got away.

During the winter, most of the gathering done by the women is for firewood. Fallen branches, twigs, anything that will burn. If they find an occasional dead tree, or one that has fallen over, they mark the spot and tell the men about it. Then both sexes form a work party to bring it in.

I was not the guest of honor that night in the mead-hall. A guy named Woritegeren, who had killed the bear, got all the kudos—which he deserved. Father Wolfslayer stood up and made a speech about his bravery and prowess, and then a little guy with a limp—a bard, I guess—made up a chant about Woritigeren that made it sound as if he'd slain a two-ton Kodiak all by himself.

Then Father Wolfslayer shouted: "Mead! Bring mead!"

A woman came from the shadows and brought Woritigeren his horn of mead, but it wasn't Brahenagenunda. This one was older and a good deal more worn looking.

Another woman, even older, came out and whispered into Vigalaf Wolfslayer's ear. He scowled.

There was tension in the air; I could tell that. The mead for the hero was supposed to be served by the Wolfslayer's youngest and prettiest daughter, and that hadn't been done.

Technically, Woritigeren had been given a social put-down.

Vigalaf Wolfslayer rose with majestic dignity. "Woritigeren Hero," he said, looking at the hunter, who was still holding his mead-horn untasted, "neither I nor my women meant insult here. I have just been told that Vigalaf's Daughter Brahenagenunda has not returned from her wood-gathering. The sun has gone to his rest, and the blizzard is over all." He turned to the little guy with the limp. "Make us a prayer to the All-Father, Song Chanter."

He made us a prayer. I didn't understand a word of it; it was in a language even older than the one they spoke. But it had a solemnity and dignity that made it a prayer.

One thing. I almost got caught out. I started to bow my head, but I saw what the others were doing in time, and looked upward, out the smoke-hole, toward the sky. I guess they believed in looking God in the face when they talked to Him.

When it was over, the Wolfslayer said: "It is her Wyrd. We shall look for her in the morning."

He was right, of course. I wanted to charge out right then and start searching, but in a blizzard, without lights, it would have been senseless. He—and we—had done all that was possible for the time being.

Wolfslayer lifted his mead horn. "Now, Woritigeren Hero, to your honor."

And the party was on again.

It may seem heartless, the way they behaved. Here was a woman—girl, really; she was only sixteen—out in the dark and the freezing cold, alone and without help, while her friends and relatives were having a merry time and getting all boozed up. But these were a practical people. When nothing can be done, do something else. She couldn't be rescued yet, so get on with the original schedule. When the time came, things would be done.

In the morning, the sky was clear again. The squads went out, this time both hunting and searching. Deer, bear, or dear Brahenagenunda, whatever we could find.

We found nothing. The snow had covered everything. It was six inches deep on the level, and deeper in the drifts. She might have been lying under the snow somewhere, but you can't search every snowdrift.

There was no party in the mead-hall that evening. Neither game nor maid had been found. It was a gloomy night. I slept only because I was exhausted.

The next morning, I went out again with Hrotokar's squad. The gloom was still with us. We didn't talk much.

It was about noon when we came across the Death Sign.

That's what Hrotokar called it.

"The Demons," he said very softly. *"They* are here."

I saw what he was pointing at. It was a human skull—the upper part, with the jawbone missing—impaled on a stake about thirty yards away.

"What does it mean?" I asked.

"War," he said simply. *"They,* too, want the bear and the deer. *They* come from the North, with their clothing of frost. This is our hunting country, but *They* want to take it from us. Drive us away or kill us. Come, let us see."

He gave orders to the rest of the squad to be on the lookout, in case this was a trap of some kind. We went up to the Death Sign without seeing or hearing any living thing around.

The skull was a fresh one. There were still shreds of boiled flesh clinging to parts of it. The stake had been thrust through the opening where the spinal column had been. Footprints led to and from the grisly thing. It had been put there sometime that morning.

Hrotokar said in a low grating voice: "All-Father curse them. A man's skull they would have kept to drink from."

Then I saw the crooked left upper lateral incisor.

I know, now, what the word *berserker* means. A red haze of absolute hatred came over me. If there had been anyone to vent that hatred against, I damn well would have done it. I don't know how long that red haze lasted. It seemed eternal from inside, but the others were still standing in the same positions when I came out of it, so it couldn't have been too long.

I had not lost the hatred; it had merely become cold and calculating instead of hot and wild. "Hrotokar," I said calmly, "what do we do next?"

"We must tell the Wolfslayer," he said. From the sound of his voice, I could tell that the same cold hatred had come over him.

"And what will he do?"

"All the fighting men will follow these tracks until we find the Eaters-of-

Men, and then we will slay them." He turned to one of the men. "Fleet-of-Foot, go and—"

"Hold, Hrotokar Squad-Leader," I said carefully. "This is a trap." Don't ask me how I knew; I just *knew*. "If Father Wolfslayer sends all the fighting men, that will leave the settlement unguarded. That is what *They* want us to do. Then, while we are following the trail, *They* will go to the settlement and butcher the women, the children, and the old ones."

He frowned. "That very well may be, Tay'or. What, then, should we do?"

"How many of the Eaters-of-Men are there?" I asked.

"Half again as many as we have in the settlement. Maybe more. Perhaps we cannot win." He shrugged. "We must try."

"We can win. Do you trust me, Hrotokar?"

He looked at me for a long moment. "I trust you, Giant Fire-Hair."

"Good. Now, here's what you do: Send Fleet-of-Foot to warn Father Wolfslayer. But Father Wolfslayer is not to send more than another squad to us. The rest should stay at the settlement to hold off the Demons. Meanwhile, we and the new squad will loop around and come upon the Demons from behind. Do you understand?"

A wolfish grin came over his face, and he nodded. "I see. It shall be done."

It took an hour for the second squad to arrive. Then we started following the tracks. But not too far. Only one of the Demons had been needed to place that skull where it would be found, and it was his job to lead us off. As soon as the tracks in the snow began leading off in the wrong direction, Hrotokar and I led the men around in an arc, back toward the settlement.

Sure enough, the place was under siege.

The besiegers had the place surrounded. Hrotokar had been underestimating when he said that there were half again as many of the invaders as there were of Father Wolfslayer's people. There were over fifty males of the Demons surrounding the log cabins. That meant that their total numbers probably exceeded a hundred.

The Demons were human, of course. There was nothing supernatural about them. They came from the far east of Asia, I think. They were big, about six feet tall, and their faces were definitely Oriental. Mongols? Huns? I don't know. You name it, and you can have it. You wouldn't want it.

They weren't Eskimos; I knew that. But they wore "frost." Polar bear skins. White, you see. And they came from the North.

That makes sense, too. Look at a map of northern Europe. In order to get down into southern Sweden, they'd *have* to come from the North. From the East, they'd have had to come up through Finland and down south again.

Whoever they were, I did not like them.

They were closing in on the settlement when I and the fourteen men with me came up behind them.

"Do we attack now, Fire-Hair?" Hrotokar asked softly. I don't know why, but he had evidently decided to give the leadership to me. He didn't sound very confident—after all, fifteen men against fifty?—but for some reason he trusted me.

"Friend," I asked gently, "how many of those could you kill in a charge?"

His eyes narrowed as he looked at me. "We come from behind. At least fifteen. Perhaps thirty."

"Good. Kill me fifteen, and the rest I shall take care of."

I only had fifty rounds of ammo, and in a firefight you can't be sure every shot will count.

His eyes widened. "Do you swear?"

"I swear by the All-Father and by my life," I said. "Go, Friend Hrotokar. Kill the cannibal sons-of-bitches!" And I added: "When you go, scream like furies! I will be with you every hand of the way."

And I was.

When the two squads charged in, screaming war cries, I was with them. The Demons heard us and turned.

They came at us, spears at the ready. When there was twenty yards between the two opposing ranks, I tossed away my spear and shield, dropped to one knee, and drew my pistol.

The thunder of that weapon echoed across the snowfield as I placed each shot. I think my own men hesitated when they heard that noise, but they charged on when they saw it was me doing the damage.

They didn't know what to make of it, but they saw the Demons, the Eaters-of-Men, fall one after another, and they knew I was doing my part, as I had promised.

Forty-five caliber hardball slugs from service ammo does more damage to living flesh than any other handgun ammo in existence. A man hit solidly with one of those bullets goes down and stays down.

I fired as if I were firing at pop-up targets, except that there was no 'friend-or-foe.' If it was wearing a polar-bear suit, it was a foe.

The cold hatred for these horrors burned in my brain. They were targets, nothing more. They were things to be shot down and obliterated. When one magazine was empty, I put in another without even thinking about it.

I still had half a magazine left when the fighting was over.

Forty-four of the no-good sons-of-bitches had fallen to me. Hrotokar and his squads had taken care of the rest.

I sat there on the ground, exhausted. Killing is not fun; it is horrible. It is something you must do to preserve your own life, or that of your loved ones.

I don't know how long I sat there, with my pistol in my hand, but the next thing I knew, there was someone towering above me.

"Giant Tay'or Fire-Hair," he began. Then he stopped.

I looked up. It was Father Wolfslayer. He looked rather frightened. He cleared his throat.

I stood up to face him. I still couldn't talk.

All of of them backed away from me—not in fear, but in reverence. I didn't like that.

"We know you now for what you are," the Wolfslayer continued. "We will—"

And then something cut him off. The world spun again.

Ulglossen, having finished the experiments necessary, prepared to return to—

But wait! In the twenty-first decimal, there was an aberration. Some life-form had been dragged from its proper space-time. Poor thing. On the way back, Ulglossen would return the life-form to its proper era. More or less. After all, one should be kind, but one need not be overly solicitous toward life-forms of the past. Still, Ulglossen was a kindly being.

There was no snow on the ground. I was alone in the forest.

Before me was the dead pine that Sten Örnfeld had drawn a target on.

I turned. There was Sten's lodge, fifty yards away.

I went toward it. It didn't fade or go away. It was solid, as it should be. Somehow, some way, I was back in my own time.

I walked to the door. I think it took me at least two minutes to decide to open it.

"Sten?" I said.

"Yah? What do you want? I thought you were going out to shoot."

"Changed my mind," I said. "I'm short of ammo."

"Dumbbell," he said kindly. "Sit down and relax. We'll have a drink together when I'm finished."

"Sure, Sten; sure," I said. I sat down on the couch.

I think I know what happened. I remember hearing Hrotokar in the background saying: "His hammer smashed them! Killed them! And then came back to his hand!"

I can see how that illusion could come about. I hold the hammer in my hand and there is a thunderbolt and the foe falls dead—his head smashed in. And then the hammer is back in my hand. Sure.

Those folk had already shortened my name from "Taydor" to "Tay'or"; why not one syllable further?

My weapon has a name now, as Sten suggested. I looked up a man who knows Norse runes, and I had another man engrave those runes on my pistol, on the right, just above the trigger.

The engraving says: *Mjolnir.*

Yah.

The original.

SUPERWINE

Harry Turtledove

The man next to Basil Argyros in Priskos' tavern near the church of St. Mary Hodegetria took a long pull at his cup, then doubled up in a terrible coughing fit, spraying a good part of his drink over the magistrianos. *"Kyrie eleison!"* the fellow gasped: "Lord, have mercy! My throat's on fire!" He kept on choking and wheezing.

Argyros' eyebrow, a single black bar that grew above his deepset, mournful eyes, went up in alarm. "Innkeeper! You, Priskos!" he called, "fetch me water and an emetic, and quickly! I think this man is poisoned." He pounded the fellow on the back.

"Sir, I doubt that very much," replied Priskos, a handsome young man with a red-streaked black beard. He hurried over nonetheless, responding to the sharp command in Argyros' voice; the magistrianos had been an officer in the imperial army before he came to Constantinople.

"Just look at him," Argyros said, dabbing without much luck at the wet spots on his tunic. But he sounded doubtful; the man's spasms *were* subsiding. Not only that, several of the men in the tavern, regulars by the look of them, wore broad grins, and one was laughing out loud.

"Sorry there, pal," the coughing man said to Argyros. "It's just I never had a drink like that in all my born days. Here; let me buy you one, so you can see for yourself." He tossed a silver coin to the taverner. Argyros' eyebrow rose again; that was a two-miliaresion piece, a twelfth of a gold nomisma, and a very stiff price for a drink.

"My thanks," the magistrianos said, and repeated himself when the drink was in front of him. He eyed it suspiciously. It looked like watered wine. He smelled it. It had a faint fruity smell, not nearly so strong as wine's. He picked up the cup. The regulars were grinning again. He drank.

Mindful of what had happened to the chap next to him, he took a small sip. The stuff tasted rather like wine, more like wine than anything else, he thought. When he swallowed, though, it was as the man had said—he thought he'd poured flames down his gullet. Tears filled his eyes. Careful as usual of his dignity, he kept his visible reaction to a couple of small coughs. Everyone else in the place looked disappointed.

"That's—quite something," he said at last; anyone who knew him well would have guessed from his restrained reaction how impressed he was. He took another drink. This time he was better prepared. His eyes watered again, but he swallowed without choking. He asked the innkeeper, "What do you call this drink? And where do you get it? I've never had anything like it."

"Just what I said," the fellow next to him declared. "Why, I—" He was off on a story Argyros did not want to listen to. Magistrianoi were imperial agents; they reported to the Master of Offices, who in turn reported directly to the Avtokrator, the Emperor of the Romans himself. Anything new and interesting Argyros wanted to hear about; his fellow drinker's tale was neither.

Luckily, Priskos was proud of his new stock in trade, and eager to talk about it. "I call it *yperoinos,* sir." *Superwine* was a good name for the stuff, Argyros thought. At his nod, the innkeeper went on, "We make it in the back room of the tavern here. You see I'm an honest man—I don't tell you it comes from India or Britain."

A good thing too, Argyros said, but only to himself: I'd know you were lying. No customs men were better at their job or kept more meticulous records than the ones at the imperial capital. If anything as remarkable as this dragons' brew had entered Constantinople, word would have spread fast. The magistrianos drank some more. Warmth spread from his middle.

He finished the cup, held it out for a refill. "And one for my friend here," he added a moment later, pointing to the man who had inadvertently introduced him to the potent new drink. He fumbled in his belt-pouch for the right coins. They seemed to keep dodging his fingers.

By trial and error, he found out how big a draught of superwine he could swallow without choking. The tip of his nose began to turn numb. Usually that was a sign he was getting drunk, but that could hardly be possible, not when he was just finishing his second cup. He could drink all night in a tavern and still handle himself well. Indignant at himself and at his nose, he waved to the innkeeper again.

He had not gone far into the third cup when he realized how tight he was. By then it was too late. He prided himself on being a moderate man, but the superwine had snuck up on him. The more he drank, too, the easier the stuff was to drink. Feeling most expansive, he ordered a fresh round for everyone in the place, the taverner included. Cheers rang out. He had never, he thought, drunk with such a splendid lot of fellows.

He fell asleep with a finger's width of drink still in the bottom of his cup.

* * *

Anthimos stuck his head into Argyros' office. "His illustriousness is here to see you," the secretary declared, and seemed to take mordant pleasure at his boss' groan. Mordant pleasure, Argyros sometimes thought, was the only kind Anthimos really enjoyed.

George Lakhanodrakon came in while the magistrianos was still pulling himself together. The Master of Offices was a bald, stocky man in his mid-fifties, ten or twelve years older than Argyros, and handsome in the big-nosed, heavy-featured Armenian fashion. "A fine morning to you, Basil," he said cheerfully; only the slightest eastern accent flavored his Greek. Then he got a good look at Argyros, and at once went from superior to concerned friend. "Good heavens, man! Are you well?"

"I feel exactly like death," Argyros replied. He spoke quietly, but his voice hurt his ears; his eyes were vein-tracked and found the sun oppressively bright. His mouth tasted as if the sewers had drained through it, and by the state of his digestion, maybe they had. He said, "I slept in a tavern last night."

Lakhanodrakon's jaw fell. "You did what?"

"I know what you're thinking." Argyros shook his head, and wished he hadn't. "Aii! I haven't had a hangover like this since—" He paused, trying to recall the last time he'd hurt himself so badly. The memory brought sudden sharp pain, though it was a dozen years old now: not since he drank with Riario the Italian doctor after Argyros' wife and infant son died of smallpox. He forced his mind away from that. "Do you want to hear something truly absurd? I only had four cups."

Concern returned to the Master of Offices' face. "And you're in this state? You ought to see a physician."

"No, no," Argyros said impatiently. "The innkeeper told me it was something new and strong." His eyes went to the icon on the wall, an image of the patron saint of changes. "By St. Mouamet, he wasn't wrong, either."

He dipped his head and crossed himself, showing respect for the image of the saint. No wonder Mouamet was the patron of changes, the magistrianos thought; his own life had been full of them. Born a pagan Arab in lands outside the Empire, he had accepted Christianity on a trading journey to Syria, and abandoned his camels for a monastery. A few years later, a great Persian invasion sent him fleeing to Constantinople, where he learned Greek: learned it so well, in fact, that even now, seven centuries later, he was spoken of in the same breath as Romanos the Melodist as one of the greatest hymnographers the church had ever known. He died, full of years, as archbishop of New Carthage in distant Ispania.

Lakhanodrakon was eyeing the image, too. He was a pious man, but one who also turned his piety to practical ends. "Just as they were in Mouamet's time, the Persians are stirring again."

That was plenty to alarm Argyros, decrepit though he felt. "Troops on the move?" he demanded. The Roman Empire and Persia, Christ and Ohrmazd, were ancient rivals, dueling every generation, it seemed, for mastery in the near east. Few wars were on the scale of the one that had forced Mouamet to Constantinople, but any attack would lay provinces waste.

"Nothing quite so bad, praise God," Lakhanodrakon answered, following Argyros' thought perfectly. "There's trouble in the Caucasus, though."

"When isn't there?" Argyros replied, and drew a cynical chuckle from the Master of Offices. Precisely because all-out war between them could be so ruinous, Rome and Persia often dueled for advantage on the fringes of their empires, intriguing among the clientkings of the mountains between the Black and Caspian Seas and the tribal chieftains of the Arabian peninsula. "What have you heard now?" the magistrianos asked.

"It's Alania," Lakhanodrakon said; Argyros abruptly realized this was what the Master of Offices had come to see him about. He wished Lakhanodrakon had named a different principality. Alania really mattered to both Rome and Persia, because the most important passes from the Caucasus up into the steppe were there. A prince of Alania who went bad could let the nomads in, and channel them toward one empire or the other.

The magistrianos asked, "Is prince Goarios thinking of going over to sun-worship, then?"

"God may know what Goar is thinking, but I doubt if anyone else does, Goar himself included." Lakhanodrakon betrayed his eastern origin by leaving the Greek suffix off the prince's name. After a moment, the Master of Offices went on, "Truth to tell, I have very little information of any sort coming out of Alania, less than I should. I thought I would send you to find out how things are there."

Magistrianoi, among other things, were spies. "Alania, eh? I've never been in the Caucasus," Argyros murmured. He glanced again at the image of St. Mouamet. His life, it seemed, was about to see one more change.

That thought led to another, as yet only half-formed. "I suppose I'll go in as a merchant."

"Whatever you like, of course, Basil." George Lakhanodrakon valued results more than methods, which made him a good man to work for.

Still thinking out loud, Argyros mused, "I ought to have something new and interesting to sell, too, to get me noticed at Goarios' court." The magistrianos rubbed his temples; it was hard to make his wits work, with his head pounding the way it was. He snapped his fingers. "I have it! What better than this popskull drink that has me cringing at my own shadow?"

"Is it really as vicious as that?" Lakhanodrakon waved the question aside.

"Never mind. I think you have a good idea there, Basil. Nothing would make Goar happier than a new way to get drunk, unless you've figured out how to bottle a woman's cleft."

"If I knew that one, I'd be too rich to work here." But Argyros, headache or no, focused too quickly and thoroughly on the problem he had been set to leave much room for jokes. "Superwine ought to be a good way to pry answers out of people, too; they're drunk before they know it—I certainly was, anyhow. The more anyone wants to talk or sing or carry on, the more I'll learn."

"Yes, of course. I knew in my heart you were the proper man to whom to give this task, Basil. Now my head also sees why that's so." It was Lakhanodrakon's turn to glance again at the icon of St. Mouamet. "When something new comes up, you know what it's good for."

"Thank you, sir." Argyros knew the Master of Offices was thinking of such things as the archetypes, the little clay letters that let a man produce any number of copies of any message he cared to write. He did not believe Lakhanodrakon knew of his role in showing that a dose of cowpox could prevent smallpox. He claimed no credit there; losing his family was too high a price for glory.

As he had before, he shoved that thought down and returned to the business at hand. "I'm off to Priskos' wineshop, then."

"Excellent, excellent." Lakhanodrakon hesitated, added, "Bring back a bottle for me, will you?"

Argyros rode east down the Mese, Constantinople's main street, from the Praitorion to the imperial palaces. There he picked up a squad of excubitores, reasoning that Priskos might need persuading to part with the secret of his new drink. Having a few large, muscular persuaders along seemed a good idea.

For their part, the imperial bodyguards had trouble believing the assignment that had fallen into their laps. "You're taking us to a tavern, sir? On duty?" one trooper said, scrambling to his feet as if afraid Argyros might change his mind. "I thought I'd get orders like that in heaven, but no place else."

The magistrianos led his little band north through the Augusteion, the main square of the city (all through the Empire, Constantinople was *The polis*—*the* city). The morning sun turned the light-brown sandstone exterior of the cathedral of Hagia Sophia—Holy Wisdom—to gold. Still, that exterior was plain when compared to the glories within.

The church of St. Mary Hodegetria lay a few furlongs east and north of Hagia Sophia. It was close by the sea wall; as he approached, Argyros heard the waves of the Sea of Marmara slap against stone. None of Constantinople was more than a couple of miles from the sea, so that sound pervaded the city, but here it was foreground rather than background.

Argyros had to use the church as a base from which to cast about a bit to find Priskos' tavern. It was not one of his usual pothouses; he'd stopped in more or less by accident while on his way back to the Praitorion from the seawall gate of St. Barbara. He got no help finding the place from the locals, who had a tendency to disappear as soon as they spotted the gilded shields and long spears the excubitores carried.

The magistrianos spotted an apothecary's shop and grunted in satisfaction—Priskos' was only a couple of doors down. He turned to the excubitores. "Follow me in. I'll stand you all to a couple of drinks. Back me if you need to, but St. Andreas"—Constantinople's patron—"help you if you break the place apart for the sport of it."

The soldiers loudly promised good behavior. Knowing the breed, Argyros also knew how little promises meant. He hoped for the best, and hoped Priskos would cooperate.

The taverner was sweeping the floor when Argyros came in. So early in the day, only a couple of customers were in the place, nodding over winecups. Looking up from his work, Priskos recognized the magistrianos. "Good morning to you, sir," he said, smiling. "How are you tod—" He stopped abruptly, the smile freezing on his face, as the excubitores tramped in and plunked themselves down at a pair of tables.

"Fetch my friends a jar of good Cypriot, if you'd be so kind," Argyros said. To remove any possible misunderstanding, he handed Priskos a tremissis, a thin gold coin worth a third of a nomisma. "I expect this will even pay for two jars, since they'll likely empty the first."

"I think it should," Priskos said dryly; for a man still in his twenties, he did not show much of what he was thinking. He brought the jar and eight cups on a large tray; while he was serving the excubitores, one of his other customers took the opportunity to sidle out the door.

Once the soldiers were attended to, Priskos turned back to Argyros. "And now, sir, what can I do for you?" His tone was wary, no longer professionally jolly.

Argyros gave his name and title. Priskos looked warier yet; no one, no matter how innocent, wanted a magistrianos prying into his affairs. Argyros said, "I'd be grateful if you showed me how you make your *yperoinos.*"

"I knew it! I knew it!" Try as he would, the innkeeper could no longer keep frustrated rage from his voice. "Just when I begin to work my trade up to where I can feed my family and me with it, somebody with a fancy rank comes to steal it from me."

The excubitores started to get up from their seats. Argyros waved them down. "You misunderstand. What stock of yours I buy, I will pay for," he told Priskos. "If you use some process only you know (as I dare say you do, for I've had nothing like your superwine, and I've traveled from Ispania to Mesopotamia), the fisc will pay, and pay well, I promise. Can't you see, man, what a boon such strong drink could be to those in my service?"

"Pay, you say? How much?" Priskos still sounded scornful, but calculation had returned to his eyes. "By St. Andreas, sir, I'd not sell my secret to another taverner for a copper follis less than two pounds of gold."

"A hundred forty-four nomismata, eh? You'd only get so much once or twice, I think; after that, people who wanted to learn would be able to pit those who knew against one another, and lower the price. Still—" Argyros paused, asked, "Do you read and write?"

Priskos nodded. A majority of men in Constantinople had their letters.

"Good. Fetch me a pen and a scrap of parchment, aye, and a candle too, for wax." When Argyros had the implements, he scrawled a few lines, then held the candle over the bottom of the parchment until several drops of wax fell. He thrust the signet ring he wore on his right index finger into the little puddle. "Here. It's no imperial chrysobull with a golden seal, but the staff at the offices of the Count of the Sacred Largesses, in whose charge the mint is, should accept it. Ask especially for Philip Kanakouzenos; he will recognize my hand."

The taverner's lips moved as he worked his way through the document. Argyros knew when he got to the key phrase, for he stopped reading. "Four pounds of gold!" he exclaimed. He studied the magistrianos with narrowed eyes. "You swear this is no fraud to deceive me?"

"By the Father, the Son, and the Holy Spirit, by the Virgin, by St. Andreas who watches over the city, by St. Mouamet whom I have come to recognize as my own patron, I swear it. May they damn me to hell if I lie," Argyros said solemnly. He crossed himself. So did Priskos and a couple of the excubitores.

The innkeeper tugged at his beard for a moment, then tucked the document inside his tunic. "I'm your man. You deal fairly with me, and I will with you." He held out his hand.

Argyros shook it. "Good enough. Maybe you'll fetch these good fellows that second jar of Cyprian, then, and show me what there is to see."

Priskos set the wine before the soldiers, then went to a door at the back of the taproom. It had, Argyros saw, a stouter lock than the one that led out to the street. Priskos took a key from his belt. The lock clicked open. "Right this way, sir."

Argyros felt his head start to swim as he stepped in. A small fire burned in a stone hearth sunk in the center of the floor. Above it hung a cauldron which, by the smell, was full of hot wine. The combination of heat and wine fumes was overpowering.

Over and around the cauldron was a copper contraption, a large one of thin metal. The hearth's high walls shielded most of it from direct exposure to the fire. The bottom of the cone had a lip that curved inward, and lay in a basin of water shaped to match it.

Priskos put out the fire. "I would have had to do that soon anyway," he told Argyros. He stuck his finger in the basin, nodded to himself. "The cooling bath is getting too warm." He undid a plug; water from the basin ran into a groove in the floor and out under a door that led, Argyros supposed, to the alley behind the tavern. The innkeeper put the plug back, lifted a bucket, and poured fresh and presumably cool water into the basin till it was full again. The water level was just below the edge of the inner lip.

"I hope you'll explain all this," Argyros said.

"Yes, yes, of course." Priskos splashed water on the copper cone till it was cool enough to touch. Then he picked it up. That inner lip also had a cork. He held a cup under it, pulled it out. An almost clear liquid flowed into the cup. "Taste," he invited.

Argyros did. The way the stuff heated the inside of his mouth told him it was superwine.

Priskos said, "I got the idea from my brother Theodore, who makes medicines."

"Is he the one with the apothecary's store a few doors down?"

"You saw it, eh? Yes, that's him. One of the things he does is boil down honey to make it thicker and stronger." Priskos paused. Argyros nodded; he knew druggists did that sort of thing. The innkeeper went on, "I thought what worked with honey might do the same with wine."

The magistrianos waved at the curious equipment. "So why all this folderol?"

"Because it turned out I was wrong, sir, dead wrong. The more I boiled wine, the less kick whatever was left in the pot had. I was boiling out what makes wine strong, not—what word do I want?—concentrating it, you might say."

Argyros ran his hands through his neat, graying beard. He thought for a moment, then said slowly, "What you're doing here, then, is getting back what you were boiling away, is that right?"

The taverner eyed him with respect. "That's just it, sir, just it exactly. Have you ever seen how, when you blow your warm breath on a cold window, the glass will steam over?" Again he waited for Argyros to nod before resuming, "That's what I do here. The wine fumes steam on the cool copper, and I collect them as they run down."

"No wonder you charge so much," the magistrianos observed. "You have the fuel for the fire to think about, and the work of tending this thing,

and I don't suppose one jug of wine yields anything like a jug's worth of
yperoinos."

"Not even close," Priskos agreed. "It's more like ten to one. Besides the
fumes that get away, if you boil the stuff too long, you see, then it starts
weakening again. You have to be careful of that. One way to up your yield a
little is to keep sprinkling cold water on the outside of the cone. But you
have to keep doing that, though, or pay someone to. I don't pay anyone—
he'd just sell the secret out from under me."

"You sound as though you have all the answers." Argyros rubbed his
chin again. "How long have you been playing around with this scheme, if I
may ask?"

"I guess it's about five years now, if you count a couple of years of
fooling about with things that turned out not to work," the taverner answered after a moment's thought. "Once I figured out what I had to do,
though, I spent a lot of time building up my stock; I wanted to make
yperoinos a regular part of my business, not just a passing thing I'd brew up
now and again. I still have hundreds of jars down in the cellar."

"Well, God be praised!" Argyros exclaimed. He was normally a taciturn,
even a dour man, but that was better news than he had dared hope for.
"What do you charge for each jar?"

"Two nomismata," Priskos said. "You have to remember, it's not like
Cyprian. Two jars would have your bully boys out there asleep under their
tables, not just happy."

"I'm quite aware of that, I assure you." Remembering how he had felt
the day before made the magistrianos shudder.

But the strength of the stuff was the reason he wanted it. "I'll give you
three a jar, on top of what I've already paid you, if I can buy out every jar
you have."

"Yes, on two conditions," Priskos said at once.

Argyros liked the way the younger man made up his mind. "Name
them."

"First, I have to get my gold from the Count of the Sacred Largess.
Second, let me keep half a dozen jars for myself and my friends. Out of so
many, that won't matter to you."

"Yes to the first, of course. As for the second, keep three. You'll be able
to afford to make more later."

"I will at that, won't I? All right, I'd say we have ourselves a bargain."
Priskos stuck out his hand. Argyros clasped it.

The caravan wound through the mountains toward the town of Dariel,
the capital, such as it was, of the kingdom of the Alans. Even in late summer, snow topped some of the high peaks of the Caucasus. The mountains

were as grand as the Alps, which till this journey had been the most magnificent range Basil Argyros knew.

"Good to be in a big city, eh?" said one of the caravan guards, a local
man wearing a knee-length coat of thick leather reinforced with bone scales
and carrying a small, round, rivet-studded shield. His Greek was vile;
Argyros was sure he had never been more than a couple of valleys away
from the farm or village where he had been born. No one who had traveled
would have called Dariel a big city.

In many ways, the magistrianos thought as the caravan approached the
walls of the town, the Caucasus were the rubbish-heap of history. Dariel
was a case in point. The Romans had built the fortress centuries ago, to
keep the nomads from coming down off the steppe. When the Empire was
weak, the Georgians manned it themselves, at times supported by Persian
gold. The Alans, the present rulers hereabouts, had been nomads themselves once. A crushing defeat on the steppe, though, sent them fleeing into
the mountains. Though they played Rome and Persia off against each
other, they were as interested as either in guarding the pass that lay so near
Dariel.

They had been, at any rate, until Goarios. Neither the Emperor nor the
King of Kings could count on what Goarios would do. Trouble was, the
King of the Alans was as lucky as he was erratic. All that did was make him
twice the nuisance he would have been otherwise.

The gate guards had been dealing with the merchants in the caravan one
by one. When they reached Argyros and his string of packhorses, he had to
abandon his musings. "What you sell?" an underofficer asked in bad Persian. Both imperial tongues, like money from both realms, passed current
all through the Caucasus, more so than any of the dozens of difficult,
obscure local languages.

For his part, Argyros spoke better Persian than the Alan trooper. "Wine,
fine wine from Constantinople," he replied. He waved at the jugs strapped
to the horses' backs.

"Wine, is it?" White teeth peeked through the tangled forest of the
underofficer's beard. "Give me taste, to see how fine it is."

The magistrianos spread his hands in sorrow. "Noble sir, I regret it may
not be," he said, using the flowery phrases that came so readily to Persian.
"I intend to offer this vintage to no less a person than your mighty king
himself, and would not have his pleasure diminished." Seeing the guard
scowl, he added, "Here is a silver dracham. May it take away your thirst."

The gate guard's grin reappeared as he stuffed the Persian coin into his
pouch. He waved Argyros forward into Dariel.

One of the magistrianos' comrades, a gray-eyed man named Corippus,
came up and murmured, "A good thing he didn't check the jars." He

spoke the guttural north African dialect of Latin, which no one in the
Caucasus would be likely to understand; even Argyros had trouble following it.

Since he could not use it himself, he contented himself with saying,
"Yes." All the jars looked like winejars, but not all of them held wine, or
even superwine. In the same way, the couple of dozen men who had accompanied the magistrianos from Constantinople looked like merchants,
which did not mean they were.

The horses moved slowly through Dariel's narrow, winding streets.
Small boys stared and pointed and called out, as small boys will anywhere.
Some of them were touts for inns. After some haggling, Argyros went with
one. From the way the lad described it, his master Supsa's place was what
God had used as a pattern for making heaven.

The magistrianos carefully did not ask which god the boy meant. Dariel
held both Christian churches with domes in the conical Caucasian style and
fire-temples sacred to the good god Ohrmazd whom the Persian prophet
Zoroaster praised. Churches and fire-temples alike were thick-walled, for-
tress-like structures; most had armed guards patroling their grounds. Nowhere but in this region that both empires coveted did these faiths have
such evenly balanced followings, nowhere else was there such strife between
them. Goarios was a Christian (or at least had been, the last time Argyros
heard), but it would not do to count on that too far.

Native Georgians and their Alan overlords were both on the streets,
usually giving one another wide berths. Language and dress distinguished
them. Not even Satan, Argyros thought, could learn Georgian, but the Alan
tongue was a distant cousin of Persian. And while the natives mostly wore
calf-length robes of wool or linen, some Alans still clung to the leather and
furs their ancestors had worn on the steppe. They also let their hair grow
long, in greasy locks.

Some real nomads, slant-eyed Kirghiz, were also in the market square.
They stared about nervously, as if misliking to be so hemmed in. By their
fine weapons and gold saddle-trappings, they were important men in their
tribe. Argyros almost wished he had not spotted them. They gave him one
more thing to worry about, and he had plenty already.

Supsa's inn proved more than adequate. The stableman knew his business, and the cellar was big enough to store the winejars. Argyros, who
from long experience discounted nine tenths of what he heard from touts,
was pleased enough. He did his best not to show it, dickering long and
hard with Supsa. If he had more money than a run-of-the-mill merchant,
that was his business and nobody else's.

The mound of pillows he found in his chamber made a strange but
surprisingly comfortable bed. The next morning, fruit candied in honey was

not what the magistrianos was used to eating for breakfast, but not bad, either. He licked his fingers as he walked toward Goarios' palace, a bleak stone pile that seemed more citadel than seat of government.

One of Goarios' stewards greeted him with a superciliousness the grand cubicularius of the Roman Emperor would have envied. "His highness," the steward insisted, "favors local wines, and so would have scant interest in sampling your stock."

Argyros recognized a bribery ploy when he heard one. He did not mind paying his way into Goarios' presence; he was not, after all, operating with his own money. But he did want to take this fellow's toploftiness down a peg. He had brought along a jar of *yperoinos*. "Perhaps you would care to see that its quality meets your master's standards," he suggested, patting the jar.

"Well, perhaps, as a favor for your politeness," the chamberlain said grudgingly. At his command, a lesser servant fetched him a cup. Argyros worked the cork free, poured him a good tot, and watched, gravely silent, as his eyes crossed and face turned red when he drank it down at a gulp. The steward came back gamely, though. "I may have been in error," he said, extending the cup again. "Pray give me another portion, to let me be sure."

Goarios' great hall was narrow, dark, and drafty. Petitioners worked their way forward toward the king's high seat. The magistrianos waited patiently, using the time in which he occasionally lurched ahead to examine the others in the hall who sought the king's favor.

He did not like what he saw. For one thing, the Kirghiz nobles he had spied in the market were there. For another, while one Christian priest, plainly a local, waited to make a request of Goarios, a whole delegation of Ohrmazd's clerics in their flame-colored robes sat a few paces ahead of the magistrianos. He could hear them talking among themselves. Their Persian was too pure to have been learned in the Caucasus.

As he drew closer, Argyros also studied the king of the Alans. Goarios was close to his own age, younger than he had thought. His face was long, rather pale, with harsh lines on either side of his mouth that disappeared into his thick beard. His eyes were black and shiny; he had somehow the air of a man who saw things no one else did. Whether those things were actually there, Argyros was not sure.

Goarios spent some time with the Kirghiz, even more with the Persian priests. The rumbles of Argyros' stomach were reminding him it was time for the noon meal when at last the steward presented him to the king. He stooped to one knee and bowed his head; only before the Avtokrator of the Romans or the Persian King of Kings would he have performed a full prostration, going down on his belly.

The steward addressed Goarios in Georgian. The king made a brief answer in the same tongue, then spoke to Argyros in Persian: "You have,
Tskhinvali here tells me, a remarkable new potation, one I might enjoy. Is
this so?"

"Your majesty, it is," the magistrianos answered in the same tongue. He
handed the jar to the steward to pass on to Goarios. "Please take this as my
gift, to acquaint you with the product."

Those opaque eyes surveyed Argyros. "I thank you. You must have great
confidence, to be so generous." Goarios still used Persian. Argyros had
heard he knew Greek, and suspected he was the victim of a subtle insult. He
showed no annoyance, but waited silently while the king, as his steward had
before him, had a cup brought. Unlike Tskhinvali, Goarios drank from
silver.

The king drank. His eyes widened slightly and he rumbled deep in his
throat, but he tolerated his first draught better than anyone else Argyros
had seen. "By the sun!" Goarios exclaimed, a strange oath if he still followed Christ. He drank again, licked his lips. Suddenly he switched languages: he *did* speak Greek. "This is something new and different. How
many jars have you to sell, and at what price?"

"I have several hundred jars, your majesty." Argyros also shifted to
Greek. "They cannot, I fear, come cheap: not only is the preparation slow
and difficult, but I have incurred no small expense in traveling to you. My
masters back in Constantinople would flay me for accepting less than
twenty nomismata the jar."

He expected the dickering to begin then, or Goarios to dismiss him to
bargain with Tskhinvali or some other palace dignitary. He would have
been satisfied to get half his first asking price. But the king of the Alans
simply said, "Accepted."

Disciplined though he was, Argyros could not help blurting, "Your majesty?" The first confused thought in his mind was that this might be the
only government-financed expedition in the history of the Empire to turn a
profit. He had never heard of any others; he was certain of that.

Goarios took another pull. "Agreed, I said. Rarity and quality are worth
paying for, in wine or women or—" He let his voice trail away, but his eyes
lit, as if for an instant his inner vision grew sharp and clear. The moment
passed; the king returned his attention to Argyros. "I have a banquet
planned this evening—I am pleased to bid you join me. Perhaps to further
the pleasure of all those present, you will consent to bring with you ten jars
of your brew."

"Certainly, your majesty." Argyros had hoped the superwine would
make him popular at court, but had not expected to succeed so soon. He
regretted having to stay in character. Any failure, though, might be noticed,

so he said, "Your majesty, ah—" He gave what he hoped was a discreet pause.

"You will be paid on your arrival, I assure you," Goarios said dryly. He added, "If you have found a companion, you may bring her to the feast. We do not restrict our women to their own quarters, as the tiresome custom is in Constantinople."

"You are most generous, your majesty." Argyros bowed his way out. The audience had gone better than he dared wish. He wondered why he was still nervous.

For the banquet, the magistrianos dug out the best robe he had brought. He had several finer ones back in Constantinople, including a really splendid one of thick sea-green samite heavily brocaded with silk thread. For a merchant of moderate means, though, that would have been too much. Plain maroon wool fit the part better.

The reputation of the *yperoinos* must have preceded it; eager hands helped Argyros remove the jars from the packhorses. Too eager—"Come back, you!" he shouted at one servitor. "Your king bade me bring ten jars. If my head goes up on the wall for cheating him, I know whose will be there beside it." That was plenty to stop the fellow in his tracks, the magistrianos noted: Goarios' men feared their king, then.

Horns, flutes, and drums played in the banquet hall. The music was brisk, but in the wailing minor key the Persians and other easterners favored. Argyros had heard it many times, but never acquired the taste for it.

The servants had not yet set out the tables for the feast. Guests and their ladies stood and chatted, holding winecups. When the chief usher announced Argyros' name and the other servants carried the jars of superwine into the hall, King Goarios clapped his hands above his head three times. Silence fell at once.

"Here we have the purveyor of a new and potent pleasure," the king declared, "than which what praise could be higher?" He used Persian. By now, Argyros had decided he meant no mockery by it; more courtiers used Persian than Greek here. Goarios beckoned the magistrianos toward him. "Come and receive your promised payment."

Argyros pushed his way through the crowded hall. He had no trouble keeping the king in sight; they were both taller than most of the people in the hall. Behind him, he heard the first exclamations of amazement as the guests began sampling the *yperoinos*.

"Two hundred nomismata," Goarios said when he drew near, and tossed him a leather purse over the heads of the last couple of men between them.

"I thank your majesty," Argyros said, bowing low when he and Goarios were at last face to face.

"A trifle," the king said with a languid wave. A woman stood by his side. Argyros had not got a good look at her before, for the crown of her head was not far above Goarios' shoulders. Her hair fell in thick black waves to her shoulders. She had bold, swarthy features and flashing dark eyes that glittered with amusement as she smiled saucily at the magistrianos. "Mirrane, this is Argyros, the wine merchant of whom I told you," Goarios said.

Recognizing her, the magistrianos felt ice form round his heart. He and Mirrane had met before, in Daras near the border between the Roman Empire and Persia, and in Constantinople itself. Both times, she had come unpleasantly close to killing him. She was a top agent of the King of Kings, the Persian equivalent, in fact, of himself. He waited woodenly for her to denounce him.

She turned her mocking gaze his way again. "I've heard of him," she said, speaking Greek with the throaty accent of her native tongue. "He is, ah, famous for the new products he purveys." Her attention returned to Goarios. "For what marvel did you reward him so highly?"

"A vintage squeezed, I think, from the thunderstorm," the king of the Alans replied. "You must try some, my dear." His hand slid round Mirrane's waist. She snuggled against him. Together they walked slowly toward the table where Goarios' servants had set out the *yperoinos.*

Argyros stared after them. He was too self-possessed to show his bafflement by scratching his head, but that was what he felt like. If Mirrane had become Goarios' concubine, she had to have influence over him. Of that the magistrianos had no doubt. The two of them had shared a bed a few times in Daras. Mirrane, Argyros was certain, could influence a marble statue, as long as it was a male one.

Why, then, was she letting him stay free? The only answer that occurred to Argyros was so she could ruin him at a time that better suited her purpose. Yet that made no sense either. Mirrane was skilled enough at intrigue to see that the longer a foe stayed active, the more dangerous he became. She was not one to waste so perfect a chance to destroy him.

He shrugged imperceptibly. If she was making that kind of mistake, he would do his best to take advantage of it.

After a while, servants began fetching in tables and chairs. Goarios, Mirrane still beside him, took his seat at the head table. That was the signal for the king's guests to sit down, too. Soon all were in their places but the group of Kirghiz, who would not move away from the superwine. One of them was already almost unconscious; two of his comrades had to hold him up. Stewards of ever higher rank came over to remonstrate with the nomads. At last, grudgingly, they went up to sit across the table from Goarios.

Back in the kitchens, Argyros thought, the cooks must have been tearing their hair, waiting for the dinner to start. They quickly made up for lost time. Grunting under the weight, servants hauled in platters on which rested roast kids, lambs, and geese. Others brought tubs of peas and onions, while the sweet smell of the new-baked loaves that also appeared filled the hall.

What was left of the superwine seemed reserved for Goarios' table, but jars from the sweet Caucasian vintages in the Alan king's cellars kept those less privileged happy. Argyros drank sparingly. He kept his eyes on Mirrane, again wondering what game she was playing.

None of his tablemates—minor Alan nobles, most of them, along with a few townsmen rich enough for Goarios to find them worth cultivating—found his staring obtrusive. Desirable though she was, the magistrianos did not think they were watching Mirrane. The Kirghiz were busy making a spectacle of themselves.

In his army days, Argyros had fought the steppe nomads near the Danube, and even briefly lived among them. He knew the privation they endured, and knew how, to make up for it, they could gorge themselves when they got the chance. Reading of the huge feasts Homer described, he sometimes thought the heroes of the Trojan War had the same talent. Maybe the Alans' ancestors did, too, when they were a steppe people, but this generation had lost it. They gaped in astonished wonder as the Kirghiz ate and ate and ate.

The nomads drank too, swilling down *yperoinos* as if it were the fermented mares' milk of the plains. The one who had been wobbling before the banquet slid quietly out of his chair and under the table. Another soon followed him. The rest grew boisterous instead. They slammed fists down on the table to emphasize whatever points they thought they were making, shouted louder and louder, and howled songs in their own language. Argyros understood a few words of it; not many other people in the hall did. It sounded dreadful.

Servants cleared away platters, except, after a snarled warning, the ones in front of the Kirghiz. Goarios stood up, held his hands above his head. Silence descended. Eventually the Kirghiz noticed they were roaring in a void. They too subsided, and waited for the king to speak.

"Thank you, my friends, for sharing my bounty tonight," Goarios said in Persian. He paused for a moment to let those who did not know the tongue have his words interpreted, then resumed: "I know this would not seem like much in the way of riches to one used to the glories of Constantinople or Ctesiphon, but in our own small way we try."

This time, being safely inconspicuous, Argyros did scratch his head.

Modesty and self-deprecation were not what he had come to expect from the king of the Alans.

Goarios continued, "Still and all, we have learned much from the Romans and from the Persians. Of all the folk under the sun"—here he glanced at Mirrane, who fondly smiled back his way (if Goarios had embraced the creed of Ohrmazd, Argyros was doubly sure now it was because he had first embraced an eloquent advocate for it)—"they are strongest, and also cleverest. That is no accident; the two qualities go hand in hand."

The king paused. His courtiers applauded. The Kirghiz nobles, those still conscious, looked monumentally bored. Argyros sympathized with them. If Goarios had a point, he was doing his best to avoid it.

Or so the magistrianos thought, until the king suddenly adopted the royal we and declared, "Though our realm is small at present, we do not see ourselves as less in wit than either the Emperor or the King of Kings." Both those rulers, Argyros thought tartly, had the sense not to go around boasting how smart they were.

Nevertheless, Goarios' words did have a certain logic, if a twisted one, behind them: "Being so astute ourself, it follows naturally that power will accrue to us on account of our sagacity, and on account of our ability to see the advantages of policies heretofore untried. As a result, one day soon, perhaps, the rich and famous in the capitals of the empires will have cause to envy us as we now envy them."

The courtiers applauded again. They seemed to know what their king was talking about—but then, Argyros thought, the poor devils had likely listened to this speech or something like it a good many times before. He had heard Goarios was a cruel man; now he was getting proof of it.

A couple of Kirghiz envoys also cheered the king of the Alans—or maybe the fact that he was done. The rest of the nomads had slumped into sodden slumber. Speaking of envy, Argyros envied them that.

Goarios was plainly convinced his address marked the high point of the evening, for no singers, dancers, or acrobats appeared afterwards to entertain his guests. Instead, the king waved to the doorway, showing that the festivities were over.

The banquet did not break up at once. As in Constantinople, the custom was for departing guests to thank their host for his kindness. Argyros joined the procession, sighing inwardly. He wished he could somehow get into Goarios' good graces without having anything to do with the king.

Still, Goarios greeted him effusively. "We are in your debt. You and your *yperoinos* have helped make this evening unique."

He used Greek, so as not to leave the name of the new drink dangling alone and strange in an otherwise Persian sentence. One of the Kirghiz understood the Roman Empire's chief tongue, and even spoke it after a fashion. Before Argyros could respond to the king, the nomad poked him in the ribs. "You this drink make, eh? Is good. Where you from?"

"Constantinople," the magistrianos replied. The Kirghiz's prodding finger distracted him from Goarios, whom etiquette demanded he should have answered.

"Ah, the city." The nomad was too drunk to care about etiquette, if he ever had. He poked Goarios in turn. "You, I, maybe one fine day we see Constantinople soon, eh?"   ·

"Who would not wish such a thing?" Goarios' voice was smooth, but his eyes flickered.

Argyros bowed to the king. "To serve you is my privilege, your majesty." He turned to Mirrane. "And your lady as well." Maybe his directness could startle something out of her, though he knew what a forlorn hope that was.

Sure enough, her equanimity remained absolute. With dignity a queen might have envied, she extended a slim hand to the magistrianos. He resented being made to dance to her tune, yet saw no choice but to take it. She said, "My master speaks for me, of course."

The magistrianos murmured a polite phrase, bowed his way out of the king's presence. Outside the castle, he hired a torchboy to light his way back to the inn. The boy, a Georgian lad, could follow Persian if it was spoken slowly and eked out with gestures. "Stop a moment. Hold your torch up," Argyros told him as soon as buildings hid them from Goarios' castle.

The boy obeyed. Argyros unrolled the tiny scrap of parchment Mirrane had pressed into his palm. He had to hold it close to his face to make out her message in the dim, flickering light. "Meet me alone tomorrow by the vegetable market, or I will tell Goarios who you are," he read.

Nothing subtle or oblique there, he thought as he put the parchment in his beltpouch. That did not mean she would not get what she wanted. She generally did.

"You're going to meet with her?" Corippus, when he heard Argyros' news the next morning, was openly incredulous. "What will the rest of us do once she's dealt with you? You can't tell me she has your good health foremost in her mind."

"I doubt that," Argyros admitted. He tried to sound judicious, and not like a man merely stating the obvious. He did bolster his case by adding, "If she wanted to bring me down, she could have done it simply last night; instead of going through this rigmarole. By the look of things, she has Goarios wrapped around her finger."

"Or somewhere," Corippus grunted. "This is folly, I tell you."

"Being exposed to Goarios is worse folly. One thing I know of Mirrane: she does not idly threaten."

Corippus made a noise deep in his throat. He remained anything but convinced. Argyros, however, headed the team from Constantinople, so the north African could only grumble.

The magistrianos tried to tease him out of his gloom. He waved round the cellar of Supsa's inn, pointing at the three *yperoinos*-cookers Corippus and his team had going. "You worry too much, my friend. Even if something does happen to me, the lot of you can go into superwine for true, and likely end up rich men here."

Corippus fell back into his harsh native dialect. "In this godforsaken lump of a town? Who'd want to?"

He had a point, Argyros thought. Nevertheless, the magistrianos turned a benign eye on Dariel as he made his way to the vegetable market. That was partly because, if he got through this confrontation with Mirrane, he would have a hold on her to counter the advantage she now held on him— he did not think, at any rate, that Goarios would be pleased to learn his paramour was arranging a secret rendezvous with another man. More important, though, was the prospect of matching wits with the best Persian Persia had. Mirrane was that, as Argyros had found more than once to his discomfiture.

To one used to the bounty of Constantinople, Dariel's vegetable market was a small, mean place. The city prefect's inspectors would have condemned half the produce on display. Argyros bought a handful of raisins and waited for Mirrane to come into the little square.

He was not sure what to expect. When with Goarios, she had dressed as a great lady, with brocaded robe and with bracelets and necklace of gleaming gold. He had also seen her, though, in a dancer's filmy garb, and once when she was artfully disguised as an old woman. Just recognizing her would constitute a victory of sorts.

He was almost disappointed to spot her at once. She wore a plain white linen dress, something that suited a moderately prosperous tradesman's wife, but she wore it like a queen. Copper wire held her hair in place; apart from that, she was bare of jewelry. Seeing Argyros, she waved and walked toward him, as if greeting an old friend.

"You have another new toy, do you, Basil?" Her voice held a lilting, teasing tone, of the sort a cat would use to address a bird it held between its paws. "What better way to swing a man toward you than dealing with him drunk, the more so if he's had so little he doesn't know he is?"

If anyone would realize why he had brought the *yperoinos,* it was she. He answered, "I'm not trying to turn a whole city on its ear, the way your handbills did in Daras."

"You turned the tables neatly enough on me in Constantinople. The trouble with the clay archetypes is that anyone can use them to make countless copies of his message. You saw that." She shook her head in chagrin, put her hand on his arm.

He pulled free. "Enough empty compliments," he said harshly. "Unfold your scheme, whatever it is, and have done, so I can start working out where the traps lie."

"Be careful what you say to me," she warned, smiling still. "Ohrmazd the good god knows how backwards Alania is, but Goarios' torturer, I think, would have no trouble earning his keep in Ctesiphon. In some things, he accepts only the finest."

"I dare say," the magistrianos remarked, recalling Corippus' sour jest.

"Oh, think what you will," Mirrane said impatiently. "I serve the King of Kings no less than you your Avtokrator. If my body aids in that service, then it does, and there is no more to be said about it." She paused a moment. "No, I take that back. I will say, Basil, that Goarios is not one I would have bedded of my own free choice, and that that is not true of you."

Ever since those few nights in Daras a couple of years before, Argyros had wondered whether the passion she showed then was real or simply a ploy in the unending struggle between Persia and the Roman Empire. He wondered still; Mirrane might say anything to gain advantage. That mixture of suspicious curiosity and anger roughened his words: "Say whatever you like. Whether or not you care a follis for him, Goarios dances to your tune, in bed and out."

Mirrane's laugh had an edge to it. "Were that so, I'd not be here talking with you now—you would have been a dead man the instant Tskhinvali called your name. But I need you alive.

For the first time, Argyros began to think she might be telling the truth, or some of it. She had no reason not to unmask him if she did fully control the king of the Alans. Trusting her, though, went against every instinct the magistrianos had, and against the evidence as well. "If Goarios is his own man, as you say, why has he turned his back on God's only begotten Son Jesus Christ and embraced your false Ohrmazd? Whence comes that, if not from you?"

"I find my faith as true as you yours," Mirrane said tartly. "As for Goarios, he is his own man, and his own god as well—the only thing he worships is himself. The words he mouths are whichever ones suit him for the time being. I saw that too late, and that is why I need your help."

"Now we come down to it," Argyros said.

Mirrane nodded. "Now indeed. What he intends, you see, is opening the Caspian Gates to the Kirghiz and as many other nomad clans as care to join them. His own army will join the nomads; he thinks he will end by ruling them all." Her sigh was full of unfeigned regret. "And to think that that was what I labored so hard to accomplish, and here I find it worse than useless."

Argyros found it appalling: it was George Lakhanodrakon's worst nightmare, come to life. The magistrianos said, "Why should you not be glad to see the nomads ravage Roman provinces?"

"I told you once—if that were all, you would be dead. But Goarios and the men from the steppe have bigger plans. They want to invade Persia, too. Goarios thinks to play Iskander." Argyros frowned for a couple of seconds before recognizing the Persian pronunciation of the name Alexander. Many had tried to rule both east and west in the sixteen hundred years since Alexander the Great; no one had succeeded.

Then again, no one had tried with the backing of the nomads. "You think he may do it, then," the magistrianos said slowly.

"He might; he just might," Mirrane answered. "He is a man who believes he can do anything, and those are the ones who are sometimes right." She hesitated, added, "He frightens me."

That admission startled Argyros, who had never imagined hearing it from Mirrane. All the same, he said, "It's hard to imagine a conquering army erupting out of the Caucasus. The mountains here are a refuge of defeat, not stepping-stones to triumph." He spelled out the chain of thought he'd had coming into Dariel.

Mirrane's eyes lit. She followed him at once. He knew how clever she was. Her wit rather than her beauty made her truly formidable, though she was twice as dangerous because she had both.

She said, "This once, though, the Alans have raised up a leader for themselves. He is . . . strange, but sometimes that makes people follow a man more readily, for they see him as being marked by—well, by whatever god they follow." Her smile invited Argyros to notice the concession she had made him.

He did not rise to it. Over the centuries, the agents who served the Roman Empire had learned to gauge when diplomacy would serve and when war was required, when to pay tribute and when instead to incite a tribe's enemies to distract it from the frontier. If a hero had appeared in Alania, that long experience told Argyros what to do. "Kill him," the magistrianos said. "The chaos from that should be plenty to keep the Alans safely squabbling among themselves."

"I thought of that, of course," Mirrane said, "but, aside from being fond of staying healthy and intact myself, it's too late. The Kirghiz control the pass these days, not the Alans."

"Oh, damnation."

"Yes, the whole damn' nation," Mirrane echoed, her somber voice belying the lighthearted tone of the pun. "Their khan Dayir, I would say, is using Goarios for his own ends as much as Goarios is using him. And where Goarios would be Iskander if he could, Dayir also has one after whom he models his conduct."

Argyros thought of the nomad chieftains who had plagued the Roman Empire through the centuries. "Attila," he said, naming the first and worst of them.

Mirrane frowned. "Of him I never heard." The magistrianos was briefly startled, then realized she had no reason to be familiar with all the old tales from what was to her the distant west: Attila had never plundered Persia. But she knew of one who had: "I was thinking of the king of the Ephthalites, who long ago slew Peroz King of Kings by a trick."

Argyros nodded; Prokopios had preserved in Roman memory the story of that disaster. "Enough of ancient history, though," he said with the same grim pragmatism that had made him urge Mirrane to assassinate Goarios. "We need now to decide how to deal with this Dayir." Only when he noticed he had said "we" was the magistrianos sure he believed Mirrane.

She accepted that tacit agreement as no less than her due. "So we do. Unfortunately, I see no easy way. I doubt we'd be able to pry him and Goarios apart. Until they've succeeded, their interests run in the same direction."

"And afterwards," Argyros said gloomily, "will be too late to do us much good."

Mirrane smiled at the understatement. "Ah, Basil, I knew one day Constantinople would get round to sending someone to see what was going wrong in Alania: Goarios *will* brag, instead of having the wit to let his plans grow in the quiet dark until they are ripe. I'm glad the Master of Offices chose you. We think alike, you and I."

A hot retort rose to the magistrianos' lips, but did not get past. Despite the differences between them, there was much truth in what Mirrane said; he was reminded of it every time he spoke with her. Certainly he had more in common with her than with some Constantinopolitan dyeshop owner whose mental horizon reached no further than the next day's races in the hippodrome. "We use different tongues," he observed, "but the same language."

"Well said!" She leaned forward, stood on tiptoe to plant a kiss on his cheek. She giggled. "You keep your beard neater than Goarios—there's more room on your face. I like it." Laughing still, she kissed his other cheek, just missing his mouth.

He knew she took care to calculate her effects. He reached for her all the same. The touch of her lips reminded him of those few days back at Daras, when they had shared a bed before trying to do each other in.

Sinuous as an eel, she slipped away. "What would be left of you, if you were caught molesting the king's kept woman?" She abruptly turned serious. "I must get back. Leaving the palace is always a risk, but less so at noon, because Goarios sleeps then, the better to roister at night. But he'll be rousing soon, and might call for me."

Argyros could say nothing to that, and knew it. He watched Mirrane glide across the market square; she moved with the grace of a dancer, and had once used that role as a cover in Daras. The magistrianos stood rubbing his chin in thought for several minutes after she finally disappeared, then made his own way back to Supsa's inn.

All the way there, his mind kept worrying at the problem she posed, as the tongue will worry at a bit of food caught between the teeth until one wishes he would go mad. Equally stubborn in refusing to leave his thoughts was the feel of her soft lips. That annoyed him, so he prodded at his feelings with characteristic stubborn honesty until he began to make sense of them.

In the years since his wife and son had died, he'd never thought seriously about taking another woman into his life. That came partly from the longing he still felt for Helen. More sprang from his unwillingness to inflict on any woman the lonely life a magistrianos' wife would have to lead, especially the wife of a magistrianos who drew difficult cases. In the past five years he had been to Ispania and the Franco-Saxon kingdoms, to Daras, and now he was here in the Caucasus. Each of those missions was a matter of months, the first close to a year. It was not fair to any woman to make her turn Penelope to his Odysseus.

With Mirrane, though, that objection fell to the ground. She was at least as able as he to care for herself in the field. And if—if!—she spoke the truth about how she reckoned their brief joining in Daras, he pleased her well enough, at least in that regard. There was, he remembered, far more to love than what went on in bed, but it had its place, too.

He started laughing at himself. Mirrane was also a Persian—enemies by assumption, in almost Euclidean logic. She worshiped Ohrmazd. She was sleeping with Goarios, and keeping his nights lively when the two of them were not asleep. The only reason she was in the Caucasus at all was to seduce the king of the Alans away from the Roman Empire, in the most literal sense of the word. Not only that, if—if!—she spoke the truth, both Constantinople and Ctesiphon faced deadly danger from Goarios' machinations.

When all those thoughts were done, the thought of her remained. That worried him more than anything.

*   *   *

Corippus scowled at the magistrianos. "That accursed potter has raised his price again. And so has the plague-taken apothecary."

"Pay them both," Argyros told him. "Yell and scream and fume as if you were being bankrupted or castrated or whatever suits your fancy. That's in keeping with our part here. But pay them. You know what we need."

"I know you've lost your wits mooning over that Persian doxy," Corippus retorted, a shot close enough to the mark that Argyros felt his face grow hot. He was glad they were in the dimly lit cellar, so his lieutenant could not see him blush. But Corippus, after grumbling a little more, went on, "However much it galls me, I have to say the wench is likely right. There'd not be so many stinking Kirghiz on the streets if they weren't in league with Goarios, and she'd've long since nailed us if she didn't think they meant to do Persia harm along with the Empire."

Argyros had reached exactly the same conclusions. He said so, adding, "I'll be hanged if I can tell how you'd know how many Kirghiz are in Dariel. You hardly ever come up out of here, even to breathe."

Corippus chuckled dryly. "Something to that, but someone has to keep the superwine cooking faster than Goarios and his cronies guzzle it down. Besides which, I don't need to go out much to know the nomads are thick as fleas. The stench gives 'em away."

"Something to that," the magistrianos echoed. Strong smells came with cities, especially ones like Dariel, which had only a nodding acquaintance with Roman ideas of plumbing and sanitation. Still, the Kirghiz did add their own notes, primarily horse and rancid butter, to the symphony of stinks.

Corippus said, "Any which way, I'm happier to be down here than upstairs with you and Eustathios Rhangabe. Worst thing can happen to me here is getting burned alive. If Eustathios buggers something up, I'll be scattered over too much landscape too fast to have time to get mad at him."

That was a truth Argyros did his best to ignore. He said, "The innkeeper thinks Rhangabe's some new sort of heretic who isn't allowed to eat, except with wooden tools. I don't know whether he wants to burn him or convert him."

"He'd better convert," Corippus snorted. He and Argyros both laughed, briefly and self-consciously. They knew what would happen if Eustathios Rhangabe struck a spark at the wrong time.

The magistrianos went upstairs to the room the man from the arsenal at Constantinople was using. He knocked—gently, so as not to disturb Rhangabe. He heard a bowl being set on a table inside the room. Only then did Rhangabe come to the door and undo the latch.

As always, he reminded Argyros of a clerk, but a clerk with the work-battered hands of an artisan. "Hello, Argyros," he said. "It goes well, though that thief of a druggist has raised his price for sulfur again."

"So Corippus told me."

Rhangabe grunted. He was not a man much given to conversation. He went back to the table where he had been busy. He had shoved it close to the room's single small window, to give himself the best possible light—no lamps, not here.

Along with the bowl (in which a wooden spoon was thrust), a stout rolling pin lay on the table. By its position, Rhangabe had been working on the middle of the three piles there, grinding it from lumps to fine powder. The pile to the left was black, the middle one (the biggest) a dirty gray-white, and the one on the right bright yellow.

Several years before, Argyros had stolen from the Franco-Saxons the secret of what the Empire called hellpowder. He was perfectly willing to admit that Eustathios Rhangabe knew much more about the deadly stuff now. Rhangabe had headed the men at the arsenal who concocted the deadly incendiary liquid called Greek fire (the magistrianos did not know, or want to know, what went into *that*). When something even more destructive came along, he was the natural one to look to to ferret out its secrets. That he had not blown himself up in the process testified to his skill.

He took the spoon out of the bowl, measured a little saltpeter from the middle pile into a balance, grunted again, and scooped part of the load back onto the table. Satisfied at last, he tipped the balance pan into the bowl, vigorously stirred the contents, squinted, wetted a finger to stick it in so he could taste the mixture, and at last nodded in reluctant approval.

He picked up a funnel (also of wood) and put it in the mouth of a pottery jug. He lifted the bowl, carefully poured the newly mixed hellpowder into the jug. When it was full, he plugged it with an unusual cork he took from a bag that lay next to his bed: the cork had been bored through, and a twist of oily rag forced through the little opening.

Only when Rhangabe was quite finished did he seem to remember Argyros was still in the room. He jerked a thumb at the jars that lined the wall. "That's forty-seven I've made for you since we got here, not counting the ones we fetched from the city. All in all, we have plenty to blow a hole in Goarios' palace you could throw an elephant through, if that's what you want."

A couple of weeks before, the magistrianos would have seized the chance. Hearing Mirrane had made him wonder, though, and made him watch the fortress to check what she said. He was certain now she had not misled him. Goarios might still rule Alania, but the Kirghiz ruled Goarios.

The comings and goings of their leaders were one sign; another was the growing numbers of nomads on Dariel's streets.

By themselves, those might merely have bespoken alliance, but other indications said otherwise. The Kirghiz nobles treated Goarios' guards and courtiers with growing contempt, so much so that Tskhinvali, arrogant himself, complained out loud to Argyros of their presumptuousness. In the markets, the men from the steppe treated traders like servants.

That sort of thing could only go on so long. The Alans were themselves a proud people, while their Georgian subjects remembered every slight and carried on feuds among themselves that lasted for generations. Dariel did not have the feel of a place about to become a world-conqueror's capital. It seemed, Argyros thought, more like one of Eustathios Rhangabe's jugs of hellpowder a few seconds before someone lit the rag stuffed in the cork.

The magistrianos wished he could see Mirrane again—partly because he wanted to get a better feel for what was happening in the palace, and partly just because he wanted to see her. He avoided thinking about which desire was more important to him. In any case, he could not casually make an appointment with the king's mistress. She had to arrange to come to him.

He thought from time to time about changing that, about letting Goarios get hold of her note to him. Each time he held off. Doing that was dangerous and, worse, irrevocable. Moreover, with endless chances she had not betrayed him. Yet he fretted every day at how little he really knew of what was going on.

As things turned out, he found out with no help from Mirrane. He had broken a bronze buckle on one of his sandals, and was in the market dickering, mostly by signs, with a Georgian coppersmith for a replacement. Another local had set out several trays of knives in the adjoining stall.

Half a dozen Kirghiz rode by. One leaned down from the saddle with the effortless ease the nomads displayed on horseback, plucked a fine blade from a tray, and stuck it in his belt. His companions snickered.

The knifesmith shouted angrily and ran after the Kirghiz. The thief, amused at his fury, waited for him to catch up, then gave his beard a hard yank. The nomads laughed louder. Then the one who had taken the knife bellowed in pain—the knifesmith had bitten his hand, hard enough to draw blood.

The nomad lashed out with a booted foot. The knifesmith reeled away, clutching his belly and gasping for breath. All the Kirghiz rode on; now they were chuckling at their comrade.

Had the Georgian knifesmith been made of less stern stuff, the incident would have been over. But the local staggered back to his stall. "Kirghiz!" he shouted as he snatched up a blade. The nomads looked back. The Georgian had known exactly what weapon he was grabbing. He threw the knife.

It went into the thief's chest. The nomad looked astonished, then slowly slid from the saddle.

The rest of the Kirghiz stared for a moment, first at their friend and then at the knifesmith. Quickly but quite deliberately, one of the nomads strung his bow, pulled out an arrow, and shot the Georgian in the face. The man gave a great bass shriek of anguish that made heads jerk round all over the market square. He ran a few steps, his hands clutching the shaft sunk in his cheek, then fell. His feet drummed in the dirt.

Argyros looked round to exchange a horrified glance with the coppersmith, but that worthy had disappeared. He was, the magistrianos decided, no fool. The locals in the square were surging toward the Kirghiz, as the sea will surge when driven by an angry wind. Argyros heard a harsh cry somewhere as a nomad on foot was mobbed. All the mounted ones near him had their bows out now.

He slipped away before any of the Kirghiz chanced to look in his direction. He had not got half a block out of the square when the noise behind him doubled and doubled again. He went from a walk to a trot. He had been caught in a street riot once before, in Constantinople. Once was plenty.

The tumult had not yet reached the inn where Argyros and his men were staying. All the same, Corippus was prowling round the courtyard, wary as a wolf that has taken a scent it mislikes. "How bad?" he asked when the magistrianos told him what had happened.

"With all the nomads in town? Bad," Argyros replied. "The Georgians hate 'em, the Alans hate 'em, and they hate everyone. I'd say we have to look to ourselves—Goarios' men will be too busy guarding the king and his nobles to pay attention to much else."

"Goarios' men will be hiding under their beds, more likely," Corippus snorted. His cold eyes raked the wall that surrounded the courtyard. He made a disgusted noise deep in his throat. "Too low, too shabby. How are we supposed to hold this place?" He shouted to a couple of stableboys, cursed them when they began to protest. They helped him close and bar the gates.

Supsa the innkeeper came rushing out at the noise of the gate panels squealing on their hinges. "What you doing?" he cried in bad Greek.

"He is trying to save you from being killed," Argyros snapped; the officer's rasp he put in his voice straightened Supsa up as if it had been a cup of icy water dashed in his face. The magistrianos added, "There's rioting in the market square, and it's spreading."

Supsa needed only a moment to take that in. "I have heavier bar in back," he said. "I show you where."

As soon as the stouter bar was in place, Argyros called all of his crew except Eustathios Rhangabe out of the inn. Like Corippus, the rest of the men were top combat troops. Some were imperial guards, others, like their leader, ex-soldiers who had joined the corps of magistrianoi. Every one was deadly with bow, spear, and sword.

"Fetch benches," Corippus ordered Supsa, "so they can see over the top of the wall to shoot." This time the taverner and his staff obeyed without question. Other traders came rushing out, clutching whatever weapons they had. Corippus put them on the wall too. "Who knows how well they'll do?" he grunted to Argyros. "The more bodies the better, though."

That got put to the test in minutes. Even while everyone in the court-yard had been working to turn it into a fortress, the noise of strife outside came closer and closer. The white-faced stableboys were just dragging a last bench against the wall when the mob came baying round the corner.

Supsa clambered onto a bench, stood on tiptoe so the rioters could recognize him. He shouted something in his native Georgian, presumably to the effect that he was just another local and so they should leave him alone.

Stones, bricks, and clods of horsedung whizzed past him. One caught him in the shoulder and sent him spinning to the ground. Argyros, less optimistic, had already ducked behind the wall. He peered over it again a moment later. A dozen rioters had hold of a thick wooden beam; the others, after much yelling, cleared a path so they could charge for the gate.

"Shoot!" the magistrianos cried at the same time as Corippus, in his excitement forgetting where he was, bellowed the identical word in Latin. Even without a command, everyone knew what to do. Argyros' men pumped arrows into the mob with a speed and accuracy that left the genu-ine merchants gasping. Screams rose. The improvised ram never got within twenty feet of its intended target. The men who had carried it were down, moaning or motionless. The rest of the rioters suddenly discovered urgent business elsewhere.

"Mobs," Corippus said scornfully. "The bravest bastards in the world, till somebody fights back." Argyros was nodding grateful agreement when shouts of alarm came from the rear of the inn. Men leaped down from their benches and rushed to help the few beleaguered fellows there. "No, damn you, not everyone!" Corippus howled. "The same bloody thing'll happen here if we all go haring off like so many idiots!"

That plain good sense stopped several defenders in their tracks. By then, though, Argyros was already dashing round the inn toward the stables and other outbuildings. The rioters had found or stolen a ladder; more dropped down over the wall every minute.

Bowstrings thrummed. One of the invaders fell, screaming, while two more cursed. Others ran forward. They waved knives and clubs. But for all their ferocity, they were only townsmen, untrained in fighting. Even the merchants who ran with Argyros had better gear and knew more of what they were about. His own men went through their foes like a dose of salts.

Part of that, he suspected, was what helped some women get through childbirth so much better than others: knowing and understanding the process would hurt, and carrying on regardless. He saw a rioter who took a minor knifewound in his forearm forget everything else to gawp at it. The fellow never saw the bludgeon that stretched him senseless in the dirt.

An instant later, the magistrianos got the chance to test his theory. A club thudded into his ribs. He gasped, but managed to spin away from the rioter's next wild swing. After that, drilled reflex took over. He stepped in, knocked away the club—it looked to be a table leg—with his left hand, thrust his dagger into the man's belly. The Georgian might never have heard of defense, and it was too late for him to learn it now.

By then, Argyros had come quite close to his real target, the ladder leaning against the rear wall. A man was climbing over the wall. The magistrianos displayed his blood-smeared knife, grinned a ghastly grin. "Your turn next?" he asked. He had no idea whether the man knew Greek, but the message got through, one way or another. The fellow jumped down—on the far side of the wall. From the curses that followed, he landed on someone. Argyros knocked over the ladder.

The last few rioters inside Supsa's compound had been pushed back against the wall of the stable. Only traders still fought with them hand to hand. Argyros' men, professional survivors, shouted for their allies to get out of the way so they could finish the job with arrows.

"A lesson the townsfolk will remember," the magistrianos told Corippus. He rubbed at his ribcage, which still hurt. He knew he would have an enormous bruise come morning. But to his relief, he felt no stabbing pain when he breathed. He'd had broken ribs once before, and knew the difference.

"Bodies strewn here and there will make a mob think twice," Corippus agreed. "I'm just glad they didn't try to torch us."

Ice walked the magistrianos' spine. He'd forgotten about that. With jar after jar of hellpowder in Supsa's inn— He crossed himself in horror. *"Mè genoíto!"* he exclaimed: "Heaven forbid!"

"I don't think even a mob would be so stupid," Corippus said. "Fire'd mean the whole stinking town would go up. Of course," he added, "you can't be sure."

Argyros told his archers to shoot anyone they saw outside with a torch. For the moment, the inn seemed safe enough. Like any other scavengers, the mob preferred prey that did not fight back. Rioters went by—at a respectful distance—carrying their loot. At any other time, Argyros would have wanted to seize them and drag them off to gaol. Now, caught in chaos in a country not his own, all he did was scan the sky to make sure no plumes of smoke rose in it.

"Night before too long," Corippus observed. "That'll make things tougher."

"So it will." The magistrianos laughed self-consciously. In his concern for fire, he had not even noticed the deepening blue above. The din outside was still savage, and getting worse. Of itself, his hand bunched into a fist. "What's Goarios doing to stop this mess?"

"Damn all I can see—probably under the bed with his soldiers." Contempt filled Corippus' voice. "I'd say our new Alexander can't even conquer his own people, let alone anybody else's."

Yet soldiers did appear. Darkness had just settled in when a heavily armed party approached the front gate of Supsa's inn. Argyros recognized its leader as an officer he had seen several times in the palace. He stayed wary even so—the fellow might be taking advantage of the riot, not trying to quell it. "What do you want?" he shouted in Persian.

The officer's answer startled him too much to be anything but the truth: "You're the wine merchant? His majesty has sent us to collect the next consignment of your *yperoinos.* Here's the gold for it." He held up a leather sack.

With a curious sense of unreality, Argyros let him come up to the barred gate. The magistrianos counted the nomismata. The proper number were there. Shaking their heads as they went back and forth, Argyros' men fetched the jars of superwine and handed them to the officer's troopers over the top of the gate. When he had all of them, the officer saluted Argyros and led his section away.

All the magistrianos could think of was Nero, singing to his lyre of the fall of Troy while Rome burned around him. Dariel was not burning, but no thanks to Goarios.

The stout defense Argyros' band and the real traders had put up gave the rioters a bellyful. They mounted no fresh assaults. The magistrianos found the night almost as nervous as if they had. All around was a devils' chorus of screams, shouts, and crashes, sometimes close by, sometimes far away. They were more alarming because he could not see what caused them. He kept imagining he smelled more smoke than cooking fires could account for.

"Who's that?" one of his men called, peering at a shadow moving in the darkness. "Keep away or I'll put an arrow through you."

A woman laughed. "I've been threatened with worse than that tonight, hero. Go wake Argyros for me."

"Who are you to give me orders, trull?" the Roman demanded. "I ought to—"

"It's all right, Constantine. I know her," the magistrianos said. He looked out, but saw little. "I'm here, Mirrane. What do you want?"

"Let me inside first. If Goarios learns I've come, we're all done for. We may be anyhow."

"Are you going to open the gate for her?" Despite Mirrane's alarming words, Corippus plainly did not like the idea. "No telling who all's lurking there out past our torchlight."

Argyros nodded. Trusting Mirrane was harder than wanting her. He remembered, though, her supple dancer's muscles. "Can you climb a rope if we throw one out to you?" he called over the fence.

She laughed again, not in the least offended. "Of course I can." A moment later she proved good as her word, dropping into the courtyard lightly and quietly as a veteran raider. She was dressed like one, too, in nondescript men's clothes, with her fine hair pulled up under a felt hat that looked like an inverted flowerpot. Few marauders, however, smelled of attar of roses.

Ignoring the curious glances the men in the courtyard were giving her, she baldly told Argyros, "Goarios knows you were in the marketplace where the riot started this afternoon. In fact, he thinks you're the person who got it started."

"Mother of God!" The magistrianos crossed himself. "Why does he think so?"

"You can't deny you were there—one of my, ah, little birds saw you." Mirrane sounded very pleased with herself. "As for why he thinks you threw that knife at the Kirghiz, well, I told the little bird to tell him that." She grinned as if she had done something clever, and expected Argyros to see it too.

All he saw was disaster. Those of his men who heard shouted in outrage. "I should have let Constantine shoot you," he ground out, his voice as icy as Corippus' eyes.

"Ah, but then you'd never have known, would you, not till too late. Now you—we—still have the chance to get away."

"I suppose you expect my men to give you an armed escort back to Persia."

Mirrane paid no attention to the sarcasm. "Not at all, because I'm not planning to go south." She paused. "You do know, don't you?"

"Know what?" Argyros' patience was stretched to the breaking point, but he would sooner have gone under thumbscrews than reveal that to Mirrane.

"That the whole Kirghiz army is through the Caspian Gates and heading for Dariel."

"No," Argyros said woodenly. "I didn't know that." With the chaos inside the town, that at first seemed a less immediate trouble than many closer to hand. Then the magistrianos ran Mirrane's words through his head again. "You're going to the Kirghiz?"

"To stop them, if I can. And you and yours are coming with me."

Argyros automatically began to say no, but checked himself before the word was out of his mouth. The pieces of the puzzle were falling together in his mind. "That's why your man fed Goarios that lying fairy tale!"

"To make you work with me, you mean? Well, of course, dear Basil." She reached out to stroke his cheek, which warmed and infuriated him at the same time. He hoped that did not show on his face, but suspected it did; Mirrane's smile was too knowing. But she held mockery from her voice as she continued, "I told you once that the nomads endanger both our states. Besides, you have a weapon we may be able to turn against them."

"The superwine, you mean?"

"Of course. The more Kirghiz who are drunk, and the drunker they are, the better the chance my plan has."

Being caught in her web himself, the magistrianos had a certain amount of sympathy for the nomads. There were some thousands of them and only one of her, but he was not sure that evened the odds. "We'll load the wagons," he said resignedly. He did not mention the hellpowder. He had used a little at Daras, but only a little. Mirrane would have trouble imagining how powerful more than half a ton of the stuff could be.

As Argyros set his men to work, Supsa came rushing up. "You leaving?" the innkeeper wailed. "No leave!"

"I fear I have very little choice," the magistrianos said. He glared at Mirrane. She smiled sweetly, hoping to annoy him further. He stamped away.

It was nearly midnight before the miniature caravan—wagons, packhorses, and all—rumbled out of the courtyard. The men on horseback looked less like traders than they had coming into Dariel. Some of them had worn mailshirts then too, but that was not where the difference lay. It was in their posture, their eyes, the hard set of their mouths. They were no longer pretending to be anything but soldiers. Even drunken rioters took one look and got out of their way.

"A good crew you have," Mirrane remarked. She was sitting by Argyros, who drove the lead wagon. It was full of *yperoinos*. In the last wagon of the four came Eustathios Rhangabe—as far as everyone else was concerned, he was welcome to baby the hellpowder along all by himself. If by some disaster that wagon went up, the magistrianos thought, it would take the flank guards and everything else with it, but sometimes the illusion of safety was as important as the thing itself.

Argyros' mouth twisted; that could also be said for the illusion of command. "They're dancing to your tune now," he growled. He would have lost his temper altogether had she come back with some clever comment, but she merely nodded. She was, he reminded himself, a professional, too.

He had worried about whether the gate crew would let them pass (for that matter, he had wondered if there would be a gate crew, or if they had left their posts to join the looting). They were there and alert, but their officer waved Argyros through. "Getting out while the getting's good, are you?" he said. "Don't blame you a bit—in your shoes, I'd do the same."

"Not if you knew where we were going, you wouldn't," the magistrianos said, once the fellow was out of earshot. Mirrane giggled.

Argyros called a halt a couple of miles outside Dariel. "This is far enough," he said. "None of the trouble from town will follow us here, and we need rest to be worth anything come morning. We also need to find out just what this scheme is that we're supposed to be following." He gave Mirrane a hard look.

So did Corippus. "Why?" he asked bluntly. "Now that she doesn't have Goarios protecting her, why not turn her into dogmeat and go about our business?" Several men grunted agreement.

Mirrane stared back, unafraid. She said, "I might point out that, were it not for me, Goarios' soldiers would have you now."

"Were it not for you," Corippus retorted, "Goarios' soldiers would never have been interested in us in the first place." Again many of his comrades paused in the business of setting up camp to nod.

"She could have given us to the Alan king any time she chose," Argyros said. "She didn't."

"Till it served her purpose," Corippus said stubbornly.

"True enough, but are you saying it fails to serve ours, too? Do you really want the Kirghiz rampaging through Mesopotamia, or grazing their flocks in Kappadokia from now on? They endanger us as well as Persia. And if you're so eager to be rid of Mirrane, let us hear *your* plan for holding the nomads back." He hoped the north African would not have one.

When Corippus dropped his eyes, the magistrianos knew he had won that gamble. His subordinate, though, did not yield tamely. He said, "Maybe we could use the *yperoinos* to get the buggers drunk, and then—" He ran dry, as a waterclock will when someone forgets to fill it.

"And then what?" Argyros prodded. "Sneak through their tents slitting throats? There are a few too many of them for that, I'm afraid. If you have no ideas of your own, getting rid of someone who does strikes me as wasteful."

Corippus saluted with sardonic precision, threw his hands in the air, and stalked off to help get a fire started.

Mirrane touched Argyros' arm. In the darkness, her eyes were enormous.

"I thank you," she whispered. "In this trade of ours, one gets used to the notion of dying unexpectedly, but I'd not have cared for what likely would have happened before they finally knocked me over the head."

Having been a soldier, Argyros knew what she meant. He grunted, embarrassed for a moment at what men could do—and too often did—to women.

"Why did you choose to save me?" Mirrane still kept her voice low, but the newly kindled fire brought an ironic glint to her eye. "Surely not for the sake of the little while we were lovers?" She studied the magistrianos' face. "Are you blushing?" she asked in delighted disbelief.

"It's only the red light of the flames," Argyros said stiffly. "You've been saying you know how to stop the Kirghiz. That's more than anyone else has claimed. You're worth keeping for that, if nothing else."

"If nothing else," she echoed with an upraised eyebrow. "For that polite addition, at least, I am in your debt."

The magistrianos bit back an angry reply. Mirrane had a gift for making him feel out of his depth, even when, as now, power lay all on his side. No woman since his long-dead wife had drawn him so, but Mirrane's appeal was very different from Helen's. With Helen he had felt more at ease, at peace, than with anyone else he had ever known. The air of risk and danger that surrounded Mirrane had little to do with the settings in which he met her; it was part of her essence. Like his first jolt of *yperoinos,* it carried a stronger jolt than he was used to.

To cover his unease, he returned to matters at hand. "So what is this precious plan of yours?" She stayed silent. He said, "For whatever you think it worth, I pledge I won't slit your throat after you've spoken, or harm you in any other way."

She watched him. "If your hard-eyed friend gave me that promise, I'd know what it was worth. You, though . . . with that long, sad face, you remind me of the saints I've seen painted in Christian churches. Should I believe you on account of that? It seems a poor reason."

"Sad to say, I am no saint." As if to prove his words, memories of her lips, her skin against his surged in him. Angrily, he fought them down.

Her lazy smile said she was remembering, too. But it faded, leaving her thoughtful and bleak. "If I tell you, I must trust you, and your land and mine are enemies. May you fall into the fire in the House of the Lie if you are leading me astray."

"I will swear by God and His Son, if you like."

"No, never mind. An oath is only the man behind it, and you suit me well enough without one." Still she said nothing. Finally Argyros made a questioning noise. She laughed shakily. "The real trouble is, the plan is not very good."

"Let me hear it."

"All right. We spoke of it once, in fact, in Goarios' palace. You said you remembered how the White Huns lured Peroz King of Kings and his army to destruction—how they dug a trench with but a single small opening, then concealed it. They fled through the gap, then fell on his army when it was thrown into confusion by the first ranks charging into the ditch. I had hoped to do something like that to the Kirghiz. They have little discipline at any time, and if they were drunk on your superwine, drunker even than they knew—"

Argyros nodded. The scheme was daring, ruthless, and could have been practical—all characteristics he had come to associate with Mirrane. "You do see the flaw?" he said, as gently as he could.

"Actually, I saw two," she replied. "We don't have enough people to dig the ditch, and we don't have an army to use to fight even if it should get dug."

"That, ah, does sum it up," the magistrianos said.

"I know, I know, I know." Bitterness as well as firelight shadowed Mirrane's features. "At the end, I kept telling Goarios he was giving his country away by not keeping a tighter check on the nomads; I was hoping to use the Dariel garrison to do what I had in mind. But he still thinks he'll ride on the backs of the Kirghiz to glory—or he did, until the riots started. For all I know, he may believe it even now. He's had less use for me outside the bedchamber since I stopped telling him things he wanted to hear." She cocked her head, peered at Argyros. "And so here I am, in your hands instead."

He did not answer. His eyes were hooded, far away.

Mirrane said, "With most men, I would offer at once to go to their tents with them. With you, somehow I don't think that would help save me."

It was as if he had not heard her. Then he came far enough out of his brown study to reply, "No, it would be the worst thing you could do." Her glare brought him fully back to himself. He explained hastily, "My crew would mutiny if they thought I was keeping you for my own pleasure."

She glanced toward Corippus, shivered. "Very well. I don't doubt you're right. What then?"

"I'll tell you in the morning." The magistrianos' wave summoned a couple of his men. "Make sure she does not escape, but don't harass her either. Her scheme has more merit than I thought." They saluted and led Mirrane away.

Argyros called Corippus to him, spoke at some length. If defects lurked in the plan slowly taking shape in his mind, the dour north African would find them. Corippus did, too, or thought he did. Argyros had to wake up Eustathios Rhangabe to be sure. Through a yawn wide enough to frighten a lion, Rhangabe suggested changes, ones not so drastic as Corippus had thought necessary. The artisan fell asleep where he sat; Corippus and the magistrianos kept hammering away.

At last Corippus threw his hands in the air. "All right!" he growled, almost loud enough to wake Rhangabe. "This is what we came for—we have to try it, I suppose. Who knows? We may even live through it."

A small wagon train and a good many packhorses plodded north toward the Caspian Gates. The riders who flanked the packhorses seemed bored with what they were doing: a routine trip, their attitude seemed to say, that they had made many times before. *If I see Constantinople again,* Argyros thought half seriously, *I'll have to do some real acting, maybe the next time someone revives Euripides.*

A glance up from beneath lowered brows showed the magistrianos Kirghiz scouts. He had been seeing them for some time now, and they his band. He had enough horsemen with him to deter the scouts from approaching by ones and twos. For his part, he wanted to keep pretending he did not know they existed.

For as long as he could, he also kept ignoring the dust cloud that lay ahead. When he saw men through it, though, men who wore furs and leathers and rode little steppe ponies, he reined in, drawing the wagon to a halt.

"We've just realized that's the whole bloody Kirghiz army," he called to his comrades, reminding them of their roles as any good director would. "Now we can be afraid."

"You're too late," someone said. The men from the Empire milled about in counterfeit—Argyros hoped it was counterfeit—panic and confusion. His own part was to leap down from the wagon, cut a packhorse free of the string, then scramble onto the beast and boot it after the mounts his men were riding desperately southward.

The Kirghiz scouts gave chase. A few arrows hissed past. Then one of the nomads toppled from the saddle; Corippus was as dangerous a horse-archer as any plainsman. That helped deter pursuit, but Argyros did not think it would have lasted long in any case. The Kirghiz scouts were only human—they would want to steal their fair share of whatever these crazy merchants had left behind.

Argyros looked back over his shoulder: cautiously, as he was not used to riding without stirrups. One of the nomads was bending to examine the broken jars the magistrianos' horse had been carrying. Some of the contents must still have been cupped in a shard, for the Kirghiz suddenly jumped up and began pointing excitedly at the packhorses and wagons.

Argyros did not need to hear him to know what he was shouting. Nomads converged on the abandoned *yperoinos* like bees on roses.

The poor fools who had provided such a magnificent windfall were quickly forgotten. Before long, they were able to stop and look back with no fear of pursuit. Corippus gave the short bark that passed for laughter with him. "After a haul like that, most of those buggers will have all the loot from civilization they ever dreamed of."

"Something to that," Argyros admitted. The thought made him sad.

One of his men put hand to forehead to shield his eyes from the sun as he peered toward the Kirghiz. He swore in frustration all the same, and turned to Argyros. "Can you get a better view, sir?"

"Let's see." At his belt, along with such usual appurtenances as knife, sap, and pouch, Argyros carried a more curious device: a tube fitting tightly into another, with convex glass glittering at both ends. He undid it from the boss on which it hung, raised it to his eye, and pulled the smaller tube part way out of the larger one.

The image he saw was upside down and fringed with false colors, but the Kirghiz seemed to jump almost within arm's length. Argyros had learned the secret of the far-seer from more westerly steppe nomads more than a decade before; his success in ferreting it out had led to his career in the corps of magistrianoi. The artisans in Constantinople still had trouble making lenses good enough to use—most far-seers belonged to Roman generals, though the savants at the imperial university had seen some things in the heavens that puzzled them and even, it was whispered, shook their faith. Only because Argyros had learned of the far-seer in the first place was he entitled to carry one now.

He watched the Kirghiz nobles, some of whom had sampled superwine in Dariel, trying to keep their rank and file away from the wagons. They were too late. Too many ordinary nomads had already tasted the potent brew. The ones who'd had some wanted more; the ones who'd had none wanted some. Even under the best of circumstances, the nomads only obeyed orders when they felt like it. These circumstances were not the best. Argyros smiled in satisfaction.

"They all want their share," he reported.

"Good," Corippus said. The rest of the men nodded, but without great enthusiasm. If this part of the plan had failed, it could not have gone forward. The more dangerous portions lay ahead.

The Romans rode back toward Dariel. Eustathios Rhangabe was bringing up the last wagon, the one so different from the rest. A couple of outriders were with him; Mirrane's horse was tethered to one of theirs. Argyros had told them to shoot her if she tried to escape, and warned her of his order. All the same, he was relieved to see her with his men. Orders were rarely a match for the likes of her.

"You have your spots chosen?" the magistrianos asked Rhangabe.

The artisan nodded. "Six of them, three on either side."

"Basil, what are these madmen playing at? They won't talk to me," Mirrane said indignantly. "They aren't following what we talked about at all. All they've done is dig holes in the ground and put jugs of your strong wine in them. What good will that—?" Mirrane stopped in the middle of her sentence. Her sharp brown eyes flashed from Argyros to the wagon and back again. "Or is that *yperoinos* in them? Back in Daras, you had some trick of Ahriman—"

Argyros would have said "Satan's trick," but he understood her well enough. He might have known she would make the connection. His respect for her wits, already high, rose another notch. He said, "Well, without that army behind us, we do have to modify things a bit."

"The good god Ohrmazd knows that's true." Suddenly, startlingly, she grinned at the magistrianos. "You won't need to worry about my running off any longer, dear Basil. I wouldn't miss seeing this for worlds." So I can bring news of it back to the King of Kings, Argyros added silently.

He said, "Let's hope there's something interesting for you to see." He knew she was clever enough to add her own unspoken commentary: if not, nothing else matters, because we'll be dead.

He told off the half-dozen men who had done the digging, sent them back to the holes they had made. He detailed two more to keep Mirrane under guard. Regardless of what she said, he took no chances where she was concerned. Eustathios Rhangabe, of course, stayed with his wagon.

That left—Argyros counted on his fingers—fifteen men. He wished for four times as many. Wishing failed to produce them. "Double quivers," the magistrianos told the men he did have. Each of them carried, then, forty arrows. If every shaft killed, they could hardly slay one of ten Kirghiz.

How long would the nomads take to get thoroughly drunk? Certainly not as long as any of them expected. Argyros gauged the sun in the sky. He could not afford to wait for nightfall. He did not think he would have to.

Corippus had spent even more time in the imperial army than Argyros. Their eyes met; they both judged the moment ripe. Argyros raised his right hand. His comrades clucked to their horses, trotted north once more behind him.

They rode in silence, alert for Kirghiz scouts. Argyros used the far-seer from horseback, though it made him vaguely seasick to do so. He saw no one. His confidence rose, a little. If the nomads were too busy soaking up their unexpected loot to bother with scouts, so much the better.

The horsemen topped a low rise. Corippus barked sudden harsh laughter. "Look at them!" he exclaimed, pointing. "They're like a swarm of bees round a honeypot."

The comparison was apt. The Kirghiz were milling in a great disorderly knot around the abandoned wagons and packhorses. Pulling out the far-seer again, Argyros saw jars going from hand to hand. He watched one nomad, wearing a foolish expression, slide off his horse. Another reached down to snatch away the jug the fellow was holding.

"They're as ripe as ever they will be," the magistrianos said. "Let's go kick the honeypot over—and hope we don't get stung."

Some of the Kirghiz must have seen Argyros and his followers approach, yet they took no alarm. Argyros could hardly blame their leaders for that. No sane attackers would approach a foe so grotesquely outnumbering them, no more than a mouse would blithely leap into the fox's jaws.

The magistrianos drew up his tiny battle line not far inside archery range. He raised his arm, dropped it. Along with his men, he snatched up an arrow, drew his bow back to his ear and released it, grabbed for the next shaft.

They had all shot three or four times before the racket from the Kirghiz began to change timbre. Some of the nomads cried out in pain, others pointed and yelled at the suicidal maniacs harassing them, just as a man will point and shout at the mosquito that has just bitten his leg and buzzed off.

A few nomads began to shoot back, those who happened to be facing the right way, who were not too tightly pressed by their fellows, and who were sober enough to remember how to use their bows. Argyros and his comrades methodically emptied their quivers into the tight-packed mass. Those who knew fragments of the Kirghiz speech shouted insults at the nomads. They were not out to strike and skulk away; they wanted to be noticed.

When the outer ranks of nomads moved away from the wagons, the magistrianos' little force retreated a corresponding distance, but kept plying the Kirghiz with arrows. More and more nomads came after them.

Argyros yelled the most bloodcurdling curses he knew, then turned his horse and roweled it with his spurs. This flight was not like the one when he had abandoned the *yperoinos* wagons; the nomads were pursuing in earnest now.

One of his men shrieked as an arrow sprouted from his shoulder. The magistrianos knew others would also perish, either because some arrows had to hit with so many in the air or because some nomads had faster horses than some of his men. With the thunder of thousands of hooves behind him, he hoped some of his men had faster horses than the Kirghiz. Were the chase longer than the mile and a half or so that lay between Argyros' men and Eustathios Rhangabe's wagon, he knew none of his people would be likely to survive.

He glanced ahead and to the right. Yes, there behind a bush was one of the men who had come from Constantinople. Unless one knew where to look for him, he was almost invisible. Only the stragglers of the Kirghiz, who were pursuing with scant regard for order, would come near the fellow.

Argyros had to keep his attention on more immediate concerns. He did not see his countryman thrust a lighted candle at an oil-soaked rag, and noticed only peripherally when the fellow leaped up and dashed for another hole not far away.

What happened moments after that was difficult to ignore, even for one as single-mindedly focused on flight as the magistrianos. The hellpowder in the buried jars ignited, and, with a roar louder and deeper than thunder, the ground heaved itself up. Earth, stones, and shrubs vomited from the new-dug crater.

Argyros' horse tried to rear. He roughly fought it down. He and the rest of the men from the Roman Empire had encountered hellpowder before, and knew what the frightful noise was. Even as the thought raced through Argyros' mind, another charge of the stuff went off, far over on the Kirghiz left. It should have been simultaneous with the one on the right, and was in fact close enough for Argyros to let out a pleased grunt.

The nomads, as much taken by surprise as their mounts, naturally shied away from the blasts. That bunched them more closely together and made it harder for them to keep up their headlong pursuit. Still, they were bold men, not easily cowed by the unknown. They kept after their quarry.

Another pair of blasts crashed forth, almost at the same instant, as the Romans dashed past the second prepared set of charges. These were nearer each other and nearer the path than the first ones had been. Argyros felt the booming reports with his whole body, not merely through his ears. Again he had to force his mount to obey his will.

He swung round in the saddle to look back at the Kirghiz. They were packed still more tightly now, wanting nothing to do with the eruptions to either side. He saw two horses collide. Both went down with their riders, and others, unable to stop, tumbled over them. Now the magistrianos' men were lengthening their lead over the nomads, except for the frontrunners out ahead of the pack. He grabbed an arrow, tried a Parthian shot at one of those. He missed, swore, and concentrated again on riding.

The Romans manning the third set of charges had their timing down to a science. They waited until their countrymen were past before touching off their stores of hellpowder. This last pair was so close to the path that dirt showered down on Argyros. His mount bolted forward as if he had spurred it. The nomads' ponies, on the other hand, balked at the sudden cataclysmic noise in front of them.

The last wagon appeared ahead. Eustathios Rhangabe dove out of it, then sprinted for the shelter of the rocky outcrop where, Argyros presumed, the last two Romans were holding Mirrane. The magistrianos hoped Rhangabe had accurately gauged the length of candle he had left burning atop one of the jars in the wagon. On second thought, hope did not seem enough. Jolts from Argyros' galloping horse made his prayer breathless, but it was no less sincere for that.

Around the wagon, invitingly set out, were open jars of *yperoinos*. None of the Romans paid any attention to them. The Kirghiz whooped with delight when they spied the familiar jars. Most of them tugged on the reins to halt their horses. Drinking was easier and more enjoyable work than chasing crazy bandits who shot back.

Several Roman riders were already diving behind the rocks where Rhangabe had found shelter; more dismounted and ran for them as Argyros drew up. He sprang from his horse. An arrow buried itself in the ground, a palm's breadth from his foot. Not all the nomads, worse luck, were pausing to refresh themselves.

The magistrianos peered over a boulder. He lofted a shot over the last few Romans at the pursuing Kirghiz. His fingers told him only three shafts were left in his quiver. He reached for one. If something had gone wrong with that wagon, saving them would not matter.

"How much longer?" Mirrane shouted at him.

"Why ask me?" he yelled back, irrationally annoyed. "Rhangabe lit the candle—why don't you ask—"

He was never sure afterward whether he said "him" or not. He had thought the blasts from a couple of jars of hellpowder loud and terrifying; this sound put him in mind of the roar that would accompany the end of the world. The earth shook beneath his feet. He threw himself facedown, his eyes in the dust and his hands clapped to his ears. He felt no shame at that; the rest of the Romans were doing exactly the same thing.

He was, though, the leader of this crew. Pride quickly forced him to his feet—he did not want his men to see him groveling in the dirt. He brushed at his tunic as he started to scramble over the rocks to find out what the blast had done.

Two others, he noticed, were already up and looking. One was Eustathios Rhangabe. Argyros did not mind that; if anyone could take hellpowder in stride, it would be a man who had dealt with the stuff for years. The other, however, was Mirrane.

He had only an instant in which to feel irked. Then she threw herself into his arms and delivered a kiss that rocked him almost as much as the hellpowder had. Her lips touched his ear. That was not a caress; he could feel them moving in speech. He shook his head. For the moment, at least, he was deaf. He was sorry when Mirrane pulled her face away from his, but she did not draw back far, only enough to let him see her mouth as she spoke. "It worked!" she was yelling over and over. "It worked!"

That brought him back to himself. "Let me see," he said, mouthing the words in the same exaggerated style she had used: her hearing could be in no better shape than his.

He peered over the piled rocks behind which he had huddled. "Mother of God, have mercy!" he whispered. Of itself, his hand leapt from his forehead to his breast as it shaped the sign of the cross.

He had been a soldier; he knew only too well that war was not the clean-cut affair of drama and glory the epic poets made it out to be. All the same, he was not prepared for the spectacle the lifting veils of acrid smoke were presenting to him.

The titanic blast had not slain all the Kirghiz, or even come close. A large majority of the nomads were riding north. From the desperate haste with which they used spurs and whips on their ponies, Argyros did not think they would pause this side of the pass. Observing what they were fleeing from, the magistrianos could not blame them.

In adapting the plan the Ephthalites had used against the King of Kings, Argyros knew he needed to force the Kirghiz to group more tightly than usual: thus the hellpowder charges that funneled them toward the wagon. Now he saw how appallingly well he had succeeded.

Close by the crater where the wagon had stood, few fragments were recognizable as surely being from man or horse. Freakishly, however, one of the jars of superwine that helped lure the nomads to disaster remained unbroken, though it, like much of the landscape there, was splashed with red.

Argyros had anticipated that central blast zone, and hoped it—and the noise that went with its creation—would be enough to intimidate the Kirghiz. He had not thought about what would lay beyond there, about what would happen when fragments of the wagon and fragments of the jars that had held the hellpowder were propelled violently outward after it ignited.

The results, especially when seen upside down in the surreal closeness the far-seer brought, reminded him of nothing so much as hell in a hot-tempered monk's sermon. Scythed-down men and horses, variously mutilated, writhed and bled and soundlessly screamed. That silence, somehow, was worst of all; it began to lift as the minutes went by and Argyros' hearing slowly returned.

Yet despite the horror, the magistrianos also understood Mirrane's delight at the scene before them. Never had a double handful of men not only vanquished but destroyed an enemy army; the stand of the Spartans at Thermopylae was as nothing beside this.

One by one, the rest of Argyros' crew nerved themselves to see what they had wrought. Most reacted with the same mixture of awe, horror, and pride the magistrianos felt. Others tried to emulate Eustathios Rhangabe's dispassionate stare; the artisan reacted to the grisly spectacle before him as if it were the final step in some complex and difficult geometric proof, a demonstration already grasped in the abstract.

For his part, Corippus looked as though he only regretted the carnage had not been greater. "Some of them will be a long time dying," he shouted Argyros' way, sounding delighted at the prospect. His eyes, for once, did not seem cold. He was savage as any Kirghiz, Argyros thought; the chief difference between him and them was in choice of masters. He made a deadly dangerous foe; the magistrianos was glad they were on the same side.

That thought brought his mind back to the woman next to him. Mirrane might have been able to see into his head. She said, "And now that they are done with, what do you plan to do about me?" She no longer sounded full of nothing but glee, and Argyros did not think that was solely concern for her own fate. She had been examining the results of the blast for several minutes now, and a long look at those was enough to sober anyone less grim of spirit than Corippus.

The magistrianos stayed silent so long that Mirrane glanced over to see if he'd heard. Her mouth tightened when she realized he had. She said, "If you intend to kill me, kill me cleanly—don't give me to your men for their sport. Were we reversed, captor and captive, I would do as much for you." Somehow, she managed one syllable of a laugh. "I hate to have to bellow to laugh, but my ears ring so, I can't help it."

"Yes, I believe you might give me a clean death," Argyros said musingly, though the ferocity of the King of King's torturers was a bugbear that frightened children all through the Empire. The magistrianos paused again; he had been thinking about what to do with Mirrane since they left Dariel, without coming up with any sure answer. Now, under her eyes, he had to. At last he said, as much to himself as to her, "I think I am going to bring you back to Constantinople."

"As you will." Mirrane fought to hold her voice toneless, but beneath her swarthiness her face grew pale; the ingenuity of the Emperor's torturers was a bugbear that frightened children all through Persia.

"I think you misunderstand me." Like Mirrane, Argyros found it odd to be carrying on this conversation near the top of his lungs, but had little choice. Spreading his hands, he went on, "If you had your henchmen here instead of the other way round, would you let me go back to my capital?"

"No," Mirrane answered at once; she was a professional.

The magistrianos had looked for no other reply from her. "You see my problem, then." She nodded, again promptly—in many ways the two of them spoke the same language, though he used Greek and she Persian. That reflection was part of what prompted him to continue, "I hadn't planned to put you in the gaol in the bowels of the Praitorion, or to send you to the Kynegion"—the amphitheater in northeastern Constantinople where the imperial headsmen plied their trade. "I meant that you should come back to the city with me."

"Did you?" Mirrane lifted an eyebrow in the elegant Persian irony that could make even a sophisticated Roman less than self-assured. "Of course you know I will say yes to that: if I slept with you for the sake of duty in Daras, I suppose I can again, if need be. But why do you think you can make me stay in Constantinople? I escaped you there once, remember, on the spur of the moment. Do you imagine I could not do it again, given time to prepare?"

Argyros frowned; here, perhaps, was more professionalism than he wanted to find. He said, "Come or not, sleep with me or not, as you care to, not for any duty. As for leaving Constantinople, I dare say you are right —there are always ways and means. I can hope, though, you will not want to use them."

Mirrane looked at him in amusement. "If that is a confession of wild, passionate, undying love, I must own I've heard them better done."

"No doubt," Argyros said steadily. "The Master of Offices writes poetry; I fear I haven't the gift."

"Battle epics." Mirrane gave a scornful sniff.

The magistrianos supposed he should not have been surprised she knew what sort of poetry George Lakhanodrakon composed; the Romans kept such dossiers on high Persian officials. But he admired the way she brought it out pat.

He shook his head. This was no time to be bedeviled with side issues. He said, "I doubt you could pry a confession of wild, passionate, undying love from me with barbed whips or hot irons. To mean them fully, I fear one has to be half my age and innocent enough to think the world is always a sunny place. I'm sorry I can't oblige. I will say, though, I've found no woman but you since my wife died with whom I care to spend time out of bed as well as in. Will that do?"

It was Mirrane's turn to hesitate. When she did speak, she sounded as if she was thinking out loud, a habit Argyros also had: "You must mean this. You have the power behind you to do as you like with me here; you gain nothing from stringing me along." She still kept that inward look as she said, "I told you once in Constantinople we were two of a kind—do you remember?"

"Yes. Maybe I've finally decided to believe you."

"Have you?" Mirrane's voice remained reflective, but something subtle changed in it: "I suppose Constantinople has its share of fire-temples."

She was, the magistrianos thought, a master of the oblique thrust, murmuring in one breath how alike they were and then hammering home a fundamental difference. He said stiffly, "I would never give up hope that you might come to see that the truth lies in Christ." Seeing her nostrils flare, he made haste to add, "Those who follow the teachings of Zoroaster may worship in the city and the Empire, however, in return for the King of Kings not persecuting the Christians under his control . . . as I am sure you know perfectly well."

That last little jab won a smile from her. "Fair enough," she said, "though how you Christians can fail to see that evil is a live force of its own rather than a mere absence of good has always been beyond me." Her smile grew wider, more teasing. "I expect we will have time to argue it out."

He took a moment to find her meaning. When at last he did, his breath caught as he asked, "You'll come with me, then?"

"Well, why not? Didn't the two of us—not forgetting your men, of course—just put paid to a threat to both our countries? What better sets the stage for a more, ah, personal alliance?" Now she was wearing an impudent grin.

Argyros felt a similar expression stretch his face in unfamiliar ways. He looked again at the blast that had ruined the hopes of the Kirghiz and of Goarios. His eye lit on the miraculously unbroken bottle of *yperoinos*. Suddenly it seemed a very good omen. He pointed it out to Mirrane. "Shall we pledge ourselves with it?"

"Well, why not?" she said.

DAVIDSON, SHADOW SLAYER

John Kelly

The black-cloaked figure dashed down the crowded streets, down a passage that a wedge of hooded gunmen forced open before him. Speed was everything. He barely heard the hissing of their sonic rifles; he didn't care how they got him down there. Speed was everything.

No, they weren't killing, just firing into the air to scare the crowds, to move them. All the better.

The streets grew less crowded as they entered the old section, then empty when they reached the gateway. They bounded down the ramps to the old, dusty rocketfield, Davidson still just steps behind his wedge of guards. The gunmen led him down the plastic-grate boardwalks, through the maze of cruisers and transports. They fled past the vast, useless City-movers, with their towering, decaying silver hulls, and past sleeker ships for smaller crowds, still too big to have a use anymore. The ships bounced up and down before Davidson's eyes as he pounded onward. Then suddenly they were there: at a small golden Needle, a sharply pointed, one-man ship already trembling with slowly growing power. The guards ran onward, shedding their guns and their masks, to lose themselves in the maze of small ships.

"Good luck," said a shorter man in a tapered grey coat. He shook Davidson's hand and took his cloak.

"I, um—" He looked into Davidson's eyes and stopped trying to speak.

Davidson climbed through the hatch on the Needle and was locked in for the journey. The Techies pulled away the giant clamps which had held the Needle in place and mechanically pulled the man in the coat away to a safe distance. The whine of the Needle's engines rose to a scream; then suddenly the Needle shot skyward.

Davidson had time to think, before the gas numbed him. He had a chance to review the escape plan one last time.

Everyone loved the irony. The irony! Hide him at the homeland, in the heart of everything. Davidson wished it was less ironic, and more obscure.

Ancient history: there was once only one Earth, back in "modern" times before the Great Expansion.

Political history: as if the Four Rebellions and the Great Repression hadn't been enough, the pirates of the Drassen Terror had left the center of the inhabited galaxy a vast ruin. The first Earth was one of the hardest-hit planets: very little was left to inhabit once the pirates had finished "punishing" the cities. In the growing resource crunch, reclamation efforts were not considered worthwhile since the ancient planet's resources were already so depleted. Like so many other planets at the time, it was simply left to its own devices.

And economic fact: as the resources wound down further, more and more planets were cut from contact, until finally, with the exhaustion of the last Fuels, all interstellar contact became extraordinary. It was then that the records about the other planets became less important, and their upkeep too expensive.

Davidson had a chance, if they sent him to one of the long-forgotten planets. No general search would find him. And he wasn't about to give himself away. Davidson rarely told tales.

So everything would have to be new. New life, new story, new man.

The newcomer looked vaguely like a Drortian, but he had been much too tall, and his eyes were blue instead of red. He had come out of nowhere, it seemed, for no one knew of him and he offered no past. But that didn't mean anything at the time; it was true not just of Davidson, but of almost all of us.

I was a farmboy then, trying desperately to become something else. Service to Jamaal had seemed perfect to me. Of course they all knew I was a farmboy despite my silence. It didn't bother them, I learned later—the less travelled the fighter, the fewer legends he or she would have heard, and the more likely he or she would be useful against the Shadows.

Others in the Scarlet Guard were criminals, I'm sure; but whether people were there because of an unsolved murder or because they had been chosen for sacrifice or because they simply sought adventure really didn't matter much. What mattered was that they wouldn't freeze on you when the Shadows began to sing fear into the air. The Shadows were attacking Jamaal because Jamaal still used the oldthings and because Jamaal didn't offer sacrifices.

Davidson was as good a fighter as any, ever. He had the fastest sword of all of us and I never saw him freeze. But that's not why he's famous now.

He's famous for the day the star dropped down from the sky to search for him, the day he killed a star. And he's famous for the day he disappeared.

But I'll tell his story from the beginning. And don't be surprised if it's my story too.

The older guards said that Davidson had been recruited because of a tavern scrap, in which he punched one of the guard captains senseless before the man could even draw his sword. But I was never sure if that story was true, for like much of what you heard about Davidson, the story seemed embellished with more than a touch of fable.

At any rate, the two of us entered Jamaal's guard the same day. I remember that because he was there, getting his uniforms, when I was being fitted. But it wasn't until we were in the bunkhouse that I had the courage to say anything to him.

"I'm Charya," I said.

He stared at me blankly.

"My name is Charya. What's yours?" He was silent, blank; and it dawned on me that he didn't speak Nadic.

"Sed Charya um," I said in Drortic, my mother's tongue. But he didn't speak that either.

I pointed to myself. "Charya."

"Davidson," he replied, in his low, soft voice.

In the days that followed, I learned just how little Davidson knew about Nada. As the only new recruits in training, we were responsible for each other; and I soon found myself teaching him everything from how to respond to a guard captain's orders to how to eat with a clawspoon. It was odd that he seemed twice my age and yet I was teaching him everything, and it was strangely comforting too, for the frightened boy that I was then.

And Davidson was a quick enough learner. Within a few weeks, he had a fair day-to-day knowledge of Nadic. And within the same time, he had grown from no knowledge of broadswords to being one of the best fighters in camp.

Then one morning a captain gave us our scarlet armor, signalling the end of our apprenticeship. Now we would be able to parade into town to all the respect and fear the other guardsmen drew; now we would be able to treat the sheriff's knights with the same scorn. For we were a fighting force too powerful even for them to challenge—and also, we had seen the Shadows, and were thus touched.

We were getting our armor several weeks early, and I was swelling with pride. Then I learned the reason: patrols were short, and no Shadows had been seen for many nights. That meant an attack was coming, but up which slope of the mountain was anybody's guess.

That Jamaal's castle was on a mountaintop made it visible for miles, especially at night when he made the oldthing sun tubes glow to light the darkness. And it also made it remote, although that was partly the villagers' doing, for they had moved off the mountainside when Jamaal refused to join in the sacrifices. But lastly, it made it defendable, which was the reason our guard existed in the first place.

For weeks, our trainers had been tired relieved guardsmen back from their patrols to teach us the woodcraft, stealth, and swordcraft in the early morning light. But that night, we too would patrol one face of Jamaal's mountain.

Davidson and I would be patrolling with Manda La, the only female guard captain. We would patrol the field, the one treeless face of the mountain, for they thought it the least likely place for the attack to come from. But if the attack was as big as they expected, we would all be called to the fight before it was over.

They lowered the bunkhouse shutters, that morning we received the armor, and all the guardsmen were preparing to sleep. I polished my armor and sharpened my sword, even though I knew it didn't have to be sharp to fight the Shadows. Davidson just stared at the wall.

"Davidson?" I asked.

"Davidson?"

His face suddenly snapped around. "What?" His eyes were hard and empty. I felt as if I'd never seen him before.

"Nothing, nothing," I stuttered. "Sorry."

Then the room was totally dark. I felt a hand on my shoulder. "I'm sorry, Charya. But I have to let him out. I have to be ready, to kill well."

It was just bright enough to see the grass waving.

"I hate the fields!" Manda hissed.

"Why?"

"Because the waving grass looks so much like the Shadows."

"But you can barely see it!"

Manda stopped walking. "You can barely see the Shadows, too. They're darker than black, I think."

"What?"

"Don't ask me to explain it. All I know is they're pure energy, and they would still seem dark in the deepest cave of Dror."

Davidson was slowly glancing around himself. "Then how will we know they're there?"

She laughed. "You'll know. Hasn't anyone told you of them?"

No, we explained. Our trainers had always wanted to put that subject off.

She sighed. "You'll learn fast enough," she said.

Then I saw more waving grass—except it was waving too high off the ground to be grass. I was suddenly struck with riveting, numbing fear. My blood felt hot; I gasped.

"Shadows," Manda hissed. "More than I've ever seen. Charya, run for help!"

Manda and Davidson stepped forward, in time to reach the first two Shadows, but all I could do was watch. And what swordplay I saw!

The Shadows flowed like water, in and around the swordthrusts of Manda and Davidson. The Shadows' goal was to reach through the visors of the fighting guards—the only opening through which they could touch skin. A touch would burn your life away—that much I'd been taught.

The swordsmen, meanwhile, tried to touch the amorphorous beings with their swords. And their touch was equally fatal: the essence of the creature would immediately flow down the furry-lined armor into the dirt, and the Shadow would be melted, gone forever.

The most experienced guards could tell of so melting up to a dozen Shadows, of making the rolling death clouds "sing down their sword" only a handful of times. Yet Davidson melted two even as I watched.

"Charya!" Manda yelled again. "Run for help, *now!*" But I was still frozen.

Then one of the shimmering black clouds was rolling towards me. It was close, and then closer, and then finally it blocked my view of even the stars. I swung just in time, and it stopped advancing to dance around my sword. It was my chance, and I sprinted up the field. The Shadows were slow in rolling, and I was able to get away.

When I returned with the other guards, Manda was lying dead, and Davidson was in the midst of his now legendary one-man-stand. Five or six Shadows surrounded him; and dozens more waited; yet he dodged, parried, and attacked when able; and Shadow after Shadow sang dead down his sword.

And I could hear the Shadows' other song now, too, the low drone, their song of fear. For it was through fear that you really sensed them, I realized: a sixth sense reserved for knowing only them.

With a yell, I led the guards running to save Davidson. He was my training partner, my pupil—and as I sensed even then, my protector. He had to be saved.

My sword jumped faster than I knew it could, but the Shadows were faster still. I felt one weave around my head; a swift upward parry drove it back. Then I swung sharply down again, and with a shrill buzz, my first Shadow died into the dirt at my feet.

"Charya!" Davidson's sword whistled by my ear, and a Shadow sang down his armor. I thought of thanking him, but I had to think more of fighting.

Twice more that battle, Shadows sang down my sword. Twice again, Davidson caught a Shadow on my back and saved my life. But finally the battle was over; the Shadows were rolling back down into the forest.

"Davidson!" I leaned against him, puffing. But he was rigid, and he shook me off. I pulled my visor up and smiled, but all I could see through his was a pair of iron eyes that seemed to be seeing nothing and everything at once.

"Davidson, thank you," I said. But he just turned and walked up towards the castle.

Just as we reached the bunkhouse we heard a shriek on the north slope, the kind of shriek you never forget. I'd heard it four times in the battle: the death cry of a man whose skin was touched by a Shadow.

Visors snapped down, and a horde of guardsmen rushed down the slope towards the corpse of one of the few scouts that had been left on the other approaches during the battle. And the Shadows were again in force; again dozens sang their low drone of fear.

Guardsmen were more tired, and though this second battle raged little more than an hour, five more died. Three were female, and their shrieks were even more wrenching. But we held them off, and Jamaal was safe for yet another night.

In this battle I counted: no Shadows melted by me, six by Davidson. When the sun came up we knew they were gone for the day, for Shadows were somehow diminished in the face of the sun's light, and never ventured into open daylight. Only in a cave or in the deepest thicket would you meet a Shadow in the daytime, I later learned.

But we didn't care about such details then. We just slumped in our bunks, some even still in armor.

When I awoke Jamaal himself stood at the next bunk. "Man," he said to Davidson, "you are the greatest swordsman I have ever seen."

Davidson was fully dressed. He always slept but briefly. "Thank you. But how did you see me?"

Jamaal laughed, a low chuckle that befitted the old man. "I have an oldthing which lets me see great distances, even in the dark."

Davidson cocked his head. "You mean a . . ." he grasped for words. "A long tube with special glass windows, that works on light different, lower, than the normal? That works on heat-light?"

Jamaal's eyebrows rose. "Yes! We call it infrared light, and the tube is called a telescope."

"I'd like to see it!"

Jamaal's face brightened. "And so you may. If you'll just do me the honor of describing how you fight so well."

The old man was crafty, I learned later. He knew that no guardsman liked to talk of his fighting, and he also knew that the private thoughts of the best would help the others fight better. But Davidson's answer surprised even him.

"I wish I could. But it's not me who does the fighting. I don't know how it's done."

And no matter how Jamaal pried, he couldn't get Davidson to explain himself any more clearly. Finally he gave up; and, turning to go, he spied me listening.

"Ah, young Charya. I was worried about you. But I believe you will turn out to be one of the best of all." He glanced at Davidson. "You'll do well to keep learning from this man." And with that, Jamaal turned to walk out.

"Please wait," I said.

"Yes?" He raised a feathery eyebrow as he turned back.

"Could you tell me . . ."

"What?"

"Could you tell us about the Shadows?" Davidson asked. "We really haven't been taught."

The old man smiled. "But surely you've at least heard some of the legends? Charya—what do you know of them?"

"Just—what the priests say. That the Shadows were born in a Great War, of tremendous light and thunder. They say that the Shadows were the souls of the evil men, the men who caused the war, trapped forever in the Devil's shadow, the nighttime. The priests say they're trapped until they have punished all those who are unrepentant, who think in the old ways and use the oldthings."

"But you don't believe them?"

"No. If they were doomed forever, then we wouldn't be able to kill them. And I can't see that prayer and sacrifice have anything to do with them at all."

"Excellent!" Jamaal said. "I think you're exactly right."

"Then what are they?" Davidson asked.

Jamaal slowly lowered himself onto an empty bunk. "Even in the better days of the Guard, when I was younger, we weren't sure. They're energy creatures somehow. That seems obvious."

"You mean, like sunlight?" I asked.

"Yes, or like the power in the oldthings. It's called electromagnetism," he said. "But as far as we know, the sunlight can't think and act the way men and Shadows can."

"Then how did these energy clouds learn to think?"

"We were never sure. They *were* born amid the thermonuclear explosions of the Great Wars, and one theory was that they arose from the minds of men caught near the centers of the explosions. Men's brains work somehow with small levels of electric charge, and maybe in the explosions that pattern was somehow reproduced at a much higher energy level. Or maybe they are an entirely separate kind of life that needed the vast amounts of energy to be born."

"And why do they attack you?"

"To get at my generators, I think. The oldthings that produce my energy, Charya. Maybe they need it like we need food. Some Shadows are bigger than others, and it's said that they like to dance on the treetops during lightning storms. One woman claimed that she saw one struck by lightning, and that it swelled to more than twice its old size.

"But if it's food to them, they don't need it very often, because they've been in existence for years and years with very few oldthings left for them to feed on. And that's why we try to keep them away: because very few oldthings are left, and some day men are going to be ready for them again. I don't want the knowledge of the past to die, so I hire you all to defend it." The old man sighed and painfully rose from the bed. "And you two shall do very well defending the oldthings, I think. A few more like you, and I could rest quite peacefully."

He turned and limped slowly out of the bunkroom, as Davidson helped me strap on my armor. The others were already assembling.

We had lost eleven of our hundred in the battle of the night before; but it seemed that the Shadows had fared far worse, for they were seldom seen in the weeks that followed. They recovered eventually, though; and soon enough some patrol skirmished every night. As time went on, Davidson saved more and more lives and performed more and more feats of brilliant swordwork.

Once, our patrol was besieged on a narrow path in the densest part of the forest. It was so dark that we couldn't see the trees, so dark that we couldn't see anything but the shimmering edges of the Shadows. They danced around us and swooped down from above; they tried to back us into trees, or trip us on the thick vines that covered the forest floor.

But Davidson stood in the midst of us, keeping us together and defending us from above. His long sword jumped with magical quickness from helmet top to helmet top. Three or four Shadows were held at bay above us; then, swiftly, two dove down together at guardsmen on opposite ends of the pack. Davidson's blade was invisible. All you could see was his wrist flick rapidly, and two sharp songs snapped the night air's silence as two

Shadows were melted on the same swordthrust. No one's life was lost in that "Battle of the Thicket."

And once he found some Shadows rolling up the very steps of the castle, having somehow slipped through the final ring of watchmen. It was dawn, and the sky was just lightening; Davidson had already removed his helmet. But he still charged forward with furious thrusts and swoops of his sword, and he drove the Shadows back. Ducking and twisting, he managed to defend his skin—and all three Shadows sang down his sword before any of us could even come to his side.

By the time a year had passed, Davidson had gained quite a reputation. When he walked into the village, he wasn't just a Scarlet Guardsman of Jamaal; he was Davidson, the Shadow Slayer. And I was Charya, "the only one that he befriended."

The title was fairly accurate, for he had time for few except me, and we spent most of our free time together. That is, except for the time he spent in the castle, with Jamaal. Somehow, Davidson knew much about old-things, maybe as much as Jamaal. But I never learned exactly why until later.

We did talk of many other things, though, and after I felt I knew him well enough I asked him about what had bothered me since the first battle.

"Davidson, what happens to you when we fight? You told Jamaal you become someone else. Just who is it that you become?" I paused, breathless, for I knew it was a subject he didn't like to discuss.

He smiled. "I was waiting for you to ask me, Charya, for you're not a natural fighter. I've seen that. You have to think, on the field, and know what you're doing at all times. For you, your awareness of yourself is never stronger, your control never greater, than when you're fighting.

"But I'm the opposite. I'm not a natural fighter, but that fighter is inside me. He's an animal, a caged tiger, with iron eyes and a ruthless quickness, that I lock in the back corner of my mind until I need him. But when a fight comes, I let him free, and he becomes me. You've met him; he knows you. But it's him and not me that fights with you on the mountainsides."

I could only nod, and he was silent for a long time. We never talked again of that subject, but I often thought of what he had said, when I found myself beside the tiger in late night silence.

By the end of that year Davidson was a guard captain; he immediately became the chief of the guard captains. And so it remained for another two years. I myself never was made a guard captain, for it was known by all that Davidson and I should always patrol together. And Davidson's stature seemed to grow every month.

We always made the longest, deepest forays, and we melted Shadows every night. Because of the distances we travelled, many of his greatest fights went unseen by anyone but myself, like the stand he made on the edge of a cliff, and the time his arms alone kept a trio of the clouds at bay, after a swing of his sword had embedded it in a tree limb. But perhaps the Shadows themselves came to recognize us, for sometimes they ran when they found us, and we had to chase them.

So perhaps he was never truly appreciated, except by myself and the Shadows; yet he was still a subject of fantastic rumors, the stories of young guardsmen who had seen or pretended to have seen his great sword flashing through one or another of his battles. And then came the events from which sprung his greatest fame.

One night at dawn a falling star catapulted down from the sky. It seemed to slow above our heads; then circled abruptly and landed softly in the hills beyond the village. The tiger ran from Davidson's eyes, and he swore in a language I had never heard before. And the other guards were also shaken, but in a way different from Davidson. They were not religious men and women—for no one could be and still challenge the Shadows the way we did—but where Davidson seemed angry, they seemed awed and fearful.

"What does a star want with us?" a guardsman softly asked.

"It wants me," Davidson said. He began to walk down the hill towards town, and I followed wordlessly. The star awed me, yes, but I was even more awed by the man in front. And to see a star up close, I probably would have gone anyway. All the others stayed behind.

At the edge of the village Davidson stopped. "There'll be men from that star craft in the village, I think." He paused. "They should look much like me. Charya—please go there, and see. Try to find out how many. I'd go with you, but they might kill me on sight."

His last words startled me, and I looked at him. I saw no iron in his eyes, but instead only fear, for the first time since I'd known him. I went.

I paused at the corner of the tavern, for I could hear strange voices inside.

"And where do I climb to arrive at this castle?" one of the voices asked. They all spoke very formal, wooden Nadic.

"The mountain. On the north end of the village. If you can't find Davidson just ask for Charya. He'll know where Davidson is." That was a local voice; a very frightened local voice. I glanced around the corner, counted, and then sprinted out of the village.

"There were three," I said to Davidson. I felt comforted, for he was the tiger again. He said nothing, but nodded, and led me up into the hills toward the star. We soon found it: it was a mechanical metal craft.

"Remember!" he said suddenly, "we'll have to do more than just touch them." Then we ran silently to the craft's edge, the kind of sure-footed, breath-held silence that only a guardsman can approach.

The port was open and we jumped in. Killing men was easy, compared with Shadows. There were two there; one each.

Davidson walked to a wall of small windows and levers, and made several complicated twists and pushes. Then he turned to me. "Let's get out of here."

He jumped out of the craft, and I followed as he ran and dove behind a small hammock. A searing roar broke the morning stillness and the ground shuddered at the noise of a thousand thunderclaps. Dirt and rubble flew all around us, and when I got up, the craft was gone.

"Now we wait for them," he said. "They'll be armed and cautious. Much harder to kill." I nodded, and we each hid in the hillocks.

I saw them first, and they paraded right by me without seeing. Then, about twenty yards away, they split, and two disappeared in different directions leaving the third slowly gazing around himself. He looked in my direction just in time to see my sword, and it bit through his throat before he could do anything else.

As the man died, he reached to his belt, and pulled off a small box. He pointed it at me, and suddenly bright light jumped out from a needle on its end. Luckily, it missed me, and disappeared into the sky, for the dying man's aim was bad. The arm fell dead before he could fire again.

I took the weapon from the dead star-man's hand, and pursued one of his comrades. En route, I discovered how to push it to make the light, and that weapon, coupled with my stealth, left the man with no chance. And even as he fell, I heard the third man's death scream also.

When Davidson found me, his eyes were no longer iron. He smiled when he saw what I had done, and asked for the light box. When I gave it to him he destroyed it, burning it to a cinder with another lightbox that he now carried on his belt.

I looked at him, and he sighed. "These are the weapons of another place, and another time. They don't belong here, Charya."

"Where do they belong?"

"Where I come from."

"The stars?"

He nodded. And he kept the box on his belt.

"They want to kill me," he said, "because I committed a great crime. It was a political crime, and a spiritual one. I was an assassin." He glanced at me, but I hadn't flinched. "You're not surprised?"

I shook my head no. "I guessed from the first that you had come from far away. And when a man comes that far to hide, he must be hiding from something very great indeed."

"Well, there was a famous man where I come from. A man some said was a savior, a messiah, who had finally arrived to deliver the people from evil. But the man used drugs, and clever trickery, and machines to convince his followers, and so others decided that he had to be stopped. They hired me. A professional. I killed the Great One, and I became one of the most celebrated men of my world; of all history." Davidson frowned. "Celebrated, or infamous."

My brow wrinkled. "World? I thought you were from one of the stars."

He nodded. "Yes, that's the best way to understand it. I'm from a star. A star much bigger than that starcraft, mind you, bigger even than this world."

"Bigger than this whole world?" My mind reeled. This world wasn't infinite—it had edges. He nodded slowly.

"Don't ask me to explain it. But the star men want me, for killing the Great One didn't stop his followers. They had started a war, and now it seems that the wrong side won. For otherwise, they wouldn't have come after me—they had promised not to. But they came. And they'll be back." Tears began to form, just very small ones at the corners of his eyes.

"We could run."

He nodded slowly. "We could." Then he sighed. "That had been my plan, when I exploded their spacecraft. But they'll catch me."

"We can fight."

"Yes. We can fight. But they'll be very strong."

He was silent for the rest of the climb.

Every morning and night after that day, Davidson went into the castle, to scan the sky with Jamaal's telescopes. And he began to carry the light weapon with him everywhere.

Then one evening I awoke and he was gone. Many stars had fallen from the sky that afternoon, the others told me. They had fallen all around the village, and were still there now. I quickly strapped on my armor, and ran down towards what all the other guards were too afraid of. Went there, even though Davidson had left me a note:

"I know you are willing, but it isn't your fight. You are my brother, but it is my crime and my punishment. I must fight alone."

And I got there too late. Even as I approached, the stars returned to the sky, one by one. And when I arrived in town, they asked *me* what had happened. I spent days searching for information, for any witnesses, but none had seen anything, and none had heard anything, for all had cowered inside at the sight of the dropping stars.

Then, weeks later, the rumors started. The falling stars had been awful, fire-breathing dragons, which Davidson drove off at the cost of his life. Or that Davidson and Charya had driven them off, as I became bound in his legend. Other rumors had us fighting golden star-men, or even golden daytime Shadows. And some said that Davidson was not dead, that he still roamed the hills. They said that he was mad, or that he was wounded, or that he was somehow transformed; but more and more men began to claim seeing him. And swiftly the rumors became legends; they made Davidson the most famous swordsman in the kingdom.

I never found his body.

Jamaal made me chief guard captain the day I returned from my search for Davidson. It was only the second time I'd seen him. He didn't ask me for news about Davidson, for he seemed to know that the man was gone anyway. And from then on, I had to live my life alone.

Alone I had to sit in the tavern, listening to the priests who always searched us out, whispering "But you must repent! The oldthings are evil. The oldthings caused the Great Wars. You must consent to join in the sacrifices, to cast your name among the lots. To appease them—or you'll end up one yourself!"

Alone I went to visit Jamaal, who now lay bedridden on some days. Alone I taught the other guards about what an oldthing was, and why they had to be protected.

And alone I felt when I went out on patrol; for being with any of the other guardsmen was not the same as being together with Davidson. And when the Shadows ran, I could no longer simply chase them, for the others needed protecting.

At first, it struck me as strange that the Shadows ran from me alone. And then it dawned on me that a transformation had taken place, that it had taken place and I hadn't even noticed. For now, I too gave way to a natural fighter inside me; I too uncaged a tiger with iron eyes.

Maybe Davidson was wrong. Maybe the tiger lives in all of us, maybe we can all be natural fighters. Or maybe it's Davidson's tiger who now patrols the mountain through me.

The work of the Guard is important; but it went on before me and it will go on after me. I had never left the Scarlet Guard before his disappearance, because Davidson had been my life. I can't leave it now, because I'm all that's left of him. Unless—who knows? Maybe some of the legends are right. I'm not very hopeful, but I never saw his body. In the midnight darkness, I search not just for Shadows; I search for Davidson. And maybe if I find him he'll take me to see one of the edges of the world.

RESCUE RUN

Anne McCaffrey

"God helps those who help themselves"—if they know what they're doing!

Ma'am?" Ross Vaclav Benden said in a surprised tone, "there's an orange flag on the Rukbat system." He swiveled from his position toward the *Amherst*'s command chair and the battle cruiser's captain, Anise Fargoe.

The *Amherst* had been assigned to conduct a determined search through the Sagittarian sector of space for any evidence of new incursions by the Nasties. The punitive war of six decades ago proved insufficient to dissuade those intruders from annexing remote elements of the Federation. There had already been incidents in the Rigel sector despite a powerful Federated force. A massive seek-and-destroy operation was now five years in progress with, mercifully, only a few infiltrations discovered. And those, outposts and two space stations, had been obliterated. Not until all adjoining space and every peripheral system had been investigated and warning devices strategically strewn would the Federation enjoy any sense of security. A second prolonged Nasties Campaign would ruin the already depleted Federation. Quick sharp thrusts now, the combined joint staffs had wisely decided, should suffice.

As the *Amherst* had so far had a very boring swing through their sector, Lieutenant Benden's unexpected comment roused everyone on the bridge.

"Orange? This far out?" Captain Fargoe asked, her eyes widening in a flare of excitement. "Didn't know we had colonies in this sector."

"Orange," signified that an investigation should be initiated by any vessel close enough to the flagged system to do so.

"I'm accessing files, ma'am," and Benden, suddenly remembering family history, breathlessly awaited the entry. He tapped his thumbs restlessly on the edge of the keyboard and got a quick repressive glance from old Rezmar Dooley Zane, the duty navigator. "Oh," he added, deflated, as the file header informed him that a distress message had been received from the colony on Pern, Rukbat's only inhabitable planet.

"Well, let's see the message," Captain Fargoe said. Anything to relieve the tedium of the fruitless search through this deserted—almost deserted—sphere of space. "Screen it."

Benden transferred the message to the main screen.

"Mayday! Pern colony in desperate condition following repeated attacks of an uncontacted enemy invasion force employing unknown organism—"

"Nasties don't *need* germ warfare," muttered brash Ensign Cahill Bralin Nev. Someone else snickered.

"—which consumes all organic matter. Must have technical and naval support or colony faces total annihilation. There is wealth here. Save our souls. Theodore Tubberman, colony botanist."

There was an almost embarrassed silence for the tone of the message.

"Hardly the Nasties then," the captain said drily. "Probably some old weapon-system has been triggered. Perhaps one of the Sixty units we ran into in the Red Sector. I thought only survivor types were chosen to be colonists. Mister Benden, what does Library say about this Pern expedition?"

Ross didn't need to search for the official documentation on the expedition. He knew most of the tale by heart, but he keyed up the file.

"Captain, a low-tech, agrarian colony was chartered for the third planet of the Rukbat system, under the joint leadership of Admiral Paul Benden and—"

"Your uncle, I believe."

"Yes, Captain," Ross replied, keeping his tone level. Proud though his entire family was of Paul Benden's most honorable service record, he had taken a lot of gibing during his first cadet year when his uncle's victory at Cygnus was telecast as a documentary, and in third year when Admiral Benden's strategy was discussed in Tactics.

"A most able strategist and a fine commander." Fargoe's voice registered approval but her sideways glance warned Benden not to presume on his uncle's sterling record. "Continue, mister."

"Governor Emily Boll of Altair was the other leader. Six thousand plus colonists, chartered and contracted, were transported in three ships, *Yokohama, Buenos Aires,* and *Bahrain.* The only other communication was the regulation report of a successful landing. No further contact was expected."

"Humph, Idealists, were they? Isolating themselves and then screaming for help at the slightest sign of trouble."

Ross Benden gritted his teeth, searching for some polite way to assert that Admiral Benden would not have "screamed for help," and he bloody well hadn't sent that craven message.

Fortunately, after a moment's thought, the captain went on, "Not Admiral Benden's style to send a distress message of any kind. So, who's this Theodore Tubberman, botanist, who affixed his name to the place? A mayday should have been authorized by the colony leaders."

"It wasn't a *standard* capsule," Benden replied, having noted that amendment. "But expertly contrapted. It was also sent to Federation headquarters."

"Federation headquarters?" Fargoe sat forward, frowning. "Why HQ? Why not the Colonial Authority? Or the Fleet? No, if it wasn't signed by Admiral Benden, the fleet would have shifted it to the CA." Then she sat, chin on one hand, studying the report, scrolling it forward from her armrest key pad. "A non-standard homing device sent to Federation HQ indicating that the colony was under attack . . . hmm. And nine years after a successful landing, forty-nine years ago.

"How far are we from the Rukbat system, Mister Benden?"

"Point 045 from the heliopause, ma'am. Science officer Ni Morgana wanted a closer look at that Oort cloud. She's interested in cometary reservoirs. That's when I noticed the orange flag on the system."

"They wanted squadrons then?" The captain gave a short bark of laughter. "Nearly fifty years ago? Hmmm. No Nastie activity was noticed that soon after the War. This Tubberman fellow doesn't specify. Maybe that's what he intended. Big unknown alien life form attack might have stirred Federation." She gave a dubious sniff. "What sort of resources does this Pern have, Mister Benden?"

Benden had anticipated that request and inserted a smaller window on the main screen with the initial survey report. "Pern evidently only had minimal resources, enough to supply the needs of a low-tech colony."

"No, that sort of ore and mineral potential wouldn't have interested any of the syndicates," the captain mused. "Too costly to use an orbiting refinery or to transport the ores to the nearest facility. Nine years after touchdown? Long enough for those agrarian types to settle in and accumulate reserves. And the EEC doesn't list any predators." She paused in her review of the data and made a slight grimace. "Have Lieutenant Ni Morgana report to the bridge," she said over her shoulder to the communications officer.

The captain tapped her fingers on her armrest, which caused the crew to exchange glances. The captain was thinking again!

"Doesn't compute that Paul Benden would send any distress message," she went on. "So where was he when this Tubberman sent off his contraption? Had the menace from outer space done for everyone in authority?"

"Internal conflict?" Benden suggested, not able to believe his resourceful uncle would have been destroyed by a mere organism after surviving all the Nastie Fleet had thrown at him. That would be ironic. And the admiral had certainly researched the colonial scheme from every aspect, but he might have relied on Rukbat's isolated position in Federated space to diminish any hostile attacks. The EEC report listed no hostile organism on the planet. Of course, no one could rule out such a bizarre possibility as an attack by a remnant weapons system. Sections of the galaxy were strewn with the unexploded minefields from ancient wars. Not necessarily of Nastie origin.

The grav shaft whooshed open and Lieutenant Ni Morgana entered, stood to attention, and snapped off a salute. "Captain?" and she tilted her head awaiting her orders.

"Ah, Lieutenant, there is only an Oort cloud surrounding the Rukbat system but it appears to be an orange tagged, distress message," the captain said gesturing for Ni Morgana to read the data which now occupied several windows on the big screen.

"Coming on a bit thick, weren't they? Alien invasion!" Ni Morgana gave a snort of disgust after a quick perusal. "Although," and she paused, pursing her mouth, "it's just possible that the 'unknown organism' has been seeded into the cometary cloud to camouflage it."

"What are the chances of it containing some engineered organism that attacked the planet fifty years ago?" Captain Fargoe was clearly skeptical.

"I am hoping that we can obtain samples of the cloud as we pass it, ma'am," Ni Morgana replied. "It is unusually close in to the system for an Oort Cloud."

"Have Oort clouds ever been found to harbor natural viruses or organisms that could threaten a planet?"

"I know of several cases where it's always been assumed that inimical mechanisms have been launched from one solar system to another—'berserkers' they were called."

"Could the organism this Tubberman mentioned be a Nastie softening agent? Destroying all organic matter seems like a weapon of some kind, doesn't it?"

"We've learned not to underestimate the Nasties, Captain. Though their methods, so far, have been much more direct." Ni Morgana's smile was tight, understandable when you knew that the science officer was the only survivor of her family, solely because she was at the Academy when the enemy had attacked her home world. "However, since the Nasties have been trying to establish bases far from well traveled space, it becomes a possibility out here."

"Yes, it does, doesn't it?" The captain said thoughtfully and then grimaced. It was the ambition of every member of Fleet and EEC from the lowliest long distance single scout to the commander of the heaviest battle cruiser to discover the Nasties's home world, and Captain Fargoe was scarcely an exception.

"Whatever the attack on Pern was, they would not have sent for help unless their situation was desperate," Ni Morgana added. "You are aware that the Colonial Authority exacts punitive payments for such assistance?"

A complex series of expressions rippled across the captain's face. "Far too high for the service they give, and the time it takes them to respond. The colonists would be mortgaged, body, blood, and breath, unto the fourth generation to repay such a debt. Also the message was not sent by Admiral Paul Benden. That's one man I'd like to pipe aboard the *Amherst*."

"He'd scarcely be alive now," Benden heard himself saying. "He was in his seventh decade when he started."

"A good colonial life can add decades to a man's span, Benden," the captain said. "So, I think we can entertain a rescue run to Pern. Lieutenant Zane, plot a course that will take us through the system close enough to this Pern to launch the shuttle. We can give the other planets and satellites a good probe on the swing past. Mister Benden, you'll command the landing party; a junior officer and, say, four marines. I'll want your crew recommendations, and calculations on projected journey to rendezvous with the *Amherst* on her turn back through the system. Allowing, say . . . how long did the EEC survey team take—ah, yes, five days and a bit—allowing five days on the surface to make contact with the colonists and establish their current situation."

"Aye, aye, Captain," Benden replied, trying hard to keep elation out of his voice. Lieutenant Zane on the navigation board shot him a malevolent glance, which he ignored, as he did Ensign Nev to his right who was all but tugging his sleeve to remind Ross that he'd had xeno training.

"I suggest you talk with Lieutenant Ni Morgana, Mister Benden, when she has completed her survey of the Oort cloud matter. There might just be some connection and these ancient weapons can produce some awkward surprises." She awarded Ross Benden a quick nod. "You have the con, Lieutenant Zane." With that, the captain slid from the command seat and left the bridge.

As Saraidh Ni Morgana took her seat at the science terminal, she winked at Ross Benden, which he interpreted as her support in his assignment.

On the 3-D globe on the *Amherst*'s bridge, the ship seemed only centimeters from the edge of the nebulosity that was the Oort Cloud. As she approached at an angle to sample a core through the thickest part of the Cloud, a great net was fired from a forward missile tube on the port side. The net would both collect debris and clear the ship's path. No ship would barrel through such a cloud where particles were as close as tens of meters.

The biggest particles were about a kilometer apart. The problem was to avoid collision of the net with anything above a ton, which would tear it and bring the ship's meteorite defense into play.

During the next two weeks, while the *Amherst* passed beyond the cloud, heading in to the Rukbat system, the science officer carefully examined the material. First she asked permission to rig an empty cargo pod with remote waldo controls and monitors. A work party towed the pod out to a point at which there was no risk to the *Amherst* and yet close enough to make frequent trips to the net feasible.

Then, with a work party, she jetted out to the net and selected fragments which might be worth examining. The cargo pod was already divided into sections. At first these were all kept in vacuum status at −270° Celsius or 3° absolute. Once back in the *Amherst*, Ni Morgana activated the monitors and began one of her legendary forty-hour days.

"I've got a lot of dirty ice," was her initial comment four days later after she'd had some sleep and a second review of her data. "Most of the stuff has identifiable intrusions, particles of rock and metal, but there are also—" there was a long pause, "some very unusual particles that I have never encountered before. Before anyone gets an idea I don't want to give, there is no evidence of any artifact."

As the science officer held five degrees in different disciplines and had landed on three or four dozen alien surfaces, that was an intriguing admission. The next morning she suited up again and jetted around the netted debris, looking for her special interest, "space worms."

Captain Fargoe had approved Lieutenant Benden's preliminary flight data, and Ross continued his study of the EEC survey reports and the two cryptic messages that were the only communications from the colony world.

"If there is a life form," Ni Morgana said at her most tentative in the weekly officer's meeting, "its response time is far too slow for us to discern. There have been some anomalies, both in superconductivity and in cryochemistry, that I want to follow up. I shall begin a series of tests, slowly warming some representative samples, and see what occurs."

The next week she reported, "At −200° Celsius, some of the larger particles are showing relative movement but whether this is driven by anomalous internal structure, or reacting to the warmer temperature I cannot as yet ascertain."

"Keep in mind at all times, Lieutenant," the captain said at her sternest, "what happened to the *Roma!*"

"Ma'am, I always do!" The 'melting' of the *Roma* when the science officer brought aboard a metal-hungry organism was the cautionary example drummed into every science officer.

The following week Ni Morgana was almost jubilant. "Captain, there is a real life form in some of the larger chunks from the Cloud. Ovoid shapes, with an exceedingly hard crust of material, they have some liquid, perhaps helium, inside. They're very strange but I'm sure they're not artifacts. I'm bringing one sample up above 0° C this week."

The captain held up an admonishing finger at her science officer. "At all times, keep the *Roma* in mind."

"Ma'am, even the situation on the *Roma* didn't happen in a day."

In the process of leaving the conference room, the captain stopped and stared quizzically at Ni Morgana. "Are you deliberately misquoting something, Lieutenant?"

"Mister Benden!" The peremptory summons of the science officer over the comunit by his ear jolted Ross Vaclav Benden out of his bunk and to his feet.

"Ma'am?"

"Get down to the lab on the double, mister!"

Benden struggled into his shipsuit as he ran down the companionway, stabbing feet into soft shipshoes. It was o-dark-hundred of the dog watch, for no one was even in Five Deck's lounge area as he raced across it and to the appropriate grav shaft down to the lab. He skidded to a halt at the door, skinning his forearms on the frame as he braked and fell into the facility. He almost knocked over Lieutenant Ni Morgana. She pointed to the observation chamber.

"Funkit, what in the name of the holies is that?" he wanted to know as his eyes fell on the writhing greyish pink and puke-yellow mass that oozed and roiled on the monitor screen. He could understand why everyone was standing well back even if the mass was, in reality, ten kilometers from the *Amherst*.

"If that is what fell on Pern," Ni Morgana said, "I don't blame 'em for shrieking for help!"

"Let me through," and the captain, clad in a terry-cloth caftan, had to exert some strength to push pass the mesmerized group watching the phenomenon. "Gods above! What have you unleashed, mister?"

"We're taping the show, ma'am," Ni Morgana said as well as prominently waving the hand she held over the "destruct" button that would activate laser fire. Benden could see her eyes glittering with clinical fascination. "According to the readings I'm getting, this complex organism exhibits some similarity to Terran mycorrhizoids in its linear structure. But it's enormous! Damn!"

The organism suddenly collapsed in on itself and became a thick viscous inanimate puddle. The science officer tapped out some commands on the waldo keyboard and a unit extruded towards the mass, scooped up a sample in a self-sealing beaker, and retreated. Lights glittered on the remote testing apparatus that analyzed the sample.

"What happened to it?" Captain Fargoe demanded and Benden admired how firm her voice was. He was very much aware that he had the shakes.

"I should be able to tell you when the analysis is finished on that sample of the residue but I'd hazard the guess that, with such rapid expansion, if it found no sustenance in the chamber—and there was none apart from a very thin atmosphere—that it died of starvation. That's only a guess."

"But," Benden heard himself saying, "if this *is* the Pern organism—"

"That's only a possibility at this point," Ni Morgana said quickly. "We must first discover how it managed to get from the Cloud to Pern's surface."

"Good point," the captain murmured and Benden was almost angry at her amused tone. There was nothing remotely funny about what they had just witnessed.

"But if it did, and it's what attacked Pern, I can't blame 'em for wanting help," said Ensign Nev whose complexion was still slightly green.

The captain gave him a long look that caused him to flush from neck to a scalp that was visible under his latest space trim.

"Captain," Ni Morgana said as she pressed the destruct button, destroying it by laser fire; "I request permission to join the Pern landing party to pursue my investigation of this phenomenon."

"Granted!" The captain paused, stepping over the lintel of the lab, with a wicked grin. "I always prefer volunteers for landing parties."

Whoever might have envied Lieutenant Benden the assignment had different feelings once the details of the "organism" became scuttlebutt. A concise report from Lieutenant Ni Morgana was published to quell the more rampant speculations and her lab team became welcome as experts at any mess.

Ross Vaclav Benden had nightmares about his uncle: the admiral, unexpectedly garbed in dress whites, great purple sash of the Hero of the Cygnus Campaign, and a full assortment of other prestigious and rare decorations on his chest, struggled against engulfment by the monstrosity of the lab chamber. Determined to do his best by his uncle, Ross studied, to the point of perfect recall, the EEC valuation of Pern. The terse all-safe message by Admiral Benden and Governor Boll and Tubberman's mayday were easy to memorize, the latter tantalizingly ambiguous. Why had the colony botanist sent the message? Why not Paul Benden or Emily Boll, or one of the senior section heads?

Although this was not Benden's first landing party command, he believed in checking and double-checking every aspect of the assignment. Since there might be hostile conditions including omnivorous organisms and other enigmas to be solved or avoided on Pern's surface, Ross Benden judiciously plotted an alternative holding orbit until the escape window opened up for their rendezvous with the *Amherst*. The landing party had five days, three hours, fourteen minutes on the surface to conduct its investigations. To his chagrin, Ni Morgana asked for Ensign Nev as the junior officer.

"He needs some experience, Ross," Ni Morgana said, blandly ignoring Benden's disgruntlement, "and he's had *some* xeno training. He's strong and he obeys orders even as he's turning green. He's got to learn sometime. Captain Fargoe thinks this could give him valuable experience."

Benden had no option but to accept the inevitable but he asked for Sergeant Greene to command his marines. That tough burly man knew more about the hazards that could embroil landing parties than Benden ever would. Having seen the organism which Saraidh had unleashed, Ross wanted solid experience to offset Nev's ingenuousness. If that was the proper word for the boy.

"Just what were you like as an ensign, Lieutenant?" Ni Morgana asked, giving him a sly sideways glance.

"I was never that gauche," he replied tartly, which was true enough, since he'd been reared in a service family and had absorbed proper behavior with normal nutrients. Then he relented, grinning wryly back at her as he remembered a few incidents that he hoped she had no access to. "This sounds like a fairly routine mission: find and evaluate."

"Let's hope so," Saraidh replied earnestly.

Ross Benden was, in another sense, delighted to be teamed up with the elegant science officer. She was his senior in years but not in Fleet, for she had done her scientific training before applying to the Service. She was also the only woman who kept her hair long, though it was generally dressed in intricate arrangements of braids. The effect was somehow regal and very feminine: an effect at variance with her expertise in the various forms of contact sport that were enjoyed in the *Amherst's* gym complex. If she had made any liaisons on board, they were not general knowledge though he'd overheard speculation about her tastes. He had always found her agreeable company and a competent officer, though they hadn't shared more than a watch or two until now.

"Did you see the tape of that thing?" Ross Benden heard the nasal voice of Lieutenant Zane saying later as he passed the wardroom. "There'll be no

one left alive down there. Ni Morgana has proved the Oort Cloud generated that life form, so it wasn't Nastie manufacture. There's no rationale for
taking a chance and landing on that planet if any of those *things* are alive
down there! And they could be with an entire planet to eat up."

Benden paused to listen, knowing perfectly well that, despite the dangers
involved, Zane would have given a kidney to be in the landing party. Nev
was at least an improvement on the sour and supercilious Zane. And when
the navigation officer added some invidious remarks that Benden was only
chosen because of his relationship to one of the leaders of the colony,
Benden passed quickly down the corridor before his temper got the better
of his discretion.

As the *Amherst*'s majestic passage through the system approached the
point where the shuttle could be launched, Benden called for a final briefing session.

"We'll spiral down to the planetary surface in a corkscrew orbit which
will allow us to examine the northern hemisphere on our way to the site of
record on the southern continent at longitude 30°," he said, calling up the
flight-path on the big screen in the conference room. "We've landmarks
from the original survey of three volcanic cones that ought to be visible
from some distance as we make our final approach. Survey report said the
soil there would be viable for hardy Earth and Altairian hybrids so it is
reasonable to assume that they started their agrarian venture there. The
Tubberman mayday came in some nine years after landing so they should
have been well entrenched."

"Not enough to avoid that organism," Nev said flatly.

"Your theory would hold water, Ensign," Saraidh said at her mildest, "if
I could figure out how the organism transported itself from the Oort Cloud
to Pern's surface."

"Nasties sowed it in Pern's atmosphere," Nev responded with no hesitation.

"Nasties are more direct in their tactics," the science officer replied with
a diffident shrug, and turned to Benden with a question.

"We taught 'em to be cautious, Lieutenant," Nev went on. "And devious. And . . ."

"Nev!" Benden called the ensign to order.

Benden kept his expression neutral but he wondered if Ni Morgana was
regretting her choice of the irrepressible Nev and his wild theories. If the
science officer hadn't found a transport vector for the organism, the Nasties
were unlikely to have discovered it. Their *forte* was metallurgical, not biological. Nev subsided and the briefing continued.

"Once we have made landfall, we may also have answers to that question

and others. It is obvious our search must begin at the site of record. We will
also have made a good sweep of the entire planetary surface and can deviate
if we find traces of human settlements elsewhere. We board the *Erica* at
0230 tomorrow morning. Any questions?"

"What do we do if the place is swarming with those *things?*" asked Nev,
swallowing hard.

"What would you do, Nev?" Benden asked.

"Leave!"

"Tut tut, mister," Ni Morgana said. "How will you ever increase your
understanding of xenobiological forms unless you examine closely whatever
samples come your way?"

Ensign Nev's eyes bugged out. "Begging your pardon, Lieutenant, but
you're the science officer."

"Indeed I am," and Ni Morgana rose, the scrape of her chair covering a
mutter of gratitude from the end of the table occupied by the four marines
assigned to the landing party.

Launched from the *Amherst,* the gig proceeded at a smart inner system
speed toward the blue pebble in the sky that was Rukbat's third planet. It
began to dominate the forward screen, serene and clear, beautiful and innocuous. Benden had plotted the gig's course to intercept the geosynchro-
nous orbit of the three colony ships to see if the colonists had left a message
to be retrieved. But when he opened communications, the only response
was the standard identification response, stating the name and designation
of the *Yokohama.*

"That might not mean anything," Saraidh remarked as Benden looked
disappointed. "If the colony's up and running, they won't have much use
for these hulks. Though I find that sight rather sad," she added as Rukbat
suddenly illuminated the deserted vessels.

"Why?" Nev asked, surprised by her observation.

Saraidh gave a shrug of her slender, elegant shoulders. "Look up their
battle records and you might appreciate their present desuetude more."

"Their what?" Nev looked blank.

"Look up that word, too," she said and, in an almost cloying tone,
spelled it for him.

"Old sailors never die, they just fade away," Benden murmured, eyes on
the three hulks, feeling a constriction in his throat and a slight wetness in
his eyes as the gig drifted away from them, leaving them to continue on
their ordained path.

"Soldiers, not sailors," Saraidh said, "but the quotation is apt." Then
she frowned at a reading on her board. "We've got two beacons registering.
One at the site of record and another much further south. Enlarge the

southern hemisphere for me, will you, Ross? Along 70° longitude and nearly twelve hundred klicks from the stronger one." Ross and Saraidh exchanged looks. "Maybe there are survivors! Pretty far south though, over mountain ranges of respectable height. I read altitudes from 2,400 rising to more than 9,000 above sea level. We'll land at the site of record first."

As the gig slanted in over the northern pole, it was obvious that this hemisphere was enduring a stormy and bitterly cold winter; most of the landmass was covered by snow and ice. Instruments detected no source of power or light, and very little heat radiation in areas where humans usually settled; the river valleys, the plains, the shoreline. There was one hiccup of a blip over the large island, just off the coast of the northern hemisphere. The reading was too faint to suggest any significant congregation of settlers. If they had followed the usual multiplication so characteristic of colonies, the population should now be close to the 500,000 mark, even allowing for natural disasters and those morality patterns normal for a primitive economy.

"We'll do another low level pass if we've time later. The settlers were determined to be agrarian but they might be using fossil fuels," Saraidh said as they plunged toward the equator, leaving the snowclad continent behind them and slanting down across the tropical sea. "Lots of marine life. Some big ones," she added. "Bigger than the survey team reported."

"They took Terran dolphins with them," Nev said. "Mentasynth-enhanced dolphins," he added, as if that altered the fact.

"I don't think rescuing dolphins is what Captain Fargoe has in mind, even if we had the facility to do so," Saraidh said. "Have either of you any training in other species' communications? I don't. So, let's table that notion for now."

"There's another consideration: How long do dolphins live?" Ross asked. "Remember, this trouble started when the colony was down eight to nine years. In your report, Lieutenant, you did mention that further tests with the organism proved that water drowned it and organic fire consumed it. Mentasynth-enhanced creatures have good memories, sure. But how many generations of dolphins have there been? Would they even be aware of what happened on land? Much less remember?"

"Would they want to, is more the case," Saraidh said. "They're independent and very intelligent. Clearly they have survived and multiplied from the complement that came with the colony. They'd cut their losses and survive on their own. I would, if I were a dolphin."

Then Saraidh started the recorders on the gig's delta wing to take a record of the plunging antics of the large marine life as the *Erica* swooped over the ocean on their final descent toward the site of record.

"Records state that the *Bahrain* brought fifteen female dolphins and nine males," Nev said suddenly. "Dolphins produce—what? once a year. There could be nearly eight hundred of 'em in the seas right now. That's a lot of terrestrial life forms we'd be abandoning."

"Abandoning? Hell, Cahill, they're in their element. Look at them, they're doing their damnedest to keep pace with us."

"Maybe they have a message for us," Nev went on earnestly.

"We look for humans first, Ensign," the science officer said firmly. "Then we'll check the dolphins! Ross, I'm not getting anything from the ship-to-ground interface that's recorded for the site. It's inoperative, too."

"Now hear this! Buckle up for landing," Ross said, opening a channel to the marines' quarters.

"Muhlah!" was Saraidh's awed comment as they saw the two ruined volcanic craters and the smoking cone of the third.

Ross could say nothing, appalled by the extent of the eruption. He'd expected nothing so catastrophic as this. Or had this devastation occurred *before* the organism had begun to fall? While he had more or less resigned himself that he was unlikely to encounter his uncle, he had hoped to chat with the admiral's descendants. He certainly hadn't anticipated this level of devastation. They flew over the landing field tower, its beacon now blinking, activated by the proximity of the gig.

"See those mounds, just coming up on portside?" Saraidh pointed. "They've got the outlines of shuttles. How many did the colonists have?"

"Records say six," Nev replied. *"Bahrain* had one, *Buenos Aires* two, and the *Yoko* three. Plus a captain's gig."

"Only three parked there now. Wonder where the others went."

"Maybe they were used to get out of this place when the volcano blew?"

"But where to? There were no signs of human habitation on the northern continent," Benden said, sternly repressing his dismay.

Saraidh let out a thin high whistle. "And those other regular mounds are —were—the settlement. Neatly, if not aesthetically, laid out. Must have built well, for nothing seems to have collapsed from the weight of ash and dirt. Lava's cooled. Ross, got a reading of how deep that ash is over the ground?"

"We do indeed, Saraidh," Ross replied with relief. "A metallic grid is present a half meter below the surface. No problem landing—it'll be nice and soft."

Which it was. While waiting for the disturbed ash to settle, both officers and marines suited up, checking masks, breathing tanks, and strapping on lift belts. These would convey them safely above the ash to the settlement.

"What're those?" one of the ratings asked as the landing party assembled to hover a meter above the ash-coated ground outside the *Erica*. He pointed to a series of long semicircular mounds, bulging up out of the ash. "Tunnels?"

"Unlikely. Not big enough and don't seem to go anywhere," Ni Morgana said, deftly manipulating her attitude and forward jets. She hovered to one side of the nearest mound and pushed with her foot. It collapsed with a dusty implosion and a stench that the filters of their masks worked hard to neutralize. "Faught! Dead organism. Now, why didn't that puddle?" She took out a specimen tube and carefully gathered some of the residue, sealing it, and putting that tube in a second padded container.

"It fed on ash or green or something?" asked Ensign Nev.

"We'll check that out later. Let's look at the buildings. Scag, stay by the gig," Benden ordered one of the marines. And then gestured for the others to follow him up to the empty settlement.

"Not empty," Ross said an hour later, increasingly more pessimistic about finding any survivors. Contact with a cousin or two would be something to write home about. So he clutched at a vain hope. "Emptied. They didn't leave a thing they could use. Nasties would have obliterated any trace of humans."

"That's true enough," Saraidh said. "And there's no evidence of Nasties at all. Merely an evacuated settlement. There is that second beacon to the southwest. There's certainly nothing here to give us any explanation. Your point about everything being emptied is well taken, Benden. They closed shop here but that doesn't mean they didn't open it up elsewhere."

"Using the three missing shuttles," Nev added brightly.

Airborne again in the *Erica,* heading directly toward the beacon, they overpassed the rest of the settlement, taping the one smoking volcano crater and the melted structures below it. No sooner were they over the river than the landscape showed another form of devastation. The prevailing winds had minimized the dispersal of volcanic dust but oddly enough, there were only occasional stands of vegetation and large circles of parched soil.

"Like something had sprinkled the land with whopping great acid drops," Cahill Nev said, awed at the extent of the markings.

"Not acid. No way," Benden replied. He keyed the relevant section of the report he knew so well. "The EEC survey team found similar circular patches and they also reported that botanical succession had started."

"It has to be the Oort organism," Nev said enthusiastically. "On the cruiser it died of starvation. It had plenty to eat here."

"The organism has to get here first, mister," Ni Morgana said bitingly. "And we haven't established how it could cross some 600 million miles of space to drop on Pern." Ross, glancing at her set expression, thought she was rapidly considering improbable transport media. "Terrain's flat enough

here, Mister Benden, try a low level pass and give us a closer look at that
. . . that diseased ground."

Benden obliged, noting once again how responsive the *Erica* was to the
helm, smoothly skimming the often uneven terrain. Not that he expected
something to pop up out of those polka dots, but you never knew on alien
worlds. Even ones thoroughly surveyed by exploration and evaluation
teams. They might not have found any predators but something dangerous
had put in an appearance nine years after the settlers took hold. And the
Tubberman appeal hadn't mentioned a volcanic eruption.

Klick after klick they passed over circles and overlapping circles and triple
circles. Ni Morgana remarked that some succession was visible on their
peripheries. She asked Benden to land so she could take more samples,
including clods of the regenerating vegetation. Across a broad river there
were swaths of totally unharmed trees and acres of broad leafed and un-
scathed vegetation. Over one wide pasture they caught sight of a cloud of
dust, but whatever stirred it disappeared under the broad leaves of a thick
forest. They spotted no trace of human habitation. Not even a dirt-covered
mound that might be the remains of a building or a wall.

The second beacon signal became stronger as they neared the foothills of
a great barrier of mountains, snow clad even in what must be high summer
in this hemisphere. Gradually the pips altered from rhythmic bleeps to a
sustained note as they homed in on the beacon.

"There's nothing here but a sheer cliff," Ross said, disgusted as he let
the gig hover over the destination, the single note acerbating his nerves.

"That may well be, Ross," Saraidh said, "but I'm getting body-heat
readings."

Nev pointed excitedly. "That plateau below us is too level to be natural.
And there are terraces below it. See? And what about that path down into
the valley. And hey, this cliff has windows!"

"And is definitely inhabited!" exclaimed Saraidh, pointing to starboard
where a doorway appeared in the cliff face.

"Put her down, Ross!"

By the time the *Erica* had settled to the smoothed surface, a file of
people came running down the plateau toward it: their cries, audible from
the exterior speakers, were of hysterical welcome. They ranged in age from
early twenties to late forties. Except for the white-haired man, his mane
trimmed to shoulder length, whose lined face and slow movements suggested a person well into his eighth or ninth decade. His emergence halted
the demonstrations and the others stood aside to allow him a clear passage
to the gig's portal, where he halted.

"The patriarch," Saraidh murmured, straightening her tunic and settling
her beaked cap straight on top of her braids.

"Patriarch?" Nev asked.

"Look it up later—if the term is not self-explanatory," Benden shot at him over his shoulder, operating the airlock release. He glanced warningly at the marines, who replaced their drawn hand weapons.

As soon as the airlock swung open and the ramp extruded, the small crowd was silent. All eyes turned to the old man who pulled himself even more erect, a patronizing smile on his weathered face.

"You finally got here!"

"A message was received at Federated headquarters," Ross Benden began, "signed by a Theodore Tubberman. Are you he?"

The man gave a snort of disgust. "I'm Stev Kimmer," and he flicked one hand to his brow in a jaunty parody of a proper Fleet salute. "Tubberman's long dead. I designed that capsule, by the way."

"You did well," Benden replied. Inexplicably, Benden suddenly did not care to identify himself. So he introduced Saraidh Ni Morgana and Ensign Nev. "But why did you send that capsule to Federation Headquarters, Kimmer?"

"That wasn't my idea. Ted Tubberman insisted." Kimmer shrugged. "He paid me for my work, not my advice. As it is, you've taken nearly too damned long to get here." He scowled with irritation.

"The *Amherst* is the first vessel to enter the Sagittarian Sector since the message was received." Saraidh Ni Morgana said, unruffled by his criticism. She had noted that Ross had not given his name. She hoped that Ensign Nev had also noted the omission. "We've just come from the site of record—"

"No one came back to Landing, then?" Kimmer demanded. Benden thought his habit of interrupting Fleet officers could become irritating. "With Thread gone, that'd be the place they'd return to. The ground-to-ship interface's there."

"The interface is inoperative," Benden said, carefully neutral as the old man's arrogance grated on him.

"Then the others are dead," Kimmer stated flatly. "Thread got 'em all!"

"Thread?"

"Yes, Thread." Kimmer's palpable anger was tinged with deep primal emotions, not the least of which was a healthy fear. "That's what they named the organism that attacked the planet. Because it fell from the skies like a rain of deadly thread, consuming all it touched, animal, man, and vegetable. We burned it out of the skies, on the ground, day after fucking day. And still it came. We're all that's left. Eleven of us, and we only survived because we have a mountain above us and we hoarded our supplies, waiting for help to come."

"Are you positive that you're the sole survivors?" Ni Morgana asked.

"Surely in the eight or nine years you had before this menace attacked you—"

"Before Thread fell, the population was close to 20,000 but we're all that's left," Kimmer said, now defiant. "And you cut it mighty fine getting here. I couldn't risk another generation with such a small gene pool." Then one of the women, who bore a strong resemblance to Kimmer, tugged at his arm. And he made a grimace that could be taken for a smile. "My daughter reminds me that this is a poor welcome for our long-awaited rescuers. Come this way. I've something laid by in the hope of this day."

Lieutenant Benden gestured for the two marines to remain on board before he followed Ni Morgana down the ramp, Nev treading on his heels in his eagerness.

The silence which had held Kimmer's small group while he had addressed the spacemen relaxed now into gestures and smiles of welcome. But Benden took note of the tenseness of the oldest three men. They stood just that much apart from the women and youngsters to suggest they distanced themselves deliberately. They had a distinctly Asian cast of countenance, jet black hair trimmed neatly to their earlobes; they were lean and looked physically fit. The oldest woman, who bore a strong resemblance to the three men, walked just a step behind Kimmer in a manner that suggested subservience: an attitude which Benden found distasteful as he and his party followed them to the entrance.

The three younger women were ethnic mixes in feature, though one had brown hair. All were slender and graceful as they tried to contain their excitement. They whispered to each other, casting glances back at Greene and the other marine. At a brusque order from Kimmer, they ran on ahead, into the cliff. The three youngest, two boys and a girl, showed the mixing of ethnic groups more than their elders. Benden wondered just how close the blood bonding was. Kimmer would not have been fool enough to sire children on his own daughters?

Exclamations of surprise were forced from each of the three officers as they entered a spacious room with a high, vaulting ceiling; a room nearly as big as the gig's on-ship hangar. Nev gawked like any off-world stupe, while Ni Morgana's expression was of delighted appreciation. This was clearly the main living space of the cliff dwelling for it had been broken up into distinct areas for work, study, dining, and handcrafts. The furnishings were made of a variety of materials, including extruded plastic in bright hard colors. The walls were well hung with curious animal furs and hand-loomed rugs of unusual design. Above those, and all along the upper wall space, a vivid panorama had been drawn: first of stylized figures standing or sitting before what were clearly monitors and keyboards. Other panels showed figures who plowed and planted fields or tended animals of all sorts; panels which led around to the innermost wall that was decorated by scenes Benden knew too well, the cities of Earth and Altair and three spaceships with unfamiliar constellations behind them. At the apex of the ceiling vault was the Rukbat system . . . and one planet was shown to have a highly elliptical, and possibly an erratic orbit from slightly beyond the Oort cloud to an aphelion below Pern's.

Ni Morgana nudged Benden in the ribs and said in a barely audible whisper. "Unlikely as it seems, I've just figured out one way the Oort organisms might have reached Pern. I'll be damned sure of my theory before I mention it."

"The murals," Kimmer was saying in a loud and proprietary voice, "were to remind us of our origins."

"Did you have stone-cutters?" Nev asked abruptly, running his hand over the glassy smooth walls.

One of the older black-haired men stopped forward. "My parents, Kenjo and Ito Fusaiyuki, designed and carved all the principal rooms. I am Shensu. These are my brothers, Jiro and Kimo: our sister, Chio." He gestured to the woman who was reverently withdrawing a bottle from a shelf in a long dresser.

With a searing glance at Shensu, Kimmer hastily took the initiative again. "These are my daughters, Faith and Hope. Charity is setting out the glasses." Then with a flick of his fingers, he indicated Shensu. "You may introduce my grandchildren."

"Pompous old goat," muttered Ni Morgana to Benden but she smiled as the grandchildren were introduced as Meishun, Alun and Pat, the two boys being in their mid-teens.

"This Stake could have supported many more families if only those who had said they'd join us had kept their promises," Kimmer went on bitterly. Then with an imperious gesture, he waved the guests to come to the table and be served of the wine he was pouring; a rich fruity red.

"Welcome, men and women of the *Amherst!*" was Kimmer's toast and he touched glasses with each of them.

Benden noticed as Ni Morgana did, that the others were served a paler red by Meishun. Watered, Benden thought. They could at least be equal to us, today of all days! Shensu hid his resentment better than his brothers did. The women seemed not to notice, for they passed dishes of cheese bits and tasty small crackers to everyone. Then Kimmer gestured for the guests to be seated. Benden gave a discreet hand signal to the two marines who took the end seats at the long table and remained watchful, taking only small sips of the celebratory wine.

"Where to start?" Kimmer began, setting his wine glass down deliberately.

"The beginning," Ross Benden said wryly, hoping that he might learn what had happened to his uncle before disclosing his identity. There was something about Kimmer—not his anger nor his autocratic manner—that Benden instinctively distrusted. But perhaps a man who had managed to survive in a hostile environment had the right to a few peculiarities.

"Of the end?" And Kimmer's spiteful expression served to increase Benden's dislike.

"If that is when you and the botanist Tubberman sent that homing device," Benden replied, encouragingly.

"It was and our position was then hopeless, though few were realists enough to admit it, especially Benden and Boll."

"Could you have got back up to the colony ships then?" Ni Morgana asked, nudging Ross Benden when she felt him stir angrily.

"No way," and Kimmer snorted with disgust. "They used what fuel the gig had left to send Fusaiyuki up to reconnoiter. They thought they might be able to divert whatever it was that brought the Thread. That was before they realized that the wanderer planet had dragged in a tail that would shower this wretched planet with Thread for fifty frigging years. And if that wasn't bad enough, they let Avril steal the gig and that was the end of any chance we had of sending someone competent for help." The recital of that forty-year-old memory agitated Kimmer, and his face became suffused with red.

"It was definitely established that the organism had been carried from the Oort Cloud?" Ni Morgana asked, her usually calm voice edged with excitement.

Kimmer gave her a quelling glance. "In the end that was all they discovered despite their waste of fuel and manpower."

"There were only three shuttles left at the landing site. D'you suppose some people managed to escape in them?" said Ni Morgana in a deliberately soothing tone. Benden could see the glitter of her eyes as she sipped calmly at her wine.

Kimmer glared at her with contempt. "Where could they escape to? There was no fuel left! And powerpacks for sleds and skimmers were in short supply."

"Barring the lack of fuel, were the shuttles still operational?"

"I said, there was no fuel. No fuel," and he banged his fist on the table.

Benden, looking away from the man's deep bitterness, noted the faint look of amusement on Shensu's face.

"There was no fuel," Kimmer repeated with less vehemence. "The shuttles were so much scrap without fuel. So I haven't any idea why there'd be only three shuttles at Landing. I left the settlement shortly after the bitch blew the gig up." He glared impartially at the *Amherst* officers. "I had every right to leave then, to establish a Stake and do what I could to preserve my own skin. Anyone with any sense, charterer or contractor, should have done the same. Maybe they did. Holed up to wait out the fifty years. Or, maybe they sailed away into the rising sun. They had ships, you know. Yes, that's it. Old Jim Tillek sailed them out of Monaco Bay into the rising sun." He gave a bark of harsh laughter.

"They went west?" Benden asked.

Kimmer favored him with a contemptuous glance and made a wild gesture with one arm. "How the hell would I know? I wasn't anywhere near the place."

"And you settled here?" Ni Morgana asked blandly, "in the dwelling built by Kenjo and Ito Fusaiyuki?"

Her phrasing was, Benden thought, a little unfortunate, for the question angered Kimmer even more. The veins in his temples stood out and his face contorted.

"Yes, I settled here when Ito begged me to stay. Kenjo was dead. Avril killed him to get the gig. Ito'd had a difficult birth with Chio and his kids were too young to be useful then. So Ito asked me to take over." Someone's breath hissed on intake and Kimmer glared at the three sons, unable to spot the culprit. "You'd all have died without me!" he said in a flat but somehow cautionary tone.

"Most assuredly," Shensu said, his surface courtesy not quite masking a deep resentment.

"You have survived, haven't you? And my beacon brought us help, didn't it!" Kimmer banged on the table with both fists and sprang to his feet. "Admit it! My homes and my beacon have brought us rescue."

"They did indeed lead us to you, Mr. Kimmer," Benden said in a tone he barefacedly borrowed from Captain Fargoe when she was dressing down an insubordinate rating. "However, my orders are to search and discover any and *all* survivors on this planet. You may not be the only ones."

"Oh yes, we are. By all the gods, we're the only ones," Kimmer said, with an edge of panic in his voice. "And you can't leave us here!" His eyes turned a bit wild.

"What the lieutenant means, Mr. Kimmer," Ni Morgana put in soothingly, "is that our orders are to search for any other survivors."

"No one else survived," Kimmer said in a flat, toneless voice. "I can assure you that." He splashed wine into his glass and drank half of it, wiping his mouth with a trembling hand.

Because Ross Benden was not looking at the old man just then but at the three brothers seated across the table, he caught the glitter in the eyes of Shensu and Jiro. He waited for them to speak up but they remained silent and inscrutable. Palpably they had knowledge that they would not communicate to their rescuers in front of Stev Kimmer. Well, Benden would see them privately later. Meanwhile, Kimmer was coming across as a somewhat unreliable opportunist. He might assert that he had the right to set off and establish a Stake when the colony was obviously in terrible straits, but, to Benden, it sounded more as if Kimmer had fled in a craven fashion. Was it just luck that he had known where to find Ito, and this Kenjo's Stake?

"My sled had a powerful comunit," Kimmer went on, revived by the wine, "and once I'd erected the beacon on the plateau here, I listened in to what was broadcast. Not that there was anything important beyond where the next Fall was. How many power packs had been recharged. If they had enough sleds able to cover the next Fall. A lot of the stakeholders had come back to Landing by then, centralizing resources. Then, after the volcanoes blew, I heard their messages as they scurried away from Landing. There was a lot of static interference and transmissions got so fragmented that I couldn't hear most of what was said. They were frantic, I can tell you, by the time they abandoned Landing. Then the signals got too weak for me to pick up. I never did find out where they planned to go. It might have been west. It might have been east.

"Oh," and he waved one hand helplessly, "I tried when the last signal died. I only had one full power pack left by then. I couldn't waste that in futile searches, now could I? I'd Ito and four small kids. Then Ito got so ill. I went back to Landing to see if they'd left any medicines behind. But Landing was covered in ash and lava, great rivers of it, hot and glowing. Damned near singed the plastic off the hull.

"I checked all the stations on the lower Jordan. Paradise River, Malay, even Boca where Benden lived. No one. Fierce waste of material, though, piled as storm wrack along the coast at one point. Looked to me as if they'd lost the cargo ships in a storm. We got bad ones blowing in from the sea— or maybe the aftermath of a tsunami. We had one of those after some sea volcano blew up to the east somewhere. Missed us though on Bitkim Island.

"Last message I ever heard, and only parts of it at that, was Benden telling everyone to conserve power, stay inside, and just let that frigging Thread fall. I guess it got him, too."

Ni Morgana's thigh deliberately pressed against Benden's and he took it as sympathy. Though the old man's rambling had been confused and sometimes he contradicted himself, his statement had the ring of truth as he sat silently contemplating his wine glass. Then he roused, raising a finger to bring Chio to his side. She refilled his glass. Then, with an apologetic smile, she offered wine to the other guests, whose glasses were barely touched. Down the table from Kimmer, the three brothers sat very close together, saying little but looking with a thinly veiled hatred of Kimmer.

"We had eight good years on Pern before disaster struck," Kimmer was saying now, casting further back in his memory. "I heard that Benden and Boll swore blind that they could lick Thread. Except for Ted Tubberman and a few others, they had half the colony behind them, too entranced by the great reputations of the admiral and the governor," and the titles were pronounced disparagingly, "to believe they could fail. Tubberman wanted to send for help then. The colony voted the motion down.

"Where we were on Bitkim Island, we didn't get much Thread but I heard what it did; wiped out whole Stakes down to the metal they'd been wearing. Ate anything, Thread did, gorged until it blew up too fast to live: but it could burrow down and the next generation would begin. Fire stopped it, and metal. It drowned in water. The fish, even the dolphins, thrived on it, or so the dolphineers said. Humph. Damned stuff only let up a couple of years back. Otherwise, we've had the frigging menace raining down on us every ten days or so for fifty fucking years."

"You did well to survive, Mr. Kimmer," Saraidh said in a flattering purr as she leaned forward to elicit more confidences, "for fifty long years. But how? It must have taken tremendous effort."

"Kenjo'd started 'ponics. Had some sense, that man, even with this fanatic thing he had about flying and being in the air. Space crazy he was. But I was better at contracting the things you need to live. I taught this whole bunch everything I knew—not that they're grateful to me," and his spiteful eyes rested on the three Fusaiyukis. "We saved horses, sheep, cattle, chickens before Thread could ooze all over 'em. I'd salvaged one of the old grass-makers they used the first year, before they'd planted Earth grass and that Altair hybrid got started." He paused, narrowing his eyes. "Tubberman had another type of grass growing before they shunned him. I'd none of that seed but enough to keep us going until we could plant out again. As long as I had power packs, I foraged and saved every scrap I could find. So we survived, and survived real good."

"Then others would live, too?" Saraidh asked mildly.

"NO!" thundered Kimmer, banging the table to emphasize that denial. "No one survived but us. You don't believe me? Tell her, Shensu."

As if making up his mind to obey, Shensu regarded first Kimmer and then the three officers. Then he shrugged.

"After Thread had stopped for three months, Kimmer sent us out to see if anyone lived. We went from the Jordan River west to the Great Desert. We did see long overgrown ruins where Stakes had been started. We saw many domestic animals. I was surprised to see how many animals had managed to survive, for we saw much devastation of fertile land. We traveled for eight months. We saw no one human nor any evidence of human endeavor.

We returned to our hold." He shot a single challenging look at Kimmer before his expression settled into its mask.

Benden had a stray thought—Kimmer had sent them out, not to search for survivors, but hoping they wouldn't return.

"We're miners, too," Shensu continued unexpectedly. Kimmer sat up, too enraged at the bland disclosure to form words. Shensu smiled at that reaction. "We have mined, ores and gemstones, as soon as we were strong enough to wield pick and shovel. All of us, my half-sisters, and our children, too. He insisted that we be rich enough to pay our way back to civilized worlds."

"You fools! You utter fools! You shouldn't have told them. They'll kill us and take it all. All of it."

"They are Fleet Officers, Kimmer," Shensu said, bowing politely to Benden, Ni Morgana, and the astonished Nev. "Like Admiral Benden," and his eyes slid and held Ross Benden's briefly. "They would not be so basely motivated as to steal our fortunes and abandon us. Their orders are to rescue any survivors."

"You will rescue us, won't you?" Kimmer cried, suddenly a terrified old man. "You *must* take us with you. You must!" and now he embarrassed Benden by beginning to blubber. "You must, you must," he kept on insisting, pulling himself toward Benden to grab his tunic.

"Stev, you will make yourself ill again," Chio said, coming to disentangle the grasping hands from Benden's clothing. Her eyes looked her abject apologies for an old man's weakness and her plea for reassurance. The other women fastened apprehensive eyes on the Fleet party.

"Our orders are to establish contact with the survivors—" Benden began, taking refuge in that protocol.

"Lieutenant," Nev intervened, his face contorted with anxiety, "we'd have a weight problem, taking eleven more aboard the *Erica*."

Kimmer moaned.

"We'll discuss this later, Ensign," Benden said sharply. Trust Nev to be loose-jawed. "It is time to change the watch." He gave Nev a quelling look and gestured for Greene to accompany him. Greene looked disgusted as he fell in behind the chastened ensign, who was flushed as he realized how badly he had erred.

As Kimmer kept on sobbing "you must take me, you must take me," Benden turned to Shensu and his brothers.

"We do have orders to follow, but I assure you that if we find no other survivors to make your continued residence viable, you will either come with us on the *Erica* or another means will be found to rescue you."

"I appreciate your constraints and your devotion to duty," Shensu said, his composure in marked contrast to Kimmer's collapse. He made a slight bow from the hips. "However," and his face lightened with the slightest of smiles, "my brothers and I have already searched all the old Stakes without success. Will you not accept our investigations as conclusive?" His dignified entreaty was far harder to ignore than Kimmer's blubbering.

Benden tried to assume a noncommittal pose. "I will certainly take that into consideration, Shensu." He was also trying to calculate just how to accommodate eleven extra bodies on the *Erica*. He'd three-quarters of a tank: if they stripped unessential equipment, would that still give him enough fuel to lift and a reserve if last minute adjustments were needed in the slingshot maneuver? Damn Nev. His orders were for search only; not rescue. One thing was certain, he trusted Shensu far more than he did Kimmer.

"This mission has another goal, Mr. Fusaiyuki," Ni Morgana said, "if, under these trying circumstances, you could find your way clear to assist us?"

"Certainly. If I can," and Shensu executed a second dignified bow to her.

"Would you have any documentation that Thread comes from the stray planet as Mr. Kimmer intimated?" she asked, pointing to the ceiling and the system diagram. "Or was that only a theory?"

"A theory which my father proved to his satisfaction at least, for he flew up into the stratosphere and observed the debris which the stray planet had dislodged from the Oort Cloud and drawn into this part of the system. He had noticed the cloud on their way through the system. I remember him telling me that he would have paid far closer attention had he any idea of the threat it would pose." Shensu's well-formed lips curled in a wry smile. "The EEC report evidently gave the erratic planet only a mention. I have my father's notes."

"I'd like to see them," Saraidh said, her voice edged with excitement. "Bizarre as it is," she said to Benden, "it is plausible and unique. Of course, this erratic planet could be a large asteroid, even a comet. Its orbit is certainly a cometary."

"No," Benden replied, shaking his head, "the EEC report definitely identifies it as a planet, though probably a wanderer drawn into Rukbat's family only recently. It orbits across the ecliptic."

"Our father was too experienced an airman to make a mistake," Jiro spoke for the first time, his voice as impassioned as Shensu's was cold. "He was a trained pilot and observed critically and objectively on those missions. We have notes of thanks from Admiral Benden, Governor Boll, and Captain Keroon, all expressing gratitude for his investigation and his selfless dedication to duty." Jiro shot a contemptuous look at Kimmer who was still sobbing, his face pillowed in his arms while Chio tried to comfort and reassure him. "Our father died to discover such truths."

Saraidh murmured something appropriate. "If you would cooperate, further information about this phenomenon would be invaluable."

"Why?" Shensu asked bluntly. "There can't be other worlds that are infested with this menace, can there?"

"Not that we know of, Mr. Fusaiyuki, but all information is valuable to someone. My orders were to find out more about this organism."

Shensu shrugged. "You're too late by several years to do the most valuable observations," he said with a wry note in his voice.

"We saw some . . ." Saraidh fumbled for an exact description of the "tunnels" they had seen at Landing, "remnants, dead shells of these Thread. Would there be any near you that I could examine?"

Shensu shrugged again. "Some on the plains below us."

"How far in terms of time?" Saraidh asked.

"A day's journey."

"Will you guide me?"

"You?" Shensu was surprised.

"Lieutenant Ni Morgana is the science officer of the *Amherst*," Benden put in firmly. "You will want to assist her in this investigation, Mr. Fusaiyuki."

Shensu made a small gesture of obedience with his hands.

"Jiro, Kimo," Chio spoke up. Kimmer seemed to have subsided into sleep. "Help me carry him to his room."

The two men rose, their faces blank of expression and picked him up, much as they would a sack, and carried him toward a curtained arch through which they disappeared, Chio following anxiously.

"I'll check on Nev," Benden said, rising, "while you arrange tomorrow's expedition with Shensu, Commander."

"A good idea, Lieutenant."

Benden motioned for the two marines to remain as he made his way out of the superb room, his eyes on the gorgeous murals and their story of mankind's triumph over tremendous odds.

"I could wish, Ensign Nev, that you would learn to think before you speak," Benden said sternly to the chagrined junior when he returned to the *Erica*.

"I'm really sorry, Lieutenant," and Nev's face was twisted with anxiety, "but we can't just leave them, can we? Not if we can actually rescue them?"

"You've made such calculations?"

"Aye, sir, I did, as soon as I got back on board," and eagerly Nev brought his figures up on the monitor. "Of course, I could only estimate their weight but they can't weigh *that* much and the inward journey only took a quarter of our fuel."

"We've a planet to search, mister," Benden said sharply as he bent to study the figures. This was going to be a command decision on his part: to abandon the search on the basis of the opinion of a few local witnesses or to carry out his original orders scrupulously.

"We weren't expected to *find* survivors, were we?" Nev asked in a tentative voice.

Benden frowned at him. "What exactly do you mean by that, mister?"

"Well, Lieutenant, if Captain Fargoe had *expected* there'd be survivors, wouldn't she have ordered a troop shuttle? They'd carry a couple of hundred people."

Benden regarded Nev with exasperation. "You know our orders as well as I do: to discover the survivors and their present circumstances. Nothing was intimated that we wouldn't find survivors. Or that we wouldn't find them able to continue their colonial effort."

"But this lot couldn't, could they? There aren't enough of them. I don't trust the old man but that Shensu's OK."

"When I need your opinion, mister, I'll ask for it," Benden said curtly. Nev subsided to glum silence while Benden continued to peer at the numbers on the screen, half-wishing they would cabalistically rearrange themselves into a solution for his dilemma.

"Establish how much we'd need to jettison, mister, without seriously affecting safety during the slingshot. Ascertain just where we can put eleven passengers and take into your weight consideration the extra padding and harness we'd need to secure them during lift-off."

"Aye, aye, sir." Nev's enthusiasm and the admiring look he gave Benden was almost harder to endure than his chastened funk.

Benden strode to the airlock and out of the ship, taking the crisp air into his lungs as if that would aid his thinking. In a sense Nev was right: the captain hadn't expected that they would find survivors in need of rescue. She had assumed that either the settlers had overcome the disaster or that all had succumbed to it. However, these eleven could not, in the name of humanity, be left behind on the planet.

The *Erica*'s remaining fuel would barely accomplish that rescue. It certainly wouldn't allow the Pernese to bring anything back with them to start again elsewhere, like metal ores. Possibly some of these gemstones Shensu had mentioned could be permitted. With no more than the usual shipwreck allowance, these people would be seriously handicapped in the high tech societies on most of the Federation planets, and financially unable to establish themselves in an agrarian economy. They have to have *something*.

If Kimmer could be believed, and possibly with the estranged brothers corroborating his statement, it was true that these eleven constituted all that remained of the original colonial complement, then further search would be fruitless as well as wasting fuel that could, really, be put to better use. Did the brothers have any reason to lie? Not, Benden thought, when they hated Kimmer so much. Ah, but they'd want to leave this place, wouldn't they, even if it meant perjuring themselves!

Unusual noises attracted his attention and he walked to the edge of the plateau to check. Some twenty meters below him he saw four people, Jiro and the three youngest, mounted on Earth-type horses, herding a variety of four-legged domestic beasts through a huge aperture in the cliff. He heard an odd call and saw a brown, winged shape hurtling after them. As he watched, a heavy metal door swung on well oiled hinges to close off the opening. The evening breeze, for the light was beginning to fail now on their first day of their five on this planet, wafted some curious smells up to him. He sneezed as he made his way across the plateau to the door to this unusual residence. They'd have to turn those animals loose. Bloody sure, there was no room on board the *Erica* for that mob.

When Benden reentered the big room, he spotted Ni Morgana and Shensu poring over maps on a smaller table to the left of the main entrance. There were cases of tapes and other paraphernalia along that section of the smooth carved wall.

"Lieutenant, we've got both the original survey maps here and those that the colonists filled in with detailed explorations," Saraidh called to him. "A crying shame this endeavor was so brutally short-lived. They'd a lovely situation here. See," and her scripto touched first one, then another of the shaded areas on the map of the southern continent, "fertile farms producing everything they needed before disaster struck, a viable fishing industry, mines with onsite smelting and manufactory. And then . . ." she gave an eloquent shrug.

"Admiral Benden rose to the challenge magnificently," Shensu said, the glow in his eyes altering his whole appearance, making him a far more likeable person. "He called for centralization of all materials and skills. My father commanded the aerial defense. He had flame-throwers mounted on sleds, two forward and one aft, and developed flight patterns that would cover the largest areas and destroy quantities of airborne Thread. Ground crews were organized with portable flamers to incinerate what did get through to the ground, before it could burrow and reproduce itself. It was the most valiant effort!"

There was an excitement and a ring in Shensu's voice that made Benden's pulse quicken—he could see that Saraidh was also affected. Shensu's whole attitude was suffused with reverence and awe.

"We were just young boys but our father came as often as he could and told us what was happening. He was always in touch with our mother. He even spoke to her just before . . . before that final mission." All the emotion left Shensu and his expression assumed its habitual taciturnity. "He was brutally murdered just when he might have made the discovery which could have ended Threadfall and preserved the whole colony."

"By this Avril person?" Saraidh asked gently.

Shensu nodded once, his features set. "Then *he* came!"

"And now we have come," Saraidh said, pausing a moment before continuing on a brisker note, "and we must somehow gather as much evidence after the fact as possible. There have been many theories about Oort clouds and what they contain. This is the first opportunity to examine such a space-evolved creature, and the disaster it causes on an uninhabited planet. You said the organism burrowed into the ground and reproduced itself? I'd like to see the later stage of the organism's life cycle. Can you show me where?" she asked, looking exceedingly attractive, Benden thought, in her eagerness.

Shensu looked disgusted. "You wouldn't want to see any stage in its life cycle. My mother said that there was only the hunger of it. Which no one should encounter."

"Any sort of residue would aid the research, Shensu," she said, reaching out to touch his arm. "We need your help, Shensu."

"We needed yours a long time ago," he said in a voice so bitter that Saraidh withdrew her hand, flushing.

"This expedition was mounted as soon as your message came up on the records, Shensu. The delay is not ours," Benden replied crisply. "But we are here and we'd like your cooperation."

Shensu gave a cynical snort. "Does my cooperation guarantee escaping from this place?"

Benden looked him squarely in the eye. "I could not, in conscience, leave you here," he said, having in that moment made his decision, "especially in view of the fact that I also cannot assure you that you would be relieved by another vessel in the near future. I shall, however, need to have the exact body weights of everyone and frankly we'll have to strip the *Erica* to accommodate you."

Shensu kept eye contact, his own reaction to Benden's decision unreadable. Benden was aware of Ni Morgana's discreet approval. "Your ship is low on fuel?"

"If we are to successfully lift additional passengers, yes."

"If you did not have to strip the *Erica* to compensate for our weight?" Shensu seemed amused as he watched Benden's reaction. "If you had, say, a full tank, could you allow us to bring enough valuables to assist us to resettle somewhere? Rescue to a pauper's existence would be no rescue at all."

Benden nodded in acknowledgement of that fact even as he spoke. "Kimmer said there was no more fuel. He was emphatic about it."

Shensu leaned his body across the table and spoke in a scarcely audible whisper, his black eyes glittering with what Benden read as quiet satisfaction. "Kimmer doesn't know everything, Lieutenant," and now Shensu chuckled, "he thinks he does."

"What do you know that Kimmer doesn't?" Benden asked, lowering his own voice.

"Spaceship fuel has not changed in the past six decades, has it?" Shensu asked in his whisper.

"Not for ships of the *Amherst*'s and the *Erica*'s class," Saraidh replied, quietly eager.

"Since you're interested," Shensu said in a conversational voice level as he rose from the table, "I'd be happy to show you the rest of the Hold. We have a place for everything. I think my esteemed father had visions of founding a dynasty. My mother said that had not Thread come, there were others of our ethnic type who would have joined them here in Honshu." Shensu led them towards a hanging which he pushed aside, gesturing them to proceed through the archway. "They accomplished much before Thread fell."

He let the hanging fall and joined Saraidh and Benden on the small square landing where stone-cut steps spiraled in both directions. Shensu gestured that they were to ascend.

Saraidh started up. "Wow! This is some staircase," she said, as she made the first turn.

"I must warn you that the living room has peculiarities—one of which is an echo effect," Shensu said. "Conversations can be overheard in the passages outside. I don't believe *he* has yet recovered from his . . . disability . . . but Chio, or one of his daughters, is always eavesdropping for him. So, I take no chances. No, continue up. I know the steps become uneven. Balance yourself against the wall."

The steps were uneven, unfinished, and several had no more than toe space.

"This was deliberate?" asked Saraidh, beginning to show the effort of the climbing. "Oh, for a grav shaft!"

Benden was in agreement as he felt the muscles in his calves and thighs tightening. And he had thought that he'd spent adequate time in P.T. to keep himself fit for any exertion.

"Now where?" Saraidh asked as she came to a very narrow landing. The thin slit of a tiny aperture did nothing to illuminate the blank walls all around them.

Shensu apologized as he squeezed past the two officers, the half smile still on his face and, to their chagrin, he was showing no signs of effort. He put his hand, palm down, on a rough, apparently natural, declivity in the wall and suddenly a whole section of the wall pivoted inward. Light came on to illuminate a low deep cave. Benden whistled in surprise because the space was full of sacks, each tagged with some sort of coded label. Sacks of fuel, row upon row of them.

"There's more here than we need," Saraidh said, having made some rough calculations. "More than enough. But . . ." and now she turned to Shensu, her expression stern, "I could understand your keeping this from Kimmer but surely this was fuel those shuttles could have used? Or did they?" For she had also noticed that some of the closer ranks were thinned where sacks had obviously been removed.

Shensu held up his hand. "My father was an honorable man. And when the need arose, he took what was needed from this cavern and gave it, willingly, to Admiral Benden, doing all within his power to help overcome the menace that dropped from the skies. If he had not been mur-dered . . ." Shensu broke off the sentence, his jaw muscles tensing, his expression bleak. "I do not know where the three shuttles went, but they could only have lifted from Landing on the fuel my father gave Admiral Benden. Now I give the rest of the fuel to a man also named Benden." Shensu looked pointedly at the lieutenant.

"Paul Benden was my uncle," he admitted, finding himself chagrined at this unexpected inheritance. "The *Erica* is also economical with fuel. With a full tank, we can lift you and even make allowance for personal effects. But why is the fuel *here?*"

"My father did not steal it," Shensu said, indignant.

"And I didn't imply that he had, Shensu," Benden replied soothingly.

"My father accumulated this fuel during the transfer from the colony ships to the surface of the planet. He was the most accomplished shuttle pilot of them all. And he was the most economical. He only took what his careful flying saved on each flight and no one took harm from his economy. He told me how much was wasted by the other pilots, carelessly wasted. He was a charterer and had the right to take what was available. He merely ensured that fuel was available."

"But—" Benden began, wishing to reassure Shensu.

"He saved it to fly. He had to fly," and Shensu's eyes became slightly unfocused as his impassioned explanation continued. "It was his life. With space denied him, he designed a little atmosphere plane. I can show it to you. He flew it here, in Honshu, where no one but us could see him. But he took each of us in that plane." Shensu's face softened with these memories. "That was the prize we all worked for. And I could understand his fascination with flight." Shensu took in a deep breath and regarded the two Fleet officers in his usual inscrutable fashion.

"I'm not sure I could live happily stuck landside forever," Benden said earnestly. "And we're grateful to be taken into your confidence, Shensu."

"My father would be pleased that his saving ways permit a Benden to save his kinsmen," Shensu said in a wry tone and with a sly glance at the lieutenant. "But we will wait until late tonight, when there are few to notice our activity. Those marines of yours look strong. But do not bring that ensign. He talks too much. I do not want Kimmer to know of our transaction. It is enough that he will be rescued from Pern."

"Have you checked these sacks recently, Shensu?" Saraidh asked and, when he shook his head, she had to crouch to enter the low cave and inspect the nearest. "Your father did well, Shensu," she said over her shoulder peering at the sack she had tilted upside down. "I was afraid there might be some contamination from the plastic after fifty-odd years but the fuel all seems to be clear, no sediment, well saved."

"What gemstones would be worth bringing with us?" Shensu asked casually.

"Industrial technology requires quantities of sapphire, pure quartz, diamonds," Saraidh told him as she left the cave, arching her back to relieve the strain of crouching. "But the major use of natural gemstones is once again decorative—for pets, high-status women, courtly men."

"Black diamonds?" Shensu asked, his lips parting in anticipation.

"Black diamonds?" Saraidh was astonished.

"Come, I will show you," Shensu said, allowing his lips to part in a pleased smile. "First we will close the cave and then descend to our workshops. Then I will show you the rest of the Hold as I said I would do," and he grinned back at them.

Benden was not sure whether going down was worse than climbing. He felt not only dizzy from the short arc of the stairs but had the sensations that he would fall forward down this interminable spiral. He considered himself competent in free fall or in space walking but this was a subtly different activity. He was only marginally relieved that Shensu was in front of him but, if Saraidh fell into *him*, was Shensu sturdy enough to keep all three from pitching down?

They passed several landings which Shensu ignored, and seemed to descend a very long way before they emerged into another large room which must be under the main living chamber. It was not as high-ceilinged or as well finished but it was clearly furnished for a variety of activities. He identified a large kiln, a forge hearth and three looms. Work tables were placed near racks of carefully stored tools. Hand tools, not a power tool among them.

Shensu led them to a plastic cabinet a meter high and wide with many small drawers. He pulled out two, evidently at random, and scattered their contents on the nearby table, the facets of the cut stones sparkling in the overhead light. Saraidh exclaimed in surprise, scooping up a handful of carelessly thrown stones of all sizes. Benden picked up a large one out of her hand, holding it up to the light. He'd never seen anything like it, dark but glittering with light.

"Black diamond. There's a whole beach full of them below a dead volcano." Shensu said, leaning back against the table, arms folded across his chest. His smile was amused. "We have drawers of them, and emeralds, sapphires, rubies. We're all good lapidaries though Faith is cleverest in cutting. We don't bother much with what Kimmer terms semi-precious though he has some fine turquoise which he says is extremely valuable."

"Probably," Saraidh murmured, still absorbed in running a shower of the diamonds through her hands. She was absorbed but not, Benden noted, covetous.

"The blacks are why I know you won't find any survivors in the north," Shensu went on, his eyes on Benden, who was less involved in the gemstones.

"Oh? Why?"

"Before the sled power packs died, Kimmer made two trips to Bitkim Island where he and Avril Bitra had mined both the black diamonds and emeralds. He brought me and Jiro with him both times to help gather the rough diamonds. I saw him leave our camp late one night and I followed him. He went into a big water cavern before he disappeared from sight. He had the light. I didn't dare go further. But, in the cavern lagoon three ships were moored, masts lashed to the decks. They were plastic hulled and their decks were badly scored by Thread. It couldn't pierce plastic but it could melt grooves on it. I went down into one of the ships and everything was neatly stowed aboard, even in the galley there were supplies in tight containers. Everything left in readiness for the ships to be sailed out of the cavern again." Shensu paused dramatically. Shensu had a feeling for the dramatic, Benden realized. But that was not a fault. "Three years later, we came back for a last load. And no one had been near the ships. There was a thick coat of dust on everything. Nothing had been touched. Except there was a lot more algae on the hulls and wind-blown debris on the decks. Three years! I say there was no one left to sail them."

Saraidh had let the diamonds drip through her fingers to the table and now she sighed. "You said there was a volcanic island? Was it active when you were there? That could account for that heat source we noticed," she added to Benden.

"Kimmer would stretch the truth every which way," Shensu said, "to make himself look good. But he desperately wanted to have a larger gene pool—for his own pleasure if not ours." The last was said with an understandable malice. "If only a few more had survived, there'd be that much more future for all of us."

That gave both Ross Benden and Saraidh Ni Morgana a lot to mull over as Shensu showed them round the additional facilities: the animal barn, the well-supplied storage areas. He paused at a locked door to a lower level.

"Kimmer keeps the key to the hangar, so I can't show you my father's plane," Shensu said. Then he gestured for them to ascend the stairs to the upper floors. Benden was relieved that these steps were wide and straight.

When they returned to the main level of Honshu Hold, they found the women busily preparing a feast: certainly a feast for those who had been five years on a mission. Not that the *Amherst* did not cater well but nothing to compare with spit-roasted lamb and the variety of Pernese hybrid vegetables and tubers. The two marines who stayed aboard, despite the slightly sarcastic assurance from Kimmer that no enemies could be lurking on Honshu Cliff, were brought heaping platters and non-fermented beverages by Faith and Charity. Within the Hold, the evening was merry and Kimmer, with a glass or two of wine, became expansive as a host. For he had recovered his composure after a long rest, and tactfully, no mention was made of his collapse.

As prearranged, Benden, Sergeant Greene, and Vartry met Shensu, his two brothers and the boys, Alun and Pat. Even with nine to tote sacks, it took four trips to top off the *Erica*'s tanks. The boys were short enough to walk upright in the low cave and they brought the sacks out to those who waited to haul them down. The marines were not above showing off their fitness and, using slings, carried eight sacks at a time. Ross Benden decided that four were quite enough and he had no reason to challenge the marines. The Fusaiyuki brothers carried six effortlessly. When the tanks were full, there were still sacks in the cavern.

The next morning, hearing Nev's cheerful morning ablutions, Ross Benden stirred and abruptly stopped. He was uncomfortably stiff and sore from the night's exertions.

"Something wrong, sir?"

"Not a thing," Benden said. "Just finish up and let me have a chance, will you?"

Nev took that in good part and shortly was out of the tiny cabin. Moving with extreme caution, and hissing at the pain of abused muscles, Ross Benden managed to get to his feet. Bent-kneed, he hobbled to the hand basin and opened the small cabinet above that contained the medical kit. A thorough search revealed nothing for muscular aches. He fumbled for a pain tablet, knocked it to the back of his mouth, and discovered that his neck was sore too. He took a drink of water. He must remember to drain the cistern and fill it with the excellent water of Pern.

A scratch at the door made Benden straighten up, despite the anguish to the long tendons in his legs, but he was damned if he'd show weakness.

"It's I," and Ni Morgana entered, taking in at a glance his semi-crippled state. "I thought this likely. Just one trip up and down those racks of a stair and my legs were sore. Faith gave me this salve . . . wanted me to test it to see if it was something of medical value. It's indigenous . . . no, lie back down, Ross, I'll slather it on. Supposed to have numbing properties. Hmm, it does," and she eyed her fingers and the generous dollop she had scooped out of the jar.

Ross was crippled enough to be willing to try anything, noxious or bizarre. He could hardly appear before Kimmer in his present shape.

"Oh, it is numbing. Whee, ooh, ahh, more on the right calf, please," Benden said, ridiculously relieved by the numbing effect of the salve. The pain seemed to drain out of calves and thighs, leaving them oddly cool but not cold, and certainly free of that damnable soreness.

"I've got plenty for later and Faith says they have buckets of the stuff. Make it fresh every year. Doesn't smell half bad either. Pungent and . . . piney."

When she finished doctoring Benden, she washed her hands thoroughly. "I'd say don't shower today or you'll lose the relief." Then she turned back to Ross Benden, with a puzzled expression. "Ross," she began, settling against the little hand basin and crossing her arms. "How much would you say Kimmer weighed?"

"Hmm," and Benden thought of the man's build and height, "about 72–74 kilos. Why?"

"I weighed him in at 95 kilos. Of course, he was clothed, and the tunic and trousers are rather full and made of sturdy fabric, but I wouldn't have thought he carried that much flesh."

"Nor would I."

"I didn't judge the women correctly either. They all weighed in a little under and a little over 70 kilos and none of them are either tall or heavy-set."

Nev mumbled figures under his breath. "All of 'em, even the kids?"

"No, the three brothers are 73, 72, and 75 kilos, which is about what I thought they'd be. The girl and the boys are also 2 or 3 kilos more than I'd have thought them."

"With a full tank, we can afford a few extra kilos," Benden said.

"I was also asked how much they could bring with them," Saraidh went on, "and I said we had to calibrate body weights and other factors before we could give them an exact allowance. I trust that wasn't out of line."

"I'll get Nev to calculate in those weights and let me know how much fuel we'll have in reserve then," Benden said. "And what we use as padding and safety harness so no one bounces all over the gig during take-off."

Folding out the cabin's keyboard, Benden ran some rough figures against the lifting power of the now full tank. "D'you have a total of their weights?" Ni Morgana gave him the figures. He added them in plus kilos for padding and harness and contemplated the result. "I'd hate to be considered mean but 23.5 kilos each is about all we can allow."

"That's as much as we're allowed for personal effects on the *Amherst*," Ni Morgana said. "Is there room for 23.5 kilos in medicinals? I gather this stuff is effective."

"It certainly is," Benden said, flexing his knees and feeling no discomfort.

"I'll just get some of this on the marines as well, then," Ni Morgana said.

"Ha!" was Benden's scoffing reply.

"I don't know about that," Ni Morgana said with a sly grin. "But then, you didn't catch sight of Sergeant Greene making for the galley. I think," and she paused reflectively, "that I'm doing some empirical tests of this junk and they just got lucky to be chosen as test subjects. Yes, that should save face admirably. We can't give Kimmer any reason to be suspicious, now, can we?" Then she left, chuckling over her subterfuge.

At 0835, when Benden left the galley and proceeded to the Hold, he found Kimmer and the women in the main room, none of them looking too happy.

"We've done the calculations, Kimmer, and we can allow each of you, the children included, 23.5 kilos of personal effects. That's what Fleet personnel are generally allowed to bring on voyages and I can't see Captain Fargoe objecting to it."

"Twenty-three point five kilos is quite generous, Lieutenant," Kimmer surprised Benden by saying. He turned to them chidingly "That's more than we had coming out on the *Yoko*."

"And," Benden said, turning to Faith, "that wouldn't include medicinal products and respective seeds to a similar limit. Lieutenant Ni Morgana is of the opinion that they could well be valuable commodities."

"For which we'd be reimbursed?" asked Kimmer sharply.

"Of course," Benden said, keeping his voice even. "We have to allow for the weight of padding and harness to keep you secure during our drop into the gravity well. . . ."

Charity and Hope emitted nervous squeaks.

"Nothing to worry yourself over, ladies," Benden went on with a reassuring smile. "We use gravity wells all the time as a quick way to break out of a system."

"Be damned grateful we're getting off this frigging forsaken mudball," Kimmer said, angrily rising to his feet. "Go on, now, sort out what you've got to bring but keep it to the weight limit. Hear me?"

The women removed themselves, with Faith casting one last despairing glance over her shoulder at her father. Benden wondered why he had thought any of them were graceful. They waddled in a most ungainly fashion.

"You've been extremely generous, Lieutenant," Kimmer said affably, as he settled himself again in the high-backed carved chair that he usually occupied at the table. "I thought we'd be lucky enough to get off with what we have on our backs."

"Are you absolutely positive that there are no other survivors on Pern?" Benden said, favoring a direct attack. "Others could have carved holds out of cliffs and remained secure from that airborne menace of yours."

"Yes, they could have but, for one thing, there aren't any cave systems here on the southern continent. And I'll tell you why I think the rest perished after I lost the last radio contact with those at Drake's Lake and Dorado. In those days I was more confident of rescue. And I'd enough power left in my sled to make one more trip back to Bitkim Island where I'd mined some good emeralds." He paused, leaning forward, elbows on the table and shaking one finger at Benden. "And black diamonds."

"*Black* diamonds?" And Benden thought he sounded genuinely amazed.

"Black diamonds, a whole beach full of them. That's what I intend to bring back."

"Twenty-three point five kilos of them?"

"And a few pieces of turquoise that I also found."

"Really?"

"When I'd enough of a load of stones, I went into a natural cavern on Bitkim's southeast side. Big enough to anchor ships in if you stepped the mast. And it was there."

"Pardon?"

"Jim Tillek's ship was there, mast and all, holes and grooves where Thread had scored it time and again."

"Jim Tillek?"

"The admiral's right hand. And a man who loved that ship. Loved it like other men love women . . . or Fussy Fusi loved flying," Kimmer allowed his malice to show briefly, "but I'm telling you, Jim Tillek wouldn't have left that ship, not to gather dust and algae on her hull, if he was alive somewhere on Pern. And that ship had been anchored there three or four years. That's one very good reason why I know no one was left alive."

"Did you find any sign of human occupation," Kimmer went on, his voice less intense, his eyes glittering almost mockingly, "when you spiraled down across the northern hemisphere?"

"No, neither on infra or power-use detection," Benden had to admit.

Kimmer spread both arms wide then. "You know there's no one there, then. No need to waste your reserves of fuel to find 'em. We're the last alive on Pern and, I'll tell you this, it's no planet for mankind."

"I'm sure the Colonial Authority will want a full report from you when you return to Base, Kimmer. I shall certainly log in my findings."

"Then do mankind a favor, Lieutenant, and tag this disaster of a world as uninhabitable."

"That's not for me to say."

Kimmer snorted and sat back in his chair.

"Now, if you'll excuse me, I must join Lieutenant Ni Morgana on her scientific survey. There are sufficient liftbelts, if you'd like to come along."

"No, thank you, Lieutenant," and Kimmer flicked his hand in dismissal of such activity. "I've seen about as much of this planet as I have any wish to."

Benden was just strapping on his liftbelt when Kimmer erupted from the Hold, the whites of his eyes showing in his agitation.

"Lieutenant!" he cried, running towards the small party.

Benden held up a warning hand as one of the marines beside him moved to intercept the man.

"Lieutenant, what power do you use for the belts? What power?" Kimmer cried excitedly as he approached.

"Pack power, of course," Benden replied.

"Regulation packs?" And, without apology, Kimmer grabbed the lieutenant by the shoulder and swung him around, just as Vartry took hold of the old man's arms.

"As you were!" Ross Benden barked at the marine but with a nod to reassure him, because he understood what Kimmer, in his excitement, did not explain. "Yes, standard power packs, and we have enough to reactivate that sled of yours, if it's in any reasonable working order."

"It is, Lieutenant, it is!" Kimmer reassured him, his agitation replaced by immense satisfaction. "So you'll be able to eyeball the remains of the colony and report honestly to your captain that you followed your orders, Mister Benden," and Kimmer stressed the name in a tone just short of malice, "as assiduously as your noble relative would have done." Ross grimaced, but his relation to the admiral would have become public sooner or later. "I thought you looked familiar," Kimmer added, smugly.

Benden took the lieutenant aside for a quick conference and she concurred that it was Benden's first obligation to search as far as he was able for survivors. She was quite willing to conduct her own scientific research with Shensu as her guide and two marines as assistants. So she wished the lieutenant good luck and lifted gracefully off the plateau, floating down in the direction of the nearest evidence of Thread, some ten klicks down the valley on the other side of the river.

That matter settled, Kimmer began to pluck at Benden's sleeve in his urgency and hurried him, Nev following, back into the Hold. Maps were still spread out on the table from the previous evening.

"I searched east as far as Landing and Cardiff," Kimmer said, prodding one map with an arthritic index finger. He dragged it back and down along to the Jordan River. "Those Stakes were all empty and Thread-ridden through Calusa, Ted Tubberman's old place wasn't." Kimmer frowned a moment, then shrugged off that enigma, moving his finger up to the coastline and west. "Paradise River must have been used as some kind of staging area because there were netted containers in the overgrowth along the shore but the buildings were all boarded up. Malay, too, and Boca," he stabbed again at those points on the map. "I went north from Boca to Bitkim but I confess that I didn't stop at Thessaly or Roma, where they had well-built stone houses and barns. And I didn't get any further west. The gauge on the power pack was jiggling too much for me to risk getting stranded."

"So there could be survivors to the west. . . ." Benden pored over the map, feeling a surge of excitement and hope. Then he wondered why Kimmer was willing to take such a risk—that enough survivors would be found for the colony to be left to work out its parochial problems. Maybe the prospect of leaving so much behind, including being the default owner of a planet, was giving Kimmer second thoughts. If fifty years of his life's endeavors was going to be crammed into a 23.5 kilo sack, living out the remainder of his life in the comforts he had achieved might indeed hold more charm for the old man than an uncertain, and possibly, pauper's existence in a linear warren.

"There could indeed be Stakeholders there, but why haven't they attempted any contact?" Kimmer asked defiantly, and his eyes quickly concealed a flicker of something else. "I got the last communication from the west but that could have been for any number of reasons. Now, if you've got a portable unit that we could bring with us, maybe closer to one of the western Stakes, we might rouse someone."

"Let's see this sled of yours," Benden didn't mention that they had opened the broadest range of communications on their inbound spiral with not so much as a flicker on any frequency. But Kimmer was right that lack of communication could have been caused by any number of reasons.

Kimmer led them to the locked door, which he opened, and proceeded down to the next level, a hangar in fact, with wide double doors at one end which opened out on the wide terrace below the Hold entrance plateau. While the sled occupied the center of the considerable floor space, Kenjo's little atmosphere underwing craft was not quite hidden in the back. Then Benden's attention was all for the sled, which was cocooned in the usual durable thin plastic film. This Kimmer energetically punctured. All four men helped peel the sled free as Kimmer enumerated his exact shut-down precautions. Although the plascanopy was somewhat darkened with age and the tracks of Thread hits, when Benden touched the release button, the door slid back as easily as if it had been opened the day before.

This was a much older model than those now in use, of course, so Benden did a thorough inspection; but the fabric of the sturdy vessel was undamaged. The control panel was one he recognized from text-tapes. When he depressed the power toggle, the gauge above it fluttered and then dropped back to zero. He walked aft to the power locker, flipped up the latches on the power trunk, and lifted the big unit out to examine the leads. Liftbelts used much smaller packs, but Benden could see no difficulty in making a multiple connection of smaller units to supply power. Moving forward again, Kimmer stepping out of his way but exuding a palpable excitement, Benden tested the steering yoke, which moved easily in his grip.

"We'll just make a link-up and see how she answers to power. Ensign Nev, take Kimo and Jiro and break out twelve belt packs, and the portable communit. We're going to take a little ride."

An hour later, once more operational, the old sled drifted under its own power to the narrower lower terrace.

When Benden returned to the *Erica* for rations and a bedroll, an earnest and anxious Nev accosted him, wanting to join the expedition.

"You don't know what that old man might try, Lieutenant. And I don't trust him."

"Listen up," Benden said in a low and forceful tone that stopped Nev's babbling. "I'm not half as worried about my safety as I am about the *Erica*'s. Kimmer goes with me. I don't trust him either. I'll take Jiro along as well. And Sergeant Greene. Neither of them could get through Greene to me. You'll only have Kimo to worry about and he strikes me as too placid to do anything on his own. Shensu is a proven ally. Present my compliments to Lieutenant Ni Morgana when she returns and relay this order. Either you or the lieutenant are to be on the *Erica* at all times. The marines are to stand proper watches until I return. Have I made that clear?"

"Aye, aye, sir, Lieutenant Benden. Loud and clear, sir." Nev's teeth were almost chattering with his assurances and his eyes were wide as he dutifully assimilated his orders.

"I'll report in at intervals so break out hand-units for yourself and Vartry."

"Aye, aye, sir."

"We'll be back in two days." He ordered Greene to collect supplies and carry them to the sled.

"If you will pardon me, Lieutenant," Kimmer said unctuously as he and Jiro entered the craft, "I think we can easily reach Karachi Camp today, stopping at Suweto and Yukon on the way. Karachi is a real possibility because, now that Thread is gone, they'd want to activate the mines."

Surprising himself, Benden gestured with an open hand to the pilot's seat. "You have the con, Mr. Kimmer." It was as good a way as any to see just how competent the old man had been: if he had actually done what he said he did, "After all, you're more familiar with this model sled than I am and you know where we're going." It would also be easier to keep the old man occupied.

So Benden seated himself behind Kimmer while the sergeant, giving the officer only a mildly reproachful look, took the seat next to Jiro on the starboard side.

The old sled purred along as if delighted by its release from long imprisonment. It answered the yoke with the smoothness of a well-maintained vehicle as Kimmer swung it to port. Kimmer wasn't all bad, Benden thought of himself, and wondered again why the old man had insisted on this search. Was it really to prove to Benden that his folk were the only ones left? Or had Kimmer some ulterior motive? And would Kimmer be surprised if they did find anyone? After overflying the snowy waste of the northern continent and the devastation of the southern lands, Benden could only be surprised that anyone had survived. It was certainly most unlikely that his uncle, who'd be well into his twelfth decade, would still be alive.

They came down from the foothills across the river, obliquely to port of Ni Morgana and her group, and then across a lifeless plain of circles in the dust. There were spots here and there of struggling plant life, but Benden wondered if the wind would scatter the topsoil before vegetation could reestablish itself and prevent further erosion. And that was the pattern for the next few hours—broad uneven-edged ribbons, about fifty klicks across of ravaged land—then broader belts of grassland or forest, even thick vegetation neither shrub or jungle, with the glint of hidden water in rivers and ponds.

The old sled purred along at about 220 klicks per hour. Benden broke out rations and passed them around. Kimmer altered the course and, over the sloping nose of the sled, a large and brilliantly blue lake could be seen. As they neared it and Kimmer obligingly skimmed low, vegetation-crowned mounds indicated the ruins of a considerable settlement.

"Drake's Lake," and Kimmer gave a sour laugh. "Damned arrogant fool," he muttered to himself. "No signs of anyone but there may be at Andiyar's mines."

They overflew more deserted housing and startled a herd of grazing animals who plunged wildly away from the muted sound of the sled.

"Livestock seems to have survived," Benden remarked. "Will you turn yours loose?"

"What else?" and Kimmer barked a laugh. "Though Chio's moaning about her pet fire-dragon having to be left behind."

"Fire-dragon?" Benden asked in surprise.

"Well, that's what some people thought they looked like," Kimmer explained diffidently. "They look like reptiles, lizards to me. It's an indigenous life-form, hatches from eggs, and if you get one then, it attaches itself to you. Useless thing as far as I can see but Chio's fond of it." He glanced over his shoulder at Benden.

"It wouldn't take up much room," Jiro said, speaking for the first time. "It's a bronze male."

Benden shook his head. "Humans, yes, creatures no," he said firmly. The captain was still likely to question his foisting eleven human survivors on her but she'd blow her tubes if he tried to impose an alien *pet*.

They reached the mine site and landed near the adits. Within was cocooned equipment—ore carts, picks, shovels, all kinds of hand tools, as well as an array of tough plas props for tunnel supports.

"You really had gone back to the lowest level of useful technology, hadn't you?" Benden said, hefting one of the picks. "But if you had stone cutters, didn't you—"

"When that damned Thread started falling, your uncle called in all power packs for use in the sleds. That was Benden's priority and we couldn't fight it."

The living quarters, unlike those at the lake, had been cocooned. Peering in through the thinner patches over windows, Benden could see that furnishings had been left in place.

"See what I mean, Lieutenant? This place is all ready to be started up again. It's nearly two years since Thread stopped falling. If they could, they'd be back here."

They spent the night there at Karachi, setting up a rough camp. While Kimmer started a fire, "to keep the tunnel snakes away" he told Benden, the lieutenant made contact with Honshu and spoke to Nev, who said the lieutenant was writing up her notes and that nothing of any significance had happened.

Just as Benden was signing off, Jiro came to the sled for a coil of rope and walked off into the forest. He returned not too much later with a fat squat avian which he had roped off a branch and strangled. He identified it as a wherry, as he neatly skinned and spitted it over the fire. During its roasting, the aroma of the meat was tantalizing, arousing a good appetite. It proved to be very tasty.

"Forest wherries are better than coastal ones," Kimmer said slicing himself another portion. "Those have an oily, fishy taste."

Greene nodded appreciatively as he licked his fingers clean of the juices. Then he excused himself and disappeared into the woods. Just about the time Benden was becoming apprehensive about his long absence, he reappeared.

"Nothing moving anywhere, except things that slither," he reported to the lieutenant in a low voice. "I don't think we *need* to set a watch, Lieutenant, but I always sleep light."

As Benden saw Kimmer already asleep and Jiro settling down on their side of the fire, he decided a watch would be superfluous tonight. The enemies of this deserted world had retreated into space.

"I sleep light, too, Greene." And he did, rousing often during the night at slight unaccustomed sounds, Kimmer's intermittent snores or when Jiro added more wood to the fire.

In the morning, Benden contacted Honshu and this time spoke with Ni Morgana, who said that her expedition had been entirely successful from the scientific point of view. She would spend the day cataloguing the medicinal plants and their properties with the women. Benden gave her the day's flight plan and signed off.

They doubled back east and slightly north of the mining site and Drake's Lake, then followed a fairly wide river as it flowed down to the distant sea. And came upon the stout stone houses and barns that had housed the inhabitants of Thessaly and Roma. They observed herds of beasts, cattle, and sheep in nearby fields, but the houses and barns had been cleared of all effects. Now just dead leaves and other debris littered the spacious rooms where the shutters had fallen from rusted hinges.

"Lieutenant," and Greene motioned for him to step a little away from the other two men, "we haven't seen any of the sleds Kimmer said they used. Nor those three missing shuttles. So, if we find them, wouldn't we find the people?"

"We would, if we could, Sergeant," Benden said tiredly. "Kimmer, how long did your sled have power?"

Kimmer's eyes gleamed as he appreciated what Benden did not ask.

"Once I reached Honshu, I didn't use the sled at all, except as a power source for the communit, for maybe five, six years. Ito got very sick and I went to Landing to see if I could get a medic out here. They'd all left and taken everything with them. I tried some other Stakes, as I told you, but they were deserted too. Ito died and I was too busy with the kids, and then Chio's, to go off. Then I made one trip to Bitkim and four years later, as I'd no way to recharge the pack, I made that last trip. But," and he held up his gnarled finger, "like I told you, just before I lost all contact, I heard part of Benden's message to conserve all power. So they couldn't have had many operational sleds. I *think*," and here Kimmer paused to search his memory. His eyes met the lieutenant's. "I think they didn't have enough power left to go after Thread anymore and they were going to have to wait." He sighed. "That'd be forty years they'd've had to wait for the end of Thread, Lieutenant, and I don't think they made it."

"Yes, but where *were* they?"

Kimmer shrugged. "Hell, Lieutenant, if I knew that I'd've hiked across the continent to find them once Thread stopped. If I'd had one whisper, I'd've tracked it down." He swiveled about then, facing west. "They were someplace in the west from the direction of their signals. Say," and his face lit up suddenly, "maybe they went to Ierne Island. That would have been easier to protect than one of these open Stakes.

So Benden called in the next destination. "We'll be back by tomorrow evening . . ."

"You'd better be," Ni Morgana said drily. "That window won't wait for anyone."

There was no question in Benden's mind that the lieutenant would delay taking that window either but he wasn't worried about that. He had to be sure—and it looked as if Kimmer's conscience required him also to be confident that there was no one else alive of Benden's group.

The run to Ierne Island took most of the rest of that day and was as fruitless as the other. Kimmer suggested one further detour, to the tip of Dorado province, to Seminole and Key Largo Stakes. On the wreckage of a storm-damaged building, they found a commast, or sections of it, and evidence of a hurried departure of the inhabitants. In another shed, still partly roofed, the remains of two sleds were discovered, obviously broken up to provide spare parts. The canopies and hulls were well scored and blistered by Thread. Benden appreciated that Kimmer was extraordinarily lucky to have survived at all.

They made their evening camp there with Jiro providing fish which he caught from the remains of a sturdy jetty. The last ten meters, projecting out into the channel, had been snapped off by some tremendous storm, or maybe many. It took a lot of force to break off heavy duty plastic pilings like that.

When Ross Benden checked in with the *Erica*, he roused a sleepy Nev, forgetting that there was a time difference across the southern continent.

"Everything's OK," Nev said, interrupting himself with a yawn, "though the lieutenant is sure something's up. She says the women are acting funny."

"They're about to leave all they've known as well as a very comfortable life," Benden replied.

"Isn't that. Lieutenant'll tell you when you get back." Nev didn't seem much concerned but Benden trusted the lieutenant's instincts.

He was wakeful that night, trying to figure out what *could* have gone wrong. Kimmer was with him. Shensu was eager to leave, too. And with five to guard the *Erica*, which was Benden's main concern, what could go wrong?

He worried about that all the way back to Honshu which was a useless activity. But he'd noticed that those who anticipated problems always seemed able to solve them faster.

When they finally reached Honshu, despite the gathering dusk, Kimmer insisted on maneuvering the sled into its garage, proving his piloting skills.

"This sled's done more than its designers ever expected, Benden," Kimmer said sardonically as he reversed it in, "so humor an old man in rewarding its service the only way he can."

Benden and Greene left him and Jiro to a ritualistic deservicing. Benden ran up the stairs to the main room. Ni Morgana was there, storing small packages in a case. Benden noticed first that some of the wall hangings were missing and then that the big room appeared to be stripped. Damn it! They only had 23.5 kilos each.

"Glad to have you back, Ross," Ni Morgana said, smiling a welcome. "We're just about packed up and ready to go." There was nothing in her manner to suggest anxiety. "There you are, Charity. If you'll stow that in the galley locker, that's the last. She consulted her notepad then, reading the last entry as Charity left with the container. "From your less than jubilant manner, Lieutenant, I gather that your time was wasted."

"You could gather that, Saraidh," Benden said, trying not to sound truculent. "In some places material was neatly stored as if the owners intended to return; in others, everything had been left open to the weather, or showed signs of hurried departure. They turned their animals loose and those have multiplied so I'd say that the meek have inherited this planet. You said you'd had more success?"

She reviewed her notepad a moment longer, then flipped it shut and placed it in a hip pocket. A nod of her head and both officers moved toward the door. Benden was relieved to see one of the marines on duty at the ramp of the *Erica,* having a word with Charity before she entered.

"When I've written up my investigations," she said with considerable satisfaction, "there's going to be some red faces. Irrefutably, the Oort cloud supports a life form which I have observed in its normal immensely sluggish metabolic, activated and defunct states. Fascinating actually, even if it also has managed to devastate a world and ruin it for further human habitation. . . ." Ni Morgana walked Bender to the far side of the *Erica,* raising her arm as if to point something out to him. "I don't know *what's* going on but something is, Ross. I don't believe it's just sorrow for leaving their home that's making the women nervous, jumpy, and accounts for a mass insomnia. The children seem fine and Shensu and Kimo have been most helpful."

"I thought taking Kimmer and Jiro with me was a sensible precaution."

"Sensible, but Kimmer's quite likely to have given those women orders before he left. I think he did. I just don't know what. We haven't left the *Erica* unattended but each of us who's stood a watch on her has been plagued with headaches. I'll admit to you, Ross, that I fell asleep on watch. I can't have dozed for more than ten to twenty minutes but I *was* asleep. I can't get Cahill, Nev or the other marines to admit that they had similar lapses but Nev had that hangdog expression I've come to know well in erring ensigns. Anyway, after my little snooze, Nev and I searched the ship from prow to the propulsion units and couldn't find anything illegally stowed. Which is what I think's been happening. Oh, we've put aboard everyone's 23.5 kilos which we thoroughly searched and weighed before I'd permit them to stow it. Nothing hidden in anyone's bundle.

"And the women . . ." Ni Morgana paused, deep in thought and then shook her head slowly. "They're exhausted although they swear blind that they're fine, just that this has all happened so fast. Chio released that little dragoney pet of hers and she bursts into tears if you glance sidewise at her." Then she gave a chuckle. "Nev and I thought to cheer them up and he's a main frame of humorous anecdotes about life in high tech. He's from a colonial family so he's been marvelous at reassuring them. You should have heard the spiel he gave on how they'll be living back on a 'civilized' planet and all the advantages of same. They cheer up a bit and then fall into the weeps again."

Then she turned briskly professional. "We've got additional safety harness for all, by the way, and pallets with a local vegetable sponge that is lightweight but cushioning. I figure that all the women should be strapped into the marines' bunks, the kids and the brothers can use the pallets and temporary harness in the wardroom, and the marines will take the extra seats in the cabin with us. Tight squeeze but there're only so many places

you can put bodies on this gig. Where *is* Kimmer?" she asked. "I think one
of us ought to keep a close eye on his movements this evening." Then she
looked out to the last of the brilliantly red and orange sunset. "Too bad.
This is such a beautiful planet."

That night a lavish feast was spread for everyone—except the man on
duty on the *Erica*. Kimmer urged the officers and the three marines to
drink as much of his fine wines as possible, for the tunnel snakes wouldn't
appreciate them. When he found the Fleet reluctant to overindulge, he
nagged the girls and the three men to "eat, drink, and be merry." Taking
his own advice, he passed out before the meal was finished.

"He'll have to be sober by . . ." and Benden consulted his digital to
check, "0900 tomorrow or he'll be nauseous in take-off and I don't want
to have to clean that up when we reach free-fall. Good evening and thank
you, Chio, for such a magnificent meal," he added and after Saraidh had
also complimented the women, the *Erica*'s complement left.

Kimmer looked none the worse for the drink the next morning as he and
the others reported on time to board the *Erica*. Nev strapped the Pernese
in but Benden made a final check himself. The women were all red-eyed
and Chio so patently nervous that he wondered if he should get Ni Morgana to give her a mild sedative.

At the exact second calculated by Lieutenant Zane, the *Erica* lifted from
the plateau, blasting her way skyward, tail rockets blazing.

A fisherman, standing the dog watch on his trawler off the coast of Fort
Hold, saw the fiery trail, vivid against the grey eastern sky, and wondered at
it. He followed the blazing lance of light until it was no longer visible. He
wondered what it was, but his more immediate concern was keeping warm
and wondering if the cook had made klah by now and could he get a cup.

"The roll rate's too low!" Benden cried over the roar of the engines,
exerting all his strength to keep the right attitude. "She's a slug," and
suddenly Benden realized that the *Erica*'s reluctance could be caused by
only one thing. "We've got too much weight on board. She's too bloody
heavy through the yoke," he said through gritted teeth. He forced his head
to look to his right at Nev, strapped in the co-pilot's seat. Ni Morgana was
in the next row with Greene beside her while the other marines stoically
endured acceleration g-forces in makeshift couches. "I've got to increase
thrust. And that's going to take one helluva lot of fuel."

Benden made the adjustments, swearing bitterly to himself over the expenditure of such much fuel. His calculations could not be wrong. They
were also too far gone in their path to abort and, if they did, there was no
way to contact the *Amherst* and arrange a new rendezvous. How in hell
could she be so heavy?

"Nev, give me some figures on what this is costing us in fuel and the estimated weight we're lugging up."

"Aye, aye, sir," Nev said, slowly moving his hand in the g-force to activate the armrest pad.

Benden forced his head to the side so he could see the bright green numbers leap to the small screen.

"Twenty-one minutes five seconds of boast, sir, was what we should have needed," Nev replied, his voice genuinely strained. "We're bloody twenty-nine point twenty into flight and still not free! We're . . . huh . . . four nine five point five six kilograms overweight! Free fall in ten seconds!"

Ten seconds seemed half a year until they were suddenly weightless. Benden swore as he read the ominous position of the fuel gauge. Still cruising, he adjusted her yaw with a burst of the port jets, swinging her nose towards the Sun. He already knew that they hadn't enough fuel to make their scheduled rendezvous with the *Amherst*. And the cruiser would currently be in the communication's shadow as it made its parabolic turn around Rukbat.

He called up Rukbat's system on the console monitor. There was no way they could use the second planet as a slingshot. But, and he pulled at his lower lip, there was a chance they could make it to the first little burnt-out cinder of a plant. They'd come awful close to Rukbat and even closer to the surface of Number One in order to use its gravity well. That would save fuel. But they'd need a different rendezvous point. That is, if they could get to the same point at the same time, at the same speed and heading in the same direction as the cruiser at some point earlier in her outbound hyperbolic orbit of Rukbat.

"Nev, figure me a slingshot course around the first planet." There was only the one option left to Benden.

"Aye, aye, sir," and the ensign's voice was full of relief.

Then in a taut hard voice, he shot out a second order. "Greene, bring me Kimmer. Tell the others to stay put."

He flipped open the harness release and let himself drift up out of the pilot's seat, trying to figure out just how Kimmer had managed to sneak 495.56 kilograms of whatever it was on board his ship. And when? Especially as the man had been under his watchful eye for over three days.

"Lieutenant," and Nev's voice was apologetic, "we can't take a slingshot around the first planet; not with the weight on board."

"Oh, we'll be lighter very soon, Nev," Benden replied with a malicious grin. "Four hundred ninety-five point fifty-six kilograms lighter. Figure a course with that weight loss."

"What I can't understand," Ni Morgana said in a flat voice, "is what they could have smuggled aboard. Or how?"

"What about your headaches, Sariadh?" Benden asked, seething with anger at Kimmer's duplicity. "And those catnaps no one else's had the guts to report to me."

"What could they possibly have done in ten to twenty minutes, Ross?" Ni Morgana demanded flatly, her nostrils flaring at his implication of dereliction of duty. "Nev and I searched for any possibly smuggled goods or tampering."

Benden said nothing, pointedly, and then scrubbed at his face in frustration. "Oh, it's no blame to you, Saraidh. Kimmer just outsmarted me, that's all. I thought removing him from Honshu would solve the problems." He raised his voice. "Vartry, you, Scag, and Hemlet will conduct a search of the most unlikely places on this ship; the missile bins, the head, the inner hull, the airlock. Somehow they've overloaded us and we have got to know with what and dump it!" He turned to Nev. "Try reaching the *Amherst*. I think it's too soon to make contact but get on the blower anyhow."

Kimmer overhanded himself into the cabin then, a smile on his face for the fierce expressions on the three marines as they passed him by.

"Kimmer, what did you get on board this ship and where is it, because we've got less than an hour to make a course correction and thanks to you, we've lost too much fuel lifting the bird off Pern."

"I don't know what you mean, Lieutenant," was the reply, and Kimmer looked him squarely in the eye. "I was with you for three days. How could I have put something on board this vessel?"

"Still stalling, man, it's your life you'll lose as well."

"I'm flattered that you've asked my opinion, Lieutenant, but I'm sure you know better than I what equipment can be jettisoned to lighten her."

Benden stared him down, wondering at the malevolence in the gaze Kimmer returned. "You know what weight I'm referring to and it was all put on at Honshu. If I don't know what that was, Kimmer, you'll be the first thing that lightens this gig's load."

Suddenly they all heard hysterical weeping from the stern and Vartry propelled himself back into the cabin.

"Lieutenant, they started the minute I said we were going to search because the ship was overweight. They know *something!*"

Benden hand-pushed himself deftly down the short companionway to the marines' quarters, the wailing rising to an eerie ululation that made the hairs on the back of his neck rise.

"Stow it!" Benden roared, but Chio's volume only increased. The others were not as loud but just as distruaght, plainly terrified and far too hysterical to reply to his demands for an explanation.

Ni Morgana arrived with the medical kit and injected Chio with a sedative which reduced the hysterics but had no effect when Benden questioned her, trying to keep his voice level and reasonable.

"They will not tell you what they have done," Shensu said, careening into the marines' quarters. Absently rubbing the arm he had bruised, he looked down at Chio. "She has always been dominated by him and so have the others. If Kimmer can be *made,*" and Shensu's voice was hard-edged with hatred, "to give them the necessary orders. . . ."

"I think Kimmer will explain, or take a long step out of a short airlock," Benden said, pushing past Shensu. There was no time for finesse or bluff with the *Erica* currently on an abortive course for the second planet. They had to make a correction soon. And do it without the excess weight or they'd be beyond rescue. He'd have the truth if he had to space Kimmer and enough of the women to get one of them to tell him what he had to know.

"Lieutenant!" Green's booming voice was urgent and Benden propelled himself as fast as he could back to the cabin where Greene was searching Kimmer roughly. "Sir, he's wearing metal. I felt it when I frisked him." And as the sergeant peeled back the shipsuit, a vest was exposed, a vest made up of panels of gold. "Shit!"

"Hardly!" Kimmer remarked, smiling smugly.

"Strip him!" Benden ordered and not only was Kimmer wearing a gold vest but a thick belt of gold cast in lozenge shapes. His underpants had pockets filled with thin gold sheets. Greene was nothing if not thorough, and even the boots on Kimmer's feet produced smaller gold plates worked into the soles and ankle leather.

"Saraidh!" Benden roared. "Search those women. Greene, you search the kids, but gently, get me? Shensu, Jiro, Kimo, in here on the double," Benden took some comfort when the three men proved to be wearing no more than their shipsuits.

Ni Morgana's yell confirmed Benden's guess about the women. All the while Kimmer kept in place his slight, amused smile. It took both Vartry and Saraidh to bring the concealed sheets and gold plates the women had secreted to the cabin.

"I'd estimate that's about ten to fifteen kilos per woman and five per kid," she said as they looked down at the pile of gold.

Benden shook his head. "Forty-five kilos is a drop! No where near four hundred ninety-five point fifty-six k's." He turned on the naked Kimmer who smiled back, all innocence. "Kimmer, we're running out of time. Now where is the rest of it? Or had you intended becoming an integral part of Rukbat?"

"You don't panic me, Lieutenant Benden," and Kimmer's eyes glittered with a vengeance that shocked Ross. "This ship's in no danger. Your cruiser'll rescue you."

Benden stared at the man in utter amazement. "The cruiser is behind Rukbat, in com shadow. We can't arrange a different rendezvous. Unless we can lighten this ship, we can't even make a course change for the one chance we have of staying alive!" Benden hauled Kimmer by the arm to the console and showed him the diagram on the screen, and the little blip that was the *Erica,* serenely heading for her original, now nonviable destination. "We certainly don't have enough fuel to make the arranged rendezvous." Then, with his finger, Benden indicated the inexorable path the *Erica* was taking. "Tell us what and where the excess weight is hidden, Kimmer!"

Kimmer contented himself with a wry chuckle and Benden wanted to smash it off his face. But Kimmer was enjoying this too much to give him that satisfaction.

"If that's the way you want to play it, Kimmer. Sergeant, get the stuff and bring it with you," and Benden hustled the naked barefooted colonist down the companionway to the airlock and palming the control for the inner hatch, shoved Kimmer inside, motioned for Greene to throw in the gold, and closed the hatch again.

"I mean it, Kimmer, either tell me what else is on board and where, or you go out the airlock."

Kimmer turned, a contemptuous expression on his face, and he folded his arms across his chest, a gaunt old man with only defiance to clothe him.

"You've more than enough fuel, Benden. Chio checked the gauge. The *Erica*'s tanks were full. Since you had to have used at least a third of a tank to get here, I'm of the opinion that Shensu knew," and his eyes traveled to Benden's left, where Shensu was standing by the window, "as I always suspected, where Kenjo had stored his pilferings." Kimmer drew himself up. "No, Lieutenant, I will call your bluff."

"It's no bluff, Kimmer, and if you had any training as a space jockey, you'd've felt how sluggish the gig was. She's heavy, too heavy. We burned too much in the lift-off. The gold on you and the women isn't enough to cause that. Dammit, Kimmer, it's your life, too."

"I'll have taken a Benden down with me," the man said in a snarl of hatred and sheer malevolence, his face contorted.

"But Chio, and your daughters, your grandchildren—" Benden began.

"They were none of them worth the effort I put into them," Kimmer replied arrogantly. "I have to share my wealth with them but I'm certainly not sharing it with you."

"Sharing?" Benden stared at him, not quite comprehending the man's words. "You think I'm blackmailing you? For a share of your *wealth?*" The disgust in Benden's voice momentarily rattled the man. "There are many people in *my* world, Kimmer, who are not motivated by greed." He gestured with contemptuous anger at the sheets and lozenges at Kimmer's feet. "None of that is worth the risk you want us to take. What have you hidden on the *Erica* and where?"

Just then, Ni Morgana beckoned urgently to Benden. He gratefully moved away from the window. His hand hovered briefly over the evac button. Kimmer could stay where he was, just a thin sheet away from space, and contemplate his situation.

"When I was looking for tanks, I came across a vial of scopalamine in the medical chest. It may be an anesthetic but the right dosage provides the truth, so Chio spilled it out. It's platinum and germanium, sheets of it, stuffed wherever they could when they came aboard on legitimate errands," she said, her voice low enough for Benden's ears only, "and when they drugged whoever was on the dogwatch. That's why we all had headaches."

"Platinum? Germanium?" Benden was astounded.

"Kimmer was a mining engineer. He found ores and we've all had to work in them," Shensu said, pushing over to them. "I wondered why the workroom smelled of hot metal. He must have had the girls melt the ingots down at night, extruding sheets. No wonder they've looked so worn out. I never thought to check on the metals because they'd be too heavy to bring."

"Where is it?" Benden demanded, looking up and down the aisle, momentarily bewildered when he thought of all the places sheets of thin metal could be unobtrusively attached within the *Erica*. "We've got to search the ship! Everywhere! Sergeant, take your marines to the stern. Shensu, you and your brothers start on the lockers."

"He knew one helluva lot about the interior of gigs," Nev remarked almost admiringly when the marines found that the missile tubes had been stuffed with metal plaques. These were immediately flushed into space.

"And I watched her, Lieutenant," Vartry said, aggrieved, when they found that the locker where the medicines had been stowed was also lined with thin slabs of silvery metal. "I stood here and watched her, heard her tell me she wanted to be sure the medicines were safe, as she slapped sheets top, bottom, and side."

The lockers in which the 23.5 kilo personal allowances had been stowed also proved to be lined with platinum.

"You know," Ni Morgana said, bending one of the thin sheets which she had found under Benden's bunk, "individually these don't weigh much but they damned near coated the gig with 'em. Ingenious."

There were sheets everywhere and still more was found, to be piled at the airlock hatch.

Nev, remembering how he'd entertained Hope and Charity by showing them the cabin, found metal glued to the bottom of the blast couches, lining the inside of the control panel, and thin rolls of metal tacked to the baseboards, looking for all the worlds like innocuous decorations. The viewports had platinum decorated seals. That sent Nev and Scag searching all the ports.

When the pile at the inner airlock door reached the window, abruptly Benden realized the airlock was empty.

"Kimmer? Where's Kimmer?" he cried. "Who let him out? Where is he?"

But Kimmer was nowhere in the ship. A gesture from Benden had the marines on his heels as they propelled themselves to the galley where the brothers were still searching.

"Which of you depressed the evac button?" Benden demanded, seething with impotent anger.

"Depressed . . ." Shensu's look of astonishment was, Benden felt, genuine. There was no regret, however, on his face or his brothers'.

"I'm not sure I blame you, Shensu, but it constitutes murder. You had opportunities enough while we were searching the ship . . ."

"We were searching the ship, too," Shensu said with dignity. "We were as busy as you, trying to save our lives."

"Perhaps," Jiro said softly, "he committed suicide rather than face the failure of that brainstorm of his."

"That is a possibility," Ni Morgana said composedly, but Benden knew she believed that no more than he did. But it was true that, although Kimmer could not have activated the inner hatch of the airlock, the evac button on the outer door was clearly marked. And the mechanisms cycled itself shut in two minutes after use.

"This will be investigated more fully when we have time," Ross Benden promised them fervently, pinning each of the three brothers with his angry glare. "I won't condone murder!" Though at just that moment, Benden had several he would like to commit.

Returning to the airlock, he found that Nev was busy with a chisel, letting out a hoot of triumph has he peeled off a paper thin sheet of platinum.

"I'm sure Captain Fargoe wouldn't mind having a platinum-plated gig . . ." His voice trailed off when he caught sight of Benden's expression. He gulped. "There'd be another twenty kilos right in here." And he applied himself to the task of removing it.

Benden signaled for two of the marines to assist Nev while he and the others piled the accumulated sheets, pipings, strips, and lozenges into the lock.

"Amazing!" Ni Morgana said, shaking her head wearily. "That ought to make up the rest of the 495.56 kilos."

She stepped out of the lock and gestured to Benden, who was at the controls. With a feeling of intense relief, he pressed the evac button and saw the metal slide slowly out into space, a glittering cascade left behind the *Erica*. It was still visible as the outer door cycled shut.

"I've half a mind to add their personal allowances," Benden began, feeling more vicious and vengeful than he thought possible, "which would give us another 100 kilos leeway."

"More than that," said the literal-minded Nev and then gawped at the lieutenant. "Oh, you mean just the women's stuff."

"No," Ni Morgana said on a gusty sigh. "They've suffered enough from Kimmer. I don't see the point in further retribution.

"If it hadn't been for the extra fuel, we wouldn't have lifted off the planet," Nev suddenly remarked.

"If it hadn't been for the extra fuel, I don't think we'd've had this trouble with Kimmer," Ni Morgana said sardonically.

"He'd've tried something else," Benden said. "He'd planned the contingency of rescue a long, long time. Those vests and pants weren't whipped up overnight. Not with everything else those women were doing."

"That's possible," Ni Morgana said thoughtfully. "He was a crafty old bugger. All alone he counted on our rescuing him. And he'd know we'd have to check body weight."

"D'you suppose he also fooled us," Nev asked anxiously, "about there being more survivors somewhere?"

That thought had been like a pain in Benden's guts since Kimmer's duplicity had come to light. And yet . . . there *had* been no sign of other survivors on the southern continent. Nor had their instruments given them any positive readings as they spiraled across the snowy northern landmass. Then there was Shensu's story and that man had no reason to lie. Benden shook his head wearily and once again regarded the ship's digital. The search had taken a lot longer than he'd realized.

"Look alive," he said, rising to his feet with as good an appearance of energy as he could muster. "Nev, try to raise the *Amherst* again." He knew beforehand that the *Amherst* was unlikely to be receiving. He also knew that he had to alter the course *now*, before they went too far along the aborted trajectory. He didn't have any option. He made his calculations for the appropriate roll to get the *Erica* on the new flight path. He'd worry about contacting the *Amherst* later. He couldn't wait on this correction any longer. A three-second burn at one-g would do it. That wouldn't take up much fuel. And he breathed a silent prayer of thanksgiving. "Nev, Greene,

Vartry, check our passengers, We've got to burn to our new heading in two minutes forty-five seconds."

He felt better after the burn. The gig was handling easily again. Like the thoroughbred she was, she had eased onto her new heading. And he had done something positive about their perilous situation.

"Now, let's be sure we got every last strip Kimmer added to the *Erica*," he said, unbuckling his seat restraints. He'd also go through the gig with an eye to what else could be jettisoned. But they'd a long trip ahead of them and precious few comforts for those on board.

"I'll check the women first," Ni Morgana said, pushing herself off deftly from the back of her couch and grabbing the hand hold to propel herself down the companionway. "And see about some grub. Breakfast was a long time ago."

Benden realized how right she was but, under stress, he never noticed hunger pangs. He did now.

"Chow's the best idea yet," he said and managed a reasonably cheerful grin for her.

When she checked the women, she found them still shaken by the emotional prelude and, though they helped her in the galley, they were apathetic. Chio wept silently, ignoring the food Faith tried to get her to eat. She seemed wrapped in so deep a depression that Saraidh reported her condition to Benden.

"She won't last the journey like this, Ross." Saraidh said. "She's deeply disturbed and I don't think it's losing Kimmer."

"Isn't it just that she was so dependent on him? You heard what Shensu said."

"Well, if it is, we ought to sort it out. We can't avoid discussing Kimmer's demise."

"I know and I don't intend to. His demise," and he drawled out the euphemism, "was accidental. I would have preferred to have him alive and standing trial for his attempt to disable the *Erica*," Benden replied grimly. "What I want to know is how he got those women to sabotage us. They *must* have known from our conversations that their extra mass would seriously burden the ship."

Shensu had floated down the corridor during the last sentence and he gave them a terse nod.

"You must explain to my sisters that the gemstones alone will provide suitably for them," he said, "that the stones will not be confiscated by the Fleet to pay for this rescue."

"What?" Ni Morgana exclaimed. "Where did they get that notion?" She held up her hand. "Never mind. I know. Kimmer. What maggots had he got in his brain?"

"The maggot of greed," Shensu said. "Come, reassure my sisters. They are so fearful. They only cooperated with him on the metal because he said that would be the only wealth left to them."

"And how did Kimmer plan to remove all that platinum from the *Erica?*" Benden demanded, knowing that his voice was rising in frustration but unable to stifle it. "The man was deranged."

"Quite likely," Shensu said with a shrug. "For decades he has clung to the hope that his message would be answered. Or else all he had accumulated: the gems, the metals, meant nothing."

They had reached the marines' quarters and heard Chio's soft weeping.

"Get the kids out of here, Nev," Benden told the ensign in a low voice, "and amuse them. Shensu, ask your sisters to join us here and, by whatever you hold sacred, tell them we mean them no harm."

It took hours to reassure the four women. Benden stuck to his matter of fact, common sense approach.

"Please believe me," he said with genuine concern at Chio's almost total collapse, "that the Fleet has special regulations about castaways or stranded persons. Stranded you were. It would be totally different if the Colonial Authority or Federated Headquarters had organized an official search; *then* there would have been staggering retrieval costs. But the *Amherst* only happened to be in the area and the system was orange-flagged—"

"And because," Ni Morgana took up the explanation, "I was doing research on the Oort cloud, Captain Fargoe ordered the gig to investigate. As she will tell you herself when you meet her, it saves you, the surviving colonists, any cost."

Chio mumbled something.

"Say again?" Ni Morgana asked very gently, smiling reassurance.

"Kimmer said we would be paupers."

"With *black* diamonds? The rarest kind of all?" Ni Morgana managed to convey a depth of astonishment that surprised Benden. "And you've kilos of them among you. And those medicines, Faith," and the science officer turned to the one sister who appeared to be really listening to what was said, "especially that numbweed salve of yours. Why the patents on that alone will buy you a penthouse in any Federation city. If that's where you want to live."

"The salve?" Sheer surprise animated Faith. "But it's common—"

"On Pern, perhaps, but I've a degree in alien pharmacopeia and I've never come across anything as mild and effective as that," Ni Morgana assured her. "You *did* bring seed as well as salve because I don't think that's the sort of medication that can be artificially reproduced and provide the same effect."

"We had to gather the leaves and boil them for hours," Hope said wonderingly. "The stink made it a miserable job but he made us do it each year."

"And numbweed can make us rich?" Charity doubted what she heard.

"I have no reason to lie to you," Ni Morgana said with such dignity that the girl flushed.

"But Kimmer is dead," Chio said, a sob catching in her throat and she turned her head away, her shoulders shaking.

"He is dead of greed," Kimo said in an implacable voice. "And we are alive, Chio. We can make new lives for ourselves and do what we want to do now."

"That would be very nice," Faith said in a low wistful voice.

"We won't be Kimmer's slaves anymore," Kimo added.

"We would all have died without Kimmer after Mother died," Chio turned back, mastering her tears, unable to stop defending the man who had dominated her for so long.

"Died because she had too many stillborn babies," Kimo said. "You forgot that, Chio. You forgot that you were pregnant two months after you became a woman. You forgot how you cried. I do not."

Chio stared at her brother, her face a mask of sorrow. Then she turned to Benden and Ni Morgana, her eyes narrow. "And will you tell this captain of yours about Kimmer's death?"

"Yes, we will naturally have to mention that unfortunate incident in our report," Bender said.

"And who killed him?" she shot the question at them both.

"We don't know who killed him, or if he cycled the lock open himself."

Chio was startled, as if that possibility had not occurred to her until then. She pulled at Kimo's sleeve. "Is that possible?"

Kimo shrugged. "He believed his own lies, Chio. Once the metal was found, he would consider himself to be poor. He was at least honorable enough to commit suicide."

"Yes, honorable," Chio murmured so softly her words were barely audible. "I am tired. I wish to sleep." She turned herself toward the wall.

Kimo gave the two officers a nod of triumph. Faith covered her elder sister and gestured for them to leave.

Over the next several days, passengers and crew settled into an easier relationship. The youngsters would sit for hours in front of the tri-d screen, going through the gig's library of tapes. Saraidh cajoled Chio and the girls into watched some of them as well, as a gentle introduction to the marvels of modern high-tech civilization.

"I can't tell whether they're reassured or scared witless," she reported to Benden, standing his watch at the gig's console. They still had not made contact with the *Amherst* though he had no real cause for worry on that score—yet. "How many times have you worked those equations, Ross?" she asked, noticing what he had on his pad.

"Often enough to know there's no mathematical errors," he said with a wry grin. "We'll only have the one chance."

"I'm not worried," she said with a shrug and a smile. "Off you get. It's my watch." And she shooed him out of the cabin.

"Lieutenant?" Nev's voice reverberated excitedly down the companion-way the next afternoon, "I've raised the *Amherst!*"

There was a cheer as Ross propelled himself to the cabin.

"Neither loud nor clear, sir, but definitely voice contact," Nev said with a grin as if he himself were responsible for the deed.

Ross grinned back at him in relief and depressed the talk toggle on his seat arm. "Ross Benden reporting, sir. We need to make a new rendezvous."

Fargoe's voice acknowledged him and, though her tone broke up in transmission, he really didn't need to hear every syllable to know what she said.

"Ma'am, we've had to abort our original course. We are currently aiming for a slingshot around the first planet.'

"You want a sunburn, Benden?"

"No, ma'am, but we have only 2.3 kps of Delta V remaining."

"How did you cut it that fine?"

"Humanitarian reasons required us to rescue the ten remaining survivors of the expedition."

"Ten?" There was a pause that had nothing to do with interference on the line. "I shall be very interested in your report, Benden. That is, if your humanitarianism allows you to make it. What is the total of the excess weight you're carrying?"

Nev handed over his pad and Benden read off the figures.

"Hmm. Offhand I don't think we can match orbits. Can you make it five kps?"

"No, ma'am."

"Roger. Hold on while we refigure your course and rendezvous point."

Benden tried not to look toward Nev or at Saraidh, who had joined them at the command console. He tried not to look nervous but felt various parts of himself twitching, unusual enough in gravity and damned annoying for freefall. He clutched the edge of the console as unobtrusively and as hard as possible to keep from twitching out of the chair.

"*Erica,* Captain Fargoe, here. What can you jettison?"

"How much is required?" Benden thought of the wealth they had just consigned to space.

"You've got to jettison 49.05 kilos. You will need to make a 10g burn for 1.3 seconds around the first planet, commencing at 91 degrees right ascension. That will put you on course, speed and direction and, we devoutly hope, in time to make a new rendezvous. Good luck, Lieutenant." Her voice indicated that he'd need it.

He didn't like a 10g burn, even for 1.3 seconds. They'd all black out. It'd be rough on the kids. But it'd be a lot rougher to turn into cinders.

"You heard the captain," he said turning first to Saraidh and then Nev. "Let's snap to it."

"What'll we toss, Lieutenant?" Nev asked.

"Just about everything that isn't bolted down," Saraidh said, "and probably some of that. I'll start in the galley."

In the end they made up the required kilos out of material which Saraidh knew could be most easily replaced by stores on the *Amherst*: extra packs, oxygen tanks which accounted for a good deal of the necessary weight, the messroom table, and all but one of the beacon missiles which the gig carried.

"If Captain Fargoe decides you weren't negligent," Saraidh told Ross, her face expressionless, as they both watched the articles sliding out of the airlock into space, "you won't have to pay for 'em."

"What?" Then he saw she was teasing and grinned back at her. "I've enough I've got to account for, thank you muchly, ma'am, on this expedition without paying for it, too." He kept trying to explain Kimmer's demise to himself and how he could have prevented it, if he could have.

"Now, now, Ross," said Saraidh, and waggled a finger at him. They were alone in the corridor. "Don't hang Kimmer about your neck. I subscribe completely to the suicide theory. Temporarily of unsound mind due to the failure of his plan. He might just have done it to be awkward, too."

"I'm not sure Captain Fargoe would buy that one."

"Ah, but she'd never met Kimmer, and I have," and Saraidh gave him an encouraging thumbs-up.

The moment of truth came two long weary weeks later. The temperature inside the *Erica* began to rise with their proximity to Rukbat's sun, reaching an uncomfortable level. Benden was sweating heavily as he watched the ominous approach of the tiny black cinder of the system's first planet. That poor wight hadn't had a chance to survive. He intended to.

"Burn minus sixty seconds," he announced over the intercom. He hadn't informed his passengers of the rigors of a slingshot maneuver. They'd all black out and, if something went wrong, they'd never know it. Meanwhile, he hadn't had to endure Chio's suspicions or the sorrowful reproaches of the other three women. He'd done slingshot passages before, both actual and in simulation. It was more a matter of timing the burn properly just as the ninety-one degree right ascension came up on the nav screen. He just hated blacking out for any reason, not being in control for those seconds or minutes.

"Nine, eight, seven," chanted Nev, his eyes glittering with anticipation. This was his first slingshot. "Five, four, three, two . . . one!"

Benden expressed the burn button, and the *Erica* lunged forward willingly. As he was slammed deep into the pads of the contour seat, he knew the maneuver would be successful and surrendered to the mighty g-forces he had just initiated.

Benden returned to consciousness, the blessed silence of space and the relief of weightlessness. His first glance was for the expended fuel. Point ninety-eight kps left. It should be enough. Provided the course corrections were accurate. He had one last burn to make as they bisected the *Amherst*'s wake and then turned back to her at a sharp vector.

"My compliments, Lieutenant," Ni Morgana said briskly, unsnapping her harness. "We seem to be well on our way now. I think the cook has something special for lunch today."

Benden blinked at her.

She grinned. "The very same thing we had yesterday for lunch."

Benden wasn't the only one who groaned. They'd added supplies at Honshu but the fresh foods were long gone and they were down to the emergency rations: nourishing but uninspired. And that's all they had for the next two weeks. When he was back on board the *Amherst* Ross Benden was going to order up the most lavish celebratory meal in the mess' well-stocked larder. "When," and he grinned to himself. That's positive thinking.

When the *Erica*'s sensors picked up the cruiser's unmistakable ion radiation trail, Benden was in the command cabin, teaching Alun and Pat the elements of spatial navigation. The boys were bright and so eager to prepare themselves for their new life that they were a pleasure to instruct.

"Back to your pads, boys. We've got another burn."

"Like the last one?" Alun asked plaintively.

"No, matey. Not like the last one. Just a touch on the button."

Reassured, they propelled themselves out of the cabin and down the companionway, dexterously passing Saraidh and Nev at the door.

"A touch being all the fuel we've got left," Saraidh murmured, taking her seat. She leaned forward, peering out into the blackness of space around them.

"You won't see anything yet," Nev remarked.

"I know it," she replied, shrugging. "Just looking."

"It's there, though."

"And not long gone," Benden added, "judging by the strength of the ion count." He toggled on the intercom. "Now listen up. A short burn, not like the last, just enough to change our course to match up our final approach to the *Amherst.*" In an aside to Saraidh he added, "I feel like a damned leisure liner captain."

"You'd make a grand one," she replied blandly, "especially if you have to change your branch of service."

"My what?" Benden never knew when Lieutenant Ni Morgana's wayward humor would erupt.

"Lighten up, Ross. We're nearly home and dry."

"Fifteen minutes to course correction." He nodded to Nev to watch the digital while he contacted the *Amherst. "Erica* to *Amherst.* Do you read me?"

"Loud and clear," came Captain Fargoe's voice. "About ready to join us, Lieutenant?"

"That's my aim, Captain."

"We'll trust it's as accurate as ever. Fire when ready, Gridley."

"Captain?"

"Roger, over and out."

Beside him, Saraidh was chuckling. "Where does she get them?"

"Get what?" asked Nev.

"Are you counting down, Ensign?"

"Yes, sir. Coming down to ten minutes forty seconds."

Why was it time could be so elastic? Benden wondered as the ten minutes seemed to go on forever, clicking second by second. At the minute, he flexed both hands, shook his shoulders to release the tension in his neck. At zero, he depressed the burn on the last point ninety-eight kps in the tank, yawing to starboard. He felt the surge of the good gig *Erica* as she responded. Then all of a sudden the engines cut out with the exhausted whoosh that meant no more fuel in the tank.

Had the *Erica* completed the course correction? Or had the engines stopped untimely? The margin was so damned slight! And the proof would be the appearance of the comforting bulk of the *Amherst* any time now. *If* the maneuver had been completed before the fuel was exhausted.

Like the two officers beside him, Benden instinctively leaned forward, peering out into the endless space in front of them.

"I've got a radar reading," Lieutenant," Nev said, and there was no denying the relief in his voice. "It can't be anything but the *Amherst.* I think we're going to make it."

"All we need is to get close enough for them to shoot us a magnetic line," Benden muttered.

Nev uttered a whoop. "Thar she be!" and he pointed. Benden had to blink to be sure he actually was seeing the running lights of the *Amherst*. He was close to adding his own kiyi of relief and victory.

Just then the comunit opened to a sardonic voice. "That's cutting it fine indeed, Lieutenant!" The blank screen cleared to a view of the captain, her head cocked and her right eyebrow quizzically aslant. "Trying to match your uncle's finesse?"

"Not consciously, ma'am, I assure you, but I'd be pleased to hear the confirmation that our present course and speed are A-OK for docking?"

"Not a puff of fuel left, huh?"

"No, ma'am."

She looked to her left, then faced the screen squarely again, a little smile playing on her lips. "You'll make it. And I'll expect to have reports from both you and Lieutenant Ni Morgana as soon as you've docked. You've had time enough on the trip in to write a hundred reports."

"Captain, I've got the passengers to settle."

"They'll be settled by medics, Ross. You've done your part getting them here. I want to see those reports."

And the screen darkened.

"Got yours already, Ross?" Ni Morgana asked with a sly grin as she swiveled her chair around.

"Got yours?"

"Oh, it's ready, too. I said that I believed Kimmer suicided."

Benden nodded, glad of her support. "It would have had to have been self-destruction, Saraidh. He would have been far more familiar with airlock controls than Shensu or his brothers," Benden said slowly, considering his words. "It's really far more likely that he did suicide, given the fact that he had failed to bring along all that metal. Damn fool! He must have known that he was dangerously overloading the ship. He could have murdered *us*." That angered Benden.

"Yes, and nearly succeeded. I think he was hoping that his death would have brought suspicion on the brothers as the most likely to wish his demise," Ni Morgana went on. "He would have liked jeopardizing their futures. And discrediting another Benden if he could." When she heard Benden's sharp inhalation, she touched his hand, causing him to look at her. "You can still be proud of your uncle, Ross. You heard what Shensu said, and how proud he was of the way the admiral marshalled all available defences."

Benden cocked his head, his expression rueful. "A fighter to the last . . . and it took a wretched planet to defeat him."

"Poor planet Pern," Saraidh said sadly. "Not its fault but I'm recommending that this system be interdicted. I did some calculations—which I'll verify on the *Amherst* computers—and rechecked the original EEC report.

That wasn't the first time the Oort organism fell on the planet. Nor will it be the last. It'll happen every 250 years, give or take a decade. Furthermore, we don't want any ship blundering into that Oort Cloud and transporting that organism to other systems."

She gave a shudder at the thought.

"There she is," Benden said with a sense of relief as the viewport filled with the perceptibly nearing haven of the *Amherst*. "And, all things considered, a successful rescue run."